THE FELL SWORD

D0278813

Also by Miles Cameron from Gollancz:

The Red Knight

THE FELL SWORD

MILES CAMERON

First published in Great Britain in 2013
by Gollancz
An imprint of the Orion Publishing Group
Orion House, 5 Upper St Martin's Lane, London WC2H 9EA
An Hachette UK Company

This edition published in Great Britain in 2014 by Gollancz

1 3 5 7 9 10 8 6 4 2

A CIP catalogue record for this book is available
from the British Library

ISBN 978 0 575 11334 3

Typeset at The Spartan Press Ltd,
Lymington, Hants

Printed and bound by CPI Group (UK) Ltd,
Croydon, CRO 4YY

www.traitorson.com
www.orionbooks.co.uk

www.gollancz.co.uk

For the reenactors

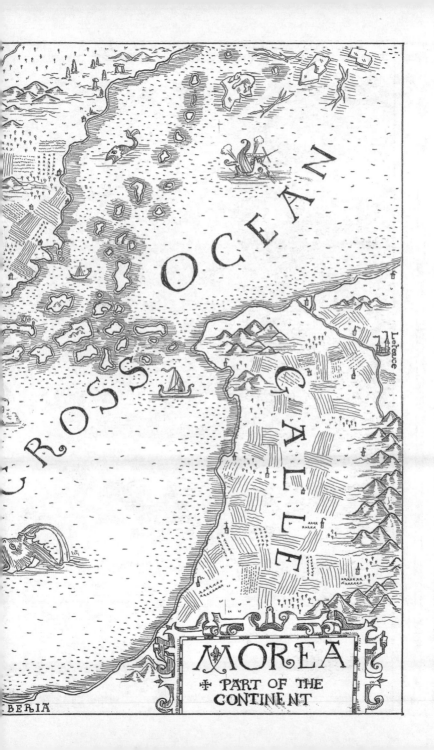

CROSS OCEAN

GALLE

Lefauce

MOREA
✝ PART OF THE
CONTINENT

BERIA

Prologue
The Emperor

The Red Knight

Chapter One

Antigonas

Liviapolis – Morgan Mortirmir

As the Red Knight left the abode of the Wyrm of the Green Hills and rode south to the Inn of Dorling, Morgan Mortirmir, late of Harndon, sat in class in the Imperial capital of Liviapolis. The classroom in which he sat was over a thousand years old; it featured dark oak benches and solid desks that sat four students per bench. The benches had, carved in so deeply you had to wonder how the professors and tutors had missed the vandalism, the graffiti of a hundred generations of would-be magisters in ten languages and in Archaic itself. The windows were mullioned and leaded and offered only the haziest glimpse of the outside world to the bored or frustrated mind.

Morgan shared his bench with three other students: two of the religious sisters from one of the great city's dozens of convents for women of noble blood, sisters Anna and Katerina, almost invisible in long brown gowns and wimples, and his sole near-friend, the Etruscan whose father was Podesta of the foreign merchants, Antonio Baldesce.

The logik master looked over the class.

'Someone who is not Mortirmir,' he said. 'Tell me why.'

Sixteen students in advanced hermetical thaumaturgy squirmed.

'Come, come, my children,' Magister Abraham said. He was a Yahadut – the first Morgan had ever met. He was one of the kindest of the masters – until he felt he had been ignored.

His eyes locked on the young Etruscan. 'Baldesce?' he asked, his voice rising a half-octave in academic impatience.

The silence was painful.

'Let me restate the problem,' Magister Abraham said in an increasingly dangerous tone. 'Why can you *not* wield the hermetical power directly inside your own memory palace?'

Sister Katerina made a slight sound – more like a moan than anything.

Sister Anna bit her lips.

Baldesce was not the sort of boy – young man – to writhe. 'No idea,' he said. He shrugged. 'But if I am permitted to guess—'

'Don't,' Abraham spat. 'Guesses do not interest me at this stage. Very well, young Mortirmir?'

Mortirmir couldn't render *potentia* into *ops*, but he had read every grimoire available and every scroll of philosophy, ethical or practical, that he could lay hands on. He met the magister's eye – and hesitated.

If he *didn't* give the answer, would they like him better?

Probably not. And sod them, anyway.

'Magister, I think you *can* manipulate the *aethereal* directly inside your own memory palace. I suspect you *shouldn't*.' Mortirmir shrugged, as Baldesce had shrugged, but it was a different gesture altogether – Mortirmir's shrug implied there was more to say rather than Baldesce's indifference to the question.

Magister Abraham scratched his chin under his long beard, his eyes on Mortirmir. 'Why do you think such an odd and heretical thing?' he asked. He was trying – and failing – to hide that he was pleased.

'Vetronius's Gladius Capitalis. Heraklitus's θανατηφόρα σπαθί.'

Sister Anna winced at his pronunciation of High Archaic, which was the Alban and not the local Morean.

Magister Abraham had the odd habit of tapping his teeth with his fingers, and he did so. When he had ink in his fingers, he sometimes stained his teeth.

He nodded. 'Yes. The Fell Sword. A weapon that will perform the same way in the real and in the *aethereal* implies that it can be forged inside the memory palace and then used – anywhere.' He allowed himself a slight smile. 'What would be the – result? – of such a use inside the memory palace?'

He paused for a heartbeat, and fifteen students paled to think of the literal destruction of the carefuly tended memories and workings.

'But you wouldn't know, would you, Mortirmir?' Magister Abraham asked. It was a rhetorical question. Now it was the magister's turn to shrug. 'Scamper off, little ones. Alchemy is waiting for you. Mortirmir, stay.'

The other students hurried out, many with heads bent to avoid catching the master's eye. He sometimes issued work at the end – massive lightning strikes of work, carefully or carelessly applied.

Mortirmir sat and fiddled with his paternoster until the last student left, and then rose as gracefully as his fast-growing body could manage and went to face the master.

The older man frowned. 'You have a brilliant mind,' he said. 'And you work harder than most of these louts.' He shrugged, and handed Mortirmir a rolled scroll. 'I'm sorry, young man. Sorry to twit you on your failings, and sorry to have to give you this.'

Mortirmir didn't even need to open it. 'Summons? From the Patriarch?'

The magister nodded, and left the classroom. As he opened the door, Mortirmir heard Baldesce's voice, and Zervas – another Morean student – say something – and they all laughed.

He had no way to know if they were talking about him, but he hated them all in that moment.

The summons in his hand meant that he would be tested one more time for powers, and if he could muster none, he'd be sent forth. He'd worked his whole life to come here.

And now, he'd failed.

Sometimes it can be very difficult to be a child prodigy.

Morgan Mortirmir was sixteen and growing so fast that none of his clothes fit properly. His face was so young that despite his size, he could, at times, easily pass for twelve. He was tall and thin, but not in the way that might have given him authority or dignity. He was gawky and, even worse, covered in adolescent acne that burst constantly into white-headed pustules all over his face, so that the Morean sisters in his Practical Philosophy class called him 'the Plague'.

And Morgan knew he was the Plague. He was too young to be at the school and worst of all – and for all his phenomenal intelligence – he lacked any ability to manipulate the world directly through *phantasmia* or even through alchemy. He had all the potential in the world.

He just couldn't get a grip on the raw stuff of power. He couldn't make *potentia* into *ops*.

But he was intelligent enough to know when he was not wanted. And no one in the great school of Higher Philosophy and Metaphysics wanted any part of him except as a scapegoat. They didn't want him to quote the authorities he'd memorised, or to explain to them the fine points of how the *aethereal* worked in terms of mathmaticka. They wanted him to wield power, or leave.

He sat in a small tavern in the greatest city in the civilised world and stared into a cup of wine.

After a while, he stared into another.

And then a third.

All day, every day, his magisters had thrust him into situations meant to unlock his powers. His ability to detect a casting – even the faintest emanations from Cravenfish, for example – earned him praise from the magisters. Every one of them agreed that he ought to have talent. His score on *potentia* was – phenomenal.

But they'd ceased to say it so loudly or so often. And today the Patriarch, who had to review each candidate for admission, and pass him as theologically reliable before granting a degree, had sent for him.

Sunday next.

Mortirmir bit his lip to keep from crying, but it didn't work and he wept. It was bitter, stupid self-pity, and he hated the sheer childishness of it even as he wept harder. The Patriarch would send him home.

Home wasn't even so bad. It simply represented the loss of everything he'd ever wanted. He wanted Liviapolis – magnificent women clad in glittering artifice talking about philosophy with men who wrote books rather than swung swords. Here, not barbaric Harndon, was where he belonged.

Or maybe not.

They didn't even send a girl to his table to pour his wine. He got a stale-faced old criminal with a leer. He waved for another.

'Pay first,' the man said, accenting his Archaic for the meanest understanding.

Mortirmir wore an Alban jupon, boots, and a sword. Hence he was a barbarian and had to be treated like a fool.

He looked down into the cup of dark red wine. Better wine, in fact, than he would ever have at home – a wine to which the wines of Alba were mere shadows of the true form.

He cursed. He had all the theories down pat. He just couldn't do the deed.

The Plague.

He'd had it as a child, or so they said – and the medical magister, who took the most interest in him, had said with terrible finality that the plague sometimes caused lesions on the brain that killed the ability to channel power.

He ordered a fourth cup of good wine and decided – again – to kill himself. It was a mortal sin and his soul would burn in hell for eternity. He thought that was fitting, because by doing so he'd *hurt God.* God who desired that sinners repent and come to him. *Take that, you fuck!*

It was a tribute to the duality of human nature as his philosophical masters taught it that on his fifth cup of wine he could see the terrible, stupid flaws in his own theology.

And then, of course, there won't be any more wine.

At which point the evening took a turn that surprised him.

A lovely young woman – older than him and more worldly, but well dressed and obviously prosperous, paused in front of his booth. She looked around nervously, then with more annoyance.

Drink bolstered him. He rose and bowed – feeling more graceful than usual. 'My lady? May I be of assistance?' he asked in his best High Archaic – which seemed even more fluid than usual. His greatest accomplishment at home in Harndon had been his ability to read and write the true High Archaic, and here even the criminals spoke it. In the Morea, it was their native tongue.

She turned, and her smile beamed like the light from a bullseye lantern. 'Ah, sir, my pardon.' She blushed. 'I am not used to speaking to a man in public,' she said, and her fan came up and covered her face, but not fast enough to cover the cavalry charge of colour that swept over her neck and—

He looked around. It was hours since he had walked in – he'd ignored the summons to evening prayer, and so had some of the other patrons, but his stomach suddenly suggested that he needed to temper his new-found hobby of drunkenness with some food. Even if he planned to jump off a bridge later. Falling on his sword was out – it was too long.

He found himself sitting again, rather like a dream. In some corner of his head, a voice said *I guess I'm pretty drunk.* He had, in fact, been drunk before – twice. But not like this.

'You could sit with me?' he said, as if it was the most natural thing in the world.

She peeped, with just her eyes, from behind her fan. 'Really, I couldn't,' she said. 'I'm waiting for my father – who is late – by the Virgin Parthenos, there is no place here for a lady to sit.'

He thought she was perhaps nineteen, but his experience of ladies – most especially of Morean ladies – was extremely limited. There were the nuns in his philosophical classes, but all of them wore full veils, and he knew nothing about them beyond their voices and the speed with which he annoyed them.

He couldn't tell whether she was beautiful or plain or ugly as wretched sin, but he already enjoyed her blush and her courtesy. 'Please – sit with me, and I will not trouble you,' he said. He stood up – wondering when he'd so rudely sat down. 'Sit here, and I will wander the room until your father comes—'

He suited action to word, and her fan shot out and pressed him back into his seat. 'You will do nothing so foolish, although your offer is gracious for a barbarian,' she said. She pushed him lightly and he was sitting again, and she was sitting, too.

It was like leafing through an illustrated Bible. He had to guess at the parts that were missing – when had she sat down? Had she been graceful?

'How do you come to be in our fair city?' she asked.

Mortirmir sighed. 'My mother sent me to University,' he said, with a little too much self-importance, he could tell.

'You must be very intelligent!' she said.

He smiled bitterly. 'Very intelligent,' he muttered.

The taverner was suddenly there – the old bastard was nearly spherical, with no hair on his head and he was pouring something from a pitcher, and the girl giggled and thanked him and the room spun a bit. 'I am,' he agreed. 'I'm so smart that...' He searched for something to say.

You are so smart that you answer every single question in any class even when you know it annoys your peers, so smart you don't understand humour, so smart that you can't talk to a girl, so smart you can't work the simplest phantasm.

She flicked her fan. 'Where is my father?' she asked rhetorically. The sober, analytical part of his mind noted that she didn't look around when she said it. He theorised that she was used to being waited on, and probably couldn't take care of herself. She smiled. 'Are you from a good family? And what is a good family, among barbarians?'

She was funny. He laughed. 'My father is a lord,' he said. 'Well – he was. Then he died. It is complicated.'

She sighed. 'What's complicated? I'm not in a hurry, especially not if you continue to serve me Candian wine and malmsey.' The fan flickered. It seemed to flick at a different rhythm, so that, although she ended hidden, he saw the whole of her face for a moment. He was thrilled.

I'm talking to a Morean noblewoman! he thought.

He tried to shrug off his excitement because he was determined on self-destruction. But few things interested him more than talking about himself, and wine did not inhibit him in any way. 'Well,' he said, 'I'm bastard born, but my father had no other children, so even though he never married my mother I'm probably his heir.' He sat back. 'He wasn't a great noble, but there's a castle and a town house in Harndon. My mother lives in the town house.' He shrugged.

The girl laughed. 'It sounds just like our court. You are not in the Church, I guess?'

He spread his hands. 'No – I'm a private scholar.' He said it with too much pride. He saw that she was amused and he resented her superiority and his own inability to make conversation without arrogance.

'And you are rich?' she asked. She poured more wine into his cup.

'Oh, no,' he said.

'In that case, she'll have nothing more to do with you,' said a deep, scratchy voice. The Morean noblewoman turned, and Morgan raised his head – surprised at the effort – to confront the palest blue eyes he'd ever seen, in a moon-shaped face as big as a soldier's breastplate. 'Eh, Anna?'

She whirled and spat, fan flying. 'Go away! You son of a mongrel dog and plague-stricken streetwalker, go swim in a sewer!'

Mortirmir rose unsteadily. 'Is this man—'

The giant beamed. 'Oh, Anna, only a crack as well travelled as your own is big enough for my member—'

Her fan slammed into his temple with the sound of lightning flashing close by. The giant didn't even flinch.

'—troubling you?' Mortirmir managed, unreasonably proud to have dragged the routine phrase out of his pickled noggin. He reached for his sword.

He wore a sword. He was much mocked for it at the University, because student philosophers didn't need swords, and by wearing one he made himself seem even more barbaric. But his failure to perform the least spell, the slightest *phantasm*, combined with a strong sense of adolescent stubbornness and some pride in his training at the art of arms left him with the most important sign of his noble status – in Alba – strapped to his side despite many warnings, some threats, and a great deal of ridicule.

He drew it.

The giant stepped away from the Morean lady and examined him with the kind of rigour usually given by the magisters to a corpse they were dissecting, when the religious authorities allowed such a thing.

'You seem to know how to draw that,' said the giant.

Mortirmir shrugged. 'Leave the lady alone,' he said.

The taverna had fallen silent. Every eye was on him, and he felt a fool – the more so as the giant was a head taller than he and would probably have his guts for garters, and he knew – with bitter remonstrance – that he was too stubborn to back down now.

'Whore,' said the giant. He shrugged. 'If you want to fight me – I like a fight. Outside, though. Inside, we'll be arrested.'

Mortirmir had never been called a whore before, but he knew it meant a fight. He wasn't walking too well, but the jolt of pure spirit that came to him as he rounded the table steadied him. With his left hand he reached ino his purse and scattered coins on the table – any gentleman would do as much.

That jolt of the spirit – was it fear? It was like the levin-power that the natural philosophy magisters produced out of the metal globes, and his fingers tingled.

The giant backed steadily away from him. 'Put the sword away, and we'll have a proper fight,' he said. 'If you insist on using it I'll probably kill you. *She's* a whore, younker. Wake up.'

Mortirmir had the sense, just, to slide the sword back into the scabbard, and he did it without much fumbling. He felt as if the giant nodded at him in approval. He looked back and saw that the Morean lady was scooping his coins off the table.

He took his time out in the yard, unbuckling his sword belt. The giant was huge. He sounded like a Nordikan, the foreigners that the Emperor kept for his bodyguard.

Dozens of men poured out of the taverna's open doors into the hot summer night, and a few women with them. The giant pulled his shirt over his head, revealing a body that seemed to be composed of sharply angled slabs of flesh-coloured rock. He had muscles on top of his muscles.

Mortirmir was wearing his best jupon, and he took it off carefully, folded it, and wished he had a friend to hold his purse. He wished, in fact, that he had a friend at all.

'I just want so say you're a brave little shit to take me on, and I intend to make you look good before I put you down,' the giant said. 'And you need to know that she's a prostitute, and even now she's watching your purse like a drunk watches a new vase of wine.' His Archaic had a strange accent. 'I like her – she's my favourite.' The huge man shrugged. 'I'd even share her with you if we were sword brothers.'

Mortirmir laughed. It was insane, but he was suddenly *released*. He was happy. His laugh rang out, and men betting in the doorway listened and bets changed a little – not much, but a little. He wanted death – no suicide required.

'I'm ready,' he said.

The big man bowed. 'Harald Derkensun,' he said. 'Of the Guard.'

Mortirmir returned the bow. 'Morgan Mortirmir,' he said. 'Of the University.'

At that, men in the crowd roared. The Academy was loved and hated in the city – a bastion of brilliance and a nest of heretics, all in one.

Mortirmir was not untrained. He began to move on his toes as his father's master-at-arms had taught him, and, with nothing to lose, his first attack was all-out. He stepped forward in mock hesitancy and kicked – hard – at his opponent's knee.

He connected – not with the giant's knee, but lower, and the giant hopped, off balance, and Morgan moved in, suddenly sober enough to do this, and landed a strong right with a right foot lunge, actually rocking the giant back half a step when he connected with the man's gut.

Mortirmir felt as if he'd punched a barn. But he changed feet and tried another kick—

And had to pick himself out of the manure heap. He'd missed the move that flung him a body length across the torchlit night, but while he was more odiferous for his fall he was uninjured, and he bounced back at his opponent, who seemed to be made of iron.

'That's one fall,' said the giant. 'Good kick. Very good, really.' The huge man grinned. 'In fact, I think we're going to have real fun. I thought I'd have to do both sides of this fight, but apparently—'

Mortirmir was thin and stringy, and his only real physical advantage was that his arms and legs were abnormally long. While the giant rattled on, he feinted another cross-body punch and kicked under it – caught the giant's arm as it shot forward defensively—

It was a near-perfect arm-lock... right until he was flying through the air again. This time, his buttocks hit the stable wall before he slid into the manure heap.

The pain was intense, and the laughter of the crowd lit him up like a lantern. He rolled off the manure, and ran at the big man.

Derkensun waited for him with stoic resignation, obviously disappointed with his adolescent rage. But just as he entered the giant's measure, Mortirmir swayed his hips, trusting to wine and luck, and then planted his foot and passed *under* the Nordikan's fight-ending blow, planted his leg firmly behind the bigger man's knee, put his head under the man's arm and threw him to the ground. It took an incredible wrenching of his body to do it – it was like throwing a house.

But Derkensun crashed to earth.

He was only there long enough to shout something, and then he rolled heels over head faster than such a big man had any right to do, and he was on his feet, rubbing his left shoulder. He grinned from ear to ear. 'Well struck, younker!' he roared. His left leg shot out and Mortirmir jumped it – more by luck than training.

Mortirmir was breathing like a bull. The giant was smiling.

'I guess that's not going to work again,' muttered Mortirmir.

The giant shook his head.

Mortirmir grinned. The sense of release was wonderful – the

physical exhilaration was a novelty. And the lightness of heart couldn't all be wine.

He stepped forward intending to feint a head punch, but he never got there. As soon as his weight shifted he was on the ground, gasping, and his back hurt.

The pain flowed into something in his head, and he rolled to his feet and grappled, perhaps the stupidest thing he could have done. The man was so large that he simply bent Mortirmir's hands back until he freed them of their lock, and then crossed his hands involuntarily. The ease of the giant's victory angered Mortirmir further, and he changed his stance and put his knee – quite viciously – into the other man's balls.

The Nordikan stumbled back, and Mortirmir kicked him hard in the middle of the gut – the man folded at the waist, and Mortirmir's right hand shot out—

The giant took it in one great paw, rolled to his left and threw the student like a trebuchet throws a stone.

Mortirmir hit the inn wall. He had time to think that he was surprised at the colour of the whole thing, and had to tell the magisters, and then . . .

'Damn Christ, you hurt me!' said a scratchy deep voice by his ear. 'But I never meant to hurt you so badly.' He felt something cold touch his head, and it hurt. But everything hurt.

'You are a very great fool,' purred a woman's voice.

'You're a big help,' said the scratchy voice.

'We could at least split his money. It is many months since you have been paid.'

'That would be dishonourable, and I would never do such a thing. Besides, when he recovers, we will be great friends. The witch woman has told me this.' The scratchy voice chuckled. 'If I didn't kill him. She said I might kill him. I tried to be careful, and then he hurt me and I lost it, as usual.'

Mortirmir tested his body, as if he was an experiment in school. His left leg moved, his left knee was full of pain, his right leg moved, his left arm moved, his left hand moved – his right hand and arm hurt like—

'*Holy* Saint Eustachios and all the venerated saints and martyrs!'

he ripped off. He sat up a little, and found that he was lying on a bed – quite a high bed.

'Holy mother of God he's awake!' The woman gave a scream and leaped from the floor, where she'd been lying naked. She had long legs and a muscular midsection and he had the impression of fine breasts high above a slightly bony ribcage and wonderful hips. The sight of her body rose above the pain of his broken hand and arm.

The giant leaned over the bed. 'You are alive! By the gods!'

Mortirmir had a pain in his head like a spike in his temple. He put his left hand to his forehead, and the whole right front of his head was spongy. 'Oh, my God, you've broken my skull.'

'Oh, I've had worse fighting with my brothers,' said the big man. 'There is a lot of blood,' he admitted.

Mortirmir forced his head back onto the pillow and the pain abated by the breadth of a hair. 'How long was I out?' he asked, trying to remember anything the medical magister had told him about head wounds.

'Almost a day – Anna? How long was he out?' cried the giant.

The woman spat something that sounded unkind. She appeared, pulling a gown over her head. Before her hair emerged, she spat, 'I suppose you don't care that I haven't eaten in two days, you Christ-cursed barbarian! And now I must be seen naked by *another* barbarian. And I'm sure you can't even pay me – Holy Mother, I open and shut for you for nothing and why? I have no idea, when you repel me so much! The ugliest man I've ever seen and I the very pearl of this city – the finest Hetaera – it's like a fine mare lying with a boar. Oh – I hate myself! Why do I do this? Perhaps it is punishment for my many sins – God curses me to rut with the very lowest form of life in the gutters. Perhaps next it will be a leper.'

Derkensun watched her with a small smile on his broad face. 'Are you finished?' he asked. 'I hate to interrupt.'

She slapped him as hard as she was able, cocking back her arm and her hand moving like the arm on a catapult. The slap echoed around the room and she clutched her hand as if the giant had struck it, when all he'd done was to stand perfectly still, a slight smile still curled comfortably in the corner of his mouth. He leaned forward very gradually, wrapped his arms around her, and kissed her. 'But,' he said slowly, 'I love you.'

'I will never come here again,' she said.

Derkensun laughed aloud. 'If you insist,' he said.

'I hate you!' she shrieked.

'Of course,' said the Nordikan.

When she was gone, the giant watched the door for a long moment, and then came back to his patient. 'Wine?' he asked.

'Never again,' Mortirmir said. There was something odd about his right hand. Flames seemed to lick at it. When he looked, there was nothing there but the warm sun coming in the room's single open window – it was still hot as hell – and falling on his hand and arm. But it felt pleasant, and it was a long chalk better than the pain. Mortirmir lay back.

His assailant came and brought him some nice water – bubbly from some underground spring. 'This will make you better. The witch woman says so. Listen – I have to go on guard. I'm on the gate of Ares today. I will be all week. I'll be back.'

Morgan nodded. 'I thought you Nordikans guarded the Emperor?' he asked.

Derkensun shrugged. 'Something must be up, for me to be on a gate. Now sleep.'

Mortirmir had the strangest sensation in his hands and his head – like flying, like finding he could read a new language. It was all—

He shrugged it off, waved at the Nordikan, and fell back into sleep.

Chapter Two

Aeskepiles

Liviapolis, the City – Aeskepiles and the Emperor

Aeskepiles, the Emperor's magister, preceded him through the reception halls of the palace with two of the axe-bearing Nordikan Guard. Their scarlet surcoats heavily embroidered in real gold showed their rank, and their great axes and heavy full-length chain proclaimed their roles. The man on the left had a scar that ran from his right eye to the left edge of his mouth and made him look like a daemon from hell. The man on the right had tattoos that ran from his brow to his neck and vanished into the hem of his fine linen shirt, just visible at the collar of his hauberk. Pages followed with their helmets, aventails and heavy riding spears.

The Emperor himself was unarmoured. He wore a purple velvet jupon over scarlet hose, and on his feet were the scarlet shoes that only he could wear. Every buckle on his shoes and belt, every lace point, every button was solid gold. Double-headed eagles were embroidered on his jupon and his shoes in gold thread as well. A page, one of the palace Ordinaries, held his great robe of purple silk embroidered with eagles and lined in tawny-gold fur.

Behind the Emperor were two more Nordikans, each with their pages, and a dozen more Ordinaries. Two carried a saddle, one carried a sword, and a pair of secretaries followed the Emperor closely, writing down his comments on the matters of state and domestic economy as read from a leather bound agenda by the Mayor of the Palace and the

Grand Chamberlain. The two men took turns to mention their issues. Behind them stood the Emperor's daughter, Irene, walking with the Logothete of the Drum, a slight man with the ascetic look of a monk.

'Item thirteen, Majesty. Arrears of pay among the palace staff and most especially the Guard.' The Mayor cleared his throat.

Emperor Andronicus had the blood of the Paleologs in his veins. He was widely accounted the handsomest man in the Empire, and perhaps the world, with darkly tanned skin and smooth blue-black hair, piercing dark eyes under arched and expressive brows, and a long, strong beard that was the envy even of the Nordikans who served him. A thousand years of breeding the most beautiful princes and princesses from all over the known world had mixed his skin to a perfect tone, and given his features the look of near perfect beauty usually saved for idealised immortals. He appeared to have been carved from old gold, or bronze.

His beauty was reflected in his daughter, who put her hand on the Logothete's arm, making the thin man flush and bow, and went to stand by her father. Irene resembled one of the pagan goddesses.

'Pay them, then,' he said, mildly.

The Mayor of the Palace bowed deeply. 'Imperator – we have no money.'

The Emperor nodded.

His daughter raised an eyebrow. 'Pater, we must find some,' she said. 'Unpaid soldiers are the bane of emperors and empires; they are to us as horseflies are to horses.'

The magister flicked a glance at the two killers who led the procession. The Guard's loyalty was legendary. But unpaid soldiers *were* the devil incarnate.

The magister had his own reasons to hate the Guard – not least of which was that they scared him. He schooled his features carefully, hiding his thoughts.

I am the greatest magister in the world, and I am trapped here in this fading, decadent court when I could be anywhere – I could be anything.

Hah! And I will be.

He caged his eyes and didn't look at the Emperor. Or at his co-conspirators.

'How many of this morning's questions hinge on money?' the Emperor asked.

The Grand Chamberlain chuckled. He was a large man – he looked like a bruiser, and his intellect was hidden behind his laughter. 'All questions turn on money,' he said. 'Except those about God.'

Any laughter was chilled by the Emperor's pained expression.

Irene turned her cold indifference on the Chamberlain. 'You presume too much,' she said.

They walked on in silence, their steps soft in the vast caverns of marble that were the outer halls of the Great Palace. Once, these halls had been packed with envoys and eager visitors. Above them, vast mosaics recorded the deeds of the Emperor's ancestors. There was Saint Aetius defeating the Wild in a battle that covered almost fifty paces of perfect mosaic tesserae. The polished stones glittered far above them, and the solid gold in the hilt of Aetius's sword gleamed like a rising sun in the near dark of early morning.

The Emperor paused and looked up at his distant ancestor, a thousand years before. The saint's gladius was stuck to the hilt in Amohkhan's breast, and the great daemon towered over him with a flint axe ready to fall. The torches of the Ordinaries at the back of their procession lit the scene fitfully, and the permanent breeze that passed through the halls of stone made the flames ripple and brought the scene to life.

'He murdered all of the old Emperor's family,' the Emperor said. 'Saint Aetius. He murdered Valens and his wife and all their children and grandchildren. He thought he would prevent civil war. Instead, he cut the head off the Empire.' He looked around him. 'He stopped the Wild at Galuns. But he destroyed the Empire. There's a lesson there.'

The Grand Chamberlain nodded sagely. The Mayor waited patiently.

Irene looked at her father with a slightly horrified expression. Aeskepiles caught it.

As soon as the Emperor started walking again, the Mayor said, 'So it seems to us, Majesty, that the solution is to implement some economies.'

The magister wanted to choke the life out of the Mayor. He glared at the man, who looked surprised – and hurt.

Why now? Today? Why not ten years ago – when we still controlled enough territory and enough taxes to rebuild? The magister's eye caught high above him in the tesserae of history. *The die is cast, indeed.*

The Emperor's eyes met the Mayor's. He nodded ruefully. 'I agree,' he said.

The two scribes wrote quickly on their wax tablets.

The Emperor held up his hand as if he'd had enough of business, which he probably had. He strode through the main doors of the outer hall, and found two Easterner servants waiting with a dozen horses.

The horses were tethered to the columns of the great portico. They looked incongruous, to say the least, and their fretting emphasised the emptiness of the massive courtyard and the two columned stoas that ran away into the distance.

'Perhaps we could invite the Etruscans to come and quarry our marble,' the Emperor said. He raised his too-perfect eyebrows. 'They own everything else.'

One of the scribes began to write. The other poked him.

An Easterner held the Emperor's stirrup and he mounted with the trained elegance of a skilled horseman. As soon as the white gelding felt the man on his back he stilled, and the Emperor backed the horse a few steps and accepted his robe for riding from an Ordinary. The morning air held a chill.

The Grand Chamberlain handed the Emperor his sword. 'Still time for me to get you a proper escort, Majesty.'

The Emperor shrugged. 'The Duke asked me to come without one. Is it time to start distrusting my officers?'

Aeskepiles hated him just then. Hated his feckless, useless optimism and his endless trust and good will.

The Emperor turned to his magister. 'You seem out of sorts this morning, scholar.'

'Your concern is gratifying, Majesty,' said the magister. 'I'm sure it is simply something I am having trouble digesting.'

The Emperor nodded. 'You have our permission to withdraw, if that seems best to you, my friend.'

The words 'my friend' struck Aeskepiles like a mace. He set his face. 'I'll manage,' he said in a harsh croak.

The Emperor looked at his daughter. 'And you, my child, seem bitten by the same fangs.'

The Princess Irene inclined her head in submission to her father. 'I *am* out of sorts,' she confessed. 'Pater, I am disturbed by a report—' She paused and the Emperor smiled benignly.

'My dear child,' he said. 'You are a princess of an ancient house and estate.'

She cast her eyes down.

At her movement, the Mayor and Chamberlain bowed deeply. Most of the servants fell on their faces. The effect was a little ruined by the steward, who unrolled a sheet of linen canvas and threw it on the ground before throwing himself on top of it.

The Emperor's daughter curtsied deep, so that her skirts spread about her like the blossoming of a silken flower.

'My dear!' the Emperor said. 'I thought you were coming with me.'

The magister had thought so, too.

'I'm most sorry, Majesty.' She remained in her full curtsey.

The magister thought *she must have magnificent legs to bear the strain. Why isn't she going with him? Does she suspect?*

The Emperor smiled beneficently at them all. 'See you at dinner,' he said, and put his heels to his mount.

Five miles away outside the walls of the city, Andronicus, the Duke of Thrake and the Emperor's cousin, was also a handsome man. He was in his mid-forties, wore his age with dignity, and while he had grey in his beard and on his chest, he clearly came from the same stock as the Emperor. He was dressed in plain blue, his favourite colour. He wore the knight's belt of an Alban – not an affectation, but the sign of his office as Megas Ducas, the commander of the Emperor's armies.

He waited for his Emperor on the Field of Ares, an enormous grass arena where sixty thousand men could be mustered. Had, in fact, been mustered, many times. He loved to be on the field – to feel the grass where Aetius might have walked – where Livia certainly walked. Where Basil II, Hammer of the Irks, had formed his great armies up and reviewed them.

Today, despite the snappish late spring weather, the sun shone on armour and colourful banners. The Duke had an army on the field – almost three thousand men. The field dwarfed them. They didn't make a brave display, but instead, seemed to suggest the opposite.

Andronicus reviewed them from habit. He always made sure the turnout was the best possible before his men were inspected by the Emperor. He rode along the front of the Latinikon – mostly Alban mercenaries, with a scattering of Galles and Etruscans.

He turned his horse and rode down a file. 'What's this man's name?' he asked in Archaic.

Ser Bescanon, an old and very tough Occitan from south of Alba who served as commander of the Latinikon, smiled. 'Ah, m'lord Duke, I'll see to this.'

The man in question had a mail hauberk and no more – no helmet, no body armour, and no shield. In fact, he had no saddle. He was sitting bareback on a warhorse.

The Duke leaned over and gave the animal a sharp poke. It backed a step.

'That is a cart horse,' he said.

'I believe Ser Raoul has had a disagreement with his landlord. His armour and horse are not, I think, currently available. I'll see to it he's ready for the next muster.'

'Dismiss him,' said the Duke.

The mercenary shook his head. 'Nah – m'lord, that would be hasty. We're not fighting anyone today – no? No need to make an example, mmm?'

The Duke raised his eyebrows.

Bescanon flinched from his gaze. 'As you wish. Ser Raoul, you are dismissed.'

Ser Raoul laughed. It was not a normal laugh. 'Pay me and I'll go, you useless sack of shit.'

The Duke backed his horse away from the man.

Bescanon nodded. 'My friend Raoul has a point, messire. None of us have been paid.' Bescanon smiled softly. 'In a very long time, messire.'

The Duke's son, Demetrius, Despot of the North, interposed his horse between the knight and his father. 'You'll be paid at the end of this parade. Ser Raoul, you are dismissed without pay. If you don't like it, I will have the skin stripped from your back and I'll sell your useless carcass into slavery.' The younger man's voice cut like a whip. He had the over-eager aggression of a young man who likes to throw his weight at obstacles.

Ser Raoul's breathing came very fast. His hair was wild – he was missing teeth and his nose had been broken many times. It was the bulbous red nose of a heavy drinker which suggested where his pay would go if he were given any.

He reached for his sword.

'Raoul!' Bescanon snapped 'Don't do it!'

Behind the Despot, two blank-faced Easterners had their horn bows at full draw. The Despot never went anywhere without his bodyguard of blood-sworn foreigners.

Horses' tails swished, and spring flies droned.

Raoul sighed. He reached behind himself and very carefully scratched his arse. Turned his horse. And rode off the grounds.

Half a mile to the east of Ser Raoul, Harald Derkensun stood tall in the sentry box at the gate of the city.

Nordikans almost *never* served as gate guards. They were far above such things. But the Logothete of the Drum had ordered that the gate guards be changed a week ago.

He had further ordered that the Nordikans stand guard in the plain tunics and cloaks of the City Militia.

Derkensun thought it was all foolishness. He was head and shoulders taller than almost any Morean and he suspected that every man passing the gate knew him for what he was, but that was the way with Morea. Wheels turned, sometimes inside wheels, and sometimes for no other reason than the turning. There were plots, and plots to cover plots, and some men, Derkensun had discovered, would plot merely to hear themselves talk.

This morning, however, the Logothete's precautions showed some sense, as Derkensun had enough experience of the palace to know that the party riding towards him was led by the Emperor. He drew his sword, and held it before his shield.

The Emperor reined in his horse. Just past him, Garald Gurnnison, the most dangerous man in the Guard, met his eye and gave a very slight nod.

The Emperor knew him immediately, of course. He knew all his guard. His fingers moved. He said, 'Good that you are on guard here. Be wary.' Then the Emperor returned Derkensun's salute. 'Guardsman Derkensun! Are you being punished for some transgression?'

Behind the Emperor, Derkensun saw the Logothete. The slim man raised an eyebrow. Derkensun allowed himself to look embarrassed. If the Emperor hadn't been told about the heightened security, it was not Guardsman Derkensun's job to inform him.

The Emperor laughed. 'Poor Nordikans. Too much discipline.' He raised his riding whip in token of farewell, and rode through the gate.

*

Ser Raoul was still scratching – mooning the Duke – when he passed the Emperor riding well out of the city without an escort. Out of habit he stopped scratching and bowed in the saddle. The Emperor gave him a little wave.

Behind them, the Despot turned to his father. 'Where are the Vardariotes?'

The pride of the household cavalry, the Vardariotes were Easterners from across the ocean, and further yet. They were a remnant of a bygone time, when the Empire ran from the steppes of Dacia across the sea all the way to the mountains of Alba and beyond. No Emperor had ridden the steppes in twenty generations, but young men and women still left their clans and came to the Emperor as their kin had done half a thousand years before. Like the Nordikans, they were loyal.

The Duke watched the Emperor approach. 'The Vardariotes were not interested in my muster,' he said mildly. 'So I ordered them to stay in their barracks.'

The Despot turned to his father. 'What are you doing?'

The Duke shrugged. 'Something that should have been done a long time ago.'

'Pater!'

The Duke whirled on his son as a tiger turns on wounded prey. 'It is *now*, you little fool. Comport yourself like my son, or die here with anyone who will not support me.'

The Despot looked for his bodyguard, and saw them fifty horse lengths away, surrounded by his father's household knights.

Father and son glared at each other.

'I'm doing this for *you*,' the Duke said softly.

The young despot met his father's eye and held it. His own eyes narrowed. He loosed a long sigh – and grinned.

'Then I want the Lady Irene. As my wife.' The Despot looked at the Emperor.

'Done,' said his father. That would have complications, but he was happy – truly happy – to have his son beside him.

The Despot shook his head. 'Why didn't you tell me?'

The Duke raised his hand. 'I didn't tell anyone. That's how you keep a secret.'

*

The magister watched them carefully as they rode up to the Duke. His men were well arrayed in ranks, their armour polished, and their pennons flapping in the late spring breeze.

Duke Andronicus's eyes met the magister's.

The magister rose in his stirrups, extended his wand, and blew the heads off two of the Emperor's guard. They continued to sit on their horses, headless, as he turned, pointed his wand at the two junior Nordikans and struck them – one with a massive *kinetikos* blow to the chest that shattered the man's ribs through his breastplate, and the other with a neat cut that opened his neck. He was showing off for his new master, and wanted the man to remember exactly what he could do.

The skill he couldn't display in the real was that every attack had to overcome the complex, layered, and in some cases quite brilliant artefactual defences that the Nordikans carried. The lead Spatharios, for example, had tattoos that should have defended him – which would have, against a lesser caster.

As far as Aeskepiles knew, no practitioner had ever succeeded in killing a member of the Guard by the art – much less four in ten heartbeats.

He allowed himself a moment of triumph, and took a dagger in the side as a result.

The Logothete.

The magister had never imagined him a man of blood. He produced a sword – quite a long one – from the air, and rode to the Emperor's side.

Aeskepiles raised a series of shining shields – too late, as the dagger's bite was deep and his side was growing cold. He could feel the poison on the blade.

It was like getting a test back in Academy and finding that he'd forgotten one small thing and, as a result, all his answers were invalid.

He knew counter-spells for poison. He just had to stop panicking for long enough to think of one . . .

The Despot saw the Logothete bury a slim dagger in the magister's side and draw a sword from the air. In the same breath, the Duke's household knights made for the Emperor's reins, and an unarmoured man sitting on a fine Eastern horse behind his father raised a light crossbow. He took a shot – and it went right past the Emperor.

The Logothete seemed to *flow* under the crossbow bolt. It should have been impossible.

His slim sword cut through a knight's vambrace – right through his wrist, so that the man's reaching hand dropped into the grass. The Logothete's back-cut took out another knight's eyes. He screamed.

The Emperor backed his horse – obviously uncertain what to do.

The Guardsman whose chest had been shattered by the showy sorcery was *not dead.* Somehow, he got his axe up – one-handed. His blow cleaved the helmet of another of the Duke's knights, spattering every man present with his brains.

The Logothete got his hand on the Emperor's bridle. He made a parry with his sword, turned the Emperor's horse—

—and the Despot's sword beheaded him. He had leaned out, horse already at a canter, and swung as hard as he could, afraid that the man had *phantasmal* protections. But the sword struck as it should have, and the Logothete's head, containing every scrap of every secret that the Emperor had, rolled away in the grass.

The Guardsman, drowning in his own blood, pitched from the saddle.

The Duke took the Emperor's reins.

The Emperor was looking at his Logothete's headless body. Tears welled in his eyes.

'Majesty, you are my prisoner,' said the Duke.

The Emperor's eyes met his. The contempt there was absolute.

'You have just killed the Empire,' he said.

Ser Raoul watched the taking of the Emperor from the edge of the Field of Ares, where rowan and quince grew wild. He'd seen the violence in the magister and in the Duke.

He shook his head. 'Son of God,' he said, and turned his cart horse towards the city gates.

He wanted to think it all through. He owed the fucking Emperor nothing – the catamite never paid him.

But he'd made a decision. He couldn't have said why, although a hankering to be more than a hedge knight with a placid cart horse might have played a role. By slamming his spurs into his mount he got it to something that might have been called a canter, and he rode for the gates.

At his back, he heard the Despot calling for his Easterners.

He turned to look back. Six of the little men on piebald horses had separated themselves from the mass and were coming after him. Their horses were no more than ponies, and they rode like centaurs.

He threw himself as low on his horse's neck as he could manage; he was halfway to the gate when his pursuers began to shoot.

The third arrow struck him squarely in the back. It hurt like hell but the mail must have taken some of the power off it, because he wasn't dead. The head had penetrated his back – he could feel it in every pace of his miserable horse.

A lifetime of tavern brawls had prepared him to bear pain, and he was an Iberian, and Iberians were famous for their ability to accept pain.

'Mother of God!' he spat.

Sometime in the next fifty paces, he was hit again.

Ser Raoul had not lived a good life. In fact, it was absolutely typical of his performance as a soldier and as a knight to appear at a routine muster without his horse or arms. He didn't pray, he didn't do penance, he scarcely ever practised at a pell or in a tiltyard. He was overweight, he drank too much, and he had an endless predilection for attractive young men that guaranteed that he could never hold on to a single copper coin.

Despite all this – or, just possibly, because of it – Raoul refused to fall off his horse despite being struck by a third arrow. It would be hard for anyone to explain how, exactly, he continued to ride for the gate, cursing all the way.

The Despot was laughing, watching his favourites track the man and hit him repeatedly. It was a lesson to every slovenly soldier, he hoped.

The tall, unarmoured man with the crossbow raised an eyebrow. 'I thought we planned to surprise the gates?' he said quietly. 'And capture the Logothete?'

The bad knight and his six pursuers were riding flat out along a quiet, morning road raising dust. His pursuers were still shooting at him.

The Duke reined in his mount, speechless with rage. His fist shot out and caught his son, who reeled away and almost fell from his horse.

The Duke spat. 'Idiot,' he said. 'Right. Attack.'

The unarmoured man shook his head. 'Too soon. None of our people are in place for another half an hour.'

The Duke whirled on him. 'You want to keep your place, spy?'

The unarmoured man met his master's eyes. 'I'll do what I can,' he said. 'But if we make a premature attack, we expose our agents and we will *fail.*'

'We will not,' said the Duke.

His spurs were drawing blood from the cart horse, which continued to rumble towards the gate.

The six Easterners were twenty horse lengths behind him and gaining. They were all shooting.

And laughing.

The outer walls of Liviapolis were as ancient as the palaces and the stoa – and just as well built. They towered three storeys high, smooth yellow fire-baked brick with decorations in red brick marking every storey; magnificent mosaics rose over every gate, and each tower – there was one every fifty paces – was capped with a red tile roof. The walls appeared impregnable. There were, in fact, two complete lines of walls.

Of course the gates were open. Wide open.

Which was more than Ser Raoul could say for his eyes, which were closing. It was as if he was looking at the gate, and it was drawing away, further and further down a long tunnel—

When he hit the ground he was already dead, and his horse shuffled to a halt, just a few paces short of the great gate.

The Easterners whooped with delight.

Derkensun was watching a pretty woman walk past while waiting for a Yahadut scholar in his little cap to cough up a passport. Derkensun did not, himself, care one way or another – the man didn't look dangerous – but while he was on the gate, rules were rules.

'My daughter warned me that this would happen,' said the scholar. He opened his leather bag and went through it. Again. 'Please, lord. It is a day's walk back to my village.'

Derkensun shook his head. 'I uphold the law,' he said.

The Yahadut nodded wearily. 'As do I.'

Derkensun saw a man riding for the gate from the Field of Ares. He was on a bad horse and riding hard.

There were men behind him.

As a Guardsman, Derkensun had participated in his share of stupid soldier pranks, and he knew one when he saw one. His attention went back to the scholar.

'Perhaps,' he said, with a little warmth, 'it is in your bedroll?'

The Yahadut were fanatics for cleanliness, and the scholar had a mattress stuffed with sheep's wool, and two thick wool blankets rolled on his back.

His face went through one of those engaging transformations that let Derkensun know he'd scored a hit.

'The blessings of the Lord be on your head!' The man put his blanket roll on the table and unlaced the thongs.

Something was very wrong at the edge of Derkensun's peripheral vision. He turned his head and took in the whole thing in one glance.

The man who fell from the horse was Ser Raoul Cadhut, an Iberian mercenary. They'd chewed on each other a few times in fights, but right now the Iberian knight had arrows in him, and half a dozen whooping Easterners were circling the corpse with arrows on the strings of their bows.

Knowing Raoul caused Derkensun to hesitate for one fleeting heartbeat, wondering if it was possible that the Iberian had got what was coming to him.

But even as he thought, he stepped back into his cupola and rang the alarm bell there. The shrill sound carried over the morning air.

He didn't draw his sword. He didn't reach for the great axe that leaned against the wall of his guard house inside the gate. Instead, he grabbed the scholar by the back of his gown and threw him into the city.

The Easterners were hesitating. One put an arrow into Ser Raoul's corpse. Another drew and aimed at Derkensun. He grinned.

Derkensun took another step, back inside his guard box, and pulled the big handle that held the iron catch on the huge gears that held the portcullis even as the arrow *thunked* home in the oak of his box. The chains holding the drum shrieked and the portcullis crashed down onto the granite lintel. The falling iron teeth powered a second drum that moved across the gatehouse from left to right while rotating rapidly against a powerful spring, and the great iron-studded oak doors began to move from their recessed silos. Less than ten heartbeats after he slapped the handle, the two huge oak doors crashed together and the bar fell into place across them.

The Yahadut's bedroll, and indeed the entire inspection table, were caught in the closing doors and crushed against the iron portcullis.

The pretty woman with the geese was frozen in shock and the scholar began to pick himself up.

Derkensun took his axe from the rack. He left his sentry box, noting half a dozen men – hard men – sitting under the olive tree in the Plataea, all staring at the gate.

He smiled. His axe rose and fell, and then he examined the edge, which was still sharp, despite having cut cleanly through the chain that would have allowed the porticullis to be raised.

The pretty goose girl was trying not to look at the soldiers.

When you are one of the Emperor's chosen Guard, you are trained to read bodies the way scholars read books. Derkensun walked boldly out of his gate, the axe casually over his shoulder, and towards the huddle under the olive tree.

One of the pock-faced hard men raised his empty hands. 'No trouble here, boss,' he said.

Derkensun smiled and nodded a polite greeting. 'I thought you'd want to know,' he said.

'Know what, Guardsman?' asked Pock Face. He was ugly. The garlic on his breath stank across ten feet which separated them.

'This gate is closed,' Derkensun said. 'I cut the chain. It will take a day to get it open.'

Pock Face looked at his companions thoughtfully. 'Reckon we ain't wanted here,' he said.

Derkensun nodded. 'I'll know you again,' he said. His Nordik grin said, quite clearly, *next time I'll just kill you.*

The sound of alarm bells spread through the great city like a fire driven by a wind. The Duke heard them, and watched the great machines that slammed the city gates in his face. He was a hundred horse lengths away. He cursed.

The Emperor sat on his beautiful Hati horse a few paces away. He shook his head in genuine sorrow.

'You! You brought us to this, you tragic abortion of a failure to rule!' The Duke vented twenty years of pent-up frustration on God's anointed representative. 'And now we'll have civil war! I should just kill you!' He whirled, drawing his sabre.

Ser Christos, the Duke's best knight, caught his lord's sword. 'We agreed not to kill him,' he said, his voice hushed.

The magister, Aeskepiles, had pushed the poison from his bloodstream, and now he was weak but back in the game. He cleared his throat. 'He should die. Now. Easier for us all,' he said.

The Emperor looked at his magister in something like shock. His pale, watery eyes met his would-be killer's eyes with a mild look, like that of a frustrated but benevolent parent watching a child. 'Do as you must,' he said. 'God has shown his will. You have failed to take the city.' He smiled. 'Kill me, and take on yourself the curse of God.'

'I have the whole of the rest of the country, thank you.' The Duke was recovering from his moment of temper. He looked back at the gates. He could see three of them from here, and all three were closed and barred, and white light had begun to reflect from mailed figures high on the walls. 'But I'll have the palace in an hour.'

'You have been foolish,' the Emperor said. 'Even now, all I require is your submission—'

Neither the Despot nor the Emperor saw the blow coming. The Duke was wearing a steel gauntlet and his fist struck the Emperor like a hammer and knocked him unconscious in a single blow.

Every man present flinched. Behind him, the magister heard a knight mutter, 'He struck the Emperor.'

And in the cogs and wheels of the magister's inner mind, he thought *just do it*. He projected his will—

Again, Ser Christos intervened. His horse seemed to slip out of his control. The stallion's head collided with the Emperor's mount, and both animals shied and the Emperor was trodden under the horse's hooves, but Duke Andronicus's face cleared and he shook himself.

Harald Derkensun watched the Duke strike the Emperor from the walls, fifty feet above the grass. He saw the Emperor collapse. He turned to his corporal, a giant with jet-black hair from Uighr, far to the north even of Nordika.

'Durn Blackhair, they have taken the Emperor,' he said. 'We are his sworn men.'

Blackhair nodded. 'If I send for horses—'

Derkensun shrugged. 'Someone needs to tell the palace. I'm not sure such a thing has ever happened before.' He looked again at the Emperor's purple-clad form lying in the dust. 'He may be dead. Then who is Emperor?'

Blackhair shook his head. 'I have no idea. Should we not ride to him and die at his side?'

The Emperor was being raised by many hands, and put across his horse. There were hundreds of mailed stradiotes coming in from the Field of Ares, and Easterners, and a large block of uniformed infantry carrying spears and bows.

'At least three thousand men there,' Derkensun said.

Blackhair tucked a thumb into his beard and pulled. 'Care to have a go?' he asked.

Derkensun smiled. 'No,' he said. 'I'm no coward, but the two of us aren't going to accomplish a fucking thing out there.'

Blackhair laughed. 'I'm not as mad as that. Very well. Fine job at the gate. Get your arse to the palace and see if you can get to the Mayor. You say the Logothete of the Drum was with the Emperor? And both of the Spatharioi?'

'He winked at me,' said Derkensun. 'And Spatharios Gurnnison nodded to me. I'd swear he knew which end was up.'

'So now we'll never be paid,' Darkhair said. 'Ja, Gurnnison put us on alert this morning, sure.' He looked out over the wall. 'You know I'm the senior corporal.'

Derkensun hadn't known that. 'So you are the new Spatharios,' he said.

'Fuck me,' Blackhair said. 'Get to the palace, now. And find someone to take rank over me. I'm too fond of wine and the song of the axe to give commands.'

Derkensun came down off the wall looking for a horse. Liviapolis was so big that a man needed a horse to cross it in a day; it was seven miles from the great gates to the gates to the palace, which was, of course, another fortress.

At the open, inner gate of the palace, the old Yahadut scholar sat, utterly disconsolate. Derkensun came to a stop by him and offered him a hand.

'Sorry, old man. But I had to close the gate. You'd have been killed.'

'I was almost killed anyway!' He raised his hands. 'Barbarian!'

Derkensun sighed. 'You know,' he began, and decided that the man was too shocked and too angry to argue with. He shouldered his axe and ran across the Plataea, looking for a horse.

He'd jogged across two neighbourhoods before he found a skinny mare between the poles of a knife-sharpener's cart. He ran straight up to the knife-sharpener, who had a set of kitchen knives on his little bench and had the wheel going so that sparks flew.

'I'm taking your horse,' Derkensun said. He smiled. 'In the name of the Emperor.'

The man rose from his spinning stone. 'Wait! I pay my tax – you can't—'

Derkensun had the horse out from between the poles in four buckles and two knots, one of which he cut through.

'I'll starve, you bastard!' shouted the knife-sharpener.

Derkensun shrugged and got on the mare's back. She was brisk enough – possibly not broken to riding. Her hooves clattered on the pavement, and the knife-sharpener was left behind, shouting imprecations.

He followed the ancient aqueducts over the hills that dominated the centre of the city – in fact, cresting the second hill, he rode past his own lodgings. The mare's knife-sharp back squashed his manhood painfully and he wished he could stop and get his saddle, but that would take time. He had no idea whether he needed to hurry or not – the city looked absolutely normal.

But it stuck in his head that Ser Raoul had died trying to bring word of whatever had happened. And they'd captured the Emperor. And the Logothete and the Spatharios had put the Guard on high alert.

He came down the last hill, and the mare, who was really quite young, began to labour, but her hooves continued to throw sparks from the streets, and the sound of his passage proceeded him, so women flattened themselves against arched buildings, and pulled their children close; men cursed him when he was far enough away not to hear.

The palace gates were closed.

The men on guard were Scholae. The Guard's inveterate rivals in brawls; and the household cavalry of native Moreans. He didn't know either of the men on the gate – both young Moreans with trimmed beards, aristocratic, and worried.

Nor was he entirely sure what to say.

He settled for Archaic dignity. 'I need to see the Mayor of the Palace. Failing that, your officer,' he said.

The two men shifted back and forth. Like most of the aristocratic scions in the Scholae they had probably never stood guard before. He leaned forward. 'Christos Pantokrator,' he said quietly.

The smaller one glowered at him. 'What?'

'It's today's password,' Derkensun said. He schooled himself not to roll his eyes or give away his contempt.

The two looked at each other.

'You *do* know the passwords?' Derkensun said. He dismounted, and in the process his axe switched hands, so that the head was under his right hand and the iron-shod butt was in his left.

'Stay back,' said the smaller one.

'I'll kill both of you if you don't give me the countersign immediately,' Derkensun said. He couldn't tell if they were fools or conspirators.

'Quarter guard!' bellowed the small man. And then, in a strained voice, 'Help!'

The taller of the two Scholae stood his ground and levelled his short, heavy spear. He looked intelligent. He was beautifully dressed in a fine Eastern kaftan and tall leather boots over his knees, tasseled in gold. Even for a courtier, he looked magnificent.

'Damn me,' he said, over his spear. 'It *is* the password, Guardsman. We were just put on duty – damn. It's – Caesar something. Caesar – Imperator.' He paused.

Derkensun relaxed his guard. 'That's right,' he said.

The taller man lowered his spear. 'I'm supposed to be getting married today,' he said. 'We were summoned to the palace half an hour ago.'

The smaller man exhaled. 'By our sweet saviour, I'll never fail to listen to the password again.' He looked behind him. 'Where's the fucking quarter guard?'

Derkensun stepped forward. 'I have no time,' he said. 'I give my word that it is a matter of the most urgency.'

The two men looked at each other a moment and the bridegroom nodded. 'He has the password,' he said.

They parted.

The bridegroom bowed. 'I'll escort you, Guardsman.'

Derkensun didn't pause to argue. He trotted through the gates and down the great courtyard, lined in marble stoas that stretched a long bowshot across the flagstones of the Emperor's Yard. It was liberally studded with statues portraying men and women who had given their lives for the Empire. Derkensun imagined Ser Raoul joining them, his cruel mouth set in marble with his drinker's nose above it.

He'd died well. Brilliantly, in fact.

They ran along the northern stoa and entered the palace through the little-used service gate which was closed but not locked, and there was no guard.

Bridegroom shook his head. 'We stationed a man here when the Chamberlain summoned us,' he said.

The gate led them into the palace over the main stable block, bypassing the Outer Court, where most of the business of running the palace was transacted – shipments of food and tradesmen and so on. Derkensun knew the palace blindfolded. Literally. Part of the Nordik Guard's training was to move about the palace with blindfolds on.

Even as he jogged across the great store room that was the upper storey of the stable block – with its hundreds of bags of grain, onions, garlic, oregano, and vats of olive oil – he tried to decide where he was going. The Mayor's office was off the stable block. Men referred to the Mayor as the Lord of the Outer Court, and it was more than a joke. But the Mayor of the Palace was not always a friend of the Guard.

He sighed and turned at the top of the storehouse steps.

'I'm ruining my clothes,' Bridegroom said.

'I don't need you,' Derkensun said.

'You're welcome, I'm sure,' said the panting man.

Derkensun leaped the last four steps and landed on the smooth flags of the stable floor, turned right, and ran past the Emperor's own mounts – sixteen stalls hung in purple, including two of the best warhorses in the world – and turned right again when he'd passed Bucephalus, the Emperor's favourite. The old horse raised its head as he ran by and out into the sun. The Mayor's office door was open and the outer office was empty, where there should have been three very busy scribes.

Far away, on the breeze that blew constantly through the main buildings of the palace, he could hear the unmistakable sound of men fighting.

Derkensun's eyes met the Scholae trooper's and he fleetingly considered hacking the other man down. Just to be sure. He had no doubt he could take him.

But the bridegroom's eyes were steady and without duplicity. 'I don't know either,' he said. 'But I'm for the Emperor and I know that something's wrong. Whatever you do, I'll back you.' He drew himself up. 'Unless you're a rebel. If you are, then let's get this over with.'

Derkensun grinned.

'Follow me,' he said.

It took them two long minutes to find the fighting.

By then, almost everyone was dead.

The Porphyrogenetrix, Irene, was curled in a corner, her long robes sodden with blood. She'd taken a blow at some point and two of her women stood over her with sharp scissors in hand, facing a dozen assailants.

The Mayor was dead. So was the Chamberlain. And so was the Scholae's quarter guard.

The princess's last defenders – besides the two women – were an unlikely pair. A monk and a bishop, one with a staff, the other with his crozier. Derkensun took them in instantly, as well as their assailants – who looked to him like palace Ordinaries with weapons.

They had more facial scars than real palace Ordinaries, though, who were selected for good looks among other qualities.

'For the Emperor!' he shouted, in Archaic, and began to kill.

His axe swept back and he cut down on a shocked assassin, shearing about a third of the man's head from the rest with an economy of effort and turning the blade in the air to cut through the shoulder of a second man as he turned. The man screamed as his right arm fell to the floor.

The Morean bishop pointed his crozier's tip and roared, 'In the name of God the Father!' and white light flashed. The monk brought his staff down on a swordsman's outstretched arms, breaking both of them.

In the far doorway, a tall man in mail raised a long sword. 'Take them, brothers!' he called. 'Kill the princess and the day is ours!'

Even as he spoke a hidden crossbowman put a bolt into the bishop's groin, and he went down screaming. The monk fell back a step and swung his staff two-handed. A swordsman tried to slip past him, and a grey-haired woman in silk plunged her long-bladed scissors into the assassin's unprotected back.

Derkensun cut twice, forward and back, and men fell back before him.

'Now the Guardsman,' said the mailed man, at the other side of the room. He raised his sword. 'And the women. Kill them all.'

The bridegroom threw his spear. He did so with an odd, hopping cast, not at all the way men learned to throw spears in the City Watch or the military. His spear was a short, broad-headed weapon almost like a boar-spear, and it went through the mailed man's armour like a hot knife through warm butter, dropping him. There was a flare of hermetical energy from the lead assassin and he got to one knee as the spear suddenly fell away from his body.

Derkensun killed another man and half-turned, having reached the monk. His axe turned a complicated pair of butterflies between his hands as he wove it in the complex pattern that the Guard learned to keep their wrists strong.

The assassins paused and the Bridegroom bellowed, 'On me, Scholae!'

Every man in the room could hear the pounding feet of the on-coming Guard.

The assassins broke and ran. Derkensun got one as he turned, and a crossbow bolt took off the lower half of his right ear as he made his cut. The monk parried two sword thrusts and made a mighty swing, but his assailant turned his staff on his side sword, pinked the monk's hand with a dagger in his off hand, and jumped back. He was as thin as a wraith and wore black, and Derkensun never saw his face – the man got through the gateway to the main audience chamber and ran in among the columns.

Bridegroom tackled another one, took a dagger in the side for it, and broke the man's arm in a wrestling lock. The desperate attacker stabbed him three more times.

The Scholae trooper fell atop his captive, and slammed the man's head into the tiles, knocking him unconscious.

The older woman – the one with blood on her shears – motioned the younger woman to stand behind her.

Derkensun met her eyes. 'The princess?' he asked.

The younger seamstress with the shears peeked out. Her face was a perfect oval, her lips full and red, her eyes an almost impossible blue.

The woman in the princess's garments kicked and gave a stifled scream on the floor.

'See to her,' snapped the younger seamstress. She nodded to her rescuers and the monk. 'Gentlemen, my thanks.' She backed away a step. 'Can *anyone* tell me what is happening?'

Derkensun recognised the older woman – one of the many minor members of the Imperial family who decorated the palace. The Lady Maria. Her son was one of Derkensun's favourite drinking companions – and wrestling opponents.

He bowed. 'Honoured Lady, the Duke of Thrake has captured or killed your father on the Field of Ares. The Logothete and the Spatharioi too.'

The young seamstress put her hand to her breast. 'Killed?' she said. Then she seemed to collect herself. 'Very well,' she said with determined calm. 'Do we hold the palace?' she asked.

Derkensun looked at the bridegroom, who was dusting himself off. He shrugged. 'Lady Irene, when I went on duty an hour ago the Scholae held all the portals.'

Derkensun turned to the princess. 'Who ordered the Scholae out, Honoured Lady?'

She pointed to the scarlet-clad corpse. 'The Mayor. Something the Logothete said.'

'Christ on the cross,' Derkensun said. 'We should ride clear, Honoured Lady.'

'Do not blaspheme in my presence,' Irene snapped. 'If we leave the palace, we will never get it back.' She glanced at Lady Maria, who nodded.

'Throne room,' she said. 'At the very least the Imperial purple will make a superior burial shroud.'

Derkensun took a moment to look at the bridegroom. He was unwounded; under his wedding clothes, he was wearing scale as fine as the scales on a big fish.

Derkensun made a face.

'I live in a tough neighbourhood,' the young man said, kneeling by the bishop, who had stopped screaming. The man was dead.

Together they dragged the bridegroom's unconscious prisoner with them as they made their way along the main audience hall and into the central throne room. There should have been six Nordik Guards on duty. Instead, there were the corpses of two Scholae.

The princess went straight to the throne. She paused, gathered her skirts, and sat.

Lady Maria gave her a slight nod.

Derkensun walked to the right-hand guard platform and stood at attention. It felt quite natural. The bridegroom went to the left platform.

The monk bowed and when Irene didn't offer him a stool, he stood. She looked around at them. 'Thoughts?' she asked.

Derkensun thought that she sounded composed, and a good deal sharper than the Emperor. In fact she sounded Imperial.

Maria looked at the two soldiers. 'We have the city?' asked the older lady.

Derkensun bowed his head. 'Madame, I sounded the gate alarm myself. But any gate may have been betrayed.'

'The army?' asked the princess. Or was she now the Empress? Her hesitation showed, despite her decisive air.

'The Vardariotes are in their barracks. Many of the Nordika...' Derkensun paused. 'Are dead.'

The bridegroom bowed in turn. 'I've seen the corpses of twenty Scholae,' he admitted.

'The Duke of Thrake has three thousand men, at least, outside the walls. Perhaps twice that.' Derkensun spoke carefully. He had only addressed the Emperor two or three times. This was the longest conversation he had ever had with royalty.

'And we have a few hundred,' said the princess. 'When it seems I need an army.'

The Lady Maria gave a curtsey. 'My lady, I happen to know where one can be found.' She gave a slight smile. 'Indeed, my lady, your father had already hired one. He sent my son to fetch them, if you recall.'

The Porphyrogenetrix Irene leaned back and sighed. 'More mercenaries? They've been the bane of our people for five hundred years,' she said. 'With what did my esteemed father intend to pay these sellswords?' she asked Maria.

'You,' Lady Maria said, offering another curtsey. 'Majesty,' she added.

'Ah,' said the princess. 'Yes, I remember.'

Part One
The Princess

Princess Irene

Chapter Three

The Red Knight

The Green Hills near Morea – The Red Knight

The Captain of the company stood almost alone in the dawn, watching the sun rise. He had one foot up on a solid stool, and his squire was buckling his leg armour on.

Toby was wise enough not to speak. So he simply went about his work; keyed the greave into the knee-cop's demi-greave, and then held the whole leg harness open to slide it on the knight's right leg.

The Captain was eating a sausage.

Toby fought the greave – it liked to close on the cloth of the Captain's padded chausse, and because they were newly laundered, they were stiff. The air was cool, almost cold – the leather was stiff, too.

Toby was above such concerns. He got the greave closed, got the lower buckle done, got the upper buckle cinched, and started on the various straps that would keep it on his master's leg all day.

The Captain finished his sausage, spat out a bit of skin, and laced the top of the harness to his arming doublet himself.

The sun appeared above the horizon – it seemed to leap up out of the east between two mountains, and the full light of the sun fell on him. Dark-haired, with a pointed beard and grey-green eyes, the morning sun made his hair almost blue and made his mail haubergeon shine and his red arming jacket scarlet.

Toby slapped the Captain's armoured thigh.

'Good,' said the Red Knight.

Toby went and got the breast and back – dented in a dozen places – from the rack and held it open while the Captain slipped into it. Even as he began to do the shoulder buckles, a dozen archers and camp servants took the twenty-four ropes of the Red Knight's pavilion in hand, loosened them, and had the whole thing down on the ground as fast as Toby could do the buckles. By the time the Captain flexed his arms, his tent was gone.

Behind them the whole camp was being struck. Rows of tents went down like pins on a bowling green. Wagons were loading at the head of every street. The pages were currying horses or leading them to the men-at-arms.

Men were pissing on fires.

The Captain watched it all, munching an apple, and he nodded at the thought. *Pissing on fires.*

Nell, his new page, appeared with his ugly warhorse. He didn't have a name for the brute – after riding one horse for four years, he was now killing a horse in every fight.

At a cost of a hundred florins a horse.

Still, he gave his apple core to the ugly brute, and the horse took it with more delicacy than his ill-bred head showed.

Nell stood nervously. Toby tried to motion her away – she was thirteen and no one knew why she'd been made the Captain's page except for Toby, who knew that horses loved her.

The Red Knight's gaze crossed hers. He raised an eyebrow. 'Yes?' he asked.

She flinched. 'Which – I don't know what to do.'

The Red Knight glanced at Toby and walked away, towards a small fire left for him by a servant.

'You don't talk to him,' Toby hissed. 'Christ almighty, girl! He'll turn you into something unnatural. Talk to me. Never to him.'

Mag handed him a cup of hippocras.

'Your usual cheerful self?' she asked.

He looked back at where Toby was gesticulating at Nell. 'I don't know why I'm saddled with the child care,' he said. Then he shrugged. 'Never mind me, Mag. Are we ready to march?'

The seamstress shrugged. 'Do I look like an officer? My wagon is packed, of that much I can assure you.' She paused. 'Except, of course, my tent and my daughter.'

The Red Knight smiled and drank her hippocras – the best in camp.

Bad Tom – six feet and some inches of unruly muscle and long black hair – appeared from the third to last tent still standing in the camp. In the doorway, Mag's daughter Sukey could be seen, as well as one attractive bare shoulder. Bad Tom was fully armed, cap-à-pied, and he gleamed in the new sun.

'I'm going to miss all yon,' he said. 'If I go to be a drover.'

Mag scowled at her daughter. 'If you are not quicker, my girl, the Captain will leave you behind!'

The Red Knight raised an eyebrow at his first lance. 'Are we ready to march?' he asked.

Bad Tom didn't even look around. 'Finish your wine, Captain. You said "matins" and it ain't rung yet.'

Seeing the two of them together seemed to act as a magnet. Ser Michael came first, fully armed. Ser Gavin was next, from the opposite direction, his great tawny warhorse held in his fist by the reins, and Ser Alison – Sauce – cantered up, already mounted.

'I don't even have to sound officer's call. Where's Gelfred?' the Captain asked.

The Forester was sent for. Nell could be seen running from wagon to wagon as if her life depended on it. She was very fast.

The Morean, Ser Alcaeus, came up with a hawk on his wrist and two small birds dangling from his belt, and he and Gavin began a quiet conversation about the bird.

The last three tents came down. The occupants of the final one, who had slept through every morning call and several volleys of orders, had cold water poured on them and were kicked. The Captain's new trumpeter, who fancied himself a gentleman, was one of them.

Cully, an archer, punched the young gentleman in the head.

There was cheering.

Gelfred came up on a pretty mare.

Sauce reached out and patted the horse on the head and then blew into its mouth. 'Sweet thing,' she said. 'What a pretty horse!'

Gelfred beamed at her.

The Red Knight drained his cup and tossed it to Sukey, who caught it.

'Everyone ready?' he asked.

'What's the plan?' asked Sauce.

The new trumpeter – soaked to the skin and with a swelling on the side of his head – came stumbling along the line of fires.

The Captain scratched under his beard. 'Gelfred is to ride for Liviapolis and find us a nice, defensible camp about a day's ride away. Two days' ride at most.'

They all nodded. Two days before, they had received word that the Emperor – their prospective employer – was missing. Liviapolis was his centre of power, one of the three largest cities in the world as well as being the home of the Patriarchate, one of the centres of the faith, and of the Academy, the very epicentre of the study of hermeticism.

Ser Alcaeus nodded. 'And then we attempt to learn what, exactly, has happened.'

Tom grunted. 'Sounds dull. Why the fucking Morea, anyway?'

The Red Knight looked over the hills to the east. 'Riches. Fame. Worldly power.'

'How are we going to deal with Middleburg?' Tom asked. The fortress city of Middleburg – the third largest in the Morea, after Liviapolis, widely known as 'The City', and Lonika, the capital of the north – was viewed as impregnable and sat astride their line of march east from the Inn of Dorling.

The Captain snorted. 'Kilkis, the locals call it. Only Alban merchants call it Middleburg.' He ate the last bite of his sausage. 'Friends have arranged our passage.' His eyes met Tom's. 'If we don't make trouble, the garrison there will let us pass.'

Gelfred winced. 'And fodder?' he asked.

'We're to meet with a party. It's dealt with, I tell you.' The Captain was impatient.'

Ser Gavin sighed. 'Easier getting in than getting out, if something goes wrong.'

The Captain glared at his brother. 'Your hesitation is noted.'

Gavin rolled his eyes. 'I only mean—'

Ser Alison – Sauce – put her hand on Gavin's shoulder and made him flinch. It was the shoulder that was now covered in fine green scales. Such things didn't trouble Sauce. 'When he's like this, there's no dissuading him,' she said.

'What about Wyverns?' asked Wilful Murder.

Gelfred laughed. 'Not a single one,' he said. 'If we fight, we'll face nothing but the hand of man.'

The archers all looked at each other. There was silence.

'Any other comments?' the Captain asked in a voice that should have stifled any such.

'I hear there's a princess,' said Sauce.

The Captain smiled crookedly. 'That's what I hear, too,' he drawled. 'Let's ride.'

Harndon – The Royal Court

The King sat comfortably in a great black oak chair, with a pair of wolf hounds at his dangling fingertips. Most of his attention was on two apprentices who were laying pieces of armour out on a heavy table in the corner of the great receiving room, under the Wyvern head he'd mounted there with his own name under it.

The King was tall, broad and blond, with a pointed beard and a thick moustache. He carried the weight of muscle required to fight in heavy harness, and his skin-tight scarlet jupon strained every time he leaned down to scratch Emma, his favourite wolfhound.

'If you'd taken the wolf, you little bastard, there'd be more meat for you, too,' he said to Loyal, his youngest male hound. He gave the dog a mock-cuff, and the young male looked at him with the kind of worship that dogs reserve for their masters.

The Master of the Staple cleared his throat politely.

The King looked up, and his eyes slid right off his Master of the Staple and went to the armour.

The Queen put her hand on the King's arm and breathed in. To say the Queen was beautiful would be to do her an injustice. She was beyond mere beauty. Her skin had a texture that made men want to touch it to see if it was real; the tops of her breasts, which showed over her tight-laced kirtle, shone as if they had been oiled, and drew the attention of every man in the room each time she moved despite the careful arrangement of her gown and her decorous carriage. Her red-brown hair was glorious in sunlight, and perhaps she had taken the time to site her chair in the best of the late afternoon sun – her salmon-pink overgown so perfectly complemented her hair that even men might have noticed it, if only they hadn't had so much else to admire.

The King's interest was instantly transferred from the armour to her. He smiled at her – beamed, even, and she flushed. 'These worthy men,' she said, 'are trying to tell you about the coinage, my dear.'

The King's ruddy face suggested he was suddenly interested in something much closer than the coinage. But he sighed and sat back, and stopped playing with his hounds. 'Say it again, Master,' he said.

The Master of the Staple was Ailwin Darkwood, and he was accounted to be the wealthiest man in Alba. He had purchased the wool staple from the King for three years – he owned the tax on wool. He also owned the most warehouses in the city, and the most ships at the docks. Despite the convention that merchants should be fat men with greedy eyes, he was tall and handsome with jet-black hair just beginning to grey and skin that had spent too many days at sea for perfection. He wore black wool hose and a black wool gown over a black wool doublet, and all his fittings – the rows of tiny buttons, the hilt of his dagger, the buckles on his belt – were of solid gold worked with red enamel. He had a pearl earring in his ear, with a ruby pendant like a drop of blood. It might have looked womanish on another man. On Ailwin Darkwood, it looked piratical. Which was apt enough, as the rumour was that his fortune had begun off the coast of Galle in a desperate sea fight.

With him were the Lord Mayor of Harndon, Ser Richard Smythe, and Master Random, whose coup with the grain wagons and boats in the late spring had catapulted him to the front rank of merchants in the city. He was missing a foot, despite which he seemed to smile all the time.

Master Ailwin smiled too, and nodded to the Queen. 'Your Grace, my wife often tells me I talk too much and too little to the point, so let me try to be brief.' He laid out on the table a dozen coins.

Behind him, the two apprentices finished laying out the armour and retired. Their master entered, bowed low to the throne, and stood decorously against the wall.

The King looked at the coins. 'Silver leopards and gold. Perhaps not our finest strikes – look how many times this one has been clipped!' He laughed. 'Sixty-four twenty-nine?' he said. 'My grandfather minted that before Chevin.'

'Just so,' muttered Master Random.

'And this one seems as fat as a ewe with a lamb in her belly,' the

King went on, picking up a heavy silver coin. His eyebrow shot up. 'Sixty-four sixty-three?' he asked. 'I haven't minted any new coins.'

Ailwin looked at his companions. 'It is not from Your Grace's mints,' he said.

'It's from Galle, or Hoek,' added the Lord Mayor.

The King frowned. 'King of Kings,' he said. 'Who dares counterfeit my coins?' Then he sat back. 'But it is solid enough. A fine coin. My father's likeness.' He spun it in the air.

'The King of Galle and the Count of Hoek are counterfeiting our coins,' Master Random said. 'Pardon me that I do not stand, Your Grace. I took a wound at Lissen Carrak.'

'Well I know it, Master Random, and you may always sit in my presence. Holding that door against all those wights – many a belted knight would have failed – aye, and more would give their left hands to have done it! Eh?' The King's eyes sparkled. He began to rise. 'That puts me in mind – I meant to—'

His wife's hand dragged him back into his seat.

'The King of Galle and the Count of Hoek are counterfeiting Your Grace's coins,' Master Random said again.

The King shrugged. 'So? They are fine coins.' He looked at the merchants. 'They are princes, not highwaymen. If they choose to make coins like ours—'

The Queen pressed his hand.

'Master Pye!' called the King.

The Master Armourer stood against the wall – short and stocky, as one would expect of a smith, with a long grey beard and clear grey eyes. He straightened and bowed. 'Your Grace?'

The Queen leaned forward. 'Your Grace needs to attend these worthy men.'

'I am attending, sweet,' said the King. He smiled at her, and then went back to his beloved Master Pye. 'Pye, unriddle me this – why is it such a mischief?' He sat back. 'I'm too simple. Money is money. Either we have enough, or we don't. I gather that we don't? Is that the root of the trouble?'

'The Captal de Ruth,' announced the herald.

Master Ailwin winced at the man's arrival.

'If you need more money,' Jean de Vrailly said, 'tax these men harder. It is a shame that any member of the lower orders dresses like this popinjay. Take all the gold fittings from his belt – that will teach him not to dress this way in public. In Galle we order things better.'

'Yes, well, Captal, in Alba we do not, and we reckon our kingdom stronger for it.' The King waved the Captal to a seat. 'Now be a good fellow and give me some room, here. These fellows are stretching my wits.'

'As I was saying—' Master Pye began. He went and stood by the coins, and Master Ailwin gave him a grateful glance.

'The King of Galle—' said de Vrailly.

The King turned the full force of his glare on the Victor of Lissen. 'Master Pye is speaking, sir.'

De Vrailly turned and stared out the window like a pouting basilisk.

'So,' said Master Pye. He tossed a much-abused silver leopard on the table and it rang like a faery's laugh. Then he tossed a fat silver leopard on the table, and it made a rude clank. He shrugged. 'More tin than silver,' he said. 'The word I hear is that the Count of Hoek and the King of Galle are attacking our coins.'

'You lie!' said de Vrailly. He was in full armour – the only armoured man in the room.

Master Pye looked him over carefully. 'That right pauldron must catch on your mail,' he observed, after a moment.

De Vrailly paused.

The Queen thought that she had never seen the Gallish knight so utterly taken aback.

De Vrailly cleared his throat. 'It does,' he admitted. 'Master Pye, you cannot attack the honour of the King of Galle in my presence—'

Master Pye didn't flinch. He looked back at the King. 'That's what I hear, Your Grace. It stands to reason – our wool is pushing theirs out the market. They don't have the kind of laws we do to support our cloth, because small men have no voice there.' His eyes flicked to the armoured man. 'So when their crafts fail, their kings must raise money by devaluing the coinage. It is like an attack.' He raised a hand to forestall the King and de Vrailly too. 'But our coinage is solid – your father made sure of that. Mmm? So everyone in the Dix Ports trades in our coin and that is our defence. They devalue their coinage, we don't, and so our trade is strong. So what have they done?' He took a deep breath, aware that the King was finally listening. 'They've counterfeited our coins but with less bullion. Right? Now they beat us in two ways: they supply their devalued coins for exchange, which makes traders believe our coins are worth less; and they most likely take our true coinage and melt it down.' He tossed the little, much clipped leopard again. 'And our coin is old, Your Grace. It's old and tired, much clipped and so lighter, but still pure silver. They've lost some of their value anyway.' He looked at Master Ailwin. 'How was that?'

'It's brilliant,' said the King. His voice was no longer bantering, but hard. 'How much has this hurt us?'

Ailwin shook his head. 'I think we all thought it was just the events of the spring, at first. But then Master Random started to chart the falling silver content and what we've lost from it.'

'How much?' asked the King.

'A hundred thousand leopards,' said Master Random.

There was silence.

'All Your Grace's revenues are down, and when people pay their taxes using these debased coins, we have even less money than we expected,' Master Ailwin said.

'Good lord, I'd rather face a charge of trolls,' complained the King. For a moment he put his face in his hands. 'What do we do?'

The Lord Mayor looked at the carefully laid-out new armour on the side table. Each piece was mostly finished, but there were no buckles or hinges yet, and in place of decoration there were careful lines in white paint.

'Cancel the tournament, for starters,' said the Lord Mayor. 'It's going to cost what the war cost, and we don't have it.'

The Queen put a hand to her throat.

The King looked at Master Pye. 'Surely we can do better than that,' he said.

Master Random raised a hand. 'I hate to see a tourney cancelled,' he said. 'Instead, why not reopen the mint and issue new coinage? Strike some copper while we're at it, and we'll hold the balances for a while.' He looked at Master Pye. 'Pye has the skills to make the dies – I know he does. We could issue copper exactly to size and weight with the Imperial coinage out of Liviapolis, and have the thanks of every merchant and farmer west of the mountains.'

Pye rolled his eyes. 'I make armour. We need to find a goldsmith.'

Master Random shook his head. 'No – saving Your Grace, we need a loyal man who is absolutely trustworthy, and that's you, Master Pye. The King's friend. Your name behind the coins will—' He looked sheepish as he realised that he was implying that men might not trust the King.

But the King had leaped to his feet. 'Well spoken,' he said. 'By God, Random, if all my merchants were like you, I'd have a corps of merchant-knights. At least I can understand you. Let it be done – Master Pye, reopen the mint and coin us some coins.'

'Commons will have to approve it,' said the Lord Mayor. But then he shrugged. 'O' course the commons asked us to bring this to council in the first place, so they'll approve.'

'Why does my cousin the King of Galle attack my coins?' asked the King. 'Much less the Count of Hoek?'

Every man present turned and looked at de Vrailly. He crossed his arms. 'This is absurd,' he said. He looked around. 'If you are short of funds, why not collect from those who owe? I hear your Earl of Towbray is very much in arrears.'

The Lord Mayor smiled. 'Great nobles are not great tax payers,' he allowed. 'Who can collect from them?'

'I can,' said de Vrailly.

Ailwin Darkwood looked at the Gallish knight with something like respect. 'If you could, my lord, this kingdom would be in your debt,' he said.

'Towbray's taxes alone would pay for the tourney,' allowed the Lord Mayor. 'And any of the northern lords' taxes would cover the cost of the war. The Earl of Westwall alone owes more taxes than all the Harndon merchants would generate in ten years. But he never pays.'

The Count of the Borders, hitherto silent, nodded. 'But it would take another war to persuade Muriens to pay his tax,' he said.

The King leaned forward. 'Gentlemen, you are on dangerous ground here. My father gave the Earl certain tax concessions for maintaining a heavy garrison in the north.'

Rebecca Almspend had sat throught the meeting in silence. Small, dark, and pretty, in a detached and somewhat *aethereal* way, she, in the Queen's words, looked like a beautiful mouse and dressed like one too.

She was not the Chancellor, but through the Queen she had access to all of that worthy man's papers. The Bishop of Lorica had died at the great battle and had not yet been replaced. Lady Almspend rattled two scrolls together and spoke in a very small voice.

'The Earl of Westwall's subjects still owe a number of taxes. None has been paid,' she looked up, 'since Your Grace's coronation.'

The Count of the Borders sat back. 'He hides behind your sister, Your Grace.'

The Captal nodded, his helmet moving heavily, more like a horse's head than a man's. 'Towbray is closer, but a campaign in the Northern Mountains would suit me very well.' The Captal, who was not known for his smiles, beamed at the thought. 'What adventure!'

'There!' said the King, obviously delighted. 'Master Pye is to be master of our mint, and the Captal shall collect taxes in Jarsay with a royal commission and a strong retinue. And I shall send a strongly worded letter to my sister's husband, suggesting that he might be next. Done! Now, before I forget – Random? Can you kneel?'

Master Random smiled, gritted his teeth, and got down on his knees. 'I pray Your Grace's mercy,' he said.

The King reached out to his new squire, young Galahad d'Acre. 'Sword!'

Galahad presented the King's sword, hilt first. It was very plain, and the gold that had once decorated the cross-guard was mostly worn off. It did have the finger joint of Saint John the Baptist set in the hilt, and it was said that no man who bore the sword could ever be poisoned.

The King drew, and the blade whistled through the air to settle like a wasp on the shoulder of Gerald Random, merchant adventurer.

'Rise, Ser Gerald,' said the King. 'No one deserves the buffet more than you. I insist you take the head of a wight as your arms. And I intend to charge you to be the master of this tournament we are planning; find the money, and account for it to the Chancellor.'

Ser Gerald rose like a man with two feet, and bowed. 'I would be delighted, Your Grace,' he said. 'But you'll need a Chancellor for me to account to.'

'Now that the Count here is Constable, I can't have him acting as Chancellor, too. And Lady Almspend cannot continue to fill the role.' The King smiled at her. 'A woman as Chancellor?' He looked at her, and for a moment, his intelligence outshone his indolence. 'Not that you haven't been the best Chancellor I've known, my lady. But it's not talent I need, but someone with enough interest in Parliament to make my laws and my coinage and my wars run smoothly.'

The Captal looked around. 'Your Grace, if—'

'Let's have Master Ailwin, then,' said Master Pye.

'A commoner fulfilling the highest office of the land?' asked the Captal. 'Who would trust him? He'd most likely steal money.'

'As a foreigner, the King's champion is no doubt unaware that the last Bishop of Lorica was born a commoner,' the Queen said, her voice light but her eyes steady. 'Captal, by now you must be aware that such statements give offence to Albans.'

The Captal shrugged, his shoulder armour rising and falling to show the strength of his shoulders and back. 'They should challenge me over it, then. Otherwise—' he favoured them with his most beatific smile '—I assume they all agree.'

As always, Jean de Vrailly's statements brought silence – in this case a stunned one as men sought to understand. *Did he just say what I think he said?*

'As this has become an impromptu meeting of the King's Grace and his private council – may I say a word?' asked the Count of the Borders. 'There are many ways in which the north has not returned to normal since the fighting in the spring. Ser John Crayford reports that the woods are full of boglins, and worse.'

The King nodded. He smiled at his Queen.

She smiled back, but nodded graciously to the Count. 'It is important to replace all the crown officers who were slain,' she said. 'Lorica needs a new bishop. His presence at our council is much missed.'

The King nodded. 'He was a good man. A fine knight.' He looked around. 'He was with us for as long as I can remember – like old Harmodius.' He looked around. 'My pater appointed him.'

De Vrailly's head shot back. 'A king, no matter how favoured by God, cannot just appoint a bishop!'

The King shrugged. 'Jean, perhaps I have the wrong of it.'

The Count of the Borders shook his head. 'Captal, our king holds the right to appoint his own bishops under the approval of the Patriarch in Liviapolis.'

De Vrailly sighed. 'The Patriarch is no doubt a worthy man, but not the rightful heir of Peter.'

Every Alban present either bridled at the words or settled his weight in boredom. The habit of Arles, Etrusca, Calle and Iberia had been to turn religious squabbles into open conflict – the investiture of bishops and the primacy of the Patriarch of Rhum were two particularly sore points. By virtue of distance and isolation, the Nova Terra was immune to such conflicts 'Perhaps—' The King grinned. 'Perhaps we might find a candidate agreeable to both worthy fathers, and thus make all men happy.' His eyes twinkled. 'Would that not be the wisdom of Solomon?'

Master Ailwin's eyes met those of the newly minted Ser Gerald.

Ser Gerald bowed from his seat. 'Your Grace – that might seem like sense, but you are abrogating a royal prerogative and asking two men who rarely even recognise each other's existence to reconcile.' He looked around, ignored a grunt from the Captal and shrugged. 'Lorica and the north need a bishop now.'

The King smiled into his wife's eyes. 'I'll look into it. Appoint a committee. Captal – you seem to know so much of religion. Will you manage this?'

'I'd be delighted, Your Grace,' said the knight, bowing with a clash.

The King whispered to his wife, and stood. 'That's enough business for one afternoon, gentles.'

The pages bustled about and the room emptied, leaving Ailwin and two servants with Gerald Random and Master Pye.

'That was well said. The Bishop of Lorica was the friend of the little man.' Pye shook his head.

'I fear the Captal will find us a Gallish candidate,' Ailwin said.

Random shrugged. 'We got the mint. We won't get the bishop. This is the life of court.' He got to his feet and tottered into the hall supported between two servants.

The Captal was there already, attended by a pair of his omnipresent squires and his new lieutenant, fresh from Galle – the Sieur de Rohan. All three were big men in full armour.

'This is the King's notion of a knight,' Rohan said, as Random passed.

He stopped. Turned his head, and smiled agreeably at the King's champion and his friend. 'Do you mean that as an insult, Ser?' he asked.

'Take it as you will,' Rohan tossed off.

Random hobbled forward and put his face in the younger man's face, very close. 'You mean, you are *afraid* to tell me what you really think?'

The Sieur de Rohan flushed. 'I mean that it is not my way to converse with a lowborn of no consequence.'

Random reached up and none too gently pulled the man's beard. 'I think you are just afraid.' He laughed. 'Come and issue me a cartel, when I'm whole. Or shut up and go home.' He smiled at the Captal. 'I hope I've made myself clear.'

The Sieur reached for his dagger.

The Captal caught his wrist. 'Ser Gerald lost a foot in a feat of arms that any of us would envy,' he said. 'You will restrain yourself.'

'I'll kill him!' Rohan said.

Gaston d'Eu materialised out of a side room and placed himself between Rohan and Random, who was standing his ground. He bowed to Random. Random returned his bow and hobbled away.

'We're in for some hard times,' he said to Master Pye.

Ten Leagues North of Albinkirk – Ser John Crayford

Ser John was not dressed in armour.

In fact, he lay on the bank of a small stream dressed in hose so old that the knees had layers of patches, and a cote he'd bought from a peasant farmer ten years before. It was a nameless colour a little lighter than the fur of a barn mouse, and very warm in the late summer sunlight.

Rain had fallen in the night, and there were drops of water caught in the streamside ferns. They caught fire in the rising sun, like tiny, magnificent jewels burning with hermetical fire against the early morning transparent black of the stream that rolled slowly by.

In his right hand he had a rod four paces long, and from it dangled a horsehair line half again as long, and at the end was a hook with a tuft of feathers. He moved cautiously, like a man hunting deer – or something more dangerous. His eyes remained on the wonder of the water-jewels caught in the ferns and he watched them, his heart overflowing, for as long as the effect lasted – a few dozen heartbeats.

And then they became mere drops of water again as the sun's inexorable rise changed the angle of light, and he moved over the low ridge at the edge of the stream, saw the rock that marked his spot, and his wrist moved, as delicate as a sword cut and as skilled, and his fly sailed back, over his head – he felt the change in tension as his line loaded – and he flicked his rod forward. The line unrolled as if from a drum, and his fly settled on the still black water with the delicacy of a faery harvesting souls.

Even as he released the breath he hadn't known he was holding, a leviathan exploded from the deeps in a deep green and rainbow-coloured explosion of power, seized its prey and fled for the depths—

Ser John stood straighter and lifted the tip of his rod, sinking his hook home.

The trout resisted the tug, fled, and then leaped clear of the water. Ser John turned the fish over, trying to keep it from putting its full weight on the braided horsehair. He felt the weight gather and stepped to the right, the way he would if facing a deadlier adversary, taking the fish off line and turning it slightly so that it couldn't get a firm purchase on the water with its fins. It tipped onto its side – and he pulled.

In a moment he had the fish on the bank – in another he'd pinned it with his left foot, and then he drew his roundel dagger and slammed the flat disc of the pommel into the back of the fish's head, killing it instantly.

Whistling, he extracted the precious fish hook – the work of a master smith – and checked his horsehair line for splits or frays before drawing another knife from the strap of his pouch. He slit the trout from anus to gills, stripped its guts out with his thumb, and tossed them into the stream.

Before they could sink, something with a large green beak snapped them down into the depths, and was gone.

Ser John's hand went to his sword hilt. It was fewer than sixty days since he'd cleared the last irks from the fields south of Albinkirk, and the new settlers were only now starting to arrive. He was still jumpy.

Just a snapping turtle, he reassured himself.

But as the sun rose over the edge of the wild, it occurred to Ser John that the snapping turtle, the otter, the beaver – and the trout – were as much creatures of the Wild as the irk, the boggle, or the troll.

He laughed at himself, put his first fish of the day into his net bag and staked it in the stream – carefully, so that he'd know if a snapping turtle was intending to take the fish. He had a spear. If he had to, he could kill the turtle.

'I love the Wild,' he said aloud.

And cast again.

*

The Manor of Middlehill had never been a great one, and the whole was held for the service of a single knight, and had been for ninety years. Helewise Cuthbert stood by the ruins of her gatehouse and her tongue pushed against her teeth in her effort not to weep, while her young daughter stood closer than she had stood in many years.

The Knights of Saint Thomas said that it was safe to return to their homes in the north, and had paid them well in tools and seed to return. Helewise looked at her manor house, and it looked like the skull of a recently killed man – the stone black from fire, the once emerald-green yard strewn with refuse that had once been their tapestries and linens. The windows, purchased with glass from Harndon, a matter of great family pride, were smashed, and the great oak door was lying flat, with a small thorn growing through its little lattice window.

Behind her stood twenty more women. Every one of them was a widow. Their men had died defending Albinkirk – or failing to defend it, or the smaller towns to the south and west of Albinkirk – Hawkshead and Kentmere and Southford and the Sawreys.

They gave a collective sigh that was close to keening.

Helewise settled her face, and gathered her pack. She smiled at her daughter, who smiled back with all the solid cheerfulness of age nineteen.

'No time like the present,' Helewise said. 'It's the work you don't start that never gets done.'

Phillippa, her daughter, gave the roll of her head that was the dread of many a mother. 'As you say, Momma,' she managed.

Her mother turned. 'Would you rather give it up?' she asked. 'A year's work, or two, and we'll be back on our feet. Or we can go be poor relations to the Cuthberts in Lorica, and you'll become someone's spinster aunt.'

Phillippa looked at her feet. They were quite pretty, as feet go, and the laces on her shoes had neat bronze points that glittered when she walked. She smiled at her feet. 'I don't think I'd like that much,' she said, thinking of some of the boys in Lorica. 'And we're here now. So let's get to work.'

The next hours were almost as bad as the hours in which they'd fled, while old Ser Hubert rallied the men of the farm to fight the tide of boggles. Phillippa remembered him a sour old man who couldn't even flirt, but he'd waded into the monsters with an axe and held the road. She remembered looking back and watching him as the axe rose and fell.

Her views on what might be useful in a man had undergone what her mother would call a 'profound change'.

Jenny Rose, one of the few girls her own age, found the first bodies, and she didn't scream. These women's screams were about spent. But other women gathered around her and patted her hands, and old crone Gwyn gave her a cup of elderberry wine, and then they all began to pull the pile of bones and gristle apart. The boggles went onto a pile to burn. The others—

They were husbands and brothers and sons. And, in two cases, daughters. They'd all been eaten – flensed clean. In some ways, that made the task easier. Phillippa hated clearing dead mice out of traps – so squishy, still warm. This wasn't as bad, even though they were the bones of people she'd known. At least one set of bones belonged to a boy she'd kissed, and a little more.

Stripped of their flesh, they all looked the same.

They found a second pile of the dead later in the day, in the apple orchard. By then, Phillippa was more hardened to it. Or so she thought, until Mary Rose spat and said, 'These is *midden heaps*.' She spat again, not in contempt, but in her effort not to retch.

Phillippa and Mary and Jenny were the youngest women, so the three of them were given most of the heavy work. They were all pretty fair at using the shovels, and Phillippa was learning to cut with the axe, although using it raised calluses on her hands that would not please the boys in Lorica. If she ever went back to Lorica.

When the sun was past midday, her mother rang the bell – the monsters didn't steal the really valuable things, the way reivers and skinners would do. So she went down the hill from the apple orchard. There was an intact rain-barrel under the eaves of the manor house, and she washed her hands.

Jenny Rose smiled. 'You have nice hands, Phillippa.'

Phillippa smiled. 'Thanks, Jen. Though I'm afraid they're going to get worse before they get better.'

Mary Rose paused to dip her own hands. 'What were the boys like in Lorica?' she asked, bold as brass.

'Mary Rose!' said her sister.

'Much like boys everywhere, I expect,' said a new voice.

Standing by the corner of the house was a tall, slim woman in a nun's black habit with the cross of Saint Thomas on it. She smiled at the girls. 'Handsome, funny, angry, preening, stupid, vain, and wonderful,' the nun continued. 'Are you Phillippa? Your mother was worried.'

The three girls curtsied together. Jenny and Mary made a stiff obeisance, the kind that the village priest taught you. Phillippa sank down, back straight and legs apparently boneless. 'Sister?' she asked.

The nun had a beautiful smile. 'Come,' she said.

Jenny whispered, 'Teach me to do that.'

Supper was ham and cheese and good bread that must have come from the fortress with the nun. The mill at Gracwaite cross was a burned-out ruin, and none of the towns around Albinkirk had had bread – fresh bread – in weeks.

There was a fine palfrey in the yard, and a mule.

The nun was a curiosity – neither particularly well bred, nor ill-bred. She was somehow too *robust* to be a noblewoman – her brown hair was rich but unruly, her lips were a little too lush, and her eyes had more of command than languor. But Phillippa admired her immensely.

The nun had a tonic effect on the gathered women. She seemed oblivious to the shadow over all of them, and she had brought seeds for late planting. The mule was to stay as a plough animal until the fortress sent oxen.

'I gather that you have found quite a few dead,' she said. She said it quite plainly, without the embellishment of false sentiment.

'Almost all the men,' Helewise noted. 'We haven't found Ser Hubert. I'd expect to know him. He had his brigandine on.'

'I saw him fighting,' Phillippa said, without meaning to. 'I saw his axe. I never liked him. I wasn't nice to him.' Her voice cracked. 'He died for us.'

The nun nodded. 'Hard times change us all, in ways that are far beyond our little knowledge,' she said. 'They teach us things about ourselves.' She frowned.

Then she looked up. 'Let us pray,' she said. When she was done, they ate in relative silence. And when she'd finished her share, the nun rose. 'When we've washed up, let's go bury the dead and say the service,' she said.

Phillippa, who had never been a great one for religion, was surprised by how moved she was by the nun's quiet prayers, her open-faced plea to heaven for the souls of the departed, and by her homily – on how deeply they'd all been touched, and how they must trust in God.

When the nun was finished, she smiled and kissed each woman on both cheeks. Then she walked to the pile of dead boggles. They didn't smell, but they didn't rot as men do – their leathery hides and the heavy cartilage of their 'shells' took time to return to the soil.

'God made the Wild, as surely as he made Man,' said the nun. 'Although these were our enemies, we pray you take them to you.'

The nun raised her face to heaven, closed her eyes, and made the sign of the cross; the entire pile turned to sand.

Twenty women lost the ability to breathe for a moment.

The nun turned to Helewise. 'The afternoon is yet young. Now, about the seed?'

Ser John had fished for too long.

He caught and killed more than ten pounds of trout – perhaps much than ten pounds – and the fishing was superb, at least in part because most of the other fishermen were dead. He didn't want to stop, but as the sun began to sink in the west he made himself pull his line off the water. He was a mile downstream from where he'd started – a mile from his horse, and, he suddenly realised, a mile from his spear.

Feeling more foolish than afraid, he plucked his harvest from the water and started back along the bank. The late summer sunlight was still strong and red, and the Wild had seldom looked less threatening but Ser John was too old in the ways of the Wild to be fooled by it, though. He moved quickly, making as little noise as he could.

He'd travelled a quarter of the distance back to his horse when something alerted him – a movement, perhaps, or a sound. He froze, and then, very slowly, lowered himself to the ground.

He lay still for a long time, watching, and the sun's angle steepened. Then he rose and began to stride rapidly along the trail. Every stream like this one had a trail along its bank – men made them, and so did the Wild. They shared the trails.

When he was just a bowshot from his horse, he climbed a tree to have a look. There were no carrion birds but there was a persistent rustling away to the south, and twice he heard the distant crash of a large animal moving too quickly for stealth. And darkness was just an hour away.

He swung down from the tree, cursing his shoulder muscles, his age, and how much all this was going to hurt the following day – but he paused to pluck his bag of fish from the ground by the tree.

To his immense relief – he hadn't even known how worried he had been – his horse was merely nervous, not boggle-food. He saddled the big riding horse – a failed warhorse – and fetched his heavy spear from the crotch of a forked tree where he'd left it at sunrise.

'I'm an idiot,' he said aloud. Calm again.

The Wild's army was beaten, but the woods were still full of danger. He had been very foolish to leave his horse. He stood with it, calming it.

He got one foot in the stirrup, powered into the saddle, and turned for home.

Two hundred feet in front of him, a young doe bolted from the trees into the meadow. She was too young to be cautious, and she turned towards him, never seeing the man or the horse.

Behind her, a dozen boggles burst from the wood line. One stride into the clearing, the lead creature paused – a slim dark figure against the light, and it took Ser John a moment to register what he was seeing. The boggle had a throw-stick.

The spear left the throw-stick as fast as an arrow and the missile took the little doe in her hindquarters. She tumbled, fell, and blood sprayed. But terror and wild determination fuelled her, and she rose and drove forward – right at the knight.

Between his knees he could feel his horse's nerves. Old Jack had failed as a warhorse because he shied at the tilt – and had done so over and over.

'Always another chance to excel,' muttered Ser John, and he lowered the spear point.

The doe saw the horse and tried to turn, but her limbs failed her and she fell sprawling, and the boggles were on her.

Ser John put the spurs to his horse, and the gelding leaped out from beneath the old tree.

The doe screamed. One of the boggles already had her open and was dragging her guts out while another sank his four-way hinged mouth into her haunch. But the boggle with the throw-stick had a long knife. The thing made a keening noise, and wrenched his throwing spear from the dying deer.

Ser John didn't have time to ride him down, and he didn't fancy facing the throwing spear without armour, so he rose in his stirrups and threw his own spear – a cloth yard of steel at the end of six feet of ash. It wasn't a clean throw but it caught the boggle in the head as it pin-wheeled through the air, and the thing shrieked.

Ser John drew his sword.

His horse put its head down as he rode straight at the doe's carcass.

I'm avenging a dead deer, for Christ's sake, he thought and then he was reining in, and four of them were dead. The one he'd knocked down with his hastily thrown spear was bubbling as the little things did when they were broken, their liquid innards emerging through rents in the carapace as if under pressure.

There was one missing.

The horse shied. It all but threw him with a sidestep and a kick – he whirled his head and saw the creature, covered in ordure, emerge from *within* the doe's guts, exploding up in a spray of blood and muscle tissue. But its claws went for the man.

The horse kicked it – rear left, rear right. Ser John managed to keep his seat as the terrified horse then trampled the boggle which had been kicked clear of the carcass and lay in the dust of the old road.

Ser John let the horse kick. It made both of them feel better.

Then he checked his fish.

Afternoon was tending to evening and the nun was in the kitchen with Phillippa's mother. Phillippa went there to help – as darkness fell, the cleanliness of the manor house chimney and the kitchen chimney had taken on paramount importance, and Helewise and the nun agreed between them to delay dinner a little longer.

There were birds' nests in the chimneys, and raccoons in the chimney pots. Phillippa thought the task was better than finding more corpses, and she pitched in with a will, climbing the roof slates in the last light with Jenny Rose and shooing the raccoons out with a broom. They didn't want to go – they looked at her over their shoulders as if to say 'We just want a nice bit of chicken, and can't we all be friends?'

She caught the flicker of movement away off to the north, and held out a filthy hand to Jenny Rose. 'Shush!' she said.

'Shush yourself!' Jenny said, but then she saw Phillippa's face and froze.

'Hoof beats,' they both said together.

'Can I light the fire, dear?' called her mother.

'Yes, and there's someone coming!' she shouted back, her voice a little higher pitched than it needed to be.

The nun was out the kitchen door in a moment, standing with her hands on her hips in the last real light. She turned all the way around, very slowly. Then she looked up at the roof. 'What do you see, Phillippa?' she asked.

Phillippa made herself do just what the nun had done. She turned slowly, balanced on the peak of the roof.

Jenny said, 'Oh!' and pointed. By the stream to the west of them, there was a flicker of light – beautiful pink light, and then another.

'Faeries!' said Jenny.

'Blessed Virgin Mary,' said Phillippa, who crossed herself.

'Faeries!' she shouted down to the nun. 'By the creek!'

The nun raised her arms and made a sign.

The sound of hoof beats grew closer.

The faeries moved gracefully along the streambed. Phillippa had seen faeries before, but she loved them, even though they were a sign of the dominance of the Wild and it was supposedly a sin to admire them. But combined with the sound of galloping hooves, they seemed more sinister.

The sun passed behind the ridge to the west.

Almost instantly the temperature fell, and darkness was close. Phillippa shivered in nothing but her shift and kirtle.

Steel glittered on the road, and the hoof beats were close now. The horse was tired, but the man rode well. He was very old, and had wild grey hair flowing out behind him, but his back was straight and his seat was solid. He was dressed like a peasant, yet he wore a long sword. She had spent the summer among men who went armed. He had a spear in his hand, too.

He reined up for a moment at the ruins of their gatehouse, stood in his stirrups, and then said something to his mount. The horse responded with a last effort, and the man passed out of sight only to reappear walking under the two old oaks on the drive.

The nun held up a hand. 'The sele of the day to you, messire,' she said in a clear voice.

The old man reined up at the edge of what had once been the yard. 'Greetings, fair sister. I had no thought that the resettlement had come this far. Indeed, I passed this way this morning and I'd wager there was no one here.'

The nun smiled. 'Neither there was, good knight.'

'*Ma belle*, you speak most courteously. Is there a bed here for an old man with an old horse?' He bowed to her from horseback. It was fun to watch them from the roof, unobserved. Phillippa gave them both high marks for courtesy – they spoke like the people in the songs of chivalry that she loved. And *not* like the stupid boys in Lorica, who were all sullen swearwords.

'We cannot give you as fair a hostel as we could in times past, Ser John,' her mother said, emerging into the door yard.

'Helewise Cuthbert, as I live and breathe!' said the old man. 'What are you doing here?'

'It's my house, I believe,' her mother said with some of her characteristic asperity.

'Christ on the cross,' said Ser John. 'Be careful. I killed three brace of boggles five miles back on the road.' He grinned. 'But I'm that glad to see you, lass. How's Pippa?'

Phillippa hadn't allowed her mother to call her Pippa in years, and while she had an idea who this man must be she couldn't remember seeing him before.

'Well enough, for her age. You'll want a cup of wine,' her mother said. 'You'd be welcome here.'

He dismounted like a younger man, kicking his feet clear of his stirrups and leaping to the ground – an effect he spoiled slightly by putting a hand in the small of his back. 'Is this to be a religious house?' he asked the nun.

The young nun smiled. 'No, ser knight. But I'm a-visiting; I'm to ride abroad to every new resettlement north of Southford.'

Ser John nodded and then caught both of her mother's hands. 'I thought you would be gone to Lorica,' he said.

She reached her face up to his and kissed him. 'I couldn't stay there and be a poor relation when I have a home here,' she replied.

Ser John stepped away from her mother, smiling. He looked away from her and then back, smiled again, and then bowed to the nun. 'I'm Ser John Crayford, the Captain of Albinkirk. Yester e'en, I'd have said "ride and be of good cheer", but I'm none too pleased with my little boggle encounter this evening. Which puts me in mind that I'd be in your debt for a rag and some olive oil.'

Phillippa was fascinated by the whole scene. Her mother was . . . odd. She'd *tossed her hair* like a young girl – it was down because she'd been working. And the old man was *old* but he had something about him, something difficult to define. Something that the boys in Lorica did not have.

'I'll fetch you a rag, John, but please stay. We're all women here.' Her mother's voice sounded odd, too.

'Helewise, don't tell me I've stumbled on the castle of maidens. I'm not nearly young enough to enjoy it.' The knight laughed.

Old Gwyn cackled. 'Hardly a maiden here, old man,' she said.

Phillippa was appalled to see the nun giggle. Nuns, in her experience, were strict, dour women who didn't laugh. Especially not at jokes that involved *sex*, even in the most harmless way.

The nun finished her laugh and she and the knight met each other's eyes. 'I can handle myself on the road,' she said.

'By Saint George, you are the Bonne Soeur Sauvage!' he said. 'Sister Amicia?'

She curtsied. 'The very same.'

He laughed. 'Sweet wounds of the risen Christ, Helewise, you don't need me here. This good sister has probably slain more boggles than all the knights west of the Albin.' He smiled at the nun. 'I have a package for you, back in the Donjon. I'll send it on to you.'

'A package?' she asked.

He shrugged. 'Arrived a month ago, by messenger from the east. Sent from the Inn of Dorling.'

She flushed.

The knight went on, 'At any rate, if you plan to ride my roads, I'd appreciate knowing what you find. The Wild is still out there – closer, I would say, than they were a year ago. These ladies are lucky to have you, *ma soeur*. They won't need me!'

Phillippa wanted her dinner, so she and Jenny Rose swarmed down the ladder to the ground and they missed Mistress Helewise saying, very softly, 'Some of us need you, ser knight.'

Ticondaga Castle on the Wall – The Earl of the Westwall and Ghause Muriens

She looked into her silver mirror for far too long.

And sighed.

Her blond hair remained as nearly white-gold as artifice and *phantasm* could make it, and it fell down her back to the rise of the swell in her buttocks. Her breasts were full and firm, the envy of women half her age.

What do I care? she thought. *I am so much more than the sum of my breasts and the length of my legs. I am me!*

But she cared deeply. She wanted to be all that she was *and* continue to beguile any man she wanted.

She picked up a fur-lined robe. The morning chill was rising, the fires weren't lit, and a rash of goose-bumps was not going to enhance her beauty. Nor was a bad cough.

She pulled the robe around her and, on impulse, cupped her breasts with her hands, and heard the movement—

'Not now, you fool!' she hissed at her husband, the Earl, but he had the neck of her gown in his hand, lifted her effortlessly and threw her on the bed, pinned her to it with a strong hand and shrugged out of his own heavy robe.

'I'm— Stop!' she said, as his weight came atop her.

He put his mouth over hers.

She writhed under him. 'You oaf! I'm rising! Can't you knock?'

'If you will preen that marvellous body of yours in front of an open door, you get what you deserve,' he breathed into her ear.

His feet were cold – he never would wear slippers. But his insistence had its own charm – his strong hands had many skills – and when his knee went to part hers, she locked his arm and rolled him over like a wrestler, and sat on his chest – leaned back and caught his prick with her hand, and he groaned.

She flicked him with a practised nail and impaled herself, and his eyes widened to have their roles so quickly reversed. He took her breasts in his hands. 'Happy birthday, you faithless bitch,' he growled into her throat.

'What did you get me, you great fool?' she asked as he sought to throw her over and get atop her again. She caught an arm and kept him pinned, and threw her hair over his face so he couldn't see. She was laughing – he was laughing, but he got one of his iron-hard arms across her back, ran it down and down, and she moaned—

—and then he was atop her, grinning like the beast he was. But he kept his hand under her, and raised her – with one hand – cradling her on his hand as they rutted so that all the muscles in her back were stretched. She locked her legs over the back of his knees and bit his shoulder as hard as she could, her teeth drawing blood. His nails bit into her back. She wriggled, clenched her knees on his sides, and moved her head – he leaned forward to fasten his mouth on her left breast—

They fell off the bed slowly, the bed-hangings holding their weight for three long heartbeats and then tearing – she caught the floor under her right foot and then she was atop him and *his* back was to the cold stone floor, *his* head was lifted to hers. He tasted the blood on her lips, and she tasted her own salt—

There was a moment when they merged with the Wild. She flooded him with *potentia*. His back arched so hard that she almost came off him.

And then they were done.

'Christ and his saints, bitch, you nigh broke my head,' he said.

She licked his lips. 'I *own* you,' she said. 'I rode you like a horse. A big warhorse.'

He smacked her naked arse hard enough to draw a cry. 'I came to tell you there's a letter,' he said. 'But there you were cupping your boobies with your hands and you looked good enough to eat.' He passed a hand over his left shoulder and it came away bloody, and he laughed. 'Jesus wept, it's me who got ate. How to you do it, you witch? Yer as old as a crone, and I want no other.'

'Fifty today,' she said. She ran her hand over his shoulder and put a tiny working into it and it closed.

He stood and ran a hand up her leg from the bottom and she purred.

'The letter will wait,' he growled, pushing her backwards.

'Aren't you too old for this sort of thing?' she asked.

An hour later, they sat on heavy chairs in the castle's Great Hall. She wore a heavy gown of blue wool as fine as velvet, spangled with gold stars embroidered by her ladies, and he wore the blue and yellow livery of the Muriens in Morean satin. They were of an age, and he had more grey than dark brown in his hair and beard. He looked like a rapacious eagle, and she looked like the eagle's mate. Their eyes met often, and their hands touched constantly, two people who'd just made love and couldn't quite let go.

Ticondaga was one of the great castles of Alba – the key to the Wall, the strongest rock against the Wild. Rising four hundred feet above the forest floor, commanding a bay on the lake with access to the Great River, Ticondaga was reckoned impregnable by Man and Wild alike. But the cold granite walls sixty feet high, the massive gatehouse, the three concentric rings of walls and the gargantuan donjon, the lower floor carved from the living rock of the mountain, while militarily magnificent, made the living uncomfortable most of the year and downright harsh in mid-winter. Late summer was merely cold in the morning. Everyone wore wool at Ticondaga.

The Great Hall seated the entire garrison for meals – sixty knights and four hundred soldiers and their wives, paramours, lemans, or whores. It was the Earl's view that seeing his men eat three times a day kept them loyal, and thirty-five years in the saddle of the greatest and most dangerous demesne in Alba hadn't changed his views. So breakfast was served to almost five hundred people – porridge, tea, scones and clotted cream and preserves and cider. When he had noble visitors, he'd serve fancier foods, but the Earl of the Westwall liked plain food in massive quantities, and he was famous as far away as Galle as a generous lord. His people *ate well*.

Once there had been six great castles on the Wall, and six lords in the north. Before that, they had been legates of a distant emperor. In the distant past, when the stones of the hall's foundations were new, the Empress herself had sat in this hall.

Times had changed, and the Earl's ancestors had sought dominion over the north, on both sides of the Wall. More, as the Wall mouldered it lost its value as either fortification or boundary. In the last hundred years, the Muriens had built their lordship at the expense of the Southern Huran across the river and the lordships to the east and west who were nominally allies and near relations.

The Earl himself had completed the job, vanquishing the Orleys in a series of pitched battles in the woods and a climactic siege of Saint Jean, once the mightiest fortress on the Wall. Young and full of vigour, sorcerously aided by his wife, the Earl had toppled the Orleys, taken Saint Jean and razed it; throwing the bodies of each and every Orley, their children, their women, and their servants into the blaze. It was a victory so total that the old King hadn't bothered to declare him forfeit, and the young King was his wife's brother and not inclined to make trouble. The old King had fought the great fight at Chevins with no help from the Muriens and died soon after, and the young King had never attempted to make his writ felt in the north.

For a while, there were the usual rumours that an Orley heir survived. Murien laughed at them in scorn and ploughed their monuments and their peasants alike under the rocky soil. As his sons grew to manhood, no one challenged his primacy as Lord of the North.

Lady Ghause stretched like a cat, showing a fine length of stocking that made her mate growl again. She ate her way through a small pile of scones and licked raspberry jam off the spoon with a curl of her tongue and then ran her eyes over him.

'Stop it, witch! I've work to do.' He laughed.

'There was talk of a letter?' she asked. 'Work? The Cock of the North? You do no work.'

'The Huran have a feud dividing their clans – they're close to war. The Sossag grow stronger and the Huran weaker, and that's my business. I've a rumour of Moreans among—'

Ghause took another scone. 'The Moreans always have men among the Huran. It stands to reason – they share that part of the Wall.'

'Woman, if you eat that many scones every morning you'll have thighs like the pillars of this hall.' He laughed at her appetite.

'Churl, if you were as fit as I the scullery maids would more willingly jump into your bed,' she said.

'The way their swains jump into yours, bitch?' the Earl spat.

'I find that older trees have harder wood,' she said, and he almost choked on his cider. He shook his head.

'Why do I love you, you selfish, vain sorceress?'

She shrugged. 'I think you like a challenge,' she said, and motioned to her third son, Aneas, who waited below the dais for her orders. He was her favourite son – absolutely obedient, charming, a fine jouster, a decent bard.

'Yes, Mother?'

'It's time we fostered this lanky by-blow,' the Earl said. 'By the virgin, he's too old to wait on our table. Let's send him to Towbray.'

'You said all Towbray's sons were lechers and sodomites,' his wife said sweetly.

The Earl poured a dollop of Wild honey onto a piece of heavily buttered new bread and ate it messily, getting the honey on his beard and hands. She could smell the latent *ops* in the honey. 'I did. That Michael – what a little hellion! Ran away! If my son did that—' He shrugged. Paused.

Her lovely violet eyes narrowed. 'Your son did do that, you fool,' she said cattishly.

He frowned. 'You tax me too hard, madam.' He half rose. 'Was he mine? Are any of them mine?' he muttered.

She leaned back. Her eyes held his pinned. 'The fourth one has a little of your look – and your piggish tastes.' She shrugged.

He laughed again and slapped his thigh. 'By God, madame.'

'By the Enemy, you mean.'

'I'll have no part in all your blasphemy,' he said. 'Here's the messenger, and the letter. It's from Gavin.'

A message from her second son was reason for interest. She pulled her robe closed, leaving just enough flesh on display to keep the Earl – and every other man in the first three rows of tables – looking, and then she crooked a finger at the stranger, a handsome man, middle-aged, in a plain red jupon and high black boots.

'What news of the southlands, messire?' asked the Earl. He was interested to see his son had access to a royal messenger. The boy must be in high favour.

The man bowed. 'I was fifteen days through the mountains, my lord Earl. Have you had word of the fighting in the south?'

The Earl nodded. 'Ten days ago I had another messenger, but well ere that the Abbess sent me from Lissen Carrak. I know that a strong force of Sossag passed the Wall well to the west – beyond my patrols, I fear.'

'Ser Gavin sent me from the Ings of the Dorring to tell you that news, and to tell you that the sorcerer Thorn was driven from the field at Lissen Carrak. Ser Gavin thinks he retreated to the north. Several of his friends – who have the fey – felt the same.'

'Thorn?' asked the Earl.

'Shush, naming calls,' said the lady, suddenly all business. 'I'll look for him later. He was once Richard Plangere. Back when we were billing and cooing.'

Her husband raised an eyebrow – they'd gone well beyond billing and cooing in their first fifteen minutes alone together, some twenty years before.

'It's an expression,' she said.

The messenger looked as if he was trying to vanish into the flagstone floor.

'How is my son?' she asked.

'He does nobly!' said the messenger. 'He won much renown in the battle. He was wounded in the great battle on the fells, and then again fighting boggles beneath the castle.'

'Ah? And how was he wounded?' she asked mildly.

'He took a great wound, but the Magister Harmodius—'

'The faker. Posturer. Yes?' The lady's eyes seemed to glow.

'Lord Harmodius healed him – although there were, er, complications.' The messenger held out a scroll tube.

'Old charlatan. And how fares my dear friend the Abbess of Lissen?' she asked. She leaned forward and her gown fell open a little.

The messenger licked his lips and raised his eyes to hers. 'She died. In the fighting.'

'Sophia is dead?' Ghause asked. She leaned back, and looked at the ceiling, thirty feet above her. 'Well, well. That is news.'

The Earl took the scroll. He opened it, read a few words, and slammed the bone scroll tube into the arm of his throne so hard it smashed. 'Son of a *bitch*,' he swore. 'Gabriel is alive.'

Ghause froze. All the colour left her face, and her hand flew to her throat. 'What?' she asked.

He picked up the scroll. His face was as red as beet.

Pater and Mater,

I must start by saying that Gabriel is alive, and I am with him.

If you have heard of the mercenary captain they call 'The Red Knight', well, that is Gabriel. He won the fight men now call 'The Fells', and he held Lissen Carrak against the devil himself. I was there.

I have left the court. It is not for me – or perhaps I liked it too well. And I have plighted my troth to the Lady Mary – yes, Pater, that's Count Gareth's daughter. I have joined Gabriel. Our company – we have a goodly company, more than one hundred lances—

The Earl looked up. 'Gabriel? My lackwit minstrel son is leading a company of lances? What sorcery is this? That ponce couldn't have led a company of maids to pick flowers.'

He met her icy stare. 'You always were a fool,' she said.

—into Morea, to aid the Emperor in his warres. I have entrusted this messenger with certain news concerning the great Enemy we vanquished at Lissen, because we are sore affeard that said Magister Traitor may attempt to recoup his fortunes north of the wall.

Gabriel has entrusted me with certain informationes which I now believe, but I will hold my peace until I have heard from Mater and from you as to how we came to be a family divided so deep. For the nonce, I ride by my brother, and we have good cheer together – better cheer, I think, than ever we had as children.

'What has Gabriel told him?' Ghause asked the air. But she could see it in her mind's eye – Gabriel, alive, had faced a power of the Wild and defeated him.

A wild joy roared in her breast like a fire just catching hold in twigs and birch bark and carefully split kindling. Gabriel – her Gabriel, her living revenge on the world of men – was alive. No matter that he no doubt hated her. She smiled.

Men quailed to see it.

Later, in the privacy of her own tower, she worked a small *phantasm*. She had known Richard Plangere well. She found him easily, cast a working to trace him if he moved, and noted that he was less than three hundred leagues away – and that he was orders of magnitude more powerful than he'd been when she had last deceived him.

She flexed her fingers. 'Oh, so am I, lover,' she said, delighted. Everything delighted her, because *Gabriel was alive.*

She wanted a look at this Lady Mary. She hadn't seen the girl since she was eleven or twelve – when she'd been gawky, hipless, and no kind of a wife for Gavin, who was moody and difficult and given to rages. Not her favourite son, although the easiest to manipulate.

This working was complex, because rumour said that the King's new whore of a wife was a sorceress, and Ghause had no intention of being caught snooping; she spent the day laying her snares, reading from grimoires with her tongue clenched between her teeth, and writing in silver on her floor.

She heard the Earl's cavalcade return, but she was almost done and she wasn't going to stop for him. She lit a faery light, and then another, and heard their little voices scream in the *aether*. She hated faeries and their soulless leeching on the world of men, and it pleased her to use their little bodies for light.

By the light of their agony, she finished her structure. She reached into her maze – an *aethereal* palace of brambles and apple trees and roses turned a little bad – and summoned the rich green power that smelled of loam and rain and semen, and pushed that power through her structures, and *saw.*

She was really very pretty – beautiful hair, fine teeth, and a good figure. Best of all, she had developed good hips for child bearing, and she was reading. A woman who could read was a find indeed.

Ghause watched her in the aethereal *for as long as a priest might say mass, studying her movements and her composure. She even watched Lady Mary take a breviary cross from her girdle and say a prayer. Her lips shaped the sounds of 'Gavin' and Ghause heard them and smiled.*

The Earl shouted for her in the hall and someone banged on her door, and *she felt another presence, and suddenly she saw the King's trull.*

Lady Mary rose and put her breviary on a side table. 'Lady?' she asked.

The Queen passed into the room, and into Ghause's ops-*powered sight. Her beauty cut Ghause like a sharp knife to the soul. And she—*

—was—

—pregnant.

Ghause slammed out of her spell and screamed.

Sixty Leagues West of Lissen Carrak – Bill Redmede

The wilderness west of Lissen Carrak was a nightmare.

Every day that the Jack of Jacks, Bill Redmede, led his exhausted and demoralised men further west, they looked at him with that mixture of trust and bewilderment that he knew would inexorably lead to the collapse of belief, and then of discipline. And he was sure – as sure as he was that the aristocrats were an evil burden on the shoulders of men – that no sanctuary lay to the east.

Every night he lay and replayed the ambush; what should have been the Day. The Day when the King and his cronies fell, when the yeomen of Alba reclaimed their freedom, and the lords fell choking on their own blood. He thought of every error he had made, every deal he had brokered. And how they'd all gone wrong.

Mostly, he lay freezing in his cloak and thought of Thorn. He'd given up his blanket to Nat Tyler, who had a fever and the runs and was worse off. They'd carried Tyler for days until he declared he could walk – but he walked in silence, and when they made camp he'd lie down and sleep. Redmede missed his council.

The worst of it was that more than a month had passed since the defeat, and he didn't really have a goal. He had heard that the Wild had a mighty lord, far to the west; an old and powerful irk who had a fortress and a set of villages where some Outwallers lived free. It was a rumour he'd gleaned when he recruited some serfs in the Brogat; he wondered now if it was just a cloud cuckoo land, a promise as false as the heaven preached by priests. A month's travel, scrounging food and killing any animal big enough to make a meal—

The immediate problem was food. It might have amused him, that his very success in saving Jacks from the wreck of defeat now meant that there were too many of them to hunt deer in the woods. His people had consumed the last of their supplies when they left their canoes at the last navigable stretch of the Cohocton, and began walking west. They followed a narrow ribbon of trail beaten into the earth by generations of Outwallers and Wild creatures – it was like a deer trail, but twelve inches wide and formed of hard beaten earth that didn't show a footprint or even the mark of a dew claw or a hoof.

And there was no game for hundreds of yards to either side of the trail. The only sign in the woods was boglin sign. Thousands of them – perhaps more – had survived Thorn's defeat, and when the sorcerer abandoned his forces he'd released thousands of the small but deadly creatures from his will. They, too, were on the trail, headed west. Headed home.

That was a frightening thought.

But this trail led somewhere. That much Redmede knew.

The woods themselves seemed more threatening then he remembered. The silence was oppressive – even the number of insects seemed reduced by the magnitude of the Wild's rout. It was a silent summer. And Bill Redmede had never travelled this far west.

A day's travel west of the Ings of the Cohocton, they found an irk village burned flat. Casual inspection showed that the inhabitants had probably done the work themselves – there were no corpses, and nothing had been left. Just the remnants of twenty-four cabins in a great circle, all burned, and the stockade around it, closely woven with raspberry canes and other prickers, black, but still thorny.

One of his men had cried to see it. 'They're ahead of us!' he said. 'Sweet Jesus, Jack, the knights are—'

Redmede wanted to smack him. But instead, he leaned on his bow and shook his head. 'Use your noggin, young Peter. How would they get here? Eh? Irks did this themselves.' He ordered men to prod the cabin foundations for grain pits, and they found ten – all empty. But they were desperate enough to pick the kernels of dried corn out of the earthen pits, one at a time, and then young Fitzwilliam found a buried pot – a great earthenware container that held twenty pounds of grain. Another hour of digging found another.

Forty pounds of corn among two hundred men was a mere handful per man, but Bill sent three of his best, all veteran Foresters, north across the stream, and they returned while the corn was being roasted on fires. They had a pair of deer.

The next morning, as if a miracle, a troop of turkeys walked boldly across the cleared fields to the south – twenty fat birds, bold as brass. In the process of killing them, the Jacks realised that the corn in the fields was ripe. The fields furthest from the woods' edge had already been picked clean – clearly the irks had harvested what they could before they burned their village – but the corn under the forest eaves was fresh, full-kernelled, and mature. Albans grew grains – oats, barley, and wheat – irks and Outwallers grew the native corn, and while the taste was unfamiliar and curiously sweet Bill knew salvation when he saw it. Twenty turkeys and four hundred ears of corn provided a second feast, and with time to think and food in his belly he decided they should rest another day and sent more hunters north and south to look for deer.

The men he sent north didn't return. He waited three days for them, and mourned the loss of his best scout, an old man everyone called Grey Cal. Cal was too good to get lost and too old to take foolish chances. But the Wild was the Wild.

A half-blood – Outwaller and Morean – offered to try to track the old man and his party. Redmede was in the difficult position of getting to know his men as he faced each challenge – the fighting at Lissen Carrak had rallied all the different cells of the Jacks, and years of patient secrecy had aided their recruitment, but it didn't help him now. He didn't know the dark-skinned man or his abilities at all.

'What'd you say your name was, comrade?' he asked.

The young half-blood crouched. He wore a feather in his hair like an Outwaller, and carried an Eastern horn bow rather than a war bow. 'Call me Cat,' he said. He grinned. 'You have any food, boss?'

'No man is boss to any other here,' Redmede said.

'That's crap,' said Cat. 'You the boss. These others – some wouldn't live a day out here withouten you.' He smiled. 'Let me go find Cal. He fed me many times. Good man. Good friend. Good *comrade*.'

Redmede had the sudden feeling he was sending his new best scout to find his old one. 'Tomorrow we go west on the trail,' he said. 'Know anything about this trail, comrade?'

The dark-skinned man looked up the trail for long enough that Redmede began to hope for an answer. But Cat grinned, suddenly. 'Goes west, I reckon,' he said. 'Can I try for Cal?'

'Go with my blessing.' Redmede handed the boy some newly parched corn.

Cat raised the corn to his forehead. 'Tara will protect me,' he said. Tara was the Outwaller goddess.

Redmede couldn't stop himself. 'Superstition will never help us be free,' he said.

Cat smiled. 'Nope,' he agreed. He ate the handful of corn in one great mouthful, picked up his bow and loped away into the gathering darkness.

The next night their camp was worse, they ate strips of badly dried venison and shivered by their fires. Redmede was sure they were being observed – he went out in person at dusk, and again at dawn, moving as silently as twenty years of outlawry had taught him to, but he didn't see so much as a bent blade of grass nor did he hear a twig snap that wasn't rightly accounted for by chipmunks and raccoons.

His men were leaner. He looked them over along the thin ribbon of trail – most of them had ruined their hose, and none of them had white cotes any more. The good wool was stained from lying flat, sleeping, crawling and living, and now their cotes had taken on the many hues of the forest. They were still too bright, but the starkness of white was being overlaid with a thousand imprints of nature, and the Wild was having the same effect on the men and the handful of women.

It was the women that caused him concern. He'd heard a couple screwing in the dark, and if he'd heard it he knew that two hundred other pairs of ears had listened with the same hunger. Men could share abstinence, but if one or two men were getting some...

He walked along the line until he reached the oldest of the female Jacks – Bess. She was as tall as he, and no kind of beauty at all in the world of men. Although here in the Wild her big-boned, heavy-breasted frame seemed as natural as a beaver dam and ten times as attractive.

Bill Redmede grimaced at himself. 'Bess?' he said. 'Walk with me a few paces, eh?'

Bess got her blanket roll on her hip, passed the cord over her shoulder, and picked up her bow. 'What's on your mind?' she asked bluntly.

'Women. Fucking.' He looked back at her. He hoped they were out of earshot of the Jacks.

She frowned. 'You have a strange way of asking a girl, Jack.'

He stopped and leaned against a tree so enormous that the two of them would never have been able to pass their arms around the trunk.

A light rain began to fall, and he cursed. He ran back along the trail and ordered the long files of Jacks into motion behind him, and then he turned and ran back to her. 'I don't mean me,' he said. 'I need you to tell the girls—'

'Fuck you, Bill Redmede,' Bess said. 'This ain't the Royal Army. Those sisters have the same rights as any Jack – right to their arms, right to their bodies. Yes, *comrade?*'

Bill plodded along for a dozen paces. 'Sister, there are ideals and then there are everyday—' He paused, looking for a word. 'Everyday things,' he said weakly. 'Every woman has the right to her own body. But plague take it, sister, we're in a tight space—'

Bess was three paces ahead of him. She stopped, turned, and put a hand on his shoulder. 'If we're in a tight space then this is when we find out what we are. All the more reason the sisters should do what they want.'

Bill thought about that a moment. 'Could end hard,' he said.

'Are you our lord? Our master? Our father?' Bess challenged him.

76

'It could end hard, and mayhap I'll say a word to a sister if it looks like it will. But it ain't your responsibility, is it, Bill Redmede?'

He looked at her, expected to find himself angry at her attitude to his authority, and instead was glad. Glad that someone else was a true believer. 'Good of the many, sister,' he said.

Bess nodded. 'That, I can understand.'

That day the hunters got nothing and the grumbling in camp was continuous. A great many men were leaning towards blaming their leader. Redmede could feel it.

Morning came after a night of rain – a night where only the most hardened veterans slept. At least it made sex unlikely – but in the morning everyone looked thinner, more pinched, and as those men who had any rolled up their sodden cloaks and blankets, they bickered over the slightest thing.

A pair of serfs from the Albin – new men, young and comparatively strong and well fed – packed their goods silently and trotted away down the trail, headed east.

Nat Tyler came up. He'd had the runs for days and keeping up had been all he could do, but he was recovering. Redmede had never known a tougher man, and his heart rose to see his most trusted friend leaning on his great bow.

'I could reach them from here,' Tyler said.

'You are feeling better, comrade. But skip it. We've never killed our own.' He watched the two men moving furtively away.

'So we have, when needs must.' Tyler spat, but he dropped his ready arrow back into his quiver, and carefully tied the thong on his arrow bag against the wet. His eyes were on Bess as she walked, head high, shoulders square. 'Fever broke in the night,' he muttered. 'And I heard a lot of shite talked.'

Redmede watched the rain. 'It'll get worse,' he said.

That afternoon, in heavy rain, he sent out three teams of hunters, one of them composed of six unwilling men, younger serfs recently escaped, with Tyler to teach them. They were resentful of authority, cold, wet, and hungry – not the ideal circumstances under which to learn how to move in the woods.

'There won't be a fucking deer moving in this,' Tyler complained.

'Then kill them in their lies,' Redmede quipped.

'If this'n was *my* woods and I knew the lies I would,' Tyler said. 'Fuck me, even then I wouldn't go out in rain like this.'

'Kills the scent,' Redmede said. 'We need meat. Needs must when the devil drives.'

'Make that up yerself, Bill?' Tyler said. But he managed a damp smile. 'I'm off then.'

They made camp too near dark, if lying in the rain under a dripping canopy of maple leaves could be accounted a camp. Everything was wet – the ground, the men, and all their clothes, all their blankets, all their cloaks.

It was dark to be gathering firewood but Redmede led the effort himself, and Bess backed him up, and before the sky overhead was black as black they had a heap of downed branches as high as a man's head, and more and more of the exhausted men were rising from their first collapse to help. But Redmede could see that they were moving like the sick; their thin-lipped, jerky wood-gathering frightened him more than outright rebellion would have done.

Bess found a treasure – a hollow apple tree full of carefully stored dry birchbark. Redmede found his fire stele and got to work, but the wind and the rain didn't help and neither did having an audience. The sky was black as a nobleman's heart when he finally had his char glowing red with a lit spark.

Even then three tries failed to get the char to light his tow, which was apparently damp despite being carried in a well-made tin, right against his skin. He cursed.

Bess shrugged. 'Stop your whining,' she said. 'I know a trick.' She rubbed some birch bark between her hands, crumpling it finer and finer as three other women held their cotes over her head to keep the rain off – and the birch dust caught the spark from the char cloth, flared to light, and lit a twist of birch bark that glared like a magic spell in the darkness. All the men and women in the dark, wet camp, cheered spontaneously – not just a gasp, but a shout. In a minute, the pile of dry birch bark caught and in ten minutes, the whole vast pile of wood was roaring, flames leaping twenty feet in the air, so high that the rain was diverted over their heads.

With fire a palpable reality, the Jacks found the spirit to get more wood, even though it had to be scrounged by feel in total darkness – armloads of sodden, half-rotten wood appeared, but by then the fire was so hot that it had ceased to discriminate. It was so hot it could dry a man's shirt in a few beats of his heart, even as that heat threatened to boil his blood. The fire was still burning encouraged to lie down, feet to the fire, in a ring close around it where the air was breathable, and they were as close to comfortable as a man could manage in the Wild.

Nat Tyler came in near to midnight. The fire was still burning like a beacon, and men were working in shifts to feed it, crashing a hundred feet or more into the surrounding darkness.

'It's like you've hung out a sign,' Tyler said. He crouched down by Redmede, and he was obviously exhausted.

'Get anything?' Redmede asked.

'Doe and two fawns,' Tyler said with half a grin. 'Wasn't pretty, but we got 'em. Funny – when we took the deer we could see your fire plain as the fingers on my hand, but when we came down the hill, we lost you – even lost the stream for a time.' He shook his head. 'Plague take it, lost in the dark is like hell come to earth, comrade.'

'They still out there?' Redmede said slowly. He didn't want the answer. He was warm and as dry as he'd been in two days and didn't want to move.

'I told the boys to sit tight and I'd come for them,' Tyler said. 'I'll go fetch 'em in.'

'I'd better come with you,' Redmede said. He hoped it didn't sound as grudging as it was.

Tyler sighed. 'I wish I could tell you to sit and rest,' he said. There was a long pause. 'But I don't think I can go out again by m'self. Fell asleep under a tree for – don't know how long. Minute? Three? Twenty?' He got to his feet. 'There's something out there, too.'

'Something Wild?' Redmede asked. 'We're allies, now.'

Tyler frowned. 'Don't you believe it, Bill Redmede. This is the fucking Wild. I know it like my own nose. They aren't even allies to each other, plague take them all. It's a world of blood and talon, and right now we're easy meat.'

Redmede shivered. He half drew his falchion in its scabbard and it caught – there was rust on the blade, rust right down into the scabbard. As it was his prized possession he felt a flare of anger and even sadness. He checked his dagger and shook his head over his bow and quiver. He hung the quiver on a spruce tree, leaned the great bow against the trunk between the dense dead branches, and made a tent for them with his cloak.

'Let's go,' he said.

His confidence lasted for ten paces, and then the sheer cold of the ever-present rain and the futility of moving in the pitch blackness hit him as if someone had thrown a pail of water over his head.

Tyler was muttering to himself, and Redmede worried he was still fevered. They crashed through the brush, making as much noise as a hundred mounted knights, and taking damage from the alder and the spruce saplings. Redmede misstepped badly and fell down the bank, putting one whole wool-hosed leg into the icy Cohocton, and when he glanced back he could see the fire burning like a mountain of light just a bowshot behind them. The heart went out of him.

'I'd never ha' gone back into the dark wi'out you, Bill,' Tyler said. 'Christ on the cross, I hope I can find the lads. They're scare't shitless and they was more a hindrance than a help. I should hae left them wi' you.'

'They've got to learn sometime,' Redmede said without thinking. One foot in front of the other – it always got him through these moments. Besides, it was Tyler doing the work, breaking trail and guessing where he'd left the runaway serfs. All Redmede had to do was follow him and keep his spirits up.

They walked and walked until Redmede's head was numb and he felt as if he was asleep and yet walking in an endless sea of rain. The downpour drowned out all other sound, the darkness was nigh total, and he tracked the shine of his friend's rain-soaked cote, the dull gleam of the leather belt that held his leather bottle, and the shape of his head against the rain. They moved from tree to tree because it was too dark to walk well, and they were far from any trail, and still low branches tripped them – it was exhausting work, and no end in sight.

And then something struck him.

He had an ill-defined warning – never fully sensed, but something made him duck and turn, and the spear haft meant to punch through his neck slapped the side of his head and came down on his shoulder instead – a flare of pain, but not a blow to stop a warrior, and Redmede had the haft in his hand. Before his head was in the fight, he'd rotated the shaft between his hands, tearing it away from his assailant, and he slammed the haft solidly into the creature and it fell away with a wet scream – the ferns under his feet were full of them—

'Boggles!' he screamed.

Tyler had a heartbeat more warning, and he used it to drag his blade clear of its scabbard. Redmede saw Tyler's blade pass so close to his cheek that he might have seen himself in the blade, with more light, and then there was a wet thump and he was sprayed with warm ichor.

He began to use the spear with ferocity. The darkness was against him, but Redmede had never quit in his life, and he put the stone spearhead into two or three of the beasts before he felt the stinging pain at his ankle that told him—

—and then Tyler was there, cutting hard. He cleared the boggles off Redmede, and then the two of them got their backs against the bole of a great tree.

The boggles were gone.

'I'm hit, Nat.' Bill Redmede was as terrified as he'd ever been in his life. He could feel the blood flowing out his ankle, and he could see the ferns moving.

Tyler spat. 'Some allies,' he said.

Chapter Four

Ota Qwan

Lutece – The King of Galle

'Jean de Vrailly?' asked the King, and his voice was high and sharp. 'He's in the Nova Terra? How lovely. For all of us.'

Courtiers laughed. A few frowned.

The Seneschal d'Abblemont laughed. 'He sent a letter, Your Grace.'

The King rolled his eyes. 'I had no idea he could read or write,' the King said. Women tittered. 'Very well, read it.'

From the Noble Knight, Jean de Vrailly, to his royal liege and master, the most puissant and powerful, Lord of the Pensey Mountains, Defender of the—

'Spare me, Abblemont.' The King's thin voice cut like a sharp eating knife.

'Your Grace. Ahem. *Greetings. In the spirit of errantry, and to prove myself worthy of the title, granted me by many, of best knight in the world* – Your Grace that's what it says.' Abblemont looked a little more like a large monkey stuffed into satin than was quite right, with too much facial hair and a curling beard, protuberant teeth, and a wrinkled forehead balancing an almost perfectly flat nose with two enormous nostrils. Wits at court debated whether he was more like a pig or a dog, but the name that stuck was 'The Horse'.

Despite a truly stunning ugliness, he remained the King's favourite.

Or perhaps because of it. His ugliness couldn't threaten the King, and some whispered that the King was a little too easily threatened – by his favourites, by his mother, and most of all by his wife and Queen.

The Horse glanced at the King, grinned wickedly, cleared his throat and went on.

Having earned the approval of the King of Alba and all the knights of his court, I accompanied the Alban King on campaign in the north country of this kingdom, where I encountered many worthy foes, to whit: daemons, Wyverns like small dragonets, irks, and a new species of adversary, called by Albans the boglin, a small creature, insignificant in arms but dangerous in great shoals and tides – and there did disport myself with such fearsomeness and prowess as to win a great victory over the forces of evil—

The King yawned. 'Does he really expect us to believe this tissue of self-delusion?'

The Archbishop of Lutece frowned. 'Irks and daemons are well-known servants of the Enemy, Your Grace.'

The King sneered. 'Has anyone seen one alive this century?' He glanced at Abblemont. 'Is there more of the same?'

Abblemont shrugged. 'Yes and no, Your Grace.' He raised his eyes from the parchment. 'I believe him.'

The King leaned forward on the arms of his throne. 'You do?' he asked, his voice suggesting delight.

Abblemont shrugged. 'First, Holy Church requires me to believe – it is an article of faith. And not one as difficult as the trinity.'

His delicate blasphemy made the ladies blush.

'Second, de Vrailly is a rash, dangerous fool, but he's not a braggart. Or rather, he is – but he isn't imaginative enough to invent this. Indeed, Your Grace, if you consider the report of the Seneschal of Outremer only this morning—'

The King shot back as if he'd received a blow. 'Silence, Horse,' he ordered.

The whole court fell silent. No lady simpered, much less tittered or giggled; no man sneered. Their faces had a certain vacuous sameness of expression. All waiting for the axe to fall.

It was hard to say if the King was young or old. He wore black – black velvet, relieved by touches of gold – a pair of gold earrings, the gold hilt of his sword, a single gold ring set with onyx on his finger, gold buckles on his shoes worth the value of a small village. Around his shoulders he wore a gold collar of linked suns. His skin was almost perfectly white, and his hair was the same impossible golden colour as de Vrailly's, which was only reasonable, as they were cousins. But there the resemblance ended. The King was, if not the smallest man in the room, then nearly so; well formed, but shorter than many of the women who gathered near the centre of power. He was not given to the practice of arms; and his ascetic devotion to religion did more to keep him thin than his time in the tiltyard. He was handsome – indeed, more than a few troubadours found themselves able to sing of him as the handsomest knight in the kingdom.

The Duchess de Savigny had been heard to say that he was beautiful, if you liked children – but having been heard to say it, she no longer attended court.

The King whistled a moment, and then shrugged. 'So – perhaps these improbable monsters exist,' he said. He looked at Abblemont. 'And perhaps there truly are witches who cast spells too?' he added, giggling.

The Horse gave a very slight nod. 'Perhaps there are, as you say.'

Conversation returned.

'Go on,' the King said.

Abblemont laughed. 'Nay, I shan't read it word for word,' he said. 'Only that they fought a great battle and slew thousands of these monsters, and now de Vrailly is named the Alban king's champion.'

The King nodded, pulling his beard.

'He says that the Queen of Alba is one of the most beautiful women in the world,' Abblemont continued, his eyes scanning the page.

'You might have mentioned that at the start,' the King said with more interest. 'Does he send a portrait?'

'And she and the King are the most perfect example of wedded bliss.' Abblemont glanced at his master, whose fist closed.

'They will give a great tournament next spring, after Lent, to celebrate his victory—'

'He's a braggart. I suspect she's beautiful as a poxed whore and just as faithful.' The King looked down at his Horse, and the Horse gazed resolutely at his parchment.

'He closes by mentioning his unshakeable loyalty to Your Grace, and stating baldly that he expects to take the kingdom for his own. And for your crown, Your Grace.' Abblemont looked up and met the King's eyes, and saw them flash almost red, as if lit by an inner fire – reviewed his last ten words and realised he'd misstepped. 'Ah – my apologies, Your Grace.'

He should not have mentioned that de Vrailly intended to conquer Alba for the King in open court.

But the King was a consummate actor, and he stretched and smiled. 'Perhaps Lady Clarissa would be kind enough to play for us, Abblemont?'

Clarissa was fifteen, pretty as a virgin in a book of hours, and a near-perfect player of the psaltery. She was shorter than the King by almost a head, and had a quiet, demure quality that affronted many of the other ladies.

'The Queen has refused to permit her in her solar,' whispered the Contesse D'Angluleme. She gave her cousin, the Vidame, a significant look.

'Poor thing, she looks underfed.' The Vidame watched her walk by, cradling her musical instrument. 'I think the Queen is cruel,' she said, her voice suggesting the exact opposite.

'I don't. The creature is brazen as a steetwalker, dear.' She leaned close to her cousin and whispered in her ear.

The Vidame's arched eyebrows still had a little room to rise, and they shot up – her handkerchief came out of her sleeve as if snapped by a crossbow, and she raised it to her lips. 'No!' she said, sounding too deeply satisfied.

If Clarissa de Sartres heard a word, it didn't crease her dignity, and she crossed the black and white marble floor, her plain brown wool overdress gliding silently over it, her head down just a little, hiding her expression. She wore an intricate net of silk and beads in her hair with a pair of linen horns rising from a base of auburn hair and pearls, and from the front hung a linen veil so fine that it was possible to see the shape of her face without distinguishing, at least by candlelight, her expression. She held her instrument the way a proud mother might hold a baby. If she was aware of the unbridled hatred she received as the King's first female favourite, she showed not the least sign of it.

And in fairness, it must be said that no woman in the whole of the great, cavernous throne room looked *less* like a royal favourite. If all the flowers of the field were not enough to adorn the rest of the women and most of the men, Clarissa de Sartres was as plain as a sleek brown mouse and about as noticeable. Without the magnificent headdress and the musical instrument, she might easily have been taken for an important female servant – complete to a small linen apron over her gown and set of keys with a pair of scissors tied to her apron strings.

Gossip and comment moved before her like a wind-blown fire in a dry forest.

She arrived at the base of the throne and curtsied so deeply that it seemed possible that she would collapse on the floor – yet so gracefully that no one ever imagined such a thing might happen.

'Your Grace,' she said.

The King smiled at her, and his gold and ivory face warmed to life. 'Clarissa!' he said. 'I didn't see you.'

'Indeed, Your Grace, I considered staying away.' Did she smile? The veil was so delicate that you thought you *ought* to be able to see her expression. Some imagined that she simpered, and some that she sneered, and a few thought she looked troubled.

'May I play?' she asked.

The King's smile grew warmer still. 'I live for it,' he said.

Abblemont permitted himself the very smallest smile.

The King waited for the notes to begin, watched his court dissolve into ill-mannered conversation – no one listened to her music but he – and turned to his other favourite. 'That was ill done, Horse.'

'Apologies, Your Grace.'

'None of us is perfect, Horse. Watch yourself. The brute may yet pull the whole – Sweet Jesu, she can play.' He smiled at the girl, and she played on, quite obviously lost in her own music.

The King watched her a moment and then nodded to Abblemont. 'When she's done, clear the room,' he said. 'I don't want to talk to any of them, and I've given them a proper target for their execrable gossip. Does de Vrailly need anything?'

Abblemont watched the girl play. He loved music, and he could all but feel her passion and the strings under her fingers. She made the rest of the women look like fools.

She made him feel a fool, too.

'There are one or two things, Your Grace.'

'We'll have a military council, then. But let her play, first.'

*

Abblemont was on all of the councils – military, civil, treasury, even Church. To be the King's favourite was to be the keeper of his time and his innermost confidant. Most of the men present – even the hard-faced professional knights like de Ribeaumont, the Marshal, tended to ask Abblemont for his opinion before approaching the King. They assembled in full armour, because that was the way of Galle, and the Rule of War applied every day. Only the King was excepted. De Ribeaumont wore elaborate armour, with sliding plates across his chest edged with bronze and plated gold, with verses from the Bible in hammered silver. Tancred Guisarme, the Royal Constable and the oldest man present by twenty years, wore the highly decorated armour of his jousting guild, made to look as if he were himself a young dragon, all in green metal and gold trim. His arm and leg harnesses were made of scales as small as the tip of a lady's finger, in alternating rows of silver, gold, and copper-bronze. Steilker, the Master of Crossbowman, wore black armour with gold lettering praising God; Vasilli, the Master of the King's Works and sometime architect of the King's castles, wore a breast- and backplate and maille. No one was likely to challenge him to fight to the death, as he was both commonly born and foreign, but it spoke volumes for the Rule of War that even he wore metal. Abblemont himself wore plain white harness – excellent stuff, utterly without adornment, the way the Etruscans made it.

As he'd already been asked about today's notion and found it acceptable, men spoke to the King with confidence. And Abblemont, true to his word, had already mentioned the whole notion to the King – that they begin exploring the northern wastes of the Nova Terra.

'The Moreans have many contacts with the Outwallers in the north,' the merchant said. He was far more than a mere merchant – he was a great owner of ships and his ships formed the flexible backbone of the navy. He had twenty great round cogs, high-sided, bluff-bowed, and impervious to weather and to all but the strongest of sea engines – almost impregnable, too, to the sea creatures of the Wild that were just as vicious as their land-based cousins. His name was Oliver de Marche, and he was dressed as plainly as the girl, Clarissa. His doublet was good black wool, and his hat, too; his hose were more of the same, and if that wool cost twenty gold leopards the ell when fulled, that was something only he and his tailor knew.

'Despite the Church prohibition on contact with the Wild,'

de Marche went on, 'the Emperor has officers appointed to deal with the chiefs of the Outwallers, and through them, he receives the very best of their trade goods – spider silk, beaver pelts, and Wild honey,' he said.

The King was given samples of all three to examine. He tasted the honey and smiled. 'Delicious,' he said.

'Apparently in Nova Terra there are small ponds of the stuff, leaking from great hives of monstrous bees the size of hummingbirds,' de Marche said. 'Men there say it is hermetical.' He shrugged as if to dispose of such notions. 'Men in the Nova Terra believe such superstitions, Your Grace.' Stony royal silence. He bowed. 'I have seen several of the bees. And—' he looked around the room '—an irk.'

Abblemont had suggested that the merchant mention this. The King was just dipping his folding silver spoon into the honey again – he looked up, and his eyebrows arched. 'You've seen one?' he asked.

'That I have, Your Grace. And a gryphon or some such creature of evil omen on the wing – far to the south of me on one of their inland seas, but I swear on my hope of heaven it was no bird. And the beaver—'

The King rubbed the fur with his thumb. It was as soft as plush, and deep, and curiously warm. 'Superb,' he said.

De Marche nodded. 'We could own the trade,' he said. 'All these things are a mere curiosity for the Emperor. For us—'

The King's eyes went to a great roll of hide – a stag or hind, tanned carefully, and with a chart drawn on it. 'I never really saw the shape of Nova Terra before,' he said quietly. 'So the Emperor has Alba to his west and these Outwallers to his north.'

'Technically, the Kingdom of Alba is a part of the Empire,' Abblemont said.

'Technically, the Kingdom of Galle is part of the Empire of Ruhm,' the King snapped back. 'And the current Emperor in Liviapolis claims to be my suzerain, by some absurd quibble of history.'

In fact, the quibble was hardly absurd or historical – every man present knew the strength of the Emperor's claim on paper. And the weakness of his armies to enforce it.

But Abblemont was the only one there who was permitted to directly dispute his word, and that was a chancy business at the best of times. Further, as it happened, Abblemont agreed with his sovereign that it was time for Galle to rule others, and cease to be ruled. So rather than suggest that the Emperor might have a point – that the King's own father had kissed the Emperor's red boots and sworn his fealty – Abblemont leaned back in his chair and said, 'Trade with the tribes north of the Wall would give us new products to tax, increase trade with the south and put us in a position to – hmm – let us say to *influence* the wild impulses of the heathen Outwallers.'

'Convert them to the true faith?' asked the Marshal.

If you define the true faith as a willingness to do the bidding of the King of Galle, thought Abblemont. 'Yes,' he said. 'Through our priests and our soldiers, and not those of the Patriarch and the Emperor.'

De Ribeaumont smiled like a wolf. 'Ahh. Yes.' He shook his head. 'My lords, I'm old and slow. If de Vrailly is only one half as successful as the bastard claims, and if we could gain any force at all in the northern Wild—' He sucked his teeth. 'Good Christ, my lords, we could crush the Emperor like a nut. Or the King of Alba.' He nodded. 'Take Nova Terra for ourselves.'

'We might not need to,' Abblemont said, tossing a scroll tube on the table with a rattle. 'You gentlemen can read that at your leisure. One of my letter-writing friends.' He leaned back.

The King extended a long black-clad arm and his delicate fingers snapped up the scroll like the sharp-tipped arm of a spider. 'Who is he?' he asked, his eyes darting rapidly over the author's elegant hand.

'I do not know myself, and I would not say his name even in this august assembly if I knew it,' Abblemont said. 'Remember our little disaster last year in Arles.'

Tancred Guisarme, the Constable, made a face as if he'd swallowed something bitter. 'Someone talked,' he said.

'The fucking herald talked,' said de Ribeaumont. 'And he's dog food now. But that's not the point.'

Abblemont nodded. 'Exactly. Do you know that in the Archaic Empire, the Master of Spies referred to every agent by the name of a flower or an animal or some such – never by their own names. Not even their sexes were known.'

'Sex?' asked Guisarme. 'We wouldn't use women as spies, would we?'

There was the briefest pause, as there always is when a dozen men realise that one of their number is a fool.

'Unchivalrous,' muttered Guisarme, in the tone of a man who's just discovered that his neighbours worship Satan.

De Marche cleared his throat. 'If Your Grace will admit of the possibilities,' he began carefully.

The King was mindful that one of his duties was not to leave his best servants blowing in the wind. He smiled and sat up. 'What do we need to start our horse in this race?' he asked.

De Marche smiled. 'Your Grace, it was in my mind to send a trade expedition, well dowered with our goods – swords and armour, which the Outwallers value above all things; wool and linen, flashy, cheap jewels such as peasant women wear, and bronze and copper pots for cooking. I'm told, by our Etruscan source, that these sell well in the north.' He nodded. 'Those have to be well made. The Outwallers like shiny things, but they are not children nor yet fools. So the Etruscan tells me.'

The King pulled at his beard and looked at his Horse.

Abblemont nodded slowly. 'I would do this thing,' he said carefully. 'But I would prime the pump first – with a mailed fist.'

That was the right kind of talk for the war council. De Ribeaumont – obviously bored and ill at ease talking to a merchant, even one who'd fought at sea and earned himself a knighthood – sat up and smiled. 'A military expedition?' he asked.

Abblemont smiled his simian smile. 'Something a trifle subtler than a charge of knights, Marshal.'

'Of course,' the Marshal said.

'Perhaps a sellsword,' Abblemont said, almost as an afterthought.

It was the King's turn to straighten up. 'Not that arrogant boy and his company of thugs,' he shot. The King had endured an unfortunate encounter with a company of lances the year before, when he tried to take Arles by subterfuge, and failed.

Abblemont smiled. *If I could hire that company then I would*, he thought, but they had apparently left for Nova Terra and vanished into its maw.

De Marche leaned forward. 'Your Grace, I have a man in mind – a very successful adventurer, one of Your Grace's own subjects. Ser Hartmut Li Orguelleus.'

'The slaver knight?' the King said, and he winced. 'The Black Knight? The Knight of Ill Renown?'

De Marche shrugged. 'They are just names, Your Grace. His loyalty is deep and entirely to Your Grace. He has sailed far to the south, landed in Ifriqu'a and come away the conqueror.'

'In the Middle Sea, he's served our purposes well,' Abblemont said. 'Though I confess I wouldn't invite him home to dinner. Nor would I allow him to address my daughter, no matter how honourable his intentions.'

'Tar sticks,' said the King. 'He has an evil name. He fought for the *Necromancer* in Ifriqu'ya!'

De Marche sighed. 'Your Grace, it takes a remarkable man to go to a distant land at the head of a tiny company, and make war for us. To make decisions—'

'Decisions that would bind us,' the King said. He looked pensive.

'The kind of decisions that the Outwallers would respect,' Abblemont said cautiously.

'He has been very successful taking slaves in Ifriquy'a,' de Marche put in.

'He almost started a war with Dar-as-Salaam that could have broken our Middle Sea trade,' hissed the King.

Abblemont shrugged. 'To be fair, he also defeated the Emir's fleet at Na'dia.'

The men around the table shared a glance. A long one. The King looked from one to another.

'Great plans require great risks, and I suspect that the employment of this terrible man is not the smallest risk we will incur to take Nova Terra,' said the King. He swirled the wine in his golden cup and stood. 'Let it be so,' he said, and de Marche smiled.

'Your Grace,' he agreed, with a bow. 'I have him waiting below.'

The King paled. He put a hand on his chest. 'I don't intend to *meet him*,' the King snapped. 'Send him to massacre heathens and bring me what I desire, but do not expect me to suffer his odious spirit in my chambers.'

The merchant recoiled. He bowed with proper ceremony. The King relented and gave him a hand to kiss, and de Marche bowed deeply.

'I approve of what you are doing,' the King said in a low voice.

Abblemont smiled very slightly – much as he had when the King had shown his pleasure to the Lady Clarissa.

If only people would simply believe me, he thought, *this would all be so much easier.* He had a strategy of campaign ready for Ser Hartmut. He had a strategy that would end in the subjugation of Alba and the Empire – and Arles and Etrusca as well. He doubted he'd see it all done in his own lifetime, but the recruitment of the Black Knight was a vital step.

'He'll need a siege train,' Abblemont added.

'Whatever for?' asked the King. De Marche was already gone.

'It would take us years to build a port in Nova Terra,' Abblemont said. 'So much easier to seize one instead.'

The King sighed. 'I sense that you have already chosen your target,' he said.

Abblemont smiled. 'One of the foremost castles in the world,' he said. 'Ticondaga.'

'I've never heard of it, Abblemont.' The King shrugged, distancing himself from the idea. He leaned back. 'May I send for the lady now, my Horse?'

Abblemont pursed his lips.

'Why target such a powerful castle, then?' asked the King.

'It will save money in garrison. And it will send a strong message to Your Grace's enemies. And rebound all the more to Your Grace's glory.' Abblemonte bowed.

'And if the Black Knight fails, or commits some hideous crime instead?' the King asked.

Abblemont shrugged. 'Then we disown him and speak much of the rapaciousness of merchants and mercenaries.' He rubbed the back of his thumb against a small hermetical instrument that looked like a stud on his sword belt. It would cause a low musical tone to play in Clarissa de Sartres' ear, summoning her. It was the Horse's method of ensuring that she always 'happened' upon the King.

The King gave his courtier a wry smile. 'Let it be so,' he said.

The Long Lakes – Squash Country – Nita Qwan

Peter – Nita Qwan – wouldn't have gone back to Ifriqu'a if he'd been offered a winged ship and a company of houris.

He had this elaborate thought as he lay on his back under a magnificent maple tree, watching his wife's round bottom as she hoed their squash, cutting weeds with the bronze-tipped hoe he'd made from a scrap of discarded armour.

She was probably pregnant, and that neither lessened her beauty nor made him feel that he should leap to his feet and hoe the ground for her. It was women's work.

Behind him three great hides stretched on frames indicated that he had pulled his weight. And the shape of her buttocks and complete lack of any covering beyond a single layer of deerskin – their rhythmic movement—

She turned and looked at him under her lashes. She laughed. 'I'm a shaman – I can read your mind.'

She went back to hoeing her way down the row. She reaped the weeds like a soldier killing boggles – efficient and ruthless. He had never imagined her to be such a good farmer, but then, when he killed her husband and took her, he'd known nothing about her but the softness between her thighs.

She was working her way back along the edge of the corn now – the head-high, ripe corn. The matrons had already harvested the first ears and all the maidens of the right age had run through the corn with young men chasing them. There had been a great deal of laughter and gallons of good cider, and Ota Qwan had taken a young wife.

His own wife stopped and pulled a ripe ear of corn from a stalk. Slowly she stripped back the husk and the silk. Her eyes met his. Her lips touched the end of the ear of corn—

He leaped to his feet and ran to her.

She stepped into the rows of corn and dropped her wrap skirt. 'Mind the baby,' she said. And laughed into his mouth.

Ota Qwan's new wife was the daughter of the paramount matron, Blue Knife. Her husband was a quiet man – a gifted hunter and a deep thinker, but without apparent interest in the politics of the people.

The girl's name was Amij'ha. She was very young – just exactly old enough to run through the corn, as the Sossag said. But she laughed well, she was prepared to ridicule her new husband like a proper wife, and she came of strong stock. She was well liked, and her marriage to Ota Qwan marked him for further advancement. And he surprised everyone by hunting deer, trapping, and even working beside his new wife in the fields. Their cabin was covered in drying hides, and when they had been home for a month from the war, he proposed to lead men to find honey – the great ponds of Wild honey that moved every year in the west, but could always be found by a party bold enough to look. When he made the proposition in front of the matrons who ruled the people in times of peace, his mother-in-law saw to it that he sounded appropriately humble, his wife supported him, and the matrons gave him the lead.

Peter had time to replace his breech clout and make tea in a fine copper kettle – almost his only loot from the summer campaign. He was still thinking how enjoyable his life was, and how much better than the fate he had expected when he was taken as a slave – when Ota Qwan's shadow darkened his door.

'Hello, the house!' Ota Qwan said. 'Hey, brother. May I come in?'

Peter threw back the deer hide and propped it open. 'My wife says it lets flies in,' he said. 'I feel it lets them out.'

Ota Qwan gave him a quick embrace. 'I suspect the Queen of Alba makes the same argument, and the King leaves the windows open anyway,' he said, throwing himself on a bundle of furs. 'You've been busy.'

'I'm happy, and I want to keep it that way,' he said. 'We're going to have a boy.'

Ota Qwan leaped to his feet and threw his arms around Peter. 'Ah! Well done. Hence all the hunting.'

Peter shrugged. 'I hear winter is nothing to laugh at,' he said.

Ota Qwan was briefly sobered. 'That's no lie, brother.' He made a face. 'I mean to make a run west for some honey.'

Peter laughed. 'Since I have a wife,' he said, 'I know all about it. And you know I'll go. Not sure I was offered a choice.'

'Honey trades well when the foreign geese come up the Great River – or even if we just trade it over the Wall.' Ota Qwan shrugged. 'But we get a better price from the geese.'

The wild geese, as the Sossag called them, were the great round ships from Etrusca that came into the river most years, in late fall, to trade. Sometimes there were only a few, and sometimes great fleets of them. They stayed to the east for the most part, but for the last decade, so the matrons had noted, the geese had come further and further up the Great River every year.

'And beaver,' Peter said. 'I have more than thirty pelts.'

Ota Qwan made a motion that suggested that he thought beaver to be too much work. 'If we're quick, we can harvest as much as we can carry,' he said. 'I did it last year.'

'And lost a warrior,' Peter said.

Ota Qwan's face darkened, but he and his brother had long since established their borders. Ota Qwan shrugged. 'Yes.' He looked at the ground. 'In fact, it was my fault.'

Peter knew more about it than he wanted to know, so he remained silent. Wives talked. Husbands heard. Finally, he said, 'I'll be with you, anyway. You know that.'

Ota Qwan stood. 'I'd take it as a favour if you'd say so at the fire,' he said.

Peter nodded. 'When do we leave?' he asked.

Ota Qwan looked at the smoke from the hearth. 'Water's boiling,' he said. 'Two days, if I can get ten men to go.'

Peter slapped him on the shoulder, stooped for the pot, and made tea.

Harfleur and the Sea of Morea – Ser Hartmut Li Orguelleus, the Black Knight

The three round ships towered over the quay, like towers over a castle wall.

The Black Knight towered over his fellows on the quay in direct proportion. He was a head taller than any Galle around him; his arm-harnesses had the circumference of a lady's waist. He was fully armed and armoured, despite being in a merchant port in the very best-protected roadstead in Galle.

He was watching his warhorse swayed by a crane driven by fifty criminals as it carried the drooping equine up, up, up the ship's side. But the dockmen knew their business, and, despite his curses, they got his horse aboard, and those of all his knights – twenty great horses, and ten more besides as spares.

At his side, Oliver de Marche looked up from a tablet. '... crossbows, mostly. They sell well among the Huran, or so the Etruscans tell me.' He shrugged. 'They've never dropped a horse, my lord.'

Ser Hartmut turned to Etienne de Vrieux, his squire. He raised an eyebrow.

De Vrieux bowed to the merchant captain. 'I must remind you that Ser Hartmut does not speak with members of the third estate.'

De Marche cleared his throat. 'But – That is – he *asked* me what we were carrying!'

De Vrieux shook his head slightly. 'No, Master Captain, if I may beg to differ, he asked the air a rhetorical question. If you would care to inform me just what you have in lading, I will pass that information on to my knight, if it proves to interest him. Otherwise, it will best become you not to address him directly.'

'And if we enter battle?' de Marche asked the squire. 'Does your Lord know I was knighted by the Lord Admiral himself?'

Ser Hartmut's eyes never left his horse. 'Battle ennobles,' he said. 'If we enter battle as companions, tell the man I will have no hesitation in speaking to him, nor even in listening to what he might have to say.' He shrugged. 'I do not know the Lord Admiral.' His eyes passed over his squire and locked on the merchant captain. 'Tell him that his unseemly staring will eventually anger me.'

In truth, the Black Knight was one of the handsomest men Oliver de Marche had ever seen. He stood a head taller than any other man on the dock, with blue-black hair and smooth, unscarred olive skin like the southerner that he was. His moustaches shone as if oiled. Perhaps they were, de Marche thought to himself. And his eyes were blue. De Marche had never seen a man with blue eyes and such dark skin.

They were also a very unlikely shade of blue – a dark blue, like lapis. *Damn me, I'm staring at him again.*

Maistre de Marche bowed to the squire. 'Please tell monsieur your master that his wishes will be complied with. And please assure him that these men have never dropped a horse.'

Ser Hartmut's eyes met his, just for a moment. 'Best they not start with mine, then,' said the giant. Rather than madness or arrogance, the dark eyes held amusement. 'And ask our captain, Etienne, while we have his attention – how well armed are your sailors?'

'I won't ship a man who can't fight,' de Marche said, waving the squire aside. 'The Etruscans are growing more outrageous every year. They won't want us in the Great Huran River, either.' He paused and bowed, again, to the squire. 'That is, please tell your master that my men are all armed with a coat of mail and most have a breastplate of the new steel; everyone has a steel cap, a sword, and a pair of spears.'

Ser Hartmut managed a thick-lipped smile. 'With three round ships and all my men-at-arms,' Ser Hartmut said, with a slow smile, 'I will endeavour to give these Etruscans an ill jest.' He nodded. 'We shall have some good adventures, Etienne.'

'Yes, my lord,' Etienne de Vrieux replied, somewhat woodenly.

The Long Lakes – Squash Country – Nita Qwan

They left in the darkness, with dawn just a murmur of orange in the east. Each man had a pair of pails made of birch bark with spruce-root handles. They weighed almost nothing, and men tied them to their spears, put bows over their shoulders, quivers on their backs, five handfuls of pemmican in their pouches, tobacco for smoking while complaining about their wives, and one blanket per man. There were women who usually ran with the warriors, but not this time.

Ota Qwan led them out at a run, and women gathered and screamed or keened farewells, sounding like irks in the warm summer morning – many affectionate farewells, most of them taunting. Peter's wife screamed that he was leaving her to bear the child alone, and Se-hum-se's wife complained that she already felt empty, so empty . . .

They left to laughter.

Running hard.

Nor did they slow. Men who went with Ota Qwan knew who he was and who he wanted to be. He made no secret of his desire to be named war chief again. Every man present had fought by his side, painted like demons, against the drovers and the Hardskins, and every man present knew that the matrons already talked of war with the Huran to the east. Another tribe of Outwallers with dangerous ideas and a penchant for expansion.

A few months with the Sossag had shown Peter they were as complex as any other people. For example, at home, his people had trained for war – a small caste of warriors within each tribe had trained hard. Among the Sossag, almost all men and no few women were warriors, and they never trained. Or rather, every other act was also training. Sossag warriors ran everywhere. There was never a time they walked, except to cross the village. Every hunt was training for war, and every war was practice for the hunt. Hunting in the Wild was war of a sort.

And so was gathering honey.

The first night, because he was fresh, Peter made a little oven from a bank of good clay and baked cornbread. Other men found rabbits and squirrels, and they were well fed, and no one needed a handful of pemmican. A young man – a distant cousin of his wife's called Ayen-ta-naga – leaned over and grinned at him.

'Men say your bread is worth coming to eat,' he said. 'By Tara's bum, it is good to call you cousin.' He laughed.

Other men nodded. In the early days no one had ever thanked him for his cooking, but now that he was fully Sossag, it seemed to be an odd, but real, fame. Nita Qwan, the life maker, was a cook. A damn good cook.

The second day it rained and he was wet, and cold. He didn't relish sleeping in a pile of other men, but he did, and he was getting better at it – he got more sleep than he'd expected, and he rose to a drizzle that hadn't quite extinguished the small fire that had warmed last night's meat. He and his wife's cousin built it big enough for the men to enjoy a little warmth. They made tea, drank it, pissed on the fire, and Ota Qwan told a sullen youngster named Gas-a-ho to carry the pot, which he did with an ill grace.

Peter stopped by the young man. 'Wash it and put it into your honey pail,' he said. 'Much easier.'

The young man narrowed his lips, looked at Peter, and shrugged. 'Fine,' he said.

Later, when he was running beside the former slave, he said, 'You were right. It's easy. Tomorrow I'll just offer to carry it.'

Peter knew he was supposed to grunt with amusement, but he nodded. 'Good,' he said. 'You know, the more work you do, the less crap they'll give you.'

Gas-a-ho ran on in silence.

They ran all day. Peter was bone tired by the end, but proud, too – when he'd first joined the people these all-day runs had nearly killed him. Now, he understood their necessity.

He still hated to run.

That night it rained so hard that there was no point in making a fire. But Ota Qwan sent two of their older men up the ridge on their left – the north – and they found a cave. Really, it was more of an overhang than a cave, and the inhabitants – a troop of coyotes – had to be driven out. They gathered wood while their muscles cooled and the shaman's son lit it with a flick of his hand. They ate pemmican; Peter – the cook – loved pemmican. Other men groaned and complained.

In the morning they ran west again. The weather cleared so that there was a lowering mist in the streambeds, low cloud rolled over their heads, but it didn't actually rain. Peter got a deer through nothing but luck, standing with his back to a tree, pissing down a hill, he saw a doe break cover. He had all the time in the world to finish his business, string his bow, put an arrow to it and watch her stop innocently almost at his feet in a little gully. He watched her sniffing the air – spooked by his urine, no doubt – and he put an arrow neatly between her shoulder blades. She fell dead without a single bound, and the other warriors pounded his back and praised him.

They spent a day there, made shelters, and ate the deer and another that Gas-a-ho brought down. They dried some surplus meat and rose on the sixth day to run again. They had a dry trail and no rain so they ran further than any day before, yet stopped earlier, made a fire, and cooked a sort of stew of half-dried meat and pemmican and raspberries picked from bushes around the campsite.

At darkness, Ota Qwan tapped him on the shoulder. 'Guard,' he said. He went from man to man, naming night guards – an hour of lost sleep.

But they were deep in the Wild, and Nita Qwan knew Ota Qwan was right. He stared into the darkness for an hour – it was an easy watch. Towards the end Ota Qwan came to him with a lit pipe, and they shared it, passing the stone and antler pipe back and forth.

They sat in complete silence for long enough that Peter could see the passage of the stars overhead. He sighed.

Ota Qwan did the same. 'Smell it?' he asked suddenly.

Nita Qwan had no idea what he was talking about. 'Smell what?' he asked.

'Honey,' Ota Qwan said. 'Sweet.'

Peter realised he'd thought it was a lingering taste of sweet tobacco. 'Ah,' he said.

'Quick strike and we turn for home,' Ota Qwan said. 'There's something out here with us. Probably boglins after the honey, too.' He shrugged. 'There's plenty for everyone.' His body rocked as he chuckled. Peter could feel him.

'Better hope so, anyway,' he said.

North and West of Lissen Carrak – Thorn

Thorn sat at the base of an immense maple tree, perhaps four or five centuries old, its branches a natural tent, its trunk home to myriad creatures great and small. A burl the size of a man projected from the trunk to make a rainproof shelter, even for a frame as large as Thorn's.

Thorn didn't mind rain, or snow, or sun. But the tree was *beautiful*, and full of power of its own, and the burl and the shelf seemed to have been made just for Thorn.

He was north of the lakes – two hundred leagues and more from Lissen Carrak. The Dark Sun could not track him here. Not that he heeded the Dark Sun.

That was all behind him.

Instead, Thorn sat in the rain, smelling the air. He had felt Ghause Muriens' sending, and he let it wash over him. She was far away, and her sending did nothing but remind him how much he disliked her and her easy carnality and her foolish passions. She had positioned herself at court as Sophia's enemy long ago, and even though the world had changed since then, still he found her easy to despise.

Sophia is dead.

Thorn shuddered.

Nonetheless, he disliked Ghause Muriens. Almost as much as he disliked moths. And butterflies. He flicked a stick-like hand to drive a large moth off his stony hide.

He disliked moths, he had since boyhood, but just now he disliked everything. Since his escape from the field of Lissen Carrak, Thorn had questioned everything – his allegiance to the Wild, the theory that supported his relationship to other creatures – even the soundness of his own mind.

He had been a fool to attempt command of an army. That way lay nothing but emptiness – it was an empty power. He wanted something more – something palpable only in the *aether*.

He wanted apotheosis. And no amount of temporal posturing would take him closer to his goal. He needed time to study, time to recover, time to evaluate. The world had proved far more complex than he had imagined – again.

If Thorn could have smiled, he would have. He rose, his immense legs creaking like trees in the wind, and put an armoured hand on the trunk of the ancient maple.

'I will go into the far west, and learn a thing or two,' he said aloud. His voice sounded harsh.

I have made myself a mockery of what I ought to be, he thought. But then the thought *I shall retain this shape to remind myself of what I allowed to happen.*

If he was having a conversation with the tree, it wasn't answering. Thorn turned to walk west, and in that moment lightning struck.

The lightning struck all around him, a moment of awesome power. The great maple was destroyed, its heartwood reduced to steaming splinters, its great trunk split as if by a behemoth's axe.

Thorn – whose body was bigger than a giant Ruk or a mighty troll – was struck to earth and pinned under the tree's ancient branches. And still the air around him was like a thick porridge of sheer power.

If Thorn could have screamed, he would have.

Thorn felt he had been *invaded*. But not destroyed. There was something in his head that he couldn't fathom – in his web of tree roots and spiderwebs, where he cast his workings and remembered the hundreds of options he had to his *potentia*, he now had a black space, like rot in the sapwood of a healthy tree.

Nothing could track him here.

And yet something so powerful that Thorn couldn't describe it had appeared, pinned him to the ground, invaded him, and vanished.

Just to the left, through the mountain of destroyed foliage, he could see an object sitting on leaves and branches as if the ruined tree was a massive nest.

It was a black egg, the size of a man's head. But not a true egg, as it was covered in scales, with curious caps on either end – like armour.

An armoured egg.

It radiated power in the *aether*.

It radiated heat in the real.

Thorn put up shield after shield – glowing hemispheres of forest green, layered like a lady's petticoats. Then he tuned, or created, *phantasmic* instruments to magnify, to probe, to explore. And as he did he used his powers and his massive strength to raise the corpse of the great tree off his body.

The egg – it was too obviously an egg to call it anything else – resisted his investigation.

Thorn had no immediate plans. He was, he suspected, in some sort of shock. He sat in the shelter of the burl, and watched and prodded the egg, and the edges of the raw blackness within himself.

He felt violated.

What was that entity? And what does it want?

An hour passed and it did not return. The armoured egg sat, generating heat, and Thorn was gradually filled with power – filled with purpose. For the first time since his defeat on the fells of Lissen Carrak, he knew what he wanted.

North of the Wall – Giannis Turkos

Giannis Turkos sat watching his Huran wife make him moccasins. He wasn't really looking at her; instead he was thinking of the council at which he would speak.

She raised her eyes. 'It is nothing,' she said. 'They will listen to you.'

He shook his head. 'It is more complicated than—' He paused. Two years among the Outwallers had killed his deep-seated belief that they were children to receive lessons, but some deep-seated prejudices remained. One was that he hated sharing his plans. And the Outwallers were not men of the Empire, nor yet even Albans. They were fickle, even whimsical, in a way that no civilised man would ever allow.

But he loved his wife. And he loved her people. Even when they were bent on a war he believed was pointless and destructive.

'There's tea,' she said, sounding oddly childlike with her mouth full of sinew.

Turkos shrugged. He was too worried to drink tea. He stood, went out of their cabin, and found that many of his political opponents in the village were sitting on the front step of the cabin across the small area of packed earth that Turkos thought of as the Plataea. Big Pine waved.

Big Pine was his inveterate enemy at council. Despite that, they had hunted together last fall, killing many deer together and gathering many beaver pelts. Life among Outwallers was a curious mixture of adversarial and cooperative.

So Turkos waved back, and smiled. But being outdoors didn't offer him sanctuary from his wife's sharp eyes and sharper tongue – or rather, it only offered sanctuary at the cost of the elusive interrogation of two hundred and fifty other Huran adults. He slipped back through the moose-hide curtain and took the copper teapot off the fire. He poured them both tea in fine, Morean-made cups, and handed one to his wife, who looked at him with a mixture of amusement and gratitude common to wives in every culture when men do exactly what women expect them to. She spat her sinew into her hand, laid it aside, and drank her tea. He put Wild honey in his.

She shook her head. 'You are like a child,' she said fondly.

He sat back on his chair, which he'd built with his own hands, as no Outwaller would use such a thing, with a small lamp full of olive oil at his side, and read through the scroll that had come a month ago. Again.

The Logothete of the Drum to his servants in the woodlands and wastes, greeting.

It has come to our ears, and sounded softly on our drum, that the Emperor's enemies are attempting to use the Outwallers as a weapon against the Empire. The drum whispers of a heavy Outwaller incursion into Alba in the spring; reliable whispers state that the culprits were Sossag and Abonaki. Any conflict between the Huran and the Sossag could spill into Thrake. Such an incursion into Thrake would have the most deleterious of effects on the economy of the Empire, and with God's will and the Emperor's beneficence, we hope to avert such calamity. Let all the Logothete's servants take note and act accordingly. Further, elements within the palace have become less enthusiastic about the Emperor's policies about land and the Outwallers than before. The Logothete's servants are required to test every assertion of this office commencing with this message for authenticity.

The message was written in a magicked ink on vellum; it was also coded using a letter-number code that was itself changed every six months, and that code translated into a form of High Archaic little used elsewhere in the world. The message had been carried by one of the Emperor's messengers; a powerful bird bred for the purpose. Yet under all these layers of protection, the Logothete – the Emperor's spymaster – had written a message that conveyed very little information and a strong hint of internal betrayal.

Turkos read it again. He'd deciphered it six times, each time looking for a new key or a chance phrase that might lead him to see a different meaning. He'd tried it with last year's key. He'd tried it with a training key he'd been taught at the University.

It said what it said.

Which was very little.

'Speak from your heart,' his wife said. 'Not from the skin of a dead animal.'

Kailin was small, her slim body hard with muscle and with a strong face, not exactly pretty by Morean standards, a little broad, perhaps, but full of character – happy with laughter, fierce with frowns. He loved her face. It had the slightly slanted eyes and sharp cheekbones that reminded him that some of the Outwallers were not, in fact, escaped peasants – many were a race apart from his own.

She leaned forward, and kissed him.

'Sinew breath,' he said, and they both laughed.

He rolled up his parchment and slipped it back into the light bone message tube in which it had come. Then he kissed her again, running a hand down her side, but she swatted him away. 'Get dressed,' she said. 'I'll have these done by the time you've got all your finery on.'

He rose and went to their bed, where they had both laid out his speaking clothes – a carefully chosen mixture of Morean court attire and Huran finery. He had a kaftan of deerskin, cut in the Morean manner but edged in porcupine quill work; instead of hose he wore Huran leggings, with Etruscan beads on every seam. He wore a Morean shirt and braes. As he finished getting the leggings on and tied to his Morean soldier's belt – some things he couldn't give up – his wife bent and offered him the new moccasins.

They were magnificent – the flaps were stiff with purple-and-red-dyed porcupine quill and edged in carefully applied purple wampum.

Purple was one of the Outwaller's favourite colours, but it made Turkos nervous. In the Empire it was a crime to wear purple without the Emperor's express permission.

Which did not prevent him from admiring his wife's work. 'You make me look like a king!' he said.

'The Huran spit at kings,' she said. 'You look like a hero. Which you are. Go speak your piece.' She helped him put his heavy *cinqueda* onto his military belt.

She pulled his cloak – which she had also made – from their sleeping pile. It was made of hundreds of black squirrel pelts stitched together invisibly and lined with bright red wool. She draped it around his shoulders and pinned it with the two pins of his Morean military rank: Stheno's immortal gorgon's head on his right shoulder in silver; Euryale's head on his left shoulder in gold.

Then she handed him his axe – a light steel head with a smoking pipe cunningly worked into the back. He had learned to rest it in the crook of his arm with affected nonchalance for the duration of council meetings, even when they lasted for many hours.

She stretched on her tiptoes and kissed him again. 'When you speak for the Emperor,' she said, 'remember that you are also my husband, and a Huran warrior. Remember that no man at the council is your foe – that all of you strive together for the good of the people.'

He smiled at her. 'Sometimes, I think you are my mother, and I am a small boy.'

She grinned. Took his hand, and felt that it was trembling.

'Oh, my dear! My strength!' She pressed his hand to her left breast. That took his mind off his worries. He smiled. His fingers moved, almost of their own volition.

'I shouldn't tell you this, but the matrons have already decided to do as you ask,' she said. 'No one wanted war with the Sossag except the Northerners.' She sighed. 'Now out!' she said. 'Your hand is making promises that the rest of you will not be here to keep!'

He tried to stoop through the deerskin curtain with all the dignity of two years practice and another twenty years at the courts of Morea.

In the street, dressed equally magnificently, was Big Pine. The man was a head taller than Turkos. They nodded to one and other and, as fate had sent them through their cabin doors together, they were forced to walk through the village together.

'Everyone thinks we've come to an agreement,' Turkos said. They could hear the whispers from every front step.

'Perhaps we should,' said the tall warrior. 'We have a hundred paces. Tell me why we should raid the Northerners and not the Sossag? The Northerners have already struck the Sossag and taken prisoners. And burned villages. They will strike back at us.'

Turkos felt as if one of Christ's own angels had come down from heaven to open his adversary's ears. Nothing like this had happened to him in three summers in the village. Usually his words fell flat; at one council, Big Pine had skilfully argued that Turkos did not speak the language of the people well enough to make his case and his wife had been summoned. Only later had Turkos realised this turned his speech into a woman's words – valuable in the council of matrons, but signifying nothing in the council of men. He'd been laughed at.

Being a laughing stock had not proved as awful as he'd expected

– indeed, in the aftermath, he seemed to have more friends in the village, not fewer.

All these thoughts and a hundred like them rode through his head while he walked silently beside Big Pine.

He wasted ten paces thinking.

Then, he shrugged. 'Peace is better for the Huran than war,' he said. 'The Sossag lost warriors this spring but they gained many weapons and much armour. The whisper of the wind is that they have an alliance with a powerful sorcerer.'

Big Pine nodded. 'It may be as you say,' he admitted.

'The Northerners want nothing but an easy victory. Their sources of beaver were hurt by the drought. Their corn crop was poor.' Understanding struck Turkos like a bolt from the blue. He stopped walking for a moment. He could keep the Huran – at least, his village and the six others that it controlled – out of direct warfare another way.

'What if we send no war party at all?' he said. He took a step. He saw from the look on Big Pine's face that his point had gone home. 'What if we send a delegation to the Sossag, disclaiming any part of the Northerners' war? And send our warriors out—' he tried to find a word to represent the Morean tactical idea of defensive patrolling '—to watch and ambush while we harvest our crop?'

The council fire was close.

Big Pine looked at him. 'No raid at all?' he asked. 'But many little parties – like hunting parties – watching every path.' He scratched the top of his head, where he had a magnificent display of heron feathers. 'Many little war parties kept close means many leaders – and much practice for the younger bloods.' He looked at Turkos. 'If you had come to me with this earlier, this might have long ago been decided.'

Turkos threw caution to the winds. 'I just this moment thought of it,' he said.

Big Pine was seen by the whole village to slap hands with Turkos before entering the council house. Both men were laughing.

The Morea – The Red Knight

'He's *actually proposing* to pay us by marrying me to his daughter?' asked the Captain. They'd stopped for a rest, bridles over their shoulders, safely past Middleburgh and deep in the Morean countryside – pale green hills and sandy rock spires stretching away into the sun-drenched distance.

The Captain chuckled and almost choked on the watered wine Ser Alcaeus had offered him.

Ser Gavin grinned. 'Men say she's the greatest beauty of our time,' he said. 'Not sure what she'd have in resale value, though.'

Ser Alcaeus had become the focus of the whole Imperial messenger service, and daily flights of the great black and white birds kept him up to date on every aspect of the princess's crisis. 'That was ill said, Ser Gavin,' he snapped.

The Captain knocked back the rest of his watered wine. 'Let me get this right,' he said. 'The Duke of Thrake has five thousand men, a powerful magister, an unknown number of traitors inside the city, and more mercenaries coming in from Etrusca, who want the Emperor gone so they can more effectively rape the rest of the Empire. Am I good so far?'

Ser Alcaeus nodded. 'Yes, my lord,' he said, his bitterness obvious.

'We have a hundred lances and our own wagon train. We can't count on the local peasants or the local lords, and now you are telling me that the princess has declared herself Empress, claims to be our employer in lieu of the Emperor who hired us, and has no money to pay us.'

Ser Alcaeus shrugged. 'There was never much money.'

Isn't that the truth, muttered Harmodius.

'So her father planned to marry her to me rather than pay us?' asked the Captain again through a spike of pain. Any conversation with Harmodius carried the possiblity of a blinding headache and a day lost. 'That was his plan?'

Ser Alcaeus made a face. 'I agree that it seems odd—'

Gavin laughed, long and loud. He rolled his right shoulder where the healed flesh continued to grow a fine crop of gold-green scales. He scratched at them too often, as if assuring himself they were real. 'Unless we're to share her,' he began.

Bad Tom slapped his armoured thigh with a gauntleted hand.

Alcaeus's face flushed with blood, and his hand went to his sword.

Ser Gavin raised both hands. 'Ser knight, I am rude in my mirth. I'm sure that the Lady Irene is beautiful above all other ladies save my own.' Lady Mary – the Queen's handmaiden – was Ser Gavin's lady; her veil fluttered from his shoulder.

Ser Michael, formerly the Captain's squire, and now known throughout the company to be the Earl of Towbray's wayward son, took the gourd of watered wine from the Captain. 'If all of us reserve our ladies, surely it diminishes the beauty of the Princess Irene? And yet, if we do not, what a sullen, unchivalrous lot we must seem?'

Ser Michael's lady was a farm girl from Kentmere, and every man present saw her every day. Despite a practical disposition, a swollen belly, and hands red from washing linen with Lis the Laundress, Kaitlin Lanthorn's beauty was not under debate, and her knight was proud to have her plain linen handkerchief adorning his shoulder.

Michael had another swig of the watered wine and handed the gourd on to Bad Tom. 'Not to mention that Kaitlin would have my guts for garters if I were to share such a plunder.'

Tom threw his head back to laugh. The Captain had to hide his face with his long trailing sleeve. Ser Gavin turned his head and his lips curled.

Ser Alcaeus gave up the struggle and shrugged. 'Later, I will kill you all,' he said.

Bad Tom slapped his back. 'You're a loon!' he said. The statement was his highest form of praise.

The Captain held up his hand, and they all fell silent.

'We're rich at the moment. There's no danger of anyone missing a day's pay. It's a fine adventure – rescuing a princess and saving the Empire.' The Red Knight turned and his eyes met his brother's. 'The Emperor assumed I was a penniless mercenary. Of course.'

Perhaps you could rescue her, arrange for her to fall in love with you, and then ride away romantically after burning her note, Harmodius whispered.

I could rescue her, arrange her father's death, and make myself Emperor. Now shut up, the Red Knight muttered in the confines of his head. Carrying a puissant mage five times his own age inside his head had become a far greater burden than he'd ever expected when he rescued the man from death. Or perhaps the man was dead. Whatever was left inside the Captain's head was beginning to hurt him all the time.

Ser Jehan, up until now silent because he was methodically eating a pair of linked sausages, spat out the casing of the last and shook his head. 'But that won't pay the bills.'

'I was hoping to anticipate Ser Jehan, just this once, and show my hard-nosed practicality.' The Captain tipped the gourd back, rolled it in his hand, stared down the neck and then handed it to Toby, his squire, who had another ready to hand.

'But yes, we need to be paid. Saving the princess is probably good advertising, but after Lissen Carrak, it should be some years before we need to do—' he looked around '—well – *anything*.' He shrugged.

Ser Alcaeus narrowed his eyes. 'We're two days' ride from the city. With respect, my lord, I feel as if you are not so much reflecting on the situation as renegotiating.'

The Captain dusted his scarlet surcoat, tugged at his haubergeon to get it to sit better under his many-times-repaired breast- and backplate, and kicked at the air until his riding shoe was better seated inside his right sabaton. Then he leaped onto his new roan warhorse. The horse grunted as he landed, swung his off leg over the high saddle and tucked his feet into the iron stirrups.

'That's right,' he said. 'Alcaeus, we're not knights set on errantry. We're mercenaries.' He looked around at his command staff. 'Besides, princes only value things that they pay enormous sums to obtain. They're like children.'

Ser Alcaeus shook his head. 'So what do you want?' he asked.

'Riches, fame, prowess and glory. I'll start with riches, though.' The Captain smiled. 'We'll make camp on that big hill I see in the distance. Gelfred said it had water and fodder for a week. So we can wait there for a week while we negotiate with the princess.'

Ser Alcaeus was growing more wroth with each exchange. 'We're close enough to raise the siege right now – by Christ's wounds, my lord, you haven't said a word about this dickering until now.'

'Everything has a season. Even dickering.' The Captain rose in his stirrups and watched his company come down the pass out of the high mountains. The mountains in Morea were more brown than green on the nearer slopes, and the foliage was a pale green at that. Below them, forests of olive trees – some terraced and tended, some wild – ran along every ridge. The cultivated patchwork – wheat, millet and barley – began very low on the ridges and ran along the base of the valleys, where narrow watercourses followed zig-zag paths among the fields.

Only the low mountains leaning over the rocky hills separated them from the heartland of the Morea, and the rich farmland. And the city, just visible as a smudge of woodsmoke and a glint of white walls, fifteen leagues distant.

And beyond it the sea.

Ser Michael shook his head. 'The Wild hasn't been here in five hundred years,' he said.

Bad Tom shrugged. 'The wine's good,' he said.

Ser Alcaeus stood at the Captain's stirrup. 'Name your price,' he said. His voice was cold.

'Alcaeus, don't take this personally. It is strictly business. I don't particularly want to marry the Emperor's daughter. Nor, despite all the levity, can I divide her up as payment. So, on balance, I need a concrete offer.' The Red Knight toyed with his sword hilt.

Ser Alcaeus sputtered. 'Tell me what you want. I'll send word immediately.'

The Captain's eyes were on the far horizon. 'I want a new breast-and backplate – one that fits and hasn't had holes punched in it. I hear there are brilliant armourers in the city.'

'You are mocking me,' said Ser Alcaeus.

'No, I'm completely serious. A nice new breast and back by a master armourer would interest me. Personally. Along with everything the Duke of Thrake possesses.'

Ser Alcaeus backed away a step. 'What? I'm sorry—'

'I assume she'll attaint him, and declare all his properties and titles forfeit. I'll take them. In addition, I'll take his office as Megas Ducas – isn't that your title for the Captain-General? Yes? And the right to levy taxes throughout the Empire to support the army.' He nodded, as if he had just that moment thought of the whole thing.

Ser Michael slapped his thigh. He looked around for Ser Alison – Sauce – to share the jest, but she was off with the outriders.

Ser Alcaeus bit his lip. 'The Duke of Thrake is a prince of the Imperial blood,' he began.

The Captain nodded. 'You know, my friend, I know a fair bit about the Empire. I understand that these little family quarrels are common, and family members are used to being immune from retribution if they revolt. Let's change the stakes from the beginning, shall we?'

Ser Alcaeus managed half a smile. 'It will certainly annoy the Duke,' he allowed.

The Lady Maria was acting as the Empress's secretary. She approached the throne – in this case, an ivory chair in the princess's solar – with a pair of message scrolls in her basket. She was pleased to note that the full complement of Nordikans were on guard – six in the outer chamber, and two in the inner chamber. Three days after the Duke of Thrake's attempted coup de main, the bloodstains were gone and the palace had a somewhat brittle air of normality, best seen in the skittishness of the palace Ordinaries who were now searched for weapons at every major doorway.

'A message from my son,' Lady Maria said, with a curtsey.

Irene held out her hand. Her other hand held a small book, bound in vellum. 'Yes?' she asked. 'Has the odious man demanded my hand in marriage? Has the gallant Ser Alcaeus dealt with that?'

'He has,' Lady Maria allowed.

Irene's attention turned to her principal adviser. 'Ah – then we have a basis for negotiation. What has he offered?'

'It is not so much what my son has offered, as what the barbarian Captain has demanded, Majesty.' She handed her Empress – opinion in the palace was deeply divided as to whether Irene was Empress or merely Regent, and the lady herself had been too astute to comment so far – the scroll tubes.

Imperial messengers were big birds, but their size was intended for speed and fighting strength against interceptors, not power in carrying heavy scrolls. The two tubes of birdbone held wisps of rice paper with only a few words on each.

'I apologise for the barbarian's insolence—' Lady Maria said softly.

Irene's face hardened. But her eyes twinkled – she turned to Maria and for the first time in three long days, she vouchsafed a slight smile.

'Duke Andronicus would be *incredibly angry*,' she said.

Lady Maria kept her eyes downcast. 'It is a shocking idea, Majesty. Let me say—'

Irene put a beautiful hand against her beautiful throat. 'I only wish I could be present when he hears. That son of a poxed heretical slut dares to raise his filthy hand against—' She paused. 'Against my father? I'll show him hell and then, with the help of this good barbarian gentleman, I'll send him there.'

As she spoke, her pale face gathered colour and her eyes glittered. Her cheeks went from the colour of old ivory to the colour of a new red rose. The Empress looked about her. 'Has the Grand Chamberlain been found?'

Lady Maria allowed her eyes to meet those of the Nordikan,

Blackhair. The man was handsome, in a tattooed, barbaric way, and she wondered idly how this bold new barbarian mercenary would look.

Blackhair met her eyes steadily and gave a very slight shake of his head.

'Majesty, we have to add the Grand Chamberlain to the list of traitors. Treasonable correspondence was found in his rooms and he has abandoned his home, wife and children to flee.' Lady Maria spoke softly, with inclined head. The crisis had reduced the amount of ceremony in the palace, but Lady Maria intended to keep up the standards of her father's day.

Irene drew herself up. 'Seize his goods and execute his family,' she said. 'Every child.'

Lady Maria nodded. 'Of course, Majesty. And yet—'

Irene turned her head. 'I dislike this phrase. You disagree with my righteous anger? Their deaths will serve to show what line we take with traitors. Did he take the Imperial seal with him?'

'He must have it. If it is in the palace, none of us can find it.' The Lady Maria shrugged. 'Your mother had a duplicate.'

Irene stiffened. 'There can be no *duplicate* of a sacred artefact!'

Maria bowed her head. 'As Your Majesty says. And yet—'

'Again that phrase!' Irene spat.

Maria nodded. 'My initial hesitation, Majesty, is because the Grand Chamberlain has openly kept a young mistress for a decade. He fathered children on her and bought her a house; this woman has gone, along with her brood. The Chamberlain chose to take her and abandon his wife. Her death, I would argue, will only please the Grand Chamberlain. In the second case, while I agree that there should not be a duplicate seal, I offer Your Majesty the evidence of her own senses.' She held out a heavy gold chain with a great ruby-coloured garnet the size of a child's fist, flat on one face, with the arms of the Empire carved into it. Red fire seemed to burn in the heart of the great crystal.

'It is the Heart of Aetius!' cried the young Empress.

'I don't think so. I think, in fact, that your mother of sainted name and spotless repute had a duplicate seal made so that, when she disagreed with your father's edicts on the true religion, she could quietly alter them.' Lady Maria kept her voice down.

Irene digested this, and for a moment, she appeared to be a sixteen-year-old girl and not an ageless pagan goddess.

'I crave your pardon, Maria. Bring the Chamberlain's wife and children to court but strip him of his titles. Purple parchment – gold ink. Make it public. And tell the barbarian we have a deal, and I will fulfil my part when the Duke's forces are broken and driven from my walls.'

The Lady Maria had not had an easy life. She had by turns been a penniless child-aristocrat, a precocious child-courtier, a royal mistress, a discarded royal mistress, the mother of an unwanted bastard, and worst of all, the old Empress's ageing rival.

And now, a train of events beyond her control had catapulted her and her son to more power than she had ever dreamed of wielding. So much power – so much influence – that instead of being concerned with enriching her relatives she had to seriously consider the good of the Empire. If she lived, and if her side won.

Her son had promised her that this barbarian mercenary was capable of working military miracles.

Her reverie was interrupted by the princess. 'Lady Maria, I gather from the Acting Spatharios, Darkhair, that a prisoner was taken during the—' she paused '—the unpleasantness in the palace.'

Lady Maria put a hand to her crucifix and curtsied. 'I know this to be true,' she said.

Princess Irene nodded several times. 'Lady Maria, this man needs to die.'

Lady Maria had suspected the same. 'Consider it done,' she said.

She had the duration of the long walk from the Empress's presence to the stables and mews to consider the ramifications of attainting the Duke of Thrake and declaring all his titles and offices forfeit. He was the most powerful warlord in the Empire. He was the Empire's most successful soldier.

He was an old rival for whom she had nothing but contempt.

She found the assassin in his cell deep beneath the palace stables, and summoned a guard – a Nordikan. They and the Scholae had taken over every armed duty in the palace.

'See that this man is served wine with dinner,' she said. She handed an amphora of wine to one of the Ordinaries.

The Nordikan bowed. 'Yes, Despoina.'

Then she walked up too many stairs to the offices of the messenger service – one of the prides of the decaying Empire. A combination of magnificent animal husbandry, a thousand years of faloncry, selective breeding and solid hermeticism combined to render the Emperor's communications both safe and efficient.

She wrote out the young Empress's answer, rolled it very small, and gave it to the master of the mews. She stood and watched as one of the great black and white birds was taken from the ready aviary, given a bone tube and instructions, and launched. A low-level adept cast a complex phantasm.

The bird rose in the air, its seven-foot wings blowing a fresh breeze over the Outer Court.

Ser Alcaeus bowed at the open door of the Captain's pavilion. Toby was polishing a sabaton with a rag dipped in wood ash. He bowed to the Morean knight and nodded. 'He's drinking,' Toby said.

The Captain was sitting with Ser Alison and Ser Thomas. On the table before them lay a second-rate piece of parchment, carefully marked up in white lead and covered with other scrawls in ink and in charcoal.

The Captain nodded to Ser Alcaeus. 'Good evening. Alcaeus – don't be angry.'

The Morean nodded his head. 'I'm not, my lord. But I'd like to say that I don't like having two sets of loyalties, with both of my masters tugging at my strings.'

Bad Tom stretched out his booted legs, filling the whole back room of the pavilion. 'Then don't have two masters,' he said.

Alcaeus flung himself into a stool. 'Every man has two masters – or three, or four. Or ten. Lords, mistresses, the church, parents, friends—'

The Captain nodded. 'Would we have any chivalric literature at all without troubled and divided loyalties?' He shrugged at Tom. 'You evade the issue by killing anything that disagrees with you.'

Tom fingered his short black beard. 'If I take the job as Drover,' he allowed.

'Just so,' said the Captain. 'Alcaeus?'

The Morean handed over a pair of scroll tubes. 'Yes, if you accept success as the only condition.'

The Captain raised his eyes. They were twinkling. 'Well, well. How desperate she must be. How *angry*. I should have asked for more.' He raised his hands. 'I can agree to payment on success only. Toby – have Nicholas sound "All Officers".'

Nicholas Ganfroy was a young man who had a fancy parchment from the Inns of Court in Harndon stating that he was qualified to serve as a herald in all circumstances. He was very thin and seemed younger than anyone else. There was almost no woman in the company he hadn't mooned after in the three short weeks he'd been attached to the household. His trumpet-playing was in no way as good as the former trumpeter, Carlus the smith, a giant of a man who had died in the final battle at Lissen Carrak.

On this occasion, however, he was awake and attentive, and after three somewhat squalid tries, he managed to sound 'All Officers' well enough to bring Ser Jehan, Ser Milus, Master Gelfred, and the new corporals, Francis Atcourt, John le Bailli, and Ser George Brewes. Ser Alcaeus ranked as a corporal, as did Ser Alison. She raised one side of the pavilion to make more room, and shouted 'Tommy!' in her streetwalker shriek across the evening camp.

Her page dropped the boot he was polishing and sprinted for the command pavilion. Once arrived, he helped Toby and a dozen other pages and squires raise an awning, spread trestle tables and lay out camp stools borrowed from the other pavilions until all the officers sat in a circle around the Captain. Two senior archers came; Cully and Bent. The two men sat with the knights in easy camaraderie that had been absent a few months before, and were served wine without comment by the squires. The last man to arrive was the notary. He nodded to the Captain and took a seat by Bad Tom.

The Captain held up a hand for silence. 'Ser Alcaeus has negotiated us a good contract with our new employer,' he said. 'I'll see to it we turn a healthy profit. So now it's time to get to work. You've all had several weeks of boredom and training. The new lances have had time to settle in. The old warriors have had time to shake the fear.' He looked around. 'Or maybe not, but we all pretend, yes?'

Sauce grinned. 'Anytime, baby,' she said.

'We could make that our motto,' allowed the Captain. 'Gelfred? Would you sum up the situation?'

Gelfred stood and unrolled the parchment that had been opened earlier. It was a whole sheep's hide, scraped very fine, and by lamplight it was transparent.

'The Duke of Thrake has about five thousand men in two main

forces. One is encamped on the so-called Field of Ares by the south-west gate of the city. Most of that force are knights and men-at-arms, although with a few exceptions, the Morean men-at-arms are not equipped or horsed like us at all. They ride lighter horses and wear coats of mail.'

Tom grinned. 'So they're what – a hundred years out of date?'

Ser Alcaeus leaned in. 'There's truth in what you say, Tom, but they are also much better disciplined than most of your Alban knights, and much more capable of manoeuvre than, say, the Galles.'

'Easy meat for a shaft, though,' Bent said.

Gelfred allowed himself a small smile. 'As you say.' He looked around as if expecting more interruptions, and then went on, 'The second force is more balanced, with northern hobilars, which they call stradiotes, to support their men-at-arms, and mounted archers. They are stationed to the south-east of the city, watching the gate where the Vardariote Regiment is quartered. It is fairly obvious that this Duke is more concerned with the Vardariotes than he is with us – if he knows we're here at all. In the last three days we've picked off more of his scouts than you'd believe.' He grimaced. 'However, he has his own force of Easterners.' Gelfred shrugged. 'Honours are about even. We haven't taken one of his Easterners, and they haven't taken any of ours, although Amy's Hob had a close shave today.'

It was well known in camp that Amy's Hob had ridden in at last light with an arrow in the fat of his arse. It had been cause for a good laugh.

'There's a powerful Etruscan squadron based on Salmis, across the bay from the city.' Gelfred looked at the Captain, who nodded. 'We have a source who suggests that the Etruscans are backing Duke Andronicus in exchange for trade concessions.'

Alcaeus nodded. 'That matches the word my mother sends,' he put in. If he was interested in the Captain having an alternate source of information inside the city, he didn't say anything.

'The Etruscans have sixteen galleys and three round ships. Almost a thousand of their marines and three hundred men-at-arms.' He looked around.

Cully whistled. 'Horn-bow archers, every man. Wicked devils, they are. Just like us.'

Bent agreed. 'Rather fight boggles and irks. Their archers ain't up to much.'

The Captain leaned back so far that his stool creaked. 'Are the Vardariotes loyal, Alcaeus?'

'No one is sure. They refused to parade for the traitor, but they haven't left their barracks. Easterners are rather inscrutable.'

'When were they last paid?' asked the Captain.

Alcaeus fidgeted. 'Not in a year.'

The Captain steepled his hands. 'Can you get their leaders to meet us?'

Alcaeus shrugged. 'I can try,' he said.

The Captain looked around. 'Offer to make good their arrears of pay. I'll cover the cost. In exchange, I want them to publicly form up on their parade in the morning and ride through the streets of the town to the—' He paused and looked at the gate. 'The Gate of Ares.'

Everyone craned forward together.

'We're going to fight on the Field of Ares?' asked Michael, the excitement plain in his voice.

'I certainly hope that the soon to be ex-Duke of Thrake thinks so,' said the Captain. 'Ser Alcaeus, I need a simple "yes", or "no" from the Vardariotes in an hour. Toby has written orders for every officer. We march in an hour.'

They sat in stunned silence.

Bad Tom laughed. 'You thought he was going to discuss strategy?' he asked. 'Come on, Sauce.'

She was reading her orders already. 'Need someone to read it to you, Tom?' she asked.

No one else would twit Tom that way. His hand went to his sword and his head shot around, but she grinned at him.

'We're going to march all night across strange ground to fight people we've never met,' she said.

Tom nodded. 'Aye,' he admitted. 'It's like a grand dream come true.'

The Court of Galle – The King, his Horse, and Lady Clarissa

The King watched Lady Clarissa play, and licked his lips.

She smiled at him and continued to play and sing.

When she finished her motet he applauded, and she bent her head modestly. The King rose from his stool – a stool of purest white Umroth bone from Ifriqu'ya, set by a fruitwood table inlaid with the ivory from the same beast – and walked to her. He put a hand on her shoulder and felt that she was trembling slightly, and he could not stop the spread of a predatory smile.

'You dress very plainly for a woman of my court,' he said.

'My lord,' she said very quietly.

'I would have you wear more elegant things,' he said. 'I suspect that you are beautiful. I desire to be surrounded by beautiful things.' His hand began to stroke her back and shoulder insistently.

She stiffened under his hand.

'Your Grace?' asked Abblemont, and the King managed not to jump.

'Yes, my Horse?' he asked.

He turned, his hands already far enough from the woman that he could pretend he'd never touched her.

'Another matter – not for the military council,' Abblemont said.

Mademoiselle de Sartres collected her lute and walked to the door of the King's private solar. Her uncle gave the slightest sign and she knew she was released, and breathed a sigh of relief. The King saw her sigh and his temper flared like the sudden shock of cold water on hot rock.

'I summon and I dismiss, Horse,' he said.

'Of course, Your Grace,' Abblemont said. 'But the matter is urgent and of importance to our policy and the kingdom.'

'I was not through with her!' the King shouted. Abblemont's blank-faced indifference angered him as much as his mother's and his elegant wife's did. He seized the first thing to hand – the stool – and threw it across the room where it struck the wall and exploded, sending shards of Umroth bone in all directions.

'Your Grace,' Abblemont said, carefully.

As usual, when the King had destroyed something, he felt much better. 'My apologies, Horse,' he said. 'You may, of course, dismiss your own niece. What is this business?'

'I want to send more knights to de Vrailly – and more men-at-arms. He is to lead an expedition on behalf of the King of Alba, so we have it in our power to place a complete army inside that kingdom's borders while appearing to be the best of friends.'

The King crossed his arms. 'The Captal? Must we? That lackwit braggart...' He looked away.

'Your Grace must see him as the tool to hand,' Abblemont said.

'While I have your private ear, I have a report that the King of Alba's Privy Council has openly accused us of counterfeiting their coin.'

He was unprepared for the King's shriek of rage. 'How dare he! As if I am some common criminal?'

Abblemont spread his arms and decided that this would be a poor time to remind the King that they were, indeed, counterfeiting Alban coinage. He stifled his sigh because it was becoming more difficult, not less, to manage the King.

'Tell me – Horse, tell me exactly – why I need to support de Vrailly's pretensions?' The King didn't shriek these words. He seemed in control of himself again.

'Your Grace, if de Vrailly can become the King of Alba's mailed fist, the kingdom will fall into our hands whenever we choose to claim it. As it is, the King of Alba is about to anger two of his key noblemen. He may drive them into a position where they are available to join us – or he may eliminate them, and thus reduce his own fighting power. In effect, he will be using our army to crush his own.' Abblemont was careful not to add that he was using de Vrailly to promote cracks in the Alban court and discredit the Alban Queen. It seemed the simplest way.

'Very well. Send more men to de Vrailly.' The King sounded like a sulky boy, and he furthered that impression by chewing on the end of his thumb.

'I had thought to send more knights to aid Messire de Rohan,' Abblemont said.

'That loathsome gossip?' the King said. He nodded. 'Perfect.' He walked over and looked at the wreckage of the stool. 'Please see that this is removed and get me another – perhaps ebony. I like to surround myself with beautiful things,' he said.

Abblemont kept his eyes down. *And you like to break them*, he thought.

Liviapolis – The Princess

Harald Derkensun hated being on duty in the prison. It was demeaning. In Nordika, no one was ever put in prison. Any Nordikan would prefer to die.

The assassin, however, was a model prisoner. He was not a contemptible weakling but a man, and Derkensun found him a pleasant surprise. He nodded pleasantly to Derkensun when he came on duty, and was otherwise silent.

At some point, a pair of men from the Logothete's office came and tortured the assassin. He said nothing – nothing at all.

The more senior of the Logothete's men shrugged. 'Early days yet. Heh – Nordikan. No sleep after this point, eh?'

Derkensun shook his head. 'Eat shit and push off,' he said. 'I do not take part in such things.'

The Logothete's men seemed immune to his anger, and the more junior man remained. He saw to it that the assassin was placed in an iron cage and he rattled a spear shaft against the bars periodically. The only other prisoner, an old man who had been taken for public blasphemy, complained about the noise.

Derkensun put a hand on the shoulder of the Logothete's interrogator. 'This is against the law,' he said.

The interrogator shook his head. 'There is no law,' he said. 'Not for animals like this one. He's a professional killer. Hired man. And his officer escaped. When he betrays his officer, we'll let him go.' He grinned. 'When we threaten to remove his feet, he'll talk. Today was like our formal introduction; don't be such a— Hey!'

'Come back with a warrant,' Derkensun said. He took the interrogator to the great iron-bound door. 'This man is certainly a criminal. So get a writ from the princess – anything. Until then, stay out of my way.' He was angry – angry to be made part of something so deeply dishonourable. And his actions had, at least, bought them all a night of sleep.

An hour later, dinner was served. The two men shared the wine.

The assassin looked up after a sip, and shook his head. 'Shit,' he said. 'Poison.'

The old man crossed himself. 'Really?' he said.

Derkensun stood up, but the assassin was already beginning to foam at the mouth in his iron cage. He babbled a bit, and Derkensun grew pale listening to his words.

And then he died.

So did the blasphemer.

An hour later, as the almost full moon rose, casting a pale white-grey light over the tents, throwing black shadows on the ground, and making armour move like liquid metal, the company had formed up. After a month on the road, even the rawest younger son knew his place in the line. They had a hundred lances, which was to say, a hundred fully armoured men-at-arms, with another hundred squires almost as well armed; two hundred professional archers, most of them carrying the great yew or elm bows that made Alba famous, but a few with Eastern horn bows or even crossbows in the mix, depending on the tastes of the archers and their knight. And another two hundred pages, for the most part unarmoured but carrying light spears, swords, and, in some cases, bows or latches. Recent successes meant that the older pages had some armour, and almost every man had a good helmet with a chain aventail.

Birds had flown back and forth from the city for the last hour – the city itself was less than fifteen miles distant. But Alcaeus had to approach the Captain and shake his helmeted head.

'No word from the Vardariotes,' he admitted. 'The Empress has sent a delegation to them but it may be hours before we hear.'

The Captain nodded. 'I don't have hours. Let's ride.'

'What if they decline?' Alcaeus asked.

The Captain shrugged in the darkness, and his harness rustled. 'Then an opportunity is lost, an easy victory sails through our grasp, and we have to do everything the hard way.' He shrugged. 'And we're out a night's sleep. Let's ride.'

Chapter Five

Ser John

Jarsay – Jean de Vrailly

The Count of Eu watched his cousin's gleaming, steel-clad back as a heavy column of knights and men-at-arms moved down the Royal Highway from Harndon through Jarsay. Behind, twenty of the Queen's new carts rolled along guarded by fifty Royal Foresters and as many Royal Guardsmen in their long hauberks, axes over their shoulders, singing. It was a small army that his cousin commanded, but it was composed of the King of Alba's finest troops, now acting as tax collectors.

Gaston scratched at the base of his beard and wished he were home in Galle. Unbeknown to his knightly cousin he'd written a letter to Constance D'Aubrichcourt's father, the Comte D'Aubrichcourt, asking for her hand in marriage. By implication, he'd have to go home to wed her. Once home, and away from his cousin's endless quest for glory, he'd pull her into bed, close the hangings, and spend the rest of his life . . .

Images of her naked body diving into the pool of icy water drove across his consciousness. All the troubadours said that good love – love with an edge – made a man a better knight, and Gaston had to admit that the image of her naked body poised to dive—

'Halt!' called his cousin.

Gaston snapped out of his reverie to find that a dozen mounted

Royal Foresters had a pair of men on horseback, seething with outrage. The older man had a hawk on his fist.

'By what right do you ride armed in Jarsay?' the hawker asked.

The Captal de Ruth smiled like the image of a saint. 'By the order of the King,' he said.

The hawker shrugged. 'Best send a rider to request my uncle's leave, then.' He leaned forward with adolescent arrogance. 'You're the foreigner – eh? De Vrailly? You probably don't know our ways—'

Jean de Vrailly's face grew red. 'Silence, boy,' he said.

The hawker laughed. 'This is Alba, sir, not Galle. Now,' he said, looking at the Royal Foresters on either side of him, 'I'll trouble you to order these fine men to release me, and I'll be back to my sport.'

'Hang him,' de Vrailly ordered the two Foresters.

The senior man, who wore royal livery, baulked. 'My lord?' he asked.

'You heard me,' de Vrailly snapped.

Gaston touched his spurs to his mount.

'Touch a hair on my head and my uncle will have you roasted alive with your prick in your mouth,' snapped the hawker. 'Who is this madman?'

'Insolence,' said de Vrailly. 'He is insolent! Hang him.'

The liveried Forester took a deep breath and then put out a hand, restraining his companions. 'No, my lord. Not without a writ and due process.'

'I am the King's commander in Jarsay!' spat de Vrailly.

Gaston had his hand on his cousin's bridle.

'And he insulted me! Very well – I see where all this is heading. You – young man. You wear a sword. I'll do you the honour of assuming that you can use it – yes? I challenge you. You have insulted me and my honour, and I will not live another moment without wiping that stain from the world.'

The hawker suddenly understood the gravity of his situation, and now he was scared – his face blotched red and white. 'I don't want to fight you. I want to go home.'

De Vrailly dismounted. 'As you are foolish enough to ride abroad unarmoured, I will take off my harness. Squire!' he called, and Stephan appeared. He ordered up two pages and a cart, and the Captal's armour began to come off – gauntlets first, then shoulders, arms, breast and back, then sabatons and finally the legs in two pieces.

The hawker finally dismounted. His companion, obviously a servant, hissed something at him, and he shook his head.

'Fuck him,' said the young man. 'I'm no coward, nor is my blade a lily wand.'

Gaston decided to try to penetrate his cousin's stubborn arrogance. 'Cousin,' he said softly. 'Do you remember how much trouble you caused killing the squires of Ser Gavin?'

'Eh?' de Vrailly asked. 'I didn't kill them, Gaston. He killed one, and you, I believe, killed the other one.'

Rage flared in Gaston, and he fought it down. 'On your orders.'

De Vrailly shrugged. 'There was no consequence, at any rate.'

Gaston was stung. 'No consequence? Did you not see the position in which you placed the King with his people in Lorica?'

De Vrailly shrugged. 'It is no business of mine if he is weak. I only act for my own honour today, no man can do more.' He was stripped to an arming jacket and hose but he still looked like an angel come to earth – or perhaps fallen to earth. 'Now leave me to this. The maintenance of my honour is my sacred duty. You would do the same.'

Gaston shook his head. 'I would not put myself in a position—'

'Are you suggesting that this is my doing? Let me tell you, cousin, that I have not found you to be as loyal as I have reason to expect as your liege.' De Vrailly met his eye.

Gaston shrugged. 'Perhaps you'd like to fight me, too?'

'Do you doubt that I am the better man?' de Vrailly asked.

Gaston stood very still, and he considered a dozen replies. Finally, he nodded. 'Yes,' he said, very slowly.

De Vrailly reacted by smiling and putting his hand on Gaston's shoulder. Gaston flinched. De Vrailly smiled. 'God has made me the best knight in the world. I am no more worthy than any other, and it is natural that even you, who love me best, should – shall I say it? – be jealous of the favours I receive. I forgive you.'

Gaston bowed his head and withdrew, as carefully as he could. His hands were twitching.

The servant was pleading with the hawker, but the boy would have none of it. He stripped off his peasant's cote – like most nobles, he dressed in simple, dull colours to hunt – and stood forth in a fustian doublet, hose, and thigh-high boots. He unbuckled his sword belt and dropped it into his man's waiting hands, and drew the sword.

The liveried Forester was shaking his head. He looked at the company of foreign knights, and then at the royal Guardsman, and finally his eyes settled on the Count of Eu.

'My lord,' he said formally. The man's hands were shaking. 'Duelling like this is illegal without express permission from the King.'

Gaston pursed his lips. 'How does the King manage to prevent duelling?' he asked, genuinely curious.

The Forester watched the preparations. 'It happens all the time, my lord, but it is proscribed and I am an officer of the law. I'll lose my place, my lord. That boy is the Earl of Towbray's nephew. My lads were foolish to pick him up, but this duel is insane.'

Gaston shrugged. 'My cousin is defending his honour.' He spoke very carefully, and his jaw was more clenched than he could control. 'I tried to stop it.'

The boy set himself in a good stance with his weight back over his hips, his riding sword in one hand, held back and across his body. Gaston knew the garde – it looked ungainly but it allowed a weaker man to block almost any cut from a stronger.

De Vrailly took his own riding sword, drew it, handed his squire the scabbard, and then walked out onto the trampled, green-brown summer grass of the crossroads. He walked towards the boy purposefully, flicked his sword up into an overhead garde and threw a cut as he entered into range – the boy covered with a rising swing. Only de Vrailly's blow was a feint, and his sword flicked around and bit deeply into the boy's unprotected neck, killing him instantly.

Without breaking stride, de Vrailly walked back to his squire and handed him the sword. Stephan produced an oily linen rag and wiped the blade clean. His face showed no trace of emotion – he might have been wiping furniture clean.

The retainer fell on his knees by the corpse and put his face in the dirt.

The liveried Forester shook his head.

De Vrailly began the process of getting back into his armour.

The Royal Forester followed Gaston back down the column. 'You know what this means, my lord? Instead of merely collecting the Earl's back taxes, and he meekly handing us the silver because we're here in force, he will instead raise his retainers and *fight*. He'll have to. Honour will demand it.'

Gaston sighed. 'I think that will suit my cousin perfectly. A nice little war to occupy the late summer.'

The Forester shook his head. 'I'm sending a rider to the King,' he said.

Harndon – The Queen

The Queen of Alba stood in front of her mirror, looking for signs of her belly swelling.

'I'm *sure*,' she said to her nurse, Diota, who shook her head.

'You had your courses—'

'Forty-one days ago, you hussy. I can tell you where I conceived and when.' She stretched. She loved her own body, and yet she was content to see it pregnant. More than content. 'When can I know if it is a boy?'

'Womenfolk aren't to be despised, mistress,' Diota snapped.

Desiderata smiled. 'Women are infinitely superior to men in most respects, but the peace of this kingdom needs a sword arm and a prick with a brain behind it. Besides, the King wants a boy.' She grinned.

Diota made a clucking noise. 'How did you get a baby off the King, sweet?'

Desiderata laughed. 'If I have to tell you, I suppose I will. You see, when a woman loves a man, she—'

Her nurse swatted her affectionately.

'I know how to make the beast with two backs, you little minx. I know how to find the sap and how to make it rise, too. None better!' Diota stood with her hands on her hips – a big woman with breast and hips ample enough to make her waist seem small. When Diota laughed, she filled a room. And there was something indescribable to her manner that led men to find her desirable, even when she belittled them.

The Queen smiled. 'I never doubted it.'

'But the King—' Diota paused, and frowned. 'I'm sorry, mistress. It's not my place.'

'Now you have me going, you coarse old woman. What do you know?'

'No more than half the court knows. That the King incurred the anger of a woman. And she cursed him to father no children.' Diota's voice grew quieter as she spoke. It was treason to speak of a curse on the King.

Desiderata laughed. 'Nurse, you speak nothing but nonsense. He has no curse. Of that, I can assure you.' She beamed. 'When he came back from the battle—' She stared dreamily off into time.

Her nurse smacked her on the rump. 'Get dressed, you strumpet. If you've kindled, you might as well enjoy these summer kirtles while you still have a flat tummy and a maiden's breasts.' But she squeezed her mistress' hand. 'I meant no harm,' she said.

'Do you think I hadn't heard the rumour?' Desiderata asked. 'Heard it, and heard other whispers, too. Two years in the King's bed and no baby?' She whirled on her nurse. 'Ugly stuff. Hurtful, ugly rumours.' She looked away, and her face settled into its habitual look of open pleasure at the world. 'But my powers are as great as any challenge. Or curse.' Her voice lowered a little, and Diota shivered. 'Who was she, Diota? This woman who cursed my King?'

Diota shook her head. 'I'd tell you if I knew, mistress. It was long ago. When he was young.'

'Twenty years ago?' the Queen asked.

Diota shrugged. 'Perhaps, sweeting. I was nursing you, not listening to court gossip.'

'And who got you with child, that you were my nurse?' Desiderata asked.

Diota laughed. 'Weren't exactly the King, if you take my meaning,' she said.

Desiderata laughed aloud. 'My pardon, I meant no such thing, and I am being indiscreet.'

Diota put her arms around her mistress. 'You're scared, sweeting?'

Desiderata shivered. 'Since the arrow struck me,' she said, 'the world seems darker.' She shook herself. 'But my baby will make it right.'

Diota nodded. 'And your tournament?'

'Ah!' said the Queen. 'My tournament – oh, my sweet Virgin, I had forgotten! I will be big as a sow at Pentecost.' She shrugged. 'Well, some other girl must be the Queen of Love. I'll be a mother.'

Diota shook her head. 'Are you growing up, pipkin? The knights will still come for you – not for Lady Mary or any of your other girls, pretty as they are.'

'I hear that the Empress's daughter is the most beautiful woman in the world,' the Queen said.

'Well,' said Diota, 'she will be in a few months, anyway.'

'Oh, fie!' said Desiderata, and smacked her.

And they both gave way to laughter.

Harndon – Edmund the Journeyman

Edmund the Journeyman – as his peers now called him – sat on a workbench with his feet dangling. He was facing three younger men, all senior apprentices. His anxieties were mostly caused by the fact that for two years he'd eaten and slept with them, and pulled pranks, stolen pies, wrestled, and been bested or triumphed, swaggered sticks, swashed and buckled—

And now they worked for him, and he wasn't sure how to reach across the sudden gulf between them.

'I see three ways of approaching the problem,' he said. 'We can cast them, like hand bells. We can cast blanks, and bore them – and that's dead slow.'

The youngest, a white-blond boy named Wat, but whom every other apprentice called 'Duke' for his aristocratic looks, laughed. 'You mean *we'll* bore it while you sit in the yard and think lofty thoughts.'

Edmund had learned a thing or two from Master Pye and he looked mildly at Duke, and said nothing.

'Sorry!' said Duke, in the same semi-demi-mock-rueful tone he used with the master.

'The third way is to build something like a barrel of iron staves, and hoop it, and forge weld the whole.' Edmund held up his first successful model. 'Everyone look at this.'

Sam Vintner, the eldest, held the octagonal tube for a few breaths. 'It failed,' he said flatly.

Edmund sighed inwardly. 'It failed after twenty shots. My forge welds weren't good enough.'

Sam pursed his lips and nodded. 'Do it on a mandril?' he asked.

Edmund had to bite a comment. He didn't like having his work questioned. But if he slapped Sam down now— Still, he was human. 'Of *course* I used a mandril,' he said.

Sam shrugged to show he meant no harm. 'A red-hot mandril? To keep the heat?'

'What do you mean?' asked Edmund, intrigued.

Sam grinned. 'I'm making this up as I go along. But it stands to reason, don't it? You need the welds to be as strong and smooth inside as out, right?'

Edmund nodded, already thinking through to the end of the argument. 'In fact, the welds *only* have to be strong and smooth inside.'

The middle apprentice took an apple out of his back and started eating.

'Tom?' asked Edmund.

Tom shrugged. 'Just tell me what to do,' he said.

'Talk about the project,' Edmund said. 'That's what we're doing. When you are an apprentice, mostly no one asks your opinion; the more senior you are, the more your master will consult you.'

Tom nodded. Took another bite of apple. 'Sure, boss. I'll bite. Why not cast 'em?'

Edmund had the first one he'd cast. He handed it around. 'Bronze,' he said.

All three boys groaned. Bronze cost twenty times what iron cost.

'Cast them in iron,' Tom said.

Edmund chewed on the idea for a moment. 'I've never cast anything in iron,' he said. 'Have you?'

All three apprentices shook their heads.

Edmund shrugged. 'I have heard cast iron is brittle. I'll ask Master Pye.'

'And I imagine that, if you cast them, the bore will be rough when you want it smooth,' said Duke.

Tom finished his apple and threw the two small bits of the core he'd left into the forge fire.

Edmund shook his head. 'Let's start with a heated mandril,' he said. The boys all nodded.

'Tom, you and Duke make a mandril. Here's my old one. One inch in diameter, no taper. Best make three.'

'Has to be steel,' said Tom.

Edmund shook his head, stung. 'Of course it does.'

'It'll deform with heat,' said Tom. 'And if it's hot enough to keep up the temperature in the welds, it'll end up welded to the barrel staves.'

Edmund was beginning to see why Master Pye had been so

willing to part with Tom. 'That can probably be controlled by careful judgement,' he said. 'And a little judicious use of water or oil.'

'Sure,' said Tom, by which he pretty obviously meant, *Wait and see. I'm right.*

Edmund ended the day feeling that Mr Smyth's hundred gold leopards might be harder to obtain than he'd expected.

But in the evening, he dressed in good wool and linen, hung his buckler – all steel, burnished like a lady's mirror – on his belt with his sword – also his own work – and after preening in Mistress Pye's glass for a moment, he walked out into the evening air. Summer was on the wane, and darkness was coming earlier – sad news for all working folks, for whom long summer evenings meant relaxation, warmth, and gossip.

He crossed the square to his sister, who stood with four other girls. They fell silent as he approached. Anne – his favourite, although nothing was settled, as one might say – smiled at him, and he returned her smile. She had full lips and large eyes; a kirtle that fit a little more tightly than most girls', in a fine burgundy. She sewed for her living, and was already fully employed, running shirts and braes for Master Keller, the tailor, to half the court. Her white linen shift had fancy threadwork at the neck and cuffs, but all her patient labour didn't catch his interest as much as the creamy white tops of her breasts and the swell of her hips.

'See something you like?' said his sister, and slapped his side – hard.

No man is a hero to his sister. He rolled away from her follow-on blow and looked rueful. 'The sele of the day to you, ladies.'

'Now he's a perfect, gentle knight,' Mary said, and laughed. 'Don't you have somewhere you're supposed to be? We're talking. Girl talk.'

'A court boy tried to put his hand down Blanche's gown!' said Nancy, who was too young to know you didn't say such things in front of a brother.

Edmund bridled. 'What court boy?'

Blanche was his sister's best friend – tall and blond and elegant. She worked at the palace, and gave herself airs. But she looked less haughty than usual today. 'I gave him no cause,' she said. 'He just – grabbed me.'

Edmund didn't like this, the more so as his sister wanted a palace position, too.

'What were you doing?' he asked.

'Ninny!' said his sister. 'It's not her fault, you gormless fool. Sod off – go hit someone with your sword.' She made a shooing motion with her hand. 'Go away!'

She threw a slight smile in the last motion – almost a wink. They were brother and sister and he got the message. 'Your servant, madam,' he said with a deep bow.

Across the square, two dozen boys took turns playing at sword and buckler. The game was a complex one with many unwritten rules. Boys and men used sharp swords – so the only target permitted was the buckler. Some games allowed the defender to move the buckler, and some specified that the buckler had to be hit a certain kind of blow, and some boys had elaborate sword and buckler chants, with each boy going through a particular rhythm of blows and blocks to a rhyme or a poem.

Edmund fancied himself a fair blade. He practised at the pell in his master's yard; he had a chance to watch real knights and men-at-arms test new weapons. Master Pye sometimes even took lucky apprentices and journeymen with him to the palace to watch the Royal Guard practise, or to see knights prepare for the tournament.

He paired up with Tom, who, despite being three years his junior, was already fully his height and weight. They started slowly, and Edmund requested a halt to take off his cote and retie his hose. Tom shook his head. 'Why wear a cote and tight hose to the square?' he asked. 'It's like you was dressed for church!'

Other, older boys rolled their eyes. Most boys over fifteen dressed up to go to the square.

Edmund smiled to himself and folded his jacket.

He and Tom had a fine bout – long enough to work up a good sweat, skilful enough that the other young men pressed around, watching them. Edmund was the better blade, but Tom was so *fast* that the exchanges were never one-sided.

Eventually, though, as the younger boy's wrist started to tire, Edmund began to strike his buckler faster and harder. And then Tom stepped back and raised a hand – at first Edmund thought it was surrender, but then he saw what Tom had seen – the other young men were watching something else.

The four new boys stuck out from the moment they entered the square. They wore bright clothing, where most apprentices wore drab or black. The leader – and there was no mistaking that he was the leader – wore hose that were striped in three colours, in the Gallish fashion, aping the look of the new foreign knights and making him look like a fool to Edmund. But he noted that all the girls turned to look at this display.

The new boys talked loudly, too, and swaggered. The thinnest of them – a boy so thin he was on the edge of invisibility – managed to take up so much space that he bumped into one of the boys watching the sword and buckler play.

The local boy stepped back and mumbled, 'Beg your pardon' automatically.

The colourful boy shoved him. 'Hey, fuckwit, watch where yer going!' he said, and his mates laughed.

The boy who'd been shoved looked resentful, but didn't take the matter up.

The thin boy whooped. 'Look at the pretty sluts,' he said.

Tom sighed. 'They want trouble.'

Edmund had just heard his sister called slut. He was doubly maddened to see several of the girls giggle and look at the brightly clad bastards. But his sister met his eye firmly.

He was a journeyman. It wasn't his place to get in brawls.

But his three apprentices were watching him. Sam smiled, Tom frowned, and Duke was picking up his buckler.

The leader had the short hair the Galles wore, and his, like Duke's, was white-blond. He had sharp features and a long dagger on his crotch, with a sword on his left hip. He rubbed the hilt of his ballock dagger. 'Which of you bitches wants it?' he asked. He laughed. 'You, sweet?' he said, stepping close to Mary.

Their behaviour was absurd. But Edmund had heard about them – gangs that acted like Galles, and kept to what they called the 'Rule of War'. Some of them really were the squires and pages of de Vrailly's men, and some just dressed to be like them.

The thin boy cackled. 'They all want it,' he shouted. 'There's not a man with balls here!'

Edmund stepped out of the crowd of apprentices. 'Get lost,' he said. It wasn't said as mildly, as drily, or as loudly as he'd intended, and worst of all, his voice rose as he spoke. His hands were shaking.

The colourfully dressed boys were scary.

'What was that, little fuckwit?' asked the leader, whom Edmund had christened Blondie. 'Go hide in your bed; the hard boys are here.' He put his hand on his dagger. 'Want some of this?'

For days afterwards, Edmund would think of witty replies. But at the time, he just shrugged.

'What's that?' said the boy, and drew both weapons.

Edmund was Harndon born and bred. He knew that lower-class boys were tough as nails and fought differently from apprentices. On the other hand, he'd used weapons since he was a boy, and he was a Harndonner – he didn't make way on the street for anyone.

He plucked his buckler onto his fist. 'He drew first,' he said cautiously, to the crowd of apprentice boys.

Blondie made a sly cut – a long, leaping cut from outside engagement range. It was a fight ender. And a move that would probably lead to a murder trial.

Edmund got it on his buckler and almost lost the fight immediately, as the other boy tried to power over the rim of his little shield and into his shoulder with his hilt. He had a feeling of unreality. The fool was really trying to kill him.

Then the reality of it hit him.

He got his sword out of his scabbard in time to stop two strong cuts to his open side, and blind luck and long training left his buckler in the way of the dagger strike – which nonetheless licked past his buckler and pricked his arm.

He backed away.

'I'm going to *fuck you up*,' Blondie said, just as one of his mates slammed his fist into Edmund from behind.

Everything happened at once.

The punch shocked Edmund – but it fell on bone, and it turned him and made him stumble to the left. Blondie attacked, stamping his foot and cutting heavily at Edmund's unshielded side – even reeling in pain, Edmund had the boy summed up. He only had three cuts.

Unfortunately, his stumble didn't save him and he fell.

But he rolled, cut low, and connected.

It was the first time Edmund had ever used a blade with intent – and even hurt and desperate, he had a heartbeat's hesitation in putting his full force into the blow. But it landed hard enough, and Blondie gasped.

Edmund got to his feet to find that a dozen apprentices were burying the thin boy in fists.

Blondie's hose were ruined, and blood was spreading over his shin.

He backed away. 'I'll be back with twenty bravos,' he said. 'My name is Jack Drake, and this square is mine. And everything in it.'

Edmund would, under other circumstances, have let him go except for the last comment. He followed the retreating boy.

'Coward,' he said. It was the first thing in the fight that went the way he wanted.

Blondie paused, and then laughed. 'I'll be back, and then you're dead,' he said, and his boys came and helped him walk. But as soon as they were clear of the ring of bystanders, the man called Jack turned and came after Edmund.

He cut at Edmund's head again – outside line, high to low.

This time, no one hit Edmund in the head and his sword licked out, picked up the cut and forced it down even faster across his opponent's body and onto Edmund's buckler as he stepped forward. He bound the man's arms under his buckler, and slammed his pommel into the man's mouth, making teeth fly.

The same motion threw the man to the ground. Edmund kicked him. The man threw up.

'Kill him!' shouted several apprentices.

The thin boy had been beaten bloody. The other two were across the square.

Edmund had every eye on him. Anne looked—

'Yield,' he said, putting his sword at the man's throat.

'You better fucking kill me, fuckwit,' Drake said. He spat another tooth.

Edmund shrugged. 'You are wode,' he said. 'Insane!'

The other man's eyes bored into him. 'This square is *mine.*'

Edmund didn't know what to do. He couldn't just kill the bleeding man in cold blood. And his insistence was as frightening as his original challenge.

'That's why I'll beat you, fuckwit,' Drake said. 'You haven't got the balls—'

A board hit Drake in the head, and his body sagged. Tom leaned on the board – a door lintel from a building site. 'My da says you have to kill 'em like lice,' he said.

'What about the law?' asked Edmund. He couldn't tell whether the man was alive or dead.

'I don't see the sheriff,' said Tom. 'Good fight, by the way. Nice move.' He laughed. He sounded a little wild, but his hands were steady. 'Let's take him somewhere – the monastery. Monks always know what to do.' He shrugged. 'He's not dead. You gonna let him live?'

Edmund found his hands were shaking hard. 'Yes,' he said. And knew he'd regret the weakness. But he also knew he couldn't kill Jack Drake in cold blood. Not and be the same man afterwards.

Albinkirk – Ser John Crayford

Ser John looked at himself in the polished bronze mirror recently mounted on the armoury wall, and laughed aloud.

His new squire, young Jamie, paused. 'Ser John?'

'Jamie, there's nothing sillier than an old man aping a younger one,' he said.

Jamie Vorwarts was a Hoek merchant's son. His whole family had died in the siege and the boy had nowhere to go. He knew more of arms than business, and he could polish steel better than any squire Ser John had ever had. He was perhaps fourteen. He was tall, a little too thin from hard rations, and his face was a little too pinched to be considered handsome.

He went back to polishing his master's new six-piece breastplate. It was an expensive miracle of steel and brass, with verses from the Bible inscribed around the edge.

'You could at least tell me I'm not old,' Ser John said.

He was standing in front of the first mirror he'd owned in twenty years, wearing a fine green doublet, three layers of heavy linen covered in silk, and laced to the doublet were a pair of hose in green and red – themselves embroidered in flowers and fall leaves. The hose were slightly padded and quilted to wear under armour, and so was the doublet, but for Albinkirk they were as good as court clothes and they made him look slim and dangerous.

And old.

'Mutton dressed as lamb,' he said with a curse.

Jamie looked at him and allowed himself a smile. 'That's damn good, my lord.'

'I didn't concoct that little saying myself, you young scapegrace.

When I was about forty years younger, that's what we called prostitutes who were too old to roll over.' The old man frowned.

'Older women are very attractive,' Jamie said carefully.

'I know somewhere you will be very popular indeed,' said Ser John.

An hour later, the two of them arrived at Middlehill Manor with a pair of donkeys laden with hampers. Ser John sat on his horse in the yard, noting that the new sheep had trimmed the yard grass, and he didn't see so much as a wayward scrap of cloth on the ground – the grass was yellower than formerly, but the house was clean and neat, the door was replaced on its pintles – he'd helped with that himself – and out in the fields, six women took turns holding a plough for winter wheat. Their furrows were none too straight but then ploughing was hard work even for a fit man.

'Jamie?' he asked. 'See those fine ladies struggling with a plough?'

Jamie leaped down and then paused. 'Is it a chivalrous thing to plough?'

Ser John frowned. He felt like a magnificent hypocrite whenever he spoke on chivalry, as he'd spent most of his life killing men for money while wearing armour. But he shrugged. 'Jamie, to the best of my understanding, anything you do to help a woman who needs help is chivalry. In this case, that's ploughing.'

Jamie stripped his cote and his doublet in the warm sun, and Ser John smiled, thinking that he would endear himself *very deeply* to the six women who now paused, favouring their backs and fully aware that they were about to be saved from more ploughing.

Helewise came into the yard and smiled. 'I ploughed yesterday,' she said. 'My pater taught me a woman can do aught a man can do. But by the wounds of Christ, he was a gentleman and never had to plough a furrow in his life.' She caught herself tossing her hair, which just happened to be down. And clean.

'I could rub your back,' Ser John said. 'It works when I've exercised too long with the sword.'

She smiled happily at him. 'I might hold you to that, ser knight. But not, I think, until all are abed.' She was already moving towards the door, and although she spoke naturally, she kept her voice low. 'And perhaps not tonight.'

He stabled his own horse and saw that the nun's palfrey had been there – her elegant shoes had left prints in the straw, and there were fresh droppings in the next stall.

He went into the house, and Helewise indicated a settle in the kitchen and went back to wrapping twine around herbs. 'I saved most of my herb garden,' she said. 'I suppose they're really wild plants, and the Wild didn't mind them too much.'

He joined her, cutting lengths of hemp twine and giving each bundle of rosemary a single twist. A very young boy – just seven or eight – took them one at a time, climbed a ladder, and hung them from the rafters.

'What brings you here this time?' Helewise asked, eyes twinkling.

'I've sent to the King for a new garrison,' Ser John said. 'Until then, Jamie and I are knights bent on errantry. You may see us more frequently than you like.'

'I doubt it,' she said, and just for a moment their hands touched.

'Sister Amicia was here,' she went on. 'She'll be back tonight, more's the pity.'

'You mislike her?' asked Ser John.

'Never say it. By the rood, John, I love her for her confidence. She makes women proud to be women and my daughter fair dotes on her. I won't say my daughter's bad, John, but she was in Lorica where it is all the fashion for young gentlewomen to play the wanton—'

John smiled.

'Don't smirk at me, sir! I'm too old to kindle and too practical to come to harm.' She blushed.

'For myself, madam, I find you very beautiful.' He reached out, greatly daring, and pushed a lock of her hair from her forehead. He smiled into her eyes. 'But it is all the Queen. She is a force of nature, and she has them all playing at it.'

'I won't hear a word agin' her.' Helewise sat back.

'I speak none. But what is right for the Queen might not sit so well with a mother,' Ser John said.

'Where was all this wisdom twenty years ago, messire?' she asked.

He laughed. 'I hadn't a grain of it, sweeting.'

She shook her head. 'I miss Rupert. Seems an odd thing to say to you, but he was solid. And he was better with Pippa than I am.'

John shook his head, leaned into the chimney corner and stuck his booted feet out towards the fire. 'I was never jealous of him. I'd never make a husband.' He looked at her. 'He'd never ha' made a knight.'

'True that,' she said. 'I crave your hands on my body,' she said suddenly.

'Now who's wanton?' he asked.

She shook her head. 'Any gate, you best not come to me tonight while the nun is here.'

He smiled and rose. 'In that case, I'll not quibble to hold the plough and work up a good sweat.'

'Though you look very fine,' she replied.

As swift as a sword strike, he bent over and planted his mouth on hers.

Three long breaths later, she broke away. 'Fie!' she said. Delight rather ruined her attempt to be severe. 'Broad daylight!'

Later the nun came into the yard, and Ser John, now stripped to his hose, took her palfrey, and then used a fork to muck the straw and put in new. She brought feed.

'I have your package,' he said. 'Right here in my saddle pack.'

She smiled. 'You needn't have. We're not much for things of this world.' She smiled more broadly. And then frowned. 'I haven't seen a Wild creature, but down towards the old ferry I saw a swathe of destruction as if a herd of oeliphants had made a dance floor. Trees are down. And there's a house I think I remember intact, now roofless.'

'By the ferry?' Ser John asked. He was rooting in his pack and it began to occur to him that he'd left her package on his work table in Albinkirk. 'How often do you get to the ferry?'

'Every week,' she said. 'I have a special dispensation to say mass at the ruined chapel there. It's the only kirk for seven mile.'

Ser John had a sudden notion. 'Wait,' he said. He reached in his belt-purse, and there it was – a package the size of a big walnut. 'Not in my saddle bag at all, I fear,' he said ruefully.

She took the package and looked at it. He thought she looked disappointed. 'Oh,' she said. 'May I borrow your eating knife?'

He drew it from the sheath of his roundel and handed it to her, and she slit the waxed linen of her package. It proved to actually *be* a walnut. She cracked it open it and gasped.

He paused and then said, 'Are you all right?'

Her face worked, and she was weeping silently. Then she gathered her wits. 'Bastard!' she spat, and hurled the walnut shell across the stable to clatter against a distant stone wall, lost in the darkness.

Ser John, provided with yet another test of chivalry, elected to slip quietly out the main stable door. Some things are too perilous for mere men, and the air around her had begun to glow a golden green, casting light in the dark stable, and he didn't think he was up to whatever she might be about to face.

But in a few heartbeats the light died away, and he heard a fragile laugh. She stepped into the dying light of the day from the darkness of the stable, and something glittered on her hand.

'He sent me a profession ring,' she said. She held out her hand, the way a woman might show a betrothal ring. The ring bore the letters 'IHS' in beautiful Gothic script.

'Who did?' asked Ser John, feeling like a man caught in someone else's story.

She frowned. 'I think you know,' she said.

Ser John bowed. 'Then I think he's a bastard, too.'

Over dinner, the women admired the ring. It was gold, and very handsome. Sister Amicia was back in control of herself – she showed the ring calmly, and admitted readily that Ser John had brought it to her.

Phillippa tried to tease her, leaning forward and saying, 'Perhaps it is from a secret admirer!'

The look she received caused her to sit silently for five whole minutes.

Helewise kept shifting in her seat, looking at the ring from various angles, and finally she reached out, almost unconsciously, and caught Sister Amicia's hand. 'It seems hermetical,' she said.

'It is!' Amicia said, obviously delighted. 'I can store *potentia* in it. It is a blessed thing.' She smiled at Helewise. 'How did you know?'

Helewise shrugged. 'It seems to change shape.'

'Change shape?' asked the nun. She grinned. 'I haven't seen that. What shape does it take?'

Helewise shook her head. 'You – a holy woman of power – accepted this token and put it on without question?'

Amicia paled. But her face cleared when she drew the ring easily from her finger, and it sat, heavy and potent, in her hand. 'You are right, Helewise, and Sister Mirim will rightfully assign me a penance for recklessness. Among other things,' she said, frowning.

'There it goes again,' said Helewise. 'It changed shape in the palm of your hand. Just for a moment.'

'What did it look like?' asked Amicia.

'Much the same, I suppose,' Helewise said, looking at Ser John for support. He smiled at her, having seen nothing.

But young Jamie leaned forward with the earnestness of the young. '*Ma soeur*, sometimes it doesn't say "IHS".'

Amicia flushed. 'It doesn't? What does it say?'

He shrugged. 'It looks to me like "G&A".'

Amicia sighed. 'Damn,' she said, and dropped the ring into her belt pouch. Then she smiled her girlish, impulsive smile at Phillippa, and said, 'I think you are right after all. A secret admirer.'

The Wild North of the Inner Sea – Thorn

Thorn had walked several hundred miles, by his own count. He had crossed the Adnacrags, and then he had crossed the Wall, and then he had crossed the river. He had gone west, and he had gone north.

His wanderings took him to the great marshes where boggles bred in the freezing headwaters of the immense river system that defined the borders of the far west. He worked his will on them, not once but five times – in a swamp so vast and desolate that there seemed nothing alive but rotting vegetation and ooze for a day's walk in every direction, and the massive mounds that bred the boggles rose like organic volcanoes at his command.

And then he started east, now on the north shore of the mighty Inner Sea. He had never been here before but he walked with confidence, and the knowledge of where to place his feet seemed to roll like a helpful poison from the black space in his head.

Somewhere to the east lay the land of the Sossag people. Beyond them was the country of the Northern Huran.

Thorn felt it would be petty for a being of his power to avenge himself on the barbaric Sossag for their failure to aid him in his hour of need. He felt such behaviour was beneath him, but he found himself plotting it nonetheless. The Huran had lost many warriors in his service. The Sossag had not. They had chosen to go their own way.

North of the Inner Sea was a different kind of country – Wild, indeed, but thickly populated with Outwallers. He had had no idea that the Great North Woods held so many men and women and children, and he moved cautiously. It was not that he lacked the power to destroy; but he had learned enough humility to know that moving undetected created fewer complications. He moved cautiously west, skirting the settlements of the great beaver and the Gothic swamps of the Kree where the Hastrenoch bred amid dead trees and brook trout. He passed to the north of the outlying Sossag villages and their northern cousins of the Messaka, and turned south into the squalid villages of the Northern Huran, whose markings he recognised. There were also ruder settlements – wild irks without a lord, and in the middle of the lakes, islands made of great logs and piled rocks by the Ruk. The giants.

The black space in Thorn's head had plans for the Ruk.

He stood on the shore of a lake in the burned lands and waited until the Ruk came to him. He gave them gifts, like children at a party, and turned them to his own ends. The Ruk were too simple for debate and argument – instead he ensnared them and sent them on his business, breaking them to his will as easily as a man disciplines a dog.

He repeated this at every lake in the burned lands that had one of the islands that the Outwallers called crannogs.

He sent other creatures to listen, and to speak, and to gather news, and he learned that the Northern Huran, having taken losses in his wars, were threatened by their southern cousins across the Great River, and from further east. And he learned that the great Etruscan ships had not come this year. He set spies to visit the distant court of the King of Alba, and to watch that blazing fire, his wife, the Queen.

He made his decisions, then. He did not help the Northern Huran simply because they had been his allies. They had been loyal. But the forests were full of potential allies and slaves and he owed the Northern Huran nothing. But now he had goals, and goals led to plans, and the Northern Huran would be his servants – willingly or unwillingly.

Thorn stopped for a day in the deep woods, and practised a new mantle – a body into which he put much skill, making it a form he could wear with ease. It was that of an old, sage Outwaller – one with clear, honest eyes and old scars. An old man with wisdom writ hard on his lined face and the name Speaker of Tongues, an old shaman. In that form he visited the smaller towns. He sat at the fires and listened to the matrons, healed children, made medicine. Many benefited from his powers. Word of him spread like wildfire among the Kree and the Northern Huran.

In each village he whispered a few thoughts, and pinned them to the minds of the men and women who were the deepest in greed. He left them like seeds, to grow with time.

Then he shed the semblance of Speaker of Tongues like an old snake shedding a skin, and he moved in great strides, passing through the endless forest like a light wind. He used his new powers sparingly – to contact a man in Lorica, a woman in Harndon, and a man deep in the Wild to the south. For them, he wore no semblance. He was a voice in the ear, and a thought, briefly tasted. It was exhausting, and he spent whole days in rest, standing exposed to the elements, before he would walk on. He had new powers to explore, new venues to work, and this ability to manipulate his shape so easily was disturbing.

He couldn't remember how he'd achieved it. Nor was he quite sure who he was.

Almost seventy days had passed since he had faced the Dark Sun.

He knew that, for his next move, he needed a secure retreat and a place of power. That without such a place there was no point to his making any further plans whatsoever. The death of the great tree in the Adnacrags had changed him, he now suspected – and the advent of the great power who had left him the armoured egg was enough to prompt him to action. Or that was how he now saw his metamorphosis.

He walked along the northern shore of the Inner Sea in his own guise, and pondered war.

Ticondaga Castle – The Earl of the Westwall

Ghause was not a woman to hesitate. But the ramifications of the Queen's pregnancy were great enough to give her pause, and she chewed on her spells for long weeks before she knew how she meant to act.

The Earl was launching his usual raids across the Great River into the Outwallers' country. He raided for slaves and information, and sometimes for Wild honey and pelts. The Earldom of the North lacked the vast resources of Jarsay or Brogat; it had sheep, and cattle, and timber and everything else, as the Muriens liked to joke, was rock. Astute raiding did a great deal to provide agricultural labour and some coin.

This year he had a dozen knights of the Order of Saint Thomas. The order had knights in commanderies along the wall, and more in Harndon – and the latest news suggested that they intended to form a new garrison at Lissen Carrak. But their power of grammerie and their deep knowledge of the Wild allowed the Earl to plan a major raid, and she lost another week to helping plan the food and baggage for it, and in welcoming fifty knights from the south – a few hard-bitten professionals, the rest knights on errantry with girls to impress.

When his raid was all but formed and he was training his conroy in the great fields south of the castle, she was finally at leisure to consider her options and plan her own battle.

She read a great deal for a day or so – delving into texts she hadn't touched for decades. Then she sent a careful probe south – an old working, called a 'scent'. From then on, nothing happened as she'd intended.

She was a careful sorceress, so her scent rode south wrapped in layers of deception and cocooned in hermetical workings that would detect any attempt by the young Queen to *see* her. And it was one of these that triggered before her scent had even reached the Queen, when it was still fluttering through the *aether*. Ghause suspected that the *aether* worked in utterly different ways than the real, so she felt – rather than knew – that the real distance between Ticondaga and Harndon had very little to do with their distance in the *aether*.

But she was jolted into action moments after releasing her precious working, the fruit of weeks of work, days of research, and a dozen amorous couplings to fuel her needs.

She ran her fingers over the threads of her casting the way a bard would caress a beautiful instrument's gut strings.

She found him immediately. She frowned.

'Richard,' she said out loud. 'You are such a man – all power and no subtlety.'

Of course, Plangere didn't answer.

If she called him Thorn he might answer, but then there'd be a fight.

She extended her sight and followed her scent as far as she could, but the *aether* was a roil of angry motions – there was a great deal going on beyond her sorceressly reinforced walls, and she withdrew.

She threw on a robe – she always cast naked, which made winter a daunting time to work – and fell into her favourite chair. From there she looked through her window, six storeys above the walls, so that she could see across the Great River, and feel the wonder of the forest rolling away unbroken to the north until it became the ice. She'd been there, and she knew the power of the land of ice.

She took a sip of wine. 'Why is the Wild so active?' she asked aloud. She looked at her cats.

They licked their paws, like cats.

'And why exactly is Richard Plangere watching the Queen?' she asked. And in the safety of her own head, she said his new name.

Thorn.

One Hundred Leagues West of Lissen Carrak – Bill Redmede

Tyler found his men. He found them amidst the flashing lightning by the bank of the stream. They were all gleaming bones and organic shapes – they'd been dismembered and eaten.

Bill Redmede retched and the lightning went on and on – faster and faster – and the rain fell harder, and the thunder and the rising stream covered all sound. The sight of the corpses, stripped to gristle, was like a shout inside his head.

He put his back to a tree and gripped his spear.

Tyler whirled, wild in the lightning. 'They're surrounding us!' he screamed.

He began to cut at the unseen enemy.

Redmede jumped to help, but even in a long series of lightning flashes, he couldn't see the enemy. Nat cut and hacked – Redmede had to duck, and leap, and finally shouted 'Nat – Nat! There's nothing there!'

Nat turned to glare at him as the thunder ended with a wild series of claps, so close that Redmede felt them like blows.

And then the thunderhead swept past, and the darkness was the more absolute for what had come before. Redmede felt Tyler step past him in the darkness, and put out a hand.

'Sweet Jesus, we're done!'

Redmede dropped his spear and threw his arms around Tyler. 'Snap out of it! They're gone. Let's get out of here.'

Tyler was frozen for a moment.

Then he started to sob.

*

Dawn was a watery grey by the time Redmede got them back to camp. He feared everything by then – feared that the camp had been hit, that the Jacks were all dead too – he was awash in fear as the rain fell and fell, and first light found him stumbling like the greenest runaway serf through the wet woods just a few hundred paces from his fire.

There was no hiding Tyler's state. The man was moaning, and Redmede cursed himself for leaning too hard on a sick man.

Somehow, with curses and cajolery and all the persuasion he could muster, he got his Jacks to pack their gear and leave the warmth of the fire and march.

By midday they were all soaked to the skin – both by the fitful rain and the wet forest, wet grass, wet ferns. There was no wool, no matter how well woven, that could repel so much water. His shoes squelched when he stepped, and when they had to cross a deep stream swollen with days of rain, every man and women simply ploughed through it, bows over their heads. No one tried to skip across the stepping stones.

By mid-morning, they had to carry Tyler again and there was some grumbling about it. Bess put a stop to it, and she and another woman carried the old ranger without complaint.

In the early afternoon, a boy from Harndon sat down by the trail and refused walk any further. 'I just want to go home!' he said.

Redmede was numb. He shook his head. 'The Wild will eat you,' he said.

'I don't care!' the boy wailed. 'I can't walk! Me feet's rubbed raw, an' I haven't had any food in days. Got the rheum. Let 'em eat me!'

Redmede hit him. The boy looked at him in stunned disbelief.

'Get up and walk or I'll kill you myself,' Redmede said.

The boy got heavily to his feet and started to hobble away. He was crying.

Redmede felt like a caitiff.

Bess stood at his shoulder and shook her head. 'That wasn't the way, Bill Redmede,' she said. 'You sounded like a lord, not a comrade.'

'Fuck you, Bess,' he spat. Then he held up a hand. 'That's only weakness talkin'. I was up all night with Nat. The boglins attacked us.'

Bess's eyes widened. 'But we're allies!'

Redmede shrugged.

And they headed west.

An hour later they came to the third stream of the day. The advance guard splashed across and the main body followed, and on the far side they found another abandoned irk village – this one with the roofs intact. In a moment they were inside, drier than they'd been in a day, and within an hour there were fires lit.

There was no food and Redmede couldn't get more than a handful of volunteers to leave the huts and stand guard, so there he was, standing silently behind a screen of leaves, when he saw movement across the stream. The irk village was cunningly placed and difficult to approach, on a bluff of packed earth with low ramparts and palisades. But Redmede had posted his guards out across the cornfields – these, unfortunately, were bereft of corn.

He watched the movement. They weren't boglins – they were both cautious and, by comparison, clumsy. He saw a flash of green – and a man emerged into the open. There was just enough light in the sky for Redmede to know him.

The man standing at the edge of the ford was Cat.

Behind him was Grey Cal.

Redmede held on to his whoop of delight and instead whistled the recognition call. Grey Cal straightened up, and whistled 'Tom, Tom the Piper's Son' in response. Redmede called like a meadowlark, and in two shakes of a lamb's tail, he was embracing his lost sheep.

Cal hugged him tightly. 'Whoa,' he said. 'That was nasty. This loon saved my life.'

Cat chuckled and smiled to himself.

'We had a deer, but we dropped it when the boggles gave chase,' Cat said. 'The little bastards are *everywhere*.'

Cal nodded. 'I lost my boys,' he admitted. 'We had to run. When they didn't run far or fast enough, they got ate.'

Redmede nodded heavily. 'We don't have any food,' he admitted in turn.

'We don't either,' Cal said. 'And a body can't hunt. It's just giving meat to the boggles.' He shrugged. 'Not to mention this fucking rain.'

Cat produced some raspberries. 'I'll share,' he said in his odd, sing-song voice.

Redmede hesitated, but decided that if he didn't eat then he might as well die. The wiry boy had filled his whole copper with the berries – they were delicious, and the three men ate their fill.

'You carried them all this way?' asked Cal. 'No offence to Bill, but we could'a stopped an et anytime.'

Cat smiled enigmatically. 'Nope,' he said. 'Not until now.'

In the morning, people were hard to wake and slow to rise. The more experienced men went and stripped sassafras by the stream to make tea. Cat, prowling the high ground north of the village, found the hives, and came back sticky and triumphant, and every man and woman had two cups of hot, honeyed sassafras tea.

And six or seven berries.

'Just enough to make you fucking *hungry*,' Bess said on behalf of everyone's thoughts.

And then they went west. Again.

The streams were coming more and more frequently, and their crossings became sloppier with each one. The advance guard no longer stayed a hundred paces ahead of the main body, not even after noon when Redmede halted them in the watery sunlight and reset the intervals.

He pointed at the low hills to the north. 'There's boglins in those hills,' he said. 'Or worse. Stop slacking off or we'll all be dead.'

'Dead anyway,' shouted someone in the crowd.

Redmede swallowed that and took charge of the vanguard for a few miles. But well before it was time to make camp, Cat appeared at his shoulder and jerked a thumb in the direction of the rear of the column. 'They're falling behind,' he said. He shrugged. 'More and more of the green ones. Some are just sitting by the trail.'

'You and Cal go and find me a campsite,' he said.

Redmede saw Bess carrying Tyler. He patted her shoulder, squeezed Tyler's hand, and headed back along the column. However far he went, the men at the end told him that they were keeping up and there were more further back.

He'd just found the same boy as the day before, sitting under a tree, when he heard shouting from the front – now far away.

The boy didn't wait to be argued with, or struck. He got to his feet and started hobbling forward, cursing. He was crying again.

'Are there more behind you?' Redmede asked, but the boy just kept going.

Redmede stood on the trail in complete indecision for a long moment – and then unslung his bow and slowly drew it from the heavy linen bags. He'd messed it up properly – he needed to sharpen up the march order and keep his people together. He needed folk he could trust at the front and back. He wasn't going to lose anyone else. He started to walk back, sure that his headcount was six men short, and equally sure that something was watching him. With practised ease he began to string his bow, the bottom nock firm against his sodden right foot. He pulled and found how weak he was when it was a struggle just to get the string in place. But his string was dry enough, and his bow was dry. He put a shaft on the great bow, and breathed a little easier as he jogged back east into the gloom.

He rounded a sharp curve in the old trail and saw boglins. There were thirty or forty, all together in a mass, and two of his people, back to back, hitting the little things with their walking staffs while a third man fought with a sword – somewhat wildly, but with effect.

Redmede had feathered three boggles before he really realised what he was seeing, and then the boggles were gone, and the thin man with the long sword stumbled – obviously wounded.

They were deep into twilight – the best time of day for boggle eyes and the worst for men. Redmede ran forward.

He saw what had happened to his other men. They were the reason the boggles had been all clumped up, and they were red ruins.

The two with staffs slumped to the ground.

'No, you fools!' Redmede shouted. 'Run!'

Then he turned to the swordsman.

It took a long moment of twilit confusion to realise that the figure with the sword was an irk. He was a man's height, wore forest colours of deerskin and wool, and his sword was almost as tall as he was and looked as if it were made of a lightning bolt. His elfin face had enormous eyes and equally prominent teeth.

The irk abruptly sat on the trail. There was blood – ichor – coming from its legs.

The bush moved. The boggles were *right there.*

Sometimes, in a moment of extreme danger, everything becomes crystal clear.

Redmede saw it all. 'Stop!' he bellowed at his two men. They hadn't run yet – he got the irk's cloak over its fanged head even as it thrashed in pain at the wounds to its feet. He laid the cloak on the ground, heard the boggles closer still, put the two staffs onto the cloak and threw the ends in over the staffs. Then he lifted the irk, who swiped a talon at his face for his pains. He'd expected that, and he dropped the foul creature into the stretcher he'd made. The creature's weight pinned the cloak against the walking staffs, and the stretcher held together as the two Jacks lifted it on the edge of panic.

The boggles were coming for them.

'Now run,' Redmede said.

The two Jacks needed no further urging.

Redmede didn't think very highly of his own leadership skills, but he knew himself to be an expert archer. Maybe the best, save his brother. He laid a shaft on his bow and had another in his fingers. He stole a moment to put five more into his belt, heads pointing up.

He was just going to try and make a break for it when the rush came, and the seven ready arrows flowed away in a steady stream – he didn't even feel the great bow bending, he released without a thought, and he scarcely noted the shaft that pinned two of the foul things to a tree, nor the one that pinned a boggle, screaming shrilly, to the ground.

His fingers fetched another arrow from his bag, but the rush was broken. Creatures of the Wild are no keener to die than men – and even as he nocked his eighth arrow, the smoothly muscled predators were gone into the cedar scrub and small spruce trees north of the trail.

He watched the bush for the count of three long breaths, and then he stooped and caught up the irk's glowing sword. It stung his hand, but he had expected it to, and held on.

And he ran.

There are times when heroism is invisible; when the effort required to do what you know to be *right* is more than your frame can bear. Redmede had fought, had used his great bow, had walked for miles and miles, and had done so with little sleep and less food. He *knew* his men needed him. He knew the ford crossing would be hard – he feared that the boglins would get in among his raw Jacks and make meat of them.

He knew that there were boggles moving behind him on the trail.

And yet, after one burst of speed, he found himself walking – striding along with his long-legged stride, but not sprinting or even jogging.

He all but ordered himself out loud, to run. And yet he walked.

'Damn you, Bill Redmede,' he said aloud. He leaned forward,

daring his own body to fail him, and his legs caught him, and he broke into a heavy, flat-footed jog. His turnshoes slapped the trail heavily, and his run lumbered more than he liked, but he was moving.

After what he estimated to be two long bowshots, he found six of his Jacks, carrying the irk.

'Move!' he shouted, as soon as he saw them.

They, too, burst into lumbering runs.

He stayed behind them. When they flagged, which they did almost immediately, he bellowed, 'Don't slow down! They're right on top of us!'

They ran. One of the younger ones looked back, and his eyes rolled in total panic.

Redmede couldn't bring himself to care.

They pounded along the trail and his breathing began to come in gasps, and he cursed his weakness and every bad decision he'd ever made. But the men in front of him kept running and he was damned if he was going to slow down when they were keeping the pace despite carrying the wounded irk.

They climbed a shallow ridge among the heavy trees, and Bill heard fighting ahead.

'Halt!' he snapped. 'Into cover – lie still.'

He ran past them, tossed the irk's sword at the weary men, and drew his own.

He crested the low ridge, and looked down into the ford. It was a scene from the priests' visions of hell.

The boglins had caught his Jacks in mid-crossing. Half his force was on the far bank, and they were holding, but only just. The men caught in the river, however, were being systematically killed and eaten – boglins lined the banks and were hauling corpses in and consuming them on the spot, and some – many – were still alive, screaming in horror as the little creatures ate them. The men in the ford were dying because they were exposed in the open, stumbling across slick round rocks where to lose their footing was death – and as they crossed, the boglins loosed a barrage of arrows on them. Flight after flight fell on the hapless Jacks, and even the weak bows the little creatures had were sufficient to wound or kill at fifty yards.

Redmede took deep breaths.

Boglins didn't usually cooperate well in groups larger than twenty or thirty. Yet there were a thousand here, at least, chewing away at his Jacks.

He unslung his bow while he looked. He expected to find a man in their midst. But irks sometimes made use of boglins. He wondered if he could even make out an irk at this range. He wondered for a moment if the irk he'd saved was, in fact, the lord of these monsters...

But the flash of white from across the stream told him that it was neither man nor irk that he faced, but one of the Priests, the rare royal caste of the boglins, with their red, black and white chitonous armour, their elongated bodies and heads that made them look, to Redmede, like vicious hornets. He watched the creature as it used two human-made swords to chop a man down. A wight.

Two hundred and twenty yards away. Some wind; the air was moist, and his bow was cold. The string was dry enough. He sheathed his sword and ran his hand almost absently up his bowstring, pulled a light arrow out of his quiver, and put three more into his belt.

Then he took a lump of maple sugar from his belt-purse and ate it. Two more of his men died – their screams went on and on while he ate but he needed the surge of energy. He couldn't afford to fail. The temptation to do something was so powerful that he could scarcely think – his body was full of the spirit of combat, and he wanted to fight.

He had a long pull of water, and corked his canteen, put the light arrow on his bowstring, and without further thought, he pulled – back leg slightly bent, his shoulders all the way into the pull – the arrowhead came up, past the target, and when his sense of the shot told him to release his fingers flew off the string almost as smoothly as the arrow leaped away in the opposite direction.

He didn't watch the fall of his first shaft, but loosed all four he'd had ready, one after another.

His third shaft struck the Priest squarely, but the range was so long and the arrow so light that his arrow didn't penetrate deeply enough. The fourth arrow struck one of its sword arms and went through it.

It fell back out of the tide of melee and began to search for him.

They don't have to talk. They communicate by magic. Or scent. Or something.

He pulled four more arrows out of his quiver. He felt strong, he had the range now, and he took out his heavy war arrows; what King's men called 'quarter pounders'. He planted three of them in the ground, and drew his bow all the way to his ear so that his back muscles strained.

He loosed – nocked, drew, and loosed, with a grunt, like a man lifting weights; and again, and finally, with his last arrow, he all but cried aloud his release was so poor.

He had time to say 'Too fucking tired' as he watched the fall of his shafts.

To reach two hundred yards with a war arrow required a big bow – Redmede's was more than six feet long. And he had to pull it to the ear, and aim it almost fifty degrees from the ground, rendering the concept of 'aiming' impossible. The archer can't even *see* the target under his arrow.

His first arrow landed at the edge of the stream, forty yards short of the target, but dead in line.

The second shaft flew true, and for a heart-stopping moment Redmede thought he'd hit the thing, but it sprang, not into the air as he hoped, but forward, and came towards the stream. The third arrow went long and to the right as the wight sprinted for the stream bank. And the fourth arrow pulled to the right, and fish-tailed, losing energy. The boglin chief changed direction to leap onto a great rock – raised its wing cases—

What does that mean? Christ – he's casting!

—and blue-white fire played along them.

His badly released arrow plummeted from the heavens like a stooping raptor. The wight stepped directly into it, and the shaft went into his extended wing case – penetrated the chitinous armour and ripped the monster's wing clean off.

Even two hundred yards away, Redmede saw the spurt of ichor as it took the wound. It stumbled and fell into the water.

A panicked Jack, Bill Alan, pinned it to the stream bed with his sword. He chopped and chopped at it, and the stream turned a green-brown around him as he cut. It landed a blow on him – he stumbled back, lost his footing, and fell. By then Redmede was running for the stream's bank and fitting another heavy arrow to his string. He had three left.

Alan got a hand under him and got to his feet, his arming sword still clutched in his fist. The wight came at him, rising heavily out of the water, still spraying ichor. It hacked through the man's guard, notching his sword and his over-cut opened Alan's cheek. But the panic had passed, and Alan cut back and his luck held – he landed a hard blow on the wight's arm. It stumbled and vanished beneath the water.

Every boglin on the bank was launching itself into the water and coming across.

It knows who I am, Redmede thought. *They're coming for me.*

He ran along the bank, skipping from rock to rock like a small boy, paused and balanced on a pair of huge boulders.

The wight errupted from the water at Alan's feet. His sword swept up—

Redmede loosed. It was less than sixty yards, and his arrow went into the soft, mammalian skin under the thing's armpit, and the thing unmade. It literally fell apart. Alan's desperate parry caught nothing; the wight was falling to pieces and the stream was already sweeping him away.

The bond that held the boglins to one another dissipated with the wight's power – Redmede watched them fall apart as well. Instead of a mass of creatures expressing a single will, they became, in three heartbeats, hundreds of individual creatures more afraid of his Jacks then determined to conquer. In the time it took a man to say a prayer they were gone.

Redmede wished he could vanish as well. He couldn't tell how bad his losses were, but they were bad enough. His men were alone in the vast Wild; exhausted, panicked, and beaten. And darkness was falling.

He sounded his great horn, gathering the survivors. Many had scattered at the first attack; Nat Tyler had held all the men and women left on the near bank and refused to let them cross, which Redmede thought a wise decision, and on the far bank Bess had crossed with Cat and Cal in the vanguard with the veterans – men and women with good swords and bows. They had held their own – indeed, they had killed quite a few boglins.

But in the centre they had lost forty men and two women. There wasn't much of them left to bury.

Any man wounded had died, save six, and Tyler, Bess, and Redmede spent the night on them, using scraps of fabric from the dead as bandages while Tyler organised watches to resist another attack. Then he came back and squatted by a fire with Redmede.

'That was bad,' Tyler said. 'We won't last another fight like that.'

Redmede sat and stared at the fire. As long as there had been something to do, he hadn't had to think. But now . . .

'It's all my fucking fault,' Redmede said. He slumped down, head on his pulled-up knees. 'We should ha' gone south, to Jarsay.'

Tyler was silent and Redmede knew the other man agreed – they should have gone south.

'Don't you believe it, Bill Redmede!' Bess emerged from the darkness, found the water bucket by feel, and began to wash her bloody hands. 'Jarsay would ha' been death for all o' us. The nobles would be huntin' us for sport. The Wild's better. It's just cold.' She smiled, collected the hot water and went back to tending her wounded.

Tyler watched her with hungry eyes. 'Even when she's dead beat and hasn't bathed in ten days, she's a beauty,' he said.

Redmede shrugged. Bess was a good companion and probably a better leader than he was. He didn't see the rest of her. He didn't allow himself to see the rest of her.

'Think she'd go for an old fuck like me?' Tyler asked.

Redmede couldn't even think of such things. 'I have to talk to the irk we picked up. We need a friend out here.'

Tyler grinned. 'I'll just go help Bess, then, won't I?'

Redmede took some time boiling water in his own small copper pot. A rout like today's had a thousand small impacts. One was that most men had abandoned any camp equipment they'd had – and pots were as precious as arrows in the Wild. Redmede had saved his – for all he knew, it was the last metal pot west of Lissen Carrak. He groaned, and waited for the water to boil. It was frustrating – they had no tapers, no rush lights, and no oil lamps, so that the darkness above the fire was absolute, and he couldn't see down into his little copper pot to see if the water was boiling. Finally he detected it by feel, through a twig. He added some sassafras – last season's – and the last of the honey. He was making a princely offering because it was all he had to give, and he needed the irk to like him.

Redmede took tea to the irk, who raised the horn cup in acknowledgement.

'Can you talk?' Redmede asked.

The creature sighed. '*Yiss*,' it said.

'What's your name, then?' he asked.

'*Tapio Haltija*,' it sang. '*I am lord of these woods, little man.*'

Redmede spat. 'I have no time for lords,' he said. But his heart rose a little.

The irk stiffened, but then looked away. '*Half a thousand yearsss I haf lorded these woodssss. But I am not ssso ungentle asss to be ungrateful. Even to a ssservant of Thorn'sss.*' He nodded. '*And your name?*'

Redmede shook his head. 'I am no servant, least of all to that bastard. He left us high and dry.' He looked away. He was too tired for this. 'Bill Redmede,' he said.

'*Ahhh, man, your ssspeech isss ever more pleasssssing. Fair Friend, let me hosst you and your men. I mean you no harm – and few men hasss ever heard sssuch an offer of me before.*' He smiled, and his fangs glittered wetly in the dark.

Bill Redmede knew too little about irks. His brother liked them – that much he knew. His brother had feasted in their halls, and traded with the bolder ones in the woods. But this one was old, and very, very dangerous, or so his instinct told him. And he had just given the creature his name. That had been foolish.

'*My people are coming. I can feel them in the blood of the earth. I would esssteem it an essspecial favour if you would give me another cup of thisss tea. And my sword. I sssee you presserved it.*'

Redmede wished he could trust the creature, but he didn't. 'I bandaged your ankles,' he said. 'You can't walk. I'll return your sword soon enough.'

The irk smiled, which was horrific. '*When you dine in my hall, man, you will sssee that I need no treachery to dessstroy the likesss of you. If I wanted you, I would meet you ssssword to sssword. I am Tapio Haltija. I do not lie.*'

Redmede found talking to the thing was tiring. He had trouble controlling his mind, his thoughts went tumbling off like the creature's sibilant esses. He went and sat on his blankets after another check on the wounded, and Bess came and sat down beside him.

'Just give my hand a squeeze,' Bess said. 'And tell me a pretty story, because I had the shit scared out of me today.' She grinned. 'And Nat Tyler is more scary than comforting. Ain't he?'

'The irk we just rescued is a figure out of legend, and he's going to save us all,' Redmede said. He took her hand and squeezed it, happy to be able to give her good news. It was no different to giving Nat's hand a squeeze when the man was sick. But the hand was cold, and he found he was holding onto it. Bess pressed up against him. There was nothing erotic in her approach. She was cold.

'A famous irk?' Bess managed a weak laugh. 'Who is he – Tapio Haltija?' she snorted derisively.

'That's what he says,' Redmede answered.

She sat up. 'That ugly monster claims he's the Fairy Knight?' she said. 'I dreamed of him as a girl. He rides a unicorn and carries a lance of solid gold.'

'Right now he's been hamstrung by boggles and he can't get a cup of tea,' Redmede said.

'Can't be,' Bess said. But her voice was calmer – happier. 'But that's a good story, Bill. You done good these last days. If'n we die. Well, hell, we stood on our feet today, din't we?'

Redmede rolled a little so that his shoulder pinned hers. 'Listen, Bess. I swear to you that we are not beaten; we're going to get through this. I'm going to kill the fucking King, and men are going to be free.'

He had the most unlikely amorous urge towards her. He never thought of Bess as a woman – and now, suddenly, she smelled like a woman, and felt like a woman. *I'm exhausted*, he thought.

'And women,' she said. She turned, and he caught a little of the look in her eyes from the firelight and the background light. That look wasn't sisterly, and so he had a moment's warning when she wriggled and put her mouth on his.

Her mouth was salty and strong, like she was herself.

'Oh, Bess,' he said, because he wanted to tell her that he was the commander, and he had to be an example. And because his body was so sore – he could fall asleep in a few heartbeats...

...only his hands had other ideas – one swept under her back, and pressed against her spine, and the other found her stomach, as hard as his own. She caught his hand and carried it away – and he found it on a breast.

All thoughts of sleep fell away from him.

Nat Tyler stood a few yards away, and his hand clenched on his dagger.

'So,' he said.

*

Tapio Haltija sighed and let go the gentle bonding he had cast.

Men were so easy. And their females, as well. So many rules, so many customs – so eager to leave them all behind. Ultimately, they were creatures of the Wild. No different from stags, or beavers.

He called to his sword, and it came.

He set a healing on his feet and ankles. Only his foolish arrogance had allowed the poor boglins to get him. It was deeply ironic that these men had rescued him. The boglins should have bowed to him, and had not – and that was Thorn's doing.

His hand wrapped around the hilt of his sword. It sang to him.

I could kill them all, he thought.

He leaned back, listening to the earth's blood. Listening to the two animals make love. It was many years since he had been among men. Outwallers had a different taste. They embraced the Wild. Nature. These were still servants of other ways.

I can kill them whenever I like, he thought. *Perhaps I'll keep them as pets. Or as hunting dogs.*

He reached out along the lines of the earth's blood, and called for his knights.

Chapter Six

Bad Tom

Liviapolis – Morgan Mortirmir

Morgan Mortirmir was days recovering from the fight. He slept and slept – slept the clock round, at one point. At another, he awoke to find the noblewoman – he had to admit she *was* a courtesan, perhaps merely a whore, but she didn't look like any whore he'd ever met in Harndon, with her exotic make-up and pouting lips – was bent over him, rebandaging his shin where it was split open and bleeding merrily. He watched her hands moving with assurance, and wondered where she had learned to wrap bandages quite so well.

'Are you planning to sleep here for ever?' she asked him. She smiled. Her eyes were deliciously tilted. 'I would like the bed back.'

'Most courteously asked, fair friend,' he said. After a pause, he realised he'd spoken in Alban, and he tried again, in High Archaic.

She smiled.

He rose carefully – he was wearing only a shirt, and it had to have been one of the Nordikan's as it hung to Mortirmir's knees. She stood close enough that he could smell the scent on her – a delicate, flowery scent with a bite at the end of it. She was wearing a deep burgundy overgown over a tight kirtle of pale green silk. At least it looked like silk to him.

He sighed. 'Where is Messire Derkensun?' he asked.

'You have your wits under control, ser barbarian,' she said. 'I have not seen him these three days. Much has happened in the city.' She sat on the bed. 'I would like to be fed, but I have no money. I would like to stop being scared. I nursed you – I hope that you will now prove appreciative.' She shrugged. 'But men so seldom are.'

'Your name, despoina?' he asked. It is difficult to manage a courtly bow while you try to get your hose on. Hose were worn – at least in Harndon – separately, not joined the way they were worn in Galle. That meant getting one on, smoothing it up over the thigh, tying it to the waist band of his braes, buckling his garter . . .

He couldn't find his garters.

'Oh,' she said, with complete falsity. 'Those were yours? I liked them.' She raised the hem of her gown, and showed him her knees – and his garters.

'They – er – they become you much better. Than . . .' He blushed, stammered, and came to a stop.

She laughed. 'How old are you, ser? What is your name and style?'

He shrugged. 'I'm sixteen, despoina, and I am called Morgan Mortirmir.' He looked about. 'Does Messire Derkensun have any leather lace? Or anything I can use as garters?'

She laughed. 'Why not just ask for your own back?' she asked.

He shrugged. 'I'm an inexperienced boy,' he said, 'but I'm quite sure that would be ungallant of me.'

Instead of giggling, she looked at him with hard eyes. 'Are you trying to bed me, ser? As a commercial matter, I could use the business, but I promise you that my Nordikan will think less of both of us for it.'

Mortirmir met her eye. This was the longest conversation he'd ever had with a woman not his mother – he felt he was doing well enough. 'I had hoped that this was flirting,' he said. 'I've been told I need practice.'

'Oh, as to flirting,' she said, 'I'm not be a good teacher, since at the end of the day I always say yes.' She looked at him expectantly, and swung her legs a little, sitting on the bed, like a much younger girl.

Mortirmir found his doublet and got his arms into it. 'And your name, despoina?'

'I'm called Anna,' she said. 'By the handful of people who know my name.' She got up from the bed and brushed her skirts. 'Will you buy me a little food, ser knight?'

'I'm not a knight yet. I'm too young,' said Mortirmir. He realised that he'd taken her too literally, and he smiled. 'I'd be delighted to feed you.'

'Then I'll teach you what I know about flirting. To begin with, if you ever want to kiss a girl, you'll need to brush your teeth.' She smiled to take a little of the sting out, and he looked away.

'You have money?' she asked. 'Please note that I didn't take your purse and run.'

'Why not?' he asked.

She shrugged. 'I like Derkensun. But he is gone, and I am hungry. Every hour, I thought of your purse. Is that too honest of me to say?'

Mortirmir was learning about the world hand over fist.

They went down the stairs of the taverna where Derkensun had rooms. The innkeeper's wife met them at the entrance to the common room. She was a handsome woman of forty, in dark clothes which were almost black; but the coral beads of her long rosary, the gold crucifix that hung from it, and the black work on her shift showed her to be a woman of property. She put up a hand, barring their entrance to the common room. She inclined her head politely at Mortirmir.

'And who might you be, kyrios?' she asked.

Mortirmir had a moment of confusion. But he realised that this wasn't his inn; he was coming from one of the landlady's rooms with a whore, however well spoken she was.

He bowed. 'Despoina, my friend Derkensun the Nordikan rescued me, and this fine young woman has been my nurse. Three days I have rested on one of your bolsters. Far from trying to evade my bill, I was on my way to take a meal with my nurse.'

The landlady inclined her head. She looked at Anna, sniffed, and said, 'I can well imagine what kind of nursing you have received.'

'Can you really?' asked Anna.

Mortirmir's hand went into his purse and emerged with a silver crown – an Alban coin, but one with value everywhere in Nova Terra. 'Might I know your name, despoina?'

The lady inclined her head a little more. 'You may call me Stella, fair sir,' she said in passable Alban. 'Come with me. I do not ordinarily allow women and men to dine together unless they are married – this is a proper inn, and we observe the laws. But as there is no one in the common room, I'll allow you to sit together.'

Anna sat in a high-backed chair and made a face. 'Now I will have to go back to climbing her gutter to get into his room,' she said. 'I hate women like that. A tavern keeper's wife? Likely she spread her legs for clients in her day – but now she pays for masses and is more virtuous than a saint.'

Mortirmir shrugged. 'I don't know any tavern keepers,' he said.

'Or whores!' she added. But she fell silent as the hostess came up.

Stella came with a pitcher of wine and another of lemon and water. 'I can make sausages and I have a good bread.'

Mortirmir realised that he was ravenous. 'Splendid.'

Anna tore through the bread, drank the wine, devoured six sausages and then tried to pretend to be dainty with a dish of figs. Mortirmir felt less ill at ease as the meal progressed; among other things, her appalling lack of table manners made him feel more confident. Eventually he leaned over and cut her sausages with his eating knife, and she watched him use his pricker to feed himself.

She ate with her fingers.

'I had a knife,' she said. 'Harald gave it to me. I had to sell it.'

'How many days did I miss? What's happened?' Mortirmir was young, and inexperienced, but a taverna with an empty common room at mid-day was an oddity anywhere, and the landlady's attentiveness spoke volumes for her desire for money.

Anna looked at him, her mouth full of figs. She chewed, and chewed, and finally they both giggled.

'You aren't any older than I am,' he said.

'That's crap,' she said. 'I'm almost seventeen.' She sighed. 'My looks will go soon.' She leaned back. 'So – here's what I know. Three days ago – the morning you went to sleep in Harald's bed – he went on duty at one of the gates. And the Emperor was taken prisoner by the Duke of Thrake. You know who he is?'

Mortirmir shrugged. 'His son was at the Academy one day. An arrogant pup.' He smiled. 'Even worse than me.'

'There was a fight inside the palace. That is all anyone knows. Rumour says Harald survived and that the Princess Irene has taken the purple and is Imperatrix.'

Without any warning, she burst into tears. 'It has been three days!' she said. 'Where is he?'

Mortirmir felt well out of his depth. 'You love him?' he asked.

She bawled for as long as a man might say ten pater nosters. It embarrassed Mortirmir, who didn't know how to deal with it, and it embarrassed the landlady who overcame her aversion to whores for long enough to bring the young woman a handkerchief.

'I don't want to be a whore!' she said. 'I want to marry him and have babies! What if he's dead? Oh, by my sweet and gentle Christ—'

'I could take you to the palace,' Mortirmir heard himself say. He swallowed, and reviewed his words. Yes, he really had said that.

Anna looked at him. 'Really? We might be killed.' She got to her feet. 'I will teach you *everything* about flirting if you will take me to the palace. And let us take wine and bread.'

The landlady, listening in, put a hand on the cross on her ample bosom. 'Take wine to the palace? Surely they have the finest wine—'

Anna used the handkerchief to wipe her face. 'They may not have received any deliveries in three days. The Mayor of the Palace is dead – everyone was saying so yesterday. Eh?'

The landlady nodded hesitantly. 'It is true. And they say that the Grand Chamberlain has left the city with his leman, abandoning his wife.' She looked fiercely at Anna. 'The markets are closed. There has been looting. And no woman is safe.' She spoke more softly. 'Not even a whore.'

Mortirmir shook his head. 'No – listen. I'll go. Stella, will you let my nurse stay here? I will take no wine. I will find Derkensun, and I will return.' In fact, he found the prospect daunting. And yet exciting, despite his throbbing temples and the ache in his gut and across his back – the long tally of bruises, abrasions, and not-quite sprains from wrestling with a giant.

Anna shook her head. 'Do you know the way from here to the palace?'

Mortirmir shrugged. 'Yes,' he said. 'I am a scholar at the University. I know how to reach the palace.'

The landlady shrugged. 'He's a barbarian,' she said. 'They will never let him in.'

Mortirmir shrugged. 'Neither of you would change that. But you'd make the risks greater.'

What has come over me?

The women agreed – too readily, Mortirmir thought. He paid for the meal and fetched his sword and went out into the empty, damp streets of the city. The inn was close enough to his own that he thought of going for his horse, but the palace was less than a mile away; the sun was high in the sky, somewhere beyond the rain clouds, and the streets were empty.

He had to cross the square of the jewellers, one of his favourite places in the city, where the craftsman sat and hawked their wares, from cheap knock-offs of court jewellery, through magnificent reproductions of such stuff, all the way up the scale to the real thing, with a sapphire ring costing more than a thousand ducats.

Not today. Today the square was empty and some broken men were gathered under the booths, hiding from the rain. Many of the booths had been smashed. There was a body lying on the cobbles.

Mortirmir edged around the square, but they saw him.

He froze in indecision. It was a foolish situation – he could kill a dozen broken men with his sword, but the cobbles were wet and he hadn't actually ever fought anyone to the death. It seemed easier to run. Except that everything hurt.

They were spreading out as they came, and hooting to one another. He had the presence of mind to look behind him, and there was another pair, their skin the unhealthy, ruddy colour that he associated with life on the streets. He ran a few steps, his boots just a little uncertain on the rain-slick cobbles, and those few steps made his head pound. He turned to put his back against a tiny stone church with brickwork decoration and an external mosaic.

He whirled, and drew. His arming sword was steady. He sank back into the guard he'd been taught for such situations, and the lead man slowed. But he had a heavy stick and didn't stop. He ran in and swung it heavily at Mortirmir.

If you practise things often enough, sometimes they happen whether you stop to consider them or not. The heavy blow rolled off his sweeping sword – he stepped forward, left foot passing right, and his free left hand slammed into the man's elbow, half spinning him, then Mortirmir's downward sword cut hit him on the crown of the head – a little flat, as the cut was too fast and a little panicked – but the effect was right. The man fell unconscious. Or perhaps just dead.

The other broken men paused.

'We can take 'im,' said the smallest, a bearded ruffian with two daggers.

'You first, dickhead,' said another, backing away.

Mortirmir was full of the spirit of prowess – he had no other words to describe it, but he felt ten feet tall, his heart thumped in his chest, and—

—and there was a bright red-gold fire burning on his left hand.

He almost lost his purse and his life right there – stunned that his left hand was cloaked in power, he missed the man coming for his left side. But he caught the incoming blow in his peripheral vision and pivoted on his hips, got his blade up and caught most of the blow, then stepped in and put his pommel into the man's face. This rogue was faster or better trained than the first, and the pommel scraped his nose and no more. Mortirmir passed him as they both stumbled.

Mortirmir raised his left hand to ward against the man's dagger – by luck and training he caught the man's wrist in the tangle, although the point of the dagger pinked his thigh.

The rogue screamed and dropped the dagger. He stumbled back, his cudgel waving between them.

Mortirmir knew the *phantasm* for fire. He knew it intimately, and yet, in that moment, in mortal combat, he couldn't summon the words for it, not even when whole bright red fire played on his hand.

The man with two daggers started at his right side.

Mortirmir seized hold of his mind and summoned the mental construct that he had memorised so pointlessly. He put his left hand at Two Daggers and said '*Poieo!*' in High Archaic.

His memory palace was a fledgling thing – well constructed, based on the temple of Minerva outside the city walls. The professors all agreed that it should be constructed of a place he loved.

The problem was that since none of his phantasms *ever worked, his impetus to construct and improve the palace had withered. So the ancient pillar – flawless white marble – was indistinct, and he could not tell for sure how many facets it had, nor could he read the graffiti he'd so carefully inscribed.*

But he focused his will, took a deep mental breath, and there it was – a fish for Pisces, an eagle – for—

Saint Mark! And the gospel, and

In the beginning was the WORD,

And an owl—

Sweet Christ, the owl stands for wisdom, and...

MINERVA...?

The man's first dagger cut almost caught his outstretched hand. He bounced back, cut with his sword—

'Athena!' he spat.

Two Daggers immolated.

The force of the *phantasm* stunned Mortirmir and he stumbled back, as much in shock as from the force of the heat. The man screamed, terribly. He wasn't dead, and three heartbeats later, he *still wasn't dead.*

Mortirmir took a deep breath, made himself step forward, and cut the man's head from his body.

The fire went out. The man was horribly burned, his skin almost melted, one of his eyeballs popped and the other—

The image of the ruined man would haunt Mortirmir for many nights. In the meantime, he spun, ready for another attacker, and they were gone he saw them vanish around corners like roaches fleeing a night candle. He took a deep breath.

His hands were shaking uncontrollably.

'I did it,' he muttered.

He stumbled a few steps, and decided, as if making the decision from a great distance, to continue his mission to the palace.

Two streets later, he realised that he still had a sword in his hand, and it was dripping blood. He stopped and expended one of his mother's linen squares on the sword. Some of the blood was dried like lacquer. He spat on the blade, suddenly far too focused on cleaning it, and another hundred heartbeats later, he realised that he wasn't thinking particularly well.

He got the blade clean enough, and sheathed it.

His right glove was soaked in blood, and there was blood running down his right leg from a hole in his thigh.

He kept going towards the palace.

He crossed the street of the lawyers, and it was empty. In the armourer's streets, there were men with swords and half-pikes – workmen. He paused at the fountain.

A man in Etruscan half-armour came up to him. 'What news, neighbour?' the man asked courteously enough.

Mortirmir bowed. 'I'm a student at the University,' he said. 'Men attacked me in the square of the jewellers.' His saliva suddenly tasted of salt – he flashed on the burned man.

The other man nodded. 'You don't look like a looter to me,' he said. But he pointed at the sword. 'Are you a barbarian?'

Mortirmir nodded. 'From Alba,' he said, ignoring his automatic resentment at the term.

'Ah. Harndon?' the man asked.

'I have that honour,' Mortirmir said. His voice sounded a little wild inside his head.

'There are fine armourers in Harndon,' the man said. 'Can you name one?'

Mortirmir saw that there were a dozen apprentices around him, armed to the teeth.

'Master Pye lives in my mother's street,' he said. 'I've been fishing with his daughters.'

The atmosphere lightened immediately. 'Ah! Master Pye!' cried the armoured man. He bowed. 'These are difficult times, ser. I had to be sure. May I ask why you are out? The watch has called a curfew and we are all supposed to be in our beds.'

Mortirmir had to struggle with his own somewhat unruly mind to come up with an answer. 'I'm going to the palace.' He shrugged. 'For a girl.'

Luckily for Mortirmir, the armourer had known a few young men, and a few girls. He smiled. 'The palace is in turmoil,' he said. 'But I will take you there for Master Pye's sake.'

An hour later, with four armed apprentices at his back, Mortirmir stood at the postern gate of the Outer Court and knocked. It was the fourth gate he had tried – his armourers were enjoying the adventure, but all five of them were tired of failure.

However, here the grate was opened – the first sign of life they'd seen in the palace. 'State your business,' said a voice.

Mortirmir had had an hour to practise his speech and calm himself from the fight in the square. 'Kyrios,' he said, 'I have come to find my friend Harald Derkensun of the Nordikan Guard. And to ascertain if the palace is in need of any food or drink that the city taverns might supply in this emergency. I have at my back members of the City Guild of Smiths, who would like to know—'

The postern opened, and revealed half a dozen ill-kept-looking Scholae guardsmen.

'Fresh bread wouldn't be amiss,' said the tallest of them, a man in magnificent, if somewhat tattered, satin and samnite clothes, with a breastplate of scales and three days growth of beard. 'As for Master

Derkensun, he's with the Empress. And I'd take it as a personal favour if you'd walk a note to my bride. If she'll still have me.' He looked at the armourer's apprentices. 'She lives in your quarter.'

'I'd like to see Master Derkensun,' Mortirmir insisted. He felt empowered. Literally. He had never felt so full of spirit, and his hands and chest felt as if they might catch fire.

The well-dressed man shrugged. 'If you'll leave your weapon and promise to take my message, I'll escort you to him,' he said. 'But if he's with the – er – Empress – you won't be allowed in.'

The palace was as empty as the streets. The Ordinaries were locked down in their barracks – a bare minimum of them walked the corridors, and those few flattened themselves against the walls when the soldiers approached.

They crossed the Outer Court and entered the Inner Court. The Scholae barracks were full, and the handsome young man took Mortirmir to the duty clerk and entered his name on a roster. Then they crossed the yard. A pair of Nordikans stood like statues in full hauberks, with great axes as tall as Mortirmir's shoulders.

'Is Master Derkensun at liberty?' asked the Scholiast.

'DERKENSUN,' bellowed the nearer of the two blond giants. He nodded. 'Just off duty after a murder. In the prison.'

A sleepy giant came to the door. As soon as he saw Mortirmir, he grasped both of his hands. 'You!' he said. 'The witch woman said we were to be bound together.'

Mortirmir might, under other circumstances, have had to proclaim his total disdain for anyone who went by the title 'witch woman', but an hour before he had caused a man to die by fire, and the universe was suddenly very strange.

'Anna sent me,' he said. It seemed a silly thing to say.

But Derkensun's smile burst over his face like sunrise after a long, dark night. 'By the gods!' he said. 'You are a true friend. Is it chaos out there?' He turned and bellowed something – the sound, to Mortirmir, very much like two dogs fighting.

'By our gracious Lord, is that what Nordikan sounds like?' he asked.

His Scholae guard grinned. 'That's what we say.'

Derkensun took the two men aside. 'I've called for my corporal. Listen. The Emperor is taken—'

'That much is all over the city,' Mortirmir said.

'But too many of the officers fell with him – or have gone over to the Duke.' The Nordikan shrugged. 'This palace is a dark place, and no mistake.'

'This man offered to bring food,' the Scholae knight said. He offered an arm. 'Giorgios Comnenos at your service, ser barbarian. You, I take it, are a student?'

'Is Maria Ekaterina Comnena your sister?' Mortirmir asked.

'First cousin,' the man smiled. 'You know her at University, I suppose?'

Mortirmir looked away, and didn't say 'she coined my nickname'. Instead he said, 'Oh, we've met. Pardon my rudeness, kyrios – I am Morgan Mortirmir, of Harndon.'

'You speak our tongue so well I'd never have taken you for a barbarian,' Comnenos said.

Derkensun put a hand on both men's shoulders. 'Listen, friends, enough pleasantries. We're all good men here – let's act the part. Morgan, can you fetch food? Do either of you know what it would take to get deliveries moving again?'

'My father's steward would probably know,' Comnenos said. 'But if I leave the palace, half of the Scholae will leave and never return.'

The only black-haired giant that Mortirmir had ever seen came out of the barracks and bows were exchanged. He was introduced as Durn Blackhair, acting Spatharios. It was a strange title – Mortirmir's pedantic young brain tended to translate every scrap of Archaic, and that one seemed to mean 'sword bearer'. Not really a title at all.

Blackhair drank off a pint of unwatered wine. 'The Duke wants a fight,' he said. 'I just had word that he's moving his camp closer to the walls, and he has threatened to bombard the city with his siege machines. We need access to the farms – without them, I guess there's no food.'

Mortirmir felt odd, speaking up when all the men around him were – well, twenty-five. Which seemed like a great age to him. 'It seems to me,' he said, and they all looked at him. 'It seems to me that the taverns and inns have food – they lay in stores.'

Blackhair nodded. 'That's good sense,' he said. 'But it won't feed the city.'

'It would feed the palace for another day,' Derkensun said.

'Long enough for . . .' The knight of the Schola shrugged. 'You know.' He exchanged a look with Derkensun.

'Three days without markets,' Comnenos said. 'By tonight, there'll be hungry people offering to open a gate.'

Blackhair took a deep breath. 'Right. Young master, if you can find us two cartloads of food, we won't waste it. I'd like to say the Empress will be grateful, but I'd say the odds aren't too good she'll still wear the purple.'

Mortirmir nodded. 'Can she pay for it?' he asked.

'If she wins,' Comnenos said. 'She's thrown her dice.'

Mortirmir laughed, caught up in it. 'Well, I can pay,' he said. 'It beats going to school, anyway.'

Blackhair slapped him on the shoulder, which almost drove him to his knees. 'I won't forget this,' he said. 'Get it done and you'll have the thanks of the Guard.'

'Those that are left,' said Derkensun.

'Let me write a note for my bride,' said the officer. He pulled a beautiful red leather cased wax tablet from his belt pouch and wrote hurriedly. Then he turned the tablet over and wrote again, and pressed the ring on his finger into the wax. 'Green side for Despoina Helena Dukas. Red side for Kyrios Demetrios Comnenos, my father.'

As it proved, delivering the tablets was as easy as returning to the square of the smiths; the Comnenoses' palace dominated the square, with four tall marble towers glistening wetly in the late afternoon rain. And the Dukas palace stood across the square. Of course, a damp and exhausted Mortirmir was not at first invited to meet the lovely despoina in person, but he heard a shriek of delight from above him, and a beautiful girl of seventeen or so with bright gold hair came down the stairs, sprinting like a professional messenger, and he had to endure her thanks, her offers of money, and a hundred questions – was he all right? Had he taken a wound? Was he a hero? What was the Empress doing?

He survived, downed a cup of wine, and suggested to the girl's father that if any supplies could be spared for the palace, they would be most welcome.

Lord Andronicus Dukas gave his bedraggled visitor a somewhat sketchy bow. 'Of course,' he said. 'But until there is a legitimate Emperor, we would hesitate to act.'

Mortirmir shrugged. 'Ah, kyrios, I am only a poor ignorant

barbarian, but it seems to me that the Empress is even now restoring order. I gather that she is victorious.'

It didn't seem to have any effect, but Mortirmir hoped it made the bastard squirm. He crossed the square, bid farewell to his escort, and passed the other note to the lord of House Comnenos. This old patriarch met him in person, and bowed politely – more than the lord of House Dukas had done.

'How is my young scapegrace?' he asked. 'Staying in trouble? Humiliating his family properly?' But he read the note, and grinned.

'I gather you are a student, and not just a messenger. I will prepare a cart and a dozen men-at-arms to escort it. May I offer you any further assistance?'

Mortirmir bowed. 'If you could provide me a shirt of mail and a horse, I'd appreciate it,' he said.

Despoina Stella filled a cart with food and wine in two hours. He spent four semesters' worth of fees on hams, sausages, fresh baked bread and lentils. Stella and her husband, who emerged with a spear in his hand, scoured the tavernas of the neighbourhood and found a wagon, a team, and an escort of spearmen raised from their own ranks. No one challenged them on their way to rendezvous with the cart provided by the Comnenos clan; they had an escort of mounted and armoured stradiotes and ten Smith's Guild crossbowmen when they crossed the Great Square and stood outside the Outer Court. Mortirmir, now utterly exhausted, had a moment of panic as the great gates remained resolutely closed.

He could hear hoof beats. They were far away – ten or twenty blocks – but there were an awful lot of them. The city was dark, there was no watch out in the streets, and all lights were extinguished. The sound of hooves was frightening.

The Comnenos men-at-arms drew together and took their lances from the leather sockets by their stirrups.

Mortirmir knocked on the gates again. His leather-clad knuckles made little noise against bronze-clad oak gates that were fifteen feet tall. Finally he drew his dagger and used the hilt to rap on the gate.

'Who goes there?' answered the sentry.

'Food!' Mortirmir replied.

The hoof beats were coming closer in the darkness, and sounded like thunder.

Above his head, Harald Derkensun leaned out. 'Morgan!' he called.
'Here!' Mortirmir called back.

'I can't open up. There's armed men in the streets – hundreds of them. If they caught the gates open—' Derkensun sounded unhappy.

'Christ on the cross!' Mortirmir shouted. 'We have two carts and twenty men. Open the gates, for the love of God. We'll be in before you can say "Ave Maria".'

Derkensun sighed audibly. 'I can't take the risk. I'm sorry, Morgan. I take my oath to the Emperor very seriously.'

From the lead cart, a voice called, 'Jesus and all the saints! Open the gate, Harald!'

The sound of horse's hooves was filling the night.

'Anna!' Derkensun said. He sounded utterly wretched.

There was a low thump, and the Nordikan landed on his feet by Mortirmir. 'I cannot open the gate,' he said. 'So I'll die by you, here.'

The Great Square of the city was itself larger than many Alban towns. It stood between the ancient arena, where chariot races were still held, and the palace, and the entire square was lined in oak trees and paved in marble slabs cunningly worked with deep grooves to run rainwater off into gutters. Seen from above, the grooves spelled out whole chapters of the gospels. In the centre of the Great Square stood a mixed group of statuary, much of it impossibly ancient; there was the great Empress Livia, in brightly gilt bronze, driving her war-chariot against the western irks; there was Saint Aetius, standing like a young David, with his sword against his thigh, apparently contemplating his conquests – the Emperor Justinian and his wife Theodora; and even more ancient men and women. Mortirmir knew them all. They had been part of one of the entrance exams.

The horsemen entered the darkened square from the south-east. They were at least three hundred strong, and as they came on the stradiotes prepared themselves like brave men. Derkensun kissed Anna.

She slapped him lightly. 'You could have just opened the gate,' she said. 'You great oaf. And I came all this way for you.'

Derkensun grinned. It was visible because Mortirmir had just cast his second ever successful *phantasm* – the first working any student ever learned. He made light, and set it on the peak of his borrowed helmet, so that it illuminated the group by him with a reddish light.

He was grinning uncontrollably.

'Perhaps you should not have made us quite so obvious?' Derkensun murmured. The professional soldiers seemed to agree.

In a rustle of hooves and harness, the house guards rode away, and the guild crossbowman cursed them.

Across the square, the horsemen came on. Mortirmir's light glinted redly off horses and harness studded in gold or brass, and their tunics were scarlet – surely that couldn't just be the light—

'Vardariotes!' said Derkensun.

They didn't form for battle. They were moving at a fast trot, and they crossed the square in a column of fours, with a small pennon at their head made of silk, with a horse's tail attached to it. The leader held a mace of what appeared to be solid gold, and he used it to salute the palace gate. The men – and a few women – were barbarians, Easterners, with black hair and slanted eyes and scraggly beards or clean-shaven, and every one of them wore a heavy horn bow in a scabbard at their waists, and a long, curved sword.

They entered the main road to the Gate of Ares, and the long column vanished into the arched gate of the Great Square as if it were being devoured by a dragon. In two hundred heartbeats, only the sound of their passage remained, echoing around the square, and floating on the night air from their new route.

When they were gone, voices inside ordered the Outer Court's gate opened, and the wagons went into the yard. Mortirmir was too fatigued to be afraid, but he could see relief on every face.

An older woman in court clothes came into the yard from the palace end – the courtyard was fully illuminated with cressets and torches – and called softly for Blackhair. The Nordikan turned the carts over to Ordinaries – he'd inspected them personally – and Mortirmir was standing to hand.

'My lady,' he said, with a bow.

The older woman nodded. 'Who were they?' she asked. Her voice betrayed nothing.

'My lady, they were the Vardariotes. They passed away to the Gate of Ares.' He spat. 'The traitors.'

'Judge them not until they are proved,' said Lady Maria.

The Court of Galle – The King, his Horse and Lady Clarissa

'My lord,' breathed Lady Clarissa de Sartres. She was leaning forward, her lute clutched against her. The King had risen from his stool in his private receiving room – and put his hand on her shoulder.

He leaned down and ran his lips across the exposed nape of her neck and she stiffened. She scrambled away, her hand straying to the amulet that her great-uncle Abblemont had given her, and her thumb touched the disc at the base of the crucifix.

The King was small but he was strong and very quick, and he had both of her hands, and then he pushed her against the fruitwood side table and pulled her veil off her head and put his mouth on hers. She stumbled, and used the stumble to cover a kick to his knee – and he threw her roughly to floor.

She screamed.

Abblemont came into the private solar without undue haste a few of her terrified heartbeats later. Clarissa was under the King, and he had her skirts above her knees and she was weeping. Abblemont left the door open.

'People are coming, Your Grace,' the Horse said. 'Let Clarissa up, please.'

The girl had enough spirit to slap the King as soon as he released her hands, and he slammed the heel of his hand into her chin.

Abblemont dragged him off her. He was a head taller, much heavier, and he trained constantly. He managed to lift the King clear of the ground and set him on his stool without doing him much harm.

'Get up and go – before the Queen comes,' Abblemont said over his shoulder to his niece.

The King sucked in a deep breath, as if he had just awakened. 'She made me!' he said.

Abblemont turned on his niece. 'I told you never to be alone with him,' he said.

She clutched her ruined dress to herself and sobbed – and reached for her instrument. But when she attempted to lift it, it became clear that it had been shattered in the struggle, and a litter of discordant strings cut her sobs.

She ran from the room.

'She seduced me,' said the King, his eyes steady. 'That strumpet.'

Abblemont contemplated regicide, and let the moment pass. 'Your

Grace, there is a letter from the Captal, and the Queen is on her way to this room. Are you prepared to receive her? She has some notion that Clarissa was present.' His words were clipped and careful. He was, at some remove, quite fond of his niece – but he was altogether fonder of the peace and prosperity of Galle.

The King sat up.

His wife came in, as if summoned. 'Ah,' she said. She was ten years older than the King, and the daughter of the man reputed to be the richest in Christendom. Her clothes and her jewels were the finest in the world, and her grace and deportment were the toast of poets in three countries. When she was fifteen, the Lady of Flowers, as she had been called then, had danced alone, accompanied only by her own voice, in front of a crowd composed of her father's friends, a thousand knights and their ladies, to open a great tournament, and the fame of that great feat remained her cloak and her armour.

Her expression was such that the exclamation 'ah' was enough to throw the King into a rage.

'You have no right to be here, you witch!' he shouted, like a boy at his mother.

The Queen of Galle came all the way into the room, her cloth of gold gown and the collar of emeralds she wore making the King *look* like a small boy. 'Abblemont,' said the Queen, with a slight inclination of her head.

Abblemont sank into a deep bow, his right knee on the floor, his eyes down.

The Queen sniffed slightly. 'I would think,' she said, 'that you would have more care for your niece.'

Abblemont kept his eyes down.

'She came after me like a bitch in heat!' said the King.

'Of course,' said the Queen quietly. In two words, she somehow expressed disbelief, and an utter disinterest. 'Abblemont, see to it that I never hear her name mentioned again.'

The Horse didn't raise his eyes. 'Of course, madame.'

Clarissa de Sartres stood on the bridge below the nunnery and watched the dark water move implacably – deep, and very cold.

An hour ago, she had considered suicide. Her immortal soul was as ruined as the rest of her – she had little interest in God, or a life of contemplation. Or anything else. And as if God had granted his permission, she found her room unlocked for the first time – and the postern gate of the nunnery unlocked as well. No one had seen her cross the courtyard. Perhaps no one cared.

But the water looked cold, and her imagination – always her bane – spun her a hell of eternal cold; dragged down to the bottom of the river and resting there for ever. With the *Bain Sidhe* of her nurse's tales.

The utter humiliation of being banished from court – for ever – for the sin of being attacked by the King. Her throat closed, and her hands shook, and she gagged and the darkness closed on her again.

Not quite raped. Her imagination supplied whatever hadn't happened, and the speed with which she'd been jettisoned by her uncle – and the sheer ferocity of the joy of the other women at court at her degradation – had been telling.

God doesn't give a fuck, she thought. And in that moment she thought of a very young man in her father's courtyard, saying those words. More than a year ago, in Arles. And how she had despised him for it.

She looked up at the nunnery on the mountain, and at the Rhun River flowing at her feet. She realised in that moment that she hadn't escaped – she had been allowed to come here, so her inconvenient version of events would perish. For a few heartbeats, she was utterly consumed in hatred – an emotion she had seldom felt before.

If I kill myself, they win, she thought.

Open Ocean west of Galle – Ser Hartmut.

The crossing itself was not without incident. Ser Hartmut had never sailed in the north, and he exclaimed with joy to see great hills of ice sailing by like so many white ships of war. But the wind was fair, and ten days sweet sailing brought them off Keos, the northernmost of the islands of Morea, and they bore north and west into the setting sun. It was late in the year, and de Marche had plotted a conservative course, making each crossing of the empty blue between islands as brief as he could allow, but no storm troubled them.

West of Keos, they saw a ship's sail – apparently a great lateen, according to the sailors – nicking the far western horizon, but when the next day dawned they were alone in the great bowl of the ocean.

Seventeen days into the voyage, and they had had no weather worse than a rain squall. The three ships were still together, well in sight; *La Grace de Dieu* was well in advance, with her two consorts trailing in an uneven line, each ship at least a mile from the last.

Ser Hartmut was on the deck, fully armed, as he appeared every day at daybreak and remained all day until the sun set. He had wrapped the mainmast in a thick linen canvas quilted hard, and he practised at this informal pell all day, cutting, thrusting, hammering away with a pole-axe. He would take long breaks in which he merely sat in the bows and watched the sea. Sometimes, Etienne or Louis de Harcourt, his other squire, would come and read to him. At other times they would spar with him, matching blunted swords or spears up and down the deck.

Ser Hartmut never spoke to the sailors but they had developed a healthy respect for him as a fighting man. Despite his size, he was as fast as a cat; despite his girth, he had excellent wind, and could usually fight long after his squires began to grow pale and raise their hands in token of submission.

His men-at-arms were no different, and they trained hard enough that every day had its tale of broken bones, sprains, and bruises.

Some of the sailors began to practise with their spears too – but never in the open glare of the Black Knight.

But this day saw nothing of the sort. It was hot, and the sailors were bored – many were in the rigging, simply hanging there, waiting for a slight breeze to cool them. After nonnes such a breeze arose, and from the east, so that the ship began to move, and the water whispered along the ship's bluff cheeks.

The sun began to set.

And then everything happened at once. Whales appeared under the round ship's counter; great leviathans rising from the deep and sounding around them.

De Marche was on deck in a moment. 'Rig the nets! To arms!'

Etienne was pale with fatigue and had a black eye. But he ran up the ladder to the aft castle in full armour and managed a good bow. 'Ser Hartmut asks – what is the purpose of this alarm?'

De Marche leaned over the side. His servant had his breast and back open on the hinges and his shirt of mail held high, and de Marche didn't wait on courtesy, but put his head into the mail and then his arms. From deep in the steel mesh, he said 'The Eeeague. They follow the whales.'

'Eeeague?' asked de Vrieux.

'Silkies, sir.' De Marche's head popped through the neck of his hauberk and he leaned out over the wall of the castle as the boarding nets went up. Crossbows were coming out to the hold at a fair speed, and men on the deck were arming.

'Land-ho!' shouted the lookout. 'Land, and three ships. Ships are hull up.' The last report was sullen – the sound of a man who knew he'd failed in his duty.

'Master Louis, the lookout is to be listed for punishment,' de Marche snapped. He sprang on to the rail, swung up into the rigging, and climbed a stay, hand over hand despite the weight of his mail, until he stood on the small platform at the midpoint of the tall, single-piece aft mast. 'Where away?' he shouted.

The lookout in the mainmast fighting top pointed. 'West-north-west,' he shouted, obviously eager to be forgiven for his dereliction. 'Bare poles,' he called. And then, almost to himself, 'And I'd have seen 'em sooner if they carried any sail, anyway.'

De Marche found them quickly enough. He watched them as long as his eyes could stand the sun-dazzle, and then he watched the water below his feet. From this height, he could see the great dark shapes of the whales, and the smaller shapes flitting in and out among them. Herdsmen? Tormenters?

The red flag burst from his own gallery. The *Grace de Dieu* heeled and began to turn; picking up the wind on her quarter she turned south – but round ships didn't turn particularly well, and the whole process was glacial.

Two miles astern, another red flag flashed; after a few heartbeats, the middle ship, *Saint Denis*, answered.

Men with crossbows were lining the sides of his fore and aftercastles. A round ship was a ship shaped like half an egg, with great towers built fore and aft to raise archers and crossbowmen, and give them the height advantage they needed, whether they fought men – or things.

Amidships, in the low waist, the men-at-arms and their squires and pages, already armed, waited with axes and spears.

De Marche picked a halyard, made sure of it, and then lowered himself to the deck, landing neatly just two Gallish cloth yards behind Ser Hartmut. The giant knight turned when he felt the wood under his feet move, and found the merchant captain, wearing his hauberk, bowing to the deck.

'Master Etienne!' he shouted. 'Ask your master if he has fought Eeeague.'

The steel giant raised his visor.

Etienne appeared. 'Never,' he admitted.

De Marche shrugged. 'Neither have I. I thought they were something that the Etruscans made up, to warn us off their trade. None in the Middle Sea? Nor Ifriqu'ya?'

De Vrieux looked a question at his master, and spread his hands.

Ser Hartmut spun his pole-axe. It was so small, compared to the man himself, that it looked like a toy. Close up, de Marche could see it was almost half again the size most of the marines carried.

'Come, sweet friends, and let us say a prayer together!' Ser Hartmut called out, and all of his men-at-arms and their people knelt on the deck. 'Let our sweet and gentle Jesus send us a good fight and a worthy enemy! Amen!'

De Marche ran back up the ladder to the aftercastle, and two of his mates got his breast and back on him and closed it. The buckles took time – too much time.

'Oh Christ,' said a sailor behind him.

Crossbows snapped – the strings sang with almost the same sound that a sword blade makes when it strikes the pell. His men had heavy arbalests, capable of putting a bolt right through a ship's side – or through a man in armour.

'Sweet Jesus Sweet Jesus ohmygodohmygod,' moaned a sailor behind him.

The tine of the last buckle under his arm slipped home, and his man Lucius slapped his back. Master Henri had his steel helmet, an open-faced bassinet with a sun-bill of steel, and a fine steel chain aventail. He got it on de Marche's head even as the sailors behind him began to scream.

Lucius put his bill-hook into his hand and he turned.

Half the sailors at the rail were already dead.

He almost missed the arm coming for him – and then he cut with the bill-hook. He had a hard time grasping the shape of the creature – it was nearly transparent, a ghastly pink and green mottling over glistening translucence.

He slammed his bill into the thing's organic centre – if that was its trunk, and not a continuation of its limbs – it was difficult to register its physiology in combat. His bill splurted into the trunk and blew out again in a satisfying shower of gore – but every splat of the thing's corporeal form that touched metal ate away at it, and Lucius tore his own helmet from his head and cursed.

The head of his bill began to deform, flaking away and rusting even as he slammed it into the thing for a second time.

The port-side crossbowmen were snapping their heavy bolts into the creature from a range of a few feet – spattering their hapless mates with the sticky, deadly gore, and sometimes with the bolts themselves, and doing the thing little harm.

It uncoiled something – an arm? A weapon? – at him, and he batted it aside with nothing but the headless shaft of his bill.

An alert ship's boy acted on a hunch and poured a helmet full of seawater on Lucius, who stopped screaming.

Ser Hartmut vaulted up the ladder and stood like a tower of steel in front of the Eeeague. It turned to face him.

He drew his great sword, and it burst into flame.

A dozen sailors shouted, 'The Black Knight!'

The thing snapped a tendril at him, and he batted it aside and cut back, right down the same line, into the monster. The thing had already endured fifty crossbow bolts and dozens of other blows, but now it screamed – and vanished down the side of the ship.

The stench of dead fish and decomposing flesh filled the air. There were six dead men on the deck, and Lucius was still having water poured over his head. He was as red as a beet and whimpering.

Just by their stern, a whale broached and a great fluke slammed into the water, showering every man on the aftercastle. The whale turned suddenly, and its great jaws opened.

Then closed.

In passing, it delivered a nudge to the great ship – one of the largest ships ever built in a Gallish yard – and the whole ship groaned, and wooden pegs carefully driven home with great oak fids sprang loose, and water sprayed in on the bales of bright red cloth.

It was too late to turn the round ship. And the whale was gone, hurtling away into the deep.

De Marche had never had to confront the three-dimensionality of the sea so forcefully, and he had a moment of vertigo as the whale vanished beneath him.

And then another of the tentacled things came at the forecastle.

*

By the fourth attack, two sailors had been thrown over the side, and the squires had fetched fire from the galley and made fire spears, wrapping dry tow dipped in oil around their boarding pikes and lighting them.

It was as well, because the fourth attack was the first one that seemed to be coordinated; six tentacled monsters came up the steep sides all together. Three of them went for the low waist of the ship as the easier target, and were greeted by Ser Hartmut. But the ship itself heeled – the things had significant weight. They were not just the spirits of damned and dead sailors, as had been shouted over the panic.

One went up the forecastle, but the forecastle was the highest point on the ship, rising sheer over the bow, and the creature, for all its hellish strength and speed, had trouble getting over the boarding nets, and was impaled with fire spears and fled.

But two of them came up the aftercastle. They screamed like dead spirits, and the Etruscans' name for them – the Eeeague – was explained. And their coming heralded a wave-front of pure terror.

De Marche stood his deck. He put a spear into one thing's trunk and severed what might have been a translucent tentacle – Lucius had an iron bucket of hot sand, and he threw it into the beast, and another sailor – Mark, an Alban – sprayed it with oil to no effect and died.

It came right over the rail and down – de Marche took a blow and the pain shocked him – whatever hit him went right through his mail.

Like water.

He screamed, stumbled back, and let go the spear.

A tendril caught a ship's boy and flipped him over the side, screaming.

The trunk seemed to open and inside it had a red-orange beak like a raptor concealed in its jelly-like flesh, and the boy . . .

De Marche drew his sword. He whipped it along the deck where the oil had been spilled, cocked it back in his strongest guard, and cut at the thing's trunk as hard as he could.

Unlike the concussive weapons, the sword cut. It felt like cutting through pig fat – but the blow was well formed, and he sawed as fast as he could even as the thing sprayed his face – he screamed, ripped the sword loose, and slammed it back again.

Lucius threw water into his face.

The smell was grotesque.

But it retreated back to the sea, leaving a great hunk of its gelatinous flesh on the deck, burning its way into the wood.

The other one had killed a sailor and paused to eat him, the beak exposed and glistening red, obscene and active. The thing had no face, no limbs. It looked like wet silk.

His blade was pitting before his eyes, but he cut into the second thing, cut and cut again. Lucius called, 'Swords,' and men drew them and hacked with the desperation of terror. A man fell screaming to the deck with a tendril wrapped around him, his flesh boiling from his body as he screeched his hopeless terror.

Two sailors, either more alert or less panicked, got the gobbet of severed flesh on their spears and flipped it over the side.

Again, Ser Hartmut charged up the ladder from the waist, his flaming sword a beacon of hope. He fell on the creature, showering it with blows, and it vented its pain with every blow, shrill screeches like birdsong. When it began to withdraw with the slickly lubricated speed with which it did everything, he slammed his sword forward in an overhand thrust that pinned it to the deck.

It dragged itself *around* the burning sword, accepting bifurcation rather than remaining.

Now, for the first time, with the sword illuminating its trunk, de Marche could see its entrails – see that it rode the side of the ship like a vast and opalescent slug, and its bulk continued over the rail and down all the way into the sea.

A whale rolled past, in easy bowshot. It showed its flukes and then, with a mighty stroke of its tail, it was alongside them – the ship shuddered and men fell to their knees. The whale ripped the silky off the hull – the ship shook again and a sailor fell from the fighting top to splash into the water.

The man vanished under the waves, dragged down by the weight of his mail.

There was silence.

Ser Hartmut stepped back from the rail. His helmet was ruined – it had holes burned right through by the thing's toxic flesh, and pitting and tendrils of rust and decay trailed all the way down his armour. His cuisses and greaves were the worst, scattered with burn holes and trails of rust brown.

He pulled the ruined helmet over his head and hurled it, aventail and all, into the sea.

He turned to de Marche. He had burns all over his face, and his hair was rucked and tufted like a patchwork gown. He was smiling.

'Now, that, monsieur, was the sort of fight a man can come to love.'

Habit caused the merchant to look for Etienne, but the squire was lying dead in his harness in the waist of the ship, his body armour ripped asunder by one of the creatures' beaks and his entrails ripped from his body to twist about the deck like obscene organic ribbon.

De Marche nodded. 'Thank you, my lord, for saving us,' he said humbly.

Ser Hartmut spat over the side. 'You saved yourselves – every one of you. You are all worthy companions, and I am honoured to command you.'

Sailors scared past their ability to comprehend – men on the brink of despair – braced up on hearing his words.

He smiled at them. 'Well fought. Nothing we find in Nova Terra will be worse than that!'

De Marche allowed himself a smile. 'By the sweet saviour, I pray not.'

'We are cut from different cloth, then, merchant. Because I pray we find worse – larger, faster, deadlier. The more horrific, the greater the honour.' He sheathed the sword that burned like a torch in his hand.

De Marche nodded, as one does when talking to a madman. He managed a smile.

Two hours later all three ships were illuminated with torches. The danger – the insane danger – of open fire on the deck of a ship was as nothing compared to the men's fears of facing the silkies in the dark. There were open buckets of seawater at every station.

They caught up with the three bare-poled ships just a mile or so off the rock-bound coast.

De Marche boarded one himself. Ser Hartmut boarded a second. The third they left until morning.

He led. He had to. Despite Ser Hartmut's words, the men were in the grip of terror – their sailors' fears of the sea now given a physical focus – and the falling darkness made it difficult for him to get a boat's crew to row him across to the bare-poled galleass. In the boat, he felt the terror himself – even the water appeared alien, black and oily, and the oar strokes were weak. The men couldn't stop looking over the side. In the bow, a man stood with a burning cresset – a huge pine torch usually expended only in emergency repairs at night.

He climbed the side – heavily, because his body was exhausted – and he had to steel himself before he threw a leg over the bulwark to look down at the deck. The rising moon revealed a macabre tangle of fallen rigging and tangled sailcloth.

He got a foot on the deck and drew his arming sword – his good fighting sword was utterly ruined, a brittle shard of its lethal self. His arming sword was light in his hand, and he got a leather buckler on his left fist after he had both feet on the deck. The buckler had been soaked in whale oil. So had his sword blade.

Oliver de Marche was a rational man. The silkies could be hurt – he'd seen it. Possibly they could be killed. Their fearsome ichor could be diluted by seawater, and to some extent defeated by oil. They hated fire.

None of that rational, military thinking helped him a jot. He stood on the deck in the moonlight, and he was so afraid that his sword hand shook. He had to force himself to move – to take a step, and then another. With each step, he poked the downed sails – they had the same fluid and organic shapes that the Eeeague had.

He crossed the deck, his heart racing when he stepped on a rope and it squirmed under his boot; he jumped when he heard movement behind him, and whirled, sword in the high guard, ready for a heavy cut—

'Just me, Cap'n,' said Lucius. He had a large, sharp axe with a spike in the base of the haft, and he did as de Marche had done, spiking each sheet of canvas as he passed it.

The waist was empty, and they climbed warily into the aftcastle, weapons at the ready.

There was no one on the command deck. It was damp, and when de Marche knelt and touched the deck with his fingers, he smelled something like fish, and something like copper, and a curious sweet, oily, tree smell. His mind struggled to identify it. It was something familiar. Even pleasant.

'Uh!' grunted Lucius, behind him.

He whirled.

The man held up a hand. 'Sorry. Look.'

Everything appeared distorted in the moonlight, and it took

de Marche a long breath to understand what he held. It was a finger, still encased in good armour – very expensive armour. The finger had been cleanly severed from a gauntlet. The man's flesh was still inside.

They went back down the ladder to the waist. There was a door in the side of the forecastle – the main hatch to the living spaces.

Something was moving in there.

The two men listened, and then de Marche moved carefully to the right of the door while Lucius moved to the left. He was a small man with heavy muscles; he raised the axe over his head.

'What's happening, there?' called the boat keeper.

The call came up over the side and echoed against the cliffs that lined the cove.

Happening there happening there hap there there.

'We could just leave it,' Lucius said.

'It is just something swaying to the rhythm of the sea,' he said. He put out a hand on the bronze-bound hatch and shoved.

It was latched.

He put his hand on the latch.

The ship swayed – the tide was rising – and he tripped the latch. The door shot back and something inside came forward as if it was flying. It had wings spread on either side of its corpse-like head, and—

Lucius's axe slammed into it with a crunch like a butcher dividing a carcass. De Marche's arming sword went into its face.

Its horrible wings swept forward, wrapping wetly around them as it fell to the deck. Both men screamed.

It was clear what had happened – the Etruscans had been caught unawares and massacred. But not by silkies. Whatever had perpetrated this massacre had claws and teeth.

And a horrible sense of drama.

The 'creature' that had 'attacked' them was the corpse of a sailor, hung from a meat hook in the doorway of the sleeping cabin. His lungs had been pulled out through his back to make wings. He had died horribly, and the marks of his agony were written across his face. His eyes bulged. His mouth was open.

De Marche took the time to recover from his fear. He used his dagger to scrape the disgusting mass of the man's lung off his shoulder, and he went to the side and threw up. After a long time, he saw that the oarsmen had moved the ship's boat all the way to the lee of his own *Grace de Dieu* and he hailed them.

They didn't want to come back.

There were twelve more bodies, but he and Lucius cleared them away like men springing traps. He offered double-shares to the oarsmen and they finally came – slowly, but they came – and backed him as he cut corpses down.

Even after a day of horror, de Marche was capable of making a profit. He took the ship's papers for their masters – there was no need to offend the men in Ruma and Gennua and Venike with whom he traded, and they would want to know what had happened to their spring fleet. Fortunes would have been lost, as well as lives, with these ships.

He took the trade goods out of the two smaller ships and put them in the larger after hearing the same tale from Ser Hartmut, and they threw all the dead over the side. His own sailors, having survived the Eeeague, were cocooned in their own fears – throwing dead men into the deep didn't trouble any of them. And every man knew he was richer by a share or two as they counted the trade goods – bales of good velvet, and fine woollens.

And bows. Bales of fine mountain yew from Iberia, carefully split and roughed into shape.

Nothing the Etruscans carried tallied with the items his sources had told him to bring for trade.

They lay to in shallow water at dark, in a small cove with a shelving rock beach. As the moon rose high and full over the greasy sea full of kelp, and the water roiled like a living thing, de Marche sat on the sterncastle as Lucius spread olive oil on his burns.

'Wasn't fucking silkies as did for the Etruscans, was it, Cap'n?' he asked.

'No, by God and all his saints, Lucius.' He winced as the man's rough fingers pressed too hard on a burn.

'How come these things live out here, and not at home? Eh?' Lucius was talking to hear himself.

'I don't know, Lucius. The King's magisters probably have something to do with it – and the power of the Emperors. And God.'

'Does that mean God's writ don't run here? Or in the Nova Terra?' asked Lucius.

'I don't know that, either.' De Marche felt himself drifting into sleep, despite his fear and pain.

'But the whales is on our side, ain't they?' asked Lucius.

'Why do you say that?' de Marche asked. 'Leviathan almost sank us all standing. Carpenter still hasn't come at the leak. If we didn't have good land under our lee—'

'I saw him,' Lucius said, with absolute assurance. 'You put that fucking thing, that Satan's spawn, over the rail, and that big fish took him in his mouth and ate 'im. And then went deep. I saw it.'

De Marche took a deep breath. 'My Etruscan friend told me that the mermen were the herders of the whales.'

'He told you to bring cheap red cloth an' crossbows, too,' Lucius growled.

'Good point,' murmured de Marche.

'What killed the Etruscans, then? Cap'n?' asked Lucius.

He thought of the man with his lungs pulled through his back. 'I have no idea,' he admitted. 'And I wonder where they are?'

'Ser Hartmut's coming up the side,' Lucius said.

The Black Knight paused to look at the horrific ruin of the dead Etruscan. His handsome face did not change expression.

De Marche tried to stand straight.

'Silkies?' Ser Harmut asked.

De Marche shook his head.

Ser Hartmut looked around. 'They would make valuable allies,' he said.

De Marche's expression made the Black Knight smile.

Beaver Lakes – Nita Qwan

The same full moon that rose over the lonely cove on the rock-bound north coast of Nova Terra rose a little later over a grassy clearing, far to the west, where Nita Qwan stood guard for the second night. He took the middle watch, because Ota Qwan played no favourites, and everyone took turns – bad watches and good.

Again, he smoked at the end of his watch – he was becoming quite fond of the smoke – and when he fell asleep, Ota Qwan was looking out into the darkness, his face just barely illuminated by the coal in his pipe.

In the morning they left their weapons, which troubled many of the men.

'We won't be able to carry honey across the swamp as well as our weapons,' Ota Qwan insisted.

After a handful of pemmican, Ota Qwan led them to the edge of a huge beaver swamp – as wide as a small lake, with beaver houses the size of men's houses.

'Tick Chuzk,' Ota Qwan said, pointing at the nearest beaver castle. 'We call it the Beaver Kingdom. Sometimes they come, and sometimes they do not. Great beavers are touchy and proud and very fierce. Do not posture. In fact, do not speak!'

Men bridled. No Sossag liked to be told what to do, even when the advice was good.

A great stream almost the size of a river flowed through the meadow, and after carefully crossing the treacherous grass – it might look like lawn, but the unwary human would find himself in water to his hips – they stood on a sandy bank looking at a crossing as wide as two boats tied end to end. Not that they had any boats.

Staka Gon, one of the youngest, plunged into the ford – where he stumbled, gave a choked scream, and fell backwards.

Ota Qwan caught him before he fell. 'Idiot,' he said. He lifted the young man, who gave a long moan.

He had a sharpened stick right through his moccasined foot. Ota Qwan pulled it out, ruthlessly, and then used his own cloth shirt to bandage the boy. 'Every tree and plant the beaver eat becomes a trap and a weapon,' Ota Qwan said. 'You *know* that.'

Nita Qwan had been told too, but he had forgotten. He looked at the stick – just a hand's breadth long and red with blood. He looked away.

Later, when they had crossed, leaving Staka Gon at the ford, they stripped to keep their leggings dry and crossed a long stretch of wet marsh, carrying their buckets over their heads. The mosquitoes were ferocious, but Sossag warriors didn't show irritation at such things.

Nita Qwan did his best to keep up appearances, but he hated insects.

After a painful league of walking and swimming across the great meadow, they climbed a low, fir-covered ridge, and lay on a great slab of limestone to dry. The smell of the honey was overpowering – almost rotten, and yet perfectly sweet.

Ota Qwan had waved into the bush. 'Easier than last year. There's a pool right here.' He pointed across the swamp. 'Gwyllch. Look – there and there. And there.'

Nita Qwan was tired. 'Gwyllch?'

Gas-a-ho lay flat. 'We have no weapons!' he said. And indeed, they had none – the spears and bows and swords had stayed in camp so that they could carry their buckets when full.

Ota Qwan crouched, unperturbed. 'Without weapons, we will simply have to be careful. Which is wiser than a pointless fight anyway.'

Nita Qwan gave half a smile. 'Who died and left you all this wisdom?' he asked.

Ota Qwan shrugged. 'Tadaio. Those are boggles, Nita Qwan, my brother. See them?'

He did indeed. They were moving like an army. And they were between the men and their weapons.

It took long minutes to fill the buckets. Wild honey was seldom pure – the great bees who made it often fouled it themselves, and the sugary stuff gave off a mighty odour of organic decay – sweet organic decay. Animals became trapped in it and died; insects became stuck and perished by the thousand – plant mould, sugar fungus, and whole dead trees fell in the honey deposits.

Gas-a-ho was expert at filling them, though, and he crouched on a sticky rock with Ota Qwan's arms around his belly and scooped each bucket full. The cleaner the bucket was at delivery, the more it would fetch in price. And the more honey a man fetched the richer the profit.

Nita Qwan heard a sound like a trumpet, and the Sossag all stiffened as one.

'Bee!' Gas-a-ho said.

Ota Qwan looked at the sky. He sprang to his feet, ran back up onto the limestone outcrop, and stared east under his hand. In Alban, he said, 'Shit.' He came back to the nervous warriors.

'Hurry,' he said. 'We need to get young Gon out of the ford before he becomes someone's lunch.'

Nita Qwan felt his brother's eyes on him. He sighed. 'I'll fetch him,' he said.

Ota Qwan flicked him a hard smile. 'Good. You won't have to carry your buckets.'

He ran – and swam – back across the meadow to the ford, after a long look at the moving line of boglins. There were hundreds of them, and they were making no attempt at concealment but were passing along the eastern edge of the meadow.

They were heading for the ford.

He beat them to it.

Despite a hard summer of constant conditioning, he was breathing hard when he splashed through the water. The boy was lying flat, already rigid with terror but doing his best to conceal it.

Nita Qwan looked at the water's edge – then at the far distant wood line to the east, and to the north, and made his decision.

'They are on their way to cross here,' he said. 'We will go north. Around them. Come – I cannot carry you.'

The boy nodded grimly and they began to burrow into the dense alders that ringed the ford. Crawling through alder was almost impossible. The sight lines were less than five yards, and in Nita Qwan's vivid imagination it seemed ideal terrain for the little boggles. He could all but see one coming, its horrible mandibles spreading wide to show its tooth-lined pink throat—

They crawled anyway, and when they had crawled for some time, they began to hear the rustling of the boglins. They were heavy enough to break the sticks forming the little beaver dams that filled the meadow, and quiet enough otherwise to make only a rustling noise as their sinewy legs passed through the grass.

'Faster,' Nita Qwan whispered. The nearest boggle was a short bowshot away.

They went down a short bank and were back at the stream – or another feeder stream. But the bottom of the stream was firm gravel, they didn't have to crawl, and the icy cold water seemed to make walking easier for Gon, who didn't complain despite the red blood he left on every wet rock as he went.

Their stream bed wound back and forth in short twists like a swimming snake. In no time Nita Qwan lost his bearings, and attempts to look over the side of the stream were fruitless – the tangle of tiny fir trees and alder bushes and fifty species of marsh grass made seeing any kind of view impossible, and the babble of the brook at the bottom of their course obscured all noise.

Nita Qwan cursed the other men, who were doubtless better at this and should have volunteered. But he kept going, as he had no other plan, back and forth up the stream bed.

Suddenly he stopped.

He could *smell* the boglins. The hard metallic scent – he remembered it from the siege of the rock.

'Down,' he hissed.

They curled up under the bank.

Even over the babble of the brook, they heard the rustling.

The boy's heart was pounding so hard that Nita Qwan could feel it in his back. He was curled tight against the boy, his feet braced against a long-dead birch log, his arms wrapped in the roots of a still-living fir that sheltered them. The two of them were pressed tight into the roots, covered in swamp mud, but the boy's foot continued dripping blood.

Nita Qwan's thighs were burning with the effort of holding the boy up against the roots. He counted to one hundred.

The rustling was close.

He smelled that sharp odour again – and another. It burned the back of his throat; metallic and yet organic, like a strong musk.

And then it began to rain. It was a gentle rain, and in his fear and his desperate effort to find them some hiding place in this open meadow Nita Qwan had missed the change in temperature and the colour of the sky. The rain fell in big drops, heralded by a gust of wind that flattened the grass to the west, and for a moment Nita Qwan could clearly see a long line of boggles walking, heads down, across the open grass, headed north and west across the ford.

And then the rain line struck harder, and he couldn't see so much as fifty feet. The rushing rain filled the stream and the swamp in moments, and banished the acrid boggle smell.

Nita Qwan didn't know if they were still there, or not. He hung from the roots, waiting, watching the river fill under his belly, feeling the boy's terror. He thought of his wife's arse when she hoed corn, and that helped him for a bit. But in the end his muscles were screaming like a man being eaten alive, and he gave a gasp and they both fell into the icy water.

It was still only a few inches deep. And if there were any boglins about, they either didn't see the two soaked men, or didn't care. Faster and faster, the two humans worked their way upstream, across a long beaver dam built by beavers of the normal size, and then they were at the northern edge of the meadow.

The dam that stood there defied belief. Even with his gut muscles protesting, freezing cold, and lashed by the rain, Nita Qwan had to stare at the beaver dam he had mistaken for the edge of the woods. It stood as tall as an Alban town wall, forty feet or more. Whole trees – big trees – studded it. Water seeped through it and under it, coming from a body of water somewhere above. It was extraordinary.

'Come on,' Nita Qwan said. Visibility was cut to a short bowshot or less, and the rain was torrential. Climbing the dam had everything to recommend it – it would be hard for the boglins to follow them, and would give them better visibility. And Nita Qwan imagined that the top of the dam would be easier walking.

Nor was he disappointed. It took them long minutes to get up the dam – all brought on by the boy's injured foot – but the top was as wide as a cart, and in some places covered in grass. And on the far side of the dam was a body of water that continued into the middle distance, covered in dead, standing trees, each one of which had a great nest in the top – and it was studded with more beaver castles.

They moved as quickly as the boy could over the top of the dam, and came down only a mile or so north of their camp. They passed two open pools of Wild honey, and Nita Qwan tried to mark them in his mind. The boy still had his buckets, so they filled them in the rain and moved on.

Twice they heard the mechanical buzzing sound of the great bees, but they didn't see one. They walked on and on, and eventually Nita Qwan lost his little remaining faith in his sense of direction and stopped. He made his way to the light that he could see on his right hand, fearing that it would not be the great meadow, but it was, and he made his way back to the boy. The boy's trust in him was total, and almost as frightening as the boggles had been. Then the light began to fade, the rain came harder, and Nita Qwan began to know real fear.

Finally, an hour or so before dark, he smelled smoke – and became conscious that he'd smelled smoke for some time. He saw a glow through the trees, and then a hard-edged flash of red-orange light, and he knew he was close. The two of them went faster and faster, and gathered more petty injuries and briar scratches in the last short distance than they had in all the rest of their long walk. At last, they came to the camp. Young Gon had his back slapped a dozen times, and he bore the teasing with dignity. Nita Qwan was amazed to see that the young man said nothing of their adventures.

Ota Qwan looked at the two full buckets of honey and nodded. 'I knew you were the right man to send,' he said, somewhat smugly.

'You know there's a dam the size of a city about a league north of here?' Nita Qwan said, when they were alone and smoking. Everyone else was asleep, which Nita Qwan had found was a good time to talk to his brother. The other man didn't bridle and resent his words so much when he didn't have an audience. Ota Qwan had doubled the guard, though, because tonight, they had more to protect. The whole camp smelled of Wild honey – twenty-four buckets of it. The buckets were so full that insects clustered on them – Gas-a-ho's buckets had already leaked a little and the smooth white birch bark was covered in needles stuck to the honey.

Ota Qwan took his pipe back. 'No. I didn't know. It's like last year – when the honey is mature, the Wild fills up with things coming to take it. Not much time to explore.'

'There's a body of water there so large you can't even see the far shore. Heron nests, and some sort of bigger bird. And huge beaver castles.' He took the pipe, put it between his teeth, and blew a smoke ring into the darkness. 'Want to check it out tomorrow?'

Ota Qwan shook his head. 'Nope,' he said. 'We've already seen boggles and golden bears. I saw a pair of them moving towards the honey, and there's never just two.'

In the morning they rose while it was still dark – ate a little honey on the remnants of their cornbread, picked up the buckets and the weapons, and started back. It took them a whole day to cross the low ground and the rocky wastes at the foot of the Beaver Kingdom, as Ota Qwan called it, and late the evening, while the scouts were looking for a place to camp and everyone else was searching for a good crossing over yet another small river, they found the dead boglins – six of them had been killed and eaten. They were all lying on the rocks of the stream.

Ta-se-ho, the oldest, crouched by the most intact corpse and rolled it over on the rocks with his spear. A cloud of bluebottles rose from the corpse and the older hunter wrinkled his nose. He was tall, with a long horsetail of dark brown hair and a scar that ran all the way up his right leg from the knee to the groin. He wore an amulet, a piece of weathered leather embroidered in quills. At some point, Peter had realised that it was a human ear.

'Golden bears?' asked Ota Qwan. Despite the fact that anyone who knew death could see the corpses were some days old, every warrior was crouched, looking at the trees.

Ta-se-ho shook his head. He walked over to a rock, and compared it to something only he saw.

Nita Qwan was picking his way across the ford. The boglins had died during their crossing. It had been two days ago, but still—

He stepped up out of the gully cut by the stream, and got one leather-clad foot on a rock. His thighs were still tired. All of him was tired. He put some will into his legs and powered up onto the rock, and gasped.

He pointed his spear at the boglins he had found, but they were all dead too. Strewn across a small clearing.

One had been cut in half.

He grunted, and Ta-se-ho climbed out of the stream bed and joined him.

'Ah,' he said. He grew pale. 'Ah.'

Ota Qwan jumped up beside him. 'What happened?'

Ta-se-ho moaned. 'Crannock,' he said. 'Crannock people. Giants.'

Ota Qwan looked south. 'The Crannock are allies of the Southern Huran.'

Ta-se-ho spat. 'Thorn, too,' he said.

North-West of the Endless Lakes – Thorn

Thorn hurried forward, excited by what he sensed, the great black egg borne on his immense trunk, secure in a web of power.

He was walking along a bay, the whole stretch of water lit in golden sunlight with pale beaches lining the deep, clear water. As he walked, the bay narrowed.

Across the bay – across a straight as wide as a river and far deeper – lay a great island. Something about that island reeked of power.

Thorn reached among the ropes and tangles of his palace of power and summoned a wind, and he spread mighty gossamer wings and flew out over the water, reckless and heedless of mere men, if any happened to see him. He rose into the setting sun, and turned south.

The island was redolent of power. And empty of other Powers.

It was not Thorn's way to ask why.

The island was the size of a great lordship in the land of men – from the air he could see that it stretched ten leagues to the south, into the Inner Sea, and as far to the west. And at the northern edge of the island, a great mountain rose more than a thousand feet above the rolling hills and shaded dells of the island.

And set into the very top of the mountain was a lake. A river rushed from it over a steep lip and down a magnificent fall, into a deep pool at its base, and then down a further short series of falls, like steps, into the Inner Sea itself.

In the midst of the mountain lake was an island, and from the island grew a single tree. He folded his vast wings and let himself fall, and then stooped towards the island – spread his wings again in the joy of flying, and coasted to a stall just a few feet above the stony surface of the island. The tree's canopy seemed to stretch high, but it was deceptive – the tree itself was only twice the height of the sorcerer. He banished his wings, and went to touch the tree with some trepidation. It was a thorn, and he put his great stony head back and croaked, the closest he could manage to a laugh.

He felt the power of the earth through his toes. Lines of power ran strong here – three crossed, and another passed deep under the lake and bubbled up like a spring. Like a well. Like Lissen Carrak.

The power boiled up from the ground and swirled around a basin carved by the raw power. Thorn dropped his staff and knelt, his heavy legs creaking with the effort – and thrust his long, skeletal hands deep into the green-gold swirl. He raised them and raw *ops* rolled down his arms.

If he had possessed the facility, he might have wept.

Instead, he forced himself to his feet, raised his dripping arms, and willed the heavens to obey him.

High in the infinite *aether*, his power fastened on something that was between a star and a stone, and he dragged it from the heavens. It fell, hurtling, burning brighter than Venus against the falling dark as it rushed through the air at an impossible speed and struck far out in the Inner Sea.

He stretched his hands to the heavens and roared at his enemies.

Petty revenge? Try this!

*

Deep in the Adnacrags, an old bear raised his muzzle against the night sky. He watched the star fall, and he didn't like what he saw. His mate growled, and he put a great paw on her back, but she felt the tremor in his paw.

Far, far to the west, Mogon saw the new star kindle and fall, and she raised her crested head and spat.

Deep in the forest, the old irk was disturbed as he plotted, and he raised his long nose and saw, amid the trees, a new star kindle, and then plunge to earth. Tapio Haltija licked his teeth and grinned at the sight, but the movement of his mouth looked more predatory than pleasant.

East and south, Aeskepiles woke suddenly from an unsound sleep full of evil dreams. He lay on the floor of a monastic church at the edge of the Field of Ares, surrounded by the Duke of Thrake's retainers. They snored, and farted, and grumbled – none of those things had wakened him.

High above him, stars twinkled in the heavens and their light seeped through the clerestory windows in the base of the dome. He watched as one grew and grew in light until it burned like a little sun, casting its radiance so brightly that it lit some of the stained glass of the chapel and cast barely perceptible and flickering shadows over the floor and his sleeping companions. And then it began to fall to earth.

'Vade retro!' spat the magister. His side ached from the wound he'd taken.

A sorcerer, somewhere, had just pulled a star down from the vault of the heavens. It was a challenge, as clearly as if he had smacked every other man of power in the world with a glove. Across the face.

Aeskepiles lay in his blankets and tried to imagine how powerful and puissant a magister had to be to pull a star from the heavens.

Then a messenger came into the chapel, calling for the Duke.

'The Vardariotes!' he whispered urgently. 'They're moving!'

The Duke grumbled like any fifty-year-old man wakened untimely. He pulled on his beard and thought for as long as a man might say a prayer.

'Order Ser Demetrios to bring his troops back to me,' he said.

Strategos Demetrios was the border-bred Morean who commanded most of their strength of men-at-arms. He had been sent with a little less than half their force to watch the Vardariot Gate, ten miles distant around the walls.

The Duke rose. 'Arm me,' he told his squires.

Their most recent defector, the Grand Chamberlain, sat up. 'Surely they will simply come over to Your Excellency,' he said. 'They haven't been paid in a year.'

The Duke shook his head as if to clear it. 'I can't take that chance. They are superb troops – no threat to us unless we're surprised, but we'd best be ready. They can make a feint and then cut through the city, while we have to ride around the outside. I fairly dread the thought of them loose beyond the gate – five hundred disciplined Easterners with horse bows!' He grunted. 'Christ Pantokrator.'

'We can take them,' said his son, now awake.

'We can,' said his father grimly. 'But I'd rather we didn't have to. If we show them serried ranks and a ready army—'

Aeskepiles nodded at the dark. 'But—' He raised his head. 'My lord, what of the Alban mercenary? Isn't he in the hills?'

'Too distant to have any effect today or tomorrow,' the Duke said. 'And no real force of men. My source in the palace says he's camped and haggles for more money.'

The Despot laughed. 'Coward,' he said.

The Duke warmed his hands on a cup of hot wine brought by a servant. 'Let's deal with these threats one at a time, and force the girl to make terms,' he said.

The Grand Chamberlain managed to sound obsequious even when exhausted. 'Ah. Well thought, my Emperor.'

'Don't call me that,' spat the Duke.

South of Harndon, the Grand Prior of the Order of Saint Thomas sipped wine on his balcony, five hundred feet above the plains of Jarsay. He looked at the middle-aged priest sitting across from him. The man's face wore the complex mask of a man both defiant and repentant – angry at himself, and angry at the world.

'What am I to do with you, sir?' the prior asked. He'd worn his harness for a day and a night as a penance, and every joint in his body ached. And last night sleep had eluded him – mostly because he was old, and had too much on his mind. Like many a sinful priest.

'Send me somewhere, I suppose,' the priest said bitterly. 'Where I can rot.'

Prior Wishart had been a knight and a man of God for almost forty years. He knew the resilience of men – and their willingness to destroy themselves. What he knew of this man, he knew only under the seal of confession. He sat back and sipped more wine.

'You cannot remain in Harndon,' he said. 'To do so would only increase the likelihood of further temptation and sin.'

'Yes,' said the younger man, miserably. He was forty years old, handsome in a rough-hewn way, with brown hair cut for convenience under a helmet. 'I meant no harm by it.'

The prior smiled grimly. 'But you did harm. And you are old enough to see the consequences. You are one of my finest knights – and a fine philosopher. But I can't have you here. The other men look up to you – what will they do when this becomes public knowledge?'

The man straightened. 'It will never become public knowledge.'

'Does that make it less sinful?' the prior asked.

'I'm not a fool, thank you, Prior.' The priest sat straight and glared.

'Really?' Prior Wishart asked. 'Can you truly sit there and say you are not a fool?'

The man recoiled as if struck.

'I could ask for release from my vows and you'd be shot of me,' the priest said. For the first time he sounded more contrite than rebellious.

'Do you wish to be released from your vows, Father Arnaud?' The prior leaned forward.

Most knights of the order were brothers – some, as Donats, were lay brothers sworn only to obey; some were religious brothers, sworn to chastity, poverty and obedience; a life of arms and prayer and serving in the hospital. A very few became priests. The order asked very little of its fighting brethren besides obedience to orders, but it required a great deal from its priests.

Father Arnaud raised his head. Tears ran down his face. 'No,' he said. 'I cannot imagine it.'

The prior's fingers played with his beard and he glanced down at the pile of scrolls and folded correspondence under his left hand – the cure of his life and his eternal penance – the paperwork. The truth was – *The truth was that Arnaud was one of the best, in the field and in council, and he'd made a terrible mistake. And Wishart didn't want to punish him. Beyond punching him a few times for being such a love-struck fool.* His eye caught on a black seal with three lacs d'amour picked out in gold leaf – a very expensive, very eye-catching seal.

He popped the seal with his thumb and read through the letter with every sign of pleasure – once he laughed aloud. When he was done, he slapped the rolled scroll against his desk with the sound a crossbow makes when it is released.

'I will send you to be chaplain to the Red Knight,' the prior said.

'That arrogant boy? The godless *mercenary*?' Father Arnaud sat back, paused, and took a deep breath. 'But – this is no punishment. Any knight would want to serve – if he could be converted!'

Prior Wishart poured himself more wine. 'Think on your own shortcomings when you preach to the Red Knight, Arnaud. Arrogance and pride. Selfish assurance. And remember the company he leads – they are men and women like any others, and need a spiritual currency.'

Arnaud knelt and kissed the prior's hand. 'I will go with all my heart. I'll fetch him in for the order, and lead him to good works.'

Wishart gave his priest a wry smile. 'He does the good works already, Arn. He merely does them while cursing God.' He leaned over. 'While you sinned while praising God.'

Arnaud raised a hand as if to deflect a blow.

When the priest was gone, the prior went out on his balcony, a hundred feet above the fecund plains of Jarsay. Close under his walls, the second cutting of hay stood in new-minted ricks; a winter's fodder for his warhorses at stud, a new generation of heavy chargers that could face the largest foes the Wild had to offer. Further away in the silver moonlight, wheat stood in dark squares, with hedgerows and fences marking field edges to the horizon. Jarsay was rich; the best farmland in the Nova Terra.

To the north, a star flared silver white and dived to earth.

He saw the star form – and saw it fall. He felt the accession of power.

He sipped a little more wine.

Thorn's latest apotheosis wasn't even his most pressing problem. The King's Champion had taken an army into Jarsay to collect taxes, and all he was collecting instead was corpses. And Prior Wishart was trying to decide what he would do if his order's home farms were threatened.

Even that paled next to the possibility that the King might allow the Captal to appoint his cousin to be the Bishop of Lorica.

'Sufficient unto the day are the evils thereof,' the prior said quietly, to the night.

Chapter Seven

Michael the Squire

North of Liviapolis – The Red Knight

Crossing a river is one of the most complicated and difficult tasks faced by an army and its commander.

Crossing at night isn't even in the books – the books by Archaics on the art of war that the Red Knight had read and reread as a boy. He thought about them, and reading the strategem while lying full length in front of his mother's fire – and while she thought he was studying a grimoire.

He smiled.

The company came down to the banks of the Meander out of the mountains, moving quickly. There were guides at every fork in the road, guides at every corner, every gap in the stone walls. The guides were all Gelfred's men; Amy's Hob and Rob the Beard and Diccon Browford and young Dan Favour, who was big enough to wear harness and clever enough to be a scout, too. They each had their own pages and archers, now – Amy's Hob laughed to be considered a leader, but he was patient and cautious and his pages learned scouting quickly enough.

They'd point the column towards its next goal, and then canter away into the darkness, looking for Gelfred, who ran the chain from the back of his horse, a league in front of the Captain, with a small sphere of red mage light perched on the point of his peaked bassinet. Only the men on whom he'd cast his *phantasm* of sight could see the light. It made him relatively easy to find – by his own scouts, anyway – and allowed him to direct them at speed. Once they rejoined him, he sent each scout to his next guide post. He consulted the chart spread over his high pommel, and he used his not inconsiderable *ars magicka* to manage all the information brought to him by forty men, pinning their reports into non-dimensional pigeon holes in his memory palace image of the terrain.

Hermeticism and good scouting and a long summer spent in harness kept the company moving through the dark at the speed of a walking horse, across strange roads and through alien country. Because these factors made it look easy, the young sprigs of nobility who made up the new men-at-arms in the company thought that it was easy.

And so the company came down out of the mountains, through the olive groves, and to the banks of the Meander at the speed of a walking horse. Which is to say that they arrived like a thunderbolt.

The company rode up to the top of the ford in a column of fours, with the men-at-arms on their warhorses mounted in the outer files, and the carts, women, archers and pages in two files in the middle. This formation had been practised for two weeks without much explanation.

The Red Knight rode past Ranald Lachlan and a pair of his drovers, who were busy belaying a heavy rope. Lachlan waved. The Red Knight saluted with a smile that was just visible in the strong moonlight. The rain clouds were blowing off.

'Gelfred?' he asked. 'This is a ford?'

Gelfred shrugged. 'If we were all twice the height of Tom, here, this would be a ford,' he said. 'In dry years, they use this. Otherwise, it's unguarded.' He met his Captain's eye in the moonlit dark. 'Best I could do,' he said.

We can do it, Harmodius said inside the Red Knight's head. *Almost five feet deep at the deepest point, just past mid-stream.*

The Red Knight nodded to his invisible companion. 'Very well. It's going to be deep in the middle. My source says five feet.'

'Sweet Jesus!' Michael cursed. 'Sorry,' he muttered, mostly to Gelfred, the only non-swearing man in the company.

'The wagons will be wet through,' Gelfred pointed out.

The Red Knight had an apple, and was eating it while watching the river.

'And it will take time. If we get beat, we won't get back across in daylight with our baggage,' he added.

Bad Tom spat. 'We won't get beat.'

A dozen men made the horned sign of aversion. Wilful Murder spat and touched the wood of his buckler. Even Ser Jehan looked unhappy.

'It would certainly be useful to know if the Vardariotes have accepted our offer and left their barracks,' the Captain said aloud.

Ser Alcaeus winced, but he had no report to offer.

White moonlight fell on glittering armour and well-disciplined horses, who stood calmly; red leather saddles were brown-grey against the dusty grey of the ground and the dark green of the olive trees on either hand. A farmhouse, shuttered tight and dark, lay silent to the right of the road – really no more than a gravel gully between the walls – that led to the abandoned ford. And the moonlight shone down on the river, reflected in ten thousand shards that made a bright white road all the way to the far shore. The effect was so powerful that a simple man might think that the water was shallow.

No one on earth has that much power, boy. Not to walk across the water.

The Captain smiled. He stripped off his gauntlets and rooted in the draw-string pouch sewn to the front of his belt-purse – the one he wore even in armour. He came up with two bone dice.

'Dice?' asked Michael.

'He's a loon,' Tom said.

Sauce shook her head.

The Captain stood in his stirrups, rattled the dice in his hand for a moment, and threw them as hard as he could out into the current of the river. If they made a splash, no one heard it.

'Go,' said the Captain.

Gelfred nodded and took the scouts across in a mass. Every man – and woman – watched them trot into the ford, up to their fetlocks and then their hocks, and then the horses were swimming – the men soaked – and then the horses were walking again. Rob's page, Tom Hall, came adrift from his horse in mid-stream, but he kept his head and his horse's mane, and despite being the smallest he got over and mounted again.

Gelfred flashed the red on his helmet three times, and the Red Knight nodded to his staff.

'They're across,' he said. Among the men-at-arms, only he, Tom, Jehan and Milus could see the red light on Gelfred's helm. It occurred to the Captain, then and there, that they should all have mage lights – in different colours – for night operations.

I'll bet the ancients used mage lights.

Harmodius grunted, in an *aethereal* way. *I never bothered with those books – but there are many on war. From the Archaic Empire, and even earlier.*

You interest me, old man. The Red Knight looked around. *But I need peace for a few hours.*

It's awfully dull in here. But very well. I'm sure you'll call me when you need me to destroy something, the old man said with some bitterness.

In the strong moonlight he could see all his scouts fanning out across the river.

'You asleep?' asked Bad Tom. 'You look half wode. And yer lips are moving.'

The Red Knight straightened, feeling the weight of command like a belt of lead on his hips. 'I must be wode. I ride with Mad Tom.' He looked around at his staff – larger since the spring, with more knights under his direct command. They were his reserve – itself an Archaic concept. Everyone was ready.

'Let's do it,' he said.

Bad Tom laughed, and put spurs to his stallion, who put his steel-horned head down and plodded into the water on the upstream side. As he walked forward into the sluggish, sparkling water, he angled to the left, out and away from the main column.

Fifty men-at-arms mounted on their warhorses walked into the current behind him, in a long single file.

Sauce led fifty more men-at-arms off to the right, downstream.

'What was that about?' Cully asked Bent.

Bent shrugged. 'Cap'n does strange things. You know that.'

Ser Michael leaned in between the two archers. 'You gentlemen are missing the benefits of a classical education. When he threw the dice, he meant, "the die is cast". As in, there won't be any going back.' He looked at the two senior archers, who stared back at him. Finally, he snorted, turned his horse, and joined Bad Tom's file in crossing upstream.

'Could have just said,' muttered Cully.

'Arrogant pup,' agreed Bent.

*

The crossing took the company less than half an hour, and then they were moving at a cart's pace along the track on the far side.

There was no crisis, but small emergencies slowed their march. Lis's cart lost a wheel and had to be repaired. That meant sending up the column for the two wheelwrights that the company retained, and they had to go back down the column with their cart and enlist twenty archers to raise the cart bed. The actual repair was the work of two minutes and a portable anvil, but all together it took longer than crossing the river had.

Twice, the whole column had to halt because Gelfred was unsure of their way in the maze of unmarked roads that criss-crossed the fields of the Morean heartland. The field walls were all at least six feet tall and in many cases twelve feet tall – or rather, aeons of use had sunk the roads six feet into the stony soil, meaning that even a mounted man on a big horse couldn't see over the walls on either side. The roads themselves were just big enough for a full-sized wagon or three horsemen abreast – sometimes narrower if an old tree grew out into the road bringing the attendant wall with it. Sometimes the old walls had tumbled down into the road and needed to be cleared, and the Captain moved the company's pioneers – in effect, his peasant labourers – to the head of the column to clear the road as he went.

The Red Knight let Gelfred have his head. The huntsman was better at understanding terrain than anyone else; if he lost his way, it was best to give him time to find it again. So he sat, reining in his frustration as hard as he reined his warhorse, a big gelding with whom he was just beginning to have a warm relationship.

Gelfred rode ahead in person, vanishing into the slate grey. He came back two very long minutes later.

'I have it,' he said. 'My apologies, my lord. Things look different in this light.' He shrugged. His stress showed clearly on his face.

The Red Knight clapped him on an armoured shoulder. 'Lead on.'

Gelfred had Amy's Hob to hand, and his page. 'Go fetch everyone in – we're too far west,' he said. To the Captain, he said, 'We need to wait until the skirmisher screen is out again.'

The Captain looked at the wolf's tail of dawn – it was a false dawn, but their time was running out. 'I misdoubt that we have the time to wait for your men to collect themselves,' he said. 'We'll have to be our own pickets.'

Gelfred nodded. 'I'll lead, my lord. You know the risk.'

The Red Knight laughed aloud. 'We could be ambushed!' he said. 'Let's go. I hear the early bird gets the worm.'

Gelfred winced.

Ranald Lachlan came up level with the huntsman. 'Why is he so fucking cheerful in the morning? But it could be worse – he could be blaspheming.'

Gelfred sighed. 'I take your point,' he muttered, and turned his horse's head.

Unfortunately their troubles weren't over.

With no scouts, there was no one to move early farmers off the road. And so it was, as they came to a major crossroads somewhere within a mile of their goal, they found the entire intersection filled from wall to wall with sheep. Hundreds of sheep.

The two shepherds were mounted on ponies, directing a dozen dogs with whistles and shaken staffs. Gelfred's Archaic wasn't up to the altercation. And the intersection was blocked as completely as it would have been if a company of armoured spearmen were standing on the same ground. Worse, the warhorses hated having the sheep close in among their vulnerable legs.

'Just kill them and have done with it,' shouted Bad Tom.

The Captain reached into his belt pouch and rode forward. 'Toby!' he called over his shoulder. 'Money!'

In a matter of moonlit moments the shepherds went from from terrified belligerence to eager cooperation. Whips cracked, dogs barked, and the vast, amorphous herd of sheep began to move back along the road and up one of the side roads. The shepherds bowed and called benedictions, and the company was finally free to move. The sky was definitely grey.

Gelfred's scouts had caught up during the delay and finally they spread out again in front, covering all three branching roads. 'Almost there,' Gelfred said. He had gone as grey as the dawn.

'Can you imagine what this would be like if we had to move and fight?' asked Michael.

No one answered.

They moved at a trot now that their flanks were secure, and as the sun crested the city in front of them, gilding a hundred church towers each topped with a dome of copper gilt that burned like a new fire in the rising sun – as three thousand monks in fifty monasteries began to chant the hymns that marked the break of a new day – as seventy thousand cocks crowed their relief that the darkness was over – as a quarter of a million people rose to face another day of uncertainty – they reached the main road. It was a circuit road a thousand years old, built from hewn and matched stone, wide enough for six carts to travel abreast, and it ran all the way around the walls from the Gate of the Vardariotes on the eastern shore of the Morean Sea, around nine miles of walls to reach the Royal Gate at the north-west end of the circuit.

The company arrived at its chosen point – where the road dipped into a low vale. There wasn't a scrap of cover for a long bowshot in any direction, except a single huge oak tree and a small villa well off the road.

The Red Knight didn't have to dispose of his troops – every section rode to their place as they had practised twice in the last week, and dismounted.

The Red Knight joined hands with Mag the seamstress and Gelfred and the three of them threw a working over the company, and then tossed in a little ground fog at the bottom of the dale. The Captain, aided by Harmodius, placed the whole working inside a deep green peridot, a fine stone he'd picked up from a peddler. A good jewel helped focus a complex casting; the crystal also gave the complex working stability and thus durability.

Half an hour later, Gelfred rode back to the Captain and opened his visor. 'Nothing behind us, m'lord. They haven't passed this way.'

Twenty long minutes later, a great black and white eagle the size of a warhorse began to circle overhead.

Ser Alcaeus rode up to the Red Knight. 'M'lord – that bird is for us. It can't see through your *phantasm*. But it will mark our place to any Morean.'

The Captain sighed.

Working with Harmodius, he extracted the working from the jewel. With careful control, he adjusted the casting to open a sight line into the top of the illusion.

The bird spied them and stooped.

He closed the working and replaced it in the jewel. 'That cost me more than half the working I can do in a day,' he said sulkily. 'The next crisis will have to be met the old-fashioned way.'

Alcaeus read the note while every horse within eyeshot shied away from the gigantic bird. 'The Vardariotes are on the move,' he said. 'Last night – after midnight. They are armed and mounted in formation at the Gate of Ares.'

The Captain nodded. 'Well, we did our part,' he said. 'Maybe we've been too subtle?'

His men had begun to fidget. The sun rose; flies came. Horses grew fractious. The women with the baggage began to talk, and a low mutter came to the command group from the soldiers.

Dan Favour rode in just as the monks in the city began to celebrate matins.

'Two thousand men,' he said happily. 'Less than a mile away.'

The Captain failed to hide his sigh of relief. He grinned ruefully. 'Of course, we still have to win the fight,' he reminded them.

The Morean stradiotes came down the road in good order, with a strong vanguard of almost six hundred men, and a hundred Eastern horse bowmen. They were late, and they were moving fast. Their main body was several hundred yards to the rear, almost two thousand horse, no infantry, no baggage. There were no banners, but in the centre of the main body were two great icons, held aloft by strong men on lances.

The Captain dismounted and put his peridot on a rock. Toby handed him a war hammer and stood by, holding his helmet and lance.

'If we stay here, I'm going to want a straw hat,' he said. The sun was hot.

The Moreans came at a trot, right along the road. From time to time, groups of Easterners would break off from the column and ride to look at something, but the column was in a hurry, and crossing safe terrain.

When the enemy vanguard was at short bow shot, the Captain raised his hammer and brought it down smartly on the peridot, which blew apart into a thousand tiny green pieces. The complex *phantasm* collapsed with the death of the stone, allowing every man covered by the working to see clearly.

Whistles sounded, and the archers nocked.

Before the Red Knight had his aventail over his head, the first flight of livery arrows leaped from his archers' great white bows. Two hundred bowmen loosed five shafts apiece in rapid succession – most men were drawing their last shaft before the first one hit home.

The arrows struck, and the Morean vanguard disintegrated.

A group of horse bowmen who had ridden clear of the column to investigate the farmhouse were greeted by the combined bolts and shafts of all of Gelfred's scouts. The survivors drew their bows from the cases at their hips and stood in their stirrups to loose, then turned and bolted for the safety of the main body, loosing further shafts over the rumps of their horses.

The battle was not quite two minutes old when the Red Knight stood in his own stirrups and roared, 'Mount!'

Expecting the order, most of the archers were already up, as were all the men-at-arms – pages scrambled to find their own mounts after passing horses to their men-at-arms and archers. Inexperience showed; the older pages were ahead of the order and the new ones were behind it, and to the left of centre, in Ser Alcaeus's lances, there was chaos. The Red Knight couldn't see what was causing it. Nor could he wait.

'*En avant!*' he called, and his whole company began to move forward in three mounted ranks, men-at-arms in front, pages to the rear.

The Morean vanguard broke. A third of them were down or dead, and they'd done their job – the ambush hadn't fallen on the main body.

The company closed up and went forward at a trot – the men-at-arms and squires were mailed leg to steel-clad leg, the line almost three hundred yards long. Gelfred's huntsmen and scouts went wide to the right, angling towards the rear of the column's main body.

'Charge me or don't,' muttered the Red Knight, inside his helmet. He had the element of surprise but he was still outnumbered three to one; he needed his opponent to lose his nerve.

As if responding to this challenge, the icons in the centre of the enemy column went up and down, and the enemy column began to unroll – very professionally – from a column to a line, companies cantering to the right and left as the line unfolded.

The Red Knight raised his lance. 'Halt!' he roared.

The trumpeter made a noise much like a mating moose – twice – but the company knew what to expect. The line halted. They began to dress, the trailing left centre catching up, the wings unbowing, the centre already dismounting.

To the untrained eye, it looked like a disordered mess.

Tom flipped up his visor. 'We could ha'e just charged them,' he said.

The Captain shrugged. At his feet, Wilful Murder was handing his horse to Toby's replacement, Nell, who got five sets of reins in her skinny little fist and led the brutes out of the line. Wilful got his bow in hand, nocked an arrow, looked left and right, and called, 'Ready!'

The horses were coming out of the ranks.

More 'ready!' calls floated along the morning breeze.

The enemy line was almost formed, and the icons were moving up into the centre.

'They are damned good,' the Red Knight said.

Wilful Murder shook his head. 'Pretty, but no plate armour and no infantry?' he said. 'It's the archer's dream.' His questing eye found Bent, far to the right – the master archer raised his bow.

Wilful raised his own bow, saw Cully off to one flank and Bent off to the other.

'Fast as you can, now, boys,' he said.

And they loosed.

The end of the fight was messy.

The heavy shafts slaughtered the Moreans, whose charge was shattered before it was fully under way. But the Moreans were veterans of hundreds of fights, and if they had never faced such concerted, disciplined longbow fire before, they had good leaders and long experience of both victory and defeat. The shredded Morean line retired out of bow shot, and reformed. Some few of the Morean stradiotes carried Eastern bows, and they returned a few shafts.

'Mount,' said the Captain. He had never dismounted himself. He turned to Bad Tom, who was close at his heels. 'This time we go right over them. I want to end this; we don't want that force snapping at our heels tonight.'

Tom grinned and motioned at Ranald, who pumped a fist in the air to show his men that this was it.

Wilful Murder demurred. 'My lord, I'd give 'em another dose of goosefeather before I put my horse's head at them. They ain't broke – look at 'em.'

The Captain watched their adversaries reforming. 'Men are so much more complicated than facing the creatures of the Wild,' he said. 'I want to leave as many of them alive as possible. We're killing our employers' taxpayers and soldiers.'

The horse holders were getting a workout – little Nell came shoving by. 'Take your fucking horse,' she spat at Wilful, who was standing at the Captain's horse's head.

This time Ser Alcaeus's division was better ordered, and they started forward together.

A hundred paces from the enemy line the Moreans turned and began to ride away, expecting another arrow shower.

'Charge!' shouted the Captain.

From a fast trot to a gallop took three strides for a trained horse, and the men-at-arms were off. The trumpeter got the call right, and it rolled on and on – clearly it was the only one he'd really practised.

The Moreans took fifty paces to understand what was happening. They were out-shot, and out-armoured, and now, all of a sudden, they were going to be out-ridden.

Their discipline came apart. It is almost impossible to rally troops who have already turned their backs on the enemy; it is harder to do it a second time, and even harder when the enemy is already charging with murderous intent. As a result, when the strategos reined in, faced his company about, and launched a counter-charge right at the Red Knight and Mad Tom's lances, his red and purple clad stradiotes were alone. The rest had scattered, leaning low on their horses' necks and riding flat out for the safety of the distant hills, or their farms, or the city.

Very few were caught. The heavier Gallish warhorses were lumbering after a hundred paces, and most were down to a canter after two hundred paces.

In the centre, however, the knights came together with the enemy general's bodyguard with a crash that they could hear in the palace.

The strategos was a small man in heavy scale armour with bright red-dyed hardened leather covering his limbs and hard horn scales over his horse. He couched his lance like a Galle and aimed for the Red Knight, who lowered his own lance in response.

The strategos did not intend a knightly encounter – two paces from impact, his lance dipped, and he plunged his lance tip deep into the Red Knight's gelding, killing the great animal instantly, but not before the Red Knight's lance caught in the Morean's shield rim and ripped him from his saddle. Knight, strategos, and horses all crashed to earth, and the dust rose as the melee spread around them.

Bad Tom unhorsed three Moreans in a row, crushing their leather armour and sending them crashing to the earth until his lance point caught in the mail of his third victim and spiked through it – mail, leather, padded linen, flesh, ribs, and lungs. The man fell, spitted like a capon, and dragged Tom's lance with him so that the big man had to let it go. He was turning his horse, drawing his great sword, when he realised that his Captain was nowhere to be seen.

He turned his horse back into the rising dust.

The Red Knight got slowly to one knee and wrenched in a breath. The fall had taken him by surprise and he'd screamed as he struck a rock – only his back armour had saved him from a broken hip or spine. His sword was gone, his belt snapped in the fall.

He realised that his purse was under his foot, and his roundel dagger, a knife like a short iron spike, was strapped to it. He got it in his right fist. Then, peering through the dust and the slits of his visor, he searched for his sword as horses pounded past him in both directions and the rising dust choked him. He only had moments – there were hoof beats all around him, and the kettlepot rattling sound of a hundred men in armour beating away at each other with swords.

He pushed with his right leg and got his feet under him. A spike of cold pain pulsed in his right hip.

The Morean strategos came out of the dust like the inevitable villain of a romance. He had a heavy short sword in his right fist and a scarred shield with a beautifully painted figure of the Virgin Mary on his left arm.

'Yield,' shouted the Red Knight in High Archaic.

The strategos stopped. 'What?' he asked.

'Your army is beaten. Yield.' The Red Knight flexed his hip carefully like a man testing a bad tooth. It wasn't good.

No, there's nothing I can do.

Thanks for that, old man.

A few feet away Ser Jehan hacked one of the icon bearers to the ground, swinging his long sword over and over into the man's guard until he slipped and took the sword in his unarmoured face.

'Heretic barbarian!' the strategos shouted. 'I am Michael Tzoukes.

My ancestors fought the infidel and the irk when yours lived in straw huts and worshipped idols. I will not yield to *you*.'

The Red Knight sighed and stepped forward into the guard called 'All gates are iron'. He crossed his wrists, held his dagger reversed in his right hand and grabbed it by the tip with his left. The roundel was a foot and a half long, triangular in cross section, and had steel rounds which neatly filled the top and bottom of his closed and armoured fist, making the hand a single, seamless steel surface to an enemy blade.

The dust of the melee was settling and sight lines were improving. The Moreans were utterly beaten – routed or, in the centre, smashed flat. More than a dozen of the Red Knight's men-at-arms were closing in on the strategos.

They were still six feet apart. The Red Knight stepped back, tried and failed to open his visor and got a nasty pain in the back of his right leg for his trouble. He had to shout from within his helmet.

'Stay back,' he managed.

The strategos looked around him, growled, and leaped. His heavy sword fell like a lightning bolt—

—onto the Red Knight's crossed hands and the steel bar that was his dagger. Cursing his hip, the Red Knight powered forward, slipped the dagger from his left hand for a moment, caught his opponent's blade, and rolled on his hips – a sudden and unintended intake of breath and a stumble marked how much pain the hip could cause – before he uncrossed his hands, stripping the sword from the Morean and breaking the man's elbow in a single fluid movement.

Ruthless to his own hip and to his opponent alike, the Red Knight stepped in again, holding the man by his broken arm, and rolled him – put a foot between his armoured legs and forced him to the ground through pain and the power of his leg lock – against his own steel-clad legs.

'Yield,' said the Red Knight, panting with pain and trying his level best to hide it.

'I yield,' spat the Morean.

Ser Alcaeus took charge of the Morean prisoners while the archers brutally and efficiently looted the Morean camp. The Captain said they had one hour and none of them intended to leave a single silver solidi behind. Trunks were dumped, clothes slit, tents thrown down.

Ser Alcaeus had the forethought to inform the Captain that the women in the camp were probably the wives of stradiotes and not trulls. The men-at-arms, under Sauce's command, rounded them up and penned them where the Moreans' spare horses had, until a few minutes before, been kept. If the women saw this as a merciful release from the threat of rape and violent death, they didn't show any thanks. Rather they screamed, heckled, and cursed. Luckily, very few of the men-at-arms spoke any Archaic.

The company took all of the carts and animals.

The Captain was almost the only man who was injured. He tried to bite down on the pain, and he soaked up the strong sunlight and filtered through his newfound medical workings, trying to use it to heal the injury, but either he was doing something wrong or it was getting worse.

'Trust you to find a good fight in the middle of a wasted day,' said Bad Tom. 'That was *pitiful*. I want to go back to fighting the Wild.'

'Tom, we were outnumbered three to one. What do you want? We surprised them. I doubt we'll be so lucky again.' The Captain winced.

'He put a lance in your horse, eh? Smart.' Tom grinned. 'Nasty fall. You weren't ready for that.'

'Clean against the laws of chivalry,' Michael said. 'Here, I just looted some really good white wine.'

'I don't think yon have quite the same laws,' Tom said.

'Did you have to break his arm?' asked Michael.

'He was trying to kill me,' said the Captain.

Tom laughed.

When the hour was up, the company marched west around the walls accompanied by a hundred prisoners and twenty new carts, chased by nothing but the imprecations of a thousand unexpectedly destitute women.

The road was excellent, but it was still late afternoon when the company came in sight of the Duke of Thrake's main army, drawn up in battle order facing the Gate of Ares. The Moreans weren't taken completely unaware, and even as the Red Knight's battle line, formed up a mile away on the move, came over the low ridge that faced the ancient field, the Morean army was wheeling back, giving ground to avoid being outflanked.

The Morean line was three times the length of the company's line, and deeper. The Duke of Thrake had four good companies of infantry, with armour, long spears, and archers in the fifth and sixth rank, and they filled the centre of his line. He had heavy Alban-style men-at-arms on his left, and stradiotes flanked by Easterners on his right.

The Despot's company of Easterners flowed further and further to the right, out on to the apparently limitless grass of the Field of Ares, galloping around the company's flank. In response, the company formed a shallow box with the baggage in the centre.

'I can feel their magister,' the Captain said to no one in particular.

Ser Jehan trotted over. 'We need to retire and secure one of our flanks,' he said.

'We should give them some ash shafts and then charge 'em,' said Ser Thomas.

The Captain rose in his stirrups and his hip screamed in protest. His ugly, borrowed horse assumed that he was at liberty to rid himself of an unwelcome rider and did a four-footed bound, which the Captain reined in savagely.

Ser Jehan coughed. 'Captain, the men are tired, we have already faced one action today, and the enemy is both more numerous and well armed and trained. I would like to respectfully suggest—'

Tom spat. 'Fuck that. We can take them.'

Jehan narrowed his eyes. 'Tom, you ain't as smart as you think you are. This is foolery. Mayhap we can win. Put a lot of our boys in the dust – and what for?'

'The Vardariotes will come into his flank and just like that, the campaign is won,' the Captain said.

'Or they don't and we get gutted. Who cares? We're paid the same either way. Christ on the cross – we're mercenaries. What got into you two? Retire now and tomorrow we'll drive him off with these whatever-you-call-them on our flanks.'

The Captain looked through him. 'We'll use the wagons to cover our flanks. Advance.'

'You just want to say you've won two battles in a day, you arrogant pup. And men will die for your – your—' Jehan was spluttering with professional rage.

Tom laughed. 'He's a loon, right enough. Save your breath to cool your porridge, boyo. We're going to fight.'

*

'Look!' shouted the Despot. He leaned out over the neck of his horse and pointed at the enemy. 'He has both of our icons! Tzoukes has betrayed us!'

The Duke had not won every battle of his career, and he smelled a rat. He rose in his stirrups. 'That's crap. And saying such things aloud does you no credit.' He looked under his hand at the glittering, steel-clad ranks of his new adversaries. The Vardariotes had thus far remained safely inside the gates of the city.

The magister began to raise power. The *ops* was rippled and strained. He was not the only workman in this brickyard, and the wound he'd taken from the Emperor's spymaster and bodyguard was a distraction that weakened his casting. 'They have a powerful mage with them,' he said through clenched teeth. 'By the crucified Christ, my lord – they have two.' He breathed, and then spoke as if he'd run a race. 'No, four. Perhaps five— Parthenos, my lord!'

'He beat Tzoukes and he has another force. He's not showing me all his spears,' the Duke said. 'Nonetheless, he's a barbarian and we are not. Let's push him.' He waved to his banner bearers. The trumpeters had horns made of wild aurochs, and they raised them, and the horns echoed like the cries of Wild creatures.

The Morean army marched. Their dressing was impressive – their own mercenary knights on the left, the five big blocks of infantry in the centre, and the Duke and his stradiotes on the right, with a thin second line a few hundred yards behind – mostly ill-mounted men and camp guards, but a second line nonetheless.

The army was small enough for a short speech so he rode to the centre of his line, tilted his steel cap back on his head, and stood in his stirrups.

'Companions!' he roared. 'These foreigners are more of the same – barbarians who come to take our wealth and our daughters and leave us with nothing but the right to be slaves when our fathers were lords. This mercenary has nothing but his arrogance to sustain him. We have God on our side. Go with God!'

His men roared. The spearmen in the centre – his veterans from his first days – raised gilded helmets on their spearheads and bellowed his name, calling him Imperator.

Duke Andronicus cantered back to his small command group and gestured to his son. 'We overlap him on both flanks. See to it that your Easterners turn his left so my Hetaeroi can finish him.'

Golden-haired Demetrius saluted smartly. 'As you say, Pater!' he shouted cheerily and cantered away to the right.

Kronmir sat comfortably on his horse's back, watching the distant city gate. 'It seems to me he is expecting help,' he said.

'He is merely arrogant. Galles and Albans – I've beaten them both.' The Duke smiled soberly. 'That sounds too much like hubris. But with God's help—' He looked west, towards his enemies.

The enemy baggage train was rolling forward.

As the Duke watched, walking his horse at the same pace that his marching spearmen were crushing the long grass, he saw the enemy baggage train split into two. There was confusion somewhere in the middle, and he smiled.

The enemy was in the process of dismounting. But their trumpet calls sounded tuneless, and the men at either end of the line were obviously unclear as to what to do. They were still three hundred paces distant, and Duke Andronicus watched his textbook attack roll into the barbarians. He looked to his left – the mercenary knights were drifting to the left, intentionally improving their flanking position and cutting the enemy off from the gate. Ser Bescanon knew his business.

On the right, his son was carefully maintaining the line. He wouldn't swing wide until the fighting had started. Barbarians never saw anything beyond immediate threat.

Two hundred and seventy-five paces. The capture of his most faithful vicar and two battle icons was annoying, but Andronicus intended to rescue all three before the sun set. The sun was beginning to set now, so if the contest ran longer than an hour the rays would fall in the eyes of his men. A small thing, but the sort of detail that Imperial commanders were careful about.

The last of the barbarians were dismounted. He had to admire the discipline of their horse holders, and he cursed that the barbarians were rich enough to mount every man while the Empire scrabbled to afford a few hundred professional cavalry of their own.

The enemy infantry were archers. He'd known it – but he was still a little surprised by the density of their first volley, especially considering the range.

Men went down.

As his men stolidly marched forward, Andronicus strove to

understand what had happened. Men in the armoured infantry had gone down.

The second, third, and fourth volley struck so close together that he lost track. The centre was staggered – it slowed, and the line bowed.

Ser Christos, one of his best officers and the Count of the Infantry, spurred out of the centre, took two arrows on his heavy shield, and still managed to raise his sword. 'Forward, companions!' he called, his high-pitched voice carrying like song, and the infantry surged forward, any momentary hesitation forgotten.

'Now *that's* an army,' said Bad Tom with satisfaction. 'Good thing irks don't react like that, eh?'

Three horse lengths in front of Tom, the company archers were grunting and releasing their shafts as fast as they could, and the Imperial infantry were soaking up the volleys on their shields. There were men down, but their huge round shields were three boards thick and formed of leather and bronze as well, and the men behind them were big, tough louts wearing heavy mail or scale, and they were still coming – close enough now that the archers could see their faces.

The Captain looked to the right, where, instead of covering his flank with a wagon wall, he had a snarl of panicked wagoners.

Even as he watched, Mag the seamstress leaped up on a wagon and began to yell at the men around her. She did something hermetical – he felt the odd hollowness that practioners could always sense before another cast – and he saw a wagon freeze in place, horses vibrating like lute strings.

He wished her well, but whatever she did was going to be too late, because five hundred enemy knights were intending to turn that flank.

She's using a great deal of power, and she's attracting the enemy magister's attention.

Shut up, Harmodius! The Captain put a hand to his head. *If you make me sick now, we're lost.*

He turned. 'Tom – there.' He pointed with his lance.

Bad Tom grinned his mad grin. 'With me, boys!' he shouted. He must have seen Sauce, because he said, 'And girls! Hah! Wedge, now – on me.'

The Captain had a third of the company's men-at-arms gathered around him – Ser Gavin, Ser Michael, Ser Alcaeus, Ranald and all the Hillmen, and others.

'Go!' shouted the Captain.

In a moment he was alone behind the line of archers, and Tom's wedge was forming, and Mag was still screaming at the men and women of the baggage train.

His hip hurt.

To no one in particular, he said, 'I've fucked this up.'

He backed his horse and turned the plug's head to look off to his left. There, the wagons had formed better, and Bent already had the end of the line covered by wagon bodies while the wagoners unhitched horses and hitched chains. They'd practised this, but it was obvious they hadn't practised it enough.

He looked at the oncoming wall of Morean infantry. There were holes in their line, and it looked a little like a waving flag. If he had another hundred men-at-arms, he could—

'Gelfred!' he called. 'Go all the way past Tom's wedge and do what you can.'

Gelfred's scouts, well behind his command, were all he had of a reserve. The rest of the men-at-arms and squires were dismounted with the archers.

Off to their front left, *ops* swelled. He could feel the working emanating from someone very powerful indeed—

Harmodius...

I knew you'd need me.

Whatever the enemy cast, it *sliced the grass* on its way to the archers' line. Men flinched, and then the great scythe was lifted as if it had never been there. A few men on the left felt an icy cold at their knees, and then they nocked and loosed.

Harmodius gathered power. Harmodius and the Red Knight had a shared problem – they seemed to have tangled whatever matrix of habit and *aethereal* training allowed them to access *ops*, so that instead of being two mages with two sets of power, they were two mages at the mercy of one another's expenditures.

The Captain watched most of his *ops* crackle off across the scythe-cut grass and crash into the centre block of enemy infantrymen. Men burst into flame. One man stumbled clear, screaming, a horrible parody of a person.

Another flight of arrows hissed into the enemy charge.

They kept coming.

*

Duke Andronicus could see his line flanking the enemy's, but he could also see the wagon wall the mercenaries had formed. He turned to Ser Stefanos, his personal champion. 'To my son. Tell him to ride further around the enemy flank.'

Ser Stefanos saluted and galloped away.

Far off towards the city, Ser Bescanon's men were starting to trot.

Andronicus began to look for the spot to place his killing blow. 'Close up, Hetaeroi!' he called.

The Captain dismounted next to Ser Milus with the standard and Ser Jehan, in the centre of the line. Ser Jehan still had his visor open, although the enemy was only fifty paces away.

'We're over-extended, and you were right,' the Captain said to his senior officer.

Ser Jehan looked at him – a glance of pure disgust that ever so briefly reminded him of his father's contempt.

He was stung by it.

'Three more!' Cully roared.

The last three flights did more damage than all the shafts loosed until then. The Captain had never, in fact, seen his company's archers loose into men at point-blank range before.

At that range, the arrows went through shields, and men's bodies. Through light helmets. Through horn scales. Through Wyverns' hide.

A hundred Morean veterans died with each flight – men who had served for ten or fifteen years. The Duke of Thrake's best men fell.

The two centre blocks of infantry shuffled, hesitated and were shredded.

On their flanks, the spearmen put their heads down and ran the last few paces into the teeth of the arrow storm.

Duke Andronicus couldn't believe the evidence of his eyes as his handpicked veterans hesitated and then broke. His position on the right wing limited his line of sight and so he couldn't see the intensity of the arrow storm, only the result – his centre breaking.

They were the men he'd commanded since he was the most junior centurione in the army, and he left his bodyguard and rode to them, rode among them. 'On me! On me, companions!' he roared – and they came. They turned and raised their heads – his men were crying in shame.

Duke Andronicus looked down the path of their charge and saw how few of them were left. 'Christ Pantokrator,' he said.

Ser Christos, wearing Gallish plate and mail and well mounted, had six arrows in his horse and two more in his breastplate. Even as Andronicus watched, the horse collapsed, feet rolling high, and the Count of the Infantry took too long to rise.

The barbarians immediately attacked from their centre, where their archery had proven so triumphant.

'Charge,' shouted the Captain. He had his sword in his fist and he started forward. Jehan shouted something, but the Captain saw their salvation and all around them archers threw down their bows and plucked out their swords and the dismounted men-at-arms went forward – the Captain ran towards the left. The men in front of him were not the immediate threat.

They caught the enemy infantrymen by surprise in their shielded flank and then all was chaos.

The Red Knight ran full tilt into the flank of the enemy block, hip forgotten. He knocked a man flat at impact, kicked him savagely with an armoured foot, stepped on the man's shield and broke his arm then lunged with the point of his sword, which went between the scales of the next man's flank, behind his shield, while he tried to turn and was hampered by the length of his own spear. He took a blow to his head, a spear blow that rocked him, and fell.

He started to rise – a spearshaft rang against his helmet and then he got his left hand on it and pulled, cut down without science, and his blade rang off the man's helmet and he stepped in and crushed the man's face with his pommel. To his right, Ser Jehan had cleared a space the length of his pole-hammer. Long Paw was cutting hands from spearshafts, and Ser Milus was using the company banner to shield himself from cuts while he crushed men with a mace. Cully tackled a spearman and Wilful Murder ran the prone man through with his side sword. Kanny fell with a spearpoint through the meat of his right leg, Big Paul died with a spearpoint in his throat, and John le Bailli stepped on his corpse and buried the point of his pole-axe in his killer... And as they pressed forward, the enemy infantry flinched back.

Bent's archers and Ser George Brewe's men-at-arms charged into the front of the spearmen and they broke.

'Halt! Halt!' roared Ser Jehan, while the Red Knight slumped, panting, to his left knee – his hip wouldn't support him any further. They were far beyond the line of the wagons and just a hundred paces away they could see the enemy commander's standard as he rallied the remnants of his broken centre.

The Red Knight looked around but Ser Jehan was herding the victors back to their own lines, leaving their dead and wounded intermingled with the enemy.

He got his feet under him, found an abandoned spear, and used it to limp back to their lines. As he turned, he saw the enemy's knights begin their own charge, into his open right flank.

And his headache began with a pulse that nearly blinded him, as Harmodius cast again.

Andronicus watched his attack fail and, like a farmer who has seen bad weather before, put his head down and kept rallying his men. To his own right he could see his son swinging wide of the enemy wagons. To his left, he watched his own mercenaries begin their charge.

But his son was going too far. Perhaps worried by the flights of arrows, his son's Easterners had gone off almost half a league in the high grass, and were only now turning their deep hook into the enemy flank.

'Steady, my friends!' Andronicus bellowed. 'Steady! We're not done yet!'

He looked around for the magister, but the man had stayed with his stradiotes, hundreds of paces away. Andronicus wished the man would *do something*.

In the *aethereal*, gouts of power spat back and forth over the battlefield like fireflies on a summer evening – and were extinguished. Aeskepiles had allowed one strike through into the Duke's precious infantry, but he couldn't be everywhere, and it was far more difficult to project a deflection than it was to deploy one closer to hand.

His adversary was nimble and subtle, and after attempting too many heavy blows Aeskepiles had to acknowledge that he was facing a peer. He prepared a layered attack, murmuring a reassuring invocation while using one of the rings on his left hand to power what he hoped would be a decisive strike.

In that moment between initiation and action, the enemy's second magus revealed himself again and laid some kind of complex working – Aeskepiles couldn't read it, but the potency of the caster caused him to alter his tactics yet again.

Self-protection was always Aeskepiles' first priority. He raised a layered shield and allowed his own complex attack to dissipate, unpowered.

Bad Tom was the point of the wedge, with almost sixty knights and men-at-arms hastily arrayed behind him – two in the second rank, three in the third, and so on. He watched the enemy knights lower their lances and come forward at a trot, then a canter, and he grinned.

'That's more like it,' he said. He put spurs to his horse.

The wedge emerged from behind the tangle of wagons Mag was trying bring to order out of equine and bovine chaos and turned east towards the charging knights. The ground shook beneath their charge.

The enemy knights had to wheel to face the unexpected threat, and their loose formation began to fall apart.

The right flank archers got several flights into the enemy, and the heavy arrows tore through them, striking the unarmoured rumps of their warhorses. Then Tom put his lance down, tucked his head, and the whole world became the point of his lance and the man in red and gold he had chosen as his target. He roared as his lance struck home, knocking his opponent down, the horse falling sideways, and Tom released his lance – hopelessly tangled in the man's guts – and took the axe from his pommel as he ducked a lance aimed at him. His axe cut, rose to cover him against the shaft of another lance, and then he was deep into the enemy, past the lance shafts, his axe smashing into them, his battlecry a palpable thing inside his faceplate. He rose in his stirrups, caught a knight unawares with a smashing blow from above that caused the welds in the crown of the helmet to split and his brains to leak out like juices from a split melon. Tom roared joy and his mad laughter rang with his battlecry. Behind him, the picked knights of the company made a hole as large as their wedge, crushing the centre of the enemy charge, and then the wedge split open like a steel bud coming to flower and the enemy mercenaries, pinned between a wagon wall and a madman with an axe, chose the better part of valour and retreated.

*

Standing on a wagon box, Mag watched the enemy charge develop, tried to cast a single working to force all the horses to her will and lost the thread of it, and then saw the company's mounted reserve hurl themselves onto the more numerous foe like a palpable salvation. The earth shook. The wagoners hid under their wagons and horses reared and kicked, bit each other – a wagon overturned, panicking the teams on either side, and somewhere a boy was screaming.

Somewhere off in the *aethereal* a familiar voice asked her to channel power and she reponded before she had time to think *but Harmodius is dead.*

'Make what terms you can,' Jehan growled. 'Now, while we've stung them.'

The Red Knight's armour was covered in dust and his red surcoat was dirty and he had several wounds he could feel. His hip didn't seem to be broken, but something was very wrong and he couldn't face mounting. He could see Duke Andronicus, patiently rallying his men.

But Tom had done it – not just held the enemy knights, but beaten them.

He looked off to his left, and saw the enemy flankers far out on the grass.

'When he comes again, he'll gut us.' Ser Jehan had his visor open, and he panted every word. 'By Saint George, Captain. Perhaps he won't. But we can't stop another charge like that.'

The Red Knight looked at his mentor in the art of war and made himself walk to his horse. 'You have to. We have to. Whatever mistakes I've made today, the company held. We have to win this thing. Hold on.'

Jehan spat.

Cully was looking at his bow. 'Sixteen shafts left, Cap'n,' he announced.

The Captain eyed his ugly gelding and then with a desperate and inelegant lunge powered by his left leg, managed to get his right leg mostly over the saddle. The horse didn't revolt – the Captain waited out the moment of agony and then got his arse into the seat and his right foot into the stirrup. He was up.

'Jehan, you're in command. I'm going for the Vardariotes. *Don't lose.*' He managed a smile. 'That's all I ask.'

*

The Duke had rallied the infantry line and men had collected their dropped shields and armed themselves. The enemy archers stood in dangerous silence, shafts visible on their bows, but loosing nothing.

The Duke watched the shattered remnants of the mercenary knights organise themselves, but he knew they wouldn't charge again. They were unpaid, and fickle at best. He could see Ser Bescanon riding towards him across the crushed grass.

He looked the other way and saw an ashen-faced Aeskepiles doing what looked like shadow boxing. He turned away in disgust.

Close at his side, Ser Christos, remounted, shook his fist at the city. 'Look! Ungrateful fools!'

The Gates of Ares had opened.

Clad in scarlet, mounted on matched bay horses, the Vardariotes were riding out of the city in a compact column of fours.

One scarlet figure detached itself from the enemy and rode, with a single companion, through the sun-drenched late afternoon, raising a line of dust. He met the red column emerging from the iron gates – and was swallowed by it.

The Red Knight rode to the head of the Vardariotes with only his trumpeter for company.

The officer of the Vardariotes was himself an Easterner – with deeply set eyes and leathery skin that had seen the endless winds and sun of the steppes. The man's kaftan was red silk embroidered in gold flowers and trimmed in dark brown fur, and he carried a magnificently laquered Chin bow in a case that seemed to be made of pure gold, as well as a gold and enamel mace surmounted with a double-headed eagle worked in blued steel.

He smiled and circled his horse, and he and the Red Knight rode all the way around each other like two birds beginning a complex mating dance.

'Your horse is crap,' said the Easterner. 'You have money?'

'Your horse is beautiful. And I have money.' The Red Knight turned his borrowed destrier's head in and rode at the other man, who did the same, so that they met in a mathematical middle.

'Radi and Vlach watched your little fight from the walls,' said the little man. 'You beat the Moreans hours ago. Where have you been?'

'Looting,' said the Red Knight. 'How do you think I can afford to pay you?'

The Easterner snorted. If it was meant to be a laugh, it sounded more like the bark of a dog. 'Just so you know, Steel Man. We are loyal to our salt. Some of my Aviladhars might choose to be offended that you think we could be bought.'

The Red Knight flipped up his visor. 'I didn't offer to buy you. I offered to cover your arrears of pay. Can we get to business? I want to hand the Duke his arse. Where have you been?'

The mace bearer grinned. 'I've been right on the other side of the gate, watching you. You have a lot to learn about war.' He barked a cruel laugh. 'But your people are brave like fuck, eh?' He extended his hand, and they embraced, hand to elbow. The Vardariotes let out a very un-Morean shriek.

'Call me Zac,' said the Easterner.

The Red Knight shook his head. 'Call me Captain,' he said.

The Easterner grinned. 'Cap-tan?' he asked. 'Strange name. But sure. Listen, Cap-tan. You want us to do something about our cousins, busy riding around your flank?'

The Red Knight stood in his stirrups, looked at the dust and nodded sharply. 'Yes,' he said.

'Kill them?' asked the Easterner. 'Or recruit them?'

The Captain smiled. 'It could be a busy summer, Zac,' he said. 'I'd rather you recruited them.'

'Sure,' said Zac. 'Listen, Cap-tan. We'll clear them away. What will you do? They have a powerful shaman.'

No argument there, Harmodius said inside the Red Knight's palace. *More puissant than the mighty Harmodius?*

You haven't seen any lightning strike your knights, have you? I'll need whatever little reserves of power you have available, if I might.

'I plan to roll straight forward into bow range, put some arrows into his horses, and make him retreat – now that I can count on my flanks. I'd appreciate your support.' The Red Knight bowed.

'Good!' said the smaller Easterner. 'I'll ride around, kill fucking Krulla, who I hate, and then I'll fall on the Duke's northern flank, may that fucking traitor rot in the ancient frozen hell of my people. Take good care of our back pay.' He saluted with his mace, raising the back of his right hand to his forehead in an oddly graceful movement.

'Krulla?' asked the Red Knight.

'My cousin's brother-in-law, over there pretending to be a great khan. It is a grass matter, not a stone house matter.' The smaller man smiled, and his eyes twinkled. 'Then we go back to the city and maybe I sell you a horse. Not a crap horse. Yes?'

'Sure,' said the Captain.

The Vardariotes moved like a flock of birds who rise all together from a tree at the approach of a predator. But they were the pack of lions, and not the prey.

Duke Andronicus watched the Vardariotes leap from a stand to a gallop in a dozen strides, flow like water along the back of the enemy box formation, and then fly like an arrow from a particularly powerful bow at his son's Easterners. The more lightly mounted Easterners turned like a school of fish and fled, hotly pursued by the scarlet-clad Vardariotes.

'Son of a fucking whore,' he spat. 'Marcos! Christos! On me. Kronmir! Take your useless trick-riders and find me a path north and east.' He backed his horse.

The aurochs horns roared out.

Kronmir turned his horse, so his mount and the Duke's were nose to tail. 'You can still beat him,' he said. 'If we march away from the city now, we will lose most of our support inside the walls. And we leave—' He looked both ways. 'She will benefit at our expense.'

Duke Andronicus shrugged. 'If I retreat today and I am wrong, I lose nothing. If I fight today and I am wrong, I lose everything. Aeskepiles says this foreigner has powerful sorcery. He's already beaten Tzoukes. Let's see what tomorrow brings.' He looked at the other man. 'As for that bitch, let her rot. She wanted to stab us in the back? Leave her to it.'

Kronmir fingered his beard. 'I fear she may have planned it this way.' He shrugged. 'We did try to kill her,' he said quietly. When the Duke had no answer, Kronmir saluted with his whip and led his scouts north, away from the battle lines.

Before the sun settled another finger, Demetrius rode up in a roil of sun-reddened dust and gold hair and gilt armour.

'We're retreating?' he cried.

Duke Andronicus shrugged, suddenly very tired. 'Look for yourself,' he said.

His son's face worked. His skin grew mottled, red and white, and his jaw jutted out like that of a very small boy whose wooden sword has just been taken away by an angry parent.

But he mastered himself with an effort. 'On your head be it,' he said.

'That's right, boy. When you are Duke – or Emperor – you can make these decisions. But today, I make them. And I say, let's take ourselves out of here.' He turned in the saddle. 'Aeskepiles! Wake up, old man.'

The magister was grey, his ascetic eyes heavily lidded as if he was near sleep.

'They have blocked my every casting,' he muttered.

The Duke shook his head. 'Don't give me that crap, Aeskepiles. I need a little help. How about a fog?'

Aeskepiles sighed. 'Not crap, my lord. I've made three efforts and failed on each.'

The Despot shook his blond head. 'Why can we never *see* these great efforts?' he asked.

Aeskepiles pursed his lips. 'Fog,' he said.

'Saint Basil and all the phalanx of saints,' said Lykos Dukas, the Duke's standard bearer and a veteran of fifty fights. He pointed with his sword.

The Vardariotes were mounted on magnificent blood horses and the Despot's Easterners had steppe ponies. The better mounted men were, even as Dukas pointed, riding down their enemy, closing on them, catching them.

There was a moment where the two forces met – a swirl of dust, and all of the horses seemed to stop altogether.

Then dust rose, obscuring the whole fight.

Duke Andronicus spat. 'We have fifteen minutes until they are around our flank and cutting us off from home,' he said. 'Lykos, get the wagons moving. Anything that can be saved. Damn it, Aeskepiles, raise me some fog! Conjure the sun from the sky! Make it dark!'

Despot Demetrius put an elbow against his waist and turned in the saddle. He was a magnificent horseman, and his body and his horse's seemed to flow together, as if they were one creature. 'This flight is unseemly. Let us fight.'

Ser Lykos ignored him and rode for the baggage wagons.

Aeskepiles entered into the cool *darkness of his basilica of power and prepared a complex working, moving from pillar to column, aligning the distant stars in his carefully ordered sky. A cooling; a force of attraction, an enhancement of moisture; binding, losing, and empowering.*

It was very complex, and Aeskepiles enjoyed building the edifice that would support it, even as another part of his working mind gathered power from his staff and his ring of lapis. He still hoarded his own reserve of power.

He's about to cast again, Harmodius said in the *aether. I could use some help, here.*

Instead of responding immediately, the Captain touched his horse's sides with his spurs and cantered up the last low, round hill – so round that it appeared artificial – at the edge of the Field of Ares. Ser Jehan and Ser Milus followed him, while just ahead of him, the sides of his shallow box formations broke open and wheeled into line, extending his front by another three hundred paces. The tangle of wagons was left behind to the right and left.

From the top of his little hill, he could see from the city wall at his right, all the way across the Field of Ares to his left, some four leagues. He spared a moment for his own awe. He was on the Field of Ares, and the Empire had once been powerful enough to fill this field with soldiers.

Closer to hand, the Duke's army was half again the size of his own, and it stretched off to the left, so that the enemy left far overreached his own right – except that out beyond the furthest fringes of the enemy line, the Vardariotes and the Despot's Easterners had merged in a single dust cloud.

He's raising a fog, Harmodius said.

Stop him.

I could use any small reserves you can spare.

Bad Tom had rallied the wedge and returned to the company's line – now he cantered up like the embodiment of war itself, his huge black horse snorting foam. He raised his bloody axe and saluted. Then he pointed at the Moreans.

'There is drill for ye and a'! Look at 'em!' Tom's waving axe sprayed droplets of brown red, but the awe in his voice spoke for them all. The Duke's cavalry was wheeling by sections and retreating. It was a beautiful manoeuvre. The still afternoon air brought the sound of trumpets.

The Red Knight slipped *into his palace and opened the door, so that a warm green breeze blew over the black and white marble floor to mix*

228

with the golden rays that soaked in through the distant clerestory windows to make a haze of power.

That's better, said Harmodius. He made no use of the Red Knight's palace – he was doubtless deep within his own working place.

Is he more puissant than you?

No, muttered Harmodius. But he's cautious, careful, and capable. And we spent potentia *like a sailor spends gold this morning on concealment, the river crossing and a dozen other extravagances—*

Spare me.

'They're going to run,' said Tom.

'Let them!' Ser Jehan managed a rare smile. 'Jesus Saviour, we almost lost the whole line. Letting them march away would be good for everyone, wouldn't it, Captain?'

'Let's see if we can fix them in place,' said the Captain. 'Double time. Trot!' he shouted. His new trumpeter managed to get the call out, but the corporals had heard his shout and the company, already remounted, surged forward.

Behind the Red Knight, his new page, Nell, swung up onto her tall pony and swore. 'On and off! On and off!' she spat in fourteen-year-old disapproval.

Across the grass, five hundred paces away, the Duke's army was wheeling into columns of march. The manoeuvre was complicated, and well executed, and despite that it was slow. Men began to look over their shoulders at the advancing wave of scarlet and steel.

'Couldn't we just let them go?' asked Jehan.

The Captain shook his head. 'If we let them go, we'll have to fight them all winter. If we smash them now, we're done.' He looked under his hand, and then roared, 'On! Canter! Dress the line!' and threw himself forward.

Duke Andronicus sighed so hard that his cheeks blew up like a bladder and then deflated. 'Why's he so aggressive?' he asked. 'Aeskepiles!'

'Watch, my lord,' said the magister. He raised his arms, carefully balancing powers in his head.

Fog began to rise from the damp grass – first wisps, and then tendrils.

'I still say that with one charge – envelop their flanks – we could roll them back to their barbarous homes,' Demetrius said. 'Pater – listen to Kronmir. We'll lose support in the city—'

'Christos Pantokrator!' spat the Duke. 'Demetrius! You are last out, since you are so full of fire.'

But even as the fog began to thicken, the mass of Easterners to the north started to move, and the hooves of their horses shook the earth. They were riding to cut the Duke off from his line of retreat. The first of his baggage wagons were only starting to move.

'Marcos! Take the last Tagma and clear the Vardariotes out of our path,' called the Duke. He turned to his son. 'Do not – I repeat, do not – die here. What I do, I do for you and your own sons. Cover us, and then ride away.'

The fog rose like smoke.

And then the wind hit. It blew straight from their enemies into their faces, picking up dust and bits of grass. The first gust was like the breath of a tired man, but the second gust was as harsh as a mid-winter storm.

The fog broke like glass.

Across the field, the enemy was dismounting. Demetrius stroked his beard. 'They're out of range,' he said aloud. 'How can they—'

'Look at their horse holders,' said his father. 'Once, the Empire put every man on a horse or mule – every infantryman, every archer.'

Just to his left, their own infantry were retreating in columns, well closed up, their shields lapped and their spears held high, the small wind-sock standards of the Thrakian border holdings suddenly rigid in the new wind.

'Draw!' roared Cully.

The better archers measured the distance by eye and sneered.

Kandy, the fattest man in the company, shook his head. 'On my best day I couldn't hit yon,' he muttered. But he grunted and got his string to his ear.

'Loose!' Cully roared. A few men had already loosed – no man could keep a great war bow at full draw for longer than a moment or two.

Twenty paces behind the archery line, the Captain felt the surge of power. It was odd, vaguely upsetting even, to be both a participant and an observer in an arcane contest.

Even as the volley of arrows leaped into the air, the gust of wind off Harmodius's working overpowered the enemy's hermetical defence.

Borne on a massive pulse of air, three hundred arrows fell like a well-aimed hail on the nearest block of retreating infantry. The heavy quarter-pound shafts punched through the scale or leather of the mountaineers. In one gust of air, forty men fell—

The enemy volley of arrows did more damage than the Duke had thought possible. More men – his men, his own trained soldiers, veterans of a dozen campaigns – died. The screams of the wounded told every other man on the field that the enemy arrows were in range, and they were caught with their shields facing away from the enemy.

His men panicked.

Far off to the right, where Ser Bescanon had rallied part of the Latinikon, the mercenary Albans and Galles and Occitans broke and ran, leaning far out over the necks of their wretched heavy horses as they galloped away.

Demetrius didn't mutter imprecations at his father. Instead, he turned to the magister. 'Do something!' he snapped.

Aeskepiles took a deep breath and flung up a hand.

A carpet of flame, so thin as to be transparent, flowed over the field from his hand to the enemy, crossing the four hundred or so paces in the time it took a man's heart to beat three times.

The carpet of white flame ran at the archers like a rising tide – a tide moving at the speed of a galloping horse.

'Stand fast! Nock!' ordered Cully. Most of the archers obeyed, but some awkward sods were flinching away.

Cully watched the fire and hoped it was an illusion.

But just short of his position it parted as if cut by a knife and flowed away to the left and right, rolling along the front of the archers' positions.

The fire was not wholly without effect, as it panicked the horses. One small page was only enough to hold six strong cobs under ideal conditions, and with a wall of fire bearing down on them, dozens of the stronger – or more wicked – horses put their heads down, pulled their reins right out of their handler's hands, and ran free over the grass.

Nell lost the Captain's wicked roan, was bitten, and punched the horse in savage frustration. The horse looked at her in surprise and she recaptured his reins. Cully's nag tried to rip free, and reared, and she was carried into the air. Then the Captain's roan pulled his head, and she was down, face first in the bloody dirt. She didn't let go, and the roan dragged her right over the corpse of a Thrakian. She screamed when the man – not yet dead – screamed.

Then Long Paw, the nicest of the archers, was dragging her to her feet. She still had the horses. He smiled at her and turned back to the line.

'Draw!' Cully roared.

'Loose!' he shouted as the wind rose behind them.

The second volley rose ragged and lost more shafts as the wind struck. The archers were shaken by the fire. But more than a hundred shafts received the full lift of Harmodius's working and they fell on the centre tagma of stradiotes; Morean gentlemen in chain hauberks, with lances and bows and small steel shields. At the range, few of them were killed through their mail, but their horses suffered cruelly and the small band seemed to explode away from the point of impact as men rode in all directions.

The Red Knight raised his hand and snapped a single coherent beam of emerald light at the source of the enemy's magery.

Aeskepiles raised a shield like a mirror, the size of three mounted men.

Very clever, Harmodius admitted, and voided the casting as it came, reflected, right back at him.

The Athanatos tagma was shattered, and the panic of the mercenaries was augmented by the stradiotes. Andronicus watched the hermetical workings – back and forth like a child's game.

'My men are dying!' he roared.

Aeskepiles reached deep and cast a working he created on the spot. He built extravagant displays for court – he could work with inanimate materials, given time. And cloth and wood had once been animate. It was a snap working – something from deep inside him created it and he let go.

Every bowstring in the front rank snapped. The bows gave an odd sound, almost like a scream. Men had their faces flayed – Cully almost lost an eye. Men flinched. A few archers fell.

'Christ save us!' said Cully, now firmly spooked and blood running down his face.

Harmodius seized control of the Captain's body and cast, breathed, and cast again, draining his master's reserves utterly. Reserves, he noted, which grew deeper every day.

Fire appeared to leap from the Captain's hand. It wasn't a beam of light, but rather a great round gout of raw fire that made a deep roaring sound as it burst into being.

Damn you! said the Captain. *Let go! Damn it!*

Us or him! Harmodius barked. He kept control of the Red Knight's body and let fly his spell.

The travel time of the fearful ball of fire was slow, by hermetical standards. The casting was terrifying – the power of the ball of fire dizzying. Aeskepiles had little choice but to shield – he left himself almost nothing, and struck the fireball with a deflection, swatting it to the north.

Even as he displaced it, he felt its insubstantial nature, and the hair stood up on the nape of his neck.

Illusion.

Got you, muttered Harmodius through the Red Knight's mouth, and he flicked a single point of light, a sphere the size of a pearl or a child's smallest marble.

Aeskepiles managed to shield himself by draining his last amulet and his secret, invisible ring, but he was blown clear of his horse, which was killed in a spectacular manner, and the magister was knocked unconscious.

But the enemy archers were dismounted, their mounts had panicked and their bowstrings were cut. Both armies were filled with dread at the unsealy exchange of powers, a sight that filled them all with fear, and if the Moreans broke for their baggage train, the company soldiers stood rooted to the spot, unwilling to advance.

Harmodius was in full control of the Red Knight's body. He flexed *his* fingers, and sighed, because he could feel that his opponent was dazed, and he himself was almost out of *potentia*.

He felt alive. He savoured it. He breathed, and watched the enemy break and run.

Bad Tom glared at him. 'Bah!' he said. 'Come on, man! We can yet have them.'

The mad Hillman wanted to charge three thousand Moreans with two hundred Alban knights.

I don't know what will happen if I smash this statue, said the Red Knight, deep inside his own palace. *But I'm willing to bet it will end you, and I want my body back.*

I just saved your army, you ungrateful whelp, Harmodius said. But with a last inbreath of the scent of grass and horses, he *let go*.

The Red Knight snapped back into full awareness, and he could see the men around him – Ranald and Bad Tom, Michael, Alison – straining in their saddles, eager to charge.

'Advance!' he ordered. At his side, the trumpeter raised his instrument and blew. The first call came out like the honking of a goose. The second rang as clear as day, and he repeated it once more.

'That's *halt* you idiot!' roared the Captain. 'Advance! Advance!' he called, and rode out to the front where men could see him, his lance held high – but the damage was done. Confusion reigned supreme in his ranks for agonisingly long heartbeats.

By the time he had his lances moving, the last company of enemy stradiotes was retreating, a thousand paces away. The Vardariotes had wrecked the enemy Easterners, or perhaps subsumed them, and the enemy's cadre of Alban mercenaries – the Latinikon – was scattered to the winds. Many were simply surrendering.

The Captain had a headache of monumental proportions, but he managed to indicate the surrendering knights to Bad Tom. 'They look like men who want a new employer,' he said.

'You look like dog shit,' Ranald said, and put a hand on his shoulder.

The Red Knight swore in a very undignified manner, and forced himself to sit upright and lead.

His knights rode forward as fast as they could in good order, and they pursued the retreating Thrakians over the Field of Ares. A mile out in the grass, they linked up with the scarlet-clad Vardariotes, and they rode side by side at a slow canter. Behind them, archers scrambled to retrieve their lost horses. Pages were cursed, but not very hard.

Cully took his horse from Nell and smiled at her.

'Ain't you goin' ta follow the Cap'n?' she asked the master archer. He and Long Paw were standing at their horses' heads, but they weren't mounting.

Cully looked down on her. 'You're a young 'un to tell me my trade, ain't you?'

Long Paw nodded. 'We've done our bit,' he said.

The sun was going down in ruddy splendour over the city to the south and west behind them. When every basilica's gilt roof was ablaze with the fire of the sun, the Thrakian infantry had to turn at bay or be ridden down in retreat. They were at the northern edge of the great field, and they halted between two of the low, round hills that defined the ancient drill field.

They faced about, got their aspides, their great round shields, off their shoulders, and they pulled their helmets down, set their feet, and prepared to give their lives. In the fifth and sixth ranks, archers restrung their bows and then moved out into the scrub on the hills and tried some long shafts at the Vardariotes.

The Red Knight watched it all with weary resignation. He formed his men-at-arms up in two companies under Ser Jehan and Ser Milus; both in broad, deep wedges.

The archers had emptied two Vardariote saddles when the scarlet-clad Easterners swept forward at the gallop – they rode all the way to just short of the enemy's spear points and then shot down into their phalanx at point-blank range – and then galloped away, exchanging ranks with a dexterity that spoke of long practice and perfect horsemanship. When the dust settled, darkness was moments away and two dozen of the Thrakians were face down in the grass – but they closed their ranks grimly. And backstepped.

The Red Knight beckoned to Count Zac, who rode up. 'I can do it again,' he said with a shrug. 'But they are not soft, these Thrakians. I don't think they will break.'

The Red Knight shook his head. 'If it were noon, we'd have them in an hour,' he said. 'But it isn't, and we won't. Let them go. I'm not willing to lose one more man-at-arms to break them. And they're just his infantry. His knights are gone.'

Sauce laughed. 'You sound like Ser Jehan,' she said.

Ser Alcaeus shook his head in turn. 'You need to learn to think like a Morean. His infantry are the heart of his army. His cavalry are not "knights". They are soldiers.'

The Red Knight scratched at his two-day beard growth. 'Let's go see if Cully found any new bowstrings,' he said. He looked at Zac. 'You feel we should try them?'

Zac watched the infantry retreat into the gathering gloom. 'No. Foolishness,' he said. 'Let's go back to the city. You pay me, I sell you a horse. We drink. '

The Red Knight looked around at his officers. He kept his tone light, although fatigue and his unspoken war with Harmodius made it hard even to think. 'I think we've come to the right place,' he managed.

Bad Tom sat watching the Thrakians, and he shook his axe at them and then hurled the weapon into their ranks and roared, 'Lachlan for aa!' like a lion baulked of his prey. He rounded on his captain.

'I want the fight! Christ damn their souls to hell—'

The Captain waved to Lachlan through a fog of fatigue. 'See to your cousin,' he said.

The sun was gone from the sky when the Red Knight rode through the Ares Gate at the head of the company. He had Ser Gavin at his side, half his men-at-arms at his back, then all the archers and pages together, and then the rest of the men-at-arms, with the wagons bringing up the rear with all the women, and finally Long Paw and a dozen veterans with Gelfred and the scouts. Moreans stood in the gate and the square on the far side and cheered them.

Sort of.

The cheers were half-hearted. Many people simply watched them ride in without a comment, and there was some heckling after they passed through the gate.

There was a strong guard of men with long-hafted axes on the gate, and they stood in rigid silence as the mercenaries rode past.

'Brother, you are a study,' Gavin said.

'I've had better days. My hip is killing me. We should have had the thrice-damned Duke today.' He observed a pair of Moreans who watched him with open contempt. 'And these people don't love us for all that we just saved them from a siege and starvation.' He was, in fact, seeing spots in front of his eyes.

Bad Tom, in the rank behind, hawked and spat. Ser Milus spurred his horse out of the column and rode right up to the two local men. 'See something you like, gentles?' he asked.

The two men looked right through him.

Ser Milus reached out with his riding whip and touched one on the shoulder. 'Tell me what we're laughing at, and we can all laugh together.'

The Red Knight reined in. 'Leave it!' he called.

Milus turned his destrier, unwillingness in every inch of his six feet of steel, and behind him, the two men smiled nastily.

'They're mocking us,' he complained.

The Red Knight sighed. 'Yes, they are. And as long as we're paid, we don't have to give a shit whether they love us or hate us.'

In the second rank of the second company, Sauce strained her eyes as they passed their third or fourth basilica. 'By all the saints. I mean *all* the saints – they must have a church for every saint in the book.'

Ser Michael shook his head. 'I had no idea,' he said. He was looking at a bronze statue of a warrior of some kind. He couldn't even identify what kind of warrior, but the quality of the statue was incredible – lifelike. The musculature – the strain on the man's face—

'Don't gape like rubes,' growled Ser Jehan. But then he smiled at Michael. 'I thought you, at least, would ha' been here afore.'

'Never,' breathed Ser Michael. 'It even smells good.'

Ser Jehan nodded. 'Sewers. From old times. See yon great bridges? I forget the word for them, but they carry water from the hills right into the city. In some houses, you turn a little tap, and fresh water you can drink flows right out. Crap goes right into the pipes and *whish*, it's gone away. At least in good houses.'

Ranald couldn't stop turning his head. 'It's huge!'

Michael leaned forward. 'You've been here before,' he said.

Jehan nodded back over the rump of his great warhorse. 'Oh, aye. Ten years and more. I served here two years. Good pay. Not much fighting. A lot of standing around in draughty halls and listening to priests sing.'

Ser George Brewes caught a rose thrown from a high balcony by a young woman and tucked the stem behind his ear. 'It's beautiful,' he said, marking the tall house with the red doors. But the street went on and on, and as they climbed the central hills, all of them realised that the city was seven miles across – fifty times the size of Harndon.

Conversation slowed.

You don't have to be angry. I was handing control back.

Were you, though? I think perhaps it is time I was rid of you, sir. You are a troublesome guest.

Give me a little more time. This city – this is the very home of hermeticism. I might learn something—

You took control of my body, Harmodius. How can I trust you now?

Don't be a fool, boy. I did it to save us both.

So you say. And you will rationalise it right up until the moment that you find yourself my master.

The Red Knight stamped down on his connection to the old mage and focused on the real, all about him. Count Zac had displaced Ser Gavin at his side.

'You talk to the spirits?' he asked, interested.

'No,' said the Red Knight. 'Yes. Maybe.'

Zac tilted his head like an interested dog. 'Which one?' he said.

'Maybe,' said the Red Knight.

The Easterner made a sign with his hands. 'Best be careful,' he said. 'Spirits are scary bastards. Listen to me.' Then he grinned. 'You know the city?' he asked.

'I've been here before,' the Red Knight admitted.

Count Zac nodded. 'The Porphyrogenetrix wants to see you.' The Easterner, who had trouble with Gothic names, got out the Morean title with fluidity. 'You know Blacharnae?'

The Red Knight shook his head. 'Not the part of town I know,' he said.

'She's going to garrison your men in the palace,' said the Easterner. 'As bad as spirits. Be careful.' He shrugged. 'When you are done at the palace, come and get that horse. Your horse—' He waved at the Captain's borrowed warhorse. Slapped his rear end, and laughed. 'Listen, you like girls?' he asked.

Through the haze of pain, the Captain had trouble following the Easterner. 'Yes. I have, in fact, been known to like girls,' he managed.

'Then watch out for the princess,' Count Zac said.

*

The gates of the palace were shut, and the company rumbled to a halt in the Great Square in front of the palace under the watchful eyes of Saint Aetius. Every man and woman in the company was looking around, gawping like the poorest peasant in a rich man's house. The archers were talking so loudly that scraps of their repartee slipped up the column to the Captain, who sat calmly looking at the gates.

Never seen... made of fewkin' money... with his parts hanging in the air... look at the tits on her! Most beautiful thing... made by gods or men... that bow's too heavy to pull... no, you stupid sod, it's a chariot... they used to wear those things... not solid gold...

Harmodius stirred, deep inside his head. *May I speak?*

The Red Knight sighed a little. *Go right ahead. How can I stop you?*

This is far more dangerous than I had imagined. The hermetical energy here is very like the Well at Lissen Carrak. I can feel the University. Across the square at the Academy are thirty men and two women each as puissant as I am – perhaps not quite, but very close.

There is a strong user in the palace, and more than a dozen competent weaker users.

I have never seen such a concentration of hermetical talent in one place... well, perhaps in my youth.

The Red Knight felt the pleasure in the other man's thought as if it was his own. *Where was that, old man?*

Harmodius laughed in his head. *Ifriqu'ya, lad. Dar-as-Salaam, the abode of peace. The very best hermetical study centre in the known world.*

The Red Knight sat on his horrible gelding and watched the gates. The horse shifted and shifted again, grunted, tossed his head and tried to spit out the bit.

At the Captain's shoulder, Ranald Lachlan spat – a more contemplative spit than the horse's. 'By all that's sacred. It is like seeing the dragon. Like rain on a mountainside and the sun over the lakes. Is that a statue of Lady Tar? By the Blessed Virgin, is that sort of thing allowed?'

His cousin chuckled. 'Boyo, I look around this square and all I see is a customer that can pay.' Bad Tom grinned. 'Mickle sly they are, to make us wait and drink yon in. Mayhap to make us know our place, eh?' Despite his words, Tom looked where Ranald had pointed – spotted the golden statue of Tar with the green emerald eyes, and made a sign.

'Christ on the cross!' Ranald said. 'We'll all be burned as pagans.'

'You spent too long in Harndon, cousin.' Tom's eyes crossed Ranald's. Neither man flinched – but both put their right hands unconsciously on their hilts.

The Captain didn't turn his head. 'Gentlemen? While I will be the first to admit that a duel here in the Imperial forum would probably excite the locals, I suspect we'll win greater love from the lady here if we behave with decorum.'

Bad Tom curbed his charger and laughed. 'Just fun, Captain.'

Ranald said, 'He didn't get enough fighting today,' and some of the archers laughed.

The Red Knight stood in his stirrups and called in his battlefield voice, 'Eyes front!'

The company stopped its bickering, its commenting, its art criticism, and stood silently in the evening air. The horses' tails swished at the late summer flies. A mule farted. A woman sighed.

Silence.

Men shifted, unlocked their knees – Sauce loosened her sword in her scabbard and her new warhorse, confused by the shift in her weight, stepped out of the column and she blushed. Wilful Murder, leading a hand of archers, tried to whisper to them about their pay, and his failed attempt to whisper floated like the sound of a small saw-mill over the column until Oak Pew leaned forward and flicked his ear with the force and accuracy of a schoolteacher. He yelped and subsided.

Silence.

A single horse hoof struck the stone flags in impatience, and rang out like a hammer blow. It echoed off the statues – across the square, in front of the Academy, stood a great bronze of the pagan god Cerberus, the multi-headed dog. It seemed to bark.

The sound of marching feet could be heard on the far side of the palace wall. They were marching in step – an art virtually unknown in Alba. The thin sound of a flute rose over the great walls.

A drum beat slowly. It was a low drum, and very large. Alien. Combined with the sound of the flute it was beautiful and wild.

Two smaller drums joined in, rattling like crazed woodpeckers. *Prrrr-thump* with the larger drums.

And the great gates began to open.

The Outer Court beyond the gates was a mass of torchlight – torches flared in more than a hundred brackets, illuminating the mosaics which adorned every flat surface – the front face of the Imperial stables, the Mayor of the Palace's offices, the barracks, the apartments of the Ordinaries. The image of Christ Pantokrator, hand raised in benison, in royal robes of purple and red; the image of the harrowing of hell, with Satan being driven from the field by a Christ armed with a longsword; the Virgin Mary dressed as an Empress, or the Queen of Heaven, in lapis and gold, glittered and seemed alive. Even the tiles underfoot were astonishing – black and white marble in a magnificent and endless geometrical pattern that stretched away from the viewer at the gate to run like a maze of mazes into the entrances.

Standing in the courtyard were hundreds of men: the Guard. A hundred Nordikans stood in knee-length hauberks, with five-foot hafted axes on their shoulders and round aspides on their left arms. Every man of them wore a magnificent helmet in the ancient style, tall helmets of bronze and steel with hinged cheekplates and tall horsehair crests in red, white and black, and long cloaks of Imperial purple with the gold double-headed eagle of the Emperor embroidered on their left shoulders.

Across the courtyard from the Nordikans stood the Scholae; almost twice the number, with spears and teardrop-shaped shields. They wore blued and gilt bassinets and coats of plate covered in scarlet leather over bronze scale haubergeons and hip-high boots of red leather. Every man had the same Imperial purple cloak that the Nordikans had.

At the back of the yard, three hundred Ordinaries stood in matching scarlet gowns with gold buckles and white leather shoes.

It looked like a vision of a particularly martial heaven.

An officer stood forth, marched briskly to the centre of the gates, and called out in High Archaic.

'Halt! Who is there? Who dares come to the gate of the Divine Emperor?'

Harmodius chuckled in the Red Knight's head. *That must be really old. I don't think we see the Emperor as divine any more – fascinating.*

Could you shut up?

Bah.

'The Duke of Thrake, Megas Ducas, commander of the Imperial Armies, and his bucellarii!' roared the Red Knight.

The sound from within the courtyard was palpable. Men murmured.

The officer in the gateway paused, obviously at a loss.

The Red Knight sat on his horse and waited, enjoying the mess he'd just made.

That's put the cat among the pigeons. Bucellarii – splendid scholarship.

Thank you, Harmodius. I was quite proud of it, I confess.

You are forcing her hand.

I am, at that. It would suit her to use me while keeping me at arm's length – to retain the option of allowing the former Duke to return to the fold. I thought I'd save us all time.

You have a plan?

Yes.

Can I be of service?

I'd like to know why the Empire commands all this hermetical talent and these superb soldiers and yet remains so toothless.

See the boy coming out of the Ordinaries?

Ah, a message.

The boy was dressed in stark black and white parti-colour. Just like the Imperial birds – an Imperial messenger. He ran to the officer at the gate, knelt, and presented him a red ivory scroll tube.

The officer bowed deeply and kissed the tube. Then he opened it. He bowed again, and returned the tube to the messenger and pivoted sharply.

In High Archaic, he called, 'General salute – the Megas Ducas enters the palace victorious!'

Six hundred feet stamped the ground. The drums rolled and rattled. Six hundred arms swept up in the Imperial salute.

The Red Knight didn't even turn his head – he shouted, 'March!'

The company – knights and squires, pages and archers and saddlers and armourers and priests and whores and wives and children and wagoners – marched neatly through the palace gates. If they lacked the formal dignity of the Nordikans or the magnificent plumage of the Scholae, they had a great deal of mirror-polished Gallish and Etruscan plate armour, and their scarlet wool surcoats and matching white ostrich plumes in every hat or helmet made them any soldier's envy.

It had been Mag and Lis who had provided every one of the company's non-combatants with a neat red surcoat and a black wool cap with a white ostrich plume. The wool wasn't the best and the boxwood dye would run in rain, but at night in a torchlit courtyard they looked like a magnificent embassage, or the retinue of a king.

The company rode to the centre of the great yard.

'Halt!' called the Captain. 'Imperial salute!'

He was two horse lengths in advance of Ser Michael, who swept his lacs d'amour banner in a great figure of eight and then laid it across the marble parquetry under his horse's hooves, the six-pointed star at the tip of the banner pole resting on the ground. Every man and woman in the company swept their right arms out straight from the shoulder, parallel to the ground and extending the line of the shoulder.

'Ave, Kaisar!' roared the company. They'd practised it in the hills, with Ser Alcaeus rolling his eyes at their bad Archaic and their lewd gestures. Tonight, by torchlight, in a two-thousand-year-old palace, it seemed – right.

'Dismount!' called the Captain, and the order was echoed by the corporals, and five hundred legs swept up and crossed five hundred saddles. The Ordinaries broke ranks and came forward to take the horses and in a moment the Outer Court appeared to be a riot of colour and movement, but it didn't last. The Ordinaries had performed this task for hundreds of years, and the warhorses and palfreys were taken into the Imperial stables faster than the Red Knight would have thought possible. Indeed, he thought it was the greatest expression of raw power he'd seen yet – perhaps would ever see – that five hundred horses could be taken and stabled as fast as a man could say, 'Hail Caesar.'

An officer of the Ordinaries appeared, along with the officer of the Nordikans who had stood in the gate and a pair of Imperial messengers – both, in this case, women.

'Durk Blackhair, my lord Duke,' said the Nordikan. His accent was thick enough to cut with a knife, even in Archaic.

The officer of Ordinaries bowed deeply. 'My lord Duke, I am to take you to the throne. This would usually be the duty of the Mayor of the Palace but I regret to say that there is no such person at this time. No offence is intended. While I am unworthy to perform this task, I will make every effort to satisfy.'

'You are the Captain of the Ordinaries?' asked the Red Knight.

'I have that honour,' answered the Imperial servant. 'May I add that your High Archaic is elegant? Bucellarii? The Imperial messengers had to consult a book.' He gave the slightest nod to the two women and then bowed deeply and walked away into the torchlight.

'Where will my people be placed?' asked the Red Knight.

'The Athanatos barracks were built for a thousand soldiers, and are currently unoccupied. As their former occupants have made some unwise choices, the Imperial will is that they be given to you. Bedding may be a trifle tight—'

The Red Knight caught Sauce's eye and indicated that he wanted her. He turned to Toby, already at his shoulder, and as his squire took his helmet and gauntlets and changed his sword, he sent Nell for Ser Gavin and Ser Michael and Ser Thomas.

'You cannot keep the throne waiting!' said the Captain of Ordinaries.

'I am not keeping the throne waiting. I'm seeing to my soldiers as quickly as I can, while preparing myself to greet the throne, which I cannot do in full armour.' He smiled as graciously as he could. 'Sauce, see to it that the wagons are only unloaded into the Athanatos barracks. Barrack by mess group; men-at-arms are responsible for the behaviour of their mess.' He saw John le Bailli. 'John! Collect the wagoners and barrack them together – draught animals to the stables. Mag – Mag!'

The seamstress was as self-effacing as usual, although when she stepped forward she was striking in her red surcoat over a black travelling gown. Her hat was – pert.

'My lord Duke,' she said with a curtsey that had just the smallest hint of mockery.

The Captain of Ordinaries grew pale.

The Red Knight, despite the throbbing at his temples, had to laugh. 'Mag, can you see to all the non-combatants? I've meant to appoint you corporal – will you accept the job?'

'At a corporal's pay?' she asked quietly.

'Of course,' he said.

She smiled. 'I'll have Kaitlin as a lieutenant,' she said.

'Place them all together. Best behaviour all round.'

His soldiers saluted with their free hands, and Mag dropped another curtsy.

'We have food for three days,' John le Bailli said quietly to the Captain of Ordinaries.

The palace officer puffed out his cheeks in relief. He turned to another Ordinary, this one distinguished by a loop of white braid or rope on his right shoulder. 'Are you following, Stephanos?'

The man saluted.

The Red Knight had light leather gloves on his hands, a small fur hat with a gold enamel brooch and a white ostrich plume on his head and the baton of his captaincy in his hand. He bowed to his officers. 'Ser Gavin, Ser Thomas, Ser Jehan, Ser Milus, Ser Alcaeus – on me.'

Toby just got his ermine-trimmed cloak over his shoulders as he turned away and followed the Captain of the Ordinaries. The Captain's leg harnesses littered the ground, but they were off, and the sabatons, and the arm-harnesses too, so that the Captain looked as if he might be wearing his breast and back by choice.

They passed together from the Outer Court to the Inner. The Red Knight turned to Darkhair. 'My pardon, Captain. I needed to see to my men.'

Darkhair was not an old man. He grinned, and showed a mouth missing a great many teeth. He was the same size as Bad Tom – the two giants were already sizing each other up. He pointed with his axe – moving the three-pound head and five-foot haft like a child flicking a straw – and beckoned six men from the rightmost two files of the Nordikans.

'Dismiss!' he roared.

The whole body of Nordikans dissolved like salt into warm water and vanished into the torchlit darkness, pouring in through their barracks' gate, which was six men wide. The Red Knight caught a glimpse of darkly carved wood, knot work, great gaping-mouthed dragons and running dogs and whitewash, and then he was past, and the six men in long chain cotes were swinging along, three on each side, every one of them the size of Tom or Ranald or the Gallish nobles.

'I'm no captain,' said Darkhair. He smiled again. 'I'm acting Spatharios. That means—'

'Sword bearer,' chorused Ser Michael and the Red Knight together. They grinned at each other. Ser Jehan rolled his eyes.

'There is no captain in the palace except the Captain of the Ordinaries,' Darkhair went on. 'The commander of the Nordikans is called – Jarl.' He shrugged. 'The Jarl was killed by the traitor.'

'But of course, your men call *you* Captain,' said the palace functionary. 'I'm sure we can arrive at some mutually beneficial—'

The Red Knight smiled. 'I'll settle for Duke,' he said.

Bad Tom grinned. 'Duke it is, then.'

The throne was occupied by one very small, and very magnificent, young woman. She was dressed in purple and gold, and her hair was so wound about with pearls that it was almost impossible to determine what colour her hair might be. A veil of gold tissue hung over her face, and the vestments she wore must have rivalled the Red Knight's armour for weight.

He walked down the purple carpet, painfully aware that his leather-soled shoes had grass stuck in them from the Field of Ares. The Imperial throne room was intended to strike barbarians dumb with wonder, and the Red Knight found it difficult to keep his gaze fixed on the princess. Over his head, the dome soared a hundred feet, with a round crystal window set exactly in the centre, through which distant stars glittered; the rest of the vault displayed a mosaic of the creation of the world, an hermetical artefact that moved as it retold the story.

Under the wonder of the dome was the Imperial throne, twice the height of a man in gleaming ivory and solid gold, with a single yellow-red cabochon ruby the size of a man's fist set high over the canopy. It was hermetical, and it glowed from within, casting a rich golden light over the princess.

Sitting on a footstool by the throne – also of ivory – sat an older woman in midnight-blue robes embroidered with stars and moons and crosses. She had a pair of shears in her hand and appeared to be cutting a thread – an act that seemed bizarre amidst the incredible opulence.

The acting chamberlain raised his staff. 'The Duke of Thrake!' he called. 'Megas Ducas of all the Imperial Armies, Admiral of the Fleets, Lord of the Mountains, the Red Knight.'

The Duke had been well briefed in his long walk through the palace – and, today, he was not interested in flouting etiquette. He made himself put one foot boldly in front of the other until he reached the edge of the throne, and then he went to one knee, sweeping his fur cap from his head, and then lay, full length, at the princess's feet.

She might have been seen to smile, and extended one red-slippered foot.

He kissed her toe and then put his forehead back against the scarlet carpet. Even at this angle, with his head almost flat against the floor, he could see that the marble under the ivory throne was perfectly clean. Further back, among the hangings that partially covered a pagan mosaic by a small door, he could see the four paws of a cat.

He smiled to himself.

He lay on the thick carpet and felt the pain in his hip, the numbness creeping into the small of his back, the fatigue in his shoulders. It was, in fact, very comfortable at the foot of the throne.

Don't say a word, he said to his annoying guest.

A mass of rattles, rustles, and clanks told him that his knights were throwing themselves to the floor as well. The cat started at the motion and put its head almost to the marble, looking under the throne to see if there was some threat to which it needed to attend.

'We gather you have driven the traitor from the walls of my city and won a great victory,' said the figure on the throne. 'Accept the plaudits of the throne. We are most grateful. We would wish to meet you and your officers in private audience for further consultations.'

The Duke and his knights lay like effigies on the carpet. One did not speak to the throne during a full audience.

He smelled her perfume – a wonderful mixture of cedar and musk and lavender – as she rose to her feet. Slim, arched feet. He wondered if all the fuss about what kind of shoes the Emperor wore stemmed from the fact that his subjects spent so much of their time seeing him from ground level.

The cat was hunting a rat. The Red Knight could now see both of them.

The princess stepped down from the throne and swept out of the Great Hall with her retinue at her heels, leaving a trace of cedar and musk and lavender in her wake.

The acting chamberlain's staff tapped the floor rapidly, and all the courtiers began to rise. The Duke gritted his teeth and got slowly to his feet, although his hip shot pulses of low, slow pain into his upper leg and torso like the thump, thump of the bass drum.

The Captain of the Ordinaries appeared at his elbow. 'Follow me. Very elegant – well done,' he said with well-practised effusiveness that the new Duke found suspect.

But he didn't have long to be suspicious. His hip gave a click of protest, and he fell – his whole leg failed to support him. He hit his head, hard.

Ser Milus shouted something about blood.

They carried the new Duke to his new suite of apartments and laid him on a bed magnificent enough to use in a pageant, and he bled on sheets of purest white linen. Palace Ordinaries buzzed around him like wasps, and Ser Thomas grabbed the Spatharios by the shoulder.

'He needs a doctor!' Ser Thomas said, his slightly mad eyes bulging.

'A doctor has been summoned,' the Captain of the Ordinaries said with a bow.

Tom didn't like the Captain of the Ordinaries. Something about the man was false – rotten to the core. Blackhair, on the other hand, might have been Tom's twin brother – black hair, a forehead like the prow of a ship, and blue eyes that looked like they could cut you. Blackhair was tattooed from knuckles to eyelids – Tom thought he liked the look. And Tom was not a man to hesitate.

'I would'na take water from him if I was dyin' of thirst,' Bad Tom said to Blackhair. 'Do ye ha' yer own doctor?'

The acting Spatharios shook his head. He turned and growled something in Nordikan at another giant, who pushed forward. 'Harald Derkensun. I speak Alban – and Archaic.'

Tom watched the Ordinaries for a moment and shook his head. 'I want these fucking slaves out of the room an' I want a doctor *you* trust,' Tom said.

Derkensun nodded. He clapped his hands and rattled orders, and surprised Ordinaries fled the room.

The Captain of Ordinaries bowed. 'I have sent for our doctor,' he began, but Tom cut him off.

'We'll get our own,' he said. 'Ye can go, now.'

The Captain of Ordinaries sighed. 'I'll have water and bandages sent.'

Ser Jehan caught Bad Tom's arm. 'Mag. I sent for her. And for Toby and Nell and fresh men to stand guard.'

Bad Tom nodded. 'Aye – thanks.'

Jehan pursed his lips. 'I didn't like the look of the pompous bastard either,' he said.

Mag had the *potentia* to heal, but it was not her strongest hermetical skill, and she settled for easing the pain and manipulating the hip until she had the cracked bone aligned and then placing a light binding on it. 'Don't let him move,' she told Toby.

Toby gave her the look that boys usually save for their mothers. 'How'm I ta do that, ma'am?' he asked, more than a little whine in his voice. He looked at Nell. Nell stared at the ground.

Mag stretched and looked at le Bailli, who was rubbing his chin. 'Christ, I need some sleep,' he muttered.

Mag turned to Bad Tom. 'We still need a doctor. A good one.'

'One of the Nordikans says he knows one – an old Yahadut with powers.' Bad Tom jutted his chin at the door, where two axe-bearing giants stood. 'In the Hills, we have great respect for the Yahadut.'

Mag shrugged. 'Never met one,' she said. 'If he's a doctor and we can trust him, then send for him. Captain's not too bad for now – but he'll want to be up, and I'm not sure I set that hip right.' She yawned.

Derkensun bowed to Mag, and grinned at Bad Tom. 'I can send a runner to my friend. He'll find the old man. But it will be morning before we see him. And the princess will be wanting to meet as soon as possible.' He looked back and forth from Tom to Mag. 'You are doing the right thing – be wary.'

Tom nodded and pulled his leather bottle over his head. 'Only water from our canteens until we're sure we're safe. Got me, boys?'

The other men in the room nodded.

Later in the night, Nell brought two of the company mutts up from the stables. It took her almost an hour to find the horses, and more time to find the stall where the dogs had been penned. Then she lost her way coming back through the endless corridors and the mutts tried to bite an Ordinary.

Everything is an adventure when you're a page.

When she presented them to Toby, the squire offered both dogs water in bowls. The younger pup drank enthusiastically. The older bitch smelled the water and whined.

In an hour, the pup was dead.

The company went on alert, and began to mount a separate guard. Exhausted men and women laid plans to defend the Athanatos barracks in case of need, and Ser Milus cleared every man, woman and child out into the night and went from room to room with ten knights in full harness and torches – sweating archers opened every trunk and every wardrobe. Beds were upended.

Two men were caught. Both struggled, and both were killed.

Bad Tom looked like a devil incarnate in the torchlight of the courtyard, his sword red with the second man's blood – a uniformed Ordinary.

The Captain of the Ordinaries refused to be summoned.

Ser Milus looked at Ser Michael's plan for the defence of the barracks and approved it. 'Where's the guardroom?' he asked.

Ser Michael indicated the room they were in – a long, open hall with access to the interior and the main hall of the building. It was floored in black and white marble, and had battle scenes on the walls.

'Well done, Youngling. You ha' the first watch.' The older knight grinned. 'Thanks for volunteering.' He nodded at Ser Michael's stylus. 'You can pass the watch making out a watchbill.'

Mag sat by the Red Knight's bedside. He was pale and and his skin had the odd clarity of the very sick, and she wondered somewhat hopelessly if she'd set the hip badly, or somehow drained his *ops* with her own working. It was one of the great risks of healing.

She knew that her hopes to find a doctor were largely to do with her own desire to see the Captain in someone else's charge. Healing was not her field.

She sat, and sewed. Worried and slept.

But when the hermetical working attacked, she felt it coming. She had time to take a breath, raise a shield over the bed, and stand up.

One of the Nordikans died – his blood boiled. The other put a hand on his sword hilt, and whatever malevolence had targeted him washed over him like a thin ink and was gone.

Mag spread her hands as she had learned from the Abbess, and the foul working cleared and the power that washed over Nell's sleeping form only made her cry out and wake.

'It eats the stars!' Nell said, and her eyes closed.

The surviving Nordikan knelt, put a hand on his partner's forehead, and rose, shaking his own head. 'Fucking cowardly witches,' he said.

Mag reached down. Workings have causes. Every stitch leaves a hole in the fabric, however small. Even when the stitches are pulled, a seamstress can see where the old work ran.

She raised her arms and spoke aloud, and the thread that tied her opponent to his working appeared, running out into the corridor.

She summoned the dog – the dead puppy – and set it on the scent. Filled it with her own *ops* to animate it for a few minutes, and sent it, mindless, to hunt for her.

Harald Derkensun watched the dead dog rise and sniff the ground with dismay; he even backed away and drew his sword against the nice old woman.

She nodded at him. 'You have nothing to fear. Not all witches are cowards.'

Her voice rang with power.

The dog leaped up like a hound and bounded down the corridor outside.

Derkensun was shaken. 'It was dead.'

'Still is, more's the pity, as it was my daughter's,' Mag said. 'Needs must as the devil drives,' she added.

The dog had only one purpose, and that was to follow the scent. It followed the working, and after running some way the scent of it grew stronger. And stronger still.

The source! It towered over him, and kicked at him.

He became – *light*.

She felt her sending subsume. She narrowed her eyes and just for a moment, the Nordikan thought he saw one of the vicious old witches of the myths of his people – feral crones who guarded an icy hell.

'Got him,' she said. And sagged into her chair.

Dawn brought the doctor.

He was old – so old that his moustache and beard had the wispy quality of bad wool. He wore a small cap on his head and carried a tall staff. He arrived with Derkensun, Ser Michael and a young man who was not introduced. Four more Nordikans came, placed the dead guard on a shield and carried him away.

The Yahadut leaned over the bed and put a hand on the Captain's head – then snatched it back.

'God of my fathers,' he said. 'What blasphemy is this?'

He started to turn, stumbled, and froze.

Ser Michael ignored the old man's antics. 'A man was killed in the kitchens, Mag. Killed hermetically – he had burns inside his skin.'

'He killed the guard – he tried to kill us all,' Mag said wearily.

'Bad Tom caught a pair of them too,' Michael said. 'This place is riddled with treason.'

*

Harmodius made a fresh, desperate effort.

Yahadut scholar!

The man halted.

We need your help!

It is blasphemy for two souls to occupy one body, the old man said. But the sheer rarity of the thing caught his interest. *I see. Ahh – I see. Your body is dead?*

It is, Harmodius said. *I need to leave my host. I'm killing him.*

So I see, said the scholar, now fully intrigued. *Ah! You are Harmodius? I am.*

Yosef ben Mar Chiyya, at your service. You know Al-Rashidi . . .

I do. I was his student. And you?

We correspond. Your host is not so badly wounded. I regret to confirm you are the source of the problem. You must leave him.

I felt it. I seized control—

This is evil! You must not!

—to save him. And myself, of course. Yosef – I am powerless in here. Can I be moved to an artefact?

Never. The soul is too complex. Only to another host. Surely you know this?

If Harmodius had had a corporeal body, he would have shrugged and sighed, too. *I have such reasons to live!*

Yosef ben Mar Chiyya's eyes opened, and he turned back to the Red Knight's body. In the comfortable, slightly shabby sitting room of his great library-palace, he fell into an armchair. *I am well armoured against you, daemon. Come and sit.*

I am no daemon.

Anything that seeks to seize control of a man's body is a daemon. But you will not tempt me. I'm too old for temptation. Who is the woman who burns like the sun?

Mag. A seamstress. She has a natural talent.

By the horns and drums of Judea, she is like an angel of fire. Unlike you, daemon. You must die.

If I must, so be it. Wait – wait. What if you drugged him? Can drugs help?

They can help – but you will still be there.

Damn it! Rashidi would find a solution!

Rashidi is ten times as powerful as I, and would yet say that the solution is easy – you will simply not accept it. Let go. Die!

I will not.

The Yahudat took a deep shuddering breath and muttered an invocation, hand on the amulet at his chest. There was a flare of pure white light.

The Captain's eyes opened.

He met the eyes of the old scholar. Took a deep breath as his friends crowded around the bed.

'He's gone,' whispered the Red Knight.

The scholar shook his hand. 'Not hardly, the wicked old thing.' He put a hand on the Red Knight's brow. 'I simply forced him down for a while. Listen – I will make you a drink. A posset. It will help for now.' He frowned. 'But in truth, you must rid yourself of this troublesome guest.'

Mag leaned forward. 'What is he talking about?'

The Captain's eyes fluttered. 'He's babbling, Mag,' he said.

The doctor met the seamstress's eyes – in an eternity of no time, they both *knew.*

'Ah, I see,' Mag said.

An hour after the Captain drank off the posset, he was up, and possessed of ferocious energy.

He reviewed their arrangements, heard about the various attacks in the night, and paced his room until Nell brought him fresh clothes and a basin in which to wash.

Nell drew the water herself, brought it to the room, and Mag heated the water hermetically.

He sent Ser Michael – who was barely able to stand from fatigue – to inform the Captain of Ordinaries that he could meet the princess at her convenience. He exchanged a handclasp with Harald Derkensun.

'Mag says I owe you for the excellent doctor and the warning, too. I'm sorry for your man.' He met the Nordikan's eyes.

The other man nodded. 'There is much you should know,' he said. 'You are the Megas Ducas of the Emperor. I have eaten the Emperor's salt and owe fealty to no other. No matter what their blood tie.'

The Captain heard the Nordikan out, and at the end, said, 'You have given me much to think on.'

'Blackhair knows,' Derkensun said. 'And Giorgios Comnena of the Scholae.'

The new Megas Ducas leaned against a wall. 'Well, well,' he said. 'Thanks. Forewarned is forearmed, they say in Westwall.' He seemed far away, then rallied. 'What can you tell us of this Aeskepiles? The Emperor's magister?'

Derkensun shrugged. 'Little. Some men call him Vulcan. He was a smith, or a jeweller, before he came to power. Or so I have heard.' He shrugged. 'In truth, we Nordikans hate witches.' He smiled a little. 'We hate what we fear.'

'You seem well informed to me,' the Megas Ducas said.

'I have a friend who is a warlock,' Derkensun volunteered. 'He would be rid of the smith. That is, Aeskepiles. We try not to say his name.'

An hour later, all of the night watch were abed. He'd left the apartments in the palace – the former Duke of Thrake's apartments, of course.

He followed Toby and Nell all the way out of the labyrinthine corridors to the Athanatos barracks, where he found that Mag – prescient, as always – had kept him an officer's suite of three rooms – sitting room, bedroom, orderly room. She already had it furnished with his camp furniture. And she was yet awake.

He took her hands and kissed both cheeks. 'You are—'

She laughed. 'I try to think ahead. Someone has to.' She leaned over and

Entered his palace. Harmodius is alive! she said.

Yes, he admitted.

She smiled. *Oh good – I liked him.*

He makes a restless companion – like a bad housemate, except inside my skull. The Yahadut's drugs are to suppress him.

Oh! she said. *Tell me if I can help.*

Her paramour, John le Bailli, handed his Captain a pair of wax tablets. 'Here's the billeting arrangements as best I understand them. Things got chaotic at the end, and this place is incredible – there's a legionary eagle over the mess hall. The building must be more than a thousand years old.' He held out a scroll. 'We caught a pair of spies, and Tom killed 'em.'

'Of course he did,' the Captain agreed.

Sauce came and leaned in the doorway of the orderly room. 'People are saying we're to call you Duke.'

He grinned at her. 'I like it. It outranks Earl.'

'Duke Gabriel?' she asked, greatly daring.

His grin faltered.

She came into the orderly room, where Toby had his field desk open on a table and his sealing wax hot. He had a stack of parchment scrolls on one side of the desk and a couple of hides' worth of cut parchment on the other side.

'It's not like the old days,' Sauce said. 'Gavin – is on your side. A fair number of people know, or suspect – Alcaeus, for one. And if he knows, the princess knows.' She shrugged. 'When it was just you, me, and Jacques... then things were different.'

He leaned back. 'Once, it was just me and Jacques,' he said.

Mag took her man's elbow and dragged him out of the room. She waved over Sauce's head.

Meanwhile, Sauce blew the newly minted Duke a kiss. 'You don't scare me. I'm a knight.' She shrugged. 'I hear you had a bad night. We all did.'

'Actually, I got the best night's sleep I've had in two weeks. Go and lie down, woman.'

She shook her head. 'Can't. Michael tagged me for this watch, and I'm the duty officer.' She grinned. 'Duty officer. Think I'll ever tire of it?'

'No,' agreed the Captain. 'How's reading and writing?'

She winced. 'Not so good.'

The Duke pointed at the stack of scrolls at his side. 'See all those? The duty officer and the corporals should be handling most of this, but Michael and I are doing almost all of it right now. Reading and writing are not optional for company officers. Clear?'

She saluted. 'Yes, my lord Duke.' She giggled. And got out the door.

Ser Michael returned. He fell into a stool. 'Now, if you can do it,' he said.

The Duke nodded. 'Fetch the officers. Leave Sauce here – we could be attacked at any time and I want a good officer on duty. I know, you already took care of it, I'm just enjoying having my mind work again.'

Ser Jehan cursed and Ser Milus looked his true age, but they came – in armour. With their pages and squires, they crossed the Outer and then the Inner Court, climbed two staircases and clanked and scraped their way along a corridor that seemed as the whole road from Lissen Carrak. Finally, they paused outside a pair of oak doors, the old dark wood richly carved.

There were two Nordikans on guard at the doors. They raised their axes and clashed them together, smiling through their long beards.

'Ave, Imperator!' they said together.

Taken aback, the Duke looked over his shoulder before he realised that they meant him.

'I, too, am something of a scholar, my lord Duke,' said a light voice from inside the room.

The Emperor's daughter sat on a low-backed oak chair set in ivory. She wore a long scarlet kirtle with an overdress of silk that seemed to change colour in the light – between dark red and pale green. She had three peacock feathers in her hair and a veil of nearly transparent silk. Her almond-shaped eyes were rich and dark like thick velvet, and her hair shone like black brocade in the light of so many candles that the room itself seemed to be on fire. The Duke realised that every double pair of candles hung in front of a bronze mirror that reflected the light over and over in a ruddy-gold profusion. It wasn't like daylight – it was like the light in the last moments of a magnificent summer day.

The Duke lowered himself again to the floor – all the way, and lay flat. There was something round and gold wedged under a bookcase behind her feet – which were still encased in the same red slippers.

Her scent was the same.

This room was not as well swept at the throne room – dust had gathered in riotous profusion under the parquetry cabinets – Etruscan work, a meticulous trompe l'oeil of books piled in bookcases, astrolabes, rolled charts and hermetical and scientific tools in gilt and carefully stained wood, so lifelike that a casual observer in the ruddy light would take the parquetry for the real thing.

The newly minted Duke thought it all needed a dusting and a coat of walnut oil.

'You need never perform the full obeisance to any but the throne, my Lord Duke,' she said. 'I am but the Emperor's daughter – it is arguable that I don't deserve it even when I sit on the throne.'

'On the contrary, Majesty, your beauty commands my utter devotion wherever I find it,' said the Duke.

The woman with the shears clapped her hands.

'I am sure that flattery will, in fact, leave the *most* favourable impression,' said the princess, a trace of amusement cutting through her controlled voice.

'That's my experience,' said the Duke. 'May I rise?'

'Perhaps I shall measure the full force of my beauty by the duration of your willingness to lie in the dust at my feet,' she said.

'Are you by any chance missing a gold button shaped like a hawking bell?' he asked.

'Where did you find the word bucellarii?' she asked. 'The capture of my father made only slightly more stir than your claim to be at the head of your bucellarii.' She smiled, and a slight glow came to her ivory face.

'But you know what it means,' said the Duke.

'I am something of a scholar. And you? Do you know why the Nordikans saluted you?' She nodded. 'It will be very difficult to converse with you if you insist on lying on the floor.'

'If Your Majesty would care to spend a day in armour on an inferior horse, smiting Your Majesty's enemies, she might find that the floor of the Imperial Library as comfortable as I do.'

Her voice was as controlled, contrived, accented and pitched as an actress's or a great singer's. It sounded almost hermetical. 'Well, as you insist on lying on the floor, I am, in fact, missing one of my favourite buttons.'

The Duke rose slowly, favouring his right hip, and knelt on one knee before her. 'If one of the Ordinaries could fetch it, I believe it lies under the middle bookcase. If there is a maid responsible for dusting this room, perhaps her eyesight should be checked.'

She smiled at him.

He had difficulty breathing for a moment.

'Can you defeat the traitor and recapture my father?' she asked.

'Yes,' he said.

He felt the probe of her hermetical enquiry.

The Duke nodded his head. Very, very quietly, he said, 'In Alba, that would be considered very rude. Or even an attack.'

Her expression did not change. 'I am quite desperate,' she said with crushing honesty. 'Where I sit, there are no rules at all.'

One by one, they introduced their officers – his mercenaries, and her palace officers, military and civil.

'It is my intention to treat you as my Megas Ducas,' she said. 'You are indeed the commander of my armies and navies, which currently consist of a single armed galley at the Imperial mole and the forces you have seen tonight in the palace, with the addition of your own men. And perhaps the Vardariotes?'

'I took the liberty of paying them a year's arrears of pay,' the Duke said. Sitting wasn't any better for his hip than standing, and his armour felt as if it was a machine built to break his body.

The Captain of Ordinaries and the acting chamberlain both coughed.

The Lady Mary looked at Ser Alcaeus, who gave her a very slight nod.

'I know that you are Earl Muriens' son,' said the princess.

'I know that you are Ser Alcaeus's mother,' the Duke said to the woman with the shears. 'And the knight at the end of the table, seated by Acting Spatharios Darkhair, is my brother. Just in case all of this becomes a family affair.'

'You paid the Vardariotes, my lord Duke. I do not have the means to make such a payment – or to repay you. Even if I did, I'd use that money to buy some of my Thrakian lord's allegiances. I would like to know what you plan to do to defeat the traitor and retake my father.'

The Red Knight – the Duke of Thrake, now – inclined his head. 'Majesty, your palace is riddled with spies and traitors, and I intend to be very careful to whom I disclose my plans.'

The princess frowned. 'I agree that my palace has spies. Palaces generally do. But those in this room can be trusted. We are only twelve people.'

'Jesus only had twelve,' the Duke said. 'Look how that came out.'

The Moreans had less experience of blasphemy than Albans, and they gasped. The princess looked physically pained.

The Duke shrugged. 'At any rate,' he said, 'I intend to win over the Academy and build you a fleet. Since both of these will require a great deal of public action, there's no sense in hiding my intentions.'

She pursed her lips. 'The Academy is loyal,' she said. It was the first sign she'd shown of hesitation.

The Duke paused. 'The Academy has enough hermetical firepower to overthrow the Emperor and the church together, if that's what they wanted. They allowed the Magister Militum to turn against your father. I suspect that they are unhappy with something.'

The princess looked away. 'I have no money for a fleet.'

Her new Megas Ducas nodded. 'I will borrow the money to build a fleet,' he said.

Lady Maria spoke for the first time. 'The Etruscans will burn your new fleet on the stocks.'

Bad Tom grunted. 'Let 'em try,' he said. He was never at his best without sleep – this morning, he looked like a black boar made into a man, with the hair at his brow curling up like a satyr's horns.

Lady Maria leaned forward, interested. 'I had assumed we would buy the Etruscans aid with trading privileges. It has worked before – offer Genua concessions, or Venike, and play them against each other like barbarian tribes.'

'When you are yourself strong, you can afford to make concessions,' the Duke said. 'With a fleet to back your Imperial will, you can dictate your terms to the Etruscans. Right now, they are blockading your ports, shutting out your primary sources of Imperial revenue.' He shrugged. 'Besides, we will need a fleet to raid the traitor's lands, as you call him, and to trade with Alba.'

'We have no trade with Alba,' said the princess. She paused, and for the first time, her hands fidgeted. 'I suppose we have a little.'

The acting chamberlain spoke up hesitantly. 'We do have trade, Majesty – over the mountains to Albinkirk. Only a trickle, I'm sure.'

'And that cut off by the Wild,' said the Duke. 'Alba is richer and more vigorous than your father or grandfather imagined, Majesty. I, too, am a scholar, at times. And I have a friend who is a great merchant. I enquired at length before coming here. Your silks – some of the finest brocades in the world, made within the walls of this city – travel all the way to Venike before they come back to Harndon, which is just a few hundred leagues along the coast.' He smiled. 'And there are other things we share. The fur trade.'

'A few bolts of brocade will not save the Imperial revenues,' said the princess. 'And the furs come from the north – Thrake lies between us and our border revenues. We will not see any furs this season.'

'Will we not?' the Duke asked.

Lady Mary put a hand on her mistress's arm.

'This is the whole of your plan?' asked the Imperial princess.

'No, Majesty. This is the very tip of my spear, and will itself serve to cloak my other activities.' The Duke smiled. 'If you'd rather, I suppose I can gather my bucellarii and ride away.'

She sighed. 'You are the very barbarian mercenary I imagined.

Your manners are better, and you speak the High Archaic, but your arrogance is staggering.'

'Majesty, your arrogant barbarian mercenary would not have a plan to restore the Imperial revenues while maintaining the quality and numbers of the Imperial Army. For fifty generations, your forefathers have squandered their inheritance and purchased foreign soldiers to protect them and maintain the rump of their Empire – and now you think I am arrogant?' The Duke met her eye squarely. 'You should get out of this palace, Majesty, and see what the rest of the world is like.'

'And you imagine that you can save me?' she asked.

'I believe I can defeat the traitor and rescue your father,' he answered.

'You failed today,' she countered.

Lady Mary put her hand on the princess's arm again, but Princess Irene brushed it off.

The Duke nodded. 'It didn't help that the traitor knew I was coming, and had already placed his right flank nearest the gate,' he said. 'Nor was I warned that he had a most puissant mage waiting to cut my men's bowstrings and fire the grass. Mmm? Majesty?'

She nodded. 'I am not responsible for these things,' she said.

The Duke shrugged. 'To me and my men, you are entirely responsible. You are the Captain of your Empire.' He met her eyes.

The princess had the look of a young man trapped in an alley by footpads. Brave enough to fight it out. But aware of the inevitable outcome. She rose. 'You accuse me, for your failure, my lord Duke? Or you imagine that I *betrayed* you?'

He shook his head. 'Let us deal with political realities, and not accusations. If you can rule – if you can hold the palace and the city – I can defeat the old Duke and the Etruscans. If you wish to be rid of me – let me stress this, Your Grace – you have only to bid me go.' He met her, eye to eye. 'There is no need to assassinate me.'

They looked at each other long enough to become lovers. The look stretched on and on, neither blinking.

Lady Maria stood. 'The princess will withdraw. We thank you for your efforts on our behalf, my lord Duke. In future, you must use a little less familiarity in dealing with the Imperial presence. Princess Irene is not used to so much confrontation and finds it irreverent and confusing.'

The newly minted Duke stood straight, his hip screaming at him now and joined by an unsealy chorus of bruises, abrasions and pure fatigue. He ignored the polyphony of pain and knelt, took a handful of her hem as she swept by and kissed it.

The princess blushed. 'You think me ungrateful,' she said. 'You find me defenceless, with a traitor at the gate. This Empire has been the bulwark of civilisation for more than a thousand years, and I fear—' her hand toyed with the diamond cross at her throat '—I fear to be the cause of its fall.'

He smiled into her gown. 'A knight can make a tolerable gate keeper,' he said. 'You are not defenceless. There is no chance that the traitor will take this city. Let us build on that.'

She smiled, reached down – cautiously – and touched his hand. Then she glided away.

Lady Maria paused in the doorway. Ser Alcaeus bowed deeply and kissed her hand. She smiled. 'You have done brilliantly,' she said to him. Then she turned to the Red Knight. 'The patents of your appointments are being drawn up even now. I love the boldness of the idea of building a fleet.' She shrugged. 'I simply cannot imagine it succeeding.'

Everyone bowed, and the Imperial party swept away, leaving only the Captain of Ordinaries. He turned to the Duke. 'She touched you!' he breathed.

The Duke ignored the man. 'Leave him, Tom,' he said, without turning around.

Tom lowered his arms and spat at the Captain of Ordinaries' feet. 'Your turn is coming, dog,' he said.

The man turned white and grabbed the cross at his breast. 'I'm innocent!' As soon as the Albans were gone, he turned to his lieutenant and murmured, 'Barbarians.'

Bad Tom appeared in the Captain's doorway. 'You two fucking, or can anyone come in?'

Sauce was leaning over the writing desk, shaping the word *omega* with her mouth, tongue in her teeth. The Duke was holding her hand as it drove the sharp stylus into the wax.

Toby fled.

The Duke looked up without releasing Sauce's hand. 'Tom, do you know that some people could find your sense of humour offensive?'

'Really?' asked Bad Tom. He sank onto a camp stool, which

groaned. 'Jehan, as usual, thinks you are selling us down the river. Could you pat him on the head?' The big man chuckled silently at Sauce's discomfiture.

Sauce glared at Bad Tom like an angry cat. 'You can go fuck yourself,' she spat.

'Does the truth hurt, baby?' Tom asked, and his eyes were hard as flint.

Sauce took a breath and smiled. 'Jealous? You just want him for yourself,' she said.

Tom's right hand shot to his sword hilt.

Their Captain had gone back to work, and ignored their exchange.

Master Random,

If you would be so kind – I need a loan of a hundred thousand ducats and two Master shipwrights. Also a table of values for brocades, silks, and northern furs on the dock at Harndon. In haste—

He tended to stick out his tongue slightly when he wrote too fast, and he sucked it in and clenched his teeth as he finished.

Toby returned as if summoned, sanded the finished document and laid it on a side table.

'You two done?' the Red Knight asked.

Bad Tom tore his eyes away from Sauce. 'You paying the archers after mass on Sunday? Also we need a cleric of some kind. A priest.'

'We have two priests, I believe. Father Peter from Albinkirk and the mendicant friar—'

'He's wode – clean mad, lost his wits.' Tom crossed his arms.

'You ought to like him, then,' said Sauce.

'A regular chaplain. It's been mentioned a fair amount by the lads.' Tom looked at Sauce. 'And the lasses.'

'I'll look into it.' The Captain went back to writing.

'I gather we're to call ye Duke.' Tom's voice was itself a warning.

'Yes. I like it. My lord Duke.' The Captain sat back.

'You ain't our lord. Y'er our Captain.' Tom shook his head. 'I mislike it.'

The Captain met his eyes for a moment over his pen. 'Your reservations are noted,' he said coldly.

'Like that, is it, boyo? Don't get to big for yer braes.' Tom got up and leaned over the table.

'I'm not. I'm tired and injured and listening to two posturing idiots puts me in a foul mood.' The Captain paused. 'I had enough of it at the palace.'

Tom shrugged. 'Aye. Well. So you'll pay the lads on Sunday?'

The Captain met his eye. 'Perhaps.'

Sauce shook her head. 'Of course he'll pay them – Tom? What are you on about?'

The two men were staring at each other.

'He gave all our money to the fucking Easterners. We don't have ten silver leopards together. Do we, my lord Duke?' Tom put both hands on the table. The action was threatening.

The Duke smiled. 'Tom, it is ten o'clock in the morning, and I'm tired and pissed off. Yes – if that's what you want to hear – I spent all our money to buy the Vardariotes. It's no matter. I can get more.'

Bad Tom shook his head. 'For once, my lord Duke, I'm with Jehan. This is a tom-fool contract with no gold and no gain and too many enemies. Let's go back to killing monsters.'

The Captain leaned back and put his hands behind his head. He closed his eyes and stretched a little, favouring his right hip. Then his eyes opened. 'Want a good fight, Tom?'

Tom smiled. He looked at Sauce. 'Anytime, baby.'

'Would you settle for catching the spies in the palace?' he asked.

Tom's smile came more slowly.

'Look around you, Tom. This is the richest city in the world. The diamond cross on the princess's neck would pay the company for a month.' The Duke stretched again. 'I have the right to *tax* this Empire for our pay. Think a little bigger, Tom. There's never been a contract like this.'

'Best pay the archers on Sunday then,' Tom said. He grinned. 'Christ's skinny knees, you bought me with hunting spies. Will there be fighting?'

'You can kill anyone you catch, but Tom, how about we extract a little information from them first, eh? Gelfred will have the bulk of the fun but, before Christmas, we'll have a good fight.' He rose. 'Friends, I have to go to bed.' He handed three scrolls to Toby. 'See these placed on the birds. Yourself.' He turned back. 'And while I'm handing out tasks: Sauce, I want you to learn everything you can about Aeskepiles. Start with the Nordikan, Derkensun. *Do not ask anyone connected to the princess.*'

Toby nodded gravely.

Sauce raised a dark red eyebrow. 'We don't trust the princess?'

The Red Knight sighed. 'We absolutely do not trust the princess.'

Tom put his hands on his hips. 'Sweet Christ, Captain my Lord High Duke Commander! We don't trust *our employer*?'

'I need sleep, sweet friends,' the Duke said. 'Our employer, for good or ill, is the Emperor. Not the princess. That's our legal and quite possibly our moral stance, as well.'

Bad Tom caught his Captain's arm. 'I can'na wait to see how this comes out. But – you know I have to go in the spring.'

'And drive the cattle? Of course you do, Tom. I'm counting on it.' The Captain smiled. And vanished through the curtain to his sleeping room.

Tom turned and looked at Sauce. 'He's counting on it? What the fuck does that mean? I hate it when he does that.'

She shook her head. 'I don't really mind that he's smarter than most folk,' she said. 'I just hate it when he rubs my nose in it.'

'Amen, sister,' Tom said.

Chapter Eight

Harmodius Magus

Jarsay – Jean de Vrailly

The Captal arrayed his little army on the hilltop and watched the Earl of Towbray's retainers form up on the opposite hillside. He'd sent his defiance to the Earl and then burned a swathe a mile wide down the Earl's principal valley; looted four of his towns and wrecked his ripe crops, and killed more than a hundred of his peasants. And that night, his angel came again.

He fell on his face. The angel was even brighter; like sapphire and emerald fire.

You will defeat Towbray, his angel said.

'Of course,' de Vrailly said into his prayer carpet.

Do your best to take Towbray alive, the angel said. *Later, he will prove useful.*

De Vrailly was human enough to feel that he didn't need angelic visitation to see these truths.

You desire to be the best knight in the world. Your triumph is at hand. At the spring tournament, all will be as we have said.

De Vrailly smiled, even under the oppressive fear of his mighty ally. 'Ah, the tournament,' he said.

But there are other ways in which this kingdom must be brought to orthodoxy. The Queen must fall. She is a pagan adultress. You must have no pity on her or her people.

De Vrailly bridled. 'Not even for the wrath of heaven would I make war on a woman.'

The angel could be heard to sigh. *You are the most arrogant mortal I have ever known.*

De Vrailly smiled into the carpet.

Very well. You are my chosen servant, and I will allow you your will. But you must not stop her fall. The angel sounded insistent. Almost wheedling.

De Vrailly shrugged. *As to that, I care nothing for the witch.*

Good. Let us add some religious discipline. There is a monk – a pious man – in Lucrete. It is the will of God he become Bishop of Lorica. And restore these heathens to the way. He is a true apostle and he will stamp out the heresy of their witchcraft.

De Vrailly sometimes found talking to his angel was tiresomely like bargaining with a merchant for a horse...

In the full light of dawn, armed and mounted, he turned to his cousin Gaston. 'He won't soon defy the King his master,' he allowed, and laughed.

Gaston was waiting patiently while a squire fixed the buckle on his visor. 'It appears to me that he's defying you and the King right now. That's his standard – and there are his knights.' He rubbed his chin. 'Quite a few more knights than we have.'

De Vrailly laughed. 'I will defeat him easily – first, because his array is weak and his men fear to be taken as rebels, and second because I am a better knight.'

Gaston sighed and bent his head while Forwin buckled his visor. 'As you say, cousin. Has your angel spoken to you?'

'Yes. He told me I will soon be king,' De Vrailly said. 'And to summon my cousin Guillaulme to become Bishop of Lorica.'

'The *angel* chose your cousin?' Gaston knew Guillaulme for a difficult man, one in whom piety had replaced both common sense and common compassion.

De Vrailly held up a gauntleted hand. 'I have told you before, cousin – to doubt my angel is blasphemy. This realm needs my cousin, so that they may be cured of their heresies and their tendency to accept things that should not be accepted.'

Gaston didn't answer – merely closed his visor and leaned forward in the saddle to allow his squire to buckle it shut.

De Vrailly rode forward to his standard.

De Vrailly was not so contemptuous of infantry as he appeared, and he'd put the Royal Guard in the centre, flanked by Royal Foresters on each side – about sixty archers on either flank. Towbray had about three hundred knights and men-at-arms, and another two hundred footmen, most of whom were merely servants. Of course, all his archers had already served throughout the spring, in the north – and they were gathering in their harvests, or protecting them against de Vrailly's raiders.

De Vrailly raised his lance and rode forward, and his knights followed him willingly. His standard bearer, Pierre Abelard de Rohan, shouted the Gallish war cry. All the Gallish knights took it up, shouting, 'Saint Denis!' at the Jarsayans, and Towbray's knights charged.

If the Earl of Towbray had expected a chivalrous encounter, he was wrong. He was the first man to discover how wrong he was when his horse tumbled into a small pit that one of the archers had dug and its guts were ripped out on a stake. In a few heartbeats, the 'battle' was over, and the Earl's surviving knights were riding for home. His footmen, such as they were, cowered in their camp or broke and ran.

De Vrailly took the Earl himself, dismounting and knocking the stunned traitor unconscious with his heavy war sword before leading his knights in hunting the footmen through the camp and into the dales beyond. They killed or captured every man they could catch, burned the crops, and took their prisoners back to their own camp.

De Vrailly had the Earl put in chains, in a wagon.

Gaston d'Eu found him standing on a low bluff, looking out over the burning fields and small hamlets of Jarsay.

'You have to take him to the King,' d'Eu said.

De Vrailly pursed his lips. 'Why, when I can punish his serfs all autumn?'

Gaston sighed. 'These people are innocent of anything but having a bad lord. And they are the King's subjects. If your angel speaks you true – hear me, cousin, and don't interrupt – they will soon be *your* people.'

De Vrailly motioned out at the fields of fire and smoke stretching off into the sunset. 'But – is this not beautiful?' He smiled. 'Our knights are flush with victory and richer with the loot of this traitor's lands. He'll pay a huge ransom – and it's all mine. The King can collect his taxes from the man while he is my captive.'

Gaston shook his head. 'All those payments will be extracted from these rich valleys – where your men have killed the men, raped the women and burned the crops. So who will pay this ransom? The crows?'

De Vrailly waved his hand in dismissal. 'You have grown soft here in Alba. This is what war is. We are servants of war. If you do not like it, strip off your spurs and become a monk.'

Gaston shook his head. 'Take Towbray to the King. Immediately, before it gets worse.'

'Ahh!' De Vrailly rubbed his beard. 'But— No. I could simply kill him. I can take his lands and make them my own.'

'That's not how Alba works,' Gaston said. 'And he has a son.'

'Bah.' De Vrailly laughed. 'He's no threat at all. A boy playing at being a knight.' De Vrailly shook his head. 'You really think that the King will not take my part in this?' he asked.

'I think he could argue you made the traitor revolt when you killed his nephew in an illegal duel.' Gaston shrugged. 'Eh?'

De Vrailly spat. 'You ruin everything,' he said. 'And I was so happy. I cannot understand this place. Everywhere, their rule of law means the strong must give way to the weak. I hate it.'

Gaston shrugged. And, wisely, said nothing.

Harndon – The King and Queen

'He did what?' roared the King. He stared balefully at the messenger, who stood woodenly before him.

The captain of the Royal Guard – and the old King's by-blow – Sir Richard Fitzroy, raised his eyebrow at Gareth Montroy, widely known as the Count of the Borders, who cleared his throat.

'The Captal can be precipitate,' the Count said quietly.

'He fought a battle with Towbray and captured him,' the King said, reading the letter. 'By Christ's passion, he burned a swathe through Towbray's lands – my lands!' The King looked at his new constable, the Count. 'He says he will set Towbray's ransom at three hundred thousand silver leopards.'

The Count struggled to maintain a straight face. 'There's not that much coin in the world,' he said.

Sir Richard made a face. "That's roughly the value of Towbray's entire demesne. I have no love for the Gallish thug, but Towbray's been a burr under Your Grace's saddle throughout your reign. That's why you sent de Vrailly to deal with him.'

The King paused and pulled on his beard.

The Count shook his head in disagreement. 'Your Grace, I believe that the Earl is a dangerous man and as changeable as a weathercock. He served you well this spring, but your other peers would not take kindly to seeing this foreigner displace one of our oldest families.' He looked at the captain of the bodyguard. 'I could see us being well rid of Towbray.'

Ser Richard shrugged. 'I'd like to have seen Towbray's face when he found himself a captive of yon loon. But Your Grace has to consider sending him back to Galle for this. The commons openly say he's a spy for the King of Galle.' He glanced around the room. 'And my lord, if we attaint Towbray, the other lords will be very afraid. Scared men make foolish choices. And they are already scared of de Vrailly and his Galles.' Ser Richard looked at the King and shrugged, as if to say that this wasn't his fault. 'And Your Grace appointed him to choose the next Bishop of Lorica,' he said. 'He has chosen his cousin – a member of the University of Lutece. A priest famous for his harsh interpretation of God's word.'

'Did I ask for your opinions?' said the King, eyes afire. 'Did I ask you—' He paused. The Queen was coming into the room, and he rose and bowed.

She had two of her ladies with her, Lady Rebecca Almspend, her secretary, in a deep blue overgown with midnight-blue stockings that she rather daringly showed through a slit of her gown, and Lady Mary Montroy, the richest heiress in the realm and the Queen's chief maid, who wore a gown of red and black check pinned with a golden dragon – her gown revealed one red leg and one black leg, and contrasting slippers. As she had black brows and deep red hair, the contrast was maintained over her entire body – a body worthy of review.

The three women curtsied, and the men bowed.

The Count smiled at his daughter. 'You may be the first woman to grace this court in a Northern tartan.' Even the King smiled.

The King leaned forward. 'By God, though, Montroy. I thought the Muriens colours were green and gold?'

They all laughed, and the Queen leaned forward, a hand on her chest, and said, 'My lord must know that the Northerners have an ancient style – a set of colours that is a badge and a vaunt all at once.'

The King smiled. 'Any man who has hunted a bear in the Adnacrags knows about tartan, my dear. And Becca – we are all informal today, I find – you are dazzling. Which, if I may, is not how I am used to see you.'

'Fie, Your Grace! And yet my stockings remain blue.' She said this with a fetching lift of her hem to show her ankles and a hint of dancer's legs. The comment was so at odds with her usually severe demeanour, downcast eyes, and profusion of stylus ends and wax tablets that the King snorted and Sir Richard, who had been quite enamoured of the secretary from time to time, felt his former feeling rush back.

The Queen smiled. 'Having a worthy lover maketh a woman bloom like a rose in summer – isn't that what the poem says?'

The Count, a simple man with simple tastes and a devoted wife, nonetheless found his throat a bit tight and his face flushed. Ser Richard caught himself leering like a gowp and shut his mouth. The King beamed at his wife with adoration. 'That might be the highest compliment you've ever paid me,' he said, voice husky.

Her lips brushed his. 'How clever of you to see that,' she said. 'The three of us are on our way to the library, but it appears that we require Your Grace's permission to open your father's letters.'

'By Saint Martin's cloak!' said the King. 'Whatever for? Be my guest. Here – Becca, write it out for me and I'll seal it.'

'Your Grace,' said Lady Almspend, and she produced, not her usual horn inkwell, but instead a young page clad in livery, who had a heavy leather bag on his shoulder. He knelt and offered her a lap desk. She received a nod from the King permitting her to sit – it was an informal day and place and not high court – and she perched on a chair meant for a man in armour and wrote in her round, clear Gothic hand. She then produced royal red sealing wax and melted it from a device.

'Is that hermetical?' asked the King.

Lady Almspend nodded. 'Approved by the old Bishop of Lorica, Your Grace. Made with the sun's energy harnessed in a matrix of prayer and held—' she produced the item '—in a cross.'

They all passed it around.

'We live in marvellous times,' said Ser Richard, looking for some little contribution to catch her attention. It was widely known that she loved a barbarian drover – a member of the royal bodyguard named Ranald Lachlan. Paradoxically, Ser Richard held Lachlan in the highest esteem, and did what he could to further the Hillman's career.

Almspend looked at him and shrugged. 'I expect all times are marvellous to those who live in them, Ser Richard.'

The King was notoriously insensitive to the feelings of his men about the ladies of court, and he leaned over to watch her seal the order and asked, 'What of your handsome drover, eh, Becca? I want my Ranald back at my shoulder.'

The Queen, in a rare display of temper, said, 'Then Your Grace has but to make him a knight and offer him a dowry.'

Almspend's hand paused.

The King laughed. 'A stiff-necked drover? He'd never accept it from me. He has to go win it for himself – aye, and he'll be a better man for it, and you'll bloom all the more.'

Almspend finished her task. 'As Your Grace says, of course,' she breathed.

The King frowned at Lady Almspend. 'Do you know as much of religion as you do of history, my dear?'

Almspend bowed in her chair. 'Your Grace, religion is nothing *but* history.'

Ser Richard laughed aloud, but the Queen frowned.

'Why do these gentlemen disapprove so strongly of the Captal's cousin Guillaulme as Bishop?' the King asked.

Almspend raised an eyebrow. 'I'm sure I am *not* the one to discuss this with the King and privy council,' she said.

The Queen put a hand on her back. 'The King asks *you.*'

Almspend shrugged. 'Guillaulme Le Penser is one of the leaders of an intellectual movement.'

The King nodded. 'Come, that sounds promising.'

Almspend raised both eyebrows. 'He is a teacher at the University of Lutece. He and the other Scholastics – as they call themselves – believe that the use of hermeticism is connected to the worship of Satan; that the miracles of God are of an entirely different order; that those who use power should be burned as witches.'

There was a stunned silence.

The King leaned forward. 'Why would they believe such a foolish thing?' he asked.

Almspend shrugged. 'I can give a politic answer, an intellectual answer, or a pragmatic answer, Your Grace.'

The King nodded. 'Let's have pragmatic, for all love.'

Almspend tried to meet the Queen's eye before she went on. 'Your Grace, the University of Lutece follows the Patriarch of Rhum. As the Academy – the centre of learning, especially hermetical learning – is in the grasp of the Patriarch of Liviapolis, it serves the needs of the Patriarch of Rhum to make his rival appear a witch. Further to that all of the Scholastics are men and none of them have access to power. They seek to create a world that they can dominate – after all those capable of using power are burned away.'

The Count of the Borders shook his head. 'Sweet Saviour, then how will we stop the Wild?'

'Lutece is a long way from any battlefront with the Wild,' Almspend replied.

The King nodded. 'Well, best to know. I'm sure he'll be difficult – look at the Captal and his heavy-handed policies. But he does get things done. Perhaps his cousin is from the same mould.'

The Queen looked baffled. 'My dear, you just heard Becca say he'll try to rid the realm of all hermeticals?'

The King patted her hand. 'Fear not, love – I know what's best for the realm. Random wants a new bishop. This man sounds very intelligent. He'll be a help at council, and we'll simply have to show him the kindly light of our hermeticals.' He nodded, dismissing the women. 'Lady Almspend, your learning lights my court like a hundred candles.'

She curtsied. 'My lord, it would be a good thing for the realm for Magister Harmodius to be replaced. A new magister could help us persuade the Bishop.'

The King nodded and waved a hand.

When they were gone, Gareth Montjoy shook his head. 'Was that poised young woman with the lovely ankles my daughter?' he asked. 'Need they pluck so much of their foreheads and show quite so much leg?'

The King laughed. 'When I was coming to manhood women wore sacks in layers. I prefer the modern taste.'

Montjoy shook his head. 'Your Grace is not a parent,' he said, and then stiffened. He'd come close to the unsayable.

The King looked at him mildly. 'I suppose someday God will bless me with a child,' he said, and his face grew tight. His sigh was heavy.

'Your Grace, I am sorry.' Gareth bowed. Reminding the King of his childlessness was not a good start to a day.

The King waved him off. 'Never mind, Gareth,' he said. 'God will provide.' He turned to Ser Richard. 'Why so long-faced, Dick?'

Ser Richard shrugged. 'I think I may need to ask a leave of absence from Your Grace and go ride about on errantry until my worth is ranked higher.'

The King frowned. 'You were at my side at Lissen. Indeed, you stood by me to the end. No man here doubts your worth, and your hand was reckoned mighty that day.'

Ser Richard bowed. 'It is kind of Your Grace to say so – but many men fought valiantly at Lissen.'

The Count nodded. 'Aye, and to brag about it, carping on all day. And every one of them Galles.' He looked at Ser Richard. 'Are you really proposing to leave court for a while?' he asked.

Ser Richard met the King's eye. 'Yes, if I have leave.'

Montjoy looked at the King. 'De Vrailly is on his way back here with the Earl, isn't he?' he asked.

The King shrugged. 'Yes.'

'We need to get all the Southerners – all the knights from Jarsay and their retinues – away from court before there is blood.' Montjoy leaned forward.

The King sighed heavily. 'Yes,' he admitted.

'And what if he gets above himself?' asked Ser Richard. 'Don't you need the Southerners to balance the Galles?'

'By Christ I hate all these factions,' said the King. 'And I'm the King, not the head of a rival faction myself. I need nothing to curb the Captal but my word.'

Montjoy's eyes met those of Fitzroy. But after a long unspoken message – pleading – he nodded. 'I'll go. Where do you have in mind, my lord Constable?'

'Albinkirk,' said the Constable, 'needs new men for the garrison, and Ser John has been fighting. He's virtually alone, and he deserves better of us.' He turned to the King and squared his shoulders as if entering combat, and said, 'Is Your Grace determined on this new bishop? I feel it is an error to give de Vrailly another boon.'

The King set his face. 'I will have nothing to do with factions,' he said.

'Your Grace, I have not asked you for *anything*. I stand for the kingdom. And I say that de Vrailly has too many men-at-arms and too much power already, and that this man should be sent back to Galle as soon as his ship touches the shore.'

'I'll consider it,' the King said.

The Queen led the way down the corridor. 'That was easier than I expected. Why do you think that the old King's writs and letters are closed, Becca?'

Almspend was already regretting her fashionable gown with its high collar – managing it required the very skills she'd spurned when other girls were learning them, so that she could instead master High Archaic. Her beautiful deep-blue slippers offered no protection at all against the cold of the stone.

Why is it the Queen never seems to be affected by these things? Almspend wondered. The Queen seemed to float along, never hot, never cold, never troubled by cramps or headaches or even a runny nose.

'My lady, I would guess that the old King said some outrageous things in his time. He certainly had lovers – women and men both, according to my father. He played favourites and while he was an excellent king, my lady, one rather has the feeling that he was not a particularly good person.' She shrugged.

The Queen laughed. 'How exciting! For the first time, I understand your interest in history. Where are we?'

'My lady, this is the donjon – we are entering by what would have been the secret passage, back in King Uthaneric's day. But when the New Palace was built—'

'Becca, is there anything you don't know?' asked Lady Mary. 'By the Virgin! I thought the New Palace had been here two hundred years and more.'

'Yes, Mary,' Almspend said, in the voice she reserved for the great number of otherwise intelligent beings who seem to have no interest in history. 'The New Palace is almost exactly two hundred years old. I can show you a foundation stone with the date. Sixty-two sixty-three.'

'How old is Harndon, then?' asked Lady Mary.

'The Empress Livia and her legions established a fortress here one thousand and fifty years ago. Or so.' Almspend shrugged. 'Actually, there's a great deal of argument among scholars about the date of the expedition, and whether Harndon was established in the first or second expedition to the Nova Terra.'

'Really?' asked the Queen. She rolled her eyes at Lady Mary, but Almspend either didn't notice or didn't care.

'At any rate, my lady, Harndon is a very old name and probably pre-dates the Archaics. When good King Ranulf returned from the Holy Land and built the New Palace, his chamberlain, Hildebald, writes that the deepest excavations found both tunnels, a temple foundation, and a road of logs laid side by side and planed flat with an adze of great antiquity. The temple still held enormous latent *potentia* and had to be cleansed by the archbishop. He died of the task, and the Patriarch had to come from Liviapolis.'

The three women walked along the corridor for a few more steps.

'How terrifying!' said Lady Mary. 'Where was this temple?'

'Oh, just behind us, about twenty paces. Some of the old stones were reused in the corridor – look – see the Green Man? That's one of their old signs.'

The Queen put a hand on the stone. She closed her eyes. 'They still have power. They called this place—' She paused. 'Harn Dum.'

'Why yes!' Almspend was delighted. 'Did you read that in Tacitus?'

'No,' said the Queen, clearly shaken. 'I just heard a voice in the stone.'

'You mean to say that our world sits atop yesterday's world, and that one sits atop another, and another? Under our New Palace is an older palace, and then a temple – what's under the temple?'

'Something wrought by the Wild, perhaps, or by the Old People.' Almspend laughed.

'The Wild cannot build anything,' said Lady Mary.

'Nonsense! The Wild makes wonderful things. The new scholarship studies these things. Irks build, they have music, and they have towns and castles.' Almspend nodded, happy to be able to discuss the things that delighted her with her friends, who too often talked about dancing.

'That is merely the imitation of man,' said Lady Mary.

'Not at all. That's a very dated theology, my dear,' said Almspend. 'In fact, it is far more likely that our works are an imitation of theirs.'

'Poppycock!' snapped Mary, who was tired of being patronised by her father and didn't intend to let Becca Almspend get into the habit. 'Rubbish!'

Surprisingly, it was the Queen who agreed. 'Before he left, Harmodius was experimenting with issues raised along these lines,' she said. Almspend nodded. 'The Archaics understood these things far better, Mary. I could—'

'By the virgin, Rebecca, in a moment you'll tell me that you worship Tara.' Lady Mary crossed herself.

Rebecca smiled. 'Mary, would it shock you to know that some scholars think that the Virgin may be the early Church's attempt to harness the worship of Tara the Huntress?'

'You only say that because we're deep beneath the earth where the lightning can't hit you,' said Mary. Her voice was light, but she was clearly mortified.

'Tar,' said the Queen.

The other two women were silent. They had come to a great oak door with iron hinges and all three women stopped.

'They call her Tar,' the Queen said, in a dreamy voice. 'She became later Tara, but her name is Tar.'

'My lady?' asked Mary.

The Queen looked at her strangely. 'Yes?' she snapped.

Almspend kicked Mary with one slippered foot and Mary squealed and stepped away from the Queen. 'Ouch, what was that for?' Her eyes met Almspend's.

'What just happened?' asked the Queen.

'You touched one of the Green Man stones and went all funny,' said Almspend in her matter-of-fact voice.

The Queen shrugged. 'And now I remember. Well. Here we are.' She produced a key, and the three women took turns working it in the lock with sweet oil until it turned.

The Queen put a strong hermetical light over the door, and the three women gaped. There were piles of scrolls spilling onto the floor, and heavy tomes piled on heavy slab tables. A large rat stood in the middle of the central table, chewing parchment with malevolent, spiky teeth.

The rat met the Queen's eye.

The Queen raised a hand and the rat turned to ash.

'Oh – very good!' said Lady Almspend. 'Well hit!'

The Queen allowed herself a smile. 'I have been practising. That animal was under someone's control – I can see the web of its hermetical owner.'

'Who would want to read these old—' Lady Mary stepped back and gave a shriek. She leaned against the door frame, a hand to her bosom. 'By the Blessed Virgin. Saints protect me.'

'By all that's holy – or unholy!' said Almspend. 'I see why this room is protected! These are Plangere's papers! In with the King's! Sweet Jesu, my lady – this is raw power for the taking! Did Harmodius know?'

'I'll guess he did not. But his own papers need to be protected as well – you wouldn't believe what I've found in his rooms. That man was far deeper than we ever realised.'

'They all are,' muttered Almspend, rifling through an enormous grimoire. 'Oooh! This stinks of Archaic necromancy.' She literally held her nose. 'My lady, what are we looking for?'

The Queen looked back and forth between her two most trusted friends. 'Do you two know what old wives whisper about my husband? That he is impotent, and cursed?'

There was a pause. Hermetical light is very white, and unflattering, and the two women looked at their Queen under its glare, each struggling to hide something.

Almspend bowed her head. 'I have heard this, yes. And worse.'

Lady Mary nodded. 'Although the Galles all say it is you, my lady. That you are barren.' Even in the cold white light, she flushed.

Almspend nodded. 'The Galles are the most vicious gossips I've ever heard, for men. I thought only women were so poisonous. Once or twice I've wished I wore a sword and could use it, so I could cut the comb of a braggart who needed it.'

The Queen put a hand to her belly. 'I'm pregnant,' she said. 'By the King, if that needs to be said.' She sighed.

In some ways, she was the most human that Lady Mary had ever seen her.

'My husband has a secret,' the Queen went on. 'It concerns the Red Knight. Beyond that, I know the older women say the King had an affair, and she is the woman that cursed him with impotence.'

Mary smiled. 'Well, if that was the case, you seem to have cured him.'

The Queen smiled. 'I have powers,' she said, her voice low. 'And after the battle – that woman, Amicia? She healed us. I think her power and mine combined sufficed to break the curse.'

To Mary, who had no access to power whatsoever, this was too much information; like hearing about another person's toilet habits. But Almspend leaned forward. 'Really!' she said. 'Fascinating!'

'I want to know who cast the curse and why,' said the Queen. 'So that I can fight it.' She shrugged. 'Among other things, it occurs to me that whoever cursed him in the first place might want to harm my baby.'

The two ladies-in-waiting nodded slowly, but Mary smiled. 'Perhaps you were just slow to kindle?' she asked.

The Queen laughed. 'I have lain with the King upwards of three times a day since we were wed,' she said with a low chuckle. 'More, when the fancy took us.' She met her maid's eye. 'I *know* by my powers that I am fecund. Absurdly so. Need I say more?'

Mary blushed so hotly that she fanned herself.

Almspend took a deep breath. 'Your Grace?' she asked quietly. As the women hardly ever addressed the Queen by title, she bowed her assent to let her secretary go on.

'Your Grace must understand that the study of history is littered with unpleasant truths,' she said.

The Queen nodded. 'Go on.'

'That's all,' Almspend said. 'You may well learn something you do not wish to know. Or need to know.'

'I intend to save my baby,' said the Queen.

Harndon – Ser Gerald Random

Random was comfortably and pleasurably abed with his wife when the wings began to beat at the window. His first reaction was annoyance, and then fear – the wings were immense and, to a veteran of combat in the Wild, portended something worse than a messenger pigeon. He rose, naked, and drew his sword from its place over his bed, knelt because hopping on one foot is not the best way to face a monster, and pushed his wife's naked flank to hurry her from the room.

Thump thump thump
Thump thump thump

Once, when he had been a boy, great luna moths had come to the horn windows of his father's house in South Harndon. His mother, a seamstress, had purchased beeswax candles to allow her to work late – a special commission – and the moths had been drawn by the light. They had been as big as his head or bigger; creatures of the deep Wild. And the thump of their alien, insectile bodies against the mullioned horn and glass windows of his parents' house had been terrifying and yet fascinating. And very young Thomas Random had watched their shadows flit and nudge and, greatly daring, he had stepped out into a summer night to watch them. The largest moth had fluttered about in its clumsy flight and come to hover just a few inches from the tip of his nose and he'd missed it at first in the dark, and then felt the breeze of its wings, each as big as his hand. He'd felt no urge to kill it. In fact, he'd wondered what it saw when it looked at him.

He'd always been curious about the Wild. He'd ignored his father's instructions, cashed out his apprenticeship and marched with the Royal Army as a young man – just to see the Wild.

And now, he used the tip of his sword to throw the catch on his bedroom window. The windows opened outward, so he pushed.

The sheer size of the thing outside took his breath away, and then he saw the colour and laughed.

The gigantic raptor was half black and half white – and every child knew what an Imperial messenger looked like. Random had never seen one before, but he knew it, even soaked with rain and desperate with fatigue, and he threw the windows wide so the poor bedraggled thing cartwheeled in and fell in a sodden mass on his bed.

By the time his wife, now decently arrayed, dared return to her bed chamber, Random had the message. He was sitting on the bed, shaking his head.

'These sheets are ruined,' Lady Alice said. 'Six weeks sewing wasted. Couldn't you have let the damned bird into the stables, or something?'

Random grinned at her.

She stepped back. 'This isn't some damned adventure— Oh, no! You are directing the Queen's tournament.' She leaned forward. 'So you can't leave.'

He caught her and kissed her. 'It's a different kind of adventure,' he said. 'All I have to do is raise a hundred thousand Etruscan ducats.'

Harndon – Edmund the Journeyman

The first corpse in the square shocked every man and woman in the neighbourhood.

The body was that of a young man – a handsome young man. His murderer meant him to be found – he was spiked to the stump of the maypole with a pair of daggers. He'd been killed with a sword. He was expensively dressed in red and yellow wool and silk.

Edmund saw the crowd around the corpse and waited his turn to see the thing itself. He'd seen enough corpses to know the look – white as milk, a slackness about him that threatened any man's belief in an afterlife. Dead was dead.

Friars came and took the man down and by late afternoon, when he and his apprentices were taking turns boring the latest barrel, a shop boy told them that the body was one of the Queen's squires.

'It was them Galles,' said Sam.

Tom and Duke kept working.

'Well, it stands to reason. Jack Drake tried to take our square, and he's the king of them Galle lovers. One of the Queen's squires dead? The Galles kilt him.' He shrugged. 'Or Jack Drake did. To warn us off.' Sam looked at his acting master, who shook his head.

'What a lot of foolery,' Edmund said. 'The Galles are knights. They don't go around killing other gentles—'

'But they do!' said Duke. 'Christ on the cross, Ed! Where've you been? Their top knight, Vrailly, kilt the Earl of Towbray's nephew in cold blood! Just hacked him down.'

Tom shook his head. 'Kilt him in a duel, fair as fair. That's the way I hear it.' He went back to turning his drill, and then paused. 'Mind you, Vrailly is as big as a house and the other was just a boy – but a fight's fair if both parties agree to fight – eh? Ain't it?'

'Galle lover,' Duke spat.

'Nope,' said Tom. 'I just like to have my facts straight.'

'Could have been Drake, though,' Sam said.

Edmund nodded. 'That's enough. Let's get this job done.'

Duke grunted, angry. The boy was often angry, these days. The city air was poisoned with the new factions – the Galles, the Jarsays, and the Northerners. Galles dressed in bright colours, wore their cotes and gowns very short, and walked about looking for trouble.

Naturally, all three of these things had appeal for young men.

The Jarsays were predominantly men and boys from the Southern farmlands. The city was full of Jarsayans after harvest, and there were more than ever this year – some with tales of brutal attacks by Royal troops. The sign of the Jarsayans was a farmer's smock.

The outer wards of the city had received an influx of Northern refugees in the late spring. Most of them were going back to their homes now, but the remnant were angry and dispossessed and very prickly.

The guilds had responded by holding an increased number of drills for all the trained bands within the city. The armourers prided themselves on being one of the best military guilds, and they drilled so often that Edmund was tired and hungry all the time. But he had become aware that the guild masters were using the trained bands to overawe the factions.

'We're armourers,' he said firmly. 'We're above faction concerns.'

'That's crap,' said Duke. 'The Galles is foreign, and they're out to get the Queen. Calling her a whore. Saying she's barren. They say she's—'

Master Pye appeared at the door, and Duke flushed.

Master Pye looked at them grimly, but he didn't say a word.

'I don't believe any of those things!' Duke said.

Master Pye nodded and beckoned to Edmund.

Edmund felt like his feet were made of lead. But he followed Master Pye across the yard to the master's office, a room as full of vellum and parchment as the royal secretary's office at the palace.

He felt like the best defence might be a good offence, so as soon as the master was seated, he bowed and said, 'Master Pye, I am sorry. The body found this morning disturbed everyone.'

Pye nodded. 'I'm glad you accept responsibility, young Edmund. What your men say reflects on you. What my men say reflects on *me*.' For a moment, his mild eyes, framed by his enormous Etruscan spectacles, magnified and enhanced, met the journeyman's, and Edmund felt a jolt of pure fear. He had only seen the master really angry once. 'I spend too much time at the palace. I need you, Edmund. How is the project?'

Edmund shook his head. 'There's no end to it, Master. But I'm making three barrels with one-inch bores. I think – *think* – they'll answer some of the specifications on Mr Smyth's contract. And the strange bell with the holes for bolts.'

Master Pye steepled his hands. 'Good. Get it done. You know something about both casting and making punches.'

Edmund bowed. 'Yes, Master.'

'I will need you to take charge of a number of projects here, Edmund. These iron barrels have done a good job of training you to run a project – you are well inside your budget and your work nears completion. I will need you to direct ever more of the work here, which is why I need you to be better at controlling the apprentices.' The master raised his hand. 'I understand that these are difficult times and, make no mistake, I understand that you used to be one of them and therefore lack that quality of awe that might give you an air of command. In the old days I'd send you to another shop.' Master Pye shook his head. 'I hate to say this, but I think I have more orders than I can possibly fill without engaging another dozen apprentices and two more journeymen – yet I lack the time to train and oversee them in a way which would make them good masters in their turn.' He looked up. 'Do you understand what I am saying?' he asked.

Edmund coughed. 'No. Yes. I'll do what I can.'

'The most important commission in the shop is the King's armour for the tournament. Yet I have done almost no work on it since we completed the hardening process, because I am cutting the dies by hand.' He looked at Edmund. 'And I need hundreds of coin blanks cast and cut.'

'I can do that,' Edmund nodded.

'No, boy, I don't need you to do it. I need you to develop a process to allow apprentices to do it, so I can cut dies and you can embellish the King's armour.' Master Pye's eye met his again.

'Tom could run it,' Edmund said. 'He's very good.'

Pye took a deep breath. 'Really?' he said. 'Young Tom is a street boy. You know that, eh?'

Guilds took on a proportion of foundlings, but they seldom amounted to anything because, even inside a guild, success required both nepotism and ready silver.

Edmund knew that. Tom tried not to be resentful of it, but sometimes his superior skills so obviously overshadowed Edmund's that he was acerbic about it.

Edmund leaned forward. 'He'd be loyal – for ever – if we give him this opportunity.'

Pye rubbed his unshaven cheeks. 'Good call. I knew my confidence in you was not misplaced. I've been too long out of the shop. Send for him this instant.'

By the time an enthusiastic young woman could have murmured an ave maria, young Tom was standing with his cap in his hand in the master's office.

'Edmund says you are ready to be a journeyman,' said the master.

Tom moved the cap round and round in his hands, as if his fingers were looking for flaws in the frayed edges. 'Oh!' he said, and looked at Edmund. Then he slumped. 'Can't pay the fees,' he said.

Master Pye nodded. 'Don't slouch, Tom. I'll pay your fees on two conditions.'

Tom sprang to attention. 'Anything!' he blurted.

'Always wait to hear what the contract holds before you sign, young man. First – will you work for Edmund?' The master leaned forward.

'Yes!' said Tom.

'Second; you'll have full wages as a journeyman, but I'll have you bound to me for two years. No leaving me for other shops or other cities.'

Tom laughed. 'Master, you can bind me for the rest of my life.'

Pye shook his head. 'Never say it, boy. Very well – go make yourself an iron ring and meet me at the guild hall. Have a cup of wine to celebrate,' he said, 'for by God, it'll be the last afternoon you spend out of the shop for many a day.'

Master Pye went out into the courtyard, and Edmund stayed to help Tom make himself a blued steel ring. While the older boy was trying to get a bezel to form and cursing over it, he said, "Thanks. I owe you.'

Edmund said, 'He's going to expand the shop. We're going to make coins.'

Tom whistled. 'That'll put the cat among the pigeons.'

Edmund was polishing the ring as if he were a new apprentice but, by tradition, when a boy got raised his friends pitched in. 'Why?'

Tom shrugged. 'Them Galles want to kill our coinage. If'n we're minting new they'll come after us too.'

Edmund nodded slowly. 'Best take some precautions.'

Tom smiled. 'After I make journeyman. Thanks again. I never thought it would happen.'

West of Lonika in Thrake – The Emperor and Duke Andronicus

They dismounted in the courtyard of a small castle. The place was no bigger than a manor house, with two stone towers and a timber-built Great Hall that filled the space between. The castle had an outer palisade wall and stood atop a high ridge. From the tallest tower, the sentry could see the snow-covered tip of Mons Draconis, sixty leagues to the west amidst the Green Hills.

Sixty stradiotes of the Duke's personal household accompanied the Emperor, and they received him with an elaborate ceremony that failed to conceal his status as a prisoner in a miserable border castle, so far from his home that rescue was impossible.

His dignity remained unmarred. He accepted the plaudits of his enemies, and their bows, and he went to the room assigned him with good grace. The guard on his door begged his blessing.

That night, he tied his sheets together and went out through the window, but a light snow was falling and horsemen took him at first light.

One of the Easterners took his steel axe, and used the handle to break both of the Emperor's legs. Then they carried him back across the frozen swamp to the castle, returned him to his room, and the guards all asked his blessing.

Southford under Albinkirk – Ser John Crayford

Another week passed before Ser John had time to ride to the ferry. There were more and more settlers arriving – the latest merchant convoy from Morea brought ten new merchant houses, come for the autumn fur trade and the Wild honey that the Outwallers would be selling at the fair in another month. Ser John bit back his usual comments on the rapacity of the merchant class. Instead, he carefully regulated their entry into his city, assigned them to empty houses and ordered them to rebuild the houses on pain of forfeiture of their goods. That was, in fact, far beyond his powers, but the mayor and council had been killed by boggles in the siege of Albinkirk and none had replaced them, and he didn't see the King appearing to order him to cease.

The merchants grumbled but they hired the surviving local men as labour. And stonemasons appeared from Lorica, lured by the promise of work.

Every day there was a new crisis, but they were all small. On Wednesday, the newly appointed Bishop for Albinkirk arrived. He had a retinue of one priest and one monk, and they rode donkeys.

Ser John missed his arrival as he was north of the town, listening to complaints about irks and Outwallers. When he returned, his useless sergeant reported that the bishop had arrived, had moved into the bishop's ruined palace and wanted the captain's attention at the earliest opportunity. Ser John rolled his eyes.

'An' he's peasant born,' said the sergeant.

Ser John laughed. 'And so am I. And so are you, knave.' He dismounted and gave Jamie his horse. 'I'll get to the low-born prelate when I have time to breathe.'

But best of all, on Thursday Sir Richard Fitzroy appeared with forty lances – all court men except for a single black-robed knight – a priest of the Order of St Thomas.

Ser John met Ser Richard in the fore-yard of the citadel, and they embraced.

'Are you here to relieve me?' he asked.

Ser Richard shook his head. 'Not a word of it – you are high in the King's favour, and I have forty archers for your permanent garrison, and these lances to bolster you for the autumn. I'm the King's Justice on Eyre for the north this season, and I'm rather hoping you have a few monsters left to kill.'

Ser John saw several men-at-arms who looked, to him, too young to be away from their mothers, but he slapped Ser Richard on his armoured back. 'Most pleased to have you. Plenty of monsters; I killed half a dozen boggles just the other day.'

The youngest man-at-arms looked as if his eyes would pop out of his head.

Over a cup of wine, Ser Richard revealed that all was not well in Jarsay, and the Constable had sent the captain of the guard with all the Jarsay knights from court to avoid unpleasantness with the returning Captal de Ruth. Ser John, whose garrison had not been reinforced in six years, whose men were three years in arrears of pay, and who had lost four of his five good surviving men-at-arms to the Red Knight when the insufferable upstart passed through in early summer, cared nothing for the politics, and he spent a delightful day organising his shire into patrol areas and assigned them to the older and more reliable knights.

On Saturday he held a feast after mass – supported by a little direct taxation levied on two Hoek merchants who came up the river. They reported that they evaded boggles and something worse at Southford, and had been succoured by a nun with miraculous powers. He taxed them for wine and gold and assigned them a house to repair, and then held his carefully planned feast. He held it in the Great Hall of the citadel, had his servants construct a dais, and on that dais he placed a golden shield with a bright red cross displayed. The Bishop of Albinkirk – the new man, Ernald Anselm – was invited, and he sat in his episcopal throne on the dais, with Ser Richard on one side and Ser John, who had some thoughts about his own hypocrisy, on the other by the priest of the order, Fra Arnaud. There were six empty seats on the dais, and when the last remove was reduced to mutton bones, and the squires were pouring hippocras, Ser John rose and the hall fell silent.

'Brothers,' he said. 'There are six empty seats here, prepared for those who best comport themselves as knights errant.' He smiled at all of them and walked to the edge of the dais. 'Listen, friends. I've watched you for most of a week. I've seen you in the tiltyard and at the pell; watched you wrestle and watched you ride. You are ready to face the foe in every way but one.'

They started to cheer when he said 'ready to face the foe' but quieted at the end.

'Most of you,' he said, 'know that I'm a plain soldier; I've served in many places in this world, in Tartary and in the Holy Land, and in Galle and Arles and a few other places. I know a little about war. And what you gentlemen are going to is *war*. So stop thinking about fucking Jean de Vrailly, forget the court, ignore whatever political situation landed you here, and stay alive. I guarantee that by this time tomorrow night, one of you will be dead or badly injured – not because the Wild is such a deadly foe, but because you fine gentlemen are off to fight the Wild with your heads in the clouds or deep in worry and hate about what is happening at home. Forget all that. Remember the woman you love, for that love will make your sword hand fast and heavy. Obey your officers, because they see more than you do. Remember your King, because it is in the King's grace we fight a just war. Remember your training. The rest is crap. Forget it. And in a few weeks, when you ride home covered in glory – well, then you can bicker about the Captal and his policies again.'

The bishop rose to speak. He had a beautiful voice, and despite being peasant born, he was highly educated and eloquent. He spoke briefly of a knight's duty to the Church, and on their opportunity to do penance for their sins by wearing armour and serving the cause of man. He bowed graciously to Father Arnaud, who returned his bow with a pained smile.

Ser John had met him once before and didn't know what to expect, so he was as surprised as everyone else when the bishop walked off the dais and among the men-at-arms. He laughed, and his laughter was a clear, bright sound. 'It is odd, is it not, to be sent to kill in the name of our Lord? He never said, "Raise me armies and fight the Wild." He said, "Turn the other cheek."' He walked on in stunned silence. 'But he also said, "Succour the little children."' The bishop paused. He was in the middle of them. 'My people are not nobles. My father tills his fields in the shadow of the walls of Lorica. My mother is a yeoman's daughter. My brothers and I are the first generation in our family to leave serfdom and be free farmers.' He looked around at them. 'Freedom to farm means that in exchange for our tax and tallage *you* protect us with your bodies. Knighthood, my brothers, is not all pointy shoes and plucked foreheads and dancing. The men and women who sweat and work on your farms do not serve you because God ordained it. It is a contract, and in that contract you receive the fine sword, the tall horse, and the admiration of all the pretty girls *and in exchange you are willing to die.* That is your duty.'

He looked around at them. The power of his voice was immense. They weren't even shifting in their seats, and Ser John had a cup of wine in his right fist and had forgotten to raise it to his lips.

'Every family in this town and the surrounding country has lost people. I administer the sacred host to a flock almost without men. Children are terrified. Women are hopeless. The reconstruction work lags. We question our faith. How can God allow this?' He looked around and thumped his crozier on the floor. Men jumped.

'You can save them!' he roared. 'Every widow who sees you ride by will feel a ray of hope. Every child who sees a knight will know that mankind is *not beaten.* Show these people who you are. Prove yourselves worthy of your knighthoods. If you are required to, die for them. That is all God asks of you, his knights. In his name, go forth, and conquer.' The young bishop walked back through the knights, blessing those closest to him, and he mounted the dais, turned, and made the sign of the cross. 'And know that if you fall, you die in the good grace of our Lord, amen.'

'And take a lot of the little bastards with you,' muttered Ser John.

'That was a marvel,' said Ser John after the bishop seated himself.

Anselm smiled. 'It was rather good,' he admitted. 'I cribbed some from Patriarch Urban, and the rest was inspiration. I prayed a great deal. But this is what these people need – the flash of armour on the roads every day. A ray of hope.'

Ser John put a hand on the young man's shoulder. 'I didn't welcome you as I should have,' he admitted.

'You were busy, and I'm only a low-born prelate,' said the younger man with a twinkle in his eye.

Ser John shook his head. 'Did I say that?' Next to him, Father Arnaud almost spat up his wine.

The bishop shrugged. 'It's all hearsay, Ser John. And I *am* a low-born prelate. But I intend to rebuild this flock, and to help you rebuild this town. By the way, Sister Amicia of the sisters of Saint John asks to be remembered to you. She has the most remarkable dispensation – there can't be ten women in Alba who are allowed to say mass.'

'She's a remarkable woman,' Ser John said.

Father Arnaud nodded. 'I would very much like to meet her,' he said.

'I gather she was instrumental in stopping the enemy at Lissen?' asked the bishop.

'Her powers are formidable,' Ser John said. He grinned. 'That's hearsay too; I was here.' Ser John looked at the other man, who was handsome in a rough-hewn, red-haired way, and looked far more like a knight than a monk. 'But she has been very helpful to me in the last weeks.'

The bishop shrugged. 'Well, she wished me to remind you to take a look at the devastation at the ferry. I saw it myself – something evil is lurking there. My own powers are in the hands of God – they come and go – but I can feel it.'

Ser John nodded. 'I'll have a look.'

Father Arnaud nodded. 'Ser John, I'm merely passing through but I'd very much appreciate it if you would let me accompany you?'

'A knight of the order?' Ser John laughed. 'I'll hide behind you if it gets rough.'

In the morning he had four patrols mounted in the yard. It made him feel as if he was a great lord; forty knights at his beck and call, and another forty men-at-arms or squires, plus pages and archers. The archers were all his own, and he'd celebrated the feast after mass by issuing his surviving veterans with all their arrears of pay. Even the new men were paid to date, an unheard of benison.

But he rode for the ford with Father Arnaud, two new archers, his own squire Jamie, Ser Richard and finally his squire, Lord Wimarc, a rich young sprig whose armour was better than Ser Richard's and Ser John's. But Wimarc's manners were exceptional, the boy obviously worshipped Father Arnaud, and he didn't condescend to Jamie in the least. They were a good team by the time they rode along the river to the ford.

It was a clear day, with a magnificent blue sky. A few trees had colour – most maples tending to yellow, and a few beeches. The river sparkled.

The corpses were covered in ravens.

Ser John hadn't even known that men were trying to rebuild the ferry, but their attempts only stirred his pity. Something had broken right through their new log walls and freshly thatched roof, and torn a baby from its cradle. It had ripped two men to very distinct shreds – an arm here, a long, horrible shred of human gristle there. The heads, arranged neatly on spikes in the ferry's yard, all pecked about by ravens.

Lord Wimarc swallowed a few times but didn't lose his breakfast. Father Arnaud dismounted, prayed over the corpse flesh, and then set about the grisly task of gathering the remnants for burial.

Ser Richard had not risen from royal bastardy to captain the Royal Guard on looks and patronage alone. 'It's big,' he said. 'Not an adversary. Even bigger.'

Ser John looked at the rooftrees. 'I can't believe this is a Wyvern,' he said. 'Nor do mammoths eat folk.'

'Troll?' asked Ser Richard. 'I fought them at Lissen,' he said, eyes suddenly moving about. 'Christ's wounds, but they scared the shit outen me.'

Ser John stood in his stirrups, raising his lance to measure the height of the arm that had torn aside the thatch to reach inside. 'That's a very large troll,' he said quietly. 'Sweet Jesu. And I had hoped to dine with a friend today.' He kept his voice low because the priest was nearby.

Ser Richard laughed. 'This must be an adventure,' he said.

Ser John raised an eyebrow.

'I'm already shit scared,' said Ser Richard, and the sound of their laughter rang out, over the ferry, and into the woods.

They crossed the Great River, and Ser John saw immediately what the nun had wanted him to – a swathe of destruction like a road made by a mad woodchopper, running west into the deep woods.

'Blessed Crispin.' Ser Richard reined up. 'We can't ride in that.'

Father Arnaud fingered his short beard and then stripped off his riding gloves and put on his gauntlets. Lord Wimarc darted about, trying to be the priest's squire.

He had a cervellieur – a much older rig than the Gallish bassinet now in favour at court. Wimarc put it over his head; a light skull cap of steel with its own aventail of chain mail.

Father Arnaud smiled at the young man. 'I'm not used to having a squire,' he said, and the younger man flushed.

Ser John studied the terrain for as long as the squire drew twenty breaths.

Grown trees had been ripped down and tossed about like matchsticks – dozens of them. It looked as if some gargantuan child had played jacks with the trees – and they lay like jack-straws in a massive tangle that stretched into the west as far as the eye could see.

'I'm going to guess this will intersect with the Royal Road somewhere,' he said. 'So much for my pleasant dinner with pretty women.' He looked over. 'Your pardon, Father.'

Father Arnaud smiled. 'I'm certainly not offended that you like pretty women, Ser John. I misdoubt God is offended either. He made them.' He grinned. 'As to dinner – I'm always in favour of dinner.'

The two archers, Odo and Umphrey, were too junior even to have nick-names, and they were both looking a little pale. Ser John smiled at the two. 'You boys like camping?' he asked, and went to check the pack horses. When he was satisfied, he changed from his palfrey to his warhorse.

Ser Richard did the same, and then both of them pulled on helmets and gauntlets.

Ser John looked at the priest. 'Isn't that skull cap a little light?'

The priest nodded. He took a full helm out of the bag at his saddle bow and put it on his head – Ser John noted with professional interest how the lugs he had scarcely noticed on the skull cap engaged with corresponding tracks inside the great helm, locking the massive steel helmet in place and creating a protective system of two layers of hardened steel. He whistled.

Father Arnaud dropped the great helm home with a click.

They rode for a mile at a cautious pace. From the Royal Road, which ran west to Lissen Carrak and then crossed the Bridge Castle and on to Hawkshead, they could see the open sky of the devastation just to the north, between the road and the river. Sometimes they lost it, but then they would spy it again and, after a mile when the road cut north, they slowed to a walk, and the road entered the devastation.

They picked their way carefully for about three hundred paces, and then they were deep in. Ser John reined up, raised a hand and shook his head. He pushed up his visor.

'Fuck it,' he said. 'We need to come back with the archers, clear the road, find whatever did this and kill it. As it is, we're in its terrain and our horses are useless.'

Ser Richard raised his visor. 'I agree. I'm already tired, and my poor Arrow will probably bite me right through my harness if I make him jump another log.' He turned his horse. Both men looked at the priest, who was perfectly still on his black charger.

He was looking past Ser John's shoulder, and he'd just drawn his sword.

There was a loud *snap* as a branch was broken. Everyone froze.

'Blessed Virgin,' Ser Richard said.

Ser John saw movement in the downed trees. 'Dismount!' he shouted.

Ser Richard didn't dismount. He put his horse at the downed tree immediately behind them and his horse made the leap – man and armour and all. Ser Richard had a royal education – so he rode like a centaur.

The archers and squires dismounted. Jamie took the horses' heads and pulled them clear of the men, but the downed trees on the road made the space so restricted that any fidgeting from the horses would crowd the men, or worse.

Ser John's eyes met his squires'. 'Get them out of here,' he barked.

Jamie began to thread his way through the fallen timbers.

The archers were still stringing their great war bows.

'What is it?' asked Ser Richard.

'No idea,' spat Ser John.

'Giant,' said the priest. Like Ser Richard, he was still mounted.

Behind him, the smell of something foul reached the horses, and they panicked. The pack horses ran – one misstepped, and its leg broke with a sickening crack. The horse screamed.

The scream acted like a signal, and two giants rose out of the downed trees and struck.

They were huge.

And, unlike legend, they were fast.

In forty years of fighting, Ser John had never seen one, and he was rooted to the spot for a fatal moment. His mouth framed the word, 'Christ.'

The priest went forward, and his horse leaped a downed spruce, despite the weight of the armoured man on his back, and the priest's sword took a finger off the giant's reaching left hand and he was by.

The monster was shaped like a man, if that man were very ugly, had legs only as long as his torso, and no neck. And only one great eye.

And carried a club roughly the size of a small boy.

But for some reason, the thing threw its blow at the screaming pack horse, as if its cries pierced the thing's enormous shell ears, or the pain of the wound to its hand disoriented it.

'It *is* a giant,' said Odo the archer, unnecessarily. And then his first shaft, thirty-five inches long and weighing four royal ounces, slammed into the giant's thigh. The livery head with a bodkin point went so far into the giant's meat that only the fletching showed.

The giant roared, and the woods shook with the sound.

Off to his left, Ser John heard Ser Richard call his war cry and heard the pounding of his horse's hooves.

Umfrey loosed a shaft and missed.

Sir John made himself move forward at the giant, which was just about three times his own height. Its club had pulped the horse's head and spattered all of them with gore.

Lord Wimarc followed at his shoulder, a fine gold-chased pole-axe in his hand.

'What— What do we do?' asked the younger man.

'We kill it,' said Ser John.

The giant was as fast as a man. It turned to face the two armoured men, and while Odo missed, Umphrey's second shaft went right through the thick muscles of its upper right arm, spoiling its blow at Lord Wimarc. Most of the blow went into the ground, but the club skipped and caught him, breaking both his legs and knocking him flat. He screamed – a nasty, choked sound. Despite the wound, Wimarc swung his pole-axe at a finger the size of his wrist, and connected despite lying flat on his back. Only then did he lie back and scream in earnest.

Ser John didn't waste his free moments. He had a hammer with a five-foot haft and a spiked back. He slammed it full force into the giant's right foot, shattering bone, and then stepped in between the reeking thing's legs and lifted his hammer, catching the giant's dangling testicles with the spike and ripping – pivoting on his hips and passing the pole-arm through a whole butterfly to slam his third strike into the giant's left knee.

Its scream sent every bird for four miles into the air. Its mate paused, turned and took Ser Richard's lance in its belly.

She cut down with her club, shattering Ser Richard's shield, breaking his hand and arm, but Ser Richard put spurs deep into the side of his beloved Arrow and the big horse responded in a rage of injured horse-friendship, plunging forward into the bad smell and pushing the lance head deep into the she-giant's belly.

Umfrey and Odo saw the male giant go down, turned together like veterans, and engaged their second target. Neither missed. They drew and loosed, nocked, drew and loosed, their bows singing every few seconds. The female giant was only ten paces distant, and she had no cover.

Ser John slammed the point at the end of his hammer into her rump as she fell, got between her legs and turned and hit again.

It made a piteous sound, and fell to hands and knees across Lord Wimarc. Ser John was behind it, and he broke its thigh with his hammer on his third blow. And then started on where its kidneys ought to be.

The female plucked Ser Richard from the saddle, breaking his collarbone and dropping him on his already broken arm and hand. But she didn't seem to be able to understand where the heavy livery arrows were coming from, and she slapped at them after they hit her, like a small child slapping insects that have already bitten and left.

Ser Richard rolled over on training alone, cut at the ankle and connected. He cut again, screaming his terror and his war cry at the giantess, and she ignored him and turned and saw the archers.

Umfrey's bow broke with a snap – he'd been drawing hard, with every shot, in something like blind panic. 'Uh-oh,' he said.

Odo put an arrow into her face, but he missed the eye and the arrowhead bounced off the bone. He reached for another shaft but there weren't any more. The rest were on the pack horse.

Umfrey drew his sword and turned to run.

Odo caught an arrow in Umfrey's belt by the head and pulled it clear. He nocked.

Ser Richard cut with everything he had at the giantess's hamstring and then fainted.

Father Arnaud appeared behind the giantess. His horse rose like it had wings, and his sword went in to the hilt – in with a long over-arm thrust, out again like a deadly needle punching living flesh, and he was past again, and her blow missed him as his horse bounded away like a deer.

Ser John's giant voided his bowels and collapsed. Ser John couldn't see Ser Richard – the other knight's horse was kicking at the giantess, and she stood stock-still on one foot. There was an arrow in her eye, and Odo was standing, watching her with a curious look of triumph on his face.

Her club pulped him.

But when she stepped forward to finish his mortally wounded mate, her right leg gave under her, the hamstring completely severed, and she fell.

Umfrey saw Odo die and went berserk. He shouted. He screamed. He wept, and his sword hacked at the downed giant as fast as a woodpecker eats insects, striking along her dangling breasts and into her shoulder. She screamed and tried to rise.

Father Arnaud hit her in the back of the head with a mace plucked from his saddle bow, full force, and the mace head broke the back of her skull with a spurt of blood and pulverised brains.

Darkness was falling when Helewise, who listened every night for such things, heard voices from the gatehouse, which had become a sort of barracks for their newer folks. She had sixty people now – far more women then men, and most of the men were older, but everyone worked and the fields had been cleared.

She wasn't yet undressed, but she ran a brush through her hair in hope and then ran down the steps from her solar to the main hall of the old manor.

'Blessed Saint Katherine, what is that smell?' she asked before she was out the door.

The yard was full of horsemen and Phillippa was there, and both the Rose girls and old Gynn and Beatrice Upton. Then there were torches.

Ser John appeared among the men. He was in full armour, and he looked *old*. But he managed a smile for her. 'Don't touch me,' he said. 'I'm covered in shit.'

She flinched back, and saw that there were other knights – a man on a stretcher between two horses, and a bundle that held the particular quality of a corpse. She put her hands to her mouth, but only for a moment.

'Hot water,' she called. 'And get Sister Amicia!'

'I'm here,' said the nun. She was dressed only in a shift, and she ran across the yard to the man on the horse-stretcher.

Ser John swung a leg over his horse and dismounted slowly. His squire came and took the horse.

'He fought a giant. By himself,' said Jamie.

'Crap I did,' said Ser John. 'Sister, Ser Richard isn't dying. This boy is.' Ser John led her to another man, also on an improvised stretcher between two pack horses.

Helewise went to the man called Ser Richard. She waved to the girls. 'Let's get him inside,' she said. 'Smartly with the stretcher.'

'I know what I'm doing,' her daughter said with her usual attitude.

She and Jen got the stretcher unlashed from the saddles and they carried the wounded man inside, grunting at his weight. He was a big man in full harness. The two young women grunted but they got him onto the hall table, while Mary Rose took the cloth and rolled it away, moving the two great bronze candlesticks that the looters couldn't break, and dropping a heavy salt-cellar on her foot and cursing.

'Christ, they stink,' said Mary.

There was a glow of gold-green light outside, and then they heard Sister Amicia praying.

'Oh,' said Phillippa. 'I want to see her miracles!'

'You can stay right here and help me with these buckles,' said her mother.

Golden light like the rising sun played outside.

'Oh! It's not fair!' said Phillippa.

'Be a help and not a hussy,' spat Helewise. 'Get his arm harness off.'

While she fumbled with the unfamiliar buckles under the man's sword arm, Ser John and the priest and Sister Amicia came in. Phillippa suddenly became very serious about her buckles.

Sister Amicia had hair going every which way, and there were lines under her eyes. Helewise had never seen her look so old.

But she put a hand on Phillippa's hand. 'You must be even more gentle,' she said. 'Look – collarbone is broken, and the arm, and all these bones in the hand. And his breastplate – see where it is bent?' Amicia took a deep breath. 'All those ribs are broken, and they can't even spring back until the breastplate is removed.' Her voice emitted a sort of warm calm, like a mother's love made palpable.

She took a deep breath and turned the collet on her ring so that the bezel was out. 'Oh, my sweet Lord,' she said.

Six hundred leagues to the east, the Red Knight paused, his breath caught, and for a moment he was sitting hand in hand with Amicia the novice, under the magical apple tree on the wall of the convent at Lissen Carrak. The feeling was so powerful that he *was* there.

She didn't seem to ask, but he gave her every scrap of his horded *ops* – the deep reserve he kept for the moment he might have to face Harmodius.

She took it all.

Ser John reached past Phillippa and undid the side-straps on the other knight's breastplate – one, two. But the third moved something inside, and Ser Richard gave a choked scream.

Ser John looked at the nun, and she shook her head.

He drew a dagger and cut the strap, and the armour hinged open, and the man's body made a wet sound.

'Helewise!' Ser John said, and she got a hand in with his and they rolled the man a little, and the priest got the backplate off as he coughed blood.

'No!' said Amicia. 'Lay him flat. Gently.'

Phillippa finally had the last straps on the arm undone, and Ser John opened the left vambrace with a sticky, wet sound.

Ser Richard's eyes opened, and he screamed and then choked and said, 'Awfully sorry.'

Sister Amicia put a hand on his shoulder. Her face grew pale, then almost leaden. The ring flared like a diamond in sunlight, and then like a small sun.

She sighed. And slowly smiled.

Her eyes opened.

Ser Richard's eyes fluttered again. He released a breath that he might have been holding for a very long time. 'I'll never doubt God again,' he said dreamily.

Sister Amicia laughed. It wasn't a strong laugh but it was a good one, and she sat heavily on the trestle bench.

Now that the crisis was past, Helewise and her daughter looked at each other. They both smiled.

The stench was truly awful.

'Everyone wash,' said Helewise. 'What in the name of heaven is it?'

Ser John shook his head. 'Giant shit,' he said. 'Pardon my Gallish, but that's what it is.'

The hall was full and so was the yard, and everyone was awake. And everything happened at once – girls got pails of water from the well, fires were lit in the kitchen and the hall fireplace and even in Helewise's solar, and every kettle they possessed was pressed into service heating water. Ben Scold, the best of the new men, started cleaning the horses, and the surviving archer joined him. Young Jamie began collecting the reeking armour – Lord Wimarc's was the worst – and by then Phillippa had some boiling water for him. He looked at her and smiled.

'Did you kill one?' Phillippa asked.

Just for a moment, he thought of lying to her – she was so pretty. But he shrugged and looked at the ground. 'I was sent with the horses,' he said. 'I didn't strike a blow.'

She smiled at him. 'Your time will come,' she said, and he fell instantly in love with her.

Everyone bathed. The knights had soap, of all things, and the women had made some more; the women bathed in the hall and the men in the kitchen, and Helewise started a fashion by wearing her kirtle without a shift under it, because there was still dirty work to do.

Ser Richard attempted to rise and was pressed back into a bed by Amicia. 'Good knight, the power of my healing, even with God's help, is greatly aided by careful rest and a great deal of sleep.'

He looked at her with worship. 'Beautiful sister, why? I feel better than I have in a long time.'

She smiled and smoothed his hair. 'Shall I tell you? When I heal – when any good healer heals – we knit the tissues just as much as we need to bring them together, and no more. The power used is greater than any other kind of casting.' She smiled hesitantly, and then shook her head. 'Think of the power you would use to cut a man's hand off with a sword. The power to put it back on is many times greater. So we fix what we can, but then we must let God and nature do the rest over time.' She shook her head. 'And nature's healing gives a greater hope of success.' she said. 'And, when it comes to healing, I really need more training.'

Ser Richard gazed adoringly at her and said, 'I'm sure you need no further training.'

Amicia had some experience being a healer – and a woman – and knew when it was time to fluff the pillow and be all business.

Lord Wimarc was moved into Helewise's solar. The smell of giant began to recede, although it continued to catch at the back of people's throats for days. Helewise broached a keg of cider, and everyone had a little – there wasn't that much of it – and Old Gwynn produced a leather flagon of wine that they all drank greedily, and Mag Hasting brought out fresh bread.

Eventually, the excitement faded. Helewise made sure that her daughter went to bed with her friend Jen and not with either of the squires – she didn't really think her daughter would, but she had to check – and then scrubbed the hall table one more time and helped Old Gwynn wipe down the kitchen where the men had slopped wash water. Amicia had passed out in the hall settle, and Helewise threw a heavy wool blanket over her. She stood in the middle of her hall, and listened to the silence. Gwynn smiled toothlessly and went laboriously up the stairs to the rooftrees, where she had a little garret.

Helewise stood there indecisively for just long enough to realise that there was someone there with her, and then his hands were around her waist.

'I think you should dress this way all the time,' he breathed in her ear.

'John Crayford, if I catch one whiff of giant on you—' she muttered. When he tried to kiss her, she ducked her head and slipped through his arms, but she caught his hand and pulled him into the yard. 'Where's your squire?' she asked.

'In the gatehouse,' he breathed in her ear. 'I kept the barn for myself.'

She put her arms around his neck. 'Was it bad?' she asked.

'Better now,' he said. He lifted her and carried her into the barn.

Father Arnaud sat in the hall and sipped from a cup of wine. His hands were shaking.

Sister Amicia came and sat by him. 'Can I help?'

He smiled at her. 'You are the famous Soeur Sauvage?' He rose and bowed. 'No one told me you were so pretty,' he added.

'Are you sure you're a priest?' she asked. But she grinned, and he had to grin back.

He drank more wine. 'I'm good at killing monsters,' he said. 'Pardon me, *ma soeur*. I am suffering a crisis of faith.' He turned his head. 'Why on earth did I just tell you that?'

She shrugged. 'People tell me things like that all the time. I suppose I'm easy to talk to – being pretty, and all.' She sat opposite him, seized a dirty cup and poured wine into it. 'I'm in a perpetual crisis of faith myself, though, so I'm of no help to you.'

He sat back. 'Mayhap I could argue that if you have many crises of faith, you must also resolve them often, and thus you are my fittest guide.' He looked away.

'What's the matter?' she asked.

'I couldn't heal. I haven't been able to because—' He paused and looked away.

They sat silently for a bit, because he was crying, and she knew better than to interrupt. After a little while, she said a prayer and then handed him her plain white handkerchief.

He dried his eyes. 'Sorry,' he muttered. 'I don't want to be a sop. I am simply so tired of failure.'

She watched him, waiting, listening.

But he surprised her by turning with a wry smile. 'And you, *ma soeur*? Why your crises of faith?'

She shrugged. She had little interest in discussion or confession; she knew her sin, and talking about it would only make her feel more vulnerable.

On the other hand, he'd confided in her.

'I'm in love,' she said. Even saying the word gave her a jolt, like touching a sacred relic.

His smile sharpened. 'Ah – love,' he said. He drank off his wine, and his hands shook.

She couldn't tell whether that was bitterness or not. 'Has anyone asked if you killed the giants?' she asked.

'Oh, yes. Both dead. Two of God's creatures, as innocent as babes, and we killed them.' He raised his eyes.

They were empty and hard for a moment. And then they softened, and he wrinkled his mouth – a particular tick. 'Bah, I am too talkative. Lift my vow of silence and I ramble on and on.'

She got up and stretched. 'You don't seem especially talkative to me, ser priest. But I think I'm too tired to drink any more.'

'Who is it?' he asked. 'Who do you love?'

She shook her head. 'It's not important. He's not around, so I cannot err.' She was quite proud of how light her voice sounded.

'I fell in love with a lady.' Father Arnaud raised his eyes. 'I ruined her life. I was proud and vain, and our love was a gift from God. Even now, I'm not sure that I repent it.' He swirled the wine in his cup. 'Isn't it interesting that God can cut me off from the power to heal, but my strong right arm can continue killing? Despite my sin?'

She sat down with a thump. 'So far, it sounds like you are more interested in being a romantic hero in a troubadour song than in being a good man. Despite which I promise you, ser priest, that the only thing that stands between you and healing is yourself.'

They sat for a moment, glaring at each other.

He shook his head, wrinkling his mouth again. 'Sometimes our situations resemble the best troubadour songs. That's why we love them, is it not? And yet – and yet, I feel a pang of something at your words, and you anger me, and that is good. I have considered that my limitations on casting must come from within me, like some kind of amnesia. But there is nothing there.'

She reached out a hand. 'Let me look,' she said.

He shook his head. 'No – pardon me, *ma soeur*, but you are too puissant for me. I will go and do my duty, and perhaps God and I will come to be friends again.' He got up. 'The worst of love is the change in habit – you know that? Years of celibacy, and now all that is overturned. I see you as a woman, not a sister. I see women all around me.'

'Not altogether a curse,' she said. 'Might it not be better if some of our order lived and worshipped with yours?'

He laughed. 'It would certainly alter our convents,' he said.

She crossed her arms. 'I'm cold. Good night to you, Father.'

He watched her climb the stairs, and then he poured himself a cup of wine, and later he prayed his beads and cried.

The next day, when the wounded men were stable and the dead man was buried, the priest took his leave.

Crayford embraced him. 'You are a fine man of arms, Father,' he said. 'I wish you were staying. Where are you headed?'

Father Arnaud was booted and spurred and had a warm cloak over his arm. He bowed to the Lady of Middlehill. 'Thanks for your hospitality, my lady,' he said.

She curtsied. 'May I ask your blessing, Father?' she asked.

'You need no blessing beyond the presence of Sister Amicia,' he said. But he held out his hand and blessed her, and her daughter, and all the manor.

'Where are you headed, Father?' asked Ser John.

'Over the mountains to Morea,' the priest replied. 'I'm off to be the chaplain to the Red Knight.' He said it lightly enough, but Ser John's brow darkened and the nun put her hand to her throat. The ring on her finger seemed to flash in the autumn sun. 'I gather he needs a chaplain. Perhaps I'll even reform him,' he said.

Ser John shook his head. 'You won't. For an upstart sprig of nobility, he's a fine fighter. Nor any worse than any other sellsword. But he stripped me of my best men-at-arms in the late spring, and now he gets you as well. Despite which, send him my regards.'

Sister Amicia coughed. 'And mine, Father.'

'You know him, I gather,' said the priest. He vaulted onto his horse.

She nodded. 'I do,' she said.

When the priest was gone, Sister Amicia thought, *There goes a man who thinks me a pious hypocrite. And who is too intelligent for his own good. They'll get along famously.* She sighed, clamped down on her regrets, and got on with her work.

Chapter Nine

Thorn

Ticondaga Castle – Ghause Muriens

Ghause spent more time on research than she had done since she was very young, reading her mother's books and her grandmother's grimoire again and again. Even as the days grew colder and wetter, and her husband's sword punished the Outwallers harder and tried to enforce his notions of peace among the Huran, she read and read, and then began one of the most complicated castings she'd ever designed.

The work began with an elaborate array of diagramata written in silver lead on the slate floor of her work chamber, high above the stone flags of the castle courtyard. The working was so dense that it required a kind of application that she normally forbore. She hated both research and diagramata, preferring to make up for each with simple power – power that she had had from birth.

But this was not a matter for power. This was a matter for subtlety.

Her intent was to discover how the King's new bedmate had snapped the curse. The kind of work required – an investigative charm that would penetrate time – was so far from her usual style that she feared even to assay it, and twice she summoned daemons to question them about how they would manipulate the *aether* in such a way.

It was dull, detailed work and summoning daemons was far more exciting even if it was cold – working sky clad in an autumnal castle had its own risks.

One of those risks was that her focus on the task might blind her to other truths. She placed a sigil on Plangere, mostly meant to remind her to watch him more carefully if he moved too quickly.

She placed a sigil on her distant son Gavin – and did so three times in as many days – and saw her working dispelled each day.

'Gabriel,' she said aloud, but she didn't press the matter.

On her fourth day, her husband summoned her by means of her son Aneas, who knocked and coughed repeatedly, being a polite young man who knew perfectly well what his sorceress mother might be doing on the far side of a closed oak door. She put on an ermine-lined gown and threw a light casting over the floor to protect – and cover – her scrawls, and opened the door.

'Yes?' she said, leaning on the door frame.

Aneas bowed. 'Pater needs you,' he said. 'There's an Imperial officer come.'

She nodded and slipped her feet into bright red leather slippers. Behind her, a dull grey moth flitted across a sunbeam and landed inside the hanging silver lamp of Morean make that dangled from a heavy iron chain in the middle of the room.

The moth caught her eye and she raised a hand and killed it with a thread of green light. Its death created a rainbow spectrum of swirling motes, like dust.

'Oh, Richard!' she said with delight. 'I didn't know you cared.' She smiled.

The Castle of N'gara – Bill Redmede

Redmede woke to find Bess curled around him, her head in the crook of his shoulder, and he remembered their coupling of the night before.

She awoke as she felt him move. Her eyes popped open, and she sat up.

'Damn me,' she said. She was naked under the blankets, and she suddenly shivered, pulled her shirt out of the chaos and pulled it brusquely over her head. 'Got to piss,' she murmured, and walked away, pulling her hose up as she went.

Redmede began to roll the blankets, fighting a barrage of conflicting thoughts. The air was damp and promised rain. His people needed to get under cover before winter came, whatever else the Wild might have in store.

Why on earth had he bedded Bess?

He got the blankets rolled tightly, and found the ties so hastily discarded the night before and tied them tight. He passed the leather strap through the bundle.

Why had he never bedded her before?

He took a long pull from his water bottle and went to piss himself, and wondered where the irk had got to.

He turned and all but ran back into the middle of the camp – except that it wasn't really a camp, but a huddle of survivors gathered around one big fire. A few men were up and armed, but most were merely gathered tight together.

Redmede started giving orders, and three more fires were started, wood was collected, blankets were rolled. Men saw to their weapons, such as they were. After the fight the day before, they were shockingly low on arrows.

Nat Tyler spat. 'We're about done, Bill,' he said, conversationally.

Bill scratched at the beard he'd grown. 'I know,' he said. 'We need food and a strong place.'

'*I can provide both, yesss. For an ally.*' The irk was suddenly right there. Mounted on a great stag with golden horns and golden hooves, it towered over them.

Redmede fell back a step. 'You—'

'*My people came and fetched me, man. But I do not forget a sservicsse. Never. Come feassst in my hallsss. It isss a true invitaissshun.*'

Redmede tried to remember anything he'd heard about the fey folk and their ways, but it all fled his mind when he looked into the irk's ancient eyes. So he turned to Tyler.

Tyler whistled soundlessly. 'Free to come and go again, Fairy Knight?'

'*Yesss. My word upon it, mansss.*'

Redmede looked at Tyler. 'A lifetime of war has taught me never to trust anything more powerful than I am.'

Bess pushed forward and gave the irk a surprisingly good curtsey. 'Tapio!' she said. Her delight was evident.

Indeed, in the grey light of an autumn dawn, the irk looked like a hero of legend. He wore an elegant red surcoat, a belt of links of worked gold like wild roses, each petal enamelled, the centres of jewels. He had flowers – real ones – like a chaplet in his hair, and his enormous blue eyes filled his angelic face. Only the tips of his fangs and his ears and overlong fingers gave away his inhuman origin.

'The fairy knight has offered us refuge,' Tyler said to Bess as she rose from her curtsey.

'We should take it then,' she said. 'My lord – will you succour our wounded men?'

'*It would be my dearessst pleasssure, lady.*' The irk bowed. It was riding a giant stag without a saddle or a bridle, and had a lance and a bow in extravagant sheaths hanging behind it across the animal's withers.

Bess smiled.

'Bill thinks it might be a trap,' Tyler commented.

Redmede shrugged. 'I don't trust lords of any kind,' he said.

'*You ssshould lisssten to your lady-love,*' sang the irk. '*Often it isss the female who hass the greater wisssdom. My love isss often all that keepsss me from folly.*'

Bess and Bill looked at each other and said 'Lady-love?' aloud in the same moment. Bess blushed. Redmede coughed. Tyler flushed and spat.

Bess grabbed at Bill's arm. 'You have no choice,' she whispered fiercely.

Redmede pursed his lips, then bowed – as if doing so hurt him – to the irk lord. 'My— My lord, if you will give us leave when we wish it, and succour our wounded, I would be—' He took in a deep breath. 'I would be in your debt.'

The irk's mount took two silent steps towards them. '*Fear isss the beginning of wisssdom, in the Wild,*' he said. '*You would haf done better to sssave your dissstrussst for Thorn.*'

Redmede nodded. 'Aye,' he admitted.

A day later, he felt as if he'd lived in the irk's castle for half his life, and some of his brother's stories – and other tales mothers told children – were well explained.

The irk's hold was not like a castle of men.

A great finger of land curled out into the body of a huge lake, and all along the finger of stone and earth, huge trees stood like cathedral spires among pillars of rock that appeared at first to be natural. Along the forest floor, hundreds of wigwams stood like oversized bundles of brush gathered by a giant and dropped almost at random. The huts seemed crude from a distance – mere stacks of twigs – but they were cunningly woven with grass mats hanging inside the walls of brush that, on close examination, were grown a-purpose, so that each hut was a single plant, or bush, or tree. The innermost layer was made of heavy rugs of carefully felted wool from the great sheep that wandered free in the woods. Every cabin had a stone hearth – most of them sat on living rock. A few had chimneys like human buildings, and others had only a smoke hole. There were sheep and goats everywhere, and the forest floor of the whole peninsula alternated pine needles and cropped grass. Every building had a carefully wrought door matched to the shape of the structure – all were organic, and none perfectly straight. Indeed, in the whole of the hold, there was not a single line that was entirely straight.

All of them, save a very few, were full of irks, who lived in an indolent comfort that Bill envied. They seemed to tend the sheep and goats as a hobby rather than as work, and parties went out to gather rice or Wild honey to hunt or dance – he saw them come or go, and the products of their labour appeared – a bucket of honey, a dead doe, a basket of kale.

He was watching through a window. His spire of rock was like a keep – he assumed the wind-cut spire had occurred naturally, but the inside was as hollow as a log full of termites and just as packed – simply with irks. The tunnels ran in every direction, up and down and at odd angles, and the warren challenged his sense of direction just to find the jakes, which, thankfully, the Wild creatures seemed to need just as much as he did.

But he knew his way to the Great Hall, and it was there that his sense of time was most ruthlessly challenged, because there was always a feast laid – irks came and went, ate, played their faery harps with a magnificent ferocity that was utterly at variance to what he'd imagined irk music would be, and walked away. They came and went very quickly, and they spoke quickly, and his host sat in a chair of what appeared to be solid gold and laughed, applauded, spoke to this one and that one and never seemed to tire. Or leave his hall.

Nor did his consort, a female irk with a face shaped like a heraldic heart, eyes as big and bright as silver crowns and hair so red that Redmede thought it must have been dyed. She wore a green kirtle with hanging sleeves dagged like oak leaves, and she had by turns the air of a child and of an abbess.

It was his third visit to the hall – he couldn't stop himself, and returned continually – when she turned and saw him, and her eyes widened, if that was possible. She sang an impossibly pure note, a high 'c', and her consort turned to her.

They sang together like a troubadour and his joglar for as long as it might take a man to say a pater noster, if he had been so inclined, and she smiled at Redmede, showing a mouth full of tiny, pointed teeth.

'*Welcome, beautiful stranger,*' she sang.

Liviapolis – Morgan Mortirmir

After the sabbath, Mortirmir returned to his classes at the Academy in a city that was rapidly returning to normal – so rapidly that the siege, the battle and the capture of the Emperor all began to seem like a dream.

Some things were not a dream.

One of the four religious sisters in his medical class on Monday curtsied, and let just a corner of her veil fall away. 'My cousin tells me you helped save the princess,' she breathed. 'I had no idea – you are so young.'

He could only see her mouth, which was a fine, perfectly normal mouth. He instantly mocked himself for imagining that the four nuns were great beauties who had to hide their faces away.

'Are you a Comnena?' he asked.

She tittered. 'Yes,' she said.

It was hardly the stuff of romance, but she didn't call him 'the Plague' even once during a half-day dissection of a pauper's arm.

In the evening, he went back to his rooms over his inn. He had twice the space that Derkensun had, and a fine hearth with its own external chimney – which was the Morean fashion. He read Galeanius for an hour and found he'd learned very little. He decided to write a poem about the Comnena girl, and found that he had nothing to say. So, instead, he read a little poetry in Gallish – all the best courtly poetry was Gallish – and found that his mind was wandering.

Summer was far advanced, but hardly over. The light was still lingering, there was no need to light his fire, and he was bored and lonely and the last three days had opened a remarkable vista of new life.

He buckled on his sword and walked out into the evening. He saw the farm carts rolling in for the Tuesday market, and he waited while a herd of sheep was driven into the butcher's market, and he sat at the edge of the Great Square near the palace and played chess with a stranger – a Moor from Ifriqu'ya who beat him after a long game. They shared a cup of tea in companionable silence and the Moor went off to his bed and Mortirmir went back to his. Nothing exciting had happened. He fell asleep wondering if the peak of his existence had been reached at age fifteen and a half.

The next morning he arose feeling adventurous, and he walked to the palace – where he had the password – and attended matins in the first light with the soldiers in the Outer Court. Giorgos Comnenos grinned at him and slapped his back. 'Good of you to join us, barbarian, but if you hang around here, I'll put you in uniform.'

Mortirmir smiled and spread his hands. 'But that would be wonderful,' he admitted.

'Aren't you a student at the University?' Comnenos asked.

'Yes,' Mortirmir said.

'You're exempt from military duty then,' Comnenos said. 'Far too important. Aren't you supposed to be in class?'

'Not for an hour,' Mortirmir admitted. 'I was bored.'

Comnenos nodded. Mortirmir had seldom had a friend so worldly and handsome – and older – and the other man's willingness to listen to him was like a tonic. 'Well, take a note to my fiancée for me, then,' he said, and beckoned to his servant for papyrus.

'Suddenly I'm an officer,' he said. 'Here, take this for her. No poaching, barbarian.'

He found Anna by the gate.

'I heard you were here,' she said. 'The palace looks enormous, but really it's just a little town full of gossip. Will you bring my clothes and things from Harald's? He will be in barracks for weeks to come.' She smiled up at him. 'I'm sure he wants to thank you for fetching the doctor.'

In two days replete with adventures, finding a Yahudat scholar at midnight had hardly made his list of events. The man was so famous in the Yahudat quarter that the guards had fetched him before the bells had rung a single change.

'And you will stay here?' Mortirmir asked.

She smiled. 'Nordikans are very direct.' She laughed. 'But I'm coming to like them. And I'm welcome here.'

He agreed to bring her things and trotted to his history lecture. He was late, but much happier. Only to find that the class devolved into a tour of the Academy Library, a collection of four thousand scrolls and books dating from the foundation of the Empire in distant Ruma. He was good at research so he scarcely attended to the lesson until they were deep in the archives below the old rostra where the Senate still met on occasion.

But the librarian had elected to take them to the map room, and when he produced a chart of the ground near Chaluns in Arles, Mortirmir snapped to attention.

'Saint Aetius himself handled this map!' said the librarian reverently. He placed a glowing globe of blue-white light over the middle of the map. When the nuns leaned in to look more closely, he courteously moved the light source to them, leaving Mortirmir to stare at it in shadowy frustration.

So he provided his own light. There was an illumination of an irk in beautiful, naturalistic strokes in his corner. He smiled at it, committing the picture to memory, and some time passed before he noticed the silence.

All of his classmates were looking at him. And the librarian pursed his lips and vouchsafed him a small nod and the barest hair's breadth of a smile.

'Oh,' he said. 'Yes. I – umm ... Yes.' He grinned in sudden triumph. He hadn't even thought about making the light. He hadn't even entered his memory palace to do it.

Antonio Baldesce, the Venike boy in his class, invited him to share a cup of wine. It wasn't epochal, and he knew he was too young to be good company, but Baldesce was friendly instead of condescending.

'You know Abraham Ben Rabbi?' Baldesce asked.

Morgan shrugged. 'I met him through a friend.'

'And you met the new mercenary?' Baldesce continued.

'Not so much met,' Morgan said. 'He was not awake when I was there. I wasn't introduced. Not to anyone.' He remembered the older woman who burned like a torch with raw *potentia*. That sight he would take to his grave.

'Don't trust the old man, that's all I'm saying. The Yahudat are venal beyond belief. Most of them serve the Wild in secret.' Baldesce nodded. 'If you go to the palace again, will you tell me? I might want to send a message to a friend.'

As Morgan emerged from his first social evening with a 'friend' from the Academy, he thought about Baldesce, who had never been particularly nice to him before now, and so obviously seemed to want something from him. A servant fetched his cloak, and Baldesce paused to answer a hermetical summons.

It occurred to Mortirmir that he might hang on to all the slights his colleagues had paid him. There were twenty-seven other students – serious, full-time hermetical students – in his study, and none of them had previously paid him the slightest heed, except to mock his failures or his efforts. He'd seen himself – too young, too arrogant, an utterly inept barbarian – so clearly through their eyes that only two weeks before, he'd contemplated ending his life.

Now he finished his cup of wine and told Baldesce that he needed to study, and the older boy nodded and went with him all the way to the door. 'They say that the later you come to your powers, the more powerful you will be,' said the scion of the Venike bankers.

Mortirmir searched his face for signs of mockery and found none, so he laughed. 'In that case, I expect be very powerful indeed,' he said. 'I'm still in shock,' he admitted.

Baldesce smiled too. 'Come for a drink again,' he said.

Mortirmir buckled on his sword and went out into the falling darkness. He walked across three squares to fetch Anna's things from Derkensun's inn and made sure that Stella and her husband had been paid for their food. In that neighbourhood, at least, he had a hero's welcome, and he had no choice but to drink three cups of wine. Back at his own inn, and a little drunk, he fell into bed without undressing.

The next morning he had rhetoric and memory, two of the most difficult classes. If he had needed a lesson in how much had changed in his studies, rhetoric was that lesson – his inability to manipulate the *ops* had forced him to work very hard indeed in classes that did not involve direct hermeticism, and rhetoric had been one of them. Yet – now that he had even the slightest command of the *aether*, he understood as never before *why* the study of logic and grammar were so essential.

'If you listen any harder, your tongue will loll out like a dog's,' said one of the nuns. He couldn't tell them apart, but from her familiarity he had to assume she was Comnenos's cousin. She had a magnificent set of lapis and ivory prayer beads on the girdle of her gown and he decided to use their fancy beads to name them – he christened the taller one 'Lapis' and the shorter one 'Coral'.

He listened to the master grammarian say exactly the same things he'd said in every other class, and yet—

He considered the logik of the grammarian's argument, and he applied it to the creation of light, and instead of the usual globe he made a perfect cube of blue-white light appear over his right shoulder.

The master grammarian didn't pause in his lecture, which was largely based on the letters of a number of early Imperial senators. He wrote his usual scurrilous, slightly naughty Archaic verse on the blackboard at the end of class, but instead of twirling his long robe and stalking away down the long halls towards his lunch, he reached out an ascetic hand and grasped Mortirmir's shoulder.

'Now make a pyramid,' he said.

Mortirmir did. His own confusion over whether it should have a square base or a triangular base made him to create an amorphous blob. It vanished in a *blop* of consternation, and he tried again, structuring his argument more clearly. It was difficult, because the threads of argument needed to be rooted in his memory palace, which was not all it should have been. In fact—

But he made a pyramid of light.

'Now make it red,' said the grammarian.

Mortirmir managed a shocking salmon pink.

'Is the creation of light a true working, or an illusion?' asked the grammarian.

Mortirmir saw that several of his fellow students had stayed behind. The question was not directed to him alone.

Two of the nuns raised black-robed hands.

'Yes?' said the grammarian.

'Obviously it is a true working, since illusionary light would cast no light?' said the nun that Mortirmir thought was the Comnena.

'Oh, it is obvious, is it?' asked the grammarian. He opened his hand, and a perfect pearl shone in the palm of his hand. 'True making, or illusion?' he asked.

'Illusion,' said Baldesce.

'Correct, young Antonio. If I could create a pearl this perfect with so little effort, I would be the richest man in the city.' The grammarian held his pearl up.

'But to make the illusion work, you must make it both bend and

312

emit light – as if it is actually there.' Mortirmir put his hand over the teacher's hand, and indeed, the pearl emitted the faintest glow.

'By God's mercy there is one of you paying attention,' said the grammarian. 'You're – Mortirmir, aren't you? Roger?'

'Morgan, maestro.'

'Of course. Barbarism piled on barbarism. There is no Saint Morgan.' The grammarian smiled – only from one side of his mouth. 'You have finally come into your powers, I take it?'

'I think so,' Mortirmir said.

'There is no such thing as illusion. Or, contrarily, everything is an illusion.' The maestro raised his wand and suddenly there was a great, horned daemon standing in the middle of the room.

Mortirmir hadn't seen so much hermeticism displayed since he arrived. 'But – I can't see any *ops*.'

'Well said. Anyone else care to admit the same?' asked the master.

There was some shuffling.

'Of course you cannot. Because I have placed the entire suggestion directly into your eyes.' The daemon vanished. 'It's an incredibly difficult manipulation, but one that is undetectable. What does it prove?'

There was a long and heavy silence.

'Well, well. Figure it out for yourselves. Mortirmir, you need to work much harder in memory.'

'Yes, maestro.' Mortirmir shook his head, still able to *see* the image of the daemon – on the back of his eyeballs, as his father used to say.

'I think I hate him,' said the smallest nun.

'You just don't like to think so hard,' said the tallest nun. 'Why did you make your light in the form of a cube, Ser Morgan?'

Mortirmir bowed. 'For fun, demoiselle.' He tried to imagine what she looked like. 'I suddenly understood what all the grammar was for.'

Baldesce laughed. 'Tell me!' he said.

'It's the code we use. I'm sure Wild workers use a different code, but we use grammar to structure the power. Right?'

The other students nodded. 'Of course,' Baldesce snorted with some of his accustomed derision.

'But in High Archaic, we can shape a sentence many ways and never change the meaning—', Mortirmir was struggling with the words to fuel his concept.

'Yes,' said Baldesce.

'But at the same time we can speak of things with such precision that—'

Baldesce all but slapped his own forehead. 'Of course,' he said. 'I had only thought to manipulate the *ops* in the mould of creation. You are speaking of making minute changes to the mould itself – and to how the power fills that mould.'

The taller nun reached out a hand and produced a glowing, scarlet pyramid that threw a strong red light.

Baldesce, stung, made his bigger.

The smaller nun made hers very small indeed, and the three of them laughed. They were – by far – the three best students.

Mortirmir rolled the logic of his argument around for a moment and produced two.

They all applauded.

In the corridor, the taller nun – Lapis – bent her head slightly. 'I'm Eugenia,' she said.

'I'm Katerina,' Pearl murmured.

'Tancreda,' said the third, whom he had called 'Coral' in the privacy of his thoughts. Now that he really looked at them, he could see other distinguishing marks.

'I'm the Plague,' he returned. But he grinned as he said it.

They all giggled.

I may yet come to be good at this, he realised.

They had two hours between rhetoric and memory, and they were walking across the square to an open-air taverna that only existed to serve the students when the Imperial gates opened and two men rode out – both wearing red.

Sister Anna watched the man ride by. 'Handsome – just as Giorgos said. That's the new mercenary. He calls himself the Duke of Thrake, but of course he's not really.'

Baldesce raised an eyebrow. 'I think he really is. He beat the former Duke pretty thoroughly last week. And my father hates him with a perfect, pure hate.'

Sister Katerina leaned out over their table in a very undignified way. 'He's going to the University!' she proclaimed.

'Why does your father hate him?' asked Mortirmir.

'My father is Podesta of the Etruscan merchants here,' he said.

'He was summoned to the palace and threatened. Or that's how he tells it.' Baldesce spoke with the amused tolerance of sons for fathers.

'I'm sure that the Patriarch will put him in his place,' Baldesce said. 'But he cuts a fine figure. He's Alban, like you, Mortirmir.'

Mortirmir resolved to like him.

Memory was a torture. In the first five minutes he learned that the master had ignored him because he had no access to Power. Now that that had changed, he was expected to catch up. Preferably by the end of the class.

That didn't happen.

He was called on more in two hours than he had been since his studies began, given odd geometric shapes and other memory objects to store in his palace, and then asked to reproduce them. He failed – sometimes he barely failed and then, as he got increasingly flustered and frustrated, he failed more and more spectacularly.

The memory master was remorseless and, at the end of class, he took Mortirmir aside. 'Your failure to memorise even the simplest form is shocking,' he said.

Mortirmir wondered, in the safety of his head, if he could turn the man to ash. He certainly had enough rage and frustration to fuel a really powerful working.

'I'll – work – on – my – memory palace,' he said through clenched teeth.

The memory master shrugged. 'Oh, do as you please,' he said. He swept out of the hall.

'He likes to do that,' Baldesce said.

'He's never picked on me before,' said Mortirmir, who was very close to crying and didn't want to give way in public. *Sweet Jesu, I can kill a man with fire, but I can't face a mocking maestro.*

'You weren't worth his time, before.' Baldesce shook his head. 'I'd invite you for wine, but I really think you'd best go work on your memory. I've been the target of his attentions myself and I really owe you – that's the easiest I've had it in that class this year. Now that he has his teeth in you, he won't let go.' The Etruscan smiled. 'It's your own fault. When you had no Power, none of them cared.'

Mortirmir decided after a moment that the Etruscan didn't mean his raillery to be offensive. The social acceptance from his classmates came at a price – now he had to pay attention to what they said. He'd been distancing himself from them for so long . . .

'After a little consideration, I'll keep my access to Power and go work on my memory,' he said, as if he'd really considered ridding himself of Power.

Baldesce slapped him on the back and laughed.

I really can do this, Mortirmir thought.

'Going to the palace today?' Baldesce asked. It was clumsily asked, and his face told them both he knew it.

But Mortirmir was starting to like the other boy, so he shrugged. 'I don't think so,' he said.

Mortirmir stopped and picked up Anna's things, and carried them to the palace, where he wasted an hour waiting because the watchword had been changed. An enormous Galle stood by the gate, watching with his hands on his hips, and Mortirmir, feeling hurt and angry, locked eyes with the man.

'Who is this little lordling?' growled the giant to the gate guards. But he spoke in Alban, and the guards spoke only Archaic. Mortirmir thought it might be too foolish to translate.

So he bowed. 'I'm Alban,' he said to the giant.

'Hah!' said the giant. He had black hair and a nose as big as a horse. 'I'm not, little man.' He looked down. 'What's your business here? Pimp?' He eyed the armful of woman's clothing.

Mortirmir considered a range of responses. 'No,' he said sullenly. 'I brought these for a friend.'

'Why are you standing here, then?' asked the giant.

'I had the password but it has been changed, and now I'm waiting for my friend to come to the gate.' Mortirmir looked around.

'Who gave you the password, then?' asked the giant with a wicked smile.

'I did,' said Harald Derkensun. He was obviously off-duty, and wore plain clothing, a long tunic with a fancy soldier's belt, and a short sword. 'He brought us food – before you came and defeated the Duke.' Harald grinned. 'Before the new Duke defeated the traitors,' he corrected himself.

The black-haired giant shook his head. 'You're the loon who killed all the assassins and cleared the throne,' he said. 'And found the doctor who helped the Captain. Which is to say the Duke.'

Harald spread his hands. 'I had help.' He smiled. 'And this young man fetched the doctor.'

The other man bowed. 'I'm Ser Thomas. You are in my "above suspicion" pile, and so is your friend. Now.' He took a playing card out of his purse. 'Name?'

'Morgan Mortirmir, of Harndon.'

'Well, Master Harndon, the password is *Parthenos* and the counter-sign is *Athena*. Your name will be on the guardroom list.' He nodded to both men and walked rapidly away to look into a wagon led by a pair of palace Ordinaries, fresh from the butcher's market.

'What an arsehole,' Mortirmir said.

Harald shook his head. 'I disagree. He was as courteous as he needed to be. He made no threats. And these mercenaries have made the gate much safer. Twice now they have taken spies. I think you were close to being taken yourself.'

Behind Mortirmir a vicious-looking Alban with red hair said, 'Let's just see your bill of lading, then, laddy,' and a young Imperial messenger translated for him. Four men began to take the wagon apart.

'I brought Anna's clothes,' Mortirmir said. In fact, he realised, anyone who looked at his bundle of faded silk would know his errand.

Harald led him into the warm darkness of the Nordikan barracks, where he was jostled repeatedly by much larger men who seemed to converse by shouting at the top of their lungs. He looked into the mess hall, where two men were rolling on the floor, locked in what appeared to be mortal combat, and he looked in wonder at the magnificent carvings – knights, dragons, wolves, irks – that festooned every beam and every wooden surface.

Anna was sitting on a bed reading by the light of a pair of glassed windows set high on the wall. As soon as she saw Mortirmir, she bounced to her feet. 'Clothes!' she said. She came and kissed the young man, who felt himself blushing to the tips of his fingers. Anna didn't give a chaste kiss. Even her kiss on the cheek carried a world of meaning.

When he had told them all the news he knew – the new Duke of Thrake had moved a permanent garrison into the old naval yard and the word on the street was that he intended to build ships there – he'd gone in person to visit the University . . .

'He's just a barbarian,' said Anna. 'He won't change anything.'

*

He had no classes on Friday, so he went out to the ruins of the Temple of Athena and worked on his memory palace. He walked the ruins and then he began to sketch, drawing each pillar from different angles. He worked all day, filling sixty sheets of heavy papyrus with charcoal sketches that weren't very good – but would serve as aide-memoires, and the very act of drawing them seemed to improve his mental image of the place.

His drawing didn't seem to disturb the middle-aged man who was sitting with his back to the easternmost column, watching the old harbour. The Temple of Athena was ideally situated to watch the old harbour – high on its own acropolis, which the history master said predated the Archaic occupation.

'Would you care for some cider?' Mortirmir asked the man.

'I'm partial to cider,' the watcher admitted. He rose, dusting off his green gown. 'Stephan,' he said. He drank off a cup of cider and gave Mortirmir a very good piece of bread in return, and went back to his watching.

Mortirmir was sketching the capital of his nineteenth column when he saw the man stiffen like a pointer seeing its prey.

Mortirmir followed the man's attention to see the approach of two lines of galleys with three tall round ships between them.

He didn't believe what he was seeing. Or rather, he was surprised to have such a very good view. His fellow students – Baldesce especially – had predicted an attack by the Etruscans, but this was somehow balder and more real than he'd expected.

The Etruscan squadron bore down on the old naval arsenal at the speed of oarsmen rowing at a regular cruising pace. The attack was unhurried, despite the lateness of the hour.

At the distance of several hundred yards, it was difficult to see exactly what had gone wrong. But suddenly the lead galley's bow fell off course, and the next ship in line collided with it – not heavily, but hard enough to make the other man wince.

A third ship carried on, straight for the gap between the two moles that guarded the entrance to the ancient naval yard.

Even across the distance, the massive volley of arrows was visible – rising like pinpoints of red light in the sunset. The third galley in line seemed to strike a barrier.

The other ships turned away – all of them, including the first two galleys and the round ships, which had to carry on into the current of the strait and then turn almost glacially to port. But the former third ship was struck – appeared to be struck – by another massive flight of arrows. The man who had shared his cider groaned aloud at the sight.

The injured ship behaved a like a hunted whale, wallowing broadside to its tormentors on the wall, oars thrashing the water like the flukes of a wounded sea-beast, unable to muster enough speed to get clear of the merciless raking of the arrows from the sea wall.

The current pressed it closer to the land.

Something grabbed it, like the hand of God, and began to pull it inexorably into the naval yard. Mortirmir found that he was standing, fists clenched, like a man watching the end of a foot race. He didn't even know which side he supported – although now that he had time to breathe, he decided that he sided with the city and the new Duke.

They had grappling irons set in the Etruscan galley. That's how it was being dragged into the yard. But *potentia* played like fire and lightning in the *aether*, and even at this distance Mortirmir was aware of the point at which the hermeticist on the galley was overcome and died.

Dark trickles had become visible where the scuppers opened. Men were dying on the oar benches, and their blood ran down the sides of the ship. Yet not a scrap of the sound carried to the ancient acropolis, and instead he heard a girl singing an Archaic song.

His companion spat angrily. 'Idiots!' he said aloud, and he gathered his pilgrim's scrip and walked away, his booted feet crunching on the ancient gravel. He was still shaking his head when he walked down the ancient acropolis.

It occurred to Mortirmir, at about the moment when the middle-aged man in green vanished through a city gate, that his presence was possibly suspicious.

Tyrin, County of Arelat, South-Eastern Galle – Clarissa de Sartre

Few things are as difficult for a young adult as a retreat to the nest.

Clarissa de Sartre was a descendant of the now lost kings of Arelat. Her father was one of the greatest lords of the mountains, with four hundred knights at his back and nine great castles.

So it did not please her particularly to walk through the gates of the family's great winter hold at Tyrin, in the relative warmth of the great highland valley of the Duria. The gates were as high as six men, and bound in iron; the road entered the castle through a massive double barbican that was viewed by the count's neighbours as impregnable.

Clarissa had walked almost a hundred leagues through late autumn into early winter. She had huddled twice under ledges with no fire, and had spent one night in a camp of men she distrusted deeply, but they had offered her neither leers nor violence. She was filthy; she had not had her mouse-brown wool kirtle or her linens off since she escaped the nunnery. Her breath stank inside her stolen wool scarf.

She was more than a little proud of having made it home, alive and unraped. She had stolen food, and noted the places from which she had stolen.

None of the gate guards knew her. Pierro, one of her father's hard men, patted her bottom absently as he reached into her scrip for a donation.

He looked at her, his watery blue eyes devoid of malice. 'A girl has some options,' he said with a smile that reeked of garlic.

Clarissa decided that she'd reached the end of impostature. She put up a hand. There were merchants behind her – the scene was public enough. 'I don't think the count would approve,' she said in her mother's tones.

Pierro stiffened. 'Oh, if you plan to be difficult—' He leaned forward, the vacant eyes suddenly focused. 'Saint Maurice! By the Virgin's cunt, Giacopo!' he shouted, and rang the alarm bell.

Clarissa sat amidst her mother's ladies. Her father was wearing hunting clothes – a quilted green pourpoint in deerskin, boots that went all the way to his hip and buckled on the sides – and her mother wore the woman's equivalent: a neat mannish cote that she rendered feminine, a pert green hat and long skirts. She wore a sword; the count wore a long knife and held a whip in his hands.

'They told me you were *dead*.' The count was not a dull man, but he said the words for the sixth time.

His wife, Anne, watched him carefully. 'We are not about to declare war upon the King of Galle. However much he may be a fool.' She was Etruscan – a cousin of the Queen of Galle. She had the long straight nose and imperious eyebrows of her line.

'They told me you were dead,' the count said.

'Please stop saying that, Papa,' Clarissa said.

He came forward suddenly and threw his arms around her. 'Jesus and Mary, my little buttercup! We thought you were dead! And you are not! This is the best news to come to me in my life!'

Anne's brow cleared. She joined the embrace, and the three of them sat for a while as the ladies shifted around them. Off in the yard, dogs barked. A trio of local noblemen, all dressed for the hunt, were nervously fidgeting in the doorway to the main hall.

Anne smiled at her husband, usually so reserved and now weeping. 'My sweet, go and see to your dogs,' she said.

He stood up from where he'd knelt by Clarissa and relinquished her hand. 'Of course, love,' he said. He took a handkerchief from one of Anne's ladies and wiped his face and beamed at them all.

'Come, gentlemen. Forgive me – it is not every day that a lost child returns.' He bowed, his gentlemen bowed, and they were off to the yard.

'Out,' Anne ordered her ladies.

They fled, after pouring hippocras and providing a tray of delicacies.

Anne sat in a cushioned chair and folded her booted legs on a stool. 'So,' she said.

Clarissa met her eye. Her mother had always been her favourite. But they fought like cats, which was one reason her doting father had sent her to court in the first place.

Anne took her hand. 'I have guesses, my dear. I grew up at court. But you do not seem ... broken.'

'The King tried to rape me,' Clarissa said. Her voice caught on the word, but she managed to go on. 'Uncle saved me, but then arranged that I be dismissed from court.'

Anne nodded decisively. 'This much I have in a dozen letters from supposedly helpful *friends*.' She sneered. 'Your father will not let me send them poison.'

It was difficult for Clarissa to know how much to believe her mother, who spoke as if she was as bloodthirsty as some Wild creature.

Anne leaned forward. 'We are told you attempted to seduce the King.' Anne put a hand on her daughter's hand and clasped it. 'Sweeting, I am a woman. I know that these things can happen—'

'Mama!' Clarissa didn't quite shriek. 'I was playing music and he tried to throw me to the floor and put his knees between mine!'

Anne sat back and smiled. 'Yes,' she said.

'He smashed my best—'

'He is, for good or evil, the King,' Anne said. 'Why Galle, which should be the greatest land in all the world, has to have a line of fools as kings . . . Well, it has been discussed by greater heads than mine or yours.' She leaned forward again and kissed her daughter. 'I didn't see you as much of a seducer, my love.'

Clarissa could writhe even at that. But the incident itself was still so sharp – so clear – that she ignored her mother's words. Her mother seemed to believe that only she, Anne of Soave, had ever possessed the ability to charm men, but Clarissa steadied herself. *My mother is trying to be on my side.*

I'll take that.

She reached out and hugged her mother, and hung on her neck for a moment.

'Now we must marry you to someone, quickly,' Anne said.

That night, Clarissa was summoned to her father. He sat in the Great Hall with a dozen of his knights, playing cards. There were women present; mostly wives, but not all. Her father called these 'camp evenings' and insisted, when he held them, that his hall became a military camp, with its relaxed etiquette and air of masculinity.

Even as she entered the hall, she felt the tension. And smelled an odd smell – a feral, musky smell.

Clarissa curtsied. Her father was sitting with Ser Raimondo, his first lance, and Ser Jean de Chablais, one of the best knights in all Galle and her father's closest friend and adviser. Raimondo's wife Catherine smiled at her.

'Come share my cup, poppet,' she said.

They were all very clingy. Catherine put a hand on her shoulder. Jean de Chablais kissed her hand.

She felt the warmth of their affecton and she needed it.

'We are considering sending a challenge to the King,' her father said.

De Chablais nodded. 'My lord, you must. My lady Clarissa I beg your forgiveness, but as your father's champion I must ask—'

Clarissa sat straight. 'Ask,' she said.

'The King—'

'Tried to force his sex on me,' Clarissa said. 'And was only prevented by monsieur my uncle.'

De Chablais coloured – he was not a soft man, and not given to blushes. He bowed his head.

'I beg your pardon, mademoiselle, even for asking.' Turning to his lord, he said, 'By God, if you will not challenge him in your own name, I will challenge him myself.'

The count sat back and made a steeple of his hands. 'Jean, you know it is not that simple.'

'It *is* simple. Sometimes, it is simple. This is what knighthood is for: to protect the weak. To war on the strong when they abuse their power.'

Ser Raimondo nodded, his red hair glinting in the firelight. There was more grey there than Clarissa remembered. 'My lord, we must. Or others will think the slanders true.'

The count frowned. 'And the other matter?' he asked.

Catherine stiffened.

Clarissa leaned forward. 'What other matter?' she asked.

Ser Raimondo made a wry face. 'Didn't your mother tell you of our family's other new affliction?' he asked.

His wife put out her arm. 'Don't!' she said, but the knight reached for a crumpled cloth on the floor and flipped it back.

Underneath it lay a thing out of nightmare – all teeth and green and yellow mottled skin and blood and entrails. The smell, the musky animal smell, filled the hall.

Clarissa shrieked. Then she stiffened and cursed inwardly, disdaining to be the kind of woman who shrieked.

'What is it?' she asked.

Her father pointed to the illustrated manuscript under his hand. 'We think it is an irk,' he said.

Liviapolis – Julas Kronmir

Kronmir lived on the edge of his own fear. He'd almost killed the boy in the ruins because he couldn't get over the notion that the boy had been sent to watch him, even when it became obvious that he was bent on sketching the antiquities in the temple.

Kronmir was a scholar, and he was not unmoved by the wonders of the temple, but his employer's entire plan depended on the pressure that the Etruscans could exert on the palace. He cursed their arrogant foolishness silently as he watched their fleet come up the channel with no attempt at diversion or surprise – and ploughed straight into the chain that the mercenary had placed across the mouth of the naval yard.

The chain's presence had been reported to him by a whore and a suborned workman, and he'd reported it three days earlier. Along with a complete rundown of the foreign mercenary's intentions towards the Academy, and towards the Etruscan merchants, gleaned from his two sources inside the palace. And his report on the unreliability of several of the company's archers and of a faction in the Nordikans troop who were willing to change sides. And his losses – four men in two days, and his only hermetical assassin.

Kronmir was a professional, and he predicted the result of the Etruscan attack even as he watched it. He shook his head.

'Is this how God feels, watching men commit sin?' he asked the gathering darkness.

He had one consolation – he hadn't killed the harmless boy sketching the ruins.

He slipped back into the city to write another report. His dockyard worker would probably never report in again – that would be the least consequence of the Etruscan defeat.

Perhaps the whore would.

North of the Great River – The Black Knight

Ser Hartmut Li Orguelleus stood on Oliver de Marche's quarter deck watching the land roll past them on both sides – forests so deep and still as to seem holy. The Black Knight was in full harness, as always, and now every sailor, every marine, and even the ship's boys wore whatever scraps of leather and mail they could muster.

'It is magnificent,' Ser Harmut said. 'I had no idea. As vast as Ifriqu'ya?' he said, turning to the captain.

De Marche shook his head. 'I don't know. The Etruscans have sent a dozen expeditions around the northern capes, and more to the south. That much I've heard from our fisherfolk, my lord. But either none of them have returned, or they keep what they have learned close to their greasy Etruscan chests.'

Early autumn had gilded the forests, so that birches and maples were just turning gold or red, and the effect in the distance was to touch the green vista with a warmth that the chill air belied. The enormous river ran between heights – vast heights – that rose from wide plains on either shore, as if they sailed in a long and narrow bowl. A west wind filled their sails, and they had white foam at their bows from the rapidity of their passage.

'Are we close to our port?' asked the Black Knight.

De Marche shook his head. 'My lord, I don't know. This expedition was based on information provided by a traitor – an Etruscan seeking refuge from a family quarrel. I had expected him to travel with us. Unfortunately, he seems to have been killed – murdered, I believe.'

Ser Harmut nodded. 'The Etruscan guilds have very long arms,' he admitted.

'There will be no port, per se,' de Marche added. 'A clearing in the woods, and a beach, is the best we can expect. But the Genuan ships we found – their destruction means we will be first to the market.'

'Market be damned. We are here for a far nobler cause,' Ser Harmut said.

De Marche took a careful breath. 'Are we, my lord?' he asked. Talking to Ser Harmut was a delicate exercise. The death of his favourite squire and the results of the combat against the Eeeague had thrown Ser Harmut into de Marche's company, but the knight was a dark and difficult man, and never a companion.

'We will take one of Alba's wall castles,' Ser Harmut said. 'And lead an Outwaller invasion.'

De Marche blinked his eyes. 'Which castle, my lord?'

'Ticondaga,' Ser Hartmut said. 'Do you know it?'

De Marche scratched his beard. 'It's much further west than I had anticipated our travelling,' he said. 'We are almost as far as I sailed on my last expedition. According to our Imperial chart, Ticondaga is another three hundred leagues up the Great River. The river will grow narrower each day, and the risk of running aground grows accordingly. Even losing a single ship—'

Ser Hartmut nodded. 'Take care, then,' he said. 'We cannot hope to succeed with any less than all three ships and all of our soldiers.'

De Marche took two full breaths. 'My lord, my men are sailors, not soldiers, and we expected to rest and—' he dropped his voice and spoke as if he was using a dirty word to a child '—trade.'

Ser Hartmut smiled. 'I know. But your men have more than proven themselves worthy of better lives. We will lay siege to Ticonaga.'

De Marche took another deep breath. 'My lord, the fortress there is reputed to be one of the strongest in the world – it was built by the ancients.'

Ser Hartmut nodded. 'All the more honour when we take it. Fear not, master mariner! God will provide.'

De Marche looked at Ser Hartmut, and his thoughts must have shown in his face, because the Black Knight smiled.

'You are surprised to hear me speak of God? Listen, master mariner, I am a knight. I kill the enemies of my king and my religion. Men hate me because, in the end, I always succeed. Men decry my methods because they are themselves jealous, weak, or foolish. War is butchery. What matter if I use alchemy? Hermetical magic? If Satan himself were to offer me his aid—' He smiled.

De Marche thought *I don't really want to get into this.* But his curiosity got the better of him, as it always did. 'Satan's aid to help God?' he asked.

'Every cause has a traitor,' the Black Knight said. 'Even Satan's.' He nodded.

Ten days sail up the Great River and they passed two Outwaller 'castles', both built on high promontories, and both walled with palisades and densely woven thorn fences. The sailors called out to pretty Outwaller girls on the banks and had arrows shot at them for their pains.

De Marche watched the Outwaller communities go by with something akin to his sailor's unrequited lust. But Ser Hartmut had a letter from the King, and despite de Marche's knowledge that he'd been used, he did as he was ordered.

But the eleventh day gave him new hope for his trade. He'd cut the rations to all his men, officers and knights included, and the resulting meals had brought Ser Hartmut on deck in an ingratiating mood, if such a thing were possible to the Black Knight.

'If I gave you leave to trade at one of these huddles of barbarian huts, would we have better food?' he asked.

'I expect we might have venison and corn, my lord. Perhaps even bread. But I would have to explore. Trade is never quick.' De Marche wanted to be off the ship with all his heart, exploring the interior, meeting the people, finding new routes. But offending Ser Hartmut was nothing but a death sentence.

The Black Knight looked over the bow for some time. 'Very well,' he said. 'Our task will only be eased by winning the trust of the peasants.'

De Marche didn't expect Ser Hartmut would win their trust, but he was willing to see him try, and so, when mid-morning of the twelfth day on the Great River revealed a third Outwaller town on a great island in the river, he anchored in the lee of the island and summoned Lucius.

'Shouldn't you be in harness?' Ser Hartmut asked. 'With a retinue? I would be delighted to accompany you.'

De Marche shook his head. 'My lord, I beg you to accept my guidance in this. If we afright or affront these folk, they will do no trade with us, nor be our allies in any way. We need to approach them with gifts, kind words and open hands.'

Ser Hartmut looked over the side at the island town. 'We have the resources to storm the town,' he said. 'Failing Ticondaga, this would make a fair base for the King.'

De Marche cleared his throat. 'I'm sure we could storm it, my lord,' he said. 'However, I'm not sure we could hold it. Perhaps I have not fully explained that just as each holding in Galle is itself part of a larger holding of a greater lord, so most of the Outwallers are vassals of Lords of the Wild.'

'Daemons of hell, you mean?' asked the Black Knight. A light kindled in his eye and his hand went to his sword.

De Marche caught Lucius's eye. 'Not exactly,' he said.

He and Lucius rowed themselves in a small open boat. As soon as they were well clear of the ship, Lucius said, 'When you told him that your Etruscan source was dead—'

De Marche grunted and pulled his oar. The river was choppy and they were rowing into a brisk headwind. There were a dozen Outwallers on the beach, and two of them wore the long squirrel robes that were the mark of noblemen, along with elaborate caps like crowns. But it was dangerous to draw parallels. Any free Huran could wear the *gustaweh*. They were not quite crowns.

'Lucius, would I shock you if I said that Ser Hartmut and I do not have the same goals for this expedition?' he asked.

Lucius looked away. 'He's terrifying.'

'If he knew how much you know,' de Marche said, 'I fear that he'd—' He paused. There were now more than fifty men on the beach. Some had spears – steel-tipped spears.

Lucius nodded. 'The Northern Huran are among the most powerful tribes. If our fleet failed this summer then there are bales of furs in every longhouse waiting for the trade. By the gentle Christ, look at them!'

They were three hundred yards from shore, and now there were a thousand Outwallers waiting for them on the shingle.

They landed, and eager hands took their boat and pulled it high up the beach so that the little coracle seemed to skim the ground the way it had skimmed the waves. When de Marche stepped over the side he was embraced, pinched, and prodded by a hundred men and as many women – mostly older women in furs, with beads and quillwork on every robe.

Lucius, who spoke a fair version of Huran, was immediately surrounded by leaders – a dozen men and four women – and de Marche made his way to the Etruscan's side.

'The thieving barbarians have taken my dagger,' de Marche said.

Lucius smiled. 'I told you not to bring a knife,' he said. 'Relax. Your dagger is a small price to pay for their love. As I thought, there has been no Etruscan fleet this year. The silkies who killed the Genuans have left these folk bereft. They are in a war with their southern cousins, and they have no bolts for their crossbows, no armour – Desontarius here was just telling me that they are on the point of making peace, and our arrival will allow them to make war.'

De Marche blew air out through his cheeks. 'It seems all the world makes war,' he muttered.

Lucius seemed taller and more commanding. 'By God, I will crush my cousins,' he said. 'We have the whole of the trade – it is God's will. We will be rich!'

Chapter Ten

Sauce

The Squash Country – Ota Qwan

Their march back through the Wild was rapid, and made the trip out look easy.

They sighted Crannog People each day. The giants didn't move cautiously – indeed, they tended to leave a path of destruction wherever they went, whether in the woods, across a marsh, or along the edge of a trail, as if they visited destruction on plants and rocks as easily as on animals or creatures of the Wild. Ota Qwan sent his best trackers out on wide sweeps, and moved them from one cover to the next with the canny precision of a soldier.

Ta-se-ho shook his head after the third day. 'I've never seen so many Ruk,' he admitted. 'Something has kicked their nest.'

The going was slow because of the heavy, sticky, ungainly buckets of honey, which the warriors carried on long yokes. A strong man could carry four buckets all day on a clear trail, but as soon as they left the main paths, the difficulty of negotiating the narrower capillaries of the Wild with yokes on their shoulders began to remind Nita Qwan of his days as a slave in the mountains east of Albinkirk.

By the time they reached their village they'd seen twenty giants, and they hadn't lost a man, and Ota Qwan's reputation as a leader had reached new heights. They had harvested almost fifty bark buckets of Wild honey, and they hadn't lost one on the dangerous journey back.

Any sense of triumph was immediately overturned by the obvious sense of crisis that pervaded the village. Ruk had devastated a pair of villages at the eastern corner of the Sossag holdings. Only a few of the People had been killed – the Ruk enjoyed general devastation too much to focus on small prey – but the survivors became refugees at the edge of winter, and the trickle of new faces threatened to consume any surplus the Sossag had gathered after a spring spent at war.

The matrons met and talked, and summoned the Horned One, the old shaman who knew the lore of the land, and his apprentice, Gas-a-ho, passed the rumour that he had been asked about the Sacred Island.

'What about it?' Nita Qwan asked his wife.

She looked around as if others might be listening in on their conversation. 'I shouldn't know – I'm not a matron yet,' she said, and patted her belly. 'Although I expect you'll see that status changed soon enough.'

'Shouldn't know isn't the same as *don't* know,' he said.

She wriggled her toes. 'To the east, just at the border of our hunting lands and those of the Huran, there is an island in the sea. On the island is a lake at the top of a mountain. In the centre of the lake is an island. It is sacred to all the peoples and creatures of the Wild.'

'Sacred?' he asked.

'No one Power is allowed to hold it,' she said, and would say no more.

The next day he asked Gas-a-ho while he and Ota Qwan mended nets, and the youth, puffed up with self-importance, said, 'That is a matter for the shaman.'

They were repairing nets because the matrons had decided to send a fishing expedition out onto the lake to gather as many fish as they could. Their plan was to salt them against winter need. Another party of men would sweep the woods to the north and west for deer – and for early warning of Crannog People.

When the boy was gone, Ota Qwan finished a repair carefully, wrapping the bark thread again and again with practised ease. When he was done, he raised his eyes. 'It's Thorn,' he said.

'You can't know that,' Nita Qwan said with some annoyance. Ota Qwan's endless sense of his own superiority was more than a little grating, despite his successes.

'My wife's mother told her, and she told me,' Ota Qwan said.

'Thorn has taken this place of power which I didn't even know we had.' He shrugged. 'I didn't expect the wilderness to be so small.'

'What do we do?' Nita Qwan asked. Thorn was more a name than a threat, but he understood that the sorcerer had been the Power behind their spring campaign. 'He can't force us to war in the winter – or can he?'

'I've learned one thing in my years with the People,' Ota Qwan said. 'Let the matrons decide. You can shape the decision by influencing the information on which the matrons act, but after that you have to accept their word.'

'And have you?' Peter asked.

'Have I what?' Ota Qwan asked, biting off a length of bark twine.

'Have you influenced the matron's information?' Peter asked. He wasn't sure exactly why his brother annoyed him, but he was growing angry.

Ota Qwan spread his hands. 'Don't make me the bad guy. All hell is about to break loose on us, brother. There are *giants* out there, smashing villages. If they hit us we'll spend the winter in the woods, and most of the children and old people will die. That's not my opinion. That's the way it is.'

'So what do we do – talk to Thorn? Is this his doing?' asked Peter.

Ota Qwan frowned. 'The matrons think so. I don't know what I think. '

Nita Qwan smiled. 'That's a first.'

Ota Qwan shook his head. 'I don't want to quarrel, brother. The matrons think we should send for allies. Allies can lead to tangles.'

'And the Huran?' asked Nita Qwan.

'The Southern Huran make war on the Northern. Nothing new there. Who knows who started it? The Southerners get trade goods from the Empire, and now the Northerners get trade goods from the Etruscans. They make war over beaver pelts and honey. The matrons say that this year the Etruscans haven't come.' He shrugged and sat back. 'These are the sorts of things my family used to watch and understand. When I was another man – with another life. Why did I think life among the Sossag would be simple? It is life!'

The matrons debated for three days. It was the longest debate that any of them could remember, and the work of the village all but came to a stop. Rumours flew – that they would pick up their belongings and move until the giants were gone, that they would launch a great raid on the Huran for food and slaves, that they would send an embassy to Thorn...

In the end the senior matron, Blue Knife, the tallest woman in the village, called them to council.

'Thorn has moved to the Sacred Island.' She looked around with the calm dignity that characterised the matrons in all their dealings. Rumour said they fought like dogs when alone, but if there were any cracks in their unity they never showed to the rest of the People.

'The Horned One, our shaman, has made his castings. He has confirmed it is Thorn on the Sacred Island, and that it is his workings that send the Crannog People into our lands.' She looked around, and Peter felt as if her eyes came to rest on him. 'We lack the strength to fight Thorn without allies,' she said. 'We have discussed sending to Tapio Haltija at N'gara, and we have discussed sending to Mogon and her people. It was Thorkhan, Mogon's brother, who claimed these lands. But he died facing Thorn, and Thorn may well feel that he is now lord here.'

Again her eyes passed over the crowd. Again, Peter felt singled out.

'We want this conflict to end. The warriors have been consulted. They say that every Ruk we kill does no hurt to Thorn, but will cost us ten men. They say Thorn can bring fire and death in the depths of winter when even men on snowshoes can do little to strike back. So had Tadaio made a decision for all the People: to ignore Thorn's demands and go our own way. He thought we were strong enough. Perhaps we were – if Thorn had not chosen to become our neighbour. Now we must find another path. Tadaio is dead. We have lost two villages. So the matrons have decided to send an embassy to Thorn.' She bowed to Ota Qwan. 'We have chosen our brother Ota Qwan to lead that embassy.'

Ota Qwan rose and bowed. 'I accept the task and the pipe of peace. I will attempt to bring Thorn to a happier disposition.'

Blue Knife frowned slightly. 'Promise him anything he requires. Surrender anything but our bodies. Offer warriors in his wars.'

Ota Qwan was clearly displeased. 'This is craven surrender!'

'The matrons have seen the rise and fall of many Thorns. We lack the strength to face him. So we will lend him the least aid we can manage without incurring his wrath. We will offer songs to his pride. We will aid him.'

'And then, when he is weak, we will strike!' said Ota Qwan.

Blue Knife shook her head. 'No. When he is weak, someone else like him will strike, and we will rejoice quietly, and grow our corn.'

The People sang three songs – all songs of the harvest season, and then they filed out. Peter was near the door, but a small hand on his arm blocked him as effectively as a giant, and he stepped aside to let others pass. Blue Knife stood there, with Small Hands and the other matrons.

'You will not accompany Ota Qwan,' Blue Knife said.

Peter had very little experience of dealing with the matrons. They did not issue orders – no one among the Free People issued orders. So he was taken aback by her tone, and he looked around. His wife was standing behind him and she nodded sharply in agreement.

'He will not like that,' Peter said.

Small Hands nodded gravely. 'He will have other followers and friends. You must not go. Please – we ask this of you.'

Peter bowed. 'I will not go.'

The next week was one of the most difficult Peter had experienced since becoming a Sossag. Ota Qwan lost no time in asking him to come, and then, once the invitation had been declined, became increasingly angry about it.

'Don't let your woman turn you into a coward,' he said in his third attempt.

Peter shrugged. 'She won't.'

'I *need* you. Men follow me for my skills – but they also follow me because *you* follow me. Ta-se-ho has declined to come. You know what he said? He said, *Nita Qwan isn't going.*' Ota Qwan was growing red, and his voice rose, and heads were turning all along the village street. It was a cold, windy day – a presage of autumn. There was rain in the air, and two Ruk had been spotted in the beaver meadow south-east of the village, which had everyone on edge.

'I'm not coming this time,' Peter said, as calmly as he could manage.

'Why? Give me one reason. I led the honey gathering *well*. I have done *nothing* to offend you. I am polite to your bitch of a wife—'

The two men looked at each other. Peter was quite calm. 'Please walk away,' he said.

Ota Qwan put his hands on his hips. 'I'm doing this all wrong. I'm sorry – I don't think your wife is a bitch. Or rather, I do, but I assume you see something in her that I don't. Listen, *brother.* I appeal to you. I admit that we have only known each other this summer. But I *need* you.'

Peter knew in his heart that the admission – that he needed Nita Qwan – had a cost.

He tried to smile. 'I'm flattered—' he began.

'Fuck your patronising shit,' Ota Qwan said with sudden rage. 'Stay here and rot.' He turned on his heel and walked away.

Peter suspected he'd just lost his friend. And his brother.

Why are the matrons putting me in this position?

Ota Qwan left the next day, with six men, all seasoned warriors from the summer campaign. The six of them – three chosen from the neighbouring village at Can-da-ga – were considered the finest warriors the People had to offer – all hot-blooded, all highly skilled.

Ota Qwan left the village carrying his best spear, wearing a sword, with a magnificent wolf cloak over his shoulders and a tunic of deerskin carefully decorated along every seam with a stiff border of porcupine quillwork and moose-hair embroidery. He looked like the Alban notion of an Outwaller king, and he walked with pride. He didn't glance to the right or left, he refused Peter's embrace, and then he was gone.

As soon as he was gone the matrons gathered in the street. There was a flare of temper from Amij'ha, and her mother spoke sharply to her.

'You have sent my husband to his death!' she shouted, and ran into her cabin.

Blue Knife set her face like stone and beckoned to Peter. 'Nita Qwan,' she called. He walked to her. Ta-se-ho followed.

He came to a stop. All the matrons were gathered in front of Amij'ha's house – among the Sossag, the woman owned the house.

'Nita Qwan, the last week must have been hard for you. But we have chosen your brother for a lesser errand. He will fail. He will go to Thorn, and Thorn will seduce him with the offer of war. This is the way of men.'

The sound of Amij'ha's sobs echoed in the cabin.

'We will send you to Mogon. She liked you – she spoke to you. You must leave immediately and travel very fast. Her people are strong, and have strong powers and many allies. Tell her the truth – that

Thorn comes for us, and that we are too weak to do anything but blow in the wind.'

Nita Qwan sighed with understanding. 'It is unfair. My brother—' He paused. The women's eyes were deep with understanding, with unspoken knowledge. He lowered his voice, and found that he was angry; in the way that Ota Qwan had never made him angry. 'If you had sent my brother to Mogon, he would have stood tall for the people. If you had sent me to Thorn, I would have crawled for the people. By sending Ota Qwan to Thorn, you condemn him.'

Blue Knife looked down her nose at him. 'This is as it must be. War will be his own choice – and that will blind Thorn to our intentions. All the men we sent were warlike, like Ota Qwan.'

'My brother could have been better than that,' Nita Qwan spat. 'Indeed, he had been trying—'

'We have sent your brother as a sacrifice to Thorn,' Blue Knife said. 'He is the husband of my daughter and the father of my granddaughter. Do not imagine that this was not much debated and discussed.'

Nita Qwan breathed in his rage, and breathed out, as his father had taught him five thousand leagues ago. 'Very well,' he said. 'I will go. But you are no different than kings and chiefs and tyrants the world over if you send men to die like this, without giving them a chance.'

Small Hands shook her head. 'You are angry and your head is big with tears, Nita Qwan. When you are on the trail, smoking your pipe in the darkness with the flames of your campfire before you, think on this: is the life of one man worth the life of all? Or this: we will not be there to choose for Ota Qwan. If he plays the part we told him to play he will return unharmed, and we will apologise and tell him how we used him.'

Blue Knife looked away. 'But he will not. He will choose Thorn. Of his own free will.' She turned back and her eyes locked with Nita Qwan's. 'Go to Mogon and beg for us. Yesterday, Thorn sent many creatures – some sort of bird or bat or moth – to kill people south of Can-da-ga. He will not end with that.'

Nita Qwan left the next morning, after some passionate lovemaking from his wife and a tearful farewell.

'Am I being sacrificed like Ota Qwan?' he asked her. 'Would you know? Would you tell me?'

She leaned over, breasts brushing his chest, and licked his nose. 'I might not know, but I'd always tell you. The matrons are all bitches. They don't like me.' She licked his nose again. 'What they did to Ota Qwan, lover, he... I'm sorry. He had it coming. He is too much about himself. He wanted to be warlord and he said so. He was not like you. You have become one of us while he was a Southerner pretending to be a Sossag.'

Nita Qwan took the comfort offered and decided not to have a fight with his wife before leaving.

He took only Ta-se-ho who knew the way, and the shaman's boy, Gas-a-ho. They took bows and pemmican and little else. Nita Qwan declined to carry the elaborate fur robe of an ambassador, and he rolled the quillwork belt that the shaman prepared for the matrons in his Alban snapsack with a blanket, and the three of them, having bowed to the matrons and kissed their women, left the village at a run, like hunters or warriors, and not at a walk like ambassadors.

For the first three days on the trail, it rained. The wind blew harder and harder, the temperature dropped, and the three men built big fires and huddled close under their brush shelters and were cold and wet most of the time. They ran almost all day – faster on the third day, as Gas-a-ho's muscles hardened. He was young and not as strong as other boys, mostly because he'd chosen the way of the shaman and didn't spend as much time hunting and fighting.

They passed south of the beaver country, right to the shore of the Inner Sea, and they spent a fruitless morning – their fourth on the trail – looking for a canoe.

'We always sink them in this pool,' Ta-se-ho said. He prodded the bottom of a deep pool in a feeder stream for an hour while the other two sat in the water sun and enjoyed being only a little damp. He didn't find a canoe.

He didn't find a canoe sunk in the deep bay of the Inner Sea, either. He shook his head. 'Now we have to make a boat,' he said.

Nita Qwan had not truly absorbed that this was alternative, and he shook his head. 'I don't even know how to *make* a boat.'

The other two men looked at him and laughed.

The boy gathered spruce root. Nita Qwan watched him for a little while, and all the boy did was wander from spruce to spruce, dig down to the wispy surface roots, and pull. When he had a good length, he'd cut the roots with his neck knife, and go to the next. He didn't strip a single tree – not even a scrubby little tree at the edge of a meadow. He simply took one length of root from each tree.

Ta-se-ho watched him for a while, too. 'He's good. The Horned One is a fine teacher. Let's go find a tree.'

Finding a tree led to hours of walking in the deep woods. It was hard to make sense of this – they were in a hurry, rushing to take a message to the powerful wardens, and yet they were wandering from tree to tree in the woods. Peter was overwhelmed with frustration for several hours, until Nita Qwan decided that this was a matter for careful deliberation.

Ta-se-ho confirmed this view. 'If the bark opens like a flower while we are on the sea, we die,' he said. 'It is worth the time to choose a good tree.'

They hadn't found it yet, but they found other things – a pair of twisted spruces that years of wind had bent almost over. Ta-se-ho cut both of them down with a light axe – a fine tool, dark steel with a white edge, from Alba.

He tapped many trees with the butt of the same axe – yellow birch, white birch, paper birch – and pulled at the bark on elm and pine and birch alike. As he walked among them, he sang.

'White birch is best,' he said.

Nita Qwan felt entirely useless, but somehow, as the day progressed, he learned – almost wordlessly, because Ta-se-ho was a silent teacher – what it was they wanted. They searched for a dead tree – recently dead – with the bark ready to peel away. They found several, all together in the afternoon. They were all a little too small, but the way that his silent companion handled them, and peeled the elm bark back from the trunks, told Nita Qwan most of what he needed to know.

The sun had come out quite strong, and the day was more like late summer than autumn. The two men were stripped to their breech-clouts by afternoon, and walking through the magnificent trees was more beautiful than anything Nita Qwan had done – except perhaps make love – for many days. He savoured the smell of the leaves, and the magnificent royal dazzle of red and gold.

As the sun began to sink, he saw a pond, and along the pond a dozen enormous birch trees like white maidens standing over a forest pool. He walked that way, confident that he could find Ta-se-ho, or that the older man could find him, and he reached the first tree

– already excited to see that the crown was dead. The bark had the loose feel he thought might be correct, and he turned to raise his voice and saw the doe standing, head turned to watch him, within easy bowshot.

He thought that she was small enough to carry, and he took his bow from its sheath and strung it while she drank warily and watched him.

Then she turned her head, ignoring him. Her ears swivelled like a horse's ears.

He loosed an arrow, and missed entirely in his hurry. The fall of his spent shaft startled her, and she whirled, white tail shooting up, and he realised that there was another animal, a small buck, even closer to him that he hadn't seen. He got a second shaft onto his string – the buck turned, and then looked back, and then leaped along the edge of the pond.

He loosed at point-blank range and his shaft went home to the feathers. The deer fell in a tangle of its own hooves, life extinguished almost instantly, and the doe swerved and ran on, ignoring him as she bounded away.

He stood there, flush with deer fever, and realised that the fading hoof beats of the doe were not the only large animal sounds he was hearing.

The *hastenoch* came down to the edge of the pool along the same path the doe had taken, its long obscene head and enormous antler rack sending a sharp jolt through his body as he realised what had actually panicked the deer.

He found that his fingers had put an arrow on his string.

A horn blew – raucous and long. The four-hoofed monster raised its snout and looked east, towards the other end of the pond – and charged. There was no warning; it went from standing still to full gallop and it screamed its uncanny cry.

Nita Qwan loosed and missed – it was too fast. He had time to loose three more shafts as the great thing raced along the far shore, and his third shaft hit it squarely just behind the armoured plates of its head and upper neck, and the shaft went deep.

Ta-se-ho shot it twice, but both shafts glanced off the bony plates of its head.

Then he seemed to disappear. It was like magic. He was there – and then he was gone.

The horned thing slammed, head first, into the tree next to which Ta-se-ho had been standing. The crash echoed off the trees standing by the pond, and again off the rock face that rose in granite splendour into the afternoon sunlight.

The great beast reared, backed, and slammed into the tree again. Now the monster had an arrow standing upright between his shoulders, like a crest, and then another.

Nita Qwan loosed again. He was shooting the length of the pond, now.

It was too far to see cause and effect, but the monster suddenly sat. It trumpeted its rage, and got its back feet under it.

It sprouted three more arrows – tick, tick, tick.

Nita Qwan's hands were shaking so hard he had to pause and breathe. But the thing seemed to be down, and he got another arrow – the one he thought of as his best, with a heavy steel head and a heavy shaft and a deep nock he'd carved himself – on the string and then ran *at* the monster. It was struggling to rise again.

Tick. It now had seven shafts in it.

Ta-se-ho dropped from the tree that the monster had rushed. He landed lightly, bounced to his feet and drew his long knife – and the *hastenoch* rolled to its feet, antlers lowered.

It rushed him – an explosion of sinew and antler – its rack caught him and he was tossed as Nita Qwan stepped in close, drew his bow to the ear, and put his heaviest shaft through its withers from so close that its carrion smell was like death incarnate in his nostrils.

It whirled on him and he fed it his bow, right into the tentacled mouth. The horn tip of the bow bit deep and then the bow bent and snapped and it was on him and he was on the ground amidst the cold leaves – a great weight on his chest – a sense of slipping – away, away—

It was dark, and he was cold.

He opened his eyes, and the stars were cold and very far, and he was small and very cold himself.

He opened his mouth and a grunt escaped – and suddenly there was movement.

Gas-a-ho had a canteen to his lips. 'Drink!' he said. 'Are you hurt?'

It seemed a foolish question. *Until you spoke, I thought I was dead,* Nita Qwan thought. He took a deep breath, and smelled only wet fur and carrion. His hand touched something cold and very slimy – a tentacle – and he flinched. And his feet moved.

'I can't get it off you,' Gas-a-ho said. The boy was fighting panic.

'Where's Ta-se-ho?' Nita Qwan asked.

'I thought he was with you,' said the boy. 'When dark was coming, I gave up that you two were coming back. I stashed my roots and followed your tracks. This thing was still twitching when I came.'

Nita Qwan could feel the marks of the tentacles on his face and arms. 'Trying to eat me,' he said aloud. 'Even while it was dying.' His memory of the last moments of the fight was skewed, and he tried as best he could to piece it together. 'Ta-se-ho was here – he got tossed by the beast.'

The boy had a fire. He could see it, and the promise of its warmth trickled through his injured spirit. He dug into the ground with his elbows – there was a shallow puddle under the small of his back – and he pushed, wriggling his feet.

The dead monster was soft and hard, and the armour plates of its head were resting just below his groin. He couldn't feel his legs, but he seemed to be able to make them move.

He fought down panic. 'Get my spear, Gas-a-ho. Is it here?' he asked.

'I have it!' the boy said proudly. He went out of Nita Qwan's field of vision and then came back.

Wolves howled. They were right across the pond devouring the buck he'd shot.

The boy came back. 'I've cast a working on my arms to make them stronger,' he said. And then, 'I hope.'

'Put the spear under the head. Put a log under the spear, and use it as a lever – no, under the head – good. Careful – don't break the spear . . . there, it moved!'

In a moment, he dragged his right leg free. He had to use his hands, but his legs were bare, and that made them slippery and, although he lost his moccasin, he got the leg out.

The wolves howled. They sounded closer.

'Hurry,' he said. There was no pain in his right leg, but neither was there any feeling in it. He wriggled, getting his back out of the pool of water, and set his hands. The boy dug the spearhead into the earth, and pulled.

The wolves bayed, shockingly close, and provided them both with an additional incentive. He got his left foot to move – an inch, another, and then a third. They were sticky, slimy inches, but once it started to move, he wouldn't stop – not to wait for the wave of pain, the crippling sick ache of a broken bone or ripped muscle. Instead, he felt nothing but a vague slipping, as if the limb was not his but the dead beast's.

And then he was free.

He crawled fifty feet to the fire, and lay full length in its warmth, heedless of the slavering wolves.

Before the warmth could lull him, the return of life to his lower limbs struck like ice and fire and the pangs of love and being eaten alive all together. He grunted, rolled, thrashed, and grunted again.

The boy looked terrified, and Nita Qwan tried to force a smile. 'I'm fine,' he muttered, sounding foolish. 'No – really – very lucky – ah!' he said.

But shortly after, when he had some control of his feet, he listened to the wolves and turned to the boy. Gas-a-ho had gathered all their kit and made a small shelter, built a fire – even butchered part of the deer he'd shot, and cooked a haunch of the meat. Nita Qwan got his short sword from his pack and hobbled to the fire.

Gas-a-ho was by him like a swift arrow. 'I made torches,' he said proudly. 'I was going to try and get you out if the wolves came – or at least fight them off.'

'I think the whole pack fed on deer meat, and now they will sleep,' Nita Qwan said. 'But we must find Ta-se-ho if we can. He may be dead. But if he is not, a night this cool could kill him.' He took a torch and went back to the corpse of the monster, which in flickering torchlight looked almost as terrifying as it had alive.

There was something to the glistening pile of its tentacles that made his stomach turn.

He forced himself to breathe, in and out, and walked past the massive rack of antlers that had miraculously not fallen on his face and killed him.

As usual, everything was bigger at night. He couldn't find the tree that Ta-se-ho had been in – he had no moccasins and his feet were being crucified by the sharp gravel and sticks.

He stepped on the older hunter in the dark – a soft resistance, a yielding—

Something grabbed his leg and threw him to the ground – he

rolled on his shoulder and turned, torch lost. He must have shouted out as he fell.

Ta-se-ho sat up. 'You almost killed me,' he said, and managed a weak laugh.

They took turns keeping the hunter warm. He had a badly broken collarbone, and he couldn't use his left arm at all. He was also in shock, and despite his attempts to fend off their help, he needed every hot cup of tea, and every blanket they had. As the feeling returned to Nita Qwan's feet, he became more mobile, and he and the boy scrounged for firewood in the damp dark.

But in the morning, the sun rose. Nita Qwan had feared rain, but it was a beautiful day. Until the effort of downing a standing dead tree in the dawn light showed that he had cracked ribs.

He returned to camp to find Ta-se-ho coaching the boy on extracting all the best parts of the deadly *hastenoch*. By daylight the monster was smaller and less terrifying than Nita Qwan could have imagined, and as the boy meticulously removed its head plates and its tendons for sinew, it became first pitiful and then merely meat.

Ta-se-ho took tobacco from his pouch, cast it over the dead thing and sang a song for its spirit. When he was done, he sipped tea. 'You up to making a boat?' he asked, and coughed.

Nita Qwan thought of protesting about his ribs, or his inexperience. But the other two seemed untroubled by the debacle. So he tried to shrug it off, too. 'Sure,' he said.

'We will have many strong things from papa here,' said Ta-se-ho. 'They eat us. We use them.' He laughed. 'Is it different, down south?'

Nita Qwan piled up his cut firewood and then sat by the wounded man, who was laboriously lighting a pipe. Nita Qwan knelt and lit his char cloth and passed a lit taper of paper birch to the other man, who sat back in what appeared to be complete contentment.

'I was never really in the south,' he said. 'I'm from beyond the sea.'

'Etrusca?' asked the old hunter. He took a deep draught of smoke and handed the pipe to Nita Qwan.

'No, Ifriqu'ya.' He took smoke himself.

'Is everyone there as dark as you?' the other man asked. 'I have always wanted to ask how you came to be so dark, but it seemed rude.'

Nita Qwan remembered Peter's youth, and smiled. 'Everyone is,' he said.

'Very handsome. Good in the woods, too.' Ta-se-ho nodded, as if this defined what was good. 'You saved my life.'

'Perhaps you drew the creature to yourself.' Nita Qwan passed the pipe back.

'Hah! I was a fool. I thought I had it – a trap, a trick, and my bow.' He shook his head. 'It should be a saying: never try to fight a monster by yourself.' He grunted, took smoke, and handed the pipe back. 'Of course there is another saying: there's no fool like an old fool.'

Greatly daring, the boy reached out for the pipe. Nita Qwan handed it to him. 'Truthfully, we both owe our lives to this boy,' he said.

The older man smiled at the boy and ruffled his hair. 'Ah – it will only make him insufferable,' he said. He pointed with the pipe's reed stem at the white birch standing at the water's edge. 'Were those what brought you here?' he asked.

'Yes – the nearest one. I thought it might make a good boat.' Nita Qwan shrugged.

Ta-se-ho nodded. 'I may make a hunter of you yet. Listen – this is what we should do. Today, you two cut firewood. Lots of it. Yes? Then, tomorrow, we cut the tree and take the bark. Next day I'll be better – we move camp to the sea. Then we build the boat.'

'How many days before we are on our way?' Peter asked.

The hunter gave him an impatient look. 'However many it takes,' he said.

Liviapolis – Ser Thomas Lachlan

The defeat of the Etruscans was a three-day wonder. Within the company, they knew that the victory was not as good as it seemed, and Bad Tom was rapidly coming to regret accepting the task of hunting spies.

The company – with a hundred Morean shipwrights and labourers – had built three heavy galleys in a week – or rather, the new ships were framed on the quays, waiting for the long work of nailing planks. The planks had to be adzed to shape, and the trees had to be felled before that, and it seemed that Andronicus, the former Duke of Thrake, controlled most of the long, straight spruce and oak in Morea. Ser Jehan took twenty men-at-arms and as many archers into the hills with orders to fetch in enough lumber to complete ten row-galleys. He went with good grace. The second day after he left, he sent a report of an attempted ambush.

In the city, Tom chased phantoms.

Every archer received a handbill written out carefully by a scribe who'd never read Alban, announcing that every man who deserted from the company would receive fifty gold nobles and a free pass to Alba – or higher wages in the armies of the *true Duke of Thrake, fighting for the true Emperor.*

Whoever had written the handbills had mistaken the archers for men who cared which side was in the right. A great deal of ink had been spent on describing the Princess Irene as a scheming usurper and Duke Andronicus as a loyal supporter of the Emperor.

Bad Tom sat in his 'office', a table in the guardroom where the senior officers stood watches, and read it carefully. Across the table, Cully sat with his hands folded.

'Cap'n – which I mean the Duke – won't think I want to run, would he?' Cully asked. The Captain's temper had been sour since they left Lissen Carrak and now verged on poisonous.

Bad Tom shrugged. 'If he does, he's fucked in the head. Where would you go? Who'd take you?'

Cully struggled to decide whether he should defend his status as a master archer or his loyalty.

Tom threw the bill back at him. 'Anyone tempted?' he asked. Long Paw had brought him the same bill, and now sat with his feet up.

Long Paw made a face. 'There's the usual awkward sods. We don't have enough choir boys, that much I can tell ye. And skipping a pay parade – well that started some mutters.' Long Paw had a low, gravelly voice that utterly belied his gentle nature and correctly warned the listener of his danger, too. He cleared his throat – half of them had colds. 'No one will run now. Miss two or three more pay days; someone will run then.'

Bad Tom nodded his agreement.

Bent came in to the guardroom, spoke briefly to the officer of the day, Ser George Brewes, who sat with his armoured feet on a table and drank wine. Brewes was, in many ways, the worst soldier imaginable – he was a terrible example and he was bad for discipline. The men loved him, so he got away with it.

Bent tossed a casual salute to Ser George and came up to Bad Tom's table. He reached into the breast of his doublet and withdrew a crumpled handbill.

Bad Tom passed his eyes over it and nodded. 'Sit,' he muttered. 'How would you three like to desert?'

Bent narrowed his eyes. 'They'd never buy it. We're master archers. Well, some of us are.' Bent shot a glance at Cully, who rolled his eyes.

Bad Tom sighed. 'I need to get a more private place to meet. For the nonce, I am assuming that everyone in the company is reliable. But listen. Whoever's up to this ain't ten feet tall. They think we care whose side we're on. They don't know us. Stands to reason we can feed them a few archers.'

Bent flexed his hands.

Long Paw studied his nails the way a woman might. 'What's in it for us?' he asked.

'A good fight?' asked Bad Tom. 'Money?' he tried.

All three men brightened up.

'Shares? Man-at-arm's shares?' Long Paw leaned forward.

Tom rolled his eyes. 'As long as you three realise I've never made one thin clipped silver leopard from my share.'

They all four shook hands on it.

Long Paw went to the taverna that was listed on his handbill. He was the only archer who spoke the Morean version of Archaic, and he dressed in a heavy linen overshirt and a broad straw hat and walked all the way around the city – outside the walls – to enter at the Vardariot gate driving a small pig.

Either his disguise was excellent or no one was watching him. He scouted the taverna, behind the Academy and in a seedy slum of small tenements and three-storey stuccoed houses with flat roofs, and returned without incident.

When he came back, the whole company was turned out in armour, standing at attention in the Outer Court. Bad Tom had already taken twenty lances to the Navy Yard.

Someone had torched their new ships on the stocks, and someone else had poisoned a great many of the company's horses.

The Captain – whose beautiful new horse was dead – walked up and down in front of his company, obviously deep in rage.

Long Paw slipped into the guardroom. Wilful Murder was the duty archer – he was leaning in the doorway of the guardroom watching the fun.

'Christ on the cross – you'll catch it,' Wilful said. He was delighted to see someone so senior as Long Paw so deeply in the shit.

'Heh,' Long Paw grunted. 'What's the Cap'n on about?'

'We turned out for the alarm, and there ain't forty horses fit to ride. Turns out he ordered the stables guarded, but they weren't. Ser Jehan ain't here to say one way or another, see?' Wilful shook his head. 'Ser Milus said – right on parade, in front of everybody – that the Cap'n clean forgot to order the stables guarded.'

Long Paw grunted, slipped into the barracks and had a nap.

The next day, a maid, one of the Princess Irene's servants and a pretty thing already chased by half a dozen Scholae, two Nordikans, and Francis Atcourt, died of poison in the palace kitchen. Bad Tom ran through the palace to get to her corpse as soon as he heard, but by the time he reached the kitchens she had been taken for burial and all of the people who might have had something to say were gone to their duties.

He did find Harald Derkensun and his pretty whore Anna. The two men clasped arms. They spoke briefly, and Anna nodded several times.

That night Bad Tom reported to his Captain, who had lines on his face and dark circles under his eyes and was sitting drinking wine with Ser Milus, who looked as bad or worse.

'Sorry, Captain – er, my lord Duke.' Bad Tom paused in the doorway of the Captain's outer office.

Ser Milus rose stiffly. 'I should go,' he said.

'You can hear anything Tom has to say. Milus – I'm *sorry*. My temper got the best of me.' The Duke put a hand on his standard bearer's shoulder, but the older knight simply bowed and withdrew – gracefully enough that it was hard to see if he was angry or not.

'You must hae' cocked up proper. Ne'er heard you speak so small to any man.' Tom grinned.

'I was an arse of the first water, and the worst of it, Tom, is that I feel as if I'm losing my mind. Nay – forget I said that. Anything saved on the docks?' The Duke mixed something into his wine with the tip of his fighting knife.

'Master Aeneas thinks we can save one hull out of the three,' Tom said. 'I doubled the guard and put him to it. For what it's worth, I accept that it's my fault and ye can do as ye like.'

There was a silence.

'Well, I accept that it was my fault too, so we can both sulk together. You won't be rid of this job so easily.' The Duke tossed off a cup of wine.

'Ye'r drinking hard these days.' Tom poured some for himself. Toby was making himself scarce – he looked like he was going to have a prime black eye, too.

'Yes, well, some days it *is like I have a fucking voice inside my head and I'm never alone*!' He spat.

Tom laughed. 'Nah, that's just Sauce.'

The Captain spat out some of his wine. 'You make me laugh, Tom,' he said. 'I wonder if that means I've lost my mind.'

'Like eno,' said Tom. 'Listen, Cap'n – I'd like to send Bent and Cully to pretend to be deserters. Long Paw will cover them.'

The Captain sighed. 'We can ill afford to lose three of our best men. But – yes. It's your command. Any word from Jehan?'

'His guides mislead him and he thinks it was done a-purpose. He killed one.' Tom shrugged.

'We could be so unpopular here, Tom.' The Duke shrugged. 'But Jehan knows what he's doing. We need that wood.' He looked up. 'Any word from Sauce?'

'She's chatting with people; people she knew here.' Tom shrugged. 'She's a strange one. She was a whore, here?'

'Right here in this city,' the Red Knight said.

'Aweel. She's off tonight to talk to an armourer. Says that this man witch was one of his father's apprentices, fifty years back.' Tom didn't sound very interested. 'She's also found me some useful people.'

'Paid informants?' the Red Knight asked. 'Spies? Whores? Tavern ruffians?'

Bad Tom nodded. 'Aye.'

The Red Knight grimaced. 'We are living in the very annals of chivalry, ain't we?'

Chapter Eleven

Thorn

The Sacred Island – Thorn

Thorn had been using the moths more and more – they were tough, agile, and very quick to breed. The spring of power, Deseronto, as the locals called it, now had so many moths and their larvae that the soft beat of their fragile wings was actually a noise when they were disturbed, and Thorn spent more time on them than on some of his more immediate projects. He told himself that they would all be useful in time, but the truth – a truth he admitted freely – was that he had fallen in love with the species and sought to redesign them to suit his many ends and for purely aesthetic expression.

He had a paradoxical thought that he had once hated moths, but he dismissed it.

In the centre of the open, unroofed chamber of natural rock from which both water and raw power gushed, he had placed a low marble table, and on it sat the two black eggs, which had altered in shape and size. They were now the size of a man's breastplate, and the eggs had developed the ridges of a pumpkin and the warts of an aged animal. Things moved within them, almost visible against the tough elasticity of the shell, and still they grew, and the marble table groaned under their weight.

They generated an effect that was, itself, the cause for concern. All the moths that gestated near the eggs were born wizened and black, as if the eggs leached their essence before they ever had a chance to feed and form a chrysalis.

But because Thorn was a careful observer, he saw that in each generation of moth larvae placed close to the eggs, a few were of remarkable dimensions and weight. The larvae were the size of earthworms or larger, jet black, and without markings.

For three patient generations, he massacred the little ones and bred the large ones – some left close to the eggs, and some given a safer berth.

As summer fled to autumn, and leaves across the Sacred Island went to red and gold, and then began to wither and fall in the driving rains and sudden winds, the black eggs grew as big as witches' cauldrons. And Thorn watched the first generations of Black Moths emerge from their cocoons – the size of a peregrine falcon, with a thousand matte black eyes and a single probiscus, like a misshapen unicorn.

He dominated them easily and sent them north. One fell victim to a windstorm. One he lost in the woods – possibly attacked by an owl. The remaining three descended on a Sossag village.

They were quick, their needle-like probiscae were deadly, their venom instantaneous, the paralysis and subsequent jellification of the victim magnificent in effect. But the Sossag were themselves agile and strong – a nine-year-old girl scored the first kill with her father's snow snake, ripping a Black Moth from the air with a practised strike even as her mother's bones disintegrated. Before he could withdraw his predators, they were dead.

Thorn reviewed their performance and decided that the Black Moths made a better tool of assassination than of terror. He worked on the second generation.

The use of insects as spies now took up a sizeable portion of his attention, but allowed him an unguessed-at level of knowledge. He could watch a person or an event from fifteen or twenty vectors, allowing him a godlike perspective on events. The effort involved was less than he had experienced with mammals but the diffuse creatures and directions required a level of minute adjustment that cost him in both power and time every day.

In return, however, he began to see things that he knew he should have ensured he saw before he attempted Lissen Carrak. The greatest limitations on his newfound powers of espionage lay in the old spells and workings built into the structures and palaces of the powerful

– and even into some shepherds' cots. It took a great warding to resist Thorn for even a moment, but it took only the will of the village witch to keep his ensorcelled insects from the door, and a new commercial hermeticism in Liviapolis – a warded amulet that prevented insects from entering a house, sold to goodwives and travellers by the University – was like to make every home in the Empire immune from his creatures.

But these were the elements that made the life and path of ascent Thorn had chosen so rewarding. That autumn he was challenged and delighted, and he worked hard to prepare his series of strokes.

Thorn waited, and watched.

He tried not to believe that he was a tool.

He watched as his eggs grew and matured, lit from within with a curious black fire that defied his own sorcery.

He watched four ships come up the Great River, their straight masts and round sides utterly alien in the world of trees. He saw them from a great height, circling as an owl, and later, as a raven with a sixty-foot wingspan. His powers had made a great leap forward, and his heart beat with renewed vitality. Once, he had been a man, and he made himself a new form. Now he could adopt many forms, and in adopting them his sense of himself altered.

It is happening he allowed himself to think.

He had access to unbelievable amounts of raw *potentia*. He swam in it – he bathed in it. He worked small things and great with reckless profusion, making tools for the future.

He went in various forms to the creatures on either side of the Inner Sea, and listened. A few he bound to his will, but now he preferred to whisper some words and let the sweetness of his suggestions work their own magics.

He watched Ghause. For every one of his sendings she destroyed he placed another, and another, until he could watch her all day, from many angles. Naked. Clothed. Working the *aether* or reading a book, rutting with her lumpen husband or preparing her revenge.

She fascinated him. Repelled him. But she was like the perfect tool, built to fit his hand. And he desired her, as a woman. It was many, many years since he had felt any such desire, and he revelled in it. It was not weakness, but strength, he told himself. He watched her work, naked, and he watched the intent rapture she displayed as she gathered *potentia* in the *aether* and cast great gouts of *ops* and he wanted her. His pale grey moths let him see her from nine directions as she rose on her toes, like a dancer, her belly moving faster and faster in her rhythmic chant—

I will take her, and have her and use her, and she will serve me. And in so doing, I will strike at the King, cripple the Red Knight, and destroy the Earl, and grow yet more powerful. And when I am tired with her, I will subsume her. And grow yet more powerful still.

He was in the body of Speaker of Tongues, and so he could smile.

He was still chuckling when the ambassadors from the Sossag found him.

They were strong men, warriors all, and they hated him. And feared him. He could smell their fear and their hesitation – indeed, he had felt their fear so far away that he'd had time to create a house in which to host them, and a table at which to sit with them, and a fire on a hearth – and to refine this body.

They introduced themselves, one by one, and he admired their courage the way a man buying slaves admires strength.

'Where is the sorcerer, Thorn?' asked the bravest. 'We have come to see him.'

Thorn bowed, the way no Sossag would ever bow. 'I am he,' he said.

'You are one of our own shamans!' said a man with the scars of nine kills on his right ear.

But the very bravest one shook his head and bent his knee. 'He is Thorn. I served him this spring, against the rock.'

The old shaman smiled. 'And we failed, you and I. And you took your warriors and left me.'

The warrior nodded. 'It seemed best, lord. You were defeated – and you were not my lord, but merely an ally.'

'Bold talk,' Thorn said.

'Now the matrons send me to make peace,' said the brave one.

Thorn brushed aside the man's protections, and skimmed his name from the muddle that was his thoughts. 'You are Ota Qwan, who took the place of Tadaio as paramount warrior,' he said. He altered the tenor of his voice to make it sound more like Ota Qwan's own voice. 'You were the bravest warrior at the fight at the ford.'

The other warriors looked at Ota Qwan with suspicion.

He glanced at them, and Thorn took their names from his surface thoughts.

'Do the Sossag offer the same sort of lies and betrayal they offered in the spring? I need them not. I have the Huran as my own.' He didn't smile, but merely leaned forward like an elder making a point. 'Ah – you were a lord among men in the south, as well.'

Now the other warriors edged away from Ota Qwan.

He shrugged. 'Mighty Thorn, we know you have sent the giants to destroy our villages.'

Thorn smiled. 'No,' he said.

Ota Qwan took a breath. The other five looked at each other.

'No,' Thorn said. 'I am not some *man* with whom you can negotiate. These are my terms. You – Ota Qwan – will come and be my captain. I need a man – a man of war – to command my forces. It was for the lack of such a man that I failed at the rock. Among the Huran there is no warrior as redoubtable as you. And you have wide experience in the south, as well. In exchange, I will give you powers beyond anything you can imagine. And I will, if you like, lift my hand from the Sossag, who are merely one hut circle of near-animals in an endless forest of them. I need no more punishment for the Sossag than to leave them to their own devices.'

The least brave of the six – and he was very brave – sprang to his feet. 'You *lie!*' he said.

Thorn laughed and stripped away his soul and subsumed it. The man's flesh fell with a thump.

'Lying is for the weak,' he said. 'I have no need to lie. You others? Will you serve as my captains?'

Ota Qwan forced a smile. He was nodding.

He has already decided to serve me, but now he will posture a little, Thorn thought. Men bored him.

'Why would I serve you? I do not crave power.' The man met Thorn's human eyes. 'You have nothing I want.'

You lie, Thorn thought. Then he skimmed along the man's thoughts again, like a man braiding a child's hair, feeling the knots, the burrs, the places where the hair hadn't been brushed. He ran tendrils of power through the man's head and he read a name.

Orley.

He laughed aloud. It was as if he was destined to attain his desire. Everything fell into his hand. Or had the black place done this?

He no longer cared.

Ota Qwan recoiled from the laughter.

Another of the six drew his short Alban sword.

Thorn cast.

An amulet on the man's chest flared – the man's blade cut, and cut well, severing Speaker's left hand. Blood spurted.

Thorn stumbled out of his chair – and then raised his left arm into the man's second slash. He sprayed blood into the man's face and blocked his sword by catching it in the bone of his left arm.

He burned the man's amulet to dust with one burst using a concoction of minor workings he had designed to baffle amulets. It was foolish of him to forget that these powerful warriors would have some protections.

He touched the man on the arm, and cast a gentle curse that excited every nerve on the man's skin. Every single nerve.

The man fell screaming, and began to thrash with no regard for his own body – bashing his head, dislocating a shoulder as he lost control of every function. His screams ripped out, one laid over the next like a shingled roof. The remaining four Sossag paled.

Thorn picked up his severed hand and put it back on the end of his arm. Healing was the least of his powers – but this he did to show them. He spent a day's power profligately, to replace the hand on his arm. It was, after all, merely a form he wore, like a cloak.

The Sossag trembled.

'I am like a god, am I not?' he said, conversationally. 'If any of you would like to try and kill me, I am here. Ready. At your pleasure, as men say.' His comments were punctuated with the screams ripping out of his victim.

'You torture prisoners – come, I know you do. You do it to prove their courage. Well – this one has failed, wouldn't you say?' He smiled.

The man on the floor had voided his bowels and bladder and still he thrashed, as if in the grip of a monster, and he screamed so fast it didn't seem that he could catch a breath. As they watched, he fetched his head against the marble table that held the eggs, and one hand was thrown out – touched the rightmost egg, and he was subsumed before their eyes, reduced to ash.

The egg flared for a moment – a purple-black light shot from it, and then it was still.

Even Thorn was taken aback. He stepped over to the eggs, paused to don his most heavily armoured semblance, and looked carefully in all the spectra he could command.

The eggs were drinking *potentia*. They emitted none.

Thorn knew a frisson of fear, and he backed away from the eggs. But he – even he – dared not show fear in front of his potential servants. So he forced a cruel laugh.

'Fascinating,' he said aloud. He whirled, keeping his skeletal tree branch arms well clear of the eggs.

The four Sossag had drawn into a corner, and a thousand moths fluttered around them.

'Anyone else? You are all free to go. But if you will stay, I will make you great.' He nodded his head.

Ota Qwan sighed, as if releasing something he held to be valuable. 'If I serve you, lord, will you hold your hand from the Sossag?'

Thorn nodded. 'If they serve me loyally.'

'Will you give me Muriens? The Earl of the North?' asked Ota Qwan. The lust that flared in him was like a moth being born from its chrysalis. This naked need for revenge – this was the true man.

'More – I will order you to take him. That will be your first task. And when he is taken, then you may have him.' Thorn nodded again.

The tallest of the three warriors was also the youngest. He shook with fear, and yet he stood tall. He stepped out of the cloud of moths surrounding Ota Qwan. 'I will not serve you,' he said. 'I have no power of arm or thought to harm you – b-b-but I will n-not serve.'

Thorn watched him, unmoved. In this form, he could shrug off a bolt from a siege engine. He had.

'Ota Qwan?' Thorn asked.

'Call me Orley,' he said, and plunged a basilard into the young warrior. He turned to the last man, a Western Door Sossag called Guire'lon, even as the younger man's heels drummed on the rock, trying to outrun death. 'Go and tell them that Ota Qwan died here, for the People. Tell my wife. Tell the matrons.' He smiled a horrible, lopsided grin. 'I will go back to being Kevin Orley now.'

Ticondaga – Giannis Turkos

Turkos left the great fortress no happier than he had arrived, and headed north as fast as he might go. He'd asked the Earl to support him against the Northern Huran, and the Earl, for his own reasons, had declined. And then ordered him off his lands.

Winter was close – three days of rain had soaked the woods. He was cold before he'd crossed the river from the nigh-on impregnable fort that covered the great castle's river gate. He paddled himself across the river, drifting almost a league on the swollen autumn current, landed, and walked back to the village that served as their northern landing – forty cabins and some lesser huts, mostly broken men and women of a dozen Outwaller clans or no clan. The Muriens had made their move to rule the Outwallers three generations earlier, and their iron fists held sway over a hundred miles of the northern bank and more of the south bank. Many of the Southern Huran, even the free villages and castles, listened to Ticondaga, served in their raids and sent headmen and matrons to council fires on the great meadow at the base of the castle walls.

For Turkos, the situation among the Huran was becoming a nightmare of divided loyalties.

His information – and gathering information was his duty – told him that the Galles, of all people, had landed a strong force among the Northern Huran. Rumour had it that a great sorcerer had moved into the Sossag lands, and Ghause, the Earl of the North's dangerous wife, had put a name on that sorcerer: Thorn.

The relations between the Northern and Southern Huran were about to grow very complicated.

He spent an afternoon in the village longhouse, listening, telling stories, and writing letters to other men like him. He hired runners in the village, and sent them off with coded messages.

Then he rode west along the river, as fast as he could go, with three spare horses, food for twenty days and two great black and white birds. As a riding officer it was his duty to report.

The woods were oddly quiet. For two nights, he put that down to the omnipresent rain; five consecutive days of rain meant that Turkos had to use his very limited hermetical talents to kindle fire.

There was a village called Nepan'ha at the place where the north bank of the Great River, which had, for twenty leagues, been mired among a hundred islands and as many swamps, at last sprang clear of all that and opened into the Inner Sea. It was not a Sossag village or a Huran village – the people there were from many Outwaller groups, and they were fiercely independent. They had withstood a siege from the Muriens. It took him five days of hard riding, with very little sleep, to make Nepan'ha and once there he bedded his horses and collapsed on a rude sleeping bench near the open hearth of a longhouse and slept for twelve hours, ate four bowls of venison stew, and enjoyed a long pipe with the headswoman.

She said Thorn's name aloud.

The longhouse grew silent.

'Naming calls,' muttered a voice in the dark upper shelves of the house, where neither heat nor light ever reached. 'Naming calls.'

'Shut up, old man,' muttered the headswoman, Trout Leaping.

'The Sacred Island was for all,' the man muttered. 'Now the magic is sucked away as if by some sorcerous leech, and soon our souls will follow until all is black and dead.'

'You see what I have to put up with,' Trout Leaping said and shook her head. 'The ones with talent – they feel it worst. He's only about seventy leagues away, across the water. Much further by land, of course.'

Later, Turkos reached out with his own art and he felt the void and the feeling of desolation almost immediately, and had the fleeting impression of moths swirling in mist.

Turkos was not a strong talent but he had been trained well. He masked his work and, in the rich garden of his memory, he marked his own location with reference to three of the University's beacons, and then he laid a vector to the desolation.

After another meal and twelve more hours' sleep he went west into another day of autumn rain, riding hard. The trail worn into the ground by fifty generations of Sossag and Abenacki and Kree was broad enough for his horse to find even in the dark – not that Turkos was foolish enough to travel in the dark.

On his third day out of Nepan'ha, he spotted a pair of Ruk on the horizon, across more than a mile of tangled beaver swamp. At first he thought they were Great Beaver, but as he picked his way closer, watching the footing not only for himself but for all his animals, he realised that they were not industrious forest giants but the dirtier, more humanoid variety. He retreated as quickly as he could, almost losing a horse in deep mud.

The three Ruk spotted him when he was almost safe, and gave their roaring hunting cry and came after him. The speed with which they could cross a swamp was matched only by the ferocity with which they crashed through heavy brush that would have been impenetrable to men.

He strung his Eastern horn bow, cursing the weather and all sorcerers everywhere, and wishing that he had a partner. Or his wife.

He remounted and rode west along a stream whose deep grass banks offered an escape route. The stream opened into a long meadow over which he cantered, standing in his stirrups and staring at the ground. There were sinkholes made by the spring run-off and he rode like a circus performer, keeping his horses moving with calls and whistles.

He was negotiating the banks of an old beaver pond when he saw the three Ruks. He turned his riding horse and loosed three arrows, but he didn't pause to see the result, and rode west again.

The problem with Ruk was not that they were particularly good trackers, but that they never gave up. The term, 'stubborn as a Ruk' referred to their tendency to prefer following their prey until they killed it, no matter what distractions or opportunities were offered.

Turkos found another trail, this one headed east-west, too. He performed a small working to determine the locations of the Academy beacons and, on comparing them, he decided he was as close as was required and cast another seeking, this one his wife's way, masking his technical skill with Outwaller charms. When he had his vector, and the sick sense of having contacted something uncanny, he walked his spare horses a league east along the new trail, and then walked his riding horse back, carefully, with an arrow on his string. The Ruk were making poor time in the open ground after his arrows – as he'd hoped – and he paused where his own tracks joined the trail and took three vermilion-dyed feathers from his pouch and tied them in an elaborate web of red yarn to a bush and cast a glamour on them. There was no working under the glamour – but to a raw talent, the whole might appear as a trap.

Then, sitting on his riding horse in a light freezing rain, he waited behind a newly downed spruce, hood up over his beaver fur cap, green cloak pulled over his bow which he held against his body to warm the sinew.

When he heard the Ruk, he cast a light illusion to cover his own scent.

He waited until they were on the trail, in the open, just the length of a large house away. He watched them as they stopped to look at his feathers. They gathered around his bush.

He stood in his stirrups and loosed the arrows he had in the fingers of his left hand – five quick shafts with barbed heads, and every one of them hit. The first three were poisoned.

The Ruk didn't even grunt when they were hit. They turned as one, bellowed, and gave chase.

He loosed over the rump of his horse four more times, and then he'd lost them. They were not as fast as a horse by any means. By the time he reached his pack horses, they were far behind – but still coming.

He rode east. He trotted for as long as his horses could manage, and then he walked – slowly, but surely – all night. The emptiness of the woods was now explained – when the Ruk walked abroad, the other big animals were cautious.

Dawn brought bright sunshine. Turkos drank water from a stream so cold that the water hurt his teeth and rode east, passed a burned village clearly destroyed by Ruk. And later in the day, another.

At evening, his trail ended abruptly in a deep swamp right at the edge of the Inner Sea. He cast north, trying to get around the swamp, and found a pair of canoes but no path and no good ground.

Just after nightfall, he heard a tell-tale crashing along his backtrail. He filled the canoes with his goods and released the pack horses. He was quite fond of his saddle horse and he tried to entice her out into the black water and, eventually, she followed his canoe as he paddled and she swam. He knew she wouldn't go far, though, and cast desperately for dry ground in the dark.

Twice, he had to balance his canoe to rest a hand on her head and offer her his store of *ops*. But as the stars rose, clear and cold, finally he heard the swishing sound of small wind-driven waves on gravel, and she was ashore before he had carefully grounded his canoes. His little mare was none too happy to find herself on a rocky islet with a little shelter and no grass, but she wasn't drowned and he'd saved all his goods. He put his small wool tent over her and when she was drier and warmer, he pulled her down, threw all his blankets over both of them, and curled up against her back. He fed her oats by hand.

They both slept, and he didn't wake until she pushed herself against him and got to her feet. The world was nothing but a grey mist; and as soon as he was awake he could hear the Ruk. They were splashing in the fog, and he was afraid – deeply afraid. He had no idea how well they moved in deep water. Could they swim? His experience of them was limited – he'd never been pursued, only read about it.

He folded his wool blankets and his small tent while his poor horse stood and shivered, and then he packed his canoe as quickly as he could. The splashing noises went on, the Ruk seemed to be all around him.

He had a notion, drew an arrow from his quiver, and used it as the basis of a very short-range spell of finding.

As quick as he cast, he felt the three, each still wearing one of his arrows. The widest gap among the monsters was to the east so he got the canoes tied together and paddled the lead east. His little horse stood on the islet for a long time, and then, with a horse noise of panic, plunged into the water and swam powerfully after him.

The fog closed in, and he paddled hard, praying to Saint Mary the Virgin and all the saints to preserve him and his horse against the cold, the water, and the giants.

Liviapolis – The Red Knight

Ser Michael had kept the journal since the opening of the siege at Lissen Carrak. He'd changed the format and moved the journal into a large volume bound in dark red leather, acquired using his restored allowance in the endless bazaars of Liviapolis, and he'd decided to count the days from their first contract and work from there. Since he didn't plan to share the journal with anyone, he didn't have to account for how he kept it.

Military Journal – Day one hundred and eleven

The defeat of the Etruscan Fleet has had every result that the Captain promised, despite our having failed to entice any part of their squadron into the arsenal after No Head loosed one of his precious engines too early. We captured a single over-bold galley, thus doubling the Imperial Fleet. But the capture of Ernst Handalo, the Etruscan captain, accomplished what his death would not – the near total capitulation of the Etruscans. Handalo is a senator of far-off Venike. Apparently, he has begun to negotiate a peace on his own behalf.

Closer to home, our little victory had procured a certain good-will – or perhaps, as the Captain likes to say, merely the foundations on which future good-will might be laid. The Captain also released all of our prisoners from our battles under the walls; he has arranged with the Princess Irene for all of the prisoners to be cleared of treason. If the knights of Morea have consequently grown to love us for our clemency, they are extremely adept at hiding it.

However, the gates are open, the markets are open, and the harvest is in. Perhaps most importantly, convoys have begun to reach us from over the mountains, via the Inner Sea and the lake country. The Captain has plans for the fur trade and for Harndon. And on that topic, the Captain has arranged a series of loans against our profits that have paid the men, which cured a good deal of grumbling.

And finally, our victory seems to have won us the approval of the Patriarch and the University. The Captain is to meet the Patriarch on Sunday after mass. We have collectively crossed our fingers.

Ser Michael leaned back and licked his fingers to get the ink off.

Kaitlin came and leaned heavily against him. 'Could you carry this little bastard for a week or so while I have a rest?' she asked.

Ser Michael turned. 'Please let's not call our child a bastard.'

'He is, you know.' She smiled. It was a pleasant smile, not a nasty one, and yet Michael knew she meant business. He'd promised marriage, and she, a peasant girl, was currently widely viewed as his whore.

'Then marry me,' he said.

'When? Where?' she asked. 'And I really don't have a thing to wear.'

'I'm sorry, love,' he said, and put his hands on her waist. He held her against him so he could feel the swell of her belly against his own stomach. 'Sorry. I've been busy.' *Christ, that sounded lame.*

'There's a rumour that the Knights of Saint Thomas sent us a chaplain,' he added. 'Why don't we have him marry us when he arrives?'

She sat heavily in his lap. She wasn't really big yet, but she felt she was the size of a horse – ugly, frumpy, and the very antithesis of all the slim, elegant, perfumed Morean ladies she saw every day in the markets. 'I suppose that when you asked, I imagined we'd have a wedding in a cathedral, and I'd be – glorious. Somehow.'

'My father hasn't said no, but he certainly hasn't said anything nice, either.' Ser Michael stared out the window for a moment. *In point of fact, the silence from home is rather ominous. I got one allowance instalment and then nothing. And no answer to my letters.*

'Could we be married by the chaplain? Set a date?' she asked. 'I think – I think I'd rather be married with a fat belly than not married at all.'

He kissed her. 'I'll ask the Captain,' he said.

'The Duke,' she said.

He paused. 'What's that mean?' he asked.

Kaitlin was both his leman and a lower-class Alban woman in the barracks. She heard things he would never hear. Being viewed as Ser Michael's whore had its positive side – women who wouldn't dare approach Ser Michael's wife would happily share hot wine with her.

She shrugged. 'He likes being called Duke, doesn't he? The archers resent it. They grumble that he used to be one of them.'

Michael shook his head. 'Sweet Christ, my love, he's the Earl of the North's son; he was born with a bigger silver spoon in his mouth than I ever had. He was never *one of them*.' But even as he said the words, he thought of the Captain loosing a bow or fighting in the sheep pens at Lissen Carrak, before the siege started. *The common touch.*

She kissed him back. 'Don't get all huffy with me, love. And do not, I pray, get your ink-stained hands on my one neat kirtle which has a belly that fits. Hands off!'

She slid off his lap. 'Just tell him.'

Ser Michael nodded.

The Duke of Thrake sat in his new office in the barracks of the Athanatoi and read through a mountain of correspondence. He had a Morean secretary named Athanasios to help Master Nestor, a perfect gentleman who seemed to know everyone at court. The Duke suspected that Athanasios spied on him for the princess, but as he didn't have anything to hide from the princess, he didn't rock that particular boat.

'I can't read this one – Nestor?'

The company treasurer pushed his black cap back and tugged at his sleeves. 'Oh! My lord Duke, another note from the Queen of Alba, accusing you of neglect in not replying to her invitation to the tournament.'

'Addressed to?' he asked.

'The warrior styling himself the Red Knight,' Nestor said, reading the outside of the scroll.

'Return it as incorrectly addressed,' said the Duke. 'Be polite and inform her of my current title. Buy me some time.'

'A set of reports from our riding officers among the Outwallers,' Athanasios reported. He had a stack of flimsy sheets – obviously carried by Imperial messenger birds.

The Duke pounced. He took the papers and then looked at his Morean secretary. 'Give the new Megas Ducas the briefest description of your contacts with the Outwallers,' he said.

Athanasios nodded. 'My lord, we have several dozen rangers, let us say, among the tribes and people outside the wall.'

'That's the Imperial wall? Or the whole length of the wall?' the Duke asked sharply. 'The Alban portion?'

Athanasios shrugged. 'My lord, we are both intelligent men. I must ask for clearer instructions if I am to give you an explicit answer. As you can, I think, surmise from my hesitation.'

The Duke smiled. 'If I thank you for your candour, which one of us is lying?'

The door opened, and Ser Michael could be seen, laughing silently, in the hall. Bent, on guard at the door, was grinning.

'Michael! Would you care to return to being my apprentice? I feel the need to discuss some plans.' The Duke smiled and took a sip of lukewarm wine.

Michael put a hand to his chest in feigned shock. 'Discuss your plans? My lord, are you ill?' He shook his head. 'I'd be delighted. And I'd like to discuss a few things myself.'

'Speak,' said the Captain.

'Do we have a chaplain on the way?' he asked.

'Any day. I have had two messages from the Grand Prior. I gather we're getting a black sheep, to match our own plumage.' He shrugged. 'If I must have a priest I'll take one of theirs, I suppose.'

'Will you come to my wedding?' Michael blurted. The two secretaries worked on, pretending to be furniture.

'To the beauteous Kaitlin?' the Duke grinned. 'Absolutely. Where?'

'Barracks' chapel?' Ser Michael asked hesitantly.

The Red Knight grinned. 'Do I get to give her away?' he asked with a leer.

Michael reacted like any young man – he glared, and their glances crossed like swords – but they both laughed.

'And some shopping?' asked the Captain. 'Cloth of gold for the bride? Michael, your father is going to have a cow.'

'Could you manage an advance against my pay?' Ser Michael asked. It was odd to ask – the Captain seemed an ageless age, but not yet old enough to be his father and pay his bills. He felt awkward and his eyes kept flitting away from the Captain's face.

'And I should mention first that Kaitlin tells me some of the lads mislike your use of your new title,' he added.

The Duke leaned back after motioning to Toby to pour wine. 'When they win themselves dukedoms, they can sport the titles, too.'

'Are you drunk?' Michael asked.

The Captain poured himself a little more wine. 'Perhaps,' he said agreeably.

'Sweet Jesus, my lord.' Michael paused and looked at the Captain – really looked at him. He had dark circles under his eyes and the eyes looked old.

His Captain – his rock of certitude – looked afraid. Troubled. Angry.

'What's the matter?' Michael asked.

The Captain looked at him – his eyes narrowed. 'Nothing,' he said, but his face worked as if the muscles by his jaw had an independent existence.

'I'm dealing with it,' he said.

'So something is wrong,' Michael said.

'My breastplate is as scarred as an old pincushion and I don't have time to visit an armourer,' the Duke said. 'That heads my list of problems. Oh – we have a city of three or four hundred thousand people but fewer than two thousand soldiers to police it and hold the walls; the population distrusts us, and there are so many spies in this palace that it is possible that every word I say to you goes straight to the former Duke, to Aeskepiles and to all of their various henchmen, grain prices are rising, the Etruscans want trading concessions to lift the blockade, I've had no letters from Alba in two weeks and the princess thinks I'm a tool, not a man or a knight.' He sat back and drained his wine cup, and Toby came and took it from his hand. 'On the positive side of the ledger, you're getting married and that means a party, and by all that's holy, our company needs a party.'

'Could you stop calling yourself Duke?' Ser Michael asked.

'No,' said the Duke. 'We're in Liviapolis, and this is the way they are. If I don't live the role, no one will take me seriously.' He looked at Michael. 'You're a thinking man, Michael – have you ever considered what victory and defeat actually are? They're ideas, like justice. Different things to different men. Yes?'

'I'm sure my tutor managed to mention this once or twice,' Michael said. He fetched his own second cup of wine. Toby was rubbing oil into the shaft of the Duke's beautiful ghiavarina, a long, heavy spear with flanges. What made this one unique was that the Captain had been given it by a dragon, and the shaft seemed to have been made from the wizard Harmodious's staff.

The Duke laughed. 'Mine, too. My point is that if we appear to be winning, we will win. If we appear to be losing, we will most certainly lose. That is the way, with men. I must be the Duke, in order to ensure obedience from Moreans and to encourage them to believe that I will lead them to victory.'

'You're not drunk after all,' Ser Michael said.

The Duke leaned back, took the ghiavarina from Toby's hands and shot to his feet. He thrust, rolled the weapon around in a long and elaborate butterfly cut and brought it back on guard – cut a candle in half, and then another. 'I love this thing,' he said.

Toby grinned.

'It's like the company,' said the Captain. 'It is so much fun to use that I want to use it. All the time, if possible.' He grinned, and cut again, and sliced a bronze candlestick in two. 'Shit,' he muttered.

'I take it back. You *are* drunk,' Michael said. 'Glorious Saint George, you just cut through an inch of bronze.'

The Duke leaned over and looked at the mirror-bright cut. 'I did, too,' he said. They grinned at each other, and the Duke cut the candlestick again, from the wrists-crossed guard of the window. The blade passed clean through the bronze again. Michael reached out to pick up the fallen piece and recoiled.

'Hot,' he said. 'Can I try?'

He took the weapon, expecting to receive a shock or a prick of poison or some eldritch punishment, but there was none. He cut – and the blade clanged on the candlestick base. It went flying across the room, deeply dented.

'It's hermetical, at any rate,' he said.

The Duke rolled his eyes. 'Considering the source—' he said. 'Listen – I suppose I need a party too. Or perhaps a fight. Or both. I'm due to meet the Patriarch tomorrow – when we're done there, let's go into the bazaar and buy some things. Pretty things.'

Michael smiled. 'Thanks, my lord,' he said. 'I agree about the fight, too.' He nodded out the window. 'The boys need a fight, too. Pretty soon they'll start fighting each other.'

The Duke nodded. 'You may get your wish. I've played a small hazard tonight.' He shrugged. 'Stay armed.'

Ser Milus shook his head. 'The Cap'n is letting you three out on a pass? While the rest of us are locked in?' He didn't snarl, but Cully, the Captain's own archer, stepped back. Like Bad Tom, Ser Milus was a force to be reckoned with, and it didn't do to cross him.

It didn't do to cross the Captain, either, so the three archers stood silent while Ser Milus looked them over and gave their passes to No Head, who sounded them out, his lips moving carefully. It was an entirely *pro forma* demonstration, as the Duke's seal hung from their passes and it was unlikely to be a fake.

'You'd think that if the Cap'n was only letting three men go and drink outside the palace, he'd pick three as was clean and well kitted,' Milus said, fingering Long Paw's threadbare doublet.

Long Paw wanted to say that it was a working evening and he didn't want to ruin good kit in a fight, but the three of them had the strictest orders about secrecy. So he stood silently.

Ser Milus made a face. 'I'll go tell the fucking gate,' he said, and walked out with the faint rattle and clash of a man in full harness.

'He's only in a state as it's not his watch,' No Head said to his mates. 'Ser Alcaeus is on the roster – didn't show to relieve his nibs.'

They were all back at attention when Bad Tom, announced by his leg armour, clanked back into the guardroom. 'All right. You're all clear. Drink for me, you bastards.' Ser Milus appeared, and Tom whispered to him, and the surly standard bearer's face cleared. He stepped back and nodded. 'I'm for bed,' he said, a little too loudly.

The three archers saluted and moved quickly out the guardroom door into the torchlit Outer Courtyard before Bad Tom could change his mind.

They passed through the gate, exchanged passwords with the Nordikans there, and Cully and Bent went immediately across the Great Square. Long Paw dropped away.

'Look impressed,' Cully hissed. 'We can't seem too sure of ourselves.'

So they drifted from statue to statue for a while, until Cully was sure. Bent was standing with his thumbs in his belt, admiring one of a naked woman with a sword.

'We're being followed,' Cully said with satisfaction. 'Let's go.'

An hour later and the two men sat in a taverna lit by oil lamps, listening to four musicians play Morean instruments. The two archers didn't know what the instruments were called, but they obviously liked the music, as well as the attention of the two young women who had attached themselves to the foreigners.

The crowd was thick – surprisingly thick for the time of night.

Bent's girl became increasingly insistent, and he looked at Cully in mute appeal. Cully looked around carefully, and shrugged. 'Stick it out a while longer,' he said.

A voice behind Cully said, 'Just go with the girls,' but when he turned his head, there was no one there.

Cully leaned forward to Bent and made a sign, and Bent grinned. He dumped his girl off his lap, tossed a silver leopard to the musicians and let her pull him up the rickety stairs to the balcony above, and the tiny rooms behind over-fancy doors.

Cully's girl took his hand in hers and all but dragged him past the music, and an elderly workman in a crushed straw hat muttered 'Lucky bastard' in surprisingly good Alban. Cully gave the man a broad wink and ran up the stairs.

Long Paw pulled the hat down over his eyes, paid for his wine, and slipped through the beaded curtain that served as a main door.

The street outside the taverna wasn't packed – but there were a dozen or more men leaning against corners and pillars, all wearing swords. He kept his shoulders stooped and shuffled his feet.

One of the bravos in the street bumped into him – hard, and a-purpose. Long Paw allowed himself to lose his footing and fall, like an untrained man.

'Fuck you, farmer,' spat the bravo. 'Stay clear of my sword.'

Long Paw crawled away, turned a corner and bolted. He'd had three days to get to know the area and he still found it difficult in the darkness. He went down an alley, got turned around, and had to climb a rickety fence. A small church gave him his bearings – he was, after all, less than a stadion from the palace.

He tossed his smelly farmer's overshirt and his straw hat, got his scabbarded sword in his left hand, and ran.

The man sitting on the whore's bed was wearing mail. His two henchmen filled the rest of the room, and they both had heavily padded jupons and heavy clubs.

'So,' the man said. 'You two want to leave the Emperor's service?'

Cully shrugged. 'Maybe, and maybe not,' he said. 'I heard there was money in it.'

Bent couldn't quite squeeze into the room. He watched the young woman slip down the corridor with real regret. He also noted that armed men were starting to fill the common room below.

'Looks to me like you plan to have us whether we want to come or not,' he said.

The man on the bed spread his hands. 'You know,' he said with a nasty smile, 'either way, your mates will think you deserted, eh, foreigner?'

The Captain had been firm – they were to play the part of greedy mercenaries all the way to the end. Cully narrowed his eyes. 'You mean there's no money?' he asked. He had a hand on his dagger.

The two thugs in jupons moved towards him, raising their clubs.

'We'll talk about money later,' said the man on the bed. 'That's not my decision to make.'

'I don't like these odds,' Bent said. He'd been leaning in the doorway, cramped by his own size and the smallness of the room. Now he seemed to uncoil. He didn't fully draw his sword, but rather he slammed the pommel into the teeth of the nearest thug, who had somewhat foolishly chosen to ignore him. The man bent over, spitting teeth, and Bent broke his nose and kneed him in the groin in a single breath while Cully drew his dagger right-handed and mystified the other thug by swapping hands – the man blocked his empty right and received the left in his right eye. He fell, dead. Bent's man fell wheezing, and opened his mouth to scream.

Cully looked at Bent. 'Now look what you've done,' he said.

Bent stepped on his fallen adversary's throat.

The man on the bed turned white as a sheet. 'Don't you touch me,' he said. 'My people are all around you.'

Cully shook his head. 'So – there's no money?'

The man bit his lip.

'If you scream, I'll gut you,' Bent said. He pulled the door closed. To Cully, he said, 'There's twenty men down there. I don't think they plan to negotiate.'

Cully shook his head. 'Fuck me. You thought you could take us down with two fat fucks?' He sounded annoyed. 'And now you're alone with us. Doesn't that seem like bad planning?'

'He's not their boss,' Bent said. 'Look at him.'

The man was terrified.

Cully reached for the heavy shutters on the window. Bent stopped him. 'Crossbows,' he said.

'Oh, fuck,' muttered Cully. 'What have we got ourselves into?'

Ser Alcaeus spent more time with his mother than with the rest of the company – not by choice, but because the princess's hold on the throne was more precarious than the Alban mercenaries seemed to imagine and his mother, the Lady Maria, was working very hard to fill the posts of the court and to get the basic machinery of justice and tax collection running properly. In their short time back in Liviapolis, Ser Alcaeus had twice had to debate a point with his mother's inner council and then sat in on one of the Red Knight's – the Duke of Thrake's – meetings and had to debate the same point again. Once, he'd found his view changed and ended up debating the opposite point of view.

Eight days of riding the tiger and Alcaeus was exhausted. He avoided his chambers in the palace – he was too easy to find there – and walked across the Outer Court to the Athanatos barracks. Alone of the men in the company, he knew what a symbolic honour it was for a company of mercenaries to take the barracks of what had once been the Empire's elite cavalry regiment.

He'd played in the neglected barracks as a child – he'd kissed a pretty Ordinary there and taken her by the hand and run into the barracks as an adolescent, on a perfumed May day.

Now the barracks were clean and full of life, and he passed the outer door as the great gates of the Outer Court were opened behind him.

Bad Tom was sitting at the duty desk. He looked up. 'Ah! Where the fuck have you been, then?'

'And a pleasant evening to you, too, Ser Thomas,' said the Morean.

Tom rose from behind the desk. 'You have the duty, ser.'

The Morean groaned.

'And you can have it again tomorrow – just to teach ye to read the roster. Eh?' Tom grinned, and got up – all six foot five inches of him – from behind the desk. 'All yours, with my compliments.'

'Oh, Tom,' Alcaeus moaned. 'I'm shot! I've done the throne's paperwork all day. I'm not even armed.'

Ser Thomas grinned. 'You need more exercise, boyo. Let's fight tomorrow.'

Alcaeus met the big man's eye and matched his grin. 'Horse or foot?'

'That's my boy. Let's be a-horse. I'll be gentle on ye, and let ye sleep in after yon stint at the night watch. Go get your armour.'

Alcaeus found Dmitry, his squire, awake, and managed to get himself armed in less than fifteen minutes. The Morean boy was all contrition. 'I tried to find you and tell you you had the duty, ser!' and so Alcaeus learned that the Imperial Ordinaries had turned the boy out of the palace. He sighed, scraped his knuckles on his vambrace, and ran back to the guard room with Dmitry following him carrying his sword and helmet.

Tom nodded. 'All yours. Long Paw is out in town on a pass with Cully and Bent. The rest are in barracks. The Captain – the Duke – doesn't want the lads and lasses loose in the fleshpots until we're better liked here so you should have a quiet night.' He paused. 'The – er – Duke ordered that the quarter guard keep their horses saddled and ready though. You might want to order the same for your own.' He smiled nastily. 'Perhaps not such a quiet night after all, eh?'

Tom clapped his shoulder and retired, sabatons snapping crisply on the stone floor. Alcaeus leaned back in the heavy chair, breathing hard, and cursing his luck. He waved Dmitry to see to his horse, and the younger man went out into the cold night. Alcaeus leaned back in the big seat – big enough for a man in armour. His eyelids were heavy and he cursed.

The last thing I need is to fall asleep on duty.

He poured himself some mulled cider, heating on the hearth, his arms heavy in harness, drank it off, and felt a little better.

No Head sat at the other table, and he was writing furiously. Alcaeus leaned over and found that the man was copying a poem from a copybook – in low Archaic.

As Alcaeus loved poetry, he began to follow along.

'Do ye mind?' No Head asked. 'I don't like to be watched.'

Alcaeus rose and apologised. He could hear commotion in the courtyard. 'That's good stuff. Where'd you get it?' he asked.

No Head looked up. 'No idea. Ser Michael gave it to me to copy.' The man stretched his right hand. 'He's teaching me to read and write.'

Alcaeus, who took literacy for granted, paused and then reordered his thoughts. 'Ah – I crave your pardon. I wasn't watching you write, I was reading the poem.'

No Head laughed. 'It is a poem, I suppose. I can't read it. I'm just copying the letters.' He leaned back. 'And it cramps my hand worse than a sword fight. But I'm keen to learn – I want to write a book.'

Alcaeus thought he should stand watch more often. He'd seldom met anyone who struck him as less bookish than No Head. 'Really?' Alcaeus asked, worrying in the same moment that he sounded a little too surprised.

No Head leaned over. 'I hear you are a writer, eh?'

Alcaeus nodded. 'I think I write all the time. In my sleep, even.' He shrugged. 'If I'm not scribbling, I'm thinking about it.'

No Head nodded. 'That's just it, ain't it? It is like a bug that bites you, and then you can't let it go. What do you write about?'

Alcaeus shrugged. 'Life,' he admitted. 'Love. Women. Sometimes war.' He shrugged. The commotion in the courtyard was growing closer. 'And you?' he asked.

'I want to write a book about how to conduct a siege,' No Head said. 'How to build the big engines – how to choose the wood, how to make the torsion ropes, how to site 'em. How to dig a trench, and how to hold it. How to make fire.'

Alcaeus laughed. 'That's a good title. *How to Make Fire*.' He sighed. 'Or maybe *Kindles Fire*. It sounds different from my books – but half the world would want a copy, I suppose. Have you thought that you might be telling someone how to lay siege to you? You could be on the receiving end of your own—'

At that moment, the doors to the guardroom opened and a pair of Nordikans stood there with a tall, bearded man in a black travelling gown.

'Your man doesn't know the passwords,' said the smaller of the two Nordikans. He grinned at Alcaeus.

Alcaeus had never seen the man before, so he shook his head. Then he thought of the latest command meeting and the Duke's instructions about spies. His mother's comments in the same vein.

'Bring him here,' Alcaeus ordered.

'I'm not a member of the company,' the man said quietly.

Alcaeus shook his head in exasperation. There was more commotion out in the courtyard, and the door was open and cold air was pouring into the guardroom.

Long Paw came through the door with three more Nordikans.

'Quarter guard,' Long Paw shouted.

Alcaeus choked. It was the company's habit to keep almost a quarter of their men in full harness, archers with bows strung, at all times when under threat, but in barracks in the palace, they'd reduced this commitment to just twenty men. And he hadn't inspected them—

But of course, Tom had. And as the shout went up, they came pounding down the corridors – Oak Pew was the first one through the double doors at the barracks' end of the guardroom. She had a war bow in her fist and she already had a steel cap on her head. Ser Michael was next, and then the Captain himself, appearing fully armed from his office with Toby at his heels, and then the rest of them – Gelfred looked as if he'd been asleep in full harness while John le Bailli looked fresh, and right behind him was one of the new men-at-arms – Kelvin Ewald, a small man with a long scar. He wore a fancy harness.

'To horse,' said the Captain.

Long Paw said, 'There are twenty or thirty men to take them. It was an ambush.'

The Captain was already getting his leg over his new gelding, bought from the Imperial stables. He cursed.

Long Paw rolled onto a small Eastern horse, and they were off, and the Nordikans had the gate open. Then they rode across the square and through the streets – first a broad street, and then a sharp corner, and then another, the street narrowing all the way, and then another turn, a Y intersection . . .

Long Paw raised his arm.

There were two more men – dead or dying – in the doorway of the tiny room, and Bent had a dagger wound in his left arm.

The man on the bed was unconscious, as Cully had punched him in the head.

'My turn,' Cully said. 'Make room.'

He and Bent switched – even this movement was the result of practice, and they changed like dance partners. Cully had his buckler off his hip, and he wrapped it around Bent from the left, caught a blow intended for the wounded man and made a short slash with his arming sword as Bent ducked away behind him. His new adversary didn't really want to be there, alone, against a much better swordsman, and he backed away, assuming that Cully wouldn't follow him from the safety of the doorway.

He was wrong, and he died for it, and then Cully was loose in the corridor, and he cut down two men – whirled, and managed to slam his buckler into the archer's head – there was an archer in the corridor, looking for a shot he never took. Cully's point sliced through the candle in a wall sconce, and a kick smashed the table with a dozen small oil lamps.

In the comparative saftey of a considerably darker corridor he got his back into the room, and took a knee.

'I'm too old for this shit,' he said.

Bent cackled.

And then a faint smell of smoke caught at the back of Cully's throat.

Long Paw sent half a dozen archers down the black maw of an alley. He turned to the Duke and shook his head. 'Never thought they'd have so many men. They have archers on two buildings, that I saw – maybe more.'

The Duke scratched under his chin. 'I'd like to take them all.'

'We'd lose Bent and Cully,' Long Paw said.

The Duke grinned. 'Can't have that. Well, Michael said he wanted a fight. If the men in harness go on foot to clear the tavern we can let the archers try and clear the roofs. Yes?'

Ser Alcaeus nodded. 'We've got a handful of Scholae. They followed us.'

The Duke whirled his horse. 'Watch them.'

'Watch them?' Ser Alcaeus asked. 'I'm related to half of them.'

The Duke wasn't to be swayed. He leaned in close. 'Alcaeus, this is all an elaborate attempt to catch a spy. This place is riddled with traitors, and the palace—'

Long Paw was motioning. 'The taverna's afire,' he called.

The Duke shrugged. 'Too late for talk. Dismount – horse holders. Helmets on, armoured men on me, unarmoured go with Long Paw. I want as many prisoners as can be taken, commensurate with not losing one of you.'

Oak Pew laughed aloud. The Duke frowned at her, and Sauce swatted the top of her steel cap with a gauntlet. 'Prisoners,' Sauce said with a nod.

Then they were off into the dark. Alcaeus knew this part of town well enough from his Academy days, but not in the dark – or rather, the streets he knew in the dark were closer to the waterfront. He followed Ser Michael, who followed Ser Alison, who followed the Duke.

They didn't have to go far. They crossed one intersection and jogged noisily down a very narrow alley full of rubbish, and then they emerged into a small square lit by a burning building.

Ser Alcaeus saw a man right where he expected to, making for the mouth of the next street, and he ran across the flagstones of the ancient square, missed his quarry but cut another man off and knocked him down with an armoured arm to the face. A sword struck his back, rang off his backplate, and then the fighting was over – Alcaeus whirled to find Ser Michael had cut his assailant's arm off at the elbow. The bravos were armed with side swords, daggers, and clubs – they couldn't stand even a moment against armoured men, and they ran or surrendered very quickly.

Ser Alison and the Duke went straight into the taverna. It wasn't fully afire – the only bright flames were coming from the roof.

A fire company appeared – forty men with buckets. The buckets went down into the cisterns, and the water started to go onto nearby houses first, to prevent the spread.

Someone slammed into Alcaeus from behind, and he sprawled on the flagstones – a crossbow bolt slammed into the stone nearest his outstretched hand. He rolled – life at the Morean court encouraged quick responses to assassination – and saw the man who'd knocked him flat. He got a knee under him, got his dagger in his right fist—

The man raised his visor. 'I'm on your side,' he hissed. He offered a hand, but Alcaeus was not quick to trust in a fight – he backed away, and an arrow struck him.

The stranger waved him away. 'Get under cover!' he shouted, and turned.

Presenting his back to Alcaeus seemed a gesture of trust – Alcaeus took it and followed him, dimly recognising the black cloak of the stranger that the Nordikans had brought to him in the guardroom, what seemed like hours before.

The black-cloaked stranger found an external staircase and pounded up it, his heavy boots making the stairs shake, but Alcaeus followed him, and felt the second-storey balcony move. Behind him, he saw that the square had emptied as more and more bolts were shot at anyone moving in the light.

Suddenly, the rooftops were *bathed* in light – a light suspended above the centre of the square, dazzling in its brightness. Even in the confines of a helmet, Alcaeus could see that there were archers on some of the rooftops. Even as he looked, they realised that they were visible. Some ducked, others took arrows from the company archers in the streets.

The stranger leaped up, grabbed a lead gutter, and swung himself onto the sill of a thousand-year-old window. 'On the roof!' he called to Alcaeus.

Ser Alcaeus had a moment to imagine that this might be a very clever plot to kidnap him, and then he followed the stranger – up onto the roof, and then, panting inside his helmet, over a roof-edge wall and down onto the next roof – a tiled roof that hadn't had its tiles changed in so long that they just peeped out from a layer of moss and lichen. He could hear old tiles breaking under his feet, but the foliage was good footing and he followed the stranger over the peak—

And into a trio of desperate men. All three wore dark clothing and facemasks. The furthest took one look at the two coming over the roofline and simply jumped over the roof edge to die on the cobbles below, or not.

The other two attacked the stranger. He absorbed a blow in his heavy black cloak, drew his sword and cut into the second man's attack. Alcaeus was fully armoured and considerably less elegant – he fell into the nearest opponent, ignored two cuts that he didn't see in the dark. The other man chose to wrestle, and Alcaeus broke his arm and then knocked him unconscious against his armoured knee.

The stranger had disarmed his man and was tying his hands with his belt.

Alcaeus opened his visor and breathed. 'Who are you?' he asked.

The man's smile shone in the bright white hermetical light that still hung over the square in front of the taverna. 'I'm your new chaplain,' he said.

The Duke went into the taverna and found Cully and Bent lying flat in the taproom with their prisoner wedged between them. He got them out the door, a bolt zanged off his helmet, and he ducked back into the doorway of the taverna.

Your men need better light, Harmodius said.

He cast that working himself, and he was surprised at the brilliance of his light. Then he added to it by putting subsidiary workings over the houses surrounding the little square – tall, stuccoed houses with a variety of rooflines perfect to hide assassins and archers.

The roar of the fire alerted him, and the fire company in the square wasn't going to accomplish anything – one or two had already been hit by arrows, and the rest were taking cover, and the bucket chain was irretrievably wrecked.

But somewhere under his feet was a cistern with thousands of gallons of water. He worked a displacement—

He was in his place of power, locating the water with one very small working while manipulating its location. On the marble plinth, Harmodius nodded.

Well done, boy. So much simpler than creating the water. No – not over the roof – under the roof. You aren't limited in your placement. Right on the fire—

The Duke cast. As he cast his working, Harmodius said, Aren't we standing right under—

The wall of water extinguished the blaze instantly.

The new Duke of Thrake was not as elegant as he would have liked to be when he met his new chaplain a few minutes later – soaked to the skin in the chill autumn air, he was already shivering under his armour, despite the heavy cloak that Ser Michael produced and threw over him. Another cloak went over Bent, who'd been knocked flat by the water and was still having trouble breathing.

The Duke sneezed again.

'So the man Cully took...?' he asked.

Bad Tom shook his head. 'He knows some names and two locations. He's paid a day-labourer in the Navy Yard, and he's used to picking up a package from the palace every day.'

'This wasn't a complete waste of time, then,' the Duke said, and sneezed again.

'You might have told me,' Ser Milus said.

The Duke nodded. 'I probably should have,' he admitted.

Ser Gavin came in and threw himself down on a stool. 'Sellswords and thugs. The two that Alcaeus and the priest caught are merely more expensive thugs. They were hired to ambush anyone who came to the taverna.'

Cully, who had been sitting listening, shook his head. 'Give me a straight-on battle anytime,' he said. 'They offered to pay us to desert, but they never meant to pay us, they only meant to kill us. We never meant to desert – we meant to capture them. They expected us to double-cross them and laid an ambush, but they didn't expect you to bring the whole quarter guard with you, so we fucked them up.'

The Duke nodded. 'That's about it. So now we follow our leads: watch part of the laundry service to see who follows the directions our captured bully is used to leaving; pick up the day-labour spy at the Navy Yard—'

'Who won't know anything,' Bad Tom spat.

The Duke shrugged, and then sneezed twice. 'It was worth a try,' he said.

Ser Gavin said, 'You should dry your hair.' He got a towel and tossed it to his brother. 'Now what do we do?'

Ser Milus was still annoyed. 'It sounds like you had a fight and I wasn't in it,' he said. 'Why didn't you tell me?'

'Three in a secret,' the Duke muttered. 'I'm sorry, Milus, I wasn't thinking clearly.' He spread his hands. 'I think I'm trying to do too many things.' To Gavin he said, 'Now let's try a poison pill.'

'What's that?' Gavin asked.

'I tell several people that I suspect a secret has been betrayed – a very hot secret. I give them each a slightly different secret, and then I see what happens. It's like dropping dye into a sewer, to see where it comes out.'

'And then what?' Ser Gavin asked.

'No idea,' the Duke answered. 'But it's time. We need to take the war to Andronicus, before he gets in here.' He sneezed. 'First we have to bring in the fur caravans.'

'What fur caravans?' Gavin asked.

The next day, the Duke of Thrake rode across the square to the tall onion-topped spires of the Academy and was admitted with much fanfare. He dismounted at the hundred steps that rose from street level all the way to the base of the ancient Temple of Poseidon – now the church of Saint Mark the Evangelist – and he walked up the steps accompanied by Ser Alcaeus and his new chaplain, Father Arnaud. He sneezed every few steps, and he didn't move very quickly.

He paused at eye level with the ancient statue to Cerberus, guardian of the underworld. The statue was enormous, and each of the dog's three great heads had its mouth open and fangs bared.

'Why does it feel so empty?' Father Arnaud asked.

The Megas Ducas patted a head affectionately. 'The statue is itself an hermetical void. Students can throw anything they like inside. And they do. This is where they rid themselves of anything that went wrong.' He grinned. 'And no questions asked.'

'Where does it go?' asked the Alban.

The Megas Ducas smiled wickedly. 'The Chancellor's office? The Patriarch's desk? Hell?' He shook his head.

Ser Alcaeus looed at him. 'Admit it! You were a student here.'

'Never,' said the Megas Ducas. 'Come! Until we reach the ante-chamber, we have not yet begun to wait.'

At the top, they were met by a pair of priests who led them along the magnificent colonnade under the heavy marble decoration of the ancient architrave and into the right-hand building, another ancient temple, smaller, but gemlike in its perfection with gold inlay in marble and a row of statues that made the Duke pause in admiration.

The lead priest smiled indulgently. 'Pagan heroes,' he said. 'The statues were brought from the old world.'

Ser Alcaeus had seen them every day of his Academy career, and he smiled to see his Captain admire one, and then the next.

'Superb,' he said.

Father Arnaud shrugged. 'Why is our ability to duplicate God's work in lifeless marble so attractive to men?' he asked.

The Duke raised an eyebrow at him. He seemed to be saying, 'Is that the best you can do?'

Father Arnaud shrugged.

They were led past the statues, through a palatial set of arches that were themselves part of one of the city's most ancient pieces of fortification, and then into a relatively modern hall of stone and timber. There were several young men and four gowned nuns sitting primly on benches. The priests bowed and waved to servitors, who brought small glasses of wine – the precise quantity that travellers were usually offered at monasteries.

The young people watched the Duke carefully, as if he might be dangerous. Ser Alcaeus leaned over. 'That's the Baldesce boy,' he breathed. 'His father is the Podesta of all the Etruscans in the city.'

Father Arnaud sat on one of the long benches. 'If I put my feet up and go to sleep, will the Patriarch be offended?' he asked. He did pull his black cloak about him.

The Duke snapped, 'As he's the most powerful prelate in Nova Terra, yes. I'd rather you were polite, Father.'

The Baldesce boy rose from his friends and came over. 'You are the new Duke of Thrake,' he said with a pretty bow.

The Duke rose. 'It's all true,' he said.

The young man smiled. 'My father hates you,' he said. 'I should hate you too, but you are cutting a fine figure here. Is the Patriarch keeping you waiting?'

Ser Alcaeus tried to throw the Duke a warning glance, but the Duke nodded. 'I suppose, but it's scarcely waiting yet. Waiting, as such, only really starts after the first hour, or that's what I'm told.'

The Etruscan boy laughed. 'Well, I just thought someone should tell you that our friend is having his examination, and it is running long over time – but the Holy Father isn't making you cool your heels.'

Noting that their friend hadn't been eaten by the Duke, the four nuns and two other young men were drifting very slowly towards the conversation.

The Duke was interested. 'Why is your friend being examined? For heresy?'

One of the nuns laughed. 'He's not a heretic as far as I know,' she said. She looked confused. 'Actually, he is. Now that I think of it, he's a barbarian like you—'

The Duke paused and then sneezed into his sleeve. 'Don't worry, sister. Where I come from, barbarian is the very highest of compliments.'

There was some shuffling of feet.

'Besides,' the Duke went on, 'almost no one is a barbarian like me.'

Baldesce laughed. 'Is it true that you are making a truce with the Merchant League?' he asked.

The Duke managed a smile. 'Are you usually this bold?' he asked.

'My father is the Podesta,' Baldesce said.

The Duke smiled. 'In that case, it will do me no harm to say that we have released all of our Etruscan prisoners. The rest is between your father and the Merchant League.'

Father Arnaud rolled his eyes.

The double doors opened.

Morgan Mortirmir wore a smile as radiant as a hot fire on a cold day. Behind him, the Patriarch stood in robes that had once been black and had faded over many years to a dark blue-grey. The Patriarch had his arms in his sleeves and he was smiling, too.

He walked out into the antechamber. The young man's friends walked over to him, shook hands, and in the case of two of the nuns, chaste embraces were exchanged. The young man continued to beam happily. 'I passed,' he said, six or seven times.

Baldesce pumped his hand. 'You really are an idiot,' he remarked. 'Of course you were going to pass.'

The Duke walked over, inserted himself among the young man's classmates – he was not more than five years older than the eldest – and shook the young man's hand. 'I gather we are countrymen,' he said. 'You are Alban?'

'Oh yes, sir,' Mortirmir said. 'I know who you are – I've seen you at the palace!' He beamed at the Duke.

Now there is power. Hermes Trismegistus, that boy has power.

Please efface yourself. How much do I need to drink, to rid myself of you?

'You are a student here, I understand?' the Duke asked.

'Yes, my lord Duke.'

'Study hard. Ever thought of a career as a professional soldier?' the Duke asked.

'Yes, my lord!' the boy said.

'I see you wear a sword,' the Duke continued.

'I've told him it's a foolish thing for a practitioner,' Baldesce said.

The Duke smiled. 'I've never found it that foolish,' he answered, and then ruined his patronising look with a heavy sneeze.

He walked from Mortirmir to the Patriarch, who allowed him to kiss his ring. 'There goes a most entertaining young man,' said the Patriarch. 'Very late to his power – very powerful, I think. Perhaps not the most powerful in his class, but very bright. A pleasure to test.' He bowed and led them down another corridor, this one a row of cloisters facing into a beautiful courtyard with four quince trees trained to heavy wooden screens. One was in flower; one was just budding, one was in fruit, and one was green and empty.

The Patriarch led them along the cloisters and into a small office with a single massive desk covered in books and scrolls. 'Find room where you can,' he said, a little absently. 'How can I help you, my lord Duke?'

'Holy father, I've come—' the Duke was looking at a scroll. 'This is an *original* copy of Hereklitus?' he said. 'But the *Suda* says he offered his book as a sacrifice to Artemis!'

The Patriarch smiled. 'The *Suda* says a great many foolish things. You read High Archaic?'

'Very slowly, Holy Father.' His finger was following his eyes.

Ser Alcaeus tried to attract his Captain's attention.

Father Arnaud stood rigid as a board.

The Patriarch looked at Father Arnaud. 'You are a knight of Saint Thomas, I think?'

'Yes, Holy Father,' the chaplain said. 'A priest.'

'A priest? That must be very difficult, Father. The teachings of Jesus are not easy to reconcile with violence.' The Patriarch leaned forward. 'Or how does it seem to you?'

Father Arnaud bowed. 'I have had struggles,' he admitted.

The Patriarch nodded. 'You would be a mere brute if you had not.' But he seemed well satisfied, and offered his ring to the priest to kiss.

'Ser Alcaeus,' he said. 'How is your lady mother? Busy hatching plots?'

Rather than taking offence, Ser Alcaeus nodded. 'Truthfully, Holy Father, she is too busy to hatch the least plot. Her only plot now is to save the Empire.'

The Patriarch raised an eyebrow at this but he chuckled warmly and turned to the Duke. 'You must pardon me, my lord, but Alcaeus was one of my students – not much of a practitioner, but a fine mind and a very able poet, when he chooses to use his powers for good. He wrote many scurrilous verses about his teachers.'

Alcaeus writhed.

The Patriarch's heavily lidded eyes fell back on the Duke.

'Surely you can read faster than that,' he said.

The Duke looked up. 'The Academy is choosing to remain neutral,' he said.

Alcaeus blanched.

The Duke went on, 'The University's neutrality is close to treason, Holy Father. The Emperor has been taken, and the traitor who took him has already offered to sell a portion of the Empire to get what he wants. The Emperor's own magister, who must have been appointed by the Academy, has proven a traitor. He is a man of exceptional power. Why is the Academy so chary of taking sides?'

The Patriarch's face gave nothing away. 'I'm sorry that you feel we've been neutral,' he said carefully. 'The Academy is at the service of the palace – now and any time in the future.'

'Couldn't you have prevented the Emperor's capture?' the Duke asked. He sat up. 'At least one of your astrologers must have predicted it.'

The Patriarch steepled his fingers. 'And we informed the palace.' He made a motion with his hands. 'Sadly, through Master Aeskepiles, who really is a traitor – to the palace, and to his training. But that is not the fault of the Church or the University.' He leaned forward. 'You are a mage yourself,' he said. 'But something about you is quite odd – as if you have two souls.'

The Duke leaned back.

Hide.

Silence . . .

'I had a tutor in the *ars magicka* who was trained here. I practise

381

when I can.' The Duke nodded. 'If I had any time at all, I'd ask to attend some classes.'

'The capture of another soul is necromancy, is heresy and is an illegal hermetical act,' the Patriarch said. He leaned forward. 'Is that another soul I sense?' he asked.

'No,' the Duke lied smoothly.

The Patriarch narrowed his eyes.

'Holy Father, if I were a daemon I'd hardly have strolled into your office...'

The Patriarch leaned back and laughed. 'I sometimes wonder. But it may just be my age. Sometimes I sense doubles in the *aethereal*.' His gaze sharpened. 'And sometimes I sense heresy where there is none. You bear the reputation as the very spawn of Satan, despite saving Lissen Carrak from the Wild.'

'Really?' asked the Duke. 'I also saved this city from treason, I believe. And my people have been attacked by hermeticism – right here, under your very nose, Holy Father.'

The Patriarch leaned back. 'I am hardly your foe, here.'

The Duke nodded. 'I never thought you were. May we speak privately?'

Father Arnaud led the procession out of the Patriarch's private office.

The two men were entirely amicable when they emerged. The Patriarch held the Duke's arm, they embraced, and then the Duke kissed the Patriarch's ring.

'Save the Emperor,' the Patriarch said.

'I'm doing all I can,' said the Duke.

Father Arnaud stepped forward. 'Holy Father, I have a message from Prior Wishart.'

The Patriarch nodded. 'I have never met him, but he has a great reputation. Yet your order has, in the past, remained aloof from us and even leaned towards Rhum.'

Father Arnaud merely held the scroll out and said nothing.

The Patriarch laughed. 'Old men will go on,' he allowed, and took the scroll. He read quickly, and then looked over the top of the scroll at the Duke. 'The King of Alba is appointing a Scholastic Bishop of Lorica?' he said.

The Duke was, for once, obviously taken aback. He glared at Father Arnaud and bowed to the prelate. 'My apologies. I had no idea.'

The Patriarch tapped the scroll on his teeth. 'I will see you in less than a week. Let me think on this.' He raised a hand and made a full benediction. 'Go with God.'

That was far too close.

Harmodius, you are becoming a liability.

I'm working on it! The old man shook the head of his statue. *I'm finally in a town where I can buy things I need. Things you need. I just need more time.*

Old man, you have taught me well; you have saved the company at least once; without you, I'd have lost the siege at Lissen Carak. But my headaches are worse every day, and I'm starting to make mistakes – mistakes that will kill people I love.

I just need more time. A few weeks. Must I beg?

No, said the Red Knight.

Harmodius made an extra effort to go deep.

When they left the Patriarch, the Duke took his friends shopping. Ser Michael and a deeply blushing Kaitlin met them at the foot of the Academy steps, as did Ser Gavin and Ser Thomas and Ser Alison. They all wore a minimum of armour – just breastplates – and carried swords and wore their jewels. They were attended by forty pages in the scarlet company livery, and even though they were riding almost every horse the company possessed, they looked very capable.

'Look rich and dangerous,' he told them.

Shopping in the city was an endless set of nested choices – tables of wares and booths and shops with polished hardwood walls and glass – real glass – in the windows, or small stalls made of hand-woven carpets from the far east, or simply a rude box of barn boards. There was a square of jewellers, a square of glovers, a square of sword smiths and a square of armourers, of silk weavers, of tailors, of veil makers, of perfumers.

The ostensible purpose of the expedition was to buy everything required for a wedding, but the Duke clearly had his own agenda, and in the square of the jewellers, he led them to the most elegant shop in the middle of the long block, where he was received like a visiting prince. He turned to Ser Michael and took him by the hand. 'You are rich,' he said. 'Buy this beautiful young woman a trinket or two.'

'With what?' Michael spat.

'Just choose some things,' the Duke said, and followed his host through a door which closed behind him.

Sauce, of all people, chose a comb with red and green enamel. The comb depicted two knights locked in mortal combat – dagger to dagger – in lovingly detailed harness, and she took off her hat, put it in her hair, and smiled into a mirror – and then closed her mouth to hide the missing teeth. 'How much?' she asked.

A shop boy was sent for sweet tea.

Ser Michael found his lady-love a wild rose in gold and garnets. She loved it, and he loved her. He put it on the padded silver tray.

Ser Gavin wandered from shelf to shelf, and finally chose a pair of bodkins for lacing and a set of buttons – cunning, tiny buttons for a lady's gown, all filigree with tiny bells hidden inside that made a lustrous sound.

The other knights tried not to damage anything.

The Duke emerged with a tight smile, and he and the jeweller embraced. He examined Ser Michael's choices and his smile grew broader.

'On my tab,' he said quietly.

Sauce paid in hard silver and softer gold, from a bag she produced.

Ser Michael noted that Sauce and the Captain exchanged a long glance as the bag was closed and she stowed it away.

In the square of the glovers, all discipline broke down, and the knights began to spend money like the mercenaries they were. Gloves were one of a soldier's most precious possessions – along with boots, an item upon which a man's comfort depended utterly. Good gloves were essential under gauntlets and just as necessary for archers.

Master Baldesce, Master Mortirmir and the nuns were also buying gloves, and by a gradual process of social osmosis, they were absorbed into the company and joined the knights, squires and pages at a tavern for wine.

The Duke walked from cup to cup, dipping the point of his roundel dagger into each pitcher before the wine was served, and the pages served it themselves. Michael could see his Captain was taking no chances.

Young Baldesce turned to Mortirmir. 'He's a magister! Look at his casting. Clean!'

Master Mortirmir watched the Duke's simple working with an avid curiosity.

After wine, they visited armourers. The Captain went from shop to shop for an hour, and while Kaitlin might have been bored, her husband-to-be entertained her by singing romances in a street-side wineshop. A pair of Morean street singers were attracted – they listened first, and then began to play accompaniment so good that all the knights who weren't avid for new armour applauded, and the pages were smitten. Then the street singers sang. The knights distributed largesse, and by the time the Captain had been carefully measured for a new breast and back in hardened steel, a small theatre had been set up and one of the ancient plays was being performed by a troupe of mimes in antic clothes.

Kaitlin, despite her pregnancy and fatigue, was delighted.

The Duke stopped by the singers and engaged them for the wedding party, and the actors as well. He paid them a fair amount of money, which was as well, because all of them subsequently received visits from Bad Tom that might have caused them to question their luck.

Every knight, man-at-arms and page had his sword sharpened in the street of cutlers, and the young Etruscan watched, delighted, as twenty mercenary swordsmen tested blades, so that wherever one looked, there was the soft slip of a balanced blade through the air – wrist cuts, overhand thrusts, imbrocattac. The sword smiths earned more hard coin in an hour than they usually saw in two weeks.

The Duke prowled the street like a predator in search of prey, swishing an arming sword through the air, admiring a brilliantly made Tartar sabre in green leather, fondling a roundel dagger – until he settled on one shop which was neither grander nor shabbier than the rest.

He went in. There were a dozen swords on the walls, and he could see the workshops built into the stone of the hillside beyond and smell the fires and the metallic odour the grinding wheels gave off. The master cutler came out in person, wiping his hands. He was small, wiry, and looked more like a schoolmaster than a smith.

Ser Michael stood at the Duke's shoulder. He was part of an impromptu conspiracy – with Tom and Sauce and Gavin – to keep the Captain under their eyes all the time. He was odder than usual; too often drunk, and too often irritable.

But not in the cutler's shop. There, he was more elated.

'You make the best blades,' the Duke said.

The cutler pursed his lips. 'Yes,' he agreed, as if it displeased him. 'That is, Maestro Plaekus makes them, and I turn them into weapons.' He frowned again. 'What is it you want?'

There followed a long exchange. Apprentices ran for wooden forms, for swords – at one point, a dagger was borrowed from a Morean nobleman's house two streets way.

In the end, the Duke settled on a length, a hilt, a pommel, blade shape, a cross section, a weight. And a matching basilard.

'Jewels?' the cutler asked.

Michael had seldom seen so much disdain packed into one word.

'No,' said the Duke. 'Ghastly idea. But red enamel. Red scabbard.' He smiled. 'Red everything. And gold.'

The cutler nodded wearily. 'Of course, gold.'

The Duke leaned forward. Michael saw the change – a subtle change in body language, a change in tone. He didn't know what it meant, but he'd seen it happen once or twice.

'May I ask a personal question?' the Duke said.

The cutler raised an eyebrow, as if the ways of the gentry and the killers who bought his wares were so alien that he couldn't be expected to know what was next. 'Let's ee, my lord,' he said smoothly.

'Wasn't the Emperor's magister once one of your apprentices?' the Duke asked.

The cutler sighed. 'Aye.' His Morean was difficult to follow, accented the way the Morean islanders spoke. 'He was here twenty years.' He frowned. 'More than an apprentice.'

The Duke nodded. 'Do you – perhaps – have anything of his?'

To Ser Michael, it was that moment when your opponent was a little too eager to draw the next card. The Duke was up to something.

'When he left—' The cutler shrugged. 'He left all his work things. When he came into his powers.' He looked away. 'He was already thirty years old. Very late.'

Wine was served, and sugared nuts.

A tall woman appeared with a bundle. 'Two work smocks, and a cap.' She smiled ruefully. 'I made him the cap, before he was so high and mighty. Kept sparks out of his hair.'

The Duke took the cap carefully – almost reverentially. 'Such a famous man,' he said.

Harmodius released control of his host and slammed his aethereal fist into his aethereal palm.

The Captain was shaken – scared, and betrayed. 'How dare you!'

Harmodius raised an aethereal eyebrow. 'You want rid of me. I want to be out of you. I have a plan. Sometimes, I need your body to make it move along.'

The Captain felt as if he might vomit. But it was – again – his body. He surfaced not in conscious control and found that he was sitting in a chair. In the moment of confusion, his body had apparently let go a cup of wine. Ser Michael was looking at him as if he'd grown a second head – Gavin was standing with a hand on his shoulder.

'Brother?' he asked. 'You were not yourself.'

The Megas Ducas grunted. 'You don't know the half of it,' he said.

He looked down, and in his right hand, wound around his index finger, he had a hair – a thick, coarse black hair.

Don't lose that! Harmodius said.

Nor was that the limit of the Duke's odd behaviour.

He made some odd stops. He spent so much time in a street of apothecaries and alchemists that the rest of the company moved on and began selecting fabrics for Kaitlin's dress, a subject on which, it turned out, every knight had an opinion. But when Kaitlin and her sisters had found a shop they liked, they went in with Mag the seamstress and Lis the laundress and didn't emerge until the Duke was long returned from the alchemists. He bought scarlet wool for the company, and brocades for others; velvet for a purse, and a few other pieces.

Quite late in the day, Father Arnaud watched him. 'Are you unwell?' he asked.

The Duke turned to Father Arnaud. 'May I refresh your clothes, Father?' He met the priest's eye easily enough. 'I've been better. But I'm hoping to – rid myself of a malady.'

Arnaud was leaning against an ancient column that helped to support a booth that sold nothing but silk gauze. He nodded. 'If you offer me charity, you gain in honour; if you mean to make me look better as an adornment of your power – well, you still gain, I suspect.' He smiled. 'Either way, I'd very much appreciate a new cloak.'

The Duke reached down and lifted the hem of his chaplain's cloak. 'It's good cloth, but something lifted the black dye—' Indeed, the whole lower half of the cloak was dun brown instead of the deep, rich black of the order.

'Giant shit,' the priest said carefully.

The Duke's eyebrows shot up.

The priest leaned in. 'I have letters for you. I assume you are spending all this money to a purpose?'

The Duke managed a thin-lipped smile. 'Yes,' he said.

Arnaud shrugged. 'I know you aren't used to having a chaplain, but I have this task as a penance and I mean to do it.' He leaned forward. 'What malady?'

The Duke's eyebrows shot up further and he furrowed his brow a moment, as if listening to someone. Then he shrugged. 'I might like having someone to bounce things off,' he said. 'As long as you aren't too talkative.' Kaitlin and Michael had their heads together and were as pretty as a picture of two saints. 'Will you marry them?'

'Saint Michael, it would be a sin *not* to wed them. Of course I will.' The priest smiled.

'We're spending money to show what nice, rich mercenaries we are. We need to win these people over, and lately I've been losing.' The Duke smiled at Sauce, who was waving a beautiful piece of scarlet velvet.

'Are you expecting to be attacked?' the priest asked. He was losing track of the number of conversational threads that his new employer could weave at one time.

'Only six people knew where we were going after the Patriarch,' the Duke said. 'If one of them has turned, I'll know it in an hour.'

'You are the only soldier I know who doesn't swear,' Father Arnaud said.

'Is that a sin? God and I have our own arrangement.' The Duke's smile was cold as ice. 'My company needs a chaplain. I do not happen to need a confessor.'

Father Arnaud leaned close. 'But you like a challenge,' he said.

'I do,' said the Duke.

'Me, too,' said the priest.

*

They made it back to the palace without being attacked, having spent a staggering sum on jewels, another on gloves, and yet more on cloth. Even the pages had new daggers. The Duke insisted on taking them back to the square of armourers so that they could all see the model for his new breast and back, in the new Etruscan style.

The priest rode with Ser Alison. She'd craved a blessing from him as soon as he joined them, identifying herself as one of the few truly devout knights in the company, not so much by her words but actions.

'I haven't seen him so happy in a long time,' she said to the priest. 'It's a little scary.'

Father Arnaud nodded. 'I met him the day after the siege was lifted – in the stable. He didn't seem this dark.' The priest looked at the woman in armour. 'You've had your hand on your sword this last half an hour. Do you know something I should know?'

Ser Alison laughed her full-throated laugh. 'See the leather bag under my right leg?' she said. 'Full of gold coin. Sixty thousand florins, give or take.'

Father Arnaud paused, and then whistled. 'Sweet gentle Jesus and all the saints. That's what he did at the jewellers.'

Sauce grinned as the guard called out their challenge and the Duke answered. 'You're quick, Father. You'll fit right in.'

They rode into the palace with all their purchases, and all their friends, intact. The group of Academy students had swelled as they went, picking up anyone they knew, and many of them returned to the Outer Court of the palace. By ancient tradition, students at the Academy were allowed in the Outer Court. The Duke broached a cask of wine and served them himself, to the scandal of the Ordinaries, and later that night there was dancing in front of the stables. Nordikans, Scholae, and the company mingled with their camp women, their wives, and their whores and a hundred Academy students.

The Princess Irene leaned against a window seat set in the walls of the Old Library, watching the Outer Court. Eventually, her ladies found her, and Lady Maria came and bowed.

'My lady,' she said carefully.

'Why can't I put on a plain dress, go down and dance?' she asked.

Lady Maria sighed. 'Because an assassin would put a dagger in your back before you crossed the yard.'

'He's right there – like a beacon. Look at him!' The Princess Irene pointed at a figure in a scarlet doublet and hose. As she pointed, he leaped a bonfire and whirled in the air.

Lady Maria sighed again. 'Yes – he is very flamboyant.' Not for the first time, she cursed her son's choice of leaders. The man was too intelligent and too charismatic by far.

Mercenaries had made themselves emperors before. And one of the easiest paths lay between the thighs of a princess.

'I *will* go,' Irene said.

Lady Maria balanced her options, as she always did. Any lover would supplant her instantly; that was a game she'd played herself. For an elderly matron to hold the position of favourite was rare, and in this case, an artefact of events.

She was bound to lose her position. But it mattered enormously to whom she lost it.

In addition, the threat of assassination was not an idle one. Two of the princess's ladies had been killed in just a week.

'If I promise to find you an occasion to attend and dance informally, will you restrain yourself tonight and go to bed, Majesty?' She tried to remember what it was like to be so *young*. The princess had skin like ivory, breasts as high as the branches of an oak, eyes without a single mark of age. Her entire being yearned for the Outer Court – for fire, and dance. And for a man.

But Irene was a warrior, in her way. She had already made difficult choices and lived with the consequences. And she'd been tutored well in the ways of the ancients. She stood straight and faced her favourite. 'Very well, Maria,' she said, so quietly that it was almost a whisper.

Half an hour before midnight the gate watch rang the alarm bell on the orders of the Megas Ducas. In a twinkling, the entire garrison formed on the square – drunk or sober, armed or stripped for dancing. Most of the Nordikans were half-naked and their muscles gleamed in the dark, while the Scholae looked like the courtiers that many of them were. The company were in all the colours of the rainbow – most of them in drab everyday clothes, a few nearly naked. They had been wrestling.

Two archers rolled a cask to the middle of the Outer Court. The Academy students were standing in a huddle by the stables, unsure what to do, and they were reassured when the Megas Ducas himself – in stripped-down scarlet – walked by and winked at them.

Then he leaped up on the barrel.

'I thought it was time we all got to know each other,' he said in good Archaic. Most of the soldiers laughed.

'Tomorrow we will start training together – all four regiments. We will march through the countryside, we will practise riding over broken country, we will practise with arms at the wooden stake, we will shoot bows and throw javelins and cut things with axes. There will be tilting and mounted archery. And I'm going to trade men around inside the guard – so that there are Nordikans who have served with the company, and Scholae who have ridden with the Vardariotes. We will ride abroad every day where people can see us. We will take our meals in roadside taverns. We will behave fearlessly, and if our enemies attempt to interfere, we will kill them.'

There was a nervous titter. Not much of one. Bad Tom said, 'That's the way!' loudly enough to sound like a shout.

'We've kept our heads down long enough. Time to do some work.' He smiled genially, but in the torchlight he looked like Satan.

No one laughed, and no one cheered.

'And next Saturday, the Feast of the Saint Martin, we will all relax and have a day of rest. During which day, we will conduct a pay parade in this very yard—' the rumbling of a cheer began '—and see to it that every man receives his back pay to one year—'

'*That's more fewkin like it!*'

'*Yes, yes!*' Men were pumping their fists in the air. Oak Pew kissed Cully. This sort of thing was repeated in all directions, and not just among the company. The Scholae seemed delighted to be paid – amazed, even. The Nordikans smiled broadly.

'And then, in the evening, we'll hear mass – said by the Patriarch, no less. After mass, Ser Michael and his lady Kaitlin will be wed, right here in the chapel of the company barracks. The Athanatoi barracks. And we'll have a little party.' He smiled benignly, and all around him soldiers cheered.

'Full discipline begins now. On parade, full kit, at daybreak. Any man who has questions about what full kit means is to ask the Primus Pilus. That's Ser Thomas. On the word dismiss, go to bed. Any questions?'

A thousand men on parade. There was silence. Not a joke, not a titter.

Even the Academy students were silent.

The Megas Ducas bowed to the students. 'You are all invited, as well,' he said. 'We will see you escorted home, unless some of you want to practise marching.'

He hopped down off the barrel, and Bad Tom emerged from the ranks. He was wearing a shirt of saffron linen over trews in black and red tartan, and he looked to be ten feet tall. He grinned at them.

'I'm just this eager for morning,' he said. He looked around in midnight silence. 'Dis – miss!'

In heartbeats, the Outer Court was empty, the guardrooms crammed with men pushing to be off parade. The same joke was repeated in three languages, as old soldiers encouraged each other to sleep fast and hard.

Daybreak – and the sun was just a streak of pink and gold above the spires of the churches.

The gates of the Outer Court opened and the Guard poured out into the square. They formed long ranks, two deep – much less cramped than parading in the Outer Court – making up three sides of a square, and stood silently, at attention, in full armour.

The Nordikans wore hauberks which came to their knees, with hoods of fine mail, mail gauntlets and arms. Many had further reinforcements of splint or scale; a few wore Morean breastplates of moulded leather, both painted and gilt, and two wore the new Etruscan style mixed with their traditional mail. Their cotes were of dark blue, and they wore cloaks of Imperial purple, many decorated in gold – with gold plates, gold embroidery, gold scales, some with pearls or diamonds.

The Scholae wore red – red leather cotes or heavy, tailored tunics under breastplates and backs of bronze scale polished like gold, or alternating steel and bronze. Many of them wore arm harnesses in the new Etruscan style, and a few had leg armour as well. They were beautifully mounted on sturdy black horses.

The company were in scarlet too, but their only uniformity was in their surcoats. Most had breast- and backplates; they wore twenty styles of helmets, from Bad Tom's towering back-pointed and brimmed bassinet to Cully's fluted kettle hat. The men-at-arms were all in plate; most of the squires had the same. The pages wore lighter armour, although Morea was already having an effect – some few pages already had curved swords and scale cuirasses. The archers were more conservative, and only one man had a turban on his open-faced bassinet. The Captain stopped during the first inspection and looked at him – Tom 'Toes' Larkin, a new man in good, clean kit and spotless breastplate.

'I like your turban,' the Duke said.

Larkin flushed. 'Sir!' he said, eyes fixed firmly on a point somewhere out in the middle of the Great Square.

'Show the rest of the archers how to make them,' the Duke said. He moved on.

Two spots to the right of Larkin, Cully said, 'That'll teach you, you fucking popinjay.' He said it without appearing to move his mouth.

If the company looked good from the standpoint of sartorial splendour, their horses didn't match the quality of their surcoats – even their old ones. Only the men-at-arms were mounted, and they rode an appalling collection of nags.

Officers conducted inspections, and then the whole of the Guard stood like additional polychromatic statues, completely at home with the other thousand bronze and marble figures in the Great Square. The Megas Ducas and his Primus Pilus rode to the centre of the three-sided square on borrowed horses and waited. They were joined by Count Darkhair and Count Giorgios Comnenos – both officers appointed to those ranks that morning.

The clock at the Academy struck six.

On the fifth strike of the wooden mallet against the great bell, the sound of hooves could be heard ringing on the frosted cobbles of the city.

As silence throbbed in the aftermath of the sixth ring, Count Zac rode into the Great Square followed by three hundred Vardariotes. They formed at the trot – formed line from street column, and then the line rode at a slight oblique – a very showy technique – to fit perfectly from the right marker of the company to the left marker of the Nordikans, facing the Scholae across the square.

Count Zac rode to the centre of the square and saluted the Megas Ducas with his heavy riding whip.

The Megas Ducas returned the salute and nodded. 'Order of march – the right squadron of the Vardariotes, followed by the Scholae, followed by the Nordikans, followed by the company, followed by the left squadron of the Vardariotes. When we reach the gate, we will turn to the left and march around the city, returning by the Gate of the Vardariotes. We will maintain a practical march order all day; we will deploy into line of battle on my commands, we will make an impromptu camp at the Plataea on the Alban road for lunch. Any questions?'

Count Zac grinned. 'Want a better horse?' he asked.

The Duke managed a smile. 'Very much. For me and everyone else in my company.'

Zac shrugged. 'Those traitors who kill your horses – they did you a favour. Get better horses!'

'You could help?' the Duke asked.

Zac smiled. 'I said I would – eh? Why have you not visited me?'

The Duke shook his head. 'I've been sick,' he said. 'I'll remedy that. Ready?' He nodded and raised his baton.

Zac pulled his horse's head around and galloped the few yards to his men, and barked commands and the right half of his regiment split off and filed away at a trot – headed south and east to the Gate of Ares. Their departure left a gap seventy files wide, and the Scholae, under orders from their new count, filed off by fours. The Nordikans simply marched – every right foot moving off together without the company's shuffling, as they all seemed to wait for their file leaders and consequently accordioned over the square.

And finally, the last eighty files of the Vardariotes closed the rear. The whole process took almost ten minutes, and there was, on balance, more shouting than was probably needed.

The next day, Ordinaries from the palace took up flagstones across the square and revealed deep cylindrical holes. They opened a storeooom in the Imperial stables and produced cedar poles more than a foot thick, hard as rock, which they fitted into the holes so that the entire square seemed to sprout dead trees. There were new, green cedar trunks, too, stacked neatly by the gate, which the Guard had fetched in on their return the evening before, footsore and armour chafed. Men who had remained behind on guard duty or as escorts or workers in the Navy Yard were cursed as slackers.

The cedar trunks were stripped of branches by Nordikans and erected. In the Outer Court, the regiments paraded in armour, but without weapons, and officers of the Ordinaries opened the Imperial Armoury and handed out wooden swords, wooden axes, and wicker shields. From the full plate and chain of Francis Atcourt to the squat leather-coated Vardariotes' youngest and slightest female archer, the whole of the Guard – again, with the exception of watch and escort detachments – formed up at the wooden posts. There were more than a hundred posts, and every one of them received ten soldiers and an officer.

Ser Milus was in his element. With a slim Imperial messenger as a translator, he strode to the central wooden post. 'This is today's enemy!' he roared, and the translator repeated his words in shrill intensity. As she was barely clear of adolescence and only five feet tall, her version of his words lost something.

'I don't want to see *this*,' Ser Milus shouted, and he took a few casual pokes at the pell with his wood and leather pole-axe. 'Any man who can cut all the way through his pell will receive an extra ration of wine tonight. So I want to see *this*!' The knight danced forward and flicked his pole-axe at the heavy cedar pole. The head struck perfectly – his second strike caused the heavy cedar trunk to move slightly. He stopped and raised his visor, which had fallen over his face as soon as he lowered his head. 'Fight the pell as you would fight a man,' he called. He backed away and danced up again, and his pole-axe licked out and the blow was so powerful that every man on parade could feel the impact. The knight leaped away, recovering his guard, and struck again – an overhand thrust to the centre of the wood. 'Make every blow count!' he roared. 'Hit his head, hit his arms, hit his thighs. Let me see you do it!' he called. 'Begin!'

They began. Each in turn would face the pell, move into range, and hit it. Some men were awkward, and some very unimaginative – some swung the same way at the pell every time. Some men understood intuitively and began to fight the pell, filling in both sides of a real fight. A few men rained blows down on it, the flurry meant to earn an extra tot of wine.

The officers bore down – singling one out for praise, and ordering another to take another turn.

The Primus Pilus went from pole to pole, taking men out of one line and marching them to another, so that by the time the most heavily armoured men were panting with exertion, there were members of all four regiments in every line. Wooden scimitars vied with wooden pole-axes to rock the heavy wood. Archers fenced with bucklered alacrity and Scholae threw blows from behind long, tapered shields while Nordikans chopped, sometimes like woodcutters and sometimes with blows as subtle as the lighter blades. The stakes were battered and rocked.

At noon, when the sun was high in the sky and there were five thousand people gathered in the square to watch, the men dispersed to tavernas and inns around the square to eat.

Ser Gavin and Count Zac sat on their horses just inside the gate of the Outer Court, at the head of a powerful troop – selected from all four regiments. As the Guardsmen ate and drank, fifty sentries watched the square, and Ser Gelfred and his huntsmen were out on the rooftops, watching.

But nothing happened.

By the time the sun began to set, most of the soldiers could no longer raise their arms above their shoulders.

That was the second day.

On the third day, there were archery butts standing in the square, and hundreds of yards of white rope to keep the spectators back. On foot, with longbow and horn bow, the men and women of all four regiments stepped up in one hundred and twenty lines at one hundred and twenty butts. As the day before, the Primus Pilus mixed every line.

Cully stood forth. 'I want to see good clean hits at each range,' he said. He walked over to a Vardariote and bowed. 'May I use your bow?' he asked.

The man drew his bow from its hip scabbard. It was horn and sinew, quite short. He also drew an arrow from his quiver on the other hip.

Cully turned to face the butts. He nocked, drew, and loosed. His shaft landed in the straw, a finger off dead centre, with a hearty *thunk*.

'Don't get fancy. Don't show off.' Behind him, a surprisingly pretty Imperial messenger repeated his words in Vardar and in Morean. 'Remember that short range has its own challenges.' He grinned. 'Every line contains a few archers and a lot of soldiers who've never loosed a bow. The line with the best score overall gets a gold florin a man. Second and third best scores get a double wine ration. So – better teach your duffers to shoot!'

He stepped out of the way. 'Begin!'

*

On Thursday, they threw javelins.

On Friday, the infantrymen ran, and the horse soldiers rode across broken country. More than a dozen horses were injured and had to be put down. Men twisted ankles, and a great many of them cursed the Duke. At noon, the tired infantrymen ate in the chilly autumn sunshine under the cover of olive trees whose fruit was so near ripe that olives fell on men's heads – they threw them at each other.

The cavalrymen arrived by a separate route, having used guides and picked up a troop of the local stradiotes – the first tentative sign of the local men showing even lukewarm support for the palace. More than a hundred men came; all of them had fought under Duke Andronicus's banner within a month. Any who represented the local regiment came.

'Half of them will be traitors,' muttered Ser Gavin.

The Duke shrugged. 'I want my new breastplate,' he said. He looked under his hand at the local troops wheeling a long line of horsemen. 'I don't think we need to care if they are traitors, Gavin. Whatever they think in their hearts, they're here.'

Under the olive trees, men of the five regiments shared apples and watered wine, almonds in honey and hard sausage.

When the trumpets sounded, they fell in with alacrity.

They marched away in column, and twice they deployed from road column to fighting columns. Then the columns themselves deployed into line – by filing, by inclining, and then, to the Duke's satisfaction, by inclining from the centre to the flanks, so that each column opened like a flower in spring and suddenly his whole little army was formed up in a long line, infantry in the centre, cavalry on the flanks.

Ser Gavin watched it happen. He rode with his brother, these days, in what had come to be known as 'the household'. Ser Milus carried the standard; the trumpeter acted as their page; Ser Gavin and Ser Michael shared some of the duties of battlefield organisation and elite messenger service, and Ser Alcaeus translated, while Ser Thomas seemed to issue all the orders – the Duke seldom spoke. Gavin worried about him, because he so often seemed to be absent. He would gaze vacantly at nothing. And he drank.

All day. Toby, his squire, provided him with a succession of flasks.

Gavin thought, *If I drank like that, I wouldn't be able to ride.*

The company had, at best, five hundred men. Today, they were commanding fourteen hundred men in three languages, and they were learning new skills at every turn.

The Duke rode across the front – he'd halted on a small hill to watch the deployment – and he pulled up by Ser Thomas. 'Wheel by companies from the right and form a column of march on the road. The Alban road.'

'Where did you learn all these commands?' Gavin asked. His brother certainly didn't seem drunk when he *did* speak.

'There's books,' Gabriel said. He smiled at his brother. 'I'll share them if you like. The Imperial Library has – fifteen? twenty? – books on strategy and tactics.'

Ser Gavin laughed. 'This is the new knighthood,' he said. 'We'll all be scholars.'

His brother made a face, as if he smelled something bad. 'Wait until we fight someone who hasn't read the books,' he said.

Meanwhile, Ser Thomas showed his surprise only in the fidgeting of his horse, and then the little army was wheeling from line into column, every company of fifty tracing a quarter of a circle and then stepping off by fours from the right – threes for the cavalry – so that the shield wall turned into a long snake with Vardariotes at its head and tail, and the snake wriggled off into the hills north and west of the city. It was mid-afternoon, and the Duke was marching the army towards Alba. Leaving the city empty.

Kronmir spread some coins out on the table. 'I want complete reports on how he deploys his forces – in what order, who is in the centre – everything you see. Nianna, I would like the muster list of the local militia who are following his banner.'

The madam shook her head. 'I might be able to get it, but if Duke Andronicus uses it to kill men then I'm dead too. I'm too exposed.'

One of the sellswords laughed at her unintended pun.

Kronmir glared at the man. Nianna was his best agent, and her other roles – as a woman, as a prostitute – were of no interest to Jules Kronmir whatsoever, except in the degree to which they made her more or less useful as a source.

'If I swear that the information will never be used for a cleansing?' he asked.

'Perhaps,' she said. 'I know who could provide it. What's it worth?'

He sucked his front teeth. 'Three hundred florins,' he said.

She shrugged.

Kronmir hated having these conversations with multiple agents – hated the loss of compartmentalisation, hated that they'd even seen each other, much less that they might start something like collective bargaining. But the foreigner moved so quickly, and made so few mistakes, that he had to strike while the iron was hot.

'You gentlemen – get in the saddle. Be wary – the Vardariotes are rumoured to be picking up every rider on the road. But bring me some information.' Kronmir motioned to the door.

'If'n the lady stands to earn three hundred florins,' said a former soldier with an Alban accent, 'mayhap me and me mates might receive a slightly more marvellous remuneration, eh?' He grinned a gap-toothed grin. 'I have information to sell, too.'

Kronmir narrowed his eyes. 'Well?'

The man shook his head. 'Well,' he said, suddenly unsure of himself. Something in Kronmir's body language scared him. 'Well – Ser Bescanon says the new Duke's going to reinstate the Latinikon. Hire back all the mercenaries.' He shrugged. 'What's that worth?'

Kronmir pursed his lips. 'Ten ducats,' he said, and counted them down.

'Fuck that! She got three hundred florins.' The Alban threw the coins into Kronmir's face.

None struck him.

Kronmir was fussy and hated waste; but he was also a craftsman, and while he might make an error in haste, he usually retrieved it. He moved under the coins, flowed around the table between them, crossed the floor to the two sellswords, and killed them. His first dagger blow – from the sheath – went into the Alban's throat, and his second blow, turning into his front leg, went into his partner's head at the temple – two blows, and both corpses fell.

'My mistake,' he said to Nianna. 'Their type is ten a florin, and I'll get more. I wanted to save time with a single briefing, and instead I endangered the whole plan.' He shook his head, cleaning his weapon on the Alban's shirt even as his dead heels drummed on the floor.

Nianna paled and put a hand to her throat. 'Blessed Virgin protect me,' she said aloud. But she paused and spat on the Alban's corpse.

*

In an hour he'd hired four men for less money – through a cut-out, of course – and dispatched them. He regretted his quick disposal of the Alban – the man had good skills and might have made a competent scout, with time. Kronmir was mentally penning a third letter requesting some Easterners from his master, who didn't seem to read his reports.

Still, Nianna had committed to providing the list.

He stayed to write a report that included a small number of triumphs: poisonings, public outrages, two deserters suborned from the Nordikans who were even now reporting on military affairs in the palace.

'At your command, I can snuff out the parvenu Duke,' he finished. 'In the meantime, he drills his troops...' He raised his pen. He'd complete the thought when his agent returned with the reports of the four hirelings. Kronmir spent an hour in the early afternoon contemplating how much easier all this might be if he did everything himself. He didn't mind taking risks. And the use of agents was painfully slow and the information second hand. And he wondered, as he had all his professional life, if the use of hermetical powers would help him. If only he could recruit an utterly reliable, skilled practitioner.

Except such men were too committed to other paths to power.

He shook his head. Spying was difficult enough.

The army turned onto the Alban road and marched at its fastest step, up into the hills. The Vardariotes swept the flanks like a curry brush on a dirty horse, making dust fly, and two of Kronmir's hirelings watched the show from a high olive grove, lying on their stomachs at the edge of an ancient stone terrace, their horses hidden away among the trees.

'He's marching away,' Antonio said.

'Our employer will want to know that,' said Alphonso.

'Duke Andronicus, you mean,' Antonio spat.

'Must be,' agreed the other. 'Who else is in this game?'

The two men wriggled back from the edge of the terrace and ran for their horses.

Both were knocked to the ground and pinned with boots against their necks by Amy's Hob and Dan Favour. Gelfred nodded to them.

'You know the drill,' he said. 'Take your report to Ser Thomas.'

They were sellswords. They didn't hesitate to talk but, as Gelfred quickly found, they had very little to say.

The Duke's army marched north almost six leagues as the shadows grew longer.

'Where the fuck are we going?' Wilful Murder spat in the autumn dust.

Toby shrugged and pulled another biscuit from his saddle bags.

Bent leaned over his horse's rump. 'Not far,' he said.

Wilful Murder glared at him.

'No wagons, no food. And Ser Michael's gettin' wed tomorrow afternoon, eh? So we won't go far.' Bent took a pull from his canteen and offered it to Toby, who shook his head.

'Fewkin' bastard would *love* to use Ser Michael's wedding to fool us and that fewkin' Andronicus. We'll have a battle – mark my words.' Wilful Murder spat. 'An' we won't get paid either.' He took the flask and drank. 'Mark my words.'

They halted in a valley between two steep ridges. There was talk all along the column – flankers went out, and the younger and faster men ran to the top of the hills.

As the church struck five, the advance guard of Vardariotes returned at a fast trot. With them came a long column of wagons and Ser Jehan with his twenty lances.

The army formed an open rectangle on the march and passed the defile at the end of the valley and then marched back towards the city. All could see what the wagons held.

It was full dark by the time the column passed the Vardariotes Gate, and the Eastern regiment dropped off on either side and saluted until the last company in the column passed them. Then, at a shrill whistle, they all dismounted together.

By then, the wagons were deep in the city, and their cargo was safe from attack or ambush.

Kronmir stood on the wall above the gate and counted forty-seven wagons. Some were merely a pair of wheels at each end with the cargo providing the wagon bed, because the forty-seven loads were all felled trees and dried lumber – an enormous quantity. Enough, in fact, to build a fleet of warships.

He also noted two of his hirelings riding with their hands bound.

Back in the Inn of the Nine Virgins, he put pen to parchment – in code. 'The parvenu has stolen a march by bringing in wood,' he admitted. 'I need trustworthy men and devices, preferably hermetical, for communications and for demolitions.' He made his sign, appended his expenses, and walked out into the cool evening air. He walked through the farmer's market, and at the third butcher's from the end of the second row he leaned for a while against the front off wheel of the butcher's wagon while he cleaned horse manure out of his boot. Then he walked around the front of the stall.

'Two cuts of spring lamb,' he said.

The butcher waited on him personally, with a wink, and the letter was on its way.

By nonnes the next day, every man and woman who could sew was sitting in the sun outside the stables, hemming Kaitlin's wedding dress. Four women had run it up the night before, after Gropf, the master tailor turned archer, cut the cloth. Now the overdress – in red and gold satin – rested on burlap sacks while thirty people sat around it in a circle. The kirtle was deep gold with gold buttons, and Mag sat with Liz and Gropf, working the buttonholes in burgundy silk twist. Squires and pages brought them wine.

The Outer Court had a festive air. All the soliders behaved as if they'd won a victory the day before. No one had opposed them, and they'd marched well out into the countryside. Fetching the wood was anything but a symbolic victory, and the archers talked about the ramifications of having a fleet with the Nordikans and the Scholae. Twenty Vardariotes stood guard at the palace gates.

Two hours later, the dress was done. Gropf and some of his cronies were tacking ermine to the sleeve openings – borrowed ermine, but there was no need for the lass to know that. The hem was done and the magnificent overdress was folded carefully into muslin and taken to the barracks.

In its place, two barrels were placed on their ends in the courtyard, and four heavy planks were laid across. Then a guard composed of two men of each regiment – two Vardariotes, two Scholae, two Nordikans, and two Athanatoi – marched into the courtyard under the command of Ser Thomas. They halted at the table made of barrels and stood behind it. All were in full harness and all had their weapons naked in their hands.

The company notary came out with Ser Michael. Chairs were brought, and the two men sat.

Francis Atcourt came out chatting with the Captain, who was dressed, not as the Red Knight, but as the Megas Ducas, in purple and gold. As he entered the yard, Ser Thomas blew a whistle, and all three regiments pushed and shoved their way onto parade. None of them were in fighting clothes – every man and woman was in their finest.

There was cloth of gold, and cloth of silver, silk brocades, rich wools like velvets, and silk velvet, too. There was an abundance of linen as smooth as cream, and a quantity of gold and silver – heavy chains, rings, brooches. Soldiers tend to wear their capital – soldiers' women much the same.

Closer attention might have revealed some paste, some gilded copper, and some tin; some brocades on their third or fourth wearer, some carefully coloured glass, and some leather tooled to look like rich embroidery.

But in general, the eight hundred soldiers present would not have disgraced some courts, albeit in a slightly more raffish manner. Clothing tended to fit more tightly and show more muscle than was usual – from Ser Thomas's padded, quilted and embroidered silk hose that showed every ripple of muscle in his thighs to Ser Alison's skin-right red silk kirtle that left almost none of her physique to a viewer's imagination, the clothing demanded attention.

Parading in their finery made them more like a boisterous crowd and less like a disciplined army. And when two heavy iron-bound chests were marched through the crowd by palace Ordinaries surrounded by fully armoured Scholae, there was outright applause.

The chests were placed on the heavy oak boards, and the escort saluted and was ordered to retire. Ser Michael produced a key and opened the two chests. Every soldier in the front two ranks could see the gleam of gold and silver. A sigh of contentment ran through the Outer Court.

High above, in the Library, the Princess Irene stood on tiptoes to be able to see the whole of the parade and the two chests. Lady Maria hovered behind her. The princess was dressed in a plain brown wool overdress – very like a nun's habit. Underneath she wore a much less plain kirtle, but it would only show at the wrists.

'That is not my money he is disbursing,' Irene said.

'I agree that he is a cause for worry,' Lady Maria said.

'My own soldiers already love him. Look at them!' she said.

'Your father's soldiers,' Lady Maria said.

An expectant hush fell over the parade. All the women who were not themselves soldiers were gathered at the corners of the square. Anna and a hundred other wives and near-wives from the Nordikan barracks, as well as some of the great ladies of the city, gathered near their husbands and brothers of the Scholae to see the fun – four nuns stood together with Morgan Mortirmir and a young despoina of the Dukae, who was greeted with respectful admiration – and some wolf whistles – by the Alban mercenaries. The new Count of the Scholae smiled at her every time he turned his head. Ser Giorgios Comnenos and his beloved were to have their long-delayed nuptials with Ser Michael and Kaitlin.

The expectant hush lasted long enough that Wilful Murder turned to his whispering colleagues and hissed, 'Shut the fuck up!'

Veterans of the company knew that no one would be paid until the Captain had complete silence.

When he had it, the Megas Ducas stood and walked in front of the table. 'Ladies and gentlemen,' he said. 'Our first pay parade together. You will be called by name, in order of the alphabet. If your pay is incorrect, you will leave it on the table and go to the end to speak directly to the notary and to me. You will not slow the process. The princess has graciously given us a hogshead of malmsey to serve when we are halfway through the list of names. If your name is missed, wait until the end of the parade to make a fuss.

'Every man and woman on this parade is looking forward to spending their pay – but no one will leave this yard until we've witnessed the weddings of Ser Michael to Kaitlin Lanthorn, and Ser Giorgios to Despoina Helena Dukas. Further to that, if you choose to take your pay into the city, be aware that there are at least a hundred men in this city hired just to kill you – that in addition to the usual crowd of ruffians who wait to rob soldiers rolling in gold. Not to mention the crooked innkeepers and whores. Caveat emptor. I expect every one of you on parade on Monday at matins.'

He smiled at them tolerantly. 'Very well, my companions. Let's get this under way.'

He leaned back and looked at the rolls. 'Archer Benjamin Aaron!' he called.

A small man in black wool with a fine belt of enamelled plaques and a little black skull cap swaggered out of the ranks. By tradition, the first man to be paid shook the Captain's hand – he grinned, the Megas Ducas grinned back, and Ser Thomas called out: 'Aaron, mounted archer: seventy-two florins, nine silver leopards, six sequins, less thirty-one leopards stoppages, four leopards, six sequins hospital, extra four leopards, four sequins, hard lying total: seventy florins, eighteen leopards, two sequins! Sign here.'

Aaron signed the book, scraped his coins – ten years wages for a peasant, or a year's wage for a highly skilled artisan, and all in cash – into his hand. He gave a little bow to the Captain and also Ser Michael and marched himself back to his place in the ranks, where he immediately settled a year's worth of small debts.

Men and women who came to the company without surnames – few runaway peasants had one – tended to adopt names that occurred early in the alphabet. Brown was a remarkably popular name, as was Able.

However, the parade also encompassed Akritos, Giorgos, and Arundson, Erik.

Ser Francis Atcourt was the first knight to collect, and conversations stopped as his wages were read out.

Ser Thomas read: 'Atcourt, man-at-arms: three hundred and sixteen florins, no leopards, no sequins, stoppages none, sixteen leopards, six sequins hospital, extra four leopards, four sequins, hard lying extra, thirty-one florins dead warhorse, total: three hundred forty-seven florins, twelve leopards, two sequins.'

Men sighed to hear how much a man-at-arms could earn. It seemed like nothing when your blood ran over the surface of your skin on a cold spring morning, facing a Wyvern with nothing but a bit of steel between you and the monster's teeth, but on a fine autumn morning in the courtyard of a magnificent palace, it seemed a fortune. All a man could ever want.

'And one share,' the Megas Ducas added.

'Put it on my account,' said Ser Francis, who was sitting at the table, and the men laughed.

From Atcourt it took almost an hour to reach Cantakuzenos. But after Dukas, the process moved faster – there were fewer mercenaries after D, and the Nordikans and the Scholae had got the rhythm of the thing so that if a man was ready, he could march up while his account was read, sweep the silver and gold into his hat, and walk back as the next lucky fellow pushed forward. A few awkward sods came out of each regiment – men disposed to debate the fine points of what was withheld for medicine, or what had been awarded as punishment – but in general, they went forward with almost three hundred men an hour.

Among the company, the pay parade was an opportunity for practical jokes and levity – wives would press forward to collect a husband's pay, and then again to collect their own, for example, and a man unlucky enough to be absent – Daniel Favour was not present when his name was called – was helped by mates who shouted, "E wants it all given to the poor!'

Shortly after, Gelfred, the Hunt Master and an officer of the company – highly paid and thus always good for entertainment – was also absent.

Wilful Murder, who had a real name and had already collected his pay, grinned at his nearest neighbour. 'None o' they scouts is on parade,' he said. 'I wasn't all wrong yester e'en. Someone's gonna cop it.'

At Hannaford the parade paused, and every man and woman present was served a fine cup of malmsey wine, heavy and sweet, by troops of Ordinaries with trays. The Megas Ducas jumped up on the table and raised his cup – everyone in the courtyard including the visiting students raised theirs, and the Megas Ducas shouted, 'To the Emperor!'

Twelve hundred voices echoed his shout.

The Imperial servants cleared away the cups – red clay with Imperial wreathes of olive leaves – and the parade recommenced at Hand, Arthur, mounted archer, and carried straight through to Zyragonas, Dmitrios, stradiotes. The sun was setting, the air was chilly, and the courtyard was packed with deeply satisfied soldiers.

In keeping with an established tradition, Dmitrios Zyragonas – a pleasant-looking man with ruddy cheeks, bright red hair and the last name on the whole parade – was greeted as he left the parade by the company's oldest camp follower, Old Tam, with every available child gathered about her. She put her arms around him before he even thought to resist, being a well-born Morean and unused to what passed for humour in Alba, he was unready when she put a hand in his pocket and equally unready when she began to kiss him, while forty children shouted and called him 'Papa' and 'Daddy' and demanded money.

'There's my honey,' croaked Old Tam. She was smiling as broadly as an escaped lunatic and licking her lips. 'So young!' she cackled. 'I only want yer better part, love!'

The Scholae, among whom Zyragonas was a staid and upright figure – were laughing themselves silly as the poor man tried to escape the harridan and the children, many of whom played their parts with touches of realism that might have chilled a less hardened crowd.

Zyragonas fled as soon as he was free of their outstretched hands – ran back into the ranks of his comrades like a one-man rout – and then had to endure the laughter as Old Tam raised high his purse, neatly cut off his belt.

'I have yer *best* part, love!' she yelled.

There were plenty of linguists to translate the jest into Nordikan and Morean.

But then, when everyone had laughed long, the Megas Ducas rose from his chair, and the old woman turned, curtsied, and handed over the blushing man's purse, and the Megas Ducas restored it to its rightful owner who couldn't meet anyone's eyes.

'Gentlemen and ladies – benches, wine, and food. Many hands make light work – let the wedding begin.' He clapped his hands, and everyone ran for their task – assigned at the morning parade.

Bent reappeared from the kitchens, where he and four men and four of Gelfred's dogs had sampled the malmsey and most of the food. Now they went into the towers around the yard, taking an early dinner and a cup of wine to the Vardariotes who were on duty so that the other soldiers could drink.

Tables appeared, and long, low benches, and a line of men went through the yard like dancers, putting beeswax candles in tall bronze sticks on every table. Men looked at the sky – darkness was coming with heavy grey clouds.

The princess's confessor came through the Outer Yard in full ecclesiastical regalia. The Scholae murmured. As the first cups and plates began to accrete on the tables, they heard the Officer of the Day shout his challenge, and after the reply the outer gate opened.

The Moreans in the yard froze.

All of them fell to one knee.

The Megas Ducas walked out into the Outer Court, and Bent whispered in his ear – and he hissed an order and fell to his knees – in his best hose, on cobbles. Most of the company didn't need the whispered order – they could see Ser Michael on his knees in his wedding clothes, and Ser Thomas too, in his magnificent quilted hose.

The Patriarch walked into the yard at the head of twenty professors of the Academy and another ten priests and bishops.

He beamed at the soldiers, and walked among them, bestowing blessings in all directions. He placed his hand on Ser Thomas's bowed black head – his chin went up as if he'd received a shock, and then he smiled like a man who has won a great prize, and the Patriarch passed to the next man. He blessed Ser Alison and, eventually, he came to the Megas Ducas, placed his hand gently on his head, and nodded.

No lightning struck.

The Megas Ducas kissed his ring.

Very low, he said, 'I hope Your Holiness is here for the wedding?'

The Patriarch's eyes twinkled. 'You mean I'm too late to get paid?' he asked.

After that, there was nothing that could have made Kaitlin's wedding any less than a great feast. She herself – when she appeared – looked sufficiently magnificent to quell the rumour among the Moreans that she was a low-born farm girl. It was obvious that she was a duchess. She and Despoina Helena vanished together and as preparations were made their giggles and snorts of laughter could be heard peeling out of the Scholae guardroom, which had temporarily been co-opted as the bridal chambers.

Ser Michael – most everyone knew he was the Earl of Towbray's eldest son – walked like an earl. It was possible, watching him, to see the Red Knight and the King in his back and his legs, in the way his right hand rested on his dagger, in the arrogance of his jaw – or in the delight of his eyes when he took back his bride's veil of seven yards of Hoek lace. Ser Giorgios was less showy, but had the dignity that most Moreans seemed to carry, and he smiled at everyone who caught his eye. And at his bride, who didn't seem to mind that her beautiful gown of golden satin and seed pearls had been upstaged.

Gropf's thin mouth smiled at those gowns and he flicked his eyes at the bride when she kissed her husband. *Five months pregnant? Sweeting, that's what the overgown is for!* He had no one to tell that his greatest triumph as a cloth cutter now came in front of a patriarch in the Imperial Palace – two years after he'd turned his back on his trade and gone to war.

But he couldn't stop smiling.

Neither could Wilful Murder, who'd just received the fullest pay day of his adult life and not a sequin in stoppages. He wandered the feast, wagering on anything that anyone would accept a wager on – the time in pater nosters until the bride next kissed the groom was a favourite. He offered odds that the whole company would march the next morning at sunrise.

Mag had a brief and sobering interview with the Captain, and took notes – but the moment the service began and she saw Kaitlin Lanthorn, whom she'd known as a puking, tiny baby not expected to live, now going to the altar to wed a man who was arguably the wealthiest young man of his generation, in front of some of the most famous people in Christendom, she cried. She cried steadily through the service. But she'd made every stitch of linen the bride was wearing, and she'd woven in every scrap of happiness she could draw from the *aether*. And she'd made a weather working too – her first – that roofed the Outer Court like a bowl of fire.

When the wine began to flow and people walked about freely, the Patriarch came and sat by her. 'They tell me you cast that,' he said pleasantly.

She smiled and looked at her feet.

'These same people tell me you've never had an education in the *ars magicka*.' He smiled.

She almost said she'd been tutored in Dar-as-Salaam – it was on her lips, one of Harmodius's memories imprinted in her head. She hadn't fully assimilated what she'd learned from Harmodius and from the Abbess in the last days of the siege, but she spent time working through what she could remember, every day. Hence her first weather working. But as usual, she found it easiest to be silent.

So she raised her eyes.

They met, eye to eye, for a moment.

The Patriarch broke the contact politely, and shook his head. 'The north of Alba must be rolling in talents,' he said.

Mag nodded. 'It is,' she agreed.

'May I invite you to visit the Academy?' he asked. 'For more than two thousand years, we have served the needs of men and women with special gifts – hermetical, or scientific, or musical, or scholarly.'

She smiled and looked at her hands. 'Do you offer a course in embroidery?' she asked, thinking that he sounded just a little like the dragon on the mountain.

After the boards were cleared, the musicians – who had eaten the dinner and watched the wedding with everyone else – came forward. While they tuned their instruments, the students gave a display of the hermetical art – air bursts of fire, tableaux of the heroes of the past striding across the yard – Saint Aetius fought a great horned irk twice his height, and fought so well that the soldiers roared their applause—

'I told you that nothing would look as good as a real fight,' Derkensun said, picking himself off the second-storey floor of the Imperial horse barn. It was not just a new working but a set of nested new workings – it had taken four of them, the two Comnena nuns, Baldesce and Mortirmir. Mortirmir had fought – sparred, at least – with Derkensun, and the working had transmitted their images – subtly altered – to the courtyard below. As the soldiers roared their approval, Mortirmir embraced the Nordikan.

He laughed his great laugh. 'Bah – it was you witches who made the glamour!' But he accepted their plaudits, and he and Anna sat with the students for the next course.

Anna put her hand on Derkensun's arm suddenly – they were being served beautiful custards, obviously the product of the Imperial kitchens. Anna was ignoring the magical shows to enjoy the food – she'd never had enough to eat in in her entire life and the custards—

But a woman in a plain brown overgown had appeared by Megas Ducas' side. Anna noticed her immediately.

She pointed, her mouth full of delicious custard.

Beside her, Derkensun was grinning at an Ordinary. 'Is that Quaveh?' he asked.

The servant bowed. 'It is, sir.'

'Anna, this is Quaveh from the *other side of Ifriqu'ya!*' he turned. 'What?' he asked.

'Who is that woman?' Anna asked.

The Megas Ducas was enjoying himself far more than he'd expected to. Some of the drugs worked – and Harmodius was obviously doing his best to hide himself. While the Duke suspected that had to do with the presence of the Patriarch – just a sword's length away in his throne of ebony and gold – a holiday was a holiday. He was alone.

Or at least, he *felt* alone.

He was considering sending Toby for his lyre when he caught a hint of scent and then she was at his side.

'I am incognito,' declared Princess Irene. 'Please call me Zoe.'

The Duke girded himself. *So much for being alone.*

Ser Gavin was sitting with the groom's party and flirting somewhat automatically with the Lanthorn girls. Ranald Lachlan was staring into darkness and drinking steadily and being a dull companion.

Ser Alison leaned back her chair. She was dressed as a woman – magnificently dressed – except for the knight's belt at her hips. 'Who's that sitting with the Captain?' she asked.

Gavin did a double-take and smiled knowingly. 'Well, well,' he said. He dug an elbow into Ranald, who looked and shrugged.

Ser Michael was an arm's length away, kissing his wife. He rose for air and caught Gavin's eye.

'Get a room,' said Gavin.

'We have one,' said Michael, brightly. 'What are you and Sauce staring at?'

Kaitlin, who looked like an angel come to earth, leaned forward, being exceptionally careful of her train and her ermine and her jewels and all the other things that didn't matter as much as the man who had just kissed her, and said, 'It's the—'

Ser Giorgios paled, and his new wife had to use years of courtly training not to spit her wine. 'The Porphyrogenetrix!' she said. 'At my wedding!'

Gavin grinned. 'Good. That's what I thought, too.'

Ser Thomas appeared and leaned down among them, bowing to – of all people – Sauce. 'May I have the honour of a dance?' he asked.

'Horse or foot?' Sauce said, automatically. She was ready to fight, and despite her gown and her tight kirtle, she looked like a warrior in that moment.

Bad Tom just laughed. 'Got you. But—' he swept a comically exaggerated bow '—but I mean it. They're about to play for dancing. Come and dance.'

'Why?' Sauce asked suspiciously. 'Ain't you doing Sukey?'

Tom raised an eyebrow. 'Not for another few hours. Come on, Sauce – come and dance.' He looked at Gavin. 'What are you all looking at?' he asked with his usual air.

'Not you,' Gavin said. He indicated the Patriarch's table without actually pointing.

'All the big hats,' Tom agreed.

'So who's sitting with the Captain?' Sauce asked. She rose to her feet and put her hand on Tom's arm. 'If you make this a mockery of me, I'll have your guts out right here, so help me God and all the saints.'

Bad Tom grinned. 'Are you like this with all the boys?' he asked. Then his half-mocking grin vanished. 'Sweet Jesu, it's the princess.'

'Got it in one, boyo,' drawled Sauce.

While Bad Tom was gawking, Ser Jehan and Ser Milus came around the wedding table and each took their turn to kiss the brides and kneel before Kaitlin, slap Michael and Giorgios on the back, and then – Jehan first – crave a dance of Sauce.

'Am I the only girl you boys know?' she asked.

Ser Jehan – almost fifty, all muscle and gristle and hard-won chivalry – blushed.

Tom pointed at the Megas Ducas, who was rising with the woman in brown – really, the girl in brown – on his arm.

'Don't point,' hissed Gavin.

Jehan smiled. He turned to Ser Milus, and whispered something.

Milus grinned at everyone. 'Suddenly, everything makes sense,' he said.

'Do you dance?' the Red Knight asked the princess.

She looked at him.

'I gather that was a foolish question,' he said. 'But as you are incognito, I assume I can ask you direct questions and get direct answers, so let's start small. What are you doing here?'

She rose. 'Dancing,' she said. 'I confess that I've never danced in public with a mercenary.'

He nodded and pursed his lips. 'It's not as hard as it looks,' he said.

'I cannot get over the quality of your Archaic,' she said, as they moved out from the tables. Just at the edge of the Red Knight's peripheral vision, the Patriarch started – sat up, turned his head, and said something that caused the young priest next to him to turn his head suddenly too.

He smiled down at her. 'I learned it right here,' he said. 'Or rather, I learned it at home from my tutor, and then practised here.'

'The Academy?' she asked.

'No,' he said enigmatically.

The musicians obviously knew who she was. There was some discordant fumbling.

'Can *you* dance?' she asked.

'No,' he said, smiling brilliantly.

One of the street musicians appeared at his elbow. He had a hat in his hands, and his hands were shaking. 'My lord. We— What— That is . . . what should we play?' he finally got out.

The Red Knight – he refused to play the Megas Ducas tonight – bowed to his lady. 'Whatever the lady asks for,' he said.

Every Morean within earshot sighed with relief.

Zoe raised her fan to cover most of her face, but allowed the musician some little bit of her smile, which was quite real. 'Something fast,' she said. She turned graciously to the brides, who stood by with their new husbands. 'Anything they ask for. You are the ladies of this merry meeting, not I.'

Kaitlin curtsied and then grinned impishly. 'Well—' She grinned at Despoina Helena. 'We have practised a Morean dance, and it's fast,' she said. 'Let's dance a *Moresca*.'

A few couples away Lady Maria gasped, and her son winced.

She leaned over to her son and said, very softly, 'What have you done?'

He stood his ground. 'What *you* told me to do.'

The music was fast. Almost a third of the couples and interested bystanders hurried off the wooden floor as soon as the music began – a combination of Albans who needed to see the dance, and Moreans who feared it.

Bad Tom and Sauce were not one of those retreating couples.

She looked up at him – not as far as other women. 'You know this?' she asked.

'No,' he said cheerfully. 'You?'

She shook her head and laughed. 'Just what I needed,' she said. 'A fearless partner.'

Mostly – with a few exceptions – the gentry of Morea and Alba shared some common tastes. The gentry often danced stately processions, in couples, or pairs of couples – while the lower orders usually danced in groups, in rings.

The dance that followed didn't fit well into either category. It featured pairs who turned with each other – not a horrifying innovation, but a daring one. It was obvious that Lady Kaitlin and Ser Michael knew the dance, and had practised with the Morean couple.

In the best traditions of weddings, and women who loved to dance, the two couples danced all the figures alone, first.

When Giorgios picked Helena up and whirled her in the air, Zoe nodded and a tiny smile played at the corners of her lips. 'Ahh,' she said, very softly.

They turned outwards from one another and clapped – their time was perfect – and the music swept them on – around, turn, clap, around, together...

Everyone applauded. The servants applauded, even the drunks applauded – they were that good. Kaitlin burst into tears and grinned at her husband. Helena threw her head back in delight.

Sauce looked at Tom. 'Got that?'

He nodded sharply, like a man going into action. 'Got it.'

John le Bailli looked down at Mag. 'Perhaps we should sit this out?' he attempted.

'Nonsense,' she said. 'Men like you have been finding excuses not to dance since the fall of Troy.'

Harald Derkensun dragged Anna by the hand to the centre of the temporary wooden floor.

'I can't dance on the same floor as the Empress!' Anna protested.

But she pivoted on her toes as she said it.

*

A dark-eyed young woman with plucked brows and a severe, elegant face cleared her throat just behind Morgan Mortirmir. He had a cup in his hand – he'd thought of asking Anna, but he couldn't, and he'd obviously been right. She looked very happy with Harald.

He turned and looked at the young woman by his shoulder.

She raised an eyebrow.

He turned back to the dancers and she kicked his ankle lightly. 'Hey, Plague,' she said.

His head shot around fast enough to leave his eyebrows behind.

He mustered up every shred of composure he had. 'Would, um … would you?' he asked. He bowed.

She sighed. 'Blessed Virgin,' she said, not at all piously, and pretended to follow him onto the dance floor while in fact leading him. 'If the princess can dance with a barbarian, I suspect it's all the fashion.'

'I don't … dance,' Mortirmir managed to say, as the music began.

'Tap your foot to the music and look elegant,' she said, rising on her toes. 'I'll do the dancing.'

'You're a nun!' he said.

She frowned. 'You *are* an ignorant barbarian,' she said.

The Patriarch indicated the young Alban mage in training to Father Arnaud. The Hospitaller nodded. The young woman danced beautifully, and the young man was – literally – suffused with light. He lit the centre of the dance floor, and she danced around him as if he was a lantern. It couldn't last, and eventually he had to move, but the effect was done well and the two laughed together when he stumbled.

But the Patriarch watched the princess as she went by – first in a ring of women, inside a ring of men, and then outside the ring of men after a complex passage of hands, and then the men shot off into the near darkness and the women danced; the women went off and the men danced, more brightly lit by young Mortirmir than by the torches. The two sexes formed chains, and the chains intertwined – leaned to the left, leaned to the right, shot around, with women's legs and men's legs flashing out. Then the women leaped and the men caught them.

The Red Knight turned a full circle with the Emperor's daughter held high above his head.

The Patriarch sat back suddenly, and then frowned, and held up his cup for more wine.

They danced for four hours. They danced until most of the men and women who fought for a living were as sober as when they had started, and as tired as if they'd fought a battle. They'd danced in lines and circles and pairs and fours and eights and every figure known to Alba, Galle, and Morea. Count Zac and his officers demonstrated Eastern dances, and the Red Knight and his officers had to try them. Bad Tom fell full length trying to kick out his legs, and laughed at his own antics, and Sauce clapped her hands and imitated the Easterners only to discover that it was a man's dance. But Count Zac put an arm around her shoulders and they drank together, and went on to another dance, and later, she went and caught Milus and Jehan by the hands and dragged them across the great circle of watchers – off-duty Ordinaries, female students from the Academy, and other unattached women.

With unerring professional sense, she marched the two knights to a gaggle of Anna's friends and peers who had made their way in under various pretences.

'Gentlemen, these women are whores. Ladies, these gentlemen are shy.' She grinned to show she meant no harm, but one of the harder women took offence anyway.

'Who you calling whore, bitch?' she said.

Sauce smiled. 'I was one, honey. I know the look.'

'Really?' the other woman said. 'And now what are you?'

'Now I'm a knight,' Sauce said. Count Zac was making eyes at her, and she walked away.

Ser Jehan looked down into the deep brown eyes of his sudden new friend. 'Is she really a knight?' the girl asked.

'She really is,' Ser Jehan agreed. And then he was dancing.

The Red Knight and Zoe danced – on and on. Once they stopped when the Ordinaries came like an avenging army bearing ice – actual ice from the mountains. The Red Knight met them well across the floor, asked who had sent the ice, and then took her some, and watched her eat it.

And again, when the servants came with a bubbly purple wine, he swept her across the floor to see that she had the very first glass.

Everyone commented on how attentive he was.

Wilful Murder sat back and drank his fifteenth jack of cider. He glared at Cully. 'Thin,' he said.

Cully rolled his eyes. 'Not hardly,' he said. 'It's just – different. Sweeter?' he asked the air.

'Mark my words,' Wilful said. 'He's going to march us all somewhere horrible in the morning. This whole party was nothing but a cover – we're going after the false Duke.'

Cully made a face, and shook his head. 'We won't have ten men fit for service in the morning,' he said.

'Mark my words,' Wilful said, and belched carefully.

The Red Knight escorted the mysterious Lady Zoe all the way to her door. If he noticed that six heavily scarred Nordikans shadowed them every step through the palace, he didn't pay them any apparent heed. If he noticed his own Ser Alcaeus or his mother Lady Maria or a long train of Imperial ladies dressed as Ordinaries – all breathless and a few perhaps a little more than breathless – following them along the marbled corridors, he said nothing.

At the doors to the Imperial apartments, he bowed over her hand, not quite touching it with his lips.

She smiled. 'I expected more boldness from the famous warrior,' she said.

'I'm only really bold when I'm paid,' he said, pressing her hand. 'Nor do I think that the audience is apt to the purpose,' he said softly.

She looked into the gloom of the long corridor and gave a sudden start. 'Ah,' she said, and vanished into the Imperial apartments. He had a glimpse of serried ranks of maids waiting to take her clothes, and a whiff of perfume, and then the door was closed in his face.

A young shepherd boy stood and gawped at the guard post on the Thrake road. There were twenty of Duke Andronicus's soldiers, a pair of armoured noblemen, and six Easterners with horn bows. The boy ate an apple and then led his sheep through the roadblock. He was dumb, and made a pantomime of it, and the men laughed gruffly, took two of his sheep for dinner, and promised to beat him if he made a fuss.

He shuffled off to stand on the next hillside, watching them.

A wagon rolled up to the post in the last light of the sun.

The shepherd boy reached into the grass and fetched out a javelin, and then another, and then a sword.

Just as the wagon – a butcher from the city – was clearing the roadblock there was the sound of hoof beats. The men at the roadblock sprang to arms, but it was all too fast, and they were captured or dead in a matter of moments.

The Easterners covering the roadblock, all hardbitten steppe men under a khan, didn't fight. They ran north, having been mounted.

The shepherd boy and a dozen other men and women who'd passed the roadblock in the last two days fell on the Easterners and the wagon, taking two prisoners and killing the rest.

Daniel Favour trotted down the hill after cleaning his spear on the dead man's cloak and taking his purse, to find Gelfred sitting on his horse on the road in the fading light.

Gelfred nodded. 'Well done,' he said.

Daniel grinned. 'I thought they was going to beat me. And I was wondering how long I'd take it before I fought back.' He shrugged.

Gelfred nodded. 'I did some praying,' he admitted.

'You see the wagon that got through?' Favour asked.

Gelfred nodded. 'He had a pass. I'll question him separately.'

Two hours later, the Duke sat with Alcaeus and Father Arnaud, playing music in the yard. A handful of diehards were still dancing, including a remarkably bedraggled Ser Jehan and a very young Morean girl.

'Will you fall in love with her?' the poet asked.

'Are you asking the Red Knight or the Megas Ducas?' the possessor of both titles asked.

'Surely you are a man, with a man's appetites and a man's desires, and not a pair of empty titles and a suit of armour,' Alcaeus said. 'Christos, I'm drunk. Ignore me.'

Father Arnaud watched him like the conscience most of his men assumed he didn't have. 'Do you fine gentlemen know *Et non est qui adjuvet*, by any chance?' he asked.

They played it, and then they all drank wine. People applauded.

'She's watching you from the Library,' Father Arnaud said.

Ser Gavin appeared with a small drum. 'If I play, am I allowed in the club?' he asked.

'A drum?' his brother asked.

'It looks easy enough.' Gavin laughed.

'Anyway, you don't need an instrument to join. You need only be celibate,' Alcaeus said.

Father Arnaud spat some of his wine. He drank a little more, wiped his chin, and shook his head.

'Someone choose a song,' the Captain said.

'It's your turn,' Alcaeus insisted.

'"*Tant Doucement*"?' asked the Captain.

'Must we?' asked the priest.

'You don't love her?' Alcaeus asked.

'Who, the princess?' asked Gavin. 'My brother is very particular. He probably has his heart set on—'

The elbow in his ribs was not brotherly, and he was unprepared for it. 'What the *fuck*!' he said in a distinctly unchivalrous and quite believably brotherly way.

'My brother was going to say that I had my heart set on the priesthood, but they insisted that I love God, and there's things I just can't lie about,' he said.

Father Arnaud looked away.

'You are an evil bastard,' Gavin said, and he laughed and slapped his brother on the back.

The Captain took a deep breath. 'That's right,' he said. 'I am.' He turned on his heel and walked away.

The priest watched him.

'We don't know, either,' Alcaeus said.

Gavin followed his brother into the stable, up the long ramp to the second storey, and his footsteps echoed hollowly on the wooden floor. His brother was standing with a horse, in near darkness.

'Only the Emperor would have a two-storey stable,' he said.

Silence.

'I'm sorry, but you know, if you have to be all strong and long-suffering and commanderly, none of us will ever know exactly why you are sad or angry or whatever in the devil's name you are.' Gavin smiled. 'And may I point out that whatever your troubles, you don't bear the actual mark of the Wild on your body? I have scales. Every day. Mary saw them and she—' Gavin paused. 'Are you listening?'

Gabriel reached out in the darkness and embraced his brother, and they stood there for the count of ten.

'Do you at least like her?' Gavin asked.

'No,' Gabriel whispered. 'As you so astutely noted, I like someone else. I need more music. Thanks for coming in after me.'

In the morning, Wilful Murder was the first man on parade, while the sun was still below the horizon. He farted repeatedly, he had a hard head, and he'd done his share of dancing, but he was ready – his horse's feed bag was full, his armour polished, oiled, and stored, his heavy winter cloak rolled behind his saddle, ready to march anywhere.

An hour later, when no alarm bells had rung, he cursed and went back to bed. In the next rack, Bent was too smart to laugh aloud.

The new week saw changes – small ones that heralded larger changes to come.

For example, a hoard of tailors descended on the company and cut new cloth delivered from the market stalls and suddenly the company had uniform scarlet hose and doublets, and new surcoats over their armour. Every man and every horse had Morean-style horsehair tufts in red, green, and white – one on each shoulder, and one atop their horse's head. A set of standards appeared in the yard, made up outside the palace. One had Saint Katherine and her wheel, and the others had three lacs d'amour in gold – one pennon on white, one on green, and one on red. In the process of learning where they were to stand by the standards, the company learned that a substantial remnant of the mercenaries – the Gallish and Iberian mercenaries – who had served Duke Andronicus were now members of their company.

Ser Bescanon, for example, was now the second standard bearer, carrying Saint Katherine. Ser Milus carried the company banner – black, with three lacs d'amour. The company was divided into three parts, of unequal numbers; the first band, of one hundred lances, was commanded by Ser Jehan, with four corporals, Ser George Brewes, Ser Francis Atcourt, Ser Alfonse d'Este and Ser Gonzago d'Avia, the last two new men from the former Latinikon. The second band, of fifty lances, was commanded by Ser Gavin, and had Ranald Lachlan and Ser Michael as corporals. The third band, also of fifty lances on parchment but smaller in reality, was commanded by Gelfred, and had two corporals, one of whom was Ser Alison, and the other Ser

Alcaeus. Ser Jehan's band was white, Ser Gavin's was red, and Gelfred's was green. Each lance had a man-at-arms, a squire almost equally well armed and mounted, a page aspiring to become a man-at-arms, and an archer or two.

The new men were cursed, and nearly everyone on the rolls declared that the company would never recover – too many new faces, with bad attitudes and personal enmities and different languages and customs. The new archers weren't any good, and the new men-at-arms were scarcely able to ride. Or so men said.

There were four new women among the new recruits – all Easterners from the steppes, all archers, on horse or foot. They kept to themselves and rebuffed any advances from Oak Pew or from Sauce. Or anyone else. The steppe men steered clear of them as well.

Bad Tom's anodyne for new recruits was work.

Men with hangovers can survive being fitted by tailors. Mag led the seamstresses to work, and if she put her head on her knees once or twice and smiled a bright and brittle smile at the world, she also looked as happy as a woman can look – perhaps not quite as happy as Lady Kaitlin, who attended her wedding breakfast and then sat and sewed hose with the other skilled seamstresses under Lis the laundress's command.

Count Zac delivered three hundred horses at the gates of the Outer Court – one he led himself. He presented it to the Megas Ducas, who accepted it with pleasure – a tall gelding, sixteen hands, jet black. Strong, but with clean lines and a fine head and a remarkably intelligent eye for a warhorse.

'He can be a bastard,' Zac said. He shrugged. 'So can I. Is your Sauce single?'

If the change of subject took the Megas Ducas by surprise, he didn't show it. 'She virtually defines single,' he said.

Count Zac cleared his throat. 'She has had lovers – yes?' His expression indicated that he was embarrassed to ask.

The Megas Ducas allowed himself the very slightest of smiles. 'It is possible,' he allowed.

Count Zac sighed. 'May I court her?' he asked.

'Will you always bring me horses like this if I say yes?' asked the Megas Ducas. He vaulted onto his new horse, bareback, and shot away.

An hour later, still bareback, he pulled up by Sauce, who was still being fitted for her hose by some very straight-faced tailors. She had just offered to strip to her braes.

'Alison? I've traded you to Count Zac for three hundred horses,' he said. 'It's not a bad deal – he'll marry you.'

She frowned, and then nodded. 'Three hundred sounds like a good price,' she agreed. 'He's short, but I fancy him.'

He grinned at her. 'Long time since you fancied anyone,' he said.

'Besides you,' she said.

He flushed, and she laughed in his face.

'Well, I'm glad it's mutual,' he said. 'Be nice to the tailors.'

He rode to find Ser Michael, who was running the remnants of a small wedding breakfast while checking the company accounts with the notary.

The Captain came in, bowed to the remaining ladies, kissed their hands and their cheeks, and took Michael by the shoulder. Michael was instantly alert.

The two men walked out of the guardroom where the guests were drinking wine, followed by Father Arnaud, who walked with them, chatting pleasantly and in an extremely artificial way until they were inside the Captain's rooms.

Ser Michael looked around. Toby poured him hot wine from a jug by the fire and walked out, closing the door.

The Captain took a deep breath. His chin went up – one of his rare signs of nerves.

'I'm sorry, Michael,' he said. 'It's not good, and I've hidden it from you so you could enjoy your wedding.'

Michael looked around. 'Sweet Jesu, what is it?'

Father Arnaud shook his head. 'Gabriel, that was not well done.' He nodded to Michael. 'Your pater has been taken as a traitor by the Captal de Ruth, acting for the King. There has been a battle, and your father lost. Badly. If he is attainted—'

Michael sat down, hard, face unmoving.

The Captain glared at the priest, who smiled beatifically.

'I've called him a traitor a hundred times,' Michael said. He looked up. 'And he used your name.'

The Captain twitched like an angry cat. 'I knew it was a mistake to get a chaplain.' He looked at the priest, and then said, 'The prior sent me a set of messages. He says Father Arnaud is to be trusted. Despite playing fast and loose with my identity. In fact, since I've discovered that my brother has written to my mother I suppose it doesn't matter any more.' He looked at Michael. 'I'm babbling. Michael, I *need* you. I plan a winter campaign here – you know what that means.'

'Par Dieu, have my pater's troubles driven you to *share* your plans?' Michael said. But he felt numb. 'I have to help my pater.'

'The King and the Constable have sent every Jarsay knight away from court,' Father Arnaud said. 'It was not done with ill will. There is some question as to whether the Captal's actions are actually within the law, or done with the King's sanction. The King is, not to put too fine a point on it, trying to keep the lid on the situation by keeping your pater's supporters away from the Galles and the men who arrested the Earl.'

The Captain poured himself some wine. 'In this, for once, I must support the King, Michael. If you insist on going – well, I won't arrest you or use force to stop you, although I did consider it. But short of force, I'll use any argument to keep you from going.'

Father Arnaud nodded. 'When I left, the rumour was that your father was going to demand trial by combat. At the tournament in the spring.' He glanced at the Duke. 'The other matter is the new Bishop of Lorica. He'll be elevated tomorrow and he has made his views plain – about the use of hermeticism, about the Patriarch here, about my order.' The priest shrugged. 'De Vrailly may be virtual master of the kingdom by summer. The Queen is virtually under siege by the Gallish faction. They hate her, and we don't even know why.'

The Captain leaned forward. 'We'll be finished here by then. We could go to the tournament.' He smiled, and it was a wicked smile. 'Visit all together, so to speak.'

Ser Michael took a deep breath. 'You plan a winter campaign, and you'll escort me to Alba in the spring?' he said. 'You don't plan to marry the princess and make yourself Emperor?'

The Captain looked out the window, wrinkling his nose in frustration at having to reveal anything of his plans. But he finally looked at Michael and grinned. 'It may yet come out that way,' he admitted. 'But it's not how I want it to go.'

Ser Michael chewed on that for a moment. 'It's not?' he asked. He looked at Father Arnaud, who looked equally surprised. In fact, he looked like a man who'd just made an important connection.

The Captain propped his chin on his hands, elbows on his knee which was in turn propped on a stool, and looked surprisingly human. 'Sometimes I have to change my plans,' he said. 'This is one of those times. For various reasons, I'd say that yes, we're going to the Queen's tournament, and no, I don't think I'll marry the princess.' He raised an eyebrow. 'I'm sorry about your pater. I liked him.'

Michael shrugged. 'I left for many reasons. I'm here because of them, and I shan't go running off. I *think* I am glad you didn't tell me until my wedding was over.' He took a deep breath. 'I think I'll go and tell my wife,' he said. He rose, found that the world was stable, and bowed. At the door he paused. 'May I call you Gabriel?' he asked.

'No,' said the Duke.

'Yes,' said the priest. 'At every opportunity.'

Ser Michael nodded. 'Got it,' he said, and withdrew.

The priest turned to his new charge. 'To the best of my understanding, you've chosen to be a human being again. Having a name is part of that.'

The Captain's face was still balanced on his hand. He was looking out the window. 'Is it an act?' he asked. 'Or do you think that if I spend enough time pretending to be a human being, I'll become one?'

Got it in one, muttered Harmodius – his first comment in days.

The priest came and stood by him.

'Who gave you power over me?' Gabriel asked, but his voice was not unfriendly.

'The *Bon Soeur du Foret Sauvage* sends her greetings,' he said.

The second day after the party, the army – now including almost two hundred local Morean stradiotes – rode into the hills towards Thrake. The Nordikans had ponies, and the entire company was remounted. They moved fast, covered almost twenty miles, and returned through the hills to the west without meeting any opposition. Selected men were counted off and practised storming a small castle that had been built to the purpose – it was only waist high, but rooms were laid out clearly.

Watchers noted too late that they went out without Gelfred's men and returned with them, as well as a wagon and twenty prisoners.

On the following day, the feast of Saint George, they drilled in the Great Square – even the stradiotes. There were sword drills, and spear drills, and tilting by the mounted men. The Vardariotes came and shot from horseback, joined by a handful of Gelfred's men and some pages who had become interested in mounted archery – or had been ordered to take an interest. Gelfred's men vanished for two hours and returned to announce that they all had new hose and new doublets – all green, not red.

Workmen came and built a toy castle – just two towers and a timber hall. None of the buildings had walls – just skeleton structures, so that the crowd could watch all the fighting inside. Forty picked men stormed the castle, to the cheers of the onlookers.

The newly recruited knights jousted with the likes of Bad Tom and Sauce and the Captain, to the satisfaction of all the old company men. Ser Bescanon was unhorsed so hard that he was knocked unconscious – Bad Tom was the culprit.

Thousands of citizens of the city watched, and cheered.

The stradiotes tilted at rings and cut fruits in half with their swords and did some trick riding.

The Nordikans cut through their drill posts with their real axes so fast that the crowd laughed to see pages and Ordinaries running about trying to fit new posts.

The Scholae demonstrated their skills, from wrestling to swordsmanship, and then a team of six of them jousted in borrowed armour. Giorgios Comnenos, who had received a fair amount of private coaching from Ser Michael, managed to keep his seat and score against Ser George Brewes. Ser Alison unhorsed Ser Iannos Dukas, deftly knocking his lance to the ground in a display of perfect martial control, and the crowd cheered her and threw flowers. Moreans were growing used to a female knight.

Morgan Mortirmir, in borrowed armour, ran three courses with Ser Francis Atcourt, scoring on the older knight's helm in the first pass, exchanging shattered lances on the second, and being unhorsed on the third. Out of practice, he fell badly.

The twenty prisoners sat alone and untended in solitary cells beneath the palace. They were not tortured on the feast of Saint George. They were merely kept awake.

Kronmir had seen the wagon coming back into the city, and he knew what that meant.

He sat thoughtfully with his fingers steepled for some time. He contemplated how long it would take for the foreigners to break his agent, and what that agent could tell them. He reviewed his message system, and assured himself from his code book that he knew the 'cease all activity' messages for his three most important agents. Then, when his inn had fallen quiet, and even the lowliest serving maids were asleep, he emptied his room, packed his valise, and pondered the deaths of the innkeeper, his wife, and the young woman Kronmir had slept with from time to time. Killing the three of them would leave the enemy with no witnesses to his presence, but he disliked such waste and he had his own rules. He smiled wryly and admitted to himself that he liked the girl and he couldn't really muster the *sang froid* to kill her. Instead, he carefully blocked the chimney in the inn's common room with flammables and relaid the fire for morning, taking care to relay it exactly the way the night maid had put it down.

He walked past Nianna's bordello and left a white cross in chalk on the door of the saddler's across the street. He walked through the deserted streets to the slums by the warehouses on the eastern shore, and left a lamda inside a circle in white chalk on a door across the street from a man who was still recovering from his wounds – the captain of the professional assassins he'd hired from Etrusca, who'd almost died storming the palace.

Then he sat in a waterfront soup house for an hour, watching his back trail, before walking uphill to the old aqueduct, removing a stone, and leaving forty silver leopards in a bag in the gap behind it. He replaced the stone, walked down the hill, and stuck a silver pin into the olive tree that stood in the centre of a tiny square near the assassin's house. He placed the pin so that it was very hard to see – but easy to find if a man leaned casually against the tree to prise a stone from his shoe.

Then he walked along the sea wall and left two more lamda-in-circle signs tucked in among the graffiti of a hundred generations.

He sat on the wall and waited to see if he had been followed. He walked right down his back trail – bad practice, but he was in a hurry and the sun would be up soon. Then he went to the drop where his Navy Yard contact left his messages – badly spelled, scrawled on leather, rolled up and fitted inside an abandoned clay water pipe from a system half a thousand years old. Kronmir knelt in the dark, felt the presence of leather, and nodded. He withdrew the report, put it in his valise, then put a bag of gold in its place, sealed the pipe, and sketched a broad black 'X' in charcoal across it.

He had other agents, but they could rot or be captured. None of them had ever seen him – nor had they ever provided him with anything worth having. And he didn't think the butcher knew they existed.

Then he walked across the city to the western walls, where the lampmaker's guild had failed for years to keep the walls in good repair. His rope – cunningly woven of grey and brown horsehair – was right where he wanted it to be. He slipped over the wall, and climbed the ditch, cursing middle age and the sword at his side. He climbed the outer wall at its most ruinous point and jumped down the far side, walked half a league across the fields to a farm, and stole a horse.

The taken wagon had told Kronmir a great deal. It told him that the Red Knight controlled access to the mountains to the north. He rode west, not north, into the hills.

Two days after the feast of Saint George, the Scholac went to two houses in the city. Both of them were empty, and the inn they had intended to raid was found to have burned to the ground. The inn staff had gone to stay with relatives.

The Duke rode through the Navy Yard gates with a handful of armoured men-at-arms led by Francis Atcourt. At his side rode an unarmoured man, who sat and watched the work of the yard with professional admiration – and some obvious discomfort.

The Duke dismounted and went into the main building, so old that it was built of the same red and yellow brick as the main walls of the city. 'Look at everything,' he said casually to the unarmoured man.

'Who is he?' asked the master shipwright, William Mortice of Harndon. He'd arrived two weeks before, overland.

The Duke smiled. 'Master Mortice, he is none other than the Mighty and Puissant Lord Ernst Handalo of Venike.' The Duke nodded.

'He'll burn my pretty sharks on their stocks!' Mortice said, rising.

'No, no. He'll go home and tell his city to ally itself with us.'

Sparrow was still getting used to the Red Knight and to Liviapolis. 'Us? Who is "us"? Alba? Nova Terra? The Empire?'

'You and me and the new navy,' the Duke said, swirling wine in his cup and adding something from a flask.

An hour later, in the biting wind on the sea wall, Handalo stood with his short cape whipping behind him. He had to shout to be heard. 'You can't sustain the expense!' he roared. 'Not without trade and a merchant fleet.'

'I agree!' roared the Duke.

'And winter is here!' shouted Handalo. 'It would be insane to put to sea this late in the year.'

'I agree!' roared the Duke.

'Then why don't you just buy us off and stop this?' Handalo said.

The Duke smiled. 'Every archer in my company carries two bowstrings in a small waxed pouch. When they are inspected, the master archers check for them. Because once, I was caught unprepared by a loss of bowstrings.'

Handalo raised an eyebrow.

The Duke looked out over the sea. 'I could make a mercantile agreement with you right here, messire. But in three years or less, it would be... inconvenient for you. And you would abrogate it – or your successor would.' He met the Etruscan's eye. 'I can defeat you militarily, but not for long. Am I correct?'

Handalo nodded. 'You have a good head.'

'Both bowstrings. I build a fleet and *then* I'll offer a trade agreement, and you and the Genuans will have every reason to keep it.' The Duke shrugged.

'The princess is lucky to have you,' the Venike captain said.

The Duke shook his head. 'The Emperor is lucky to have me,' he said.

Two weeks later, the first Morean galley built in the city in twenty years slipped down the ancient stone slipway and splashed stern first into the ocean, watched by the Etruscan squadron from across the strait. The next day the captured Etruscan galley was repaired, and by week's end the new Imperial Navy had four hulls in the water.

There followed the first winter storm, a vicious display of nature's power over water, when all work in the yard had to be halted and a small fortune in lumber, left uncovered, was blown into the sea and lost. The new Imperial ships uncrossed their yards and were stored in covered ship sheds – sheds built a thousand years before.

The Etruscans didn't have thousand-year-old stone ship sheds, so they had to strip their ships, turn them over, and store them under temporary shelters for the winter. Morea got snow and ice despite its warmer clime and the warm current off the straits, and winter was brutal for galleys.

Two days after the storm, the Etruscans had all their ships stowed safely away. They could only watch in horror in the cold and watery sunlight, as the new Imperial squadron put to sea and cruised to the mouth of the gulf unopposed. The Imperial fleet returned from a day at sea with a trio of great Alban round ships. As there was no blockade, the Alban ships docked without danger, packed to the gunwales with wool, leather and other Alban wares, and a hundred grateful merchants met the Alban traders on the docks. Meanwhile the Imperial ships dashed across the strait under the command of the Megas Ducas, landed marines, and burned the whole Etruscan squadron in their sheds.

Before the fires were out, Ser Ernst Handalo led a deputation of the Merchanter League to the palace from which he had so recently been released. That afternoon, the Etruscans abandoned their alliance with Duke Andronicus and signed a peace with Princess Irene and her father, the Emperor, and a document demanding that 'The traitorous usurper previously known as the Duke of Thrake' immediately restore the Emperor to his throne. They paid an indemnity and their Podesta signed a set of articles guaranteeing their tax rate – a rate on which they made a sizeable initial payment. All of the Etruscan officers were released.

The Imperial Army continued to drill. Every day, more of the local stradiotes reported. And every day, a few more merchant ships appeared in the gulf – all from Alba. The round ships were at less risk in the late autumn than galleys. But someone was taking a risk nonetheless.

On the next Monday, the whole of the Imperial Army formed on the Field of Ares; almost a thousand of the company, almost five hundred Scholae, three hundred Nordikans, and as many Vardariotes with nearly a thousand Tagmatic infantry from the city and four hundred stradiotes cavalry from the countryside. Most of the army was clothed in white wool – fresh, new Alban wool, heavy as armour, the colour of snow. The new winter gowns were the products of feverish sewing by every tailor and sempter in Liviapolis.

Ser Gerald Random sat on a horse with the Red Knight and his staff and watched them. He shook his head in wonder. 'You have your own army!' he said.

'You should know,' the Red Knight said. 'You're paying them.' He smiled. 'And bringing the wool.'

Random laughed with all the knights. 'You realise that if this doesn't work, I'll be broken – I have, in effect, risked the entirety of my fortune on you.'

The Red Knight looked over his army with satisfaction. 'It looks like a good bet so far,' he said. He looked around. 'The Etruscan indemnity should have paid your bills.'

'But she spent it elsewhere,' Random said.

The Red Knight shrugged.

Random glared. 'While you continue to spend money like a drunken sailor in a whorehouse.'

The Red Knight shrugged again. 'You can't buy happiness, but you can buy skill with weapons, bravery, and fine equipment.' He scratched his beard. 'They aren't cheap.' And he looked back at the merchant. 'Anyway, you are made of money. Why will this break you?'

'I agreed to manage the Queen's tournament. That reminds me – here's your official invitation. I'm to tell you to your face that you are required, as a knight and a gentleman, to open it and answer her. What happened to the others?' Random was playing with his reins and trying to judge how much the lack of a foot was going to change his balance if he rode hard.

'I ignored them.' The Red Knight opened the scroll tube, unrolled the scroll, and a small working took place and flew off in the form of a tiny dove which hovered like a white hummingbird.

The Queen is gaining in skill, Harmodius said.

'You've been knighted, and now you are in charge of the Royal Tournament?' the Red Knight asked.

Gerald nodded. 'Yes.'

'And the cost is staggering?' the Red Knight asked.

Random grimaced. 'Yes.'

'And you are fronting the money,' the Red Knight continued.

Random shrugged. 'She's the Queen. The King knighted me.' He grinned. 'I love a good tournament,' he added.

The Red Knight glared at him. 'And yet, despite that, you came here and risked your fortune to pay my bills.'

Random met his eyes squarely. 'That's right, Captain.'

The Red Knight looked at Ser Michael. 'I think that I'm learning the meaning of largesse from a merchant,' he said.

'I plan to joust, at the tournament,' Random said. 'I'll take it out of you in lessons.'

The Red Knight looked at the hovering dove. 'I will attend, with all my knights, fair Queen,' he said formally.

The little dove bobbed, and flew away.

The Red Knight – the Megas Ducas, the Duke of Thrake, Gabriel Muriens – turned his horse and made it rear slightly, and raised his baton. Every eye followed him.

'Now let's show this so-called Duke Andronicus how to make war,' he said.

Chapter Twelve

Prince Demetrius

Lutece, Galle – The King of Galle and his Horse

The Seneschal d'Abblemont tapped a parchment scroll against the great oak table for attention, and the war council gradually came to order.

Tancred Guisarme, the Royal Constable, was not in his magnificent dragon armour, but wore a plain brigandine covered in deerhide and a pair of Etruscan steel arms; Steilker, the Master of the King's Crossbowman, still wore his black armour with gold lettering praising God; Vasilli, the architect of the King's castles, wore only a maille shirt. Ser Eustace de Ribeaumont, one of the Marshals of the realm and once a famous mercenary, wore black armour with golden edges and bronze maille – very elegant. Abblemont himself wore his plain Etruscan white harness. The only unarmoured man was Messire Ciamberi, a man whose role on the council was almost always left undiscussed.

D'Abblemont waved at his secretary, and the man began to read off a scroll.

Item — The Sieur de Cavalli and four hundred lances have passed from the service of Genua and are now available for employ.

Item — The Senate and Council of Ten of Venike have come to terms with the Emperor and consequently the order for sixty galleys placed to the Arsenal. The man looked up.

D'Abblemont nodded. 'I have a note from our last meeting – it was the largest order they have ever placed, eh?'

Vasilli fingered his beard. 'And now cancelled. A lot of out of work shipwrights.'

'Mayhap the Emperor can employ them,' Abblemont quipped and they all laughed.

'And is our man in place to trim the Emperor's feathers?' asked the Constable.

D'Abblemonth looked around. He waved at his secretary to sit. 'Yes. If my sense of the timing is correct, he should be ready to storm Osawa today or tomorrow. I could be off by as much as a week.'

The Constable looked pained. He looked around like a guilty child and muttered, 'Before the Church got so high and mighty about hermeticism, we used to be able to communicate with our – missions.'

Every head turned to Messire Ciamberi, who raised both eyebrows in mock surprise.

'My lords – if anyone were to practise such heresy, I would have to remind you that a communication covering a thousand leagues *and penetrating the Wild* would require more power than—' He shrugged. 'Than the pagan ancients ever mustered.'

Abblemont waved a hand. 'I trust that in this case, our agent is on our timetable.'

Men nodded. The Constable shuffled on his seat. 'Then why are we here?' he asked.

Abblemont tossed the parchment in his hand onto the table. 'The Count of Arclat has sent a cartel to the King, challenging him to single combat.'

Guisarme winced. 'Bound to happen. Of course, the old Count will eat the King up like a snack – one of the best lances in the world.'

Abblemont shook his head. If the subject pained him – and it did – he hid his complete disgust well. 'The King will not fight,' he said.

All the men startled. 'This is Galle!' de Ribeaumont said. 'He has to fight.'

Abblemont sighed. 'Gentlemen, the King sees in this challenge an obvious ploy by the Count to re-establish the lapsed kingdom of Arelat. Defeat of the King in single combat would probably be construed that way in the Arela – don't you agree?'

'Christ, spare me another mountain campaign,' Steilker said.

It was clear from their faces that neither of the knights approved.

'Wait until de Vrailly hears that the King refused a challenge,' de Ribeaumont said.

There was silence.

Abblemont shook his head. 'That's not really the core of the difficulty,' he said and smoothed out the parchment. 'You see, while sending us a cartel of defiance, the Count has *also* sent us a detailed description of a skirmish – or rather, a series of skirmishes – in which his men-at-arms seem to have faced irks.'

'Preposterous,' said de Ribeaumont. 'Now I think that our young King has a head on his shoulders. The Count de Sartre is merely using this absurd pretext to rally troops. And besides, Abblemont, did you not give us your word that your niece was at fault in the little contretemps with the King?'

Abblemont didn't wriggle. His face retained the bland, affable look that the Horse wore at all times. 'This matter is delicate,' he admitted. 'Perhaps most delicate is this piece of evidence.'

At his wave, a servant opened a sack and put a severed head on the table. It reeked of rot.

It was, palpably, an irk, fangs and all.

Messire Ciamberi leaned forward. 'Could it be faked?' he asked.

Steilker shook his head. 'Holy *fuck.*'

Guisarme leaned forward. 'I would hate to take you for a liar, my friend. But the Queen tells a different tale. She says that the little chit was innocent as a saint. In which case, the Count is in the right – isn't he?' The Constable had never been an ally of the King's Horse. 'He sends this head to prove he's loyal. And he is. Isn't he?'

Abblemont ignored the Constable's tone. 'It seems to me that whether the Count is loyal or not, we need to be ready in the spring with an army.'

De Ribeaumont leaned forward. 'My lords! If we field an army in the south – that's no men for de Vrailly and precious little for our effort in Nova Terra's northlands.'

'Money?' asked the Constable.

Abblemont shrugged. 'Not enough to buy a second army. Not even enough, I think, to pay Cavalli's lances.'

Steilker smiled. 'Ah, but my lords, once he's on a ship for the Nova Terra, we don't ever have to pay him again.'

*

That evening, the King listened to music with his Etruscan Queen. After the music, he went to this private solar with his Horse and was entertained with the news of the world. Finally, he was laughing as he liked. All was well with the world.

'Did I miss a meeting of the military council? he asked suddenly. Abblemont nodded. 'Yes, my liege.'

'Bah – that foolishness of the Queen's – that I had to see her new wardrobe. Was anything important discussed?' the King asked.

'No,' Abblemont said. 'No, Your Grace.'

N'gara Castle – Bill Redmede

'We're losing them,' Nat Tyler said. He was sitting in the Great Hall, watching the irk musicians play fairy tunes. Two hundred men and women watched, faces rapt.

Redmede had thought the same thing a hundred times. And he thought it of himself, because Bess's hand lay comfortably in his under cover of the table.

'If we're still in this fight, we need to leave,' Tyler spat. He glared at Redmede. 'Or are you sorcelled too?'

Redmede sat up straighter, like a schoolboy accused by a teacher. But Bess shook her head.

'We ain't sorcelled, Nat Tyler. This is as close to heaven as mortal men ever get. A little work and a lot o' play. An' such play!' She shook her head. 'What's it for? I never been so happy as the last days. Not ever. Not even—' She paused, and a cloud passed over her face. 'Not even as a girl.'

Nat stood up. 'I'm for leavin',' he said. 'I'm healed. I don't want to sit in a dream. I want to kill the King and make men free.'

Redmede sat back. 'Nat,' he said.

'What?' the older man asked. 'I'm still true, even if you ain't.'

Redmede shook his head. 'Winter is falling out there,' he said.

Bess looked at both of them.

Tyler leaned forward. 'If you said you was coming with me, the rest of 'em would come.'

Redmede heard the faery music as if it was playing inside his head, and he looked at the art on the walls – the spidery tracery that defied his human eyes on the tapestries, the rich layers of colour in the felt hangings – and he sighed. 'Give me a day or two to think,' he said.

And then some days passed.

He shared a little house with Bess, and she was all he wanted. They played games, and they guarded sheep, and they made love. The other Jacks became friends – sometimes they gathered at each other's little houses for a meal, and sometimes, they sat in the Great Hall.

Parties of Outwallers came and went, and sometimes they brought women. The Jacks had had few women. Now they had a few more – or rather, perhaps there were fewer Jacks.

One frosty afternoon, Redmede went out to gather wood. The men's iron axes and strong muscles made them the premier gatherers of wood in the whole community, and they had gradually taken the chore upon themselves, in the irkish way – the best at any task took it, and taught it.

Redmede was a canny firewood gatherer – skilful and lazy, too. He liked to find one tree – preferably a good, big maple, dead and still standing, or dead and newly fallen, before its upper branches could rot on the ground. He liked to wander with his axe on his shoulder, enjoying the dusting of snow, the cold on his almost bare arms, the smell of the woods.

And he wore his sword, because this was, truly, the Wild of children's stories. The *hastenoch* walked these marshes; the great rock trolls prowled the hills to the south, and boglins tunnelled where they didn't run, while great beaver built six-feet-high dams that lasted a hundred years, and herds of bison moved in the clearings, watched by Guardians, the daemons of the woods. They, too, came and visited the Faery Knight. Redmede was growing more used to them. But he suspected that if he met one in the woods, alone, he would be prey, and not friend.

So he walked with pleasure, but warily. And despite his wariness, Tapio Haltija took him unawares, as he stood in silence contemplating the ruin of a great oak.

'*Ssso. Man.*' The irk was his own height, and moved without a sound.

Redmede nodded pleasantly. 'Ser Tapio,' he said.

The Faery Knight looked at the fallen oak. '*Thisss issss how we will all end,*' he sang. '*No matter how many wintersss we passs firssssst.*'

Redmede nodded.

'*Man, I have many guesssstsss coming.*' Ser Tapio met his eyes, and the irk's eyes were a fathomless dark blue like a summer night lit by stars, with no whites.

Redmede never found it easy to communicate with the irk. The other creature's mind did not work like a man's. 'What guests?' he asked.

'*Alliesss,*' Tapio said. '*The cold in the air is the firsst bite of war.*'

Redmede was startled by the turn of conversation, but then, talking to the lord of the irks was never easy. 'War?' he asked. 'What war? Against the King?'

The Faery Knight shrugged – a very human gesture. '*I care nothing for any king of men,*' he said. His voice sounded like a dozen stringed instruments playing together in harmony. '*I consssider a war with a rival. I consssult thossse who I sssee asss alliesss.*'

Redmede broke off gazing at the irk and looked back at his fallen oak. 'Am I an ally?' he asked.

The irk's smile was hard for a man to get used to. It meant something different among irks, and it involved a great many teeth. Tapio further complicated communications by using his smile both the irk way – as aggression – and the human way, for pleasure.

'*That isss for you to tell me, man.*'

The next day brought a retinue of Wardens – or Guardians, or daemons, depending on your point of view. They had tall red plumes, which Bill knew to be natural and not worn as decorations, although the magnificent gold and silver and lead and bronze and tin inlay in their beaks was all craft. Redmede watched two young daemons receive their first inlays by a pair of irk craftsmen who worked with their hands and magic alike. A year before he'd have fled. Now he watched in fascination.

The next day, Nat Tyler caught him by the shoulder as he entered the worm's nest of corridors of the great central keep.

'I'm gone,' he said. 'You comin'?'

Redmede took a deep breath. 'Nat – I kept you alive,' he said. 'I dragged your weary arse out of the battle, and I carried you out here – most of the way. Now I want a winter off.'

Tyler shook his head. 'Man and women are being worked to death by lords in Jarsay,' he said. 'The fuckin' Church will celebrate Christmas on the backs of the poor. Outwallers will be hunted like vermin. You want a *rest*.' He leaned in close. 'You've found a *lord*, just like your turncoat brother.'

'Nat, will it kill us to be happy for a while, and rest? Listen to music? Lady Tamlin nursed you herself – do you owe her nothing for that?' He had no trouble meeting Tyler's eyes, which he found slightly mad.

He had the oddest feeling, because they'd switched roles. He had always been the driven one, the committed one.

'Mayhap you need a girl,' he assayed.

'Jarsay is in flames and Alba is on the verge of civil war, you fool! This is *our time*. The nobles are fighting each other.' Tyler was shouting, and irks paused to look at them, or drew back against the walls. A blue-crested daemon was framed against the snow outside.

Redmede's eyes narrowed. 'What do you say?' he asked.

Tyler shrugged. 'Nothing. Come or don't. The cause is bigger than you, Bill Redmede. Stay here and rot.' He avoided Redmede's attempt to restrain him and pushed past.

Redmede turned to catch him and found himself face to snout with the elegantly inlaid beak and tall blue crest of Mogon, the Queen of the western daemons. He knew her. Not well, but they had been—

alliesss.

The thought slipped into his head.

'Mogon,' he said. She smelled like burning soap, and filled the tunnel from side to side. She had to crouch to fit.

'Jack,' she said. 'Not your true name, I will guess.'

He stood his ground. 'I'm Bill Redmede, daemon,' he said, fighting an urge to turn and flee. All the daemons projected a sort of wave front of fear – as did many of the other Wild creatures, but the daemons were the most powerful in every way. Even at rest, in a quiet hold, surrounded by other creatures, she emanated menace.

She made an effort – the blue feathers on her crest went flat. 'Why must your little men require me to pretend to be dominated?' she asked.

Her beak had surprisingly little effect on her speech.

He found himself released from terror. He forced himself to speak. 'Are you an ally? Of Tapio?'

She sighed and stretched herself in the confined corridor. 'We'll see, Master Redmede. May I say: it is a pleasure to find a former ally here?'

'I am only a guest,' he spat. 'I lead no men,' he added. 'But the men I brought here remember you. You left us to die, at Lissen.'

'Really?' she asked. 'My brother sent me to warn the Outwallers. Were you not warned? We are a chivalrous people.' The stench of burned soap increased.

'Chivalrous? Lady, a hundred of my Jacks died *for nothing* when you turned tail and ran.' People – irks, men, even a winged faery – were gathering to watch them.

'Ran?' she breathed. 'You insult my brood.'

Redmede realised that her gold-inlaid beak was less than a finger's width from his nose. He was angry enough that he didn't care.

'Your brood is alive to be insulted,' Redmede said.

The crest on her head sprang erect, and the wavefront of terror crashed around him. He stepped back – a faery vanished with a *pop* and most of the men in the corridor flinched as she raised a heavy forefoot and flexed the vicious talons that could slice through maille.

'You say words that would end in your death outside the sanctity of this hold,' Mogon barked. 'But I will *explain*, Master Redmede. Let it not be said that Mogon Fairweather of the Bluecrest People was ever less than fair, even to vermin and men. My brother *hated* Thorn. He distrusted him. And when he found that we had been posted – and I mean no offence, but speak simple truth – had been posted with only the weakest of allies, he assumed we'd been sent to die.'

Redmede released the breath he'd held through her whole speech. He ducked his head clumsily – the best he could manage of a bow. 'Lady Mogon, you exceed me in courtesy,' he growled. 'I am but man, and vermin. But I love my people as you love yours, and to see them die in defeat fair turned my stomach. Perhaps you are right. I have no time for Thorn and his schemes. But... well perhaps if you had charged into the flank of the King's men, we'd have carried the day. And killed the King.'

Mogon nodded. 'Mayhap. But killing the King of Alba is worth nothing to me. Not worth the life of one Warden. Every year, there are fewer of us.'

He could feel the heat coming off her, and the stench of burning soap filled the air.

'But I can feel the loss of your people.' She, too, inclined her head. 'I hope we may again be allies. We should not be held to blame for refusing to serve Thorn.'

Redmede tried to keep his knees from shaking. 'I am just a man,' he said, offering nothing.

Her hard black eyes glittered in her round sockets. He found it difficult to meet both eyes at once.

'All the other men and the females, they will follow you when the war comes.' Mogon nodded again. 'We will talk again.'

Redmede took another breath. 'Aye, like enough, lady.'

Ticondaga Castle – Ghause

The closer she grew to the decisive moment with the Queen's unborn baby, the more concerned Lady Ghause grew with Richard Plangere.

Her unease had begun the day she found his spy-moth fluttering in her casting chamber, but the gradual infestation of the castle with moths – minute, pale silver moths – made her angry.

But anger, for Ghause, was power. And while she had no way to strike back at Plangere – whose power she could feel like a distant lamp in a cold room – she had many weapons in her arsenal. She used her favourite.

Her body.

It had seldom failed her since her breasts budded. Had Plangere been a woman, she would have had to use other wiles, but in his case . . .

She danced naked, throwing gouts of power into the *aether*. She walked about her chambers naked. She stroked her flanks, ran hands over her own breasts and between her thighs, stretched, bobbed, stripped and dressed. Moths gathered in veritable clouds, and while she made violent love to her husband or teased a groom, she postured for Plangere, while thinking, *You always were a fool. Look at me, and devour me, and you'll never see what I'm doing.*

The moths made her laugh – he was always so proud of his toys.

In a space in the cellars, heavily defended by runes and sigils and her own workings and some ancient webs too complicated even for her, she killed moths with various techniques until she perfected a method of killing them that was efficient and absolute, because a single survivor would mean the end of her plan. And she moved her great working there. The floor of her tower room was a web of silver and alum chalk, while the floor of her cellar sanctum had only a simple pentagram and ten words in High Archaic.

Then she built another spell – simple to power, labyrinthine in is complexity. It was a layered illusion.

Of her.

Naked.

She watched it critically, several times. She'd only get one chance at this. She made different versions.

She'd cast her curse on the Queen's foetus, Plangere would come to watch, and she'd ensnare him. Or not. He was very strong. Either way, he'd know to keep his distance.

She was eating honey cakes and stretching – there were moths aplenty – when Aneas came to the door and informed her that the Earl needed her.

Her son stayed to lace her kirtle and pull her velvet gown lined in ermine over her head. She twirled a few times – for herself – and put her feet into slippers with wool felt soles.

'What does your pater want, sweeting?' she asked Aneas.

He shrugged. 'He's planning a war,' he said. 'He's going to take me with him.'

She climbed out of the cellars and walked along the corridor that was lined with cells. The Earl inclined more to outright murder than to cruel confinement, and the only men in the cells were a soldier taken for rape, a second taken for theft, and a woman accused of killing another woman. Ghause peered into each cell.

The woman had power. She hadn't noted that before.

She followed Aneas up the guard's stair, smiled lasciviously at the two men on duty, received the attention which was her due, and passed up a second flight of stone steps to the yard.

Aneas's weapons' tutor was waiting in the yard with two saddled warhorses, a great deal of kit, and a small train of servants. She smiled at him.

'Ser Henri!' she said, and waved.

He dismounted and knelt. 'My lady,' he said, in his attractive Etruscan accent. 'How may your most humble servant indicate his devotion?'

'Oh, you will turn my head, you flatterer!' she cooed. 'Please – take my son out to the tiltyard and make him a great knight. I can ask no more.'

Ser Henri had the good grace to appear disappointed. 'No one I can kill for you, Madonna?'

'I have my husband for that,' she said. 'Aneas, pay heed to your tutors.' She swept past, and crossed the yard on the cobbles – some considerable distance, and there was the bite of snow in the air. But when she passed the kitchen she smelled new-baked bread. She paused and inhaled deeply, and grinned like a girl. She went into the kitchen and stole a new loaf, because when she was tempted, she succumbed, and she entered the Great Hall from the kitchens, chewing bread.

The Earl was surrounded by soldiers – a dozen of his officers. She knew them all, in a vague way – much the same way she knew all his horses, even when she didn't know their names. He loved to make war, and he did it with flare and with cunning, but she thought he did it for his own entertainment and all the talk of goals and strategy were just so many rationalisations for a boy who wanted to hit things.

'Ghause, my beauty. You said something about this sorcerer.' The Earl was the kind of man who had little interest in sorcery. Sometimes she suspected that he didn't believe in the power of the hermetical. It was an absurd position, but he was always surprised – surprised in a way she didn't like – when she displayed her powers.

Sorcery in others he liked even less. And understood not at all. She suspected he thought it was all tricks – like a montebank's show at a carnival.

She smiled. 'You mean Thorn?' she asked. Every moth in the hall rose from their rest and fluttered towards the high clerestory windows.

Some of the soldiers paled, and two of them made horn signs with their fingers.

The Earl shrugged. 'Richard Plangere. That's who you said he was.'

She nodded. 'He was. I don't think he is any more.'

The Earl sat back and scratched a dog's head. 'I just received a year's worth of reports, sweeting. Your sorcerer, whoever he is – is getting reckless. He's raising armies and playing power with the Outwallers.'

One of his soldiers – Edward? Edmund? She couldn't remember – drank off his wine and set his cup on the big trestle table with a click. 'My lord, with respect, he'll be a tough nut. The Outwallers are clearly terrified of him.'

The Earl crossed his legs. 'That island. Can we flush him out and take it?'

Ghause shook her head. 'I don't recommend it. He's taken a place of power. He'll be very strong there.'

'Why – is it well defended?' her husband asked. 'I never heard of a stone castle further north than this one.'

In some ways, he was quite brilliant. With the hermetical, it was as if he was wilfully blind. 'He has much power, my lord,' she said deferentially.

The Earl threw up his hands. 'I've faced the Wild all my life, love! He'll have beasts and boggles and some lightning, I have nae doubt. I'll have a fleet and trebuchets.'

She tried again. 'I think that he has the power to sink a fleet, my lord.'

'When you call me *my lord*, I know you're trying to hide something. Is he a friend? One of your special friends?' The Earl grinned, and the officers all looked away.

Ghause rolled her eyes. She turned to one of the sergeants-at-arms who guarded the Great Hall.

'There's a woman in the dungeon. Bring her here.' Ghause smiled.

The man saluted – looked to his lord for confirmation – and marched away.

'Ten ships?' Edward said. 'At least. There'll be ice on the lakes in a month.'

'What about the report of Galles at Mont Reale, Ser Edmund?' asked another man.

Edmund she tried to remember.

Ser Edmund shrugged. 'I'd like to say it can't be true,' he said. 'But I have three reports – and yon Imperial officer – saying there's no Etruscan fleet this season. Instead, there are Galles. They have a powerful squadron and too damned many soldiers – that much all reports agree on.'

The Earl sat back and put a thumb behind his beard and pulled on it. 'Why?' he asked. 'Why here?'

Ser Edmund shook his head. 'Above my pay grade,' he jested.

'Will they give aid to the Northern Huran?' the Earl asked.

All the soldiers looked blank.

The Earl grunted. 'Best we settle this Thorn quickly and get back here. If the Southerners and the Northern Huran fight – if that Morean was right – then we're for it.'

Two guards appeared with the woman between them.

The Earl looked at her incuriously, and then at his wife.

'She's guilty,' Ghause said.

The woman stiffened.

The Earl frowned. 'You're sure?' he asked. He prided himself on his justice.

'She killed Wren with hermetical workings.' Ghause turned and smiled at the woman, who froze in terror.

She fell to her knees. 'Your Grace – you don't know what she did to me—'

Ghause nodded. 'Get her a priest.'

The Earl motioned the woman away. 'I'm busy. What's this about?'

'I want to show you what Thorn can do.' The moths milled about. There were far too many of them. The officers murmured at the sight.

Father Pierre came. The woman wept, and the priest shrived her and heard her confession. He turned pale. Ghause waved a hand.

The priest gave her communion. He was far more afraid of his mistress than he was of his God.

Ghause walked over to the woman. She put a hand on her bent head, and then looked at the men at the high table, planning their infantile war.

'Watch,' she said. She raised a hand. 'By my right to the High Justice of the North,' she said. Just to have the formalities done.

'Is this going to be a trick?' her husband asked. But he took his feet off the table and leaned down to watch her.

She reached out and touched the other woman's power.

And she devoured it.

The condemned woman turned to ash – all at once. And the ash held its shape for the time it took a silver moth to beat its wings once. And collapsed.

No one moved.

'Thorn is more powerful than I will ever be,' she said into the silence.

She only wished she could have been naked. She'd certainly said his name often enough to gain his attention. Inside her head, she was laughing.

The Earl stroked his beard and growled in his throat. 'Not the fleet this winter then.'

Ser Edmund was slower to recover. 'This is pure sorcery,' he said.

He rallied himself and took a deep breath. 'This – sorcer is more powerful?'

'He is far more puissant,' Ghause said.

'And yet Gavin says he was defeated by the King in springtime. Anything the King can do, I can do. Better.' The Earl rose to his feet.

Ghause curtsied. 'My lord Earl, I fear that the Thorn we face now as a dangerous neighbour is ten times the warlock that our sons faced in the spring.' She didn't add, *he's a mere pawn of something greater than himself.*

The soldiers around the table looked at each other, but none of them looked at her except her husband. 'Well, love, you've put the cat among the pigeons again. If it's not a winter campaign on the lakes, my bones tell me we'll face these Galles and their Huran allies in the spring.' Muriens sat back. 'My old tutor used to tell me that nature abhors a vacuum. And look – the lands north of the Inner Sea were a vacuum, and now they all come rushing in.'

Ser Edmund drank off his wine. 'If it please Your Grace – we could do worse than to make an alliance with the Moreans. And we need to trade all the furs we have.'

The Earl was not a man to forget the value of money. 'True, Ser Edmund. We'll need every farthing to pay the garrison if we have a siege. Unpaid men serve too many masters.' He strode to the edge of the platform and stirred the dead woman's ashy remains with a toe. 'Damn it, woman, you've cost me a good war.'

She laughed. 'You can still do it. I'll just have to plan on a cold bed for the balance of the winter.'

'Meaning I'll die, witch?' He locked eyes with her.

'Meaning just that, lover,' she said. 'And I'd rather not train up another husband. I'm an old woman.'

That night, she licked the nice salty place on the Earl's neck and bit his ear and whispered, 'He can watch us, even in this castle. The moths.'

He was no fool. Despite being deeply engaged in his favourite pastime – after war – he understood immediately. He didn't pause his stroke, or fumble. But a moment later, he put both arms under her shoulder blades, lifted her a little, and breathed into her ear:

'Son of a bitch.'

Mont Reale, One Hundred Sixty Leagues East of Ticondaga – Ser Hartmut Li Orguelleus, the Black Knight

Ser Hartmut stood at the stern rail of the command cabin of the *Grace de Dieu*, a cup of Veneti glass in his hand, drinking sweet Candian wine and looking at the fortifications and strong wooden houses of the Outwallers at the town he'd christened Mont Reale – the King's mount.

'We will land our soldiers and take this town as a secure base,' he said.

Lucius remained silent with an effort.

De Marche shook his head vehemently. 'My lord, we must not. That would alienate the very men and women whose favour we need. They are at war with their cousins to the south. We need to give them material aid.'

Ser Hartmut scratched his chin. 'And get what in return?'

'Control of the trade. A secure base—' De Marche was ticking his points off, and Ser Hartmut laughed.

'You two are trying to teach me how to make war.' He laughed. 'We can land and take the town and all the trade. And send it home to the King. At a fine price. There – I can think like a merchant!'

De Marche pursed his lips. 'And next year?'

'Next year we'll be masters of Ticondaga and the whole of the river. We can take whatever we want and sell the rest into slavery. You, sir, are too modest, and you do not know the aims of our lord King, to which I am privy.' He looked around. 'You want a small profit that continues. I offer you an enormous profit, for a few years. Think of the slaves.'

De Marche blew out his cheeks, mustering arguments. As an apprentice seaman, he had shipped in the forecastle of a slaver – a big round ship out of Genua bound for the Hati lands, where once-great nations had been ground to savagery by waves of the wild off the Great Steppes. People in Hati would sell their own children as slaves. De Marche had seen it. And smelled it.

There were many things he would not do for money.

He changed directions. 'You need soldiers for Ticondaga,' he said. 'These Huran will help you – if we help them first, against their enemies.' He leaned close. 'You heard what the Huran warrior said.

Ticondaga has a garrison bigger than all your men and all my sailors combined.' He looked at Lucius.

Lucius nodded. De Marche wasn't sure whether Lucius had arranged the story as a fabrication or not, but he needed the Etruscan.

Ser Hartmut scratched again. De Marche felt that he looked too long at Lucius, but in the end he turned to his second squire – now his only squire. The young man – in full armour – poured more wine.

'Very well,' he said. 'I'll try your way. In truth, if it doesn't work, we can always storm the town. Their palisades are pitiful.'

With the promise of military aid, the skins flowed fast, and de Marche had his hold stowed in pelts and Wild honey in five days – days which Ser Hartmut spent training his soldiers to paddle the light bark boats the natives used, and to make war on water. He had three small row-galleys – broken down into numbered beams and pre-cut strakes in Galle – and the sailors knocked them together. All three of them had a heavy ballista on the bow and a pair of crossbows.

Just below the island, three great rivers joined, two flowing in from the north, carrying the scent of a place even wilder than where they were – pine needles and rock and snow. In the great pool below the falls, Hartmut drilled his soldiers on paddling and rowing.

After a week, he met de Marche for dinner in the aft cabin of the flagship.

'How is trade, Master Merchant?' he asked.

De Marche raised an eyebrow. 'Since you are kind enough to ask, ser knight, we have done well – but we might have done better. The conflict between the Northern Huran and the Southern has kept many of the Outwaller fur merchants away. And there is a rumour that the Moreans are offering high prices and better goods. I have fewer giant beaver than I want – almost none of the white bears so prized at court.'

Ser Hartmut poured wine for the captain. The stern cabin was as small and neat as a lady's solar, with fine oak panels set in a lattice of oak frames, so that the panels could expand and contract with weather and heat and still look splendid. A bronze-banded barrel of fortified wine gleamed like an embodiment of hospitality, and the low oak table was covered in glasses – real glass, cunningly made to be easy to hold onto at sea. The luxury of the small room contrasted utterly with the conditions that could arise outside. It was like a sliver of court, or a chapel of comfort.

Ser Hartmut seemed immune to the luxury, but de Marche had decided that the fearsome knight merely took the luxury for granted, as his due.

'The Southern Huran have more furs?' he asked nonchalantly. 'And they are failing to bring them here?'

De Marche decided not to deliver an essay on the fur trade. 'The Southern Huran are not required to trade here,' he said, with a shrug.

Hartmut leaned back and laughed. 'But we can oblige them to do so, surely. A few hundred barbarous savages – cursed by God? You wish to convince me to make war on these Southerners – very well, I am convinced. Let us do this thing. The season is very advanced – we'll have to be quick.'

De Marche nodded. 'We have the boats, your soldiers and my sailors, and the Northern Huran will give us another two hundred warriors. May I propose a plan of campaign?' he asked.

Ser Hartmut gave him a jovial smile. 'No. This is my business. See to your furs and bills of lading. This is war.' He rose with a care, for he was a big man in a small cabin. 'Let us drink a toast – to the King.'

The two men drank.

'And another – to a profitable war!' He laughed. 'Send me the Huran lords, so they can hear my orders.'

De Marche nodded. 'One doesn't issue orders to Outwallers, Ser Hartmut.'

The knight nodded. 'You don't. I do. Send them to me.'

Giannis Turkos – Near Mont Reale

The onset of winter was so close that every gust of wind seemed like a warning from God to spur him on. Turkos rode as quickly as he could, once he reached dry ground, and pushed his mare harder than he had ever pushed another horse. But she responded gallantly, as if thanking him for saving her from the Ruk.

Turkos never named horses, because they died so fast under him, but she had earned a name, and by the time he made it back to Nap-na, he called her Athena.

'You are the smartest horse I've ever known,' he said, and fed her everything she could eat – slowly, so she wouldn't gripe or bloat.

He met with Big Trout again, and they smoked. She was of the Old People, like his wife, and her Huran was fluid and difficult at first for him to understand in his current fog of fatigue. But she was patient and hospitable, and when he got a cup of her tea inside him, he found her quite fluent.

'None of my men have made it so far,' she said, when he described his route. 'Long Swamp is less than ten miles from Sacred Island. Sossag land.'

He nodded. 'I don't know the castle I came across on a point of land facing Sacred Island,' he said. He drew her a sketch on birch bark.

She looked at it for a moment. 'Ba'ath,' she said. 'A big Sossag town.'

'It's been destroyed. The corpses lie in the streets.' He looked away, because the images of desolation – of ice in the puddles and burned rafters and the wolf-gnawed corpse of a child too small to even seem like a person – were still with him.

'He has been here,' Big Trout said suddenly. 'He comes as an elder – called Speaker of Tongues.' She looked at him, and her eyes were narrowed. 'He thinks we are children, and fools. But he has made threats. And the young people love what he promises. He makes very specific promises.' She sighed. 'If we fight him we will be exterminated. But if we do not fight him—' She shrugged.

'What of the Sossag?' Turkos asked, with some urgency. He needed to be moving. But he also needed every scrap of information.

'They have sent him warriors,' she said. 'They had to, to save themselves. Now he walks wide under the trees, and the wind tells me he visits the Northern Huran.'

Turkos had been hearing that for two months. 'And?' he asked her.

She shrugged. 'You would know better than I, Empire Man. The Northern Huran have a new ally – there are new ships on the Great River and many canoes full of warriors. Men coming back from the market at Mont Reale say that the Galles buy any furs brought to them, but not at the prices paid by the Alban merchants at Ticondaga, and the goods aren't as good as your Morean produce. But there *are* no Alban merchants this year. And Westerners don't like to go all the way to the Empire's trading posts to sell their furs. But some will.'

Turkos nodded. 'That's why I'm here,' he admitted.

She made a face. 'I know, Empire Man. I didn't think you rode west to look for Thorn because we are friends – eh?'

He nodded and poured more tea. 'But I did. And I shared what I learned.' He leaned forward. 'Tell me what you learned from those who went east.'

She shrugged. 'Not much more. Little Bow over there went all the way to the Empire's post at Osawa.'

Osawa was the town on the Great River closest to Turkos's own town. He quickened with interest, having been away for more than a month.

Big Trout beckoned to the hunter, who came and sat with them. The longhouse was a combination of a tavern and hostel – it had sleeping benches for sixty adults, and more if some could be convinced to share. It had three great hearths running down the centre, and Big Trout and her several husbands served food and heavy, dark beer to those who could pay. They even had a little wine. It was built of hides and straw mats, and was very comfortable even at the edge of winter. There was always a layer of smoke inside, but it was warm.

Little Bow proved to be a small, wiry man who looked Alban. He had a ready smile and a firm handshake.

Turkos listed Alban among his dozen languages, and he offered to buy the hunter a cup of wine.

'That's neighbourly of you,' Little Bow said, and sat on a stool.

'I'm interested in the fur trade,' Turkos said.

'You're a riding officer for the Emperor,' Little Bow said. 'We all know what you do, Morean.'

Turkos shrugged.

Little Bow nodded. 'I'm half Alban and half Outwaller, and neither half of me has any quarrel with the Empire,' he said. 'I took my wife and all my furs downriver to Osawa because I heard a rumour that it was the best money this year. There was a big fight down on the Cohocton – the Wild against Alba—' He looked at Turkos, who nodded.

'I hear the same,' he said. 'You may know more about it than I do.'

Little Bow nodded. 'I met some Sossags who fought there. They said that the Wild took a fair lickin'. No matter – but the Alban merchants were stung pretty bad. You know that the Alban trade goes up to Lissen Carrak for the fair, and then the fur merchants take caravans over the mountains to Ticondaga—'

Turkos was now scribbling furiously on his wax tablets.

'You didn't know that?' asked the hunter.

Turkos smiled. 'I did and I didn't,' he admitted.

The man accepted wine from Big Trout. Morning Porcupine, her surly older husband, poured himself a tankard of heavy ale and sat with them.

Little Bow was obviously a man who liked an audience. His gestures grew, and his voice lowered. 'So there's no trade to be had at Ticondaga now, and anyway, the Earl, who is a cantankerous old cuss at the best of times, is getting ready to make war.'

Turkos nodded. 'I know. I was just there.'

Little Bow nodded. 'So I went to Osawa. On the way back, we landed at Mont Reale. There's Gallish ships there – three big round ships and an Etruscan war galley.'

Turkos began writing again. 'You said there was no Etruscan trade this year,' he said.

Big Trout nodded. 'I said that,' she admitted.

'Nor is there,' Little Bow said in a know-it-all tone of voice. 'There wasn't an Etruscan to be seen. The scuttlebutt around the trading beach said the Galles had killed the Etruscans, but a Galle merchant who was decent enough to my wife told her they'd found three Etruscan ships all taken by silkies.'

The temperature in the longhouse seemed to plummet.

'Silkies is a myth,' Turkos said.

Big Trout had a pipe out. She took a taper over to the hearth and lit it, used it to light a heavy candle in a finely made bronze stick – Alban work – and used the big candle to light her pipe. She cradled the pipe bowl in her left hand and used her right to cup the first smoke and pull it back over her head. The smoke made signs in the air.

'Silkies ain't no myth,' she said, in a matter-of-fact tone. She handed the lit pipe to her husband. He puffed silently. 'They come every twenty years. This ain't their year. Next year is their year.'

Little Bow pursed his lips. 'Well,' he said. 'I didn't know that, either.'

'Nor I,' said Turkos. He took a flask out of his shoulder bag and poured some malmsey for each person at the table. 'In fact, this is a summer's worth of information in a single dinner.'

'I'm not to the good part yet,' said the hunter. 'Them Galles has one hell of a lot of soldiers. My wife's pretty. Soldiers talk.' He nodded. 'They claim they want to take Ticondaga.' He paused for effect. 'For Galle.'

'Holy Mary mother of God,' muttered Turkos.

'That's after they smack the Southern Huran around a bit,' the man added, and took the pipe.

Turkos had to fight the urge to stand up and head for the door.

'Relax – I only heard that three days back. They ain't left yet,' said the man. 'But it's a big force. More'n a hundred canoes. A lot more armour than we're used to seeing here.'

Turkos shook his head. 'And I'm here.'

'You can get around Mont Reale fast enough,' the hunter said. 'Get ahead of 'em on the river and they'll never catch you.'

'I've always coasted the Great River,' Turkos admitted. 'I don't know a route around the town.'

Little Bow smiled, showing a mouth remarkably free of teeth. 'Well – for a small fee—'

Turkos nodded. 'Can you leave in the morning?'

Little Bow nodded back. 'Money first. No offence, partner – but the wife likes to see the colour of the silver.'

Turkos leaned back. 'I don't carry silver in the Wild,' he said. He counted down three heavy Morean gold byzants. He gave a fourth to Big Trout, who nodded her appreciation. Even her husband grunted.

Come morning, the water was warmer than the air, and the Great River was hidden in mist. Little Bow met him in the yard of the longhouse. He had a string of pack animals, all loaded with furs.

Turkos had purchased two more pack horses, and he was booted and spurred. He raised an eyebrow at the furs. 'I thought you sold yours?' he asked the hunter.

The man nodded soberly. 'Took your money and bought every hide in the village, and paid a good rate for them,' he admitted. 'If I'm guiding you to Osawa, I might as well make a profit.'

Turkos laughed and showed the small man his two pack horses – loaded with buffalo robes and white bears and one great wolf hide. They laughed together.

'Let's get going,' Turkos said.

They rode off into the northern woods, at the edge of winter. The wind cut across open ground like a great sword, and nights were so cold that the warmth of a fire could only be felt from an arm's length, but no snow had fallen yet and the ground was hard, and they travelled fast. They could ride across a marsh, and the lack of leaves on the trees or undergrowth in the deep woods gave them a security that would have been absent in summer. They saw Ruk to the north on the first day, but they were going too fast to be worried. On the third day they spotted ustenoch mixed with moose in a swamp, breaking the ice with their great antlers, but they stayed on a knife-edge ridge and the great beasts didn't bother with them.

The days were short but they rode hard, changing horses at every stop. After three days, Turkos stopped changing his clothes. The little hunter was one of the toughest men Turkos had met – his saddle endurance was incredible, and he could make camp as fast as any Outwaller Turkos had known.

He admired Turkos' little oilskin tent. 'Cute,' he said, but after a night in it, he helped fold it and said, 'Not bad. You have all the best toys,' he added, admiring the Morean's matching sword and pipe-axe.

They were three days to Mont Reale, which they passed on the north bank.

'Pull your cloak over all your metal,' Little Bow said. Then they tethered their horses and crawled to the edge of a bluff.

'That was all canoes and row-galleys a week ago,' Little Bow said softly. 'They've moved on.'

Turkos also noted that the ship reports were accurate – he drew sketches of the three great round ships, and of the new fortification being built on the headland of the island where the ships were moored.

'Come on, partner,' Little Bow said. 'Lots of daylight left.'

Two days later, they came up with the fleet of canoes just turning out of the Great River for the Morean posts along the lakes.

'He could be going for Ticondaga,' Turkos said, but he didn't believe it himself. There were far more than a hundred canoes – in fact, he counted almost three hundred. It was the largest force he'd seen in the north country since he became a riding officer, and it was aimed at his people and his trading posts. He felt an overwhelming sense of failure. He'd read the signs incorrectly.

Little Bow shrugged. 'You know there's an old road along the east bank of the lake,' he said.

Turkos scratched his head where it itched. 'The old Wall road. I am a soldier of the Empire, huntsman. I know the road.'

Little Bow nodded. 'We'll beat them to Osawa,' he promised.

Turkos waved at the mile-wide Great River. 'And are we going to swim our horses across?' he asked.

Little Bow smiled his gap-toothed smile. 'I sure hope you've got more o' them pretty gold coins,' he said.

Turkos had commanded a post on the wall for two years before becoming a riding officer, and he thought he knew the border as well as any Morean. He'd passed up and down the Great River dozens of times, and always found it an endless adventure – the life he loved.

But he was more than a little surprised to find a hidden Outwaller town just east of the entrance to the lake and so well hidden that he didn't see it until they were all but in its streets.

He shook his head. 'How've I missed this?' he asked.

'Abenacki rebuilt it twenty years ago.' Little Bow showed the burned pilings out in the Great River. 'You never looked past them, I reckon.'

'I won't be lynched for seeing the secret?' Turkos asked.

Little Bow laughed. 'No one's afraid of the Empire,' he said. 'If you was one of Earl Muriens' men, that would be different. But an Imperial? No worries.'

Turkos digested that slowly.

The owner of a serviceable boat charged two gold byzants for ferrying them and their horses across the river. He coaxed the riding horses aboard, made them unload all their furs, and then dragged their pack horses into the icy water.

Turkos swore. 'No horse can survive that swim,' he spat.

Little Bow put a hand on his arm. 'Ye of little faith,' he said. 'She's a witch,' he said, pointing at the ferryman's wife.

She was small and pretty and she sat in the stern and fed the horses gouts of power. She laughed and called them strange names and they showed no signs of lagging. Halfway across she lit a pipe and joined the men amidships. She patted Athena, blew into her nostrils, and raised her eyebrows at Turkos. 'What do you call her?' she asked.

'Athena,' he said. 'She was a goddess of wisdom.'

The witch smiled. 'She is a fine god,' she said. 'So is Tar. Your Athena was one of the dresses Tar wore for man.' She patted the horse. 'Tar is in this one. Your name is good. Your horse says you are a good man, so go well, good man.'

Turkos watched her wriggle through the bales of furs to the stern. 'Tar is an old name,' he said. The witch woman frightened him a little – made him uncomfortable, even though he could all but feel her goodness. Or her lack of evil. Having tasted Thorn, he had new standards.

Little Bow grinned. 'Not here, Empire Man. Here, Tar is our aid and our support, as the Church says in the south about Christ.' He made the sign of the cross. 'Not that I have anything against Christ,' he added piously, and chuckled.

They had to take enormous care getting around the Gallish fleet. Whoever was in charge was a professional – there were scout parties on both banks of the lake, and while the fleet made camp on the western shore every night, there were parties ahead, behind, and on the opposite shore.

The second night after the ferry boat, they led their horses – in the dark – across a moonlit frozen swamp, climbed a tall bank, making far too much noise, and got onto the road – two wagons wide, interlocking flagstones laid over a deep roadbed of rock and crushed gravel. It must have been fifteen hundred years old. There were trees down on the road, and potholes deep enough to swallow a horse and rider, but there was sufficient road left to allow a man to ride in the dark at a reasonable speed.

They camped in the ruins of a watch tower. In the morning, Turkos saw signs of irks – a small party, moving fast.

He pointed them out to Little Bow.

'Far from home,' the small man said. He shrugged. 'Nothing to do with us.'

Turkos wrote a note on his tablets and then they were away, trying to ride off the cold. Athena didn't seem herself – too many nights without a fire and not enough grain, or so Turkos suspected. But he couldn't pause to investigate, and he rode south.

It was late afternoon, and they had sacrificed caution to move quickly. They were moving at a fast trot down the road, less than twenty leagues from Osawa, when the road ahead of them sprouted warriors with cocked crossbows and bright red paint.

Nita Qwan – The Shore of the Inner Sea

It took Nita Qwan and Gas-a-ho many days to make a canoe that Ta-se-ho would accept. He rejected their first bark skin and made them harvest another. He was a poor patient, endlessly demanding, and yet a pleasant companion, smoking, offering them tea and a pipe when they were tired of cutting big trees with small axes.

Nita Qwan's ribs bothered him more and more, until, after a sleepless night, he got the boy to use his fledgling powers on him, and then used most of their available animal hide to wrap his midsection.

They moved camp on the third day, choosing a sand bluff like a small fort with a deep old fire pit and three comfortable benches built by other hands.

'Irks,' Ta-se-ho said. He sat comfortably, with his back in a backrest grown from a gnarled tree. 'This is their land. N'gara is only a few days paddle away, south and west.'

The younger man had rebuilt the older shelter, piling brush atop it until it was nearly weatherproof. The skin of the *hastenoch* had made it windproof, at least.

In the evening of the fifth day, he looked at their third try and nodded. 'Tomorrow we lace on the gunwales,' he announced. 'You two have done well.'

By noon, their boat was complete, and their camp was packed. Ta-se-ho made them tidy away their scraps of deer meat and the litter of days of occupation.

'Leave it the way you'd like to find it,' the old hunter said. 'Many men hate irks, but I'm not one of them. There's enough woods for all of us.'

That afternoon they paddled west, and made camp in another lean-to left by irks.

'Tapio's kingdom,' he said. 'Mogon lives in the lands north of here. We're in the border country. Be alert. Both sides keep soldiers here.' He smiled an evil smile and rubbed his collarbone. 'They call them soldiers, anyway,' he added.

Their progress was painfully slow – broken bones and knitting ribs made paddling into the steady western wind a dull nightmare, despite the beauty of the sun on the water and the flocks of geese and ducks heading south, the crisp white clouds of late autumn racing overhead, the glorious profusion of red-gold leaves on the shore. Ta-se-ho took to smoking constantly. Their food ran low, and then the tobacco was gone and, finally, near the place where the Upper River flowed into the Inner Sea, they had to land and hunt and dry meat to be able to continue.

They landed late in the day, on a beach of good sand, heavily scuffed by other boats and other feet. After a fruitless evening hunt, the three of them sat, eating pemmican around a very small fire. Gas-a-ho spat out some gristle. 'Not much wood,' he said. 'I scrounged what I could, but it is all women's wood.'

Ta-se-ho nodded. 'Wardens were here,' he said. He pointed to the tracks that they'd all seen, and shrugged. 'I can smell them.' he said. 'Fifty warriors. They stayed a day – maybe two. Killed all the deer, and burned all the wood.'

Nita Qwan looked west at the setting sun. 'A war party?' he asked.

Ta-se-ho shook his head. 'I don't think so. In the morning, we'll find their campsite, and have a look.'

They went to bed almost as soon as darkness fell, and woke, very cold, before first light, to a steady snowfall. They had little wood to burn, and that was spruce. Nita Qwan ran down the long beach almost a mile, found some cedar driftwood, and carried it back. His ribs hurt but the exercise felt good, and he felt warm for the first time in hours. The cedar driftwood burned beautifully – the scent was almost magical, and the three of them ate their pemmican and drank sassafras tea.

Soon after first light, the three of them walked along the beach a short way, until they found where the wardens had beached their boats, and then walked up the beach to the forest edge. There, just inside the cover of the big birches, was a plashed wood fence that stood twice the height of a man. They followed the fence cautiously until they came to a gate.

'There's no one here,' Ta-se-ho said, but even his voice held tension. They crept inside, looking with some awe at the big sleeping platforms and the woven mats.

'Human work,' Ta-se-ho said. 'They have slaves – sometimes they trade.' He shrugged. Then he pounced like a cat on a mouse.

Under a sleeping mat was a beautiful otter skin. The skin was sewn shut and had a cunning pocket in it, and the opening and part of the back were decorated in beads and quillwork – beads of solid gold, and quillwork in red and purple, the colours of royalty. He opened the bag, sniffed the contents, and let loose a piercing yell of triumph.

'Tobacco!' he shouted. He opened his own bag and took out his smallest pipe and filled it with shaking hands. He went to the fort's hearth – dug with his knife in the ashes, and then lifted a live coal, on which he blew. He lit his pipe with the kind of satisfaction that men usually save for food and other passions, and sat on the edge of the stone hearth.

Then he looked around carefully. 'If this was not Mogon herself,' he said, 'it was one of her brood mates – the royals of the lake Wardens. And I would warrant that they are not a war party. The tobacco pouch almost settles it – no one would take such a thing to war.'

Nita Qwan raised an eyebrow. 'My people and the Albans both tend to take all their most precious things to war,' he said.

'There were men with them – and at least two irks. See the prints? That's a woman, or I'm a heron. So – not a war party.' The old man shrugged, pleased with himself and smirking.

'They could be captives,' Nita Qwan said.

Ta-se-ho grinned. 'If we had come from the land side, they could be captives,' he said. 'Tracks must be read in *tehsandran.*'

Nita Qwan's command of Sossag was very good, but he had never heard this word before. '*Teh-san-dra-an?*' he asked.

Gas-a-ho looked at the older hunter. The two men had a wordless exchange.

'Is this – hermetical? Magical?' asked Nita Qwan.

'No! It is an idea,' said the older man. 'It is like – when I say something by the campfire, in jest, it might have one meaning, and if I say it when we are hunting, it might have another meaning. Meanings change depending on who says the words, and how he says them, and where he says them. Feelings change.' He flailed the air with his hands. '*Tehsandran* is that thing. The change. The place. If we had come from the landward side, this might be a raiding party. But we came from the east, on the inland sea. All the people – the humans – live in the east. So they did not take a woman prisoner in the east, because they would have paddled right past us.' He spread his hands. 'See?'

Nita Qwan thought hard and then laughed. 'I do see. At first, I was afraid you were trying to tell me that if we came from the land, that would change the reality of your observation. Instead, you are saying that it changes your perception.'

Ta-se-ho shrugged. 'Yes,' he said. 'And I'm not *sure*. Tracking is never about *sure*. It is about a vast range of possibilities, bigger than a herd of fallow deer on the plains.'

'You are a philosopher,' Nita Qwan said, using the archaic word.

Ta-se-ho said the word several times and chewed the stem of his pipe while he smiled. 'Yes,' he agreed. He walked around the enclosure for another minute, leaving a trail of pungent smoke – then walked out the gate and vanished for some minutes before he returned and emptied his pipe. 'Eight boats. Fifty warriors, and two irks, both wearing shoes – and one man and one woman, barefoot and in moccasins.' He narrowed his eyes. 'If they went east, we'd have seen them. If they go west, they reach Mogon's realm in a day or two – her caves in eight days' travel. But they came here by boat. So the natural assumption is that they came *from* Mogon's caves and dens in the west. They did not pass us. Hence they went south – to Tapio at N'gara. It is an embassy – the irks were sent out by Tapio as guides. The man and woman are slaves – but trusted slaves.'

Nita Qwan followed the logic. 'Why trusted?'

'They went far to defecate,' Ta-se-ho said. 'Humans are far more fastidious about this than Wardens. They were allowed to walk off with no guards.'

'Perhaps they are not slaves?' Nita Qwan said.

'They cooked all the food,' Ta-se-ho said. He shrugged. 'But yes – perhaps they are well paid, or merely content.'

'How sure are you?' Nita Qwan asked.

The old man was repacking his pipe. He met Nita Qwan's eye with a wry smile and a raised eyebrow, and went back to packing his pipe.

'How much time do we lose if we go to N'gara and they aren't there?' Nita Qwan asked.

'A week,' Ta-se-ho said. 'More, if Tapio kills us.'

He and Gas-a-ho barked their laughter, and it rang from the rocks and low bluffs around them in the still autumn air.

Natia Qwan had to smile. 'You think that's the right thing to do,' he said.

Ta-se-ho shrugged. But he relented. 'Yes,' he said. 'If Tapio and Mogon bury the axe and make friends, they will be the most powerful allies in the north country, and we could not do better than to offer our people to them. Mogon's brother and father were never bad to the people.' He made an odd motion with his head. 'They were never particularly good, either,' he admitted.

'And this Tapio?' Nita Qwan asked.

Gas-a-ho leaned forward. 'The horned one says he is a deeply cunning shaman – almost like the old gods. He says you must never go to sleep in the halls of Tapio, or you wake to find a hundred years have passed.' He realised he had probably said too much for a young person, and looked at the ground.

Ta-se-ho lay back on a giant sleeping bench meant for a daemon nine feet tall. 'Tapio fought a war against our forefathers,' he said, dreamily. 'All the stories about the faeries under the earth and the war underground are about that war. He is very old.'

Nita Qwan had never heard such stories. 'Does he hate the Sossag?' he asked.

Ta-se-ho cocked one moccasined foot over the other. 'I doubt he even remembers us. But we most definitely remember him. We used to hold all the land around N'gara. This was Sossag – the people of the western door. Tapio took our great towns and sent us to flee into the Burned Lands in the north.'

Nita Qwan sighed. 'So much for our embassy, then,' he said.

Ta-se-ho shook his head. 'No. We have a good life now. Tapio might help us – he took what he wanted, and we survived. Not unlike the sorcerer who wants our Sacred Island. Listen, Nita Qwan. These Powers happen. It is best to accept the change and avoid death. If we can lead them to fight among themselves—' The old man chuckled. 'Well, all the better. If Tapio and Thorn destroy each other, the Sossag will laugh.'

'And be stronger,' said Nita Qwan.

The hunter shook his head. 'That's your brother talking. Stronger is for those who seek strength. The people want to live. Life is not about strength. Life is about living. The matrons know this – you need to know this, too. We do not seek an alliance to make us *strong*. We seek an alliance to avoid as much trouble as we can avoid, so that hunters can hunt, and mothers can raise children.'

Nita Qwan looked at the old hunter with new eyes. 'You sound as if you hold the Powers in contempt.'

The old man puffed rapidly on his pipe to keep it lit. 'You know the kind of child who must keep showing other children how smart he is? While other children run and play and eat and love their mothers, this little boy or girl cannot stop being smart. You know this child?'

Nita Qwan laughed. 'All too well.'

'Powers. Mostly, they are people who never learned to live.' Ta-se ho leaned back and chuckled. 'Mind you, I'm an old man with no magic. If I could kill a deer a mile away with a flick of my fingers, I'd be a different man. But I'd never learn to *hunt*. And I love to hunt.' He sat up. 'I lack the words to explain better.'

'You are a philosopher,' Nita Qwan said again.

The older man nodded. 'I could learn to like this word. But let me tell you a cold fact. The Inner Sea will freeze in a week. If we are going to paddle, we'd best paddle fast.'

An hour later, they were paddling south, for N'gara.

Lissen Carrak – Abbess Mirim and Sister Amicia

The Abbess read the latest message from Harndon carefully while Sister Amicia waited patiently, hands in her sleeves.

The Abbess winced once, and then her face stilled. Careful observation indicated she was reading the whole message a second time. This time she bit her lip.

She made a face – a very un-Abbess-like face. 'Do you know anything about the contents?' she asked Amicia, who shook her head.

'*Madame*, I was at my place by the Southwark ferry, in the chapel, when the royal messenger came. As his message was for here and the sabbath was passed, I brought it directly. He had other stops to make.'

Mirim tapped the arm of her chair. 'The King has appointed a new Bishop of Lorica who believes that the whole of the Order of Saint Thomas falls within his remit.' She smiled – not a real smile, but a combative one. 'I suspect that Prior Wishart and I will agree that he has no power over us, but equally I can see some trouble looming.'

'The new Bishop of Albinkirk is a fine priest,' Amicia said.

'He called!' Mirim said. 'Hah, and caught us all in our shifts. Washing day, and the new Bishop comes to the gate! But Ser Michael turned out the guard for him, and we put on a passable show, and got the washtubs into the kitchen. He really is a very pleasant man, and his theology is refreshingly modern.' Mirim took a scroll of the table under her elbow. 'He issued you a further license to say mass whenever there is no priest present. And he appointed us a new chaplain – Father Desmond. A scholar, no less! We've all been on our best behaviour.'

Amicia curtsied again. 'I'll look forward to meeting him.'

'You must be tired, dear sister.' She paused. 'There is a good deal of muttering about the liberties you are accorded. Please be at mass tonight, and at matins, so that all here can see you at your devotions.'

Amicia flushed with instant anger, and fought it back down.

'And we need you to help us knit the defences back together. The choir – the hermetical choir – needs to practise while you are here.' Mirim put a hand on her head. 'Who ever thought that convents were places of rest?'

The Sacred Island – Thorn and Ota Qwan

When the moths hatched into larvae, it was incredibly disturbing for Ota Qwan. When the larvae hatched in the hung-up corpses of men who had been his companions, it made him think about things he didn't want to, so he busied himself on errands. He gathered the early crop of young warriors of half a dozen tribes who had been inspired by Speaker of Tongues' vision, and he led them on a short campaign – first, to overawe the Abenacki, and then further east.

No Abenacki force rose to meet him. South of the chain of streamside villages that lay in the heart of the Abenacki nation, he rested his war party and met with a delegation of elders. He demanded warriors and threatened them with destruction, and the two older warriors who had held senior commands that spring reacted with fierce words.

He shrugged. 'Thorn will be your lord, now,' he said. 'Submit and grow in power. Fight and be destroyed.'

He left them to decide, and turned south and east. He had a branch from Thorn that allowed him to control the Ruk who suddenly infested the low country by the Inner Sea, and six of the lumbering giants followed him. The rest stayed clear of his path. He had expected to feel the power flowing through him; instead, there was nothing but the sight of the Ruk doing his bidding.

After six days' travel the war party emerged from the rock-strewn marshes near the town of Nepan'ha. He walked forward on the first snow of the season and met with the headwoman, Big Trout, who was up on the catwalk of the palisade wall, holding a spear and wearing a fancy caribou-hide coat.

'Thorn demands your submission,' he shouted.

'He should come and make that demand in person,' she said, 'and not send some witling to do it for him.'

'He will destroy you,' Ota Qwan promised.

The old woman turned, raised the hem of her coat and showed him her bare buttocks. She launched a long fart, and all her people laughed.

'Tell your sorcerer to go pleasure himself with a birch tree!' she shouted.

Ota Qwan allowed his anger to take control of him. He felt taller – stronger – and indeed he was. He raised the branch that Thorn had given him, and pointed at the wall.

From far away, there was the sound of bellowing. The ground began to shake.

A dozen Ruk lumbered forward.

The men and women on the wall had bows and spears, and the Ruk suffered much as they attacked. Four of them died outright.

But it takes a great deal to kill a Ruk. Those who withstood the withering barrage of missiles ripped the palisade down with their bare hands and went into the town. They launched themselves on an orgy of destruction, ripping buildings to the ground and killing anything they could catch – sheep, horse, or child.

Ota Qwan followed them through the breech with his fifty warriors. He pointed a hand in either direction, and ordered his senior warriors to clear the walls.

'And then?' asked one of the young Abenacki.

'Then kill them all,' Ota Qwan said.

That was not the Outwaller way. But the men were young, and they already saw much in Kevin Orley that they wanted to emulate.

Ten hours later, the last desperate mother was found huddled in a root cellar and had her child ripped away and killed. She was raped, and beheaded. His young warriors were covered in blood, and some were sick with what they had done and others curiously elated. Rape was new to the Abenacki and the Sossag – in Outwaller warfare, women were taken home, adopted and made wives. Otherwise, the matrons punished you.

Only Thorn had no matrons.

And he was there. Thorn came, wearing Speaker of Tongues.

'What you have done, you have done for me, and for your people,' he said. He went and knelt gracefully by the corpse of the last woman killed. 'It is horrible, is it not? She was a person, and you took that and made her a thing.' He rose. And smiled. 'Listen, my warriors. We do this to save the rest. After Nepan'ha, no other town will resist me. This will save many lives – yours included. But also the lives of other women, and other babies.' He walked through the rubble and the burning hides of what had been the central longhouse, to where Big Trout's corpse lay in the doorway, her big axe still in her hands. 'She was a fool to insult Ota Qwan, and doubly a fool to resist, and the deaths of all these people lie on her, not on you. When a leader accepts the responsibility of command, she accepts that she will bear the guilt. This fat woman owns the guilt you feel. So piss on her – pour your fluid on her and rid yourself of what is hers.' He smiled beatifically. 'For many years, you Outwallers have honoured the corpses of your enemy dead. Stop that. Desecrate them as fools and traitors. Our way is The Way. Be soft no longer. Be hard. Trust me on this.' Speaker did as he said – he paused and pissed a long stream on the corpse, and the fat woman seemed to melt a little, and suddenly the warriors crowded around to do the same – and as they did, found their memories of the obscenity clouding over.

Speaker of Tongues smiled. *Men are so easy to use*, he thought. *I will make them animals, and then they will be fit to live in the Wild.*

He swirled his great cloak of wolf skins and vanished.

All the warriors cheered, and the Ruk bellowed.

Kevin Orley would have liked to have been satisfied. But he couldn't help but wonder why the sorcerer didn't pause to heal his wounded. And *his* memory of the taking of the town was untouched.

Thorn left his men with a slight shudder of revulsion, rather like a surgeon closing a jar of leeches, and returned through the *aether* to his place of power.

He then passed a day in casting and watching. The first of his special moths was about to hatch, and he had to catch it at just the right moment to finish its accession of power. Or so he told himself, while another part of his great and web-filled mind confessed that he simply wanted to be present when his creation hatched.

He watched Ghause and the Earl. He watched her dance naked,

spending power like water. He watched her cast, and was annoyed and transfixed and transformed. He sent more moths, and then more still, to observe her from every possible angle in every possible part of her life.

Sometimes he heard her speak his name. It was as if she was already calling to him, over the leagues that separated them.

He watched her subsume a witch woman, and he groaned with pleasure.

She was, in her earthy way, much more complex than he had imagined, and much more powerful, and he chuckled and increased the power of his own wards.

He looked to his defences in case of material attack against her husband.

He watched other scenes, as well, through other moths and other beasts – but what they told him was not enough to build a whole scene. His creatures in Harndon gave him fragments of a picture that he couldn't understand – a sea of angry faces in fire-lit darkness; the Queen shouting at a young woman. The Queen weeping. The Queen, reading old parchment.

And in the subterranean corridors beneath the old palace, his other creatures were all dead. He had lost every moth, every rat, every living thing that he had created or recruited, seduced or suborned to enable him to read his own notes – or Harmodius's notes.

In the safety of his island, he'd begun transforming other creatures – some badgers, for example, as underground spies – but he had nothing when he needed it, and this caused him immense frustration. Even the cats he had used to maintain his spells binding Harmodius were lost to him – killing mice and roaming the castle corridors, their feline minds locked against him.

Without context, his moths alone were not useful, and he cursed the time it took to move them over vast distances and the power he had to expend to monitor them. Moths could take two months – and several generations – to reach their targets.

His attempt to plant moths on the Red Knight had failed, and all the insects he sent west to watch his nearest neighbour – the famous Tapio, who had refused to be his ally in the spring – were dead.

Thorn stood and thought in unmoving, superior indignation. If Tapio killed his sendings, then the arrogant irk was going to continue to keep his distance, or worse. *Why will the Wild not unite?* he asked himself. *Because each individual seeks only his own good.* Thorn sat in the dark, watching the chrysalis case of a caterpillar as long as a man's arm, embedded in the corpse of a man, and nodded to himself. *I will unite the Wild by force, and save it. If they cannot see to benefit of my idea, I will shove it down their foolish, ruggedly individualistic throats.*

Unbidden, the picture of the Red Knight standing against him at Lissen Carrak, and seizing control of his boggles, rose before him. 'You are just some parvenu merchant's son trying to ape the manners of his betters.'

He tried to focus his rage the way he would focus power for a working. His father had been a merchant – what of it? *I will be God,* he thought at the distant figure. *And you will be nothing.*

He managed his hate – massaged it and relived each petty humiliation of the siege – he dwelled on the moment in which he mis-sited his trebuchet batteries, and he savoured how completely he'd been out-thought the night of his great attack.

He took all that hate, and channelled it into the caterpillar like a man giving a scrap of wool to a scent hound.

When he was done, he felt lighter by the weight of much fear. It was a powerful working – akin to the spell he'd thrown on the men who had raped Nepan'ha. Hermetical workings that altered the internal reality of the sentient mind were so delicate that manipulating the life force of a moth was child's play by comparison, but he was beginning to see how he could perform such miracles.

After a while, he ceased his efforts to monitor the world, and turned to his preparations to deal with the Earl.

Near Osawa – Giannis Turkos

The men who surrounded them were all Outwallers – all Northern Huran and Kree, with topknots and dyed deer-hair in bright red. But they had crossbows – heavy, steel-bowed weapons, all new made.

It was the crossbows that decided Turkos, although his decision was almost too fast to be described as thought.

Even as they emerged from the shadows to gloat over their prisoners, he reared his horse – his precious horse, that he loved, Athena.

She reared obediently, and her broad stomach and long neck took all six of the crossbow bolts meant for him. And because she was all heart, she landed on four feet and continued forward after her iron-shod forefeet crushed the skulls of two warriors.

And then she fell.

Turkos landed on his feet and drew the heavy sabre he wore – as long and heavy as an Alban knight's sword, but slightly curved and with a reinforced point that added authority to every cut.

Two more warriors fell – one with an arm cleanly severed and the other with the whole side of his face caved in from the backbone of the blade – cheekbones shattered, jaw broken.

His reckless charge into their midst created more chaos than he had any right to expect – one Kree put a heavy bolt into a Huran from behind in his haste to engage the foe. But these weren't boggles – the older warriors were already recovering, drawing weapons, or standing clear and taking aim.

Turkos threw his best offensive working from the amulet at his neck. It was a sheet of lightning that flickered blue in the sunlight, and he laid it like a carpet, running close to the frozen earth, as his grandfather had taught him to. Men with protections wore them high, and no one can ignore a sharp blow to the ankle.

The warriors fell like puppets with their strings cut.

None of them were injured in any meaningful way, and it was the only hermetical protection he had. But knocking men down changes their view of a fight, and the veteran warriors began to consider sheer survival. He dispatched the man who fell closest to him, a sloppy blow that nonetheless buried his point in the man's skull.

A warrior near to him got to one knee and reached for him, and he seized the man's arm as the *armatura* taught and broke it and slammed the pommel of his sabre into the man's face, knocking him unconscious and waiting for a crossbow bolt between his shoulder blades. He whirled – his time of grace was over, and he was praying to God and Jesus and the Virgin Parthenos and all the legion of saints—

The old man had put an arrow in the nearest Kree, and the rest of them were mere crashing noises running into the woods.

'Best ye get on my horse,' the old hunter said. He managed a laugh, but it was obvious he was shaken. 'Glad I didn't try an' rob you,' he said.

Turkos put the point of his sabre carefully on a dead man's deerskin coat and leaned on it and breathed. He felt as if he'd run a mile.

Athena gave a great kick, and sighed. Bloody foam poured out of her mouth, and she died.

Turkos sat on his haunches by her and wept. He had a long cut across the base of his left thumb and he could see the layer of fat beneath the skin – where had that come from? And there was something in his lower leg. And Athena was dead. He had to discover her death anew, three or four times, like a man touching the stump of a missing tooth. He didn't want her to be dead. He didn't want to have sacrficed her.

'Do you think there is a paradise for animals?' he asked.

The old hunter nodded. 'Lady Tara has a place for animals,' he said. He looked around. 'We should keep moving.'

Turkos mastered himself, but his eyes were hot and full. 'I loved that horse,' he said.

'Then look for her in Tara's fields, running with the deer and the foxes – no predators and no prey.' The old man was all but chanting the words. 'Now get your arse on my horse and let's ride.'

In an hour they made the first of Osawa's outposts, and Turkos gave the password and the alarm was sounded, and mounted messengers went off to the villages of the Southern Huran with news of the coming attack. With a day to prepare, none would be taken by surprise.

Turkos returned to the ancient wall tower at Osawa to read months' worth of news as quickly as he could manage. But attempting to prepare a small fortress for siege by a vast and better-armed army precluded examining much beyond the surface knowledge that the Emperor was a prisoner of the Duke of Thrake, and that his immediate commander, the Logothete, was dead.

While his precious store of mangonels were winched onto the walls and corner towers, he read the two most recent dispatches.

The new Megas Ducas was an Alban mercenary, and – Turkos read the most recent dispatch several times with growing excitement – he was marching towards the border with an army. He – Giannis Turkos – was ordered to collect his mobile garrison and march to meet the Megas Ducas, escorting any fur merchants in Osawa and surrounding villages and their wares.

Of course he was. He was intent on protecting the Empire's share of the fur trade.

Turkos read both dispatches one more time and then stood at his work table, a dirty bandage around his left hand which was held high in the air to stop the flow of blood, while with his right he tried to write as small as ever he'd learned from the monks in Eressos. He wrote the detailed dispatch in the latest code he had available and sent off four copies, one each for all the birds in the tower. As the last great black and white messenger bird soared away, he closed the shutters of his office against the cold and walked down the curving interior steps to the ground floor, where the hunter lay napping on the guardroom bed.

Turkos woke him. 'I'd let you sleep, but you'll want to be gone before the fighting starts,' he said. 'Here's your gold,' he added, and extended his hand to clasp the hunter's, 'and here are my thanks.'

The old man smiled sleepily. 'I won't miss the show,' he said. 'But I'll take the gold.'

Later that afternoon, the first war canoes slipped ashore a few miles north of Osawa. A Kree chief stepped out of the first canoe and received Big Pine's arrow in his throat. He died, thrashing, in the icy water. Big Pine's war party screeched—

—*and the war began.*

Part Two
The Winter War

The King

Chapter Thirteen

Ranald Lachlan

North of Liviapolis – Mag

When the army marched north from the parade ground, they marched in their new white wool cotes with their best weapons and gear, and they made a fine show. Most men had water in their canteens, and the provident had a length of sausage and some hardtack in their scrips.

They marched away west, up the road to Alba, and the further they went, the more men worried.

Mag had never held any kind of command before. She had the natural power of an older woman – the wisdom that comes with the end of youth's ambition, plus a little more from her hermetical talents. She had led the altar guild of her small town, and she had helped manage supplies in a castle under siege.

She had sixty women and a dozen lances under John le Bailli, her lover, under her command. She had lost sleep over their preparations. The wagons were loaded to the tops of their steep, outward-jutting sides, and the carts were loaded, and there were water casks and spare sewing needles and tents and mess kettles and dried meat and thread and horseshoes—

None of that caused her a moment's concern. She could read, and she could write well enough.

But when the train – fifty great wagons and twenty carts and sixty-six mules – passed under the arch of the palace gate and rolled noisily into the gathering dusk, she felt more alone than she had ever felt in her life. She clung to le Bailli's hand when he mounted the lead wagon box with her in a very uncommanderly way, and he smiled at her in the dark and kissed her lips.

'I'm terrified,' she muttered.

Le Bailli laughed. 'It does me good to see it, woman of wonders.' He leaned back to stretch his legs and ease his back, caught his spurs on the wagon's front boards and almost fell off.

She guffawed.

He laughed with her.

'Listen,' he said. 'Command is easy when you are young, and harder and harder as you get older.'

'Oh, shut up with your scary philosophy,' she said, and hugged him a moment. 'What have I forgotten?'

'Spare earwax?' he asked.

For a moment she fell for it . . .

. . . and then she swatted him.

He laughed. 'Put it away. Whatever you have forgotten, we will now live without.' He looked back along the line of wagons. 'How many are new?'

'All but six,' she confessed. The wagons had been built at the Navy Yard to hide them from prying eyes – she'd used hermetical means to hide them still further.

'Best military wagons I've ever seen. He's spent a great deal of money on this,' le Bailli said.

Mag nodded. 'Yes.'

Le Bailli nodded. 'You're a company officer and I'm a lowly corporal. I don't need to know, I'm sure.' He grinned. 'But by God, woman, it seems we're marching into the mountains in winter. What's he doing?'

Mag laughed. 'He's being himself. Mysterious, arrogant, and probably victorious.' She kissed le Bailli. 'We're about to pass the gates, Corporal. Go defend my wagons from the enemy, before I use your handsome body for a distraction from the stress of command.'

'Anytime,' he said, and gave her a little interest on the investment of her kiss before stepping off the wagon into the saddle of his horse, who grunted as if to disapprove of all this showmanship.

*

Mag's convoy rolled into a camp prepared by Gelfred's men – stakes and lines laid out for tents, and a strong picket of cavalry covering their arrival. When the army arrived half an hour later, they found their tents up and most messes had cooked food waiting.

The Morean volunteers ate their hot food, slept in their prepared tents, and didn't desert.

And the next morning, they rose before dawn in the foggy cold, and marched away over the mountains towards the Green Hills.

The weather was superb. The roads were frozen and hard, but the sun was bright, and every man was mounted.

On the third day, as they jogged along at a fast walk over rolling downs full of sheep and cattle, the army passed corpses – little knots of men.

Ser Michael turned to Ranald Lachlan. They were climbing a tall ridge dominating the main road into Thrake. Mountains rolled away to the north and west. Off to the north-west they could see the looming walls of Kilkis, which the Albans called Middleburg. It was a mighty fortress dominating the crossroads where the North Road and West Road met. At the foot of the fortress sat the last town east of the Inn of Dorling.

Lachlan was watching the hills the way a man watches his love pull her dress over her head. With both love and lust. 'My hills ain't far,' he said. He looked down at the dead man – stripped naked, and already dead white – on the ground. There were patches of snow.

'Gelfred caught their outposts asleep,' Ser Michael said. 'I heard it this morning in the command meeting.'

'Blessed Virgin,' Ranald said, and crossed himself. As a man who had been dead, he took the deaths of others very seriously.

'Captain – that is, the Duke – says we've a clear run until we encounter his scouts,' Ser Michael said.

'Sweet Christ,' Ranald said. 'Poor Andronicus.' He laughed aloud, and that particular laughter spread like wildfire as the army raced across the hills, headed north. 'Tom and I thought the Castellan at Middleburg would hold against us.'

Ser Michael shrugged. 'He didn't. I don't know the story, but the gates were open and the Duke expected it.' He looked back. 'I don't know what he's doing, but he's been planning it for months.'

Ranald nodded. 'Aye. He's a canny bastard.' He caught Michael's glance and put a hand on the younger man's shoulder. 'Michael, lad, he'll plan as carefully for your da.'

Michael spat carefully in a patch of snow. 'Ran, I don't know what I want for my pater. I'm not convinced I shouldn't ride away and leave him to his dungheap.' He touched the favour he wore at his shoulder. 'I have other concerns than him.'

Ranald fingered his beard. 'Aye. As do I.'

It was Michael's turn. 'Don't fret – he'll knight you. Just give him an excuse. Ranald, I know him. He's chancy to cross, he's the devil when he's angry, he's as vain as a popinjay and he loves to show us all how smart he is – but he stands by his friends.'

Ranald nodded, obviously unhappy. 'Aye, that's what Tom says.'

'We'll have a fight in the next ten days.'

'Or we'll all freeze waiting for it,' Ranald said. 'But aye.'

There was no break for midday food. The whole column rolled along and took the north fork in the Imperial road without pausing under the walls of Kilkis – and now they were marching along the old legion road. Instead of marching west over the last pass into the Green Hills, they continued north, passing well east of the Dragon's Mountain and crossing the Meander River at a stone bridge so ancient that Ser Alcaeus dismounted, read the inscription, and laughed aloud. He cantered along the jingling column – men were eating in the saddle, and the Nordikans, who were probably the worst riders, were leaving a trail of uneaten food – dropped sausages and cheese – and they roared with laughter at each other's riding. Men fell off. They all drank steadily.

Alcaeus reined in by the standard. 'I know why you left Darkhair and half the Nordikans,' he said. 'By our avenging lord – how many wagons of wine do they have with them?'

The Red Knight grinned. 'A better question would be – what will they be like when we run out of wine?'

Ranald leaned out over his cantle. 'What did it say? I've crossed the Stone Bridge in the Hills a hundred times. I can read, but I can't read that!'

Alcaeus nodded to the Red Knight. 'A few of us can still read Old Archaic,' he said. 'For such a grand structure – out here in this waste of green grass and rock – you might expect an oration from the Empress Livia—'

All the educated men nodded.

Alcaeus straightened his back where the tug of harness and four days in the saddle grated on his hips. 'It says "Iskander, Deckarch of Taxis X Nike, and his mess group built this bridge in fourteen days."'

Tom Lachlan and his cousin turned their horses to look back, and for a moment, the whole command group – Ser Milus, and Nicholas Ganfroy, who was four fingers taller and a much better trumpeter, Bad Tom and Ranald, Toby with his master's spare warhorse and Nell, who had suddenly started to look more like a woman and less like a skinny irk, Father Arnaud, Ser Alcaeus and Ser Gavin and the Megas Ducas himself by Ser Gerald Random nursing his ankle – all sat in their saddles, munching sausage and contemplating a three-arch stone bridge built by ten soldiers in fourteen days.

'They conquered the world, or most of it,' the Duke said.

Bad Tom spat some sausage rind. 'I would ha' loved to fight them.' He nodded at his cousin. 'They'd hae gi'en us a mickle fight. Kiss the book on that.'

The Duke gave his largest man-at-arms a crooked grin. 'I don't know if they were great warriors, Tom,' he said. 'They built great roads and bridges and made damn sure they weren't outnumbered when it came to a fight.'

'Oh,' said Tom, losing interest. 'How do you know that?'

'They left books behind,' the Duke said. 'And I read them.'

Liviapolis – The Princess Irene

'What!' The princess lost control of her voice very briefly and shrieked like the girls selling fish on the docks.

Lady Maria stood her ground with the long practice of a wife, a mother, and a courtier. 'The army has marched away, Majesty.'

Irene put her bare feet into sheepskin slippers – even in the grip of terrified rage, she could not help but notice how unseemly it was that a princess born in the purple birthing room of the Great Palace would wear peasant slippers to keep her feet warm. The ancient floors of the palace had hypocausts, and should have been warmed by furnaces in the lowest cellars. But none of that had worked for many years, and only rats lived in the tunnels that had once funnelled warm air.

'Do you mean that my barbarian heretic has taken *my* army and marched away without informing me?' she spat.

Lady Maria nodded and curtsied deeply. 'So it would appear, Majesty.'

'Leaving me naked to the traitor?' Irene said. She was wearing only a thin linen shift in a very cold room, and the concept of being naked before her enemies was rather real and immediate.

'Acting Spatharios Darkhair remains with more than half of the Nordikan Guard. There are two maniples of the Scholae in the palace and our walls are manned.' Lady Maria curtsied again. 'The new sailors in the Navy Yard have been paid, and are armed. We are not utterly wretched.'

Irene went to the great arched doors that gave on her balcony. There was snow in the air, but she looked north, towards the tall mountains of Thrake. 'What is he doing?' she asked.

Lonika, Northern Thrake

A black and white bird the size of a large dog alighted on the arm of a green-clad man. He was sitting on a fretting horse in a field of snow studded with snow-covered pines, and the weight of the bird on his arm threatened his seat, but he managed it. He slipped the message cylinder out of the bird's harness of wool yarn, fed it most of a chicken, which act left him covered in bloody scraps, and then tossed the bird as high as he could manage into the air for the return journey to the city, more than a hundred leagues to the south.

Jules Kronmir read the message with what passed for panic on his face, which was registered by the very slightest downward twitch of his mouth.

He turned his horse and raced over the first snow of the season for the Palace of Lonika.

Aeskepiles sat across a big oak table from Jules Kronmir, drinking good cider and scowling.

'We have to kill him,' he said with a shrug. 'You need to convince Duke Andronicus.' He read the message again.

'Andronicus is convinced that the only way to deal with the usurper is to meet him in the field.' Kronmir raised his cup and

478

drank. 'Pray do not delay in taking this to the Duke, Magister. Time is everything.'

'You are so reserved, Master Kronmir, I can't decide what you are saying.' Aeskepiles stretched his booted legs out towards the open hearth. 'I hadn't expected to spend a winter in Thrake,' he admitted. He tossed the small confession on the still water of the spymaster's face.

Nothing rose to the surface. 'Would you do me the kindness to take this news to the palace?' asked Kronmir, displaying a deliberate patience, like a parent with a child.

'An hour won't hurt the cause. I never get a chance to speak to you, and yet you are at the heart of our organisation in the city.' The mage leaned forward. 'Is there anything you need?'

Kronmir thought for a moment. If he was frustrated at the magister's delay, he hid it well. 'I wonder if you could make me some small devices,' he asked.

Aeskepiles shrugged. 'Most men exaggerate the capabilities of hermetical devices,' he said. 'And I don't make fire-starters. What would you like?'

'I'd like to have the ability to warn an agent. Something like a ring or a pendant that would buzz, or grow warm or cold. Preferably something that would be utterly inconspicuous.'

Aeskepiles drank more cider. 'Warn them for what purpose?'

'So that they could escape. You must know that one of my best messengers was taken. I lost only one agent, but in the process of warning the others I was very exposed.'

Kronmir said this with such flat disinterest that the mage had to say the words again in his head to understand their import. 'We wouldn't want you to be captured,' Aeskepiles agreed.

'That would be most – unpleasant. For me, and for your cause.' Kronmir drank more wine. 'The capture of either of my principal agents would be just as disastrous.'

'How much do they know?' the mage asked.

Kronmir made an odd face. 'Excuse me?' he asked.

'I mean, if they are too well informed, ought we just to be rid of them?' asked the hermeticist.

'Is this how you see the world?' Kronmir asked. 'These are people who have served the Duke well.'

Aeskepiles shrugged. 'Of course.'

Kronmir rose. 'I find it odd that I – the spy, the hired killer – care more about the people we use than you or Demetrius do, the noble supporters of a noble cause.' Kronmir's delivery continued to be so flat that it was possible he was speaking ironically, and the mage chose to take him that way.

He laughed. 'Be that as it may, I will make you these devices. That is well within my art. And I ask you again – do you hold the Red Knight's life in your hand?'

Kronmir didn't smile. His cold eyes, like the eyes of falcon or a lizard, bored into the hermeticist's eyes, and for a moment Aeskepiles felt a shudder of revulsion.

'Yes,' said the spy.

'No possibility of error – your agent is that sure he can get close to the usurper?' Aeskepiles asked.

Kronmir looked at him. 'There is always the possibility of error,' he said. 'We don't call this the game of kings for nothing.'

'Your agent is reliable?' asked Aeskepiles.

Kronmir leaned back. 'You are not as far advanced in the confidence of the Duke as I would have expected, Master Mage. I will not tell you any more.' He looked away. 'The Duke needs this information.'

Aeskepiles risked some of his stature with the rebels and shook his head. 'Damn it, Kronmir, I'm not the enemy. I just want to know if there's any chance of winning this thing. I had good reason to betray the Emperor. My agenda is not advanced at all by a failed rebellion.'

Kronmir's face finally registered an emotion – surprise. He leaned forward again. 'Well,' he said. 'That was honest, Master Mage. For my part, I can provide you no assurances. I am a mere mercenary, hired under contract. I have some history with the Duke, and was willing to work on this project under certain conditions.' He shrugged. 'It is of little moment to me who is Emperor.'

Aeskepiles spread his hands in frustration. 'I thought that you were deep in the councils of the Duke!' he said.

Kronmir rose, and threw his cloak around his shoulders. 'If I were, I wouldn't admit it to you. And if I were not, I wouldn't admit it to you. So I must demur, and say nothing at all. Good day, Master Magister.' He took a step away from the table and then, with a swirl of his cloak, reappeared by the sorcerer's side.

'How are your relations with the Academy?' he asked suddenly.

Aeskepiles raised an eyebrow. 'Much like yours with the Duke,' he said. 'And with the same codicil.'

Kronmir laughed. Aeskepiles thought it might have been the first time he heard the spy laugh.

'I had that coming,' the spy admitted. 'The message?'

'Immediately, spy.'

Kronmir bowed, and was gone.

Aeskepiles spent far too much time getting the snow off his hood while incompetent servants fussed over his boots.

'Damn your eyes,' he snarled at a maid. 'I need to see Duke Andronicus.'

The major-domo of the Lonika Palace bowed deeply. 'Magister, the grand Duke is with the Despot in the Room of Embassies.'

The Palace of Lonika mirrored the Great Palace of Liviapolis in any number of ways – it had magnificent mosaic ceilings, gilt pillars, rooms full of furniture inlaid in ivory and bone and precious gems. But it was all on a far more human scale – the palace itself was the size of a Harndon guild hall, and there were only a hundred servants. Moreover, the relative wealth of the Dukes of Thrake and the smaller scale of the palace meant that the hypocausts worked, the floors were heated, the flues of the Alban-style inside chimneys were clear and warmth trickled even into outside halls, while the main rooms on the three main floors were positively pleasant.

The palace major-domo led the magister up two grand staircases to the Great Hall, which was dark – but warmer than the world outside. They moved silently across the warm marble floors. In the silence, Aeskepiles could actually hear the sound of distant fires roaring in the cellar furnaces.

They crossed the marble floor, passed through a low, arched corridor, and the major-domo knocked at a small inlaid door. A beautiful young man opened it and bowed deeply.

Aeskepiles entered a wood-panelled room – every panel was itself an inlaid trompe l'oeil, a picture of the same panel open to reveal helmets and sextants and paint brushes and daggers and scrolls – a masculine fantasy of the ideal collection, rendered in fine woods and ivory and gilt. It was, indeed, a facsimile of the Imperial study in the Palace of Blacharnae.

Aeskepiles thought it a remarkable piece of vulgarity and, because he hated it, it drew his eye every time he entered the room.

Duke Andronicus and his golden son sat at a magnificent table in northern cherry, mammoth ivory and gold, on ivory stools. They were playing chess, a set of pieces carved by an artist from Umroth ivory and the rare black bone of the non-dead.

'Aeskepiles!' said Andronicus with an enthusiasm that came across as patently false. A life of palace political life had robbed the Duke of normal human reactions – it was very difficult to determine what he thought about anything.

Demetrius, who had been kept away from court, scowled contemptuously at the mage. He didn't hide his feelings.

'We're playing chess,' he said. 'Why don't you respect our privacy and return at a mutually convenient time?' The words were polite, but the intent was anything but.

Hating Demetrius was a city-wide hobby, and one that Aeskepiles disdained. 'My lord, I would not interrupt, but that I have two pieces of news. The first is that I fear for the loyalty of the spy, Kronmir.'

Andronicus shrugged. 'He's his own man, I agree. But that was part of our arrangement. He has brought some remarkable tools to the table.'

Aeskepiles settled at the table. 'He claims he can kill the Red Knight at any time, but he will not discuss his methods or the source of this message.'

Duke Andronicus caught sight of the message tube in palace colours and he reached for it.

'I feel sometimes that I am not in your confidence, my lord Duke, despite being one of the engines of our shared rebellion. And despite having placed the Emperor in your hands.' Aeskepiles plucked the message cylinder out of the Duke's hands and placed it high above them with a whisper and a thought. 'I, too, am an ally of convenience, my lord Duke, and I do not feel that my convenience has been consulted very often. I have certain goals. I would like to know the state of play.'

Duke Andronicus crossed his arms like a man in a fight with his wife. 'Are you done?' He turned his head to where his son had just drawn his short sword. 'Do not threaten our guest.'

'He's a useless old fuck. I could gut him and we'd be the better for it.' Demetrius stood up.

His magnificent sword – blued and gilt with a scene of the crucifixion – rusted away to flakes in a single breath, leaving only the gilt – for a moment – before the whole fell like a dirty orange snow to the floor.

He dropped the hilt as if the rust were a contagion he might catch. 'Fuck you, you bastard,' he spat.

'Your son is our single greatest liability,' Aeskepiles said, effectively muffling the boy with another small working. 'Even your own people hate him.'

Andronicus shrugged. 'That's as may be. He's my flesh and blood, and a fine cavalry officer. And I can trust him with anything. Unlike a certain mage.'

'Don't be a fool, Andronicus. You can trust me – I have no other place to go. Kronmir admitted that two of his agents know how we planned the coup. And who was in it with us.'

Andronicus stroked his short ginger beard. 'They need to die, then,' he said.

'I'll see to that. In the meantime, be wary of the spy. He knows too much.' The magister brought the cylinder down from the ceiling and gave it to the Duke, who read it greedily and cursed.

But when he was done, he met the mage's eye and smiled. 'I know you want him killed,' he said. 'But he's ridden from the city with an army, and I'll have him in a week. In my own country? The thing's as good as done. Can you handle his hermetical?'

'I was the Imperial mage,' Aeskepiles said. 'I can handle a mercenary company from Alba.' He leaned forward. 'Should we move the Emperor?'

'Why?' asked the Duke. 'He's leagues west of here, with people I trust. The usurper will never get that far. Our report says he's headed east!'

Harndon – The Queen

Desiderata dismounted from her horse and rushed across the frozen ground, but it was too late.

The Sieur de Rohan stood with a bloody sword, and one of her favourites, Ser Augustus, lay bleeding. The blood pumped from his side and flowed out of his mouth, and it ran on and on, and he lay there. His eyes found hers, and of all things, he smiled.

He opened his mouth, and more blood came out – gouts of it.

She knelt, regardless of the blood and the ordure, and took his head in her lap. 'What is this?' she asked.

Rohan laughed. 'One of your lovers? One fewer, then.' He bowed his head. 'My lady Queen,' he said with a smile.

Ser Augustus looked at her as if she was his hope of heaven, and she reached inside to try—

He was slipping away, like a guest leaving a party without saying goodbye to the hostess, and she tripped after him – through the open woods where they'd been riding, across the open field where the wagon waited with all their hawks, and then into the woods and he flitted on ahead of her, and suddenly she was in dark and broken country. She stopped, and watched Ser Augustus go on – up the dark slope and away from her best effort to throw her golden light to him.

She rose, covered in blood – her white wool dress now scarlet and dark brown. She stalked regally after the Sieur de Rohan. 'Explain yourself, sir, before I have you arrested.'

'Arrested? On the word of a woman?' He laughed in her face. 'Unlike these others, I merely defend your husband's honour – as my lord, the great Captal, does on a larger field.'

She was quite calm. 'Are you accusing me of something, messire?'

'That is for a greater baron than I,' he said, and his eyes were lit as if from within. 'I will merely content myself with cutting the evil weeds from his garden.'

Lady Mary stood at the Queen's shoulder. She stepped between the murderer and the Queen. 'I think you are a coward and a murderer,' she said.

The Galle's smile slipped into blank rage. His hand twitched.

'Mary!' cautioned the Queen.

'I think you are a coward who seeks to torment the Queen when all of our best knights are away – fighting the Wild.' Mary took a step towards him.

'*We* are your best knights. There is no knight in this beggarly country that can stand against us. Coward? I? I challenged him and I beat him. You Albans pretend that black is white. It is not. He was a coward. His hand shook when he drew his sword.'

'And you enjoyed that, did you not? I say you are a false knight, a poltroon—' She leaned forward—

His hand, uncontrolled, shot out and struck her, and she fell backward.

'Arrest the Galle,' said the Queen.

'You bitch,' Rohan said softly.

Desiderata's eyes met his for a moment, and she said, 'You want open war between us? *So be it.*'

The King sat on his throne with all of his officers present and scratched the ears of his wolfhound. 'Are you a pack of complete idiots?' he growled. 'I demand my officer be released immediately. He committed no crime—'

'He struck my daughter in front of fifty witnesses!' roared the Constable. 'By God and all the saints—'

De Vrailly turned to him. 'If you desire satisfaction, challenge me, and we will settle this.'

The Count faced the Captal with an icy bow. 'Whatever odd customs you Galles keep at home, my lord, here in Alba we have laws which bind all men. Your man has broken a slew of them – lese majestie, and assault against an innocent woman—'

'Who called him a coward, in public, before witnesses – for a woman to do that! That she should dare to even raise her eyes to such a man!' said the Captal. 'In Galle, women know their places.'

There was a particularly icy silence while Gaston d'Eu, the usual peacemaker, glared at his cousin with ill-concealed distaste. 'Do they really, cousin? I think you fantasise.'

The Captal turned his glare on his cousin. 'Withdraw that,' he said.

The Count d'Eu settled himself. 'No. I, the Comte d'Eu, declare that you lie. Women in Galle are every bit as free to speak their minds at court as men. You create a world that suits yourself, rather than observing reality. I will maintain my point of view with my reality.'

The King shot to his feet. 'Damn the lot of you!' he roared.

Even the Captal backed away a step.

The King walked past the Queen, who sat in silence, her hands crossed.

'Your daughter behaved like a fishwife, yelling insults at a knight,' said the King to his Count. He walked another few steps to the Captal. 'Your man used a duel as a pretext for murder, and made broad allegations about my wife's fidelity – did you know about this, Captal?'

The Captal had no trouble meeting the King's eyes. 'It is commonly reported,' he said. And he shrugged. 'But my man killed your gentleman over a private matter – nothing to do with the Queen or the law. They are both knights – only the Law of War covers them. Ser Augustus was found wanting.' The Captal shrugged. 'I have read your laws. If my man made an accusation against the Queen, let her bring her witnesses forth. Otherwise, he was arrested for a provoked attack on a woman.'

'Do Galles hit women so very often?' asked the Count of the Borders. 'None of my training in chivalry covered such a point. Is it a particular part of the Law of War?'

The Captal turned but found the King was standing by the Count d'Eu. 'And I have been to Galle, and I agree with the Count. So – Captal. Will you face the two of us in the lists?'

The Captal took a deep breath. 'Of course.'

'Your cousin and your King – you'll fight us both?' asked the King. 'If you win, you'll be banned from this court. If you lose, you'll have been proven false.' The King was often bluff and easygoing. Some of the men in the room had never heard him take this tone. 'Captal, you are a fine knight, but sometimes you are a fool. You seem to believe that we are all peers, merely gentlemen with swords, in a sort of endless tournament. Eh?'

The King stood nose to nose with the Captal.

Their eyes locked.

'Back down, Captal,' he said. 'I am not some other knight. I am your King.'

You could hear men in the room breathe. The two men were of a size – the King was older, his golden hair a darker bronze, and his features were less fine, but you could see that they were cousins, however distant, and you could see that they were men who were not used to being said nay.

A political eternity passed. The Count of the Borders, despite his rage, had to consider what war with the Galles would mean and how much of Harndon they held; Gaston d'Eu tried to imagine being dead, or losing his cousin's faith and going home in disgrace.

'Very well,' said the Captal. 'I do God's work here. My own angers are of no moment. I submit, Your Grace, and I confess that the women of Galle are as likely to be pert and forward and rude as the women of Alba.'

The silence was more stirred than broken by the Captal's apparent submission.

'The Sieur de Rohan is banned from court for Christmas,' the King continued. 'As is the Lady Mary.'

The Queen's sharp intake of breath was as audible as the flat crack of a crossbow bolt releasing from the string.

An hour later, she turned on her husband. 'Two of my knights are dead, my lord, and you banish my best friend from court? At Christmas?'

The King sat quietly, hands folded in his lap. 'I'm sorry, my love. Sometimes the appearance is more important than the reality – that's being King. The Galles must feel I'm even-handed—'

'Must they?' she spat. 'Why not just order them from court, embrace Towbray, and tell the Captal to sail home and trouble us no more?'

He nodded slowly. 'Can I tell you a hard truth, love?' he asked. 'Only the Captal's knights kept us in the war in the spring. Three hundred steel-clad lances were the margin. Without them, I'd probably be dead on the field at Lissen, and this kingdom would be split in two or worse. I fear to send him home. And he says he was sent by God...'

She stood up. 'He's deluded – some false demon whispers in his ear. He is a fine knight, but his ways are not ours, and his knights – especially the new men – they all but hunt me with poisonous words. I have never had a lover but you, my husband. You know this. You know that they slander me every day.' She was breathing deeply. She had never felt so alone, and she was tempted to play on her pregnancy, but she had Diota's word that most women who miscarried did so in the first three months. She wanted to present the King with a swollen belly and a fact, not a supposition and a disaster. And yet the rumours of her infidelity were like a poison against her baby.

He looked away. 'He brought Towbray to heel fast enough.'

The Queen leaned over. 'He will end by bringing you to heel and making himself King,' she said.

He shook his head. 'My ruling stands. At this point, I cannot appear weak.'

Desiderata paused. She was as angry as she had ever been, and the words that formed on her lips were: *If you cannot appear weak, then you are weak.*

An hour later, still flushed with rage, she walked down the long corridor under the Old Hall with Becca Almspend. Lady Mary was with her father, and unavailable.

'Are you sure this is wise, Your Grace?' Almspend asked.

'I am done with wise,' the Queen answered.

They passed the Green Man on the stones, and the stone dedicated to the Lady Tar. Further along the corridor they came to the place where the stones were cold, and this time it was Becca who lingered, running her hand over a stone with carving worn almost smooth, and another where lettering had been effaced.

'This is where the cold is born,' Almspend said.

The Queen crossed her arms over her bosom. 'Let's be quick.'

'A moment, Your Grace. I've wondered since we were last here.' Almspend knelt, took a silver pencil from her belt. 'Do you ever consider that these other worships must have been based on something? Natural magic must have worked.'

'I think you are very close to heresy, my dear. What are you doing?' asked the Queen. 'I do not like this place.'

'Testing a small suspicion, my Queen.' Almspend frowned and drew a short invocation in letters of fire – but they paled immediately and flickered, and she had trouble speaking the words.

Trouble saying them – but speak them she did.

The stone flared, and for a moment the words, carved more than two thousand years before, were visible even where the chisel had destroyed them.

'This is not for the Green Man,' Almspend said, her voice suddenly hoarse. 'This is for a darker entity entirely.'

The two women read the name, and the Queen put her hand to her throat – then raised it, and poured raw sunlight on the stone. It seemed to grow blacker. The Queen grew taller – her skin took on a remarkable bronze hue, and her hair suddenly seemed to be made of raw metal.

Becca Almspend took a step back. 'Desiderata! Stop!'

The Queen was almost as tall as the corridor. The stone was as black as night and the very ground rumbled.

The stone made a pop like overheated stone.

Almspend turned her head, and the Queen was her normal self.

'What was that?' Rebecca asked.

'Something that the Archbishop should have seen to long ago. A tunnel that needed to be closed.' The Queen put her hand to her head. 'I have been reckless.' She was trembling, and Almspend put her shoulder under the taller woman's armpit and supported her.

'Come – there's a bench in the store room,' she said.

The Queen went, but she shook her head. 'I no longer want to know. I think I know the answer, and I can't – face it.'

Almspend, to whom history was like a law, shook her head. 'What's past is past. Whatever the King did, it was done before he met you.'

The Queen nodded. She was obviously unconvinced. But she sank onto the bench after Almspend opened her own hermetical wards and the great iron-bound door.

Almspend set a mage light, and then a second. The first trip, they'd only made a hasty catalogue of the papers. The librarian in Rebecca Almspend made her take time to neaten each pile, and riffle through them, sorting paper and parchment scrolls by date and author – Harmodius, Harmodius, Plangere – her fingers skimmed over them. The Queen's colour improved and her head came up.

'Ah! I have found Plangere's papers for sixty-four forty-two.' Almspend smiled. 'That wasn't so hard – I think he was better organised than old Harmodius.'

'I never knew how much I would miss Harmodius,' said the Queen. 'I miss him now.' The Queen stood. 'Becca, I was reckless just now, and I am nearly drained. Let us get above ground, to the light, before something evil comes.'

'The Wild?' Almspend said, her guards coming up.

'Older and far more wicked.' The Queen raised her own wards. 'Come!'

Almspend swept all of Plangere's private notes for the year into an ancient willow basket and nodded. 'After you, my lady.'

The shadows in the corridor were deep. Too deep. It was as if light itself had begun to leach away from the edges of the tunnel, despite the cressets they'd lit as they advanced.

'There's something nasty here,' the Queen said. 'Mother Mary, stand by me.'

She raised her hand and it again glowed a soft gold. The shadows retreated.

'What's happening?' asked Almspend.

The Queen shook her head. 'I have no idea,' she said, and the two of them passed rapidly down the corridor, pursued only by fear. Yet something whispered in the darkness and, behind them, the cressets guttered out without their quenching them. The darkness behind them became absolute – and began to close on them.

The Queen turned and stood her ground. 'Fiat lux!' she called.

The light she called blazed around her like a rallied army.

Almspend put her left hand on the Queen's right and gave her every scrap of *potentia* she could muster. With her own right, she raised her strongest shield and held it in opposition to the onrushing darkness.

It came like the fall of night – and whatever it was slammed into the workings of the two women and folded them, compacted them, collapsed some, evaded others—

But it did not overwhelm them. It was slowed, and the very slowing of its apparently implacable rush fuelled their resistance. They spoke no words and thought no thoughts, their wills locked together as only two friends of the heart could be locked, and the warm gold light of the Queen's power rolled, earthy and fresh as sunlight on a summer's day, into the darkness, where it was swallowed, but not without result.

The darkness pushed past Almspend's strongest shield, and her right hand vanished in icy cold – and her will was not shattered. She stood her ground, and continued to work, deep in the labyrinths of her white marble palace.

The Queen sighed, and offered her embrace to the darkness.

And it fled.

The two women stood trembling with spirit and suppressed fear for a long set of heartbeats, fast or slow.

'Oh, Blessed Virgin! Becca – your poor hand.' said the Queen.

Almspend's hand was dead white, and the place where the darkness had been turned – the borderline of their victory – was marked as if by sunburn.

Becca Almspend looked at her hand – and knew the name of the malevolence from the stone.

Ash.

*

Edmund had delivered three shipments of cast bronze tubes, and the odd bells. Apparently they were satisfactory, as he had been abundantly paid. He'd begun to do mint work with his master, and then, on a Thursday evening while he was at mass, thugs attacked the shop, killed two apprentices, and burned his shed. A gang of apprentices had driven them off, killing two.

One of the two was a Galle.

It was odd that out of all the sheds in the yard they might have burned, destroying his had the least effect – he'd made the little bronze *gonnes* and his apprentices were now working directly for the master in Shed One, setting up the dies to make the new coinage.

He found Master Pye in the yard, crouched over a dead apprentice, a boy only ten years old.

'Damn Random for running off to the city when we need him here,' he said. Edmund understood his words, but little of his sense.

And the next day, when a Hoek merchant – one of the richest men in the west, or so men said – came to their forge, all the apprentices rushed about like servants to bring wine and candied fruit. The man wore black head to toe, with gold buttons, gold eyelets, and a gold order of knighthood. He sat, still wearing his black hat, and leaned on the golden hilt of his sword in the master's office. Edmund entered carrying wine, and Master Pye nodded and extended a hand to him. 'Stay,' he said.

The Hoek merchant bowed in his seat. 'I am Ser Anton Van Der Coent. I have come to see if perhaps my alliance and yours might arrive at an accommodation.' He smiled with assurance.

Master Pye looked frowsy and ill-tended next to the groomed perfection of the Hoek merchant prince. 'I have no truck with politics, messire, and I have a shop to run and a great many commissions under way. And you may know that we had troubles yesterday – two apprentices killed.' Master Pye leaned back, his watery eyes apparently unfocused.

'Ah, I am very sorry to hear of such a thing. The law in Harndon is not what it once was,' said Ser Anton. 'Such incidents are an insult to the majesty of the realm, and a terrible pity.'

Master Pye's watery eyes seemed to transform. Edmund had seen it in the near darkness of the forge, but never over a tray of sweetmeats. 'Do you know something of them?' he asked sharply.

'I?' asked Ser Anton. 'Honestly, messire – I could be offended by such a suggestion. What would I have to do with such things?'

Edmund thought he sounded smug.

'At any rate, Ser Anton, I have nothing to do with any combine.' Master Pye nodded. 'So I must wish you a good day.'

Ser Anton smiled. 'Are you not the new master of the King's mint?' he asked.

Master Pye cocked his head to one side. 'Ahhh,' he said. 'So that's what this is about.'

'I'm prepared to offer you an order for seventy full suits of your plate and four hundred helmets,' Ser Anton said. He took a wax tablet – a beautiful thing, all figured in black enamel and gold – from his belt pouch and flipped it open. 'I estimate that you would take a little over a year to fill the order even with an expanded shop. I have customers waiting for the order – so I'd pay a premium for immediate work.' He nodded.

Master Pye scratched behind his ear. 'You're talking a hundred thousand florins,' he said. 'A fortune.'

Ser Anton smiled. 'So I am,' he said. He leaned forward. 'I would even undertake to guarantee that there would be no further interruptions of your shop's work.'

Master Pye was nodding along. 'Of course, I'd have to give up the mint,' he said.

Ser Anton nodded. 'So we understand each other.'

Master Pye nodded again. 'I understand you perfectly. Get out of my shop, before I kill you with my own hands.'

Despite being armed with a beautiful sword and facing a small, hunched-over man with watery eyes, the Hoek flinched. 'You wouldn't dare. I can buy you—'

Pye barked his curious laugh. 'You just found ye can't buy me. Now get out of my shop.'

The man shrugged. He rose elegantly, and walked to the door like a great black and gold cat. 'In the end, you know, you'd have been better this way,' he said. But something about his smoothness was broken, for Edmund. Now he appeared vulgar.

When he was gone, Pye turned to Edmund. 'Stop all work,' he said. 'All the boys, girls, everyone in the yard. But listen, Edmund—'

Edmund stopped at the door.

'If I die suddenly, you keep the mint going. Understand?' Master Pye looked more than a little mad.

But Edmund nodded.

There were almost forty of them in the yard, with shop servants, house servants, apprentices and journeymen together.

Master Pye stood before them on a small crate. 'Listen up,' he said. Then he was silent, and looked at them.

'We're in a war,' he said. 'It's hard to explain our war, because it's like a fight in the dark, and without a flash of lightning we don't even know who we're fighting. We're fighting for our King – that much for certain – but we're not defending land, or keeping our churches free of the infidel. It's hard to explain exactly what we're doing.'

He looked at them, his mild eyes more curious than inflamed.

'This kingdom endured a mighty blow this spring, from the Wild,' he said. 'And now – unless we have a few successes – it looks as if we'll lose the fur trade, and that's a blow. And men are trying to forge the King's currency – which is like robbing the King – and that's a blow, too.' He shrugged. 'We're going to make new coins for the King. It may not seem to you lads and lasses like some gallant last stand on a stricken field under a silken flag – but by Christ's blood, my young ones, it *is*. If we fail here, and God send we do not, if we fail at this, the King takes another blow. And eventually it will all fall apart, and we'll have nothing.' He stood very straight. 'When the world goes to shit the great do well enough in their fancy armour and their strong castles. It's we who suffer. The men in the middle. In cities and towns, making things and trading things. What do we eat? How do we defend ourselves?' He pursed his lips. 'When I was your age, I was sometimes known to say, "Fuck the King."'

That got a guilty titter from the apprentices.

'Aye – for a bit I was even a Jack.'

Hush.

'But the Jacks haven't given us anything, and the King gives us law. So we're in a fight. For law. The law that keeps us and the commons in the game. Not slaves. Not serfs. Now – in the next month, we're going to be attacked. I'm guessing, but it's going to be rough. Maids attacked when they go to buy milk. Boys beaten on their way to the Abbey for letters. Fire in the yard.' He looked around. 'We'll have to work all day and stand guard, too.' He paused. 'I pay the highest wages in Harndon, and I'll add some hard-lying money. Who's in?'

Everyone was in.

'They're brave today,' Pye said to his journeyman. 'Wait a week or two, when a few of them are dead, and then we'll see.'

Two days later, thugs attacked a party of girls going to the well behind the Abbey at the end of their square. Lizz Person had her face slashed, and only the chance interruption of a knight of Saint Thomas bringing winter clothes to the poor at the church saved the girls from rape or slavery.

The young knight took wine with Edmund and Master Pye in the shop's office.

'Ser Ricar Irksbane,' he said. His eyes twinkled.

Out in the yard, a dozen apprentices jostled each other to sharpen his sword.

'We all owe you our thanks,' Edmund said, as well as he could. The worst of being on the knife edge between adulthood and childhood was in dealing with mature adults, he'd found. So he stammered more than he wanted to, and his bow was clumsy.

Ser Ricar was young, bluff-faced, and had the largest nose that Edmund could remember seeing on a man. He looked like a caricature of Saint Nicolas – an armed Saint Nicolas with broad shoulders and thighs the size of most people's waists.

The heavy young man drank two cups of wine while his sword was being sharpened, and beyond his name and some beaming smiles said nothing.

Master Pye laughed eventually. 'Ser knight, are you perchance under a vow of silence?'

The twinkling eyes blinked, and Ser Ricar rose and bowed.

Master Pye nodded. 'Ser Ricar, have you by any chance been set to watch over us?'

Ser Ricar smiled into his wine, and just for a moment he looked a good deal sharper than he had a moment before. Then he looked the master in the eye and shrugged. And grinned like a village idiot.

Edmund walked him to the gate, and the knight nodded cordially to him and produced a slip of parchment from his belt purse. He pressed it into Edmund's hands and smiled. Edmund noted that the young knight's eyes were everywhere. They never stopped moving, now that the two of them were outside.

He saw the knight out into the street with his newly sharpened sword, and then he opened the parchment.

It said *Be on your guard*.

Edmund gave it to Master Pye, who nodded. 'Bad times,' he said. 'The Queen's handmaid is to be banished from court.'

Through the local girls employed in the Tower, all the neighbourhood knew how things went with the royals. Edmund sighed. 'What can we do?' he asked.

Master Pye all but snarled, 'Nothing.' Then he sat heavily. 'I hate all this. I like metal. People are fools.' He poured himself a cup of hippocras and splashed some into another cup for Edmund. 'What men call politics is, to me, foolery. All this – why doesn't the King banish the Galles? Why doesn't he stand by his wife?' He shrugged. 'He's my friend, but in this he's a damn fool.' He sighed again. 'I'm writing out a note for Master Ailwin, and another for Ser Gerald Random. Talk to Random's wife – she's got all the sense in that house anyway. He's hared off on some wild scheme, and she'll know when he's back. If the knights of Saint Thomas are standing with us, things are not as bad as they might be. But we need to pull together, or the Galles will take us all separately.

Blanche Gold curtsied to her Queen and held out a basket of clean and perfectly pressed linen. The Queen had a book of hours open on her lap and was sitting in the full, if thin, light of the winter sun as it blazed through the mullioned window of her private solar. Her hair was down, and it blazed like a bronze-brown sun around her.

'Speak to Diota,' the Queen said in a friendly voice. She knew Blanche – which was to say, she knew of the girl's existence, knew she was pretty and trustworthy and knew, too, that she had had some trouble at the hands of the Gallish squires. But the Queen didn't speak directly to servants – she let Diota handle that.

So she sat, reading, for a whole minute while the pretty blond girl knelt in front of her.

'Sweeting?' the Queen murmured.

Blanche reached into her basket and handed the Queen a beautifully scented handkerchief. Folded within it was a note.

The Queen found that her hands were shaking. But she unfolded the stiff parchment and her heart rose in her breast. 'Ahh. Thank you, child,' the Queen breathed.

Blanche rose, her duty done, and slipped away. And an hour later, when a Gallish squire tried to pin her to a wall and get his hand down the front of her kirtle, she thought, *we will bury you*. She tried to put a knee in his groin but his wrestling master had covered that. So she settled for letting him put his hand into the top of her dress, and then rammed the index finger of her left hand into his nostril and ripped with her nail as her mother had taught her.

Then she slipped through his arms before the fountain of his blood could foul her nice gown.

She skipped a little as she went down the long palace corridors to the kitchens. A good day.

Lady Emota was afraid when two of the Gallish squires cornered her. And less than relieved when they parted and the Sieur de Rohan stepped between them.

'Ah,' he said with a bow. 'The most beautiful of the Queen's ladies.'

She blushed. 'My lord is too gracious.'

'I could not be too gracious to a flower such as you.' He leaned over her, raised her hand and kissed it. 'Is there by any chance some man at this court you detest, so that I can kill him and win your love?'

She fought off a smile. He was so insistent – she felt her heart beating twenty to the dozen. She knew the Queen hated him, but then, the Queen treated her as if she was none too bright and her own mother said the Queen was merely jealous of her looks.

'My lord, I am too young to have such enemies. And I fear no one,' she said. 'But the respect of a knight such as yourself is – a worthy—' She was trying to think of a pretty speech.

He took her hand and kissed it – on the palm.

Her whole body reacted. She snatched the hand away, but she was suddenly warm. Her wrists tingled.

'Oh!' she said, and then backed away.

'Give me but the smallest token, and I will guard the shrine of love wearing it as a gage,' he said.

Emota had watched the older girls play this game. Holding his eyes, she untied the lace point on her left sleeve, and unlaced it, grommet by grommet. It was blue silk, made by her own hand, with a pretty silver point. She laid it across his palm. 'Warm from my body,' she said – shocked at her own daring, but she'd heard another of the Queen's ladies use the phrase.

The Gallish knight flushed. 'Ah – *ma petite!*' he said. 'I had no idea you were so practised in the game of love.'

Her heart was ripping along like a ship under full sail – she was overwhelmed, and at the same time that she felt like bursting with his attentions, she also wanted free of him. It was clingy, or sticky or merely—

His mouth descended towards hers, and she got a hand up, brushed his face lightly and ducked through his arms.

She ran.

Behind, she could hear him laugh. And no sooner was she free of him and a corridor away than she wanted him back. When she attended the Queen later, and they began the table arrangements for the Christmas feast, she glowed a little in her heart. And when the Queen cursed the perfidy of the Galles, Emota began to wonder.

Lonika – Duke Andronicus

Duke Andronicus looked at a table tiled to look like a chart of Thrake. 'You say he's east of Mons Draconis, at the edge of the Green Hills,' he snarled. 'Not on the coast to the east?'

Master Kronmir and Captain Dariusz, his master of scouts, stood before him. Dariusz kept glancing at the green-clad Thrakian with the traditional distrust of the scout for the spy. Seeing nothing on the other man's face, he turned back to the Duke.

'He's got half the regiment of Vardariotes with him, my lord, and I've lost men.' He stood stiffly, as soldiers do when forced to admit failure. 'He passed over the mountains like a spring flood in full spate, and I can't put men over the passes after him – they'll be snapped up.'

Demetrius nodded. 'So? Now the city is open to us by the coast road,' he said.

The Duke scratched his beard. 'Where is he going, do you think?' He whirled and faced Kronmir. 'And how could our special source be wrong?'

Kronmir shook his head. 'He's taken most of the guard troops – and some militia and stradiotes we lost in the fall.' He shrugged. 'He's surprised us. Not much use in assigning blame over it.'

The Duke looked at his son. 'How soon can we have a western

army together?' he asked. 'As Master Kronmir says – let's not trouble ourselves as to how we came to believe he wouldn't leave the city, or that he'd turn east to the coast.'

Demetrius shook his head. 'It'll be ten days before we have enough force to take him.'

The Duke shook his head. 'Make it five. And where does he get all this money? Christ Pantokrator, if the Emperor had this much ready silver, we'd never—' He paused.

Demetrius looked at the maps, 'He must be going for the fur caravans. That must be it. He'd have access to the Riding Officer's reports. Someone's talked. He may even know about the Galles.'

The men around the table looked at each other for as long as it took a winded man to draw a breath.

'Demetrius – go. Take all your guards, Kronmir, Aeskepiles. Do whatever you have to keep them from getting to Osawa.' The Duke made a face. 'Mother of God. I took for granted that he wouldn't march through Thrake. Kronmir, your palace report—'

'What if he goes for the Emperor?' Kronmir asked.

'Should we kill the Emperor?' Demetrius asked.

The Duke turned to Kronmir, and the two exchanged a long look.

'No,' Kronmir said. 'That would, at this point, only make *her* stronger. But move him to the coast, so that he's far from the scene of action.'

Albinkirk and the North Woods – Ser John Crayford

Ser Richard dismounted heavily and all but fell. When he walked from the mounting block in Albinkirk's citadel's main yard, he walked like an old man, with his left hand pressing against his backplate.

Ser John Crayford sat – fully armed – in his 'hall' with the Bishop of Albinkirk, two Hoek merchants, an Etruscan named Benevento Amato, and representatives of most of the fur trade companies in Alba. They all fell silent when Ser Richard entered.

Ser John stood. 'More giants?' he said, reaching for the mace that lay on the oak table.

Ser Richard shook his head. 'Boggles this time,' he spat. He collapsed into a chair brought by Ser John's squire. 'By the Lord's grace, gentles. I offer my apologies for the smell.'

Ser John met Ser Richard's eyes. 'Any losses?'

Ser Richard shook his head. 'We caught them well outside of the settlement area.' He sighed. 'I'm not the only knight who is tired. Ignore me, gentles. It was a small passage of arms, and we were victorious.'

The Bishop came over, placed a hand on him, and blessed him, and Ser Richard felt – *something*. Since being healed by Sister Amicia, he'd felt closer to God than he'd ever felt in his life, but...

'The Bishop was just saying we must take a convoy into the mountains to take the year's furs,' Ser John said.

Messier Amato rose and bowed. 'With all due respect to the church, my lords, I am not a rich man but I know this trade. My cousins are even now reaping the richest part of the trade at Mont Reale. But Ticondaga is an old centre for furs and other goods – Wild honey in particular.'

Ser John looked out the window. 'Albinkirk and Lissen Carak receive most of that trade,' he said.

'Ah, but this year that will not be the case. War will push the furs back north. And all of us here will go broke.' The Etruscan smiled. 'But if you will help us with soldiers – this has been done in the past, my pater assured me – if you would be so very kind as to assist us—'

Ser John nodded slowly. 'No,' he said. 'Next item of business?'

The Bishop came and sat by Ser John. 'I'd like you to reconsider, John.'

Ser John smiled a thin, don't-fuck-with-me smile. 'My lord Bishop, I'm quite positive that you know a fair shot of theology and perhaps some new learning, too. But right now, in case you aren't paying attention, we're fighting something close to a war. If the King hadn't sent half the court up here to wet their lances, we'd be in a sore straight. As it is, look at Ser Richard. Look at me. We're a-horse *every day.*'

The Bishop nodded. 'And you are uniformly victorious.' He nodded. 'I'd go so far as to say that this is more like a drill for your knights than a war.'

Ser Richard made himself sit up. 'By God, Bishop – fighting boggles is like child's play, but only until one gets its mandibles in behind your knee.'

The Bishop spread his thin hands. 'I mean no offence. But hear me. This town needs trade to live. Without that trade, the small farmers have no reason to farm and no town to sell their produce. You've taxed the foreign merchants to pay for new walls and new defences and *they've paid*. Now they need guards to go into the Adnacrags.'

'It's a month too late,' Ser John said flatly.

Amato spread his hands. 'Must I beg, ser knight? The ground is frozen, there's a little snow, and with good equipment and brave men we can be at Ticondaga in two weeks.'

'No,' said Ser John. But he had less conviction in his voice.

Men now prayed in the ferry chapel, reroofed. The ferry itself had a small fort on either side, with walls higher than a Ruk could scale, and signal towers. The work was all done in wood from the destruction wrought by the Ruk on the nearby forests, and the posts were built by the Captain of Albinkirk's archers.

As soon as they had the two forts finished there was a queue of men to man the ferry, and Ser John made it a military position and raised the toll. That money now went to the town.

He garrisoned the ferry forts, and left detachments of archers at six manor houses along the valley of the Cohocton, each with a knight or a senior squire, including Middlehill.

Helewise stood in the yard looking at Lord Wimarc. 'He's awfully young. Wouldn't you rather stay and help me hold my house yourself, old man?'

Ser John leaned down and took one of her hands, and she blushed. 'For shame – my daughter is watching. And what she sees from me is what she'll do.'

'I'd love to stay and help you hold this house,' he said. 'But I'm off north to Ticondaga. The Bishop convinced me it was my duty.'

'A pox on him, then.' She was going to cry.

He smiled. 'I wonder if you'd marry me. When I come back.'

She shook her head. 'You're just saying that.'

'Well, try it on your daughter. Listen, sweet – I must away. Wimarc's a good lad. If he says run for the town, you do that.' He bowed.

'I did last time, didn't I?' she answered, pertly enough. She stuck her chin in the air and kept being brave until he was out the gate.

Phillippa came and stood by her mother. 'He fancies you, Mama,' she said, with an air of troubled wonder.

Helewise laughed aloud. 'That he does, *ma petite*. He just offered to marry me.'

Phillippa watched the broad steel back riding away. 'But he's so old!' she said.

Ser John met Sister Amicia on the road, and they both dismounted. She had two other sisters with her and a pair of large men with axes. She grinned. 'I had what you might call a "passage of arms" and decided that a couple of large lads with axes were going to be easy on my conscience,' she admitted. 'Boggles. More than I was really ready to handle.'

He nodded, shook hands with the young men, who stammered and shifted their weight and looked nervous, and bowed to the two nuns.

'Thanks for the garrison at the ford,' she added. 'I've put far too much on Helewise, and I'm eating Middlehill Manor out of house and home.'

'I have offered to marry her,' Ser John said.

Amicia grinned. 'Good! It will make her happy, and help Phillippa. I love it when people are happy.' She raised an eyebrow. 'I hear dark things from the court,' she said. 'I'm worried for the King and Queen.'

Ser John shrugged. 'I can't lift my eyes off the problem at hand,' he said. 'It is all I can do to protect this place. And now I'm off to the Adnacrags.'

'The court's troubles are coming here,' Sister Amicia said. 'The Queen's best friend – Lady Mary – is coming to Lissen Carak. She's been sent from the court, and she doesn't want to go home to her father's lands out west. She's coming to stay with us.' She shrugged. 'The price of my celebrity, I think,' she said.

'Lady Mary? Hard Heart herself?' Ser John whistled. 'Here? Sweet Christ, my knights will all kill themselves and each other in a flood of glory. Best I get them on the trail.' He smiled. But the lines around his eyes and his mouth suggested that she'd added to his burdens.

'You are worried,' she said, somewhat uselessly.

He shrugged. 'In the spring, we fought the Wild, and bested them.' He gave her a wry smile and started walking back to his horse. 'I thought we'd won. I assumed we'd have time to recover. Now I think it was merely the first skirmish.' He looked at her, and said, his voice very low, 'Can you feel him?' he paused. 'Thorn?'

She paled, and then laughed unsteadily. 'Just for a moment, I thought you meant someone else. Yes, I can feel him – every moment. He thinks of us often.' She looked at the older knight, trying to decide how much to tell him. 'He has sent most of the things your knights are so busy killing. Is that what you wanted to know?'

Ser John shook his head. 'No – I mean, I assumed as much, sister. But I would like to know why? If he was, say, the lord of a nearby town – or the King of Galle – I could send him a herald, protest his war, and ask what might allow us to make peace. What does he want?'

Amicia was playing with the crisp linen of her wimple. 'As with most things, Ser John, it is complicated. And I see only through a glass darkly, and anything I say is only my own inference and deduction. But...'

She actually bit her lip.

'Try me,' said Ser John.

She leaned against her donkey's withers and the animal shifted and grunted. 'I don't think he knows himself,' she said. 'And worse yet, I think he's under the control of something else.'

Ser John kissed her ring and nodded. 'Thank God,' he said, 'I don't even know what that means. So I'll just go back to killing boggles. Pissing on fires. That sort of thing.'

'You are taking a convoy to Ticondaga?' she asked.

'Yes,' said Ser John.

She looked around. 'May I come?' she asked. 'I have a small matter to look into. And if you go so far north, you will need me.'

He didn't have to think that over. 'Come and welcome, sister.'

She laughed and he laughed with her, and they went their way.

The fur convoy left for the north after the sabbath. Ser John took ten lances and left Ser Richard to command Albinkirk. There were twenty heavy wagons in his convoy, all full of trade goods – some for Outwallers, to which he turned a blind eye, and some for the Earl and his people.

For fifteen leagues, they travelled on roads – good, for the first day. The second day, the roads began to narrow, and when they made camp thirty leagues north of Albinkirk in the foothills of the Adnacrags, on the south side of the West Kinatha ford, they were far enough into the Wild to listen to the wild wolves howl, to see eyes around their fires when the early darkness fell, to fear every noise on sentry duty, and to wear full harness on watch.

The West Kinatha roared down out of the High Peaks, full of new snow, and in the morning the younger men, already hesitant to leave warm blankets and big fires, stared with loathing at the rapid flow of icy water and the distant, snow-capped mountains.

Sister Amicia laughed at them, and her very graceful derision moved them faster than Ser John's curses.

Ser John got them all together, and their breath rose like the steam from their cauldrons of porridge. 'Listen up! Crossing a river in winter is ten times as dangerous as facing a charging boggle. If you fall in you could die. If you get your feet wet and you don't change your stockings and hose then you'll be uncomfortable for an hour, and then a little cold, and then very cold indeed – and then it can be bad. Take precautions. Keep your spares dry, and we'll keep fires on this bank until the last man is across. Be wary – and take as good care of your horse as of yourself.' He looked around. They seemed suitably awed.

His two advance lances crossed first – cleared a space by riding about in the dead grass of an old deer lie, and waved their success. Ser John put a line of experienced horsemen upstream to break the current for the greener men, and the nuns, and he and four veteran knights from Harndon rode into the rapids just south of the ford to catch the unlucky sod who went down in the rapid flow.

The wagons began to roll at full light, and an hour later the last supply horse was across, and the men in the river allowed their patient horses to pick their way over – then dismounted and rubbed their mounts down, drying them carefully before changing their own hose.

By the time nonnes would have been sounding in a monastery, they were across, and his squire, Jamie, rode up by him. The boy was grinning. 'That went well, didn't it, my lord?' he said. 'We're through the ford!'

'Aye,' said Ser John. 'Now we're in the Wild. With a winter river between us and safety.'

Northern Morea – The Red Knight

The Red Knight waved goodbye to most of his army at sunset and headed east into the low, wooded hills, snow-dusted and cold. He took Gelfred and the scouts and a handful of his household, Count Zakje and two dozen Vardariotes.

He handed over command to Bad Tom and Ser Jehan with a

casual wave of the hand. 'We know Demetrius and his cavalry are somewhere east of us.' He grinned. Gelfred smiled, too, and glanced at the hawk on his wrist. 'I intend to make contact with the Thrakians and brush them back.'

'Meaning you get a fight and we don't,' Tom said. 'Take me with you.'

The Duke shrugged. He wore only his breast- and backplate and his beautiful gauntlets and a steel cap with an aventail and a white wool hood. 'You keep everyone warm, Tom. I'll be back in a day.'

'Wouldn't it be better to ride by daylight?' Ser Jehan asked.

The Duke nodded. 'Yes. But also no. *A demain, mes braves!*' he said, and sixty mounted men leading sixty spare horses trotted off into the snow-covered hills.

The next morning, Mount Draconis rose to the west, a near-perfect cone, covered in snow, almost bare of trees. At their feet, the icy rocks of the Meander represented a barrier to advancing further. The arrival of an Imperial messenger bird at first light occasioned the impromptu officer's call.

'How many times do we have to cross this fucking river?' muttered Bad Tom. He was cold and tired and deeply frustrated by the lack of fighting. The night had been long, the wolves had howled, and already the growing feeling was that they should turn back. Six men had frostbite.

Ser Thomas sat with Ser Jehan and Ser Alison. Their horses were head to head, and their breath rose like smoke. Ser Gerald Random and Ser Bescanon sat off to one side, with the Imperial messenger.

Jehan looked at the Imperial messenger, an attractive young woman in black and white furs holding the newly arrived bird on her wrist. 'Where do they find them?' he asked wistfully.

Ser Milus laughed. 'Most attractive people, Moreans. But Christ, who would send a girl that young with an army?'

Bad Tom was rereading the message, sounding out the words. Reading was not his strongest suit.

Ser Alison leaned over and read aloud.

Gallish Army within one day's march. Cannot protect the Fur convoy. Request immediate assistance. Gallish Army five hundred men, with Outwaller allies. Assume siege train. Two hundred canoes, four large war galleys. Turkos–Osawa.

They had marched impossible distances in eight days – and found camp sites pre-scouted, and supply dumps of food in stone cairns. The company had lost two wagons, and crossed almost three hundred leagues of ground.

And now they had to cross the Meander for the third time, and there was no bridge.

'Anyone seen the Duke?' Sauce asked.

Ser Jehan shook his head. 'Gone with Gelfred at last light yesterday.'

Tom looked at the icy ford, the ruins of the old bridge, and the good road just a few hundred yards away on the other side.

'He ordered us to wait for him,' Ser Jehan said.

Tom looked at Gerald Random. 'Ser Gerald – I'm no big thinker, but mayhap this is your call to make and not mine.'

'Everything depends on those furs,' Random said. 'The Duke would say the same.'

Tom raised both eyebrows. 'Everything?' he asked.

'Your Captain's been spending all the profits of the spring on the Moreans, and betting *that* against having a monopoly on the fall furs to sell me,' he said. 'I backed his play. We need those furs, Tom. It's not just a fight.'

Bad Tom grinned in the way that made men uncomfortable – when all his teeth showed. 'All the better,' he said. 'Get me Mag.'

Mag looked at the wide river. 'A bridge?' she said.

Bad Tom grinned at her.

'I can't,' she said.

He looked away. 'Is this about me and Sukey?' he asked quietly.

'No, sir, it ain't, although if you want to have a quiet word about how I feel about the way you treat my daughter, I am, as John says, at your service.' She met his mad glare with her own.

Sauce shifted uneasily. 'Time's wasting, gentles. Tom, if we push half the horses into the stream—'

He shook his head. 'We'll lose too many lads, Sauce.'

Ser Milus laughed bitterly. 'Sauce, just think what it means when *Tom* hesitates to do something.'

Random scrunched up his face. It was cold, there was snow coming, and this was not a place to camp. 'Who here has built a bridge before?' he asked.

None of them had.

Random nodded. 'I have. Mag, all we need is three piers. I could mark them for you with flags. If you can put – I don't know, a pile of rock, a pillar? – fifteen feet wide, flat on top – on each spot then the lads can cut wood on the slopes over there and we have a bridge by nightfall.'

Mag measured it by eye. 'I'll try one, and we'll see.'

They made a miserable camp half a league back from the river, and built enormous fires, and ate dried food and drank hot water. Men heated rocks in the fire and put them at their feet to sleep. Men slept three under each blanket, in long rows like salt mackerel packed in crates. The army's women found themselves in high demand – for warmth.

Mag had two piers in place, but they required so much more effort than any casting she'd ever worked that she needed a night's rest to work on a third.

The sun rose, somewhere beyond the snow clouds. Her first pier had half-collapsed into the water. She hadn't built the web of the working clearly enough in her mind, and there were voids and soft spots in her rock.

Random sat by the riverbank with Bad Tom when she came out, rubbing her eyes and cursing the tight lacing of her second and third kirtles and the new pains in her hips which kept her from a good night's sleep. And the collapse of her pier. She was looking at it when she put her foot on an icy rock and down she went.

She was undamaged by the fall, but she rubbed her hip ruefully as the two knights helped her up. 'I've gone about this all wrong,' she said. 'The answer is ice.'

'Ice?' Random asked.

'The water wants to be ice already,' Mag said. 'All I have to do is stitch it together. I tried using one of Harmodius's workings – and I'm far from mastering it. But this is my old milk bucket in winter. In reverse.'

She raised her hands. In her right hand was the silver bodkin from her sewing kit, and she waved it, and the river flowed upwards, stilled and then froze into the form of three uneven piers supported a roadbed of solid ice. It was more organic than regular. But it was there. The two nearer piers were even supported by her earlier work with stone.

'I'll hold it until we're across. I'm sorry, Gerald. I should have thought of it yesterday.'

Random grinned.

Bad Tom grinned. 'Now we fight!' he said happily.

An hour later, the army was rolling across the bridge. Mag paled a little as the last three heavy wagons crossed, but the ice didn't crack.

'There they are,' Gelfred said. It was entirely unnecessary, as Demetrius's men did not have white wool cotes or horse blankets to hide them. They did have multiple horses, and they were moving fast along the valley floor below, raising a haze of fine snow as they went.

They had a baggage train with them – sixteen wagons and pack animals.

The Duke watched for as long as it took the sun to climb another finger, and then he belly-crawled back over the ridge and ran to his horse. A dozen Vardariotes were there, and Count Zac, and Ser Michael.

'He's a hot-head, yes?' the Duke asked.

White-clad horsemen swept over the low ridge that the road was climbing and loosed arrows from carefully warmed bows into the front of the Despot's fast-moving column. Three men went down, and their blood was like red smoke on the white snow.

An hour later, it happened again. This time six arrows went home. The enemy were all in white, with horse blankets and wool gowns that covered their weapons and armour. They were almost silent, and very hard to spot in the sunlight.

Demetrius took a nip of fortified wine and shook his head. The bright sun made it hard to see *anything* among the bare trees on the ridges. If he slowed down, he had no chance of winning the race to the crossings of the Meander. If he ignored these pin-pricks, he was going to lose men.

'Sabres,' he said aloud. 'Listen, Hetaeroi. When they come again let them come in close, and then charge. Everyone at them. Take me a prisoner.'

His own Thrakians nodded soberly. The Eastern mercenaries grinned.

An hour passed, as if the enemy had heard his plan, and he grew angry. When he halted to let his men eat, a single bolt from a crossbow – launched from high above – killed a pack horse. All the men took cover at once, but there were no more bolts.

As they mounted after their hasty meal, silent arrows fell like sleet from the increasingly cloudy sky, and there was no enemy on which he could vent his rage.

He gritted his teeth and led his men forward, putting a vanguard party almost five hundred paces ahead and another as far behind the wagons.

Count Zac shook his head. 'This is taking too long,' he said. 'Let's just fall on him.'

The Duke grinned. 'I'm enjoying myself, Zac. This is art. There's no hurry – the wagon trains will roll today, and the army is at the Meander. All we have to do is keep Demetrius off the ford.'

'Is waste,' Zac said. 'Waste of arrows. We have good ground and better horses.'

The Duke frowned. 'But why lose anyone? You know as well as I that almost every wound in this weather is a kill.'

Zac shrugged. 'But it's boring?'

The sun was starting its long slide to a bitterly cold darkness when the valley narrowed. Demetrius could feel the ambush coming, and he loosened the long, curved blade under his left thigh. His Easterners had kept their bows under their saddle blankets for a league.

His vanguard vanished into a hollow, and then turned, with two empty saddles, and galloped in a spray of snow back towards him. Just as they'd been told.

The apparently victorious enemy took the bait and followed, whooping, losing shafts at the rapidly retreating vanguard.

Demetrius's Easterners waited as the vanguard pounded back along the frozen road. The white-clad enemy came closer and closer to the column—

Demetrius winded his horn and the whole column exploded into motion – the Easterners swinging wide to the right and left, the Thrakian stradiotes galloping down the road. Captain Dariusz rode with his lord, watching the ridge to the south with obvious suspicion.

They pounded along the snow-covered road, but in fifty horse lengths it became obvious that the enemy were better mounted, and even in the cold, they fled over the snow faster than the Thrakian horses could catch them. And their arrows, loosed over the backs of their saddles, were deadly.

They pursued the enemy – Vardariotes, Demetrius was forced to conclude – over the next ridge. Then their horses were winded. So were the horses of the men they were pursuing, but Demetrius had played this game before. He had to ignore the insults shouted in three languages from the men he'd just chased. His three hundred men had failed to catch them.

A single man detached from the distant enemy raiders and trotted his horse across the open field towards the Despot and his men. The wind whipped at them and raised a fringe of blown snow, which burned men where it struck, and then the white-clad man was much closer. He had a red lance pennon and red horse furniture.

'Demetrius!' he called. 'Come and break a lance with me!'

Ser Tyranos put a hand on his sleeve. 'Do not!' he said.

Demetrius looked for his scout Prokrustatore. The man nodded. 'That's their Captain,' he shouted.

'What a fool,' Demetrius said. 'Tyranos, go kill him. Vardek, Vugar – either side. Take any shot you are offered.'

Ser Tyranos saluted. He took a lance from a stradiote and rode slowly towards the distant white figure. The two Easterners began to trot their horses out to the front, right and left, fitting arrows to their bows.

The enemy knight did not wait for Tyranos's arrival, but waved his lance – and charged.

His horse's hooves threw up spurts of snow, and the sound of the horse's hooves came, somewhat delayed, across the almost perfectly flat field. The wind had blown all but the frozen snow away, and the frozen ground was hard as rock, and the horse's hooves seemed to ring like distant bells.

Ser Tyranos realised the immediacy of the threat, lowered his lance, and put his own spurs to his tired horse.

They came together so fast that Demetrius couldn't see what happened. Except that the foreigner put Ser Tyranos and his horse down in the snow. And suddenly his figure seemed to blur – there was snow all around him, and a gust of wind struck the two Easterners and their first shafts were literally blown away.

The gust of wind raised a wall of blown snow that seemed as if it was full of ghostly figures.

'Ware sorcery!' Demetrius shouted. He had two decent practitioners, and the two men raised their shields, which glowed a ruddy hue in the setting sun. They were bright against the snow, and they sparkled.

Many of Demetrius's troopers made the sign of the cross, although other men made a different sign, like a pair of horns.

The front of blown snow opened to reveal a dozen Vardariotes led by Count Zac – ten horse lengths away, at full gallop. A ripple of scarlet shafts ripped into the front of Demetrius's force – and then they turned back into the arms of the convenient snow squall and vanished.

The sound of men's laughter licked at Demetrius like fire at a dry log. They were mocking him. But his force was intact, and the dozen men and horses he'd just lost were a small price to pay for the fifteen leagues he'd made. He turned his horse, and the hermetically driven blowing snow fell again to earth to reveal Ser Tyranos being led away in the distance, a prisoner.

Demetrius ripped his golden bassinet off his head and threw it in the snow in disgust. 'God damn it!' he said. 'Jesus *fucking* Christ! Change horses! Change horses! You – mage – what the fuck was that? Do I have to order you to do something about that?'

The two hermeticists stood silently by their horses. They both looked grey.

'Well!' he said, raising his sword.

'We daren't even try,' whispered the nearest.

Demetrius snarled. He was enough in possession of himself to know that killing half of his military sorcery might was not going to win him any battles. He snorted, whirled his horse, and trotted back to the remounts where Dariusz and three of his scouts were watching their back trail.

'What now?' he shouted.

Dariusz merely pointed.

In the valley behind them, fifty mounted men were leading their pack animals away. In the road, the wagons were afire, and the draught animals were all dead.

Count Zac shook his head. 'I agree – it is the very model of steppe fighting. But – it's dull. Now we wait until his horses starve?'

The Duke shook his head. He had a certain smug satisfaction about him that won him no friends – on the other hand, the little victory had been fun and most of the men had a warm place to sleep and free wine, courtesy of the Despot. 'No – now we get two hours' sleep and ride back to the army. Demetrius is done. Without baggage, he must retreat. We bring in the furs, and he goes home with his tail between his legs. And our prisoner – well the things we just learned!'

Zac laughed. 'You should let some of my girls have him, and you'll see a man tell a story!' he said.

The Duke shook his head. 'No – that would be unsporting. He had the balls to face me, and I won't see him tortured.' The Duke smiled and leaned back. 'Not exactly tortured,' he said. 'The fact that he clearly believes that's what he has coming will, of course, be used against him.'

'You like this too much,' Zac said. 'You think you are so smart.'

'Have some more hot wine,' said the Duke.

They rode back to the Meander, changing horses three times – all the horses were tired, and cold, and the temperature dropped off a precipice a little after moonrise. An enormous pack of coyotes shadowed them in the open ground just to the north, so that every man and woman in the little force could see what awaited a straggler – the coyotes were a byword for starving desperation, this time of year.

Men put on garment after garment – Count Zac displayed a marvellous kaftan of Vardariotes red, lined entirely in fox fur, with a hood.

The Duke hadn't had his drugs in two days. It was a fact of his military life – he couldn't be half-drunk and function as a commander, so he had to conserve his power and be prepared to contend with Harmodius. But the old magister had been polite, and fairly silent.

Around midnight, he spoke up.

Order a break, and we can warm the air. Air is easy. You are all but overflowing with ops. You used your powers very sparingly against Demetrius – that was well done. You are truly growing strong.

Is this a peace offering, Harmodius?

I have found another solution, Gabriel.

You have? How – you wouldn't lie to me?

I'd rather not. For that reason, I will not tell you my solution, but I guarantee that it will do you no harm, and that it will help your cause.

How could I object to that?

There was a pause so long that the Duke began to fear that the old man was gone. Fear?

Listen to me, Gabriel. I'm a selfish bastard, and I don't want to die – but there's more at stake than that. When I leave you, try and remember that we're allies. And as bona fides of my good intentions, you might take a look at your memory palace. I have – hmmm – ordered it.

Once, it would have been at the very limit of the Duke's abilities to ride through the snow and watch the ground around him while holding a conversation in the immaterial and focusing his will in the *aether* but his powers were magnitudes greater, and he plunged *into his palace.*

It had grown dark and shadowy the last few months, as he used more and more of the drugs to keep the old man at bay. Now it was clean and clear. And on the marble plinth in the centre of a rotunda the size of Hagia Sophia's in Liviapolis stood a statue of a woman – almost certainly Prudentia. She smiled.

Only a simualcrum, said Harmodius. *But when I am gone, I thought you might miss having something there. I had time on my hands. But I had access to many of your memories, and I made her as life-like as I dared.*

Gabriel looked at the sigils on the walls. *I see more than five hundred potential workings,* he said.

I arranged everything we know for you.

You terrify me, old man. Even now, I think I should drink the potion and shut you out.

Listen, boy. I have learned so much from living inside your head that I shouldn't— Bah. Suffice it to say, I could have taken possession of your perception of the universe any time I wished. But why? I wouldn't. I thought about it. But – I wouldn't do it. There are things to which even I will not stoop.

You don't want to become Thorn.

Not even Thorn wanted to become Thorn. That poor bastard is becoming nothing but a shell – a tool.

For whom?

There was another pause.

Call your halt, Harmodius said.

*

The Duke gathered all his force around him, and they packed the snow down with their horses' hooves, and then gathered all the horses in a dense pack at the edge of spruce woods that blocked the wind. It was so cold that breath caught in men's throats, and the coyotes gathered under the eaves of the ancient trees and howled. The horses shifted restlessly.

'Let's keep moving,' Count Zac said. 'It is too cold to rest.'

'Wait,' the Duke said.

The temperature rose in little jumps.

The air became warm enough to breathe comfortably, and then soldiers were pulling off their mittens and pulling feed bags over the horses' heads.

I didn't even know I could use the working this way, the Duke admitted.

Harmodius laughed. *So you believe me?* he asked.

The Duke bowed in the clean magnificence of his private rotunda. Not completely, Harmodius. But enough to enjoy this moment and accept your teaching with some humility. I want to cast it again.

Again?

For the coyotes.

What a strange man you are.

He put them to sleep, lest they run. Then he raised the temperature around them too.

I feel a certain kinship with them, the Duke said.

In the morning, the Duke's raiding party arrived at the edge of the Meander to find the remnants of a camp – felled trees, an abattis of beach and spruce, a palisaded citadel. There was a stone bridge abutment a third of the way across the Meander, and enough remnants of a collapsed ice bridge to suggest the means of crossing.

The Duke rubbed his two days' growth of beard. He glanced at Zac and shrugged. 'Mag built them a bridge. I can feel it. She froze the river and the whole army crossed.'

'We're out of food,' Zac said.

The Duke nodded. 'Best catch them today, then,' he said, and waved his sword hand.

The Meander froze, the ripples of his power moving at the speed of a swimming otter, the ice visible against the black of the water.

'Let's move,' the Duke shouted, and spurred his black charger down the bank.

Sixty men; one hundred and twenty-five horses. They crossed in minutes, and the Duke released his working.

'You are one scary fuck,' Count Zac said. He grinned. 'I'm glad you are on our side.'

The Duke looked pale. 'I'm not feeling very scary right now, Zac. Let's go.'

They caught the army at sunset, when they were already too cold, when men who'd hoarded a little dry sausage could have sold it for its weight in gold. The horses needed water, and two had already fallen and been left for the coyotes and the wolves – now they had the coyotes' larger cousins following them on the road.

But the army was encamped in an ancient legionary fort, four good earthen walls that the army had dug free of snow in the last hour, and there were tents lit orange by chimneys of stacked turf hacked from the ground with axes. An old fort like this one often had big piles of loose stone ready to be laid up into shelters or hearths.

The hillsides rang with the sound of axes as half the army gathered wood.

The Duke dismounted in the central parade and was embraced by Bad Tom.

It took less than a minute for him to understand the situation.

He winked at Random across the huge fire that lit the command area. He felt better immediately, for no other reason than that he was surrounded by friends. He found time with Harmodius very wearing.

Because the old magister scared him. *He could have me any time. I wouldn't even know.*

But surrounded by friends and warmth it didn't seem so bad. He reviewed Tom's decisions and found them good.

'If we push through, we can be at Osawa tomorrow by sunset,' Random said.

The Duke looked around. 'Well then – let's get what sleep we can.'

'Did you get a fight?' Tom asked. Heads turned – men looked at their Captain, or their Megas Ducas.

Father Arnaud frowned.

'Not really,' the Duke said.

Count Zac laughed. 'He rode off alone, right in among them, and challenged Demetrius to single combat. Oh, you should have seen him!'

Bad Tom glared at his Captain. 'But you didn't get to fight?'

Ser Michael laughed. 'Didn't he? He unhorsed Demetrius's uncle and took him prisoner in front of Demetrius's whole army!'

Bad Tom grinned. 'You're a loon. But you steal all the good fights, and that's not the place for a chieftain.'

The Duke shrugged. 'Tom, I wanted to take a highly ranked prisoner. That's all.'

Count Zac laughed aloud. 'Bullshit, Cap-tan! You want a fight – you ride out and fight!'

Tom crossed his arms. 'The Galles will gi' us a fight, anyhap.'

The Duke raised a hand. 'Not if I can help it. I plan to leave them a golden bridge to their boats.'

'What?' Tom roared.

'Is good *taktika*,' Zac said.

Tom's face twisted up in frustration. 'He's taking all the fun out of war,' he complained.

The Duke nodded. 'In the lists I'm happy to oblige another gentleman. But this is war. And while the Galles may want a fight, we want them to go home so we can save our furs for the Emperor.'

Ser Giorgios scratched at his beard. They were all dirty – no one changed clothes in that cold. 'I mean no insult,' he said. 'But men say that mercenaries avoid combat.'

The Duke shrugged. 'Sauce – can we have a little demonstration for these Morean gentry?'

She smiled. 'Anything. What do you want?'

The Duke drew his sword, and Sauce drew hers.

'You watching, Giorgios?' He lifted his sharp blade in a gliding thrust, two-handed, and Sauce's blade moved to slap the Duke's blade aside – but he slipped under her parry and the point of his sword just touched her chest. 'Did my blade avoid her blade?' he asked.

Ser Giorgios nodded. 'The better to win the fight,' he said.

The Duke nodded. 'Most warriors are amateurs,' he said. 'It should come as no surprise that they are threatened by those who make war a profession. We don't need to be manly or brave. All we have to do is win. There is no second place, and we get paid just as well whether we lose half our men or lose no men. Thanks, Sauce.' He nodded to the men and women in the fire-circle. 'Go to bed. Despite my best efforts, Tom may get his wish in the afternoon.'

Gelfred's scouts located the Gallish force by noon. Zac took both squadrons of the Vardariotes, less only a single file who guarded their remounts, and they vanished into a snow squall to the north while the army, all mounted, advanced up the coast of the unfrozen lake at a trot. The road was broad and paved in heavy stones, and even covered in snow was an easy surface for rapid travel.

They could see smoke rising in a dozen places.

By mid-afternoon, a pair of Zac's warriors had reported that the Galles were headed for their boats. There were no Outwallers with them, and the Southern Huran who lived in the towns near the northernmost Morean post were harrying the Galles every step of the way.

The Duke endured several hours of Tom's growing anger and then laughed aloud. 'Very well, Tom – take your pick of the men-at-arms and go bloody the protuberant Gallish nose.' He leaned forward. 'If it's not too much to ask, get some prisoners.'

Tom lit up like a lantern with fresh oil. He took a quarter of Ser Jehan's company and a quarter of Sauce's company – and another dozen chosen knights, including Ser Gavin, Ser Alison, Ser Michael, and Ser Alcaeus. And all the drovers.

They galloped away, headed north, behind Count Zac's screen of light horse.

The army continued, alternating their pace between the trot and the walk. It was cold, and speed meant less caution – most of the troopers had wet feet and some were wet through from exertion and a series of creeks and streams that they'd crossed without their usual precautions.

Jehan trotted at his Captain's side. 'What are we after?' he asked.

The Duke raised his eyebrows. 'Glory? Better pay?'

'You have that smug look of triumph,' Jehan muttered.

'Does it ever occur to you that in five hundred years they'll sing songs about us?' the Duke asked.

'Silence for the "Chanson of the Red Knight and the Adventure of the Avoided Battle"!' said Ser Jehan. He laughed. 'I think that this is your best work – taking Demetrius's baggage? Brilliant. And now – why even let Tom loose?'

The Duke nodded. The tower of Osawa was just visible on the horizon. 'Because he could be an unmanageable brute all winter if I'm not careful. And he has taken most of the men and women of his own stripe with him, and they'll tangle with the Gallish rearguard – Jehan, what the *fuck* are the Galles doing in Nova Terra?'

Jehan trotted along a few more paces. 'Here I was thinking that you knew,' he said. 'Silly me. You seem so well informed.'

'There have been reports. I wish the Emperor's spies extended to Galle.' The Duke nodded. 'I wish I had my own spies, and damn it, Jehan, I mean to have them! Anyway, you asked what I want. I want to find out what's happening – to get Gerald his furs and save our wages. And get the fuck out of the Morea, before it eats us alive.'

Bad Tom had taken a third of the best men-at-arms and their archers, and he was determined to press the Outwallers and their reputed allies as hard as he could – hard enough to provoke them to make a stand.

The Vardariotes made the first contact, north and west of him, fighting a stiff skirmish with crossbow-armed Huran and losing a man. Stefan Drusc, a tall, thin man who looked like a monk and had a beard to match, saluted with his long steel mace and made a face.

'Not for us, lord,' he said to Bad Tom. 'Formed infantry, big crossbows.'

Tom grinned. 'That's right, laddie. Just stay on our flank!'

He led the men-at-arms forward, angling to right across snow-covered Outwaller fields. The Drover and his clansmen had regular contact with this part of the world – the Green Hills were behind, them, the Wall just to their left. He'd traded cattle here, and raided for them, too. The Outwallers lived inside the Wall – but they were Southern Huran and no man's vassals.

By his side, Ranald shook his helmeted head. 'The Duke says there's Galles with them – that'll be heavy horse and drilled infantry in good armour—'

'Stop that noise, cousin. Let's have us a fight.' Bad Tom was watching the distant woodline intently, aware that he'd already made a mistake in letting his mounted scouts outrun his heavy column, eager for a fight.

He saw the crossbowmen before they loosed bolts.

'At them before they span!' he shouted, and his horse leaped forward.

The Hurans in the treeline broke the moment his cavalry charged them. The woodline was too open to stop the horses, and it was winter. They ran into the woods, and the knights and men-at-arms pursued them.

Ranald had the archers – led by Twinter and Long Paw and with a dozen veterans in enough armour to be called men-at-arms. He shook his head.

'Keep your visors open and watch the flanks,' he said. 'I mislike this.'

As they crossed the great snow-covered field, Tom and his men-at-arms vanished in the trees. The the north and south, he could see the red-clad Vardariotes trotting across the snow, watching their flanks.

All told, they had sixty men. Ranald waved his men forward faster, afraid he'd lose touch with his cousin and afraid, at the same time, of an ambush.

'Steady!' de Marche said.

The enemy cavalry – knights, they looked to be – were spread as thin as butter on bread, every man picking his own way through the deep woods. De Marche's sailors were two deep behind a low barricade of fallen trees. They watched the Huran run past them.

As arranged.

'Prepare to loose!' de Marche called.

The leader of the enemy, a huge man on a big black gelding, made his horse rear.

'Shoot!' he called, and forty crossbows crouched together.

The effect on the knights was not as shattering as it should have been, but the big man went down, his horse thrashing and turning the snow red.

'Span!' he called.

'Deus Veult!' called the Black Knight, and he charged at the head of a dozen of his own men-at arms.

Bad Tom was already fully aware of his folly before he saw the felled trees. Tom's creed didn't include pretence – he'd been had.

He reared his horse as he saw the Galles. They looked like professionals—

Damn, I loved this horse, he thought as six quarrels struck the gelding. The horse crashed to earth, already mortally wounded.

Tom rolled clear, armour causing him more injury than the fall. He got to his feet and found his sword was still by his side.

They had cavalry.

Tom shook his head at his own foolishness even as the enemy knights shouted their war cries.

Then he grinned. It was, after all, a fight.

Francis Atcourt – easily identifiable with his red panache – rode to his rescue. The enemy men-at-arms – all appallingly well mounted for a fight in the wilderness – were coming from the left, and Atcourt joined three more company men-at-arms at a canter.

Tom watched them with solid satisfaction, as, badly outnumbered, they couched their lances and picked their men, closing from a spread pursuit formation to a compact melee formation in fifty strides of their horses.

The Galles – he assumed they were Galles – struck. They had about a dozen knights, and at the moment of impact, Ser Francis Arcourt and one of the company's few Gallish men-at-arms, Phillipe le Beause, each cleanly unhorsed a man. Chris Foliak killed his opponent's horse and then swept his lance unsportingly sideways like a toll gate, taking another Gallish knight down. But Ser John Gage was unhorsed by a man as big as Tom himself.

Foliak, a canny fighter, didn't slow his horse, but burst through, dropped his lance, and rode back south, away from the fight.

Atcourt hesitated, and was surrounded in a moment and unhorsed by three different men catching his bridle and wrestling him from his saddle.

Phillipe de Beause managed to put his dagger into another man and his horse – bigger, or perhaps better exercised – pulled him clear of the stour by main force. He saw Tom and rode to him—

Twenty crossbows spat together, and Beause died in an instant.

Tom's other men-at-arms were rallying to the north. He could hear Ser Michael's voice.

One of the enemy knights raised his visor and pointed his lance at Tom. 'Yield,' he said.

Tom laughed. 'Usually we fight first,' he said. He wished he had an axe.

The Galle charged him immediately, his great horse sending gouts of snow into the still air. His lance tip came down like a swooping falcon, and Tom uncurled and cut the last three feet right off the lance. His backhand carved a hand's breadth of meat off the horse, and it turned, panicking at the pain.

Tom cut again, ignoring the rider and cutting deeply into his horse's near side back leg.

The horse toppled.

Another Galle charged Tom.

Bad Tom set himself in a new guard to wait the lance, but this man had seen his trick, and he didn't couch his lance at all. He rode forward, and he only lowered his lance at the last second.

Tom batted it aside and cut into the horse's neck and was knocked flat as the rider moved the horse to his own right. But the cut landed – the horse slouched and fell.

Tom got up.

A thrown lance hit him like a thunderbolt in the side, the head piercing his mail. He staggered.

'*Deus vault!*' roared the big knight as he thundred by. He turned his horse and came again, this time with a long-handed steel mace.

He cut – the expected cut, a heavy fendente from his right hand, and Bad Tom caught it on his sword and was staggered by the sheer strength of the man – but not so staggered as to not let the blow slide off his parry like rain off a steep roof, and counter-cut as the horse went by. Again, he struck the horse, who screamed.

The other knight reined in. Crossbowmen were coming up.

'This is a mere butchery of horses,' he said.

'Get off yours and we'll make it a butchery of men,' Bad Tom said.

'You are a fine man of arms. May I ask your style?' asked the enemy knight.

'I'm Ser Tom Lachlan of the Hills,' Bad Tom said.

'I am Ser Hartmut di Orguelleus,' the other man said. He waited. 'The Black Knight.'

Tom shook his head. 'I think you're waiting for your crossbowmen to come and kill me,' he said.

Ser Hartmut laughed. 'Of course!' he said. 'Why would I not? There is no such thing as a fair fight.'

Tom charged him. He roared, 'Lachlan for Aaa!' and ran as fast as his injured hips would allow.

But Ser Hartmut only let him come two paces and then pricked his horse into motion. The Black Knight's mace cut – Tom's blade rose.

Both were deceived, and thus, both struck.

Tom took the mace in his left pauldron, and was knocked to the ground.

Ser Hartmut took Tom's thrust on his breastplate, and was unhorsed. The difference was that Ser Hartmut rose uninjured beyond the blow to his dignity.

Bad Tom had taken the worst wound of his life.

Ranald entered the woods at a walk, his archers in a compact mass behind him. He could hear the fighting now – hear it in three places. But even winter woods blocked enough of his sight to keep him from understanding.

He heard Tom's battle cry and went at it. But even then he didn't surrender his caution. He trotted, visor open, looking left and right.

He saw the crossbowmen first, and then he saw Tom, alone, on one knee.

He turned to Long Paw. 'Cover me!' he yelled, but most of the archers were already sliding off their mounts, valets taking the horses in their fists even as the archers pulled their stung bows over their heads.

Ranald took his lance out of the bucket in his right stirrup and put his spurs to his charger.

Just off to the right, he saw the flash of winter sun on metal.

There were three knights – in a glance, he knew that none of them were company. And they were between him and his cousin.

He rode at them – reached up and slammed down his visor, and all four of them went to a gallop – no mean trick in snowy woods.

Six strides from contact, Ranald changed targets – his horse took a beautiful cross-step to take both of them a yard off line – and Ranald leaned forward as if he was in a Harndon tiltyard and his man went flying. A spearpoint struck his breastplate, but it didn't bite – and the tip rode up the V-shaped reinforcement and shot past over his right shoulder, ripping the round pauldron from his body as it passed but doing no other damage.

Ranald didn't turn.

Ten yards behind him, Chris Foliak's lance unhorsed a second man before Foliak's horse lost its footing in the now and went down in a spectacular spray of snow and dead leaves.

Ranald raced for his cousin.

Tom was on one knee, apparently unable to rise, defending himself with two-handed parries. A huge knight – at least as big as Tom himself – cut again and again with a mace – paused and hurled it like a lightning bolt.

Tom missed his parry and the thrown weapon struck his visor, deforming it.

The big knight drew his sword, and it burst into flame, and the crossbowmen yelled a cry, revealing themselves.

Ranald had time to think, *Christ, there's a lot of them.*

The first ranging arrow from Long Paw's bow struck a crossbowman. Behind him, Ranald could hear Foliak fighting, sword to sword.

There were fights scattered all over the woods, now – the Vardariotes were rolling in from the flanks, and suddenly it was his to win. But he needed to get the giant off his cousin, first.

Ranald put his lance at the big knight's back, but, a heartbeat from impact, the man writhed like a snake. He was still struck, but it was uncanny how he avoided most of the blow.

But his great burning sword never touched Tom, who managed to get back to his feet as Ranald swept past, reining in all the way.

Tom cut, a rising cut from a low guard, and the Black Knight snapped his own sword contemptuously at the blow – and severed Tom's sword at the midpoint.

Tom stepped off line and hurled his ruined weapon like an axe at the Black Knight, who had to step back and parry – and still took a ringing blow to the head from the hilt.

Tom drew his dagger.

A full flight of arrows from the company bowmen fell like a snow squall. The enemy soldiers stood their ground, took hits, and replied with a volley of bolts.

The Black Knight raised his burning sword—

'Get out of the way, you loon!' Ranald roared, and hip-checked his cousin.

He had a great axe – a long-hafted axe with a beard so long that it had its own poll on the shaft, the great vicious thing like a half-moon of steel on a five-foot haft. It was the axe Master Pye had made him.

Tom collapsed to one knee.

Ranald stepped past his cousin as the Black Knight threw a heavy blow – a simple fendente from his right shoulder, but with the power of a warhorse.

Ranald parried, the axe close to his body.

The two weapons met with a *clang* that rang through the woods.

'So!' the Black Knight said from inside his helm.

Ranald stepped forward, the axe out behind him like a long tail. As the Black Knight didn't flinch, Ranald cut.

Fast as a leaping salmon, the Black Knight's blade leaped to meet the axe—

Ranald rolled the great axe head – his blow a feint – and thrust with the butt spike, striking the Black Knight's hand, and locking his own haft across the Black Knight's left wrist.

He stepped forward and used the lever of the axe haft to throw the bigger man to the ground.

Quick as a cat, the Black Knight cut – flat on his back – and his burning sword cut deep into Ranald's left greave.

The Black Knight *rolled backwards* over his own head like an acrobat and came up on his feet.

Ranald could scarcely think from the pain.

The Black Knight flicked a salute. 'I think my archers have been bested by yours,' he said. He was backing away. 'And my useless dogs of allies have all run home. I'll see you another day, sir knight.' He took another step back, and another.

Ranald wanted to follow him, but there was blood all over the ground, and it wasn't Tom's.

The crossbowmen broke.

Their leader, a man in good armour, tried to rally them until he saw Ser Michael coming with a dozen men-at-arms and as many Vardariotes, and then he threw a leg over his own horse and rode for it.

Ranald tried to wrap his own wound, and, eventually, Francis Atcourt joined him.

'What happened to you?' Ranald said.

Atcourt smiled. 'Someone hit me on the head,' he said. 'Luckily, he didn't stay around to take me prisoner.' He watched the Galles. 'Who were they? They were – very good.'

'Better than me,' murmured Tom. 'Christ risen, who was that loon?'

Five leagues to the west and two days later, Bad Tom stood atop the main tower of Osawa's fortifications, peering through the light snow down the lake as if to summon the Galles back to their duty. In the yard below them, the largest fur convoy Morea had mustered in twenty years shook itself out and started into the hills, carefully watched by most of the Imperial Army.

Bad Tom stomped his feet and frowned.

'Cheer up, Tom,' the Duke said. 'We'll find someone else to fight.'

Tom swore and strode down the many steps to his horse. The Duke followed him down.

'War of manoeuvre? I'm no fool – you out-manoeuvred the Galles and only the ambush gave them a fight. But—' He shrugged. 'A war without fighting?' Tom spat the words. 'And Ranald got everything yesterday, and I got beat.' He looked down. 'And lost Phillipe.'

Ranald had been magicked and bandaged and he was still pale. Bad Tom had bounced back. But Ranald was the hero of the hour, and Tom was public in his thanks.

'You saved me, cousin, and there's not many men as can say that.'

Ranald looked sheepish.

'I want another go at that Black Knight. Nor will you beat the Thrakians with fancy manoeuvres.'

The Red Knight laughed and put a hand on his friend's shoulder. 'Tom, there will be plenty of fighting in the spring. For which, I need you to go home to the hills and raise your kern. Bring every thane and kern you can muster and the whole of the drove to the Inn of Dorling when the ice clears the roads. Spend the rest of the winter healing. You're hurt.'

Lachlan nodded. 'That I am.' He could walk, but both hips hurt; he could move his right arm, but his left arm – even after powerful magery – felt like ice.

'You giving me an order?' Bad Tom scowled.

The Duke shook his head. 'No. No, I'm not. I'm asking – as Megas Ducas to the Drover.'

Bad Tom nodded. 'There's many a slip. But I'll go. There has to be a Drover. And if I can, I'll be there.'

'The Wyrm will help,' the Duke said.

'My cousin'll help, I hope.' Tom turned to Ranald.

The Duke sighed. 'Tom, Ranald may feel he needs to go west to

Lissen Carak. Lady Mary has been sent from court, and is even now riding up the Albin to spend Christmas at the nunnery.' He handed Ranald a dispatch and smiled. 'It's good to have a spy service. I'm going to miss it. Kneel, Ranald.'

Ranald looked at him. 'Why?' he asked. He looked at the snow, which looked muddy, and cold. His leg hurt.

'Because it's customary when being knighted,' the Duke said.

Chapter Fourteen

Princess Irene

Liviapolis – The Princess

Lady Maria stood in the informal throne room with the scrolls in her sewing basket.

'The Megas Ducas is – apparently – on his way home,' she said. 'He sends word that he'll be back in a week.' She raised her eyes. 'He bids you prepare for Christmas.'

'My father is still a hostage?' the princess asked.

'He has been treated very badly,' Lady Maria said. 'The Megas Ducas bids you not lose hope. The Emperor has been moved further into the mountains, he says.'

The princess turned her head and sobbed, 'What!' and then burst into tears.

Acting Spatharios Darkhair pushed forward. 'What's happened? And where?'

Maria opened a chart. 'It is fiendishly complicated. The Megas Ducas went west almost to the Green Hills and outmarched Andronicus to western Thrake. He defeated Demetrius, who retreated. Andronicus raised an army and then dispersed it.'

Ser George Brewes nodded. 'Of course. He didn't have a supply train.'

Darkhair chortled. 'But we did!' he said.

Lady Maria permitted herself a small smile. 'We did.'

Brewes whistled. 'So – the furs were a feint all along.'

Lady Maria raised her voice so the princess, sitting disconsolate on her throne, could hear. 'No, gentlemen. The main army marched north along the lake and will – apparently – escort the furs south.' She ran her eyes over a fourth dispatch, and shrugged. 'This says there is a Gallish force on the Inner Sea that our Megas Ducas expects will retire at the sight of our banners, but I have difficulty believing there are Galles on the lake. At the edge of winter? There have been reports, but this still seems to me to be a scribal error.'

The princess shook her head. 'But he said he was going east!'

Ser George Brewes bit his tongue. He managed a smile and said, 'Either way, it's a neat campaign. And we'll have a bonny Christmas.'

Far, far to the north, Ser Hartmut watched bitterly as his galleys raced into the light snow. Already, the mouth of the lake had ice that needed to be broken.

They'd burned two towns of wicker huts and hide houses. He had nothing else to show for all his military might, and he'd been forced to retreat when an army – a magnificent army – had appeared over the hills to the south.

'Three lacs d'amour,' he said to de Marche, shaking his head. 'Who was that?'

De Marche groaned. 'Do you know the story of the King's attempt on Arles?' he asked.

Ser Hartmut looked back through the snow. '*That* captain? Ah, Master de Marche. I will need to look to my arms in order to teach him some manners. That will win me the King's love.' He rolled his shoulder against the stiffness. 'Those were good men-at-arms. As good as my own.'

'You didn't lose a man. I lost six sailors.' De Marche was fed up with war.

Ser Hartmut shrugged. 'Fortuna. If their horse-archers had pressed harder, we'd all have been taken. The ambush was a pointless fanfaronade – I admit it.'

De Marche let go the breath he'd gathered to speak his mind. Instead, he asked, 'I assume that operations are done for the winter?'

'You mean, if we are not all caught in the ice and crushed like bugs by the winter?' Ser Hartmut said. 'You wouldn't try sailing home at this time of year?'

'Christ on the cross!' de Marche said. 'No, my lord, I would not. I'll pull my ships off the water and brace them and perhaps even build them sheds, if the weather allows me.'

'Good. And we'll train the natives. They have much to learn from us,' Ser Hartmut said. 'We"ll teach them to be braver.'

De Marche knew that fully two-thirds of their Outwallers had left them after two days of fruitless combat, leaving only the Galles and a handful of loyal stalwarts to face the rising Morean tide. By Outwallers standards, they had been exceptionally loyal allies, fighting after it was clear that the Moreans and the Southern Huran had the upper hand.

But he looked at Ser Hartmut, and said nothing.

Liviapolis – Master Kronmir

It had been one of the coldest rides of his life. Kronmir lost the little finger from his left hand as soon as he found a doctor, and it took him three long days to get warm again, even among the civilised hypocausts of Liviapolis.

Master Kronmir posed as a wealthy merchant this time, and he rented rooms at the Silver Chalice, an inn much frequented by Etruscans and other foreigners.

The army was still absent from the city, and he made his rounds as soon as he felt warm and secure. He spent half a day making purchases, merely to assure himself that he was not being followed, and then he visited his best agents and left them Christmas presents – amulets fashioned by Aeskepiles. He left them coded instructions for the use of the amulets and his warmest wishes for the New Year, and then he began cautiously probing for a malcontent among the newly recruited sailors at the now-thriving Navy Yard.

The malcontent was a fool, and a dangerous, malicious fool – the worst sort of agent. But Kronmir had little choice. He used the tool to hand. And he had to meet Snea, the fool, in person – he couldn't be trusted to a cut-out – and that was dangerous.

Kronmir was taking chances. And he knew, as few men really did, where that path had to lead.

South of N'gara – Nat Tyler

Tyler left the Faery Knight's castle at the break of day, well aware of what kind of trek awaited him. There was no force to hold him, and he walked free of the hold's magicks, not quite fleeing. When he crossed the hold's not-quite-visible sanctuary line – the border of the lord's power – he saw moths out in the snow, a hundred or more of the things fluttering weakly against the bitter cold among the trees, like snowy owls without heads. He didn't like them much as an omen, and he liked them even less when two followed him.

Perhaps it helped him that he didn't particularly care whether he lived or died.

At some point in the past, he'd known how much of this was on his own head, but he'd had weeks to revisit his version of events, and by the time his feet were crunching along on frozen snow, supported by the web of rawhide thong on rackets that the Outwallers used, he no longer thought about Bess, or how long he'd loved her. He kept his thoughts fixed firmly on the uselessness of the younger generation of Jacks, not one of whom had wanted to accompany him.

I'll free the poor serfs if'n I have to do it myself, Tyler said. *And a pox on Bill Redmede and that harlot.*

He made it a day on anger, and another. Anger burns very clear in the winter. And the weather was as kind as winter can be – clear and cold, yes, but without the sudden thaw that might have killed a man travelling alone. Tyler was no fool, for all that he was consumed with jealousy and rage, and he made camp early, gathered immense piles of brush and dry wood – easy enough with the snow four feet above the forest floor. He camped under downed spruce trees, or built shelters of spruce bows, and he had his Outwaller sleigh – he pulled it himself – on which to lie on a thick pallet of skins. The wood of the sleigh and the layers of fur and the warmth of the fire kept him alive, and every morning he fried a piece of his frozen bacon and prepared to face another day. He expected to be fifteen days crossing the Wild, if he was lucky; by the time he reached the villages around Albinkirk he'd be out of food and desperate.

If he lived that long, it would be a wonder. But he couldn't stay and watch the remnants of the Jacks betray everything they stood for. They would soon turn Bill Redmede into a lord and follow the Faery Knight into servitude.

On his third night on the trail, he downed a deer with his bow and tracked it by blood spore across a ridge. He was late making camp and not as careful as he might have been – worried, more than anything, that he'd felt something give in his bow when he drew to his ear in the deep cold. He gathered firewood in a near frenzy, and sweated too much into his clothes, for which he'd pay in the deep darkness of midnight when the slick of sweat next to his skin turned to a pool of ice water.

But full darkness found him cooking deer meat in front of a respectable fire, and he'd made a good shelter in the lee of a downed, dead tree that had fallen in a windstorm and taken its roots with it, so that the roots made a wall and an overhang, studded with rocks big enough to split his skull if they fell on his head. But there was room enough to wedge his little sleigh in place and he sat on it, eating hot meat and drinking hot water.

He heard the crunching of footsteps on the snow when it was far too late. He rose to his feet, wondering who, or what would be out in this weather, at this time of year, and then there was a man – tall and straight, with thick white hair tied back with a quill-wrapped thong. The man wore a heavy robe of squirrel skins that was as black as the night around them, and he bore a staff that seemed to be made of iron, and he had no gloves.

'May I be welcome at your fire?' asked the man.

Nat Tyler had walked the world a long time. He got his sword hilt under his hand and then turned. 'You ain't no man, to need my fire. Whatever you are – if you are a guest, take a guest's oath.'

The black-clad man bowed. 'You are wise. I will do no harm at this fire, or indeed, to the fire's maker,' he said.

Tyler nodded. 'I've sassafras tea, if'n you have a mind to it,' he said.

'Do you know who I am?' asked the figure.

Tyler nodded. 'You smell like Thorn, to me,' he said.

The figure rose and bowed again. 'You *are* wise. Wiser than your comrade, who betrayed me.'

Tyler crossed his fingers inside his mitten. 'I ain't no friend o' Bill Redmede's just now, Warlock, but he never *betrayed* you. You wanted dominion. We want *no one* to hold dominion over others. We was allies. And you wasn't much of an ally to us.'

Thorn's gaze was steady across the fire. 'Nonetheless, you are leaving Redmede. With plans of your own.'

'I am,' Tyler admitted.

'I could use you,' Thorn said.

Tyler smiled toothlessly. 'Aye, Warlock. I imagine you could *use me*. But I'd rather not be used.'

Thorn laughed mirthlessly. 'You are a bold rogue, and I am out of practice in such converse. What do you want, to do my will?'

Tyler took a deep breath. He let it out slowly, and watched as it turned to white mist. He wondered how many breaths he had left. 'I doubt you have anything I want,' he said.

'What if I told you that your Bess only loves Bill Redmede because the irk lord has cast a glamour on her? And on your friend? They aren't even acting under their own wills. They are puppets.'

A stick snapped. Something let out a very animal-like grunt and Tyler stood up and drew his sword – an absurd motion when he was sitting across the fire from Thorn, who was unmoved.

A third figure glided into the firelight.

'*Ill met by firelight, tressssspasssser.*' Tapio's fangs glinted like metal. '*You are a fine one to ssspeak of puppetsss. Man, you accept ssstrange guessstsss at your fire.*'

Thorn turned his head. 'Tapio. You are very foolish, coming out of your circle of power.'

'*Not-a-man, you are very far from your own, do you not think?*' The irk stood easily on the snow.

Thorn rose and faced it, holding his staff before him. 'Shall we have our contest now?' he asked.

The irk shrugged. '*I would regret killing this man, who is my guest friend.*'

Thorn didn't move, even so much as an eyebrow. The shape of Speaker of Tongues was his perfect cloak – it looked like the body of a man, and yet had a thousand pockets to hold surprises.

He drew one and threw it.

Tapio flicked it away in the twitch of an eyebrow. '*I could help you, Thorn,*' he said.

'Help me? We are foes!' Thorn said, reaching for a more subtle preparation to cast.

Tapio gestured again, a slight wind passed, the fire flared, and Thorn's casting dissipated among the stars, impotent. '*I have had thoussandsss of yearsss to perfect thiss,*' he said. '*We need not be foesss.*'

Thorn's staff crackled and a wave of green and black shot out, mottled like mould. It passed through Tapio, who vanished.

'That was far easier than it should have been,' Thorn said. 'I distrust even victory.'

'*You have gained in wisssdom, then, Thorn.*' Tapio's voice seemed to come out of the air. '*Master Tyler, I came to keep you free of thisss – entanglement.*'

'Yes, this cruel little elf has made your lady-love a strumpet and broken your friendship and has come to help you,' Thorn said.

The irk's laughter rang on the clear, cold air. '*Cruel little elf! Ah, my pooor friend. You reek of Asssh.*'

Thorn moved, and the irk was suddenly outlined in a pale green light. Thorn's staff shot out – there was a flash, and then another – a sound like distant thunder, and the tree behind Thorn burst into a thousand splinters – some of them quite large. One penetrated right through Thorn's man-form. But it was a form, not a man, and Thorn paid the wound no heed as he worked again, and the very air became pellucid – Tyler could not breathe, but only watch. It seemed that only Thorn could move, and the tongues of his dark fire licked at the irk's form . . . and then something gave. It felt to Tyler as if the whole world missed a beat, and suddenly he was alone at his fire, heart in his throat, choking.

Well off to the east, perhaps ten miles away in the rugged hills he'd crossed on the way from the disaster at Lissen Carrak, there was a rumble like a mighty avalanche, and the flash of green-tinted lightning was followed by pulses of lavender lightning, and then the thunder carried – crack, crack and then a rumbling like the sound of a mighty army on the march.

Tyler threw more wood on the fire. He shivered, pulled his blankets closer, and sat with his sword across his knees. He was reasonably sure it wouldn't stand him in any stead against either foe, but he felt more comfortable having it ready.

Distant thunder mocked him. He had time to ponder Thorn's words. To imagine Bess, ensorcelled, locked in Redmede's embrace.

I'll show them, though.

He threw more wood on his fire, and then Thorn was back – the long spruce splinter still transfixing him. The warlock gestured. 'I will show you a secret,' he said.

'I want none of your secrets,' Tyler said. 'Did you defeat the irk?'

'Of course,' Thorn said. 'What a foolish question. Listen, man. You will die here. Or at your next camp, or your next. Winter is a more formidable foe than either Tapio or Thorn and you have neither the training nor the fortitude to defeat it. I, too, seek the death of Alba's King. Let me help you live to try it.'

Tyler felt the cold all around him. Sometimes, even when you know you are being manipulated, you have very few options. *Flow with the river.*

'Very well,' he said. 'I've got a long spoon.' He managed a brave grin. 'Like I always say, needs must when the devil drives.'

Thorn's human form seemed to frown. 'Yes,' he admitted. 'Come.' He held out his hand.

'I'll need my kit,' Tyler said.

Thorn's face remained unchanged. 'Very well.'

Tyler gathered his blankets and what remained of his food, including frozen portions of venison. His cold fingers were not quick, and the darkness hindered him at every turn. 'I could use some light,' he muttered.

'Make a torch, then. I do not make light.'

Eventually he was done, and he pulled his toboggan to where the sorcerer stood with a four-foot length of wood through his body. Some of his entrails had been blown out of his back and a length of spine showed.

Tyler shuddered.

'Take my hand,' Thorn said.

'Where are we going?' Tyler asked.

'An excellent question. We are going through the *aether* to an entrance to the Serpent's Walk.'

Mont Reale – Ser Hartmut Li Orguelleus, the Black Knight

The Gallish fleet turned into the Great Huran River out of the lake in good order. They camped for three days, built great fires, got warm and ate sparingly. The Black Knight took every precaution to prepare his men, and he ignored de Marche's whining, assembled his men, and gave his orders.

The fleet sailed after mass on a Sunday, and he kept them moving through the night, with oil lamps in the sterns of his four war galleys and exhortations and occasional trumpet calls, and as the sun rose on Monday, he looked over the stern of his own *Saint Michael* and counted the boats, and reached a satisfactory number.

'Now, we will see something, I think,' the Black Knight said.

Oliver de Marche elected to try one more time. The loss of his servant left him without a confident translator – Lucius had been killed by the Imperial troops who'd materialised out of the snow and wrecked the Black Knight's already precarious campaign against the Southern Huran. With Lucius at his side, he could have attempted to contact the Northern Huran leaders directly.

But de Marche had little choice, so he put on a bold face and climbed the steps to the quarter deck. 'Ser knight?' he asked. 'Ser Hartmut?'

The Black Knight gave him a hard smile. 'Ah – merchant. Come to dissuade me? Eh?'

De Marche nodded. 'Ser knight, it cannot help the King or your own reputation to do this.'

Ser Hartmut laughed aloud, and the sound was fell. 'Merchant, I am called the Black Knight for a reason, and what I am about to fashion will suit my reputation exactly. Indeed, what I do, I do in part so these beasts of the woods will know me – and fear me.'

'They will fear you, and being brave, then they will make war on you,' de Marche said.

'Brave? De Marche, I would have had the Southern Huran in the palm of my hand if those cowards had done my bidding. Even without them—'

De Marche bit the end of his moustache and planted his feet. 'Either way, you never had a chance against a professional army and a string of well-supplied forts. Seizing Osawa was beyond you, so taking Ticondaga is a goal as far over our heads as that bird. We would not have taken Osawa, even if the Outwallers had thrown themselves at its walls like automatons. You seek to make them bear the weight of your – of *our* – own failings.'

De Marche braced himself for death.

The Black Knight's rage passed over his face like a shower on a sunny day – passed over, and was gone. Ser Hartmut fingered his beard, 'You are a good blade, de Marche. I have learned to respect you – you are not one of us, but you are no coward. But in this, you are a complete fool. These Outwallers are not worth a fart, as my men – and yours – will demonstrate in an hour. And in the spring I will take some of them and train them as soldiers – real soldiers – as I did in Ifriqu'ya. They will learn, and they will obey.'

De Marche fought an urge to shout, or tremble. 'You cannot storm Mont Reale. It is the largest Outwaller settlement in the north. Even the armies of Alba have never attempted it, not at the height of the old King's power. Nor the Moreans.'

'More fool they. Watch and learn, merchant. Your way might work, but it is too slow.' The Black Knight brushed a pair of moths away from his helmet. 'When the ice clears in spring, we will have another fleet coming down the river bringing me more soldiers. Men who will follow me willingly, for loot, for plunder – perhaps even for God.' He smiled, and his smile was the final nail.

'You will get us all killed!' de Marche shouted. The moths flitted away. 'You will incur the wrath of God and every decent man!'

Ser Hartmut laughed. 'Listen to me, merchant. I am a man of honour, and I live by the rule of war. I will do this openly, not in the dark, and my message will be loud. I do exactly what the Moreans have done, what the Albans have done – indeed, what every *man* has done since men first came to Nova Terra. Outwallers are not men. They are outside the walls of the church and of civilisation. Their deaths will not even leave a stain on our blades.'

'You are insane!' spat de Marche.

A pair of marines grabbed him from behind.

'This has been said to me before,' said the Black Knight. 'Yet kings continue to employ me. So which of us is really insane, do you think?'

Mist was still rising from the Great River when the fleet drew even with the island at Mont Reale, and Ser Hartmut took the flag of Galle from one of his squires and was the first man over the bow, splashing through the shallow water and up the beach. A handful of early risers from the massive Outwaller town came down to help the Galles land, and Ser Hartmut brushed past them as his marines formed up behind him and de Marche's sailors, as eager as the soldiers, knelt in the gravel, were blessed by a priest, and then picked up their weapons.

An Outwaller boy threaded in among the sailors. He saw something he liked, and a quick hand darted out – he took a dagger, and ran, laughing.

One of the marines raised a crossbow and casually shot him in the back. The bow was one of the new steel varieties and the bolt ripped through the boy and tossed his small body several yards. The shamefaced sailor retrieved his knife.

Up on the bluff above the beach, the boy's sister began to scream.

At a nod from Ser Hartmut, another marine silenced her with an arrow.

'I claim this island, the river, and the land along its shores for the King of Galle,' said Ser Hartmut. He began to walk up the broad path towards the town.

His squires and men-at-arms walked behind him in a loose wedge, and the marines spread out on either side.

The crossbows coughed, and the Outwallers who had made the mistake of waking too early died first.

Mont Reale had sentries. They were, however, normal men who had trouble believing that their allies would betray them. It was not until the first flames were licking at the longhouses kept for visitors that they screamed the alarm.

Mont Reale had almost a thousand warriors.

They came from their houses and cabins half armed, and were shot down in the slushy mud of the streets. Or they attempted, unarmoured, to face Ser Hartmut and his knights as they cleared small knots of resistance. Ser Hartmut had divided the town into four quarters, and his troops cleared a quarter at a time, emptying a street, torching a few houses. As the red ball of the sun peeked above the distant mountains, Ser Hartmut clambered over the palisade of the citadel, helped by the snow already piled against the walls. The last organised resistance was crushed.

Officers moved through the town, ordering sailors to put out the fires, assigning houses to soldiers and ejecting their occupants into the snow. The survivors stood, stone-faced, watching their snug cabins turned into housing for their former allies. Then they were gathered into groups and chained together.

An old man had his squirrel robe ripped from his body. He turned with the dignity of an emperor and spat at Ser Hartmut's feet.

Ser Hartmut met his eye. 'You would not serve alongside me as allies?' he said. 'So be it. In God's name, you will serve me as slaves.'

Kilkis, in Western Thrake – The Red Knight and Bad Tom

The ride south was almost a triumphal procession, despite the increasingly bitter weather. Mag and the Red Knight combined to lay bridges of ice over the Meander, and when the Captain laced his with turrets, Mag added rearing horses of wind-blown frost to hers. Tom affected to shudder with revulsion, but many of the soldiers were delighted. They were more delighted when the two casters placed a great shining hemisphere over them during a vicious snow squall.

They reached Kilkis, the westernmost settlement on the road to the Green Hills and the last village in Morea before the Inn of Dorling, at vespers. The town was fully prepared to receive them, and the Megas Ducas paraded his full force under the walls of the snow-capped fortress.

'No rape, no plunder, no thieving. The man who steals or rapes will be executed, and the men who watch and do nothing will go to hell with him.' He looked out over his little army, and they were silent. 'Christmas is coming, and these people fear us like Satan come to earth. Prove them wrong, and I promise you will see a reward come pay day. And perhaps even in the next life.' He grinned. Off to his left, Gelfred winced. 'There is more to winning a war than defeating your enemies in the field. Go and behave. Or suffer the consequence. Dismissed.'

Bad Tom rolled his eyes when they were done and riding up the winding stone street to the citadel. 'Good Christ, Captain. They ain't choirboys nor little bairns. This town hates us.'

The Megas Ducas didn't even turn his head. 'They can obey me, or be killed.'

'You're becoming a right bastard,' Tom said. 'Why don't you get off your high horse and shag Sauce. Or find some pert thing that takes your eye and get it done so the rest of us can relax.'

The Duke dismounted with his household officers by him, and together they went into the Great Hall, which was so warm that the air seemed thick, and men who had worn four layers of wool over their armour for twelve hours now couldn't get it all off soon enough. Squires and pages stabled their horses or handed them to servants and then ran to their masters' sides to disarm them, and the Great Hall echoed like a battlefield as the armour came off – first helms and bassinets, and then gauntlets, then arm harnesses, carefully unlaced and unbuckled, and then the breastplates, or the cotes of plates, or the heavy brigantines, tossed to the carpeted floors. A legion of very young servants served wine while men stood enjoying the heat in sweat-stained arming cotes and plate leg harnesses, and gradually they, too, were unlaced and unbuckled, the squires and pages – still in their own armour – kneeling or crouching to get at buckles behind thighs and knees.

The men-at-arms grew louder.

Father Arnaud spoke briefly to one of the young attendants and then muscled his way to the Duke.

'They've sent us their children,' he said. 'It is a sign of trust. Would you say a few words?'

The Duke sighed. 'More than I've already said?' he asked. But he motioned for Toby to finish, stepped out of his right leg harness, and grinned at Father Arnaud. 'I feel as if I could fly, anyway,' he said, and leaped on a table.

His acrobatics got near-instant silence.

'Gentlemen,' he said. 'If you look at the pages serving wine, you'll find that the people of this town have sent their children to wait on us. Please pay them every courtesy. Don't treat them the way you'd treat your own children.'

They laughed obediently, and Father Arnaud introduced him to the Castellan, an elderly Morean captain named Nikolas Phokus.

'I gather that we share a mutual friend,' the Duke said, offering his hand.

The Castellan bowed and then clasped his hand. 'We do, my lord. He instructed me to open my gates to you, and so far I have no cause for complaint. But my lord, I must tell you that my garrison is unpaid in twenty-eight months, and there is some ill-feeling about it.'

The Duke nodded. 'Gerald!' he shouted over the raucous atmosphere, and Random limped his way to the front of the hall near the mammoth fireplace. 'My lord?'

'Am I good for another twelve thousand florins?' the Duke asked his financier.

Gerald Random rolled his eyes and nodded to the Castellan.

'Ah – Lord Phokus, this is Ser Gerald Random, the prince of merchant adventurers. Gerald, without Lord Phokus, there would be no furs. Can we afford to pay his garrison?' The Duke nodded amicably.

Random indicated a chair. 'May I sit?' he asked. 'Yes, you can. It won't help your spring campaign or your fleet, but you can. Remember, my lord, that when the fur money is spent, you don't have another increase in capital until – well, you know.'

The Duke turned to the Castellan. 'I can pay two years' salaries,' he said.

Lord Phokus bowed. 'My lord, I would say that would dissipate any – ahem – hard feeling.'

The Duke inclined his head. 'Just so that we understand each other,' he said, 'I expect that once paid, your troops will remain loyal. Or put it another way – once bought, they should stay bought.'

The Castellan's cheeks burned. 'My lord,' he said, his words clipped.

The Duke nodded. 'I know it is crass to discuss such things. But Lord Phokus, I will execute – quite publicly – any of my soldiers who commits a crime in the streets of this town. So please have your men think on how I will treat a garrison who takes my wages and betrays me.'

'You, or the Emperor?' Phokus asked.

'A fair question. The Emperor, naturally. But as I am now the Duke of Thrake, you may be saddled with me for some years.' The Duke sipped his wine. 'Is our mutual friend joining us?'

'I don't know – will you bully me, too?' asked a plainly dressed man. He was smaller than the Duke and had dark hair and dark eyes and most men ignored him. Ser Ranald, on the other hand, plucked Mag's sleeve and pointed, and her eyes widened.

The Duke bowed. 'Sir,' he said. 'I mean no bullying.'

The nondescript man smiled. 'I trust you found all your food.'

The Duke nodded again. 'It was beyond splendid, sir.'

'Lord Phokus has his own issues with the former Duke of Thrake and does not need to be threatened into this alliance. Likewise, Lord Phokus, Ser Gabriel here threatens you only because he is tired, and not because he is one of nature's bullies. He has, in fact, worked surprisingly hard for the restoration of the Emperor. Where is Thomas Lachlan?'

Bad Tom came forward with Ranald at his side.

'Do you recognise me, Thomas?' asked the man.

'Aye. I'd know you whatever skin you wore.' Tom towered over the smaller man, and nonetheless didn't seem the bigger man.

'I have a private solar for our ease,' said Lord Phokus.

'Then let us retire,' the Duke said. He took Lord Phokus's arm. 'I apologise if I laid it on too thick.'

Phokus smiled a crooked smile. 'I ask myself every hour if I have indeed sold this castle to you. It is painful to be reminded of it.' He shrugged. 'But my men need to be paid. The whole town depends on their wages.'

They went through a door to a low room with a ceiling worked in dark blue paint and bright gold stars, with tapestries of hunting along one wall and nine worthy women along the other wall. Father Arnaud joined them, and Mag, and Ser Gavin.

Toby slipped through the door and put a cup of something on the table in front of their guest, who took the head of the table. He lifted it and tasted.

'Ah – cider. Well chosen, Toby.'

Toby flushed and all but ran from the room.

'Call me Master Smythe,' said the nondescript man. 'Listen, friends. I am here only briefly. Tom, I have looked into your matter.' Master Smythe spread his hands wide, and then folded them together – an inhuman gesture, as his steepled fingers met the way an artist might draw them, folded perfectly flat and pointing straight at heaven.

In fact, watching Master Smythe was a little liking watching a puppet show.

'In brief, then. Hector – the Drover – was killed by Sossag Outwallers. They were, at the time, in the service of the entity who now calls himself Thorn and was formerly the magister Richard Plangere. But my investigations have shown that Thorn himself is merely the tool of one of my kind.'

Tom smiled, although the smile never reached his eyes. 'Lovely, then. Show me to the bastard.'

Master Smythe shook his head. 'It is a great deal more complicated than that, Tom.' He sighed. 'I think one of my kin has decided to break a certain compact that our kind has made. That is all I will say just now. Even saying this much – that my kind have a compact with some of yours, and that this compact is threatened – forces me to take sides in this matter.'

Smoke trickled out of Master Smythe's nose.

The Duke nodded. 'I'm sorry, Master Smythe, but please remember that we are not at fault.'

Smythe looked down the table. 'I was going to say that no one is innocent. But that is the merest casuistry, and we're better than that. So I will say that I have taken certain precautions. Gabriel, you have done well, but you will need to push your timetable forward. Tom, I know that you mislike me but I must ask you to follow me west and take up the duties of Drover. Lord Phokus, your help was, and will remain, instrumental – Ser Gabriel will need to be able to move east and west on this road for more than a year to come, and this fortress may become the focus of several armies. Which, despite their very different agendas, are being moved by a single will. Gabriel, I have brought you some interesting materiel. Use it wisely. My friends – when I must finally tip my hand I will come under attack, and then things will become very difficult. I apologise for all of the ambiguity and the cloak and dagger, but if I show my hand early the consequences would be most dire.'

The Duke laughed. 'And they accuse me of having a flair for the dramatic. Master Smythe, what kind of consequences are you thinking of?'

Master Smythe raised his eyebrows. 'The extermination of humankind in this sphere,' he said. He smiled, and his eyes locked with the Duke's. 'Are those stakes high enough to interest you, Gabriel?'

The Duke nodded. 'Yes,' he said.

'Good. Because, while we are, in every possible way, the underdog, the enemy has no idea who you are. Or what I can do.' Master Smythe nodded, and his smile was as natural as his hand gestures were false. 'It is exciting to have a true adversary after aeons of neutrality. It will require one of your God's miracles for us to triumph.' He nodded. 'But I have always found that it is far more entertaining to be the underdog. There is more honour if you triumph, and no censure if you fail.'

'Not my God,' the Duke said, somewhat automatically.

Father Arnaud snorted. And Mag nodded.

And Harmodius said, *Ahh. How I feared this.*

The Sacred Island – Kevin Orley and Thorn

Orley had ordered a castle built, and instead he had a series of sheds, each fouler than the last. The young men who followed him – a growing number – lacked the inclination to build in hardwood, or to rig latrines or shingle a roof properly. He could terrify them, but he had a hard time motivating them unless there was a town to plunder. They had dead eyes and preferred raw violence to any semblance of discipline.

The sheds angered him every day.

He had more than three hundred warriors, now, who ranged in age from eleven to seventeen. A few of the older boys were fully trained warriors, and whenever he had the spirit to rouse himself from the fire, he made the older men take the boys out in the snow where he drilled them as Southern soldiers were drilled. From Nepan'ha he had crossbows, and he begged Thorn for bolts until the sorcerer made him so many that he could have used them as tent stakes – a massive outpouring of the sorcerer's power, but one that allowed Orley to turn his least useful boys into silent killers.

He made them build a long shed for target practice, and another in which to sleep, and every time he had fifty more boys, he forced them to build another shed.

He wanted to dig a well, but in the end he had to settle for water brought from the sacred lake. That made all the boys afraid, for a while. But familiarity bred contempt so they drank the sacred water every day, fought among themselves, and the results were brutal.

There were girls as well as boys among his recruits, and they were used regularly and none kindled – some dark magery, no doubt, but nothing that Orley needed to concern himself with, although their blank eyes and lank hair felt like accusations every day. They didn't scream, and they didn't complain any more than the rest of his child soldiers, and he went among them like a war god, ordered them to train, to wash, to strip, to dress... and eventually they obeyed. The older boys seldom obeyed unless he killed one of them.

Orley grew taller. It shocked him – he'd have said he was past his last growth. He was, in fact, standing looking at the bottom of his beaded leggings, and his bare anklebones, and wondering why he'd suddenly grown four fingers, and what this portended, when suddenly the human skin of Thorn was with him.

'Choose me your two most useless mouths,' Thorn said.

'Too easy,' Orley said. He led the mage out into the main shed, and found a big boy with slabs of muscle like hams on his legs and arms. The boy was pissing on another boy while three others held him down.

'Tail!' Orley called.

The big boy raised his breach clout. 'Hah! What?' he whined.

'You are wanted.' Orley cuffed the boy and then grabbed the other – the runt being held by the others. 'And the Squirrel. The master wants you both.'

The two boys were immediately silent, and their fear stank.

'Things will begin to move, now,' Thorn said. 'Your warriors do not impress me, Orley.' His voice was hoarse and low. The warriors cringed away from him.

Perhaps the long shard of wood that transfixed his abdomen and the curl of intestine protruding from his lower back was the reason. Or perhaps it was the smell.

'You are injured?' he asked.

'No,' said Thorn.

Orley had never found the sorcerer so alien as in that moment. But he made himself shrug. He made himself stand up, like Orley. 'Pulse and Dragonfly tell me that the Galles have sacked Mont Reale.' He paused to watch his master, but the effort was wasted. In the skin of Speaker of Tongues, Thorn gave nothing away. 'We will have many more recruits if we make war on them,' Orley asserted.

Thorn didn't even shrug. 'No,' he said. 'We will use them as allies. They have broken the Northern Huran. There is nothing to be had from broken people.'

Orley's eyes encompassed the boys and girls who made his 'army'. 'I see,' he said.

Not for the first time, Orley wondered how fickle his new master was, and how easily discarded his little force might be.

'When I am done with a project here, I will go to the Galles and help them determine their next course of action.' Thorn nodded. His face was perfectly blank. It was like communicating with a stone.

Orley stood his ground. 'I need armour, swords, more crossbows – helmets. Perhaps horses. Space to train.'

Thorn nodded. 'Good. I can find these things.'

'When will we fight?' Orley asked. 'You were going to deliver Muriens to me.'

'His wife did well to warn him against me.' Thorn sounded distant. 'It will all happen in the spring. Train well, Orley. Be worthy. Because with the Galles, I may not need you, as you do not need this pair, even though this one is of the strongest.'

Both boys began to weep.

They were still weeping when Thorn fed them to the eggs, which ate their souls.

N'gara – Redmede, Mogon, and the Faery Knight

Insistent knocking at his door, and Redmede threw on a robe and went to open it. The whole house shook – the straw mats let in gusts of cold air. He drew his falchion, opened the door—

Mogon stood there, as tall as a warhorse, her plumes erect on her head. 'Come,' she said. 'I need you. Dress warmly.'

Redmede looked back at Bess, who was sitting up on their snug pallet, throwing a heavy wolf fur around her shoulders.

'I'll come,' Redmede said. It was a complex decision. She might eat him. Even now, he could feel the wave front of her rage. But she had more control than any of the other Wardens and her urgency communicated itself even through the medium of her alien body.

He pulled on two pairs of hose, one over another, and then deerskin leggings over all, and took Outwaller shoes – heavy moose hide, lined in fur – off the wall and laced them high on his legs. He had a good wool gown in Jack white, and he wore his falchion and took his bow, which he strung in the warmth of his little hut. He buttoned his old hood onto his head and put a fur cap atop it, and then pulled light gloves over his hands. Bess pulled heavy mittens like a knight's gauntlets made in wool and leather over his gloves.

Bess was more than just his partner, now. He saw the Hold through her eyes, sometimes – she loved to see the faeries, the irks, and the Wardens. To her, they were childhood tales made real, and she was living in some sort of paradise. He only saw the Wardens as monsters, and her vision of them steadied him.

'Help her,' Bess whispered. 'If Mogon seeks your aid, it can only help all of us.'

He kissed her, and went out into the brutal cold and snow.

The tall daemon was wrapped in furs, so that she was twice as big in girth as usual. 'My kind broadcast all our heat,' she admitted. 'Winter is very dangerous for us.'

'What's this about, lady?' he asked.

'Can you ride?' she asked.

He made a face. 'There's not a horse in this town,' he said.

She trotted off, her mighty three-toed feet crushing the snow flat for him, and he could walk easily except where she went through a drift. But she led him only as far as the cavernous main gate of the Hold. 'Tapio keeps war elk. Tamsin has one saddled for you.'

'What is this about?' Redmede asked.

'Tapio is missing in the snow,' she said. 'I can find him, but I need help. And this is not something he, or I, will wish to have known.'

'Shit,' Redmede said. He felt hopelessly over his head but he clung to how much Bess liked these ... monsters. And Tamsin had ever been like a creature out of a faery tale to him. He plunged into the cavern, through the curtain of warmth, some mighty working that protected the dooryard, and just inside, a pair of small irks held a sharp-faced animal like a moose but with back-swept antlers. The animal had the complete tack of a horse, although oddly shaped, decorated with tiny bells over mottled green leather.

The two irks bowed.

Tamsin, who Bess called the Faery Queen, was standing on the other side of the animal. He felt her presence – and smelled her, too. She smelled like sunlight and cinnamon and balsam of Gilead all together. He bowed. It was reflexive – he, Bill Redmede, every man's equal, had no hesitation in bowing to the Faery Queen.

'Find him, ser knight,' she said.

'I'm no knight,' he said.

Her sad smile told him that his opinion held no weight.

'What of your own people?' he asked.

'Please go,' she begged.

He had no resistance against her. He got a foot into the near-side stirrup and the great beast grunted.

'*You aboard?*'

Redmede gave a little shriek.

Tamsin held out an amulet. 'It will find him. Even if he is dead.'

The bull elk trotted out into the storm.

'*Can you hear me, boss?*'

Redmede fought his trembling hands – everything in irkdom seemed to scare him. 'I'm – how do you do that?'

'*Who knows? Good seat. Don't worry, I won't drop you. You do your part and I do mine. And don't use that fucking bit unless you have to, or we'll see which of us is stronger. Understand me?*'

Redmede put the reins carefully on the warm beast's neck and left them there, tied together. The elk increased his pace, and Mogon trotted alongside.

Too soon, they'd left the warm darkness of the Hold and the surrounding huts behind.

'Why?' Redmede asked. 'I'm not unwilling, lady. But why me?'

Mogon ran on. She ran for long enough that Redmede thought he wasn't going to get an answer, and then she crossed a series of downed trees and paused.

'We're in the Wild, man. If his own nobles suspected that he was alone in the snow, badly injured – well. Suffice it to say that his mate asks a Warden and a man to save her lord.' She turned, far more agile than a creature of her bulk had any right to be, and headed into the open woods.

Thrake – Aeskepiles

'My father will never agree to outright assassination,' Demetrius said.

Aeskepiles poured him more hippocras. 'This is the time, Your Grace. If we allow the usurper to hold the city through the winter, we have lost.'

Demetrius sat back. Despite his temper, he had the quick eyes of the thinking man, and they rested on Aeskepiles' own. 'My father said we had already lost. That all that remained of our cause was to see how much of the north we can hold.'

Aeskepiles shook his head. 'You father is merely despondent. It was a local defeat – a mere matter of marching—'

Demetrius cursed. 'Listen, Magister. Perhaps the person we needed most was you. This Red Knight – he had all sorts of sorcery. He tied my two *praeceptors* in knots as soon as the action started. He moved a storm front the way a goodwife moves a curtain.'

Aeskepiles nodded. 'I agree. So let's be rid of him.'

Demetrius took another drink. 'The world is full of sons who plot against their fathers. I am not one such. I dislike to betray my father's trust.'

Aeskepiles could feel his audience wavering. 'We are not betraying your father, but saving his cause. Was the Emperor a good ruler? No. He was a weak fool who made concessions to every foreigner. May I be frank? Even the usurper is better at ruling the Empire than the Emperor. I know it is blasphemy, but listen, Your Grace. I did not join this rebellion to win more power, or wider estates. There are *greater issues* at hand. We must win. So let's send that message. When the usurper is dead, we can cry *mea culpa* to your father.'

Demetrius drank again. 'We'll need his signet.'

Aeskepiles nodded. 'And the messenger leaves tomorrow for the city. We must be quick.'

Liviapolis – Kronmir and Mortirmir

More than a week after his return to the city, Kronmir stood at the Gate of Ares and watched the Imperial Army march in from the snow. They had been announced the night before, and it was widely held that they had won some great victories and had with them a fortune in furs. He might have cursed, but he didn't bother. Kronmir lived his life successfully by concerning himself only with elements that he could control. However, it must be said that the Megas Ducas' month-long winter campaign and its results had caused Master Kronmir to think certain thoughts about his employer and the likely durability of the cause which he was representing, and Kronmir had spent a day or two taking certain precautions.

The army, led by the Megas Ducas, looked triumphant, and far warmer than they should have. The troopers looked thin; a month of winter campaigning had shed any fat they might have had. But their white surcoats hid any deficiencies of clothing, their animals looked healthy enough, and the long train of wagons behind them spoke volumes for their triumph – Kronmir counted a hundred and sixty wagons. Enormous wagons, many drawn by oxen.

The master spy stood in the frozen evening, his hands deep in the sleeves of his fur-lined cote, and pondered how much advance planning and logistics his agents had missed which had allowed this army to march a thousand miles in winter.

He also couldn't help but notice that the crowd – ten deep at the gate and six deep even in the squares – cheered the army like madmen. They cheered the weather-beaten stradiotes, who looked proud as Pilate, every one of them, and they cheered the spry Vardariotes and their wind-reddened faces that matched their cotes, and they cheered the magnificent Scholae, who looked a little less magnificent in white wool, but still bore themselves like elven princes. They roared for the Nordikans, who rode by, hauberks swinging, tattoos almost black

547

against their winter-white and sun-reddened skin, and singing a hymn to the Virgin Parthenos. And, most disturbing, they roared themselves hoarse for the Megas Ducas on his tall black horse, wearing what appeared to be a cloak of white ermine – entirely of white ermine. He had a rod in his hand – a command staff – and he used it to salute the crowd, like an emperor of old.

At the back of the convoy of wagons there were forty further vehicles – just pairs of axles carrying heavy loads of lumber, pulled by oxen.

Kronmir went back to his inn, closed the door on his expensive private room, and wrote a long coded missive for his new communications service to carry. He went out towards evening and dropped the whole parchment scroll into a lead pipe strapped to the underside of a farmer's cart – right where it was supposed to be.

After latching the pipe closed, Kronmir walked back to his inn through the falling snow and listened to the sound of a city triumphant. He ordered a cup of mulled wine, sat down with his back to a wall, and warmed his feet on a stool while he contemplated the new reality.

And wondered if it was time to change sides.

Kronmir sat in the common room of his inn, enjoying a steaming tankard of hot cider and warming his toes at the fire. His tall boots hung over a frame with a dozen other pairs, and one of the inn's urchins turned them from time to time for a copper sequin.

He'd had a busy week, and a fruitful one. His most reliable palace contact had what might prove a useful resource among the Nordikans. The Nordikans were almost impossible to seduce from their allegiance, but he suspected that there must be some disaffection with the Emperor a prisoner. Although their payment by the Megas Ducas had killed the interest of the two who had considered his earlier offers. Or perhaps all that had been a trap.

He sighed. It was worth a try, although the latest victories by the Megas Ducas had solidified his support almost beyond saving. The Alban merchants had sailed away in the hardy round ships despite winter storms, loaded to the gunwales with the cream of the fur market – but the Etruscan League, having paid its fine, had been allowed to pick and choose among the furs, and had even made private deals with the Alban merchants. Kronmir didn't have a first-rate source, but his impression was that the Etruscan houses had avoided ruination, and now owed the Megas Ducas for their survival.

He took his eating knife from his purse and stirred his cider.

He felt someone's regard, and lifted his eyes to see the young artist from the temple outside the city. He remembered the boy well, and his own impulse to kill him.

The boy smiled on meeting his eyes.

Kronmir returned the smile. No spy or hired bravo would flash such an ingenuous smile on his way to strike his target. Nonetheless, Kronmir flipped a slim blade out of the back of his belt and held it along his left arm.

'Stephan!' called the young man. He had the air of a student, but he wore a sword on a belt of silver and gold plates, like an Alban knight or a mercenary.

Kronmir knew a moment's confusion before he settled that he had, indeed, told the young man his name was Stephan. He rose and bowed.

A potboy brought a second chair and bowed to the student.

'Are you a resident in this inn?' Kronmir asked.

The student nodded. 'Red wine – Candian, if possible. What I had yesterday? Yes?' His Archaic was superb – far better than anything Kronmir had heard from other mercenaries, and that further suggested the boy was a student. He sat. 'Yes, this is my inn. And you, sir?'

Kronmir groaned. Killing the boy would only lead to complications. But he couldn't share an inn with a person of wealth and property who could identify him to a magistrate. 'Just another day or two,' he said with an inward sigh. *I liked it here.* 'You are, I take it, a student at the Academy?'

The young man bowed again, while seated. He had very good manners. 'Yes. I am Morgan Mortirmir, Esquire, of Harndon. I am *Scholasticus Affector* at the Academy. And you?'

Kronmir knew the title meant he was a genuine adept – a wizard in training. He wondered if the young man was young enough to seduce to spying, but that was mere wheel-spinning. He would recruit his spy-mage only when he was confident of his own place and security, and this was not such a moment. 'I am a mere merchant, my lord,' Kronmir said.

'Ah!' Mortirmir said. 'I had you pegged as a fellow practitioner.'

'Whatever for?' Kronmir allowed himself a genuine laugh.

'The amulet you wear shines like a beacon in the *aethereal*. Ah – I beg your pardon, good sir. I know that some people mislike all discussion of the immaterial.'

Kronmir toyed with the amulet that the Emperor's former wizard had given him. 'Really?' he asked.

'It must be very powerful,' Mortirmir continued. He leaned over, and Kronmir flinched back. 'Sorry. Curiosity killed the cat, and all. I'll desist.'

A pretty young woman in a fine Morean gown and wimple brought a wine glass, a tumbler worked with tiny tendrils of decorative glass in blues and greens, and the small flagon. She curtsied. He raised his glass to her.

Kronmir fought his rising fear and made a snap decision – the kind he made every day. Sometimes, it was easier to know things than to live in a world of fear. So he took the chain over his head and handed it to the young man. 'My master paid handsomely for it,' he said. 'It is supposed to allow us to communicate. Over great distance.'

Mortirmir smiled, a little shy now that he was engaged. He took a sip of wine and turned the amulet over. It was a silver pendant in the shape of a praying man. He looked at the base of it, and frowned, weighed it in his hand, and something about his shift in his seat made Kronmir deeply uneasy. He began to look at the exits – his automatic reaction to threat.

Mortirmir flicked his thumb over the base of the amulet, and there was a minute flare of fire – blue fire.

Mortirmir dropped the amulet. 'Well, well,' he said with the enthusiasm of the young and passionate for an intricate device. 'It's very powerful. How far away is this master of yours? Etrusca?' He laughed.

Kronmir stood up. 'You unmask all my secrets,' he said, taking back his device. 'You are very clever.'

Mortirmir met his eye. 'I'd be hesitant to hang all that unshielded *potentia* around my neck. What if the man who directs your business dislikes you, sir?' He laughed. 'I'm only being a ninny. Here you go.'

Kronmir raised an eyebrow. 'Good to know,' he said.

He changed inns later that afternoon with a minimum of fuss, but the damage was done – the boy would know him anywhere, and the amulet was like a badge. Kronmir was suddenly obscurely afraid of the power of the thing – as if the young scholar's fear was a disease he'd caught. He put it in his pocket.

Thrake – Gelfred

'This is not how I'd planned to celebrate the nativity,' Gelfred complained.

Amy's Hob laughed aloud, and even Daniel Favour grinned.

They had six small huts of branches leaning against carefully constructed sapling frames. The lean-tos ran either side of a fire trench that warmed both sides, and the result was like a long, very low Outwaller house. The men – a dozen of them – could lie with their feet to the fire's warmth and their heads under the lowest and snuggest part of the shelter.

The lean-tos were covered in snow – indeed, they were buried in it, but the deep snow only made the shelters warmer. Every deer they brought down added a hide to the refinements they had worked on the openings, and every hour of daylight added to the immense pile of firewood that formed the north wall of the shelters; a barrier against the wind.

Favour's two hounds lay with their heads on their paws near the entrance. They had their own hides to lie on, and men collected bits of food to try and lure them as sleeping companions, but they mostly slept with the young wagoner from Harndon. Even now, at the edge of night, they raised their heads when he moved.

'He's the youngest, and he must look most like a dog,' Amy's Hob said with a rare smile. The other men laughed.

Gelfred fetched his pot off the fire and served out mulled wine. 'I'd like to do something for our Saviour's birth,' he said.

Young Daniel nodded. 'Not until tomorrow though, Ser Gelfred.'

'Wouldn't hurt us none to sing a carol,' Wha'Hae said. Amy's Hob cuffed him and Wha'Hae elbowed the man. 'What? I like to sing.'

Ginger snorted. 'I know "God rest Ye",' he said.

'Ain't we hiding in enemy territory?' Amy's Hob said plaintively.

Young Daniel gave a snort of derision. 'There's nothing moving out there but us and the deer,' he said. 'And the deer ain't moving much,' he added, and got a laugh of his own. Young he might be, but Daniel Favour was the elite hunter among an elite of woodsmen. His patience was legendary, and his arrows flew true.

Gelfred swirled his hot wine and poured a cup for Amy's Hob, who took it with a surprisingly civil inclination of his head, as if they were all lords. 'Besides,' he said in his cultured voice. 'We have sentries well out, on the road and on the hill.'

'Sweet Jesu, Master Gelfred, that hillside is cold as a witch's tit,' added Will Starling, their newest scout, a former Royal Forester.

Gelfred glanced at the man. They were of an age, and the former Forester liked to swear hard and talk bawdy, which did not sit well with Master Gelfred.

'Cold as a virgin's—' he added with relish.

Gelfred handed him a cup of hot wine. 'Master Starling, life is hard enough without reminding these men of the women they do not have among them. And it is my pleasure, while you serve with me, not to hear my Saviour's name taken in vain, or even the parts of a woman's body. Here. Have some wine.'

Starling was interested in being provoked, but it is difficult to maintain a resentment against a man with mild manners and a cup of hot, sweet wine for you on a winter's day, and he subsided muttering something about priesthood.

Young Daniel took his horn cup and nodded. 'But he has a point, Ser Gelfred. We ought to build a blind. A lie. Like we was hunting deer, or duck. The wind on that hillside goes through my cloak and my cote and my gown and my boots all together.'

'Cuts me to the prick,' Starling said, but his heart wasn't in it.

The oil lamp that burned by the entrance flared, and there was a slight buzz, like that of a hornet in high summer.

'Company!' Gelfred said, and every man had a blade in his hand. They piled into their winter gear – most had their boots to hand. Favour threw his white wool gown over his head, picked up a boar spear, and emerged into the freezing sunset air. He got his feet into the loops of his snow rackets and trotted towards the road.

The sentries each had a device rigged by Gelfred, who had command of the *ars magicka*. The buzzing meant the road, and a high, clear tone meant the hillside. Favour trotted well to the north of the sentry's position – it was Short Tooth who had the road, and he wasn't given to false alarms. Favour moved quickly, but he stayed clear of what little undergrowth stood proud of the snow and he didn't give his position away. When he crested the low bluff which dominated the road, he fell flat in the soft snow and wriggled forward.

'I *have* a pass, you nitwit!' shouted the man on the wagon. 'It's *fucking* cold and I want to get over the pass before it snows again.'

Short Tooth moved slowly clear of the huge wagon, which towered twice the height of a man, and whose wheels sank all the way to the roadbed through three feet of snow without putting the wagon body near the surface. They were exceptionally tall wheels.

'What you carrying?' Short Tooth asked.

Favour saw Wha'Hae drop into the snow a few yards to his left, closer to the wagon. He worked the action on a crossbow – a latchet – while rolling on his back. Across the road, Will Starling glided up behind a dead tree and froze.

'Grain for farmer's market,' the driver said. 'Hey, you for the old Duke or the new Duke?'

'Why don't you shut your trap and we'll just see your grain,' Short Tooth said. He had worked his way to the rear of the tall wagon and he carefully cocked his own crossbow. It was a very expensive weapon – another steel latchet.

The man on the wagon box saw it.

Favour jumped down into the road and ran lightly along the surface in his rackets.

Short Tooth spared him a glance and waited for him.

'There's another one!' shouted the man on the wagon box, and everything went to shit.

The back of the wagon seemed to lift off, and Short Tooth shot a man on instinct. His bolt vanished into the man's coat-of-plates and blood splashed the snow.

Behind him, another man spanned a crossbow, but the bow itself was yew and he hadn't warmed it so it cracked. Favour's spearshaft caught him alongside the head.

The driver fell face first into the snow with Starling's arrow in the back of his neck. Blood poured out of him, and he thrashed, leaving an obscene snow angel in red agony.

But there were more men in the wagon body, and Favour caught a shaft – right through his abdomen. The pain doubled him up and he fell, the snow cold against his face, and there was a cold wetness ruining his cote.

Gelfred worked – the air grew warm, there was a flash above his head, and then the men on the bluff began to pour shafts down into the wagon bed. Favour knew he was hurt badly, but he was still fully aware – he could hear Short Tooth, the man's latchet clicking away as he pulled the cocking handle back against the weight of the steel bow and then slapped it forward.

The man was *under* the wagon, loosing his quarrels up into the wagon bed. And the canvas roof of the wagon provided no cover to the men inside. Blood began to drip out from between the boards.

'Surrender,' Gelfred called. 'Or we will surely slay you all.'

Favour heard the men in the wagon, and heard the sound of someone throwing something heavy in the snow.

Gelfred was at his side in a dozen heartbeats. 'Stay with me, boy. It's Christmas. No one dies on Christmas. Everyone lives.'

Favour coughed, and blood came out.

Suddenly, everything seemed further away.

'Right – clear them out of the wagon. Disarm all of them. Get young Daniel in the wagon. Starling, come with us. Keep him warm. Hob – you take the post.'

Then Gelfred leaned over him and passed his hands across Favour's eyes, and that was all—

Gelfred turned to the wounded prisoner. 'I'm in a hurry. I won't make threats.'

The man was an Easterner, and he shrugged.

'He won't talk, even if we cut his fingers off,' Starling said. 'This one will.'

The young Thrakian whom Favour had bashed with his spear shaft held his head and retched.

The other rangers took the rest of the Thrakians away, leaving Gelfred and Starling, Wha'Hae and the Thrakian boy.

'Just tell me,' Gelfred said.

The boy looked at him. His pupils were enormous.

'He can suck the soul out of your body,' Starling said. It might have been a terrifying threat, except that the boy spoke only Morean Archaic and no Alban at all.

Gelfred leaned over. 'You're only six miles from the city in the worst weather in ten years. And you're coming out of the hills with a guard of Easterners.'

The boy put his head in his hands.

'Do you serve Duke Andronicus?' Gelfred asked gently.

'Yes,' the boy answered, and was undone.

In a moment, he poured his fears out, while Starling watched in contempt.

Finally, Gelfred motioned for Wha'Hae to take the young man to the other prisoners.

'The Duke will want to meet all of them,' he said. 'Leave Amy's Hob and Wha'Hae and Short Tooth here. Watch the road and forget the hillside. The rest of you get to sleep warm tonight. Horses!'

There was a cheer, and in a handful of minutes, they were off.

'Bring us back something nice,' Amy's Hob said. 'It being Christmas.'

'We'll settle for the boy's life,' Wha'Hae said. 'And some ale.'

Chapter Fifteen

The King

Harndon – Christmas Court

The Queen loved Christmas above all things, and she decorated the Great Hall of the palace the way her mother had decorated her childhood hall – with wreaths of ivy and balls of mistletoe. She visited jewellers and tailors and made herself as busy as she might to keep away her darker thoughts.

'You'll hurt your bairn,' Diota said. 'You've no business keeping yon secret from the King.'

The Queen shrugged. 'I am my own mistress, I think,' she said with some of her old spirit, but in truth, the daily sickness and the bloated feeling sapped her interest in sparring with her nurse. And her temper was sharp – sharper than usual. Weary anger was the mood of her Advent, and she resented this wicked intrusion on her life.

'Baby is his business, too,' Diota said. 'And with the wicked lies I hear told every day in these halls, I would think you'd want to tell him he's going to be a papa.'

'There are things I want to know first,' Desiderata said.

'Beware lest the King want to know some things as well,' Diota rumbled.

'Nurse, are you – what—' Desiderata spluttered.

Diota gave her a quick hug. 'I ain't impugning your bairn's paternity, if that's what you mean. I'm saying: just tell him.'

So a few days before Christmas Eve, after they shared a loving cup and he kissed her under the ball of mistletoe, she led him away to their bed, snug amidst a veritable castle of tapestries and warming pans.

The King moved quickly along his usual course of events and she laughed into his beard and slowed his rush to conclusion and finally forced his hand onto her belly.

'Listen, love. There's something stirring in there,' she said.

'Dinner?' he asked with a low laugh.

'A baby,' she said.

His hand stiffened. 'Are you – sure?'

She laughed. 'I know what a milkmaid knows – and a little more. He's a boy. He'll be born in June.'

The King breathed silently by her in the darkness.

'Say something, love,' Desiderata said.

'I cannot make a child,' he said grimly. He rolled away from her. She caught at his hip. 'Yes, you can. And did.'

'Madam, I am not a fool,' he spat.

'My lord, that court is still out. For I have never lain with any man but you.'

'No?' he asked.

'Do you question me?' she asked, and felt the root of her being and the foundation of her love melt like wax in a fire.

He sat up. 'We should not have this conversation. Not now,' he said carefully.

She sat up beside him. She found a taper, leaning across him so that, quite deliberately, her breasts trailed across his chest. She conjured the taper to light and set it in a small stick so that she could see his eyes.

He looked like a wounded animal.

Tears welled up, but she fought them, because something told her that she would only have *this one chance* to convince him they had a child before he would armour himself away – the bluff King, untouchable.

'Love, look at my tummy. This is me. I would never lie with another – nor would I quicken unless I chose to.' She leaned close. 'Think of who I am. *What* I am.'

'I *cannot* make a child. I am – *cursed*.' He sobbed the last word.

She put a hand on his chest and he didn't resist. 'Sweet, I have power. I am as God made me. And I think – I think that I have overcome your curse.' She smiled. 'With God's help, and the novice's.'

'Not my curse!' he groaned.

'Whose, then?' she asked.

He shook his head and would not meet her eyes.

'Husband, when the *belle soeur* worked her will on us – and made us whole—' She paused, remembering the moment, and trying to grasp a little of the glory she had felt. The sense of release. She kissed him. 'She cracked your curse, or shattered it. I can feel this.'

The King put his head on her chest. 'If only you might be right,' he said.

He fell asleep, and she lay awake, running her hand over his chest and trying to find the jagged ends of the curse, but the breaking had happened too long before, and she felt only the edge of the wound that the curse left in the world.

Later he awoke, and they made love.

And when she awoke with him, it was a day nearer Christmas, and she thought that perhaps everything would be healed.

A hundred rooms away, the Sieur de Rohan laid Lady Emota on a bed, and she sighed.

'It is sin,' she said. She pushed him away. 'Can't you just kiss me?'

'What sin, when two lovers make one soul?' he asked. He ran a tongue lightly across the top of her exposed breast, and she clenched her hands on his shoulders, which were hard with muscle – and he slid into the bed next to her, warm and solid and smelling only of cinnamon and cloves.

She kissed him, and breathed in the scent of him. And let his hands roam.

It was beautiful – and then it wasn't.

He put a knee between hers and she didn't like that. She pushed him away – hard.

'Make way, slut,' he said. 'You want it.'

He pushed her down. She bit him, and he struck her.

She tried to fight him.

She cried.

He laughed. 'What did you think you were here for?' he asked her. She turned to weep into the pillow, which smelled of him, and he slapped her. She pulled the bed clothes around herself, and he pulled them off again. 'I'm not done with you yet, *ma petite*.'

'You!' she managed. 'You – false—'

'It is no crime to fuck a whore,' he said.

She choked.

'Like mistress, like maid,' de Rohan said. 'Don't worry, my little *putain*. When the court finds out what your mistress has done, no one will even notice your fall from grace. Besides – you have a body made to satisfy a man.' He cooed over her, using warm love terms again.

For a little while.

N'gara – Mogon and Bill Redmede

The woods were full of snow, and there was something else there – something that moved at the very edge of Redmede's senses, something too fast to see, too small, or too quiet.

Mogon ran east, her heavy feet carving great triangular holes in the snow. The elk ran lightly, and sometimes he skimmed the surface of the snow. They would stop from time to time, and Redmede would hold the amulet in his hand and watch the fire in its depths. They followed the spark – east and north.

After full dark, they crossed tracks that showed clearly in moonlight – tracks of a man with a hand sleigh. Redmede rubbed his beard. 'That's Nat Tyler,' he said. 'I know his tracks.'

Mogon waggled her mighty head. 'It is too cold for me to think well, man. Does this other man mean something?'

'No idea,' Redmede admitted, but when he tested the amulet, he found that Tyler's tracks diverged at a sharp angle from the true line to Tapio.

They ran on.

By the height of the moon, Redmede estimated it was midnight by the time they found Tapio. His body hung high in a tree, because he was impaled on one of its shattered branches. His blood flowed down the old oak.

'Sweet Christ,' Redmede said.

'*Very like,*' Tapio whispered. '*Onssse again, Man, I will owe you my life.*'

Mogon shook her head. 'What will we do?' she asked. 'I can manipulate the powers. But how to reach him down from the tree?'

'Can you lift him?' Redmede asked. 'With sorcery?'

Mogon nodded. 'If I can make my sluggish brain work, yes.'

In the end, Redmede climbed the tree and cut the branch that impaled the Faery Knight while the red blood flowed over the old wood and didn't freeze. He put the irk – tall as a man but light as air – across the rump of the great elk, who grunted.

'Can't carry the both of ye. Sorry.'

Redmede got his rackets off his saddle and put them on his feet. He already missed the warmth of the beast.

Tapio raised his head. *'You both have my thanksss.'*

Mogon bowed her head. 'It was Thorn?'

Tapio Haltija laughed, and something bubbled in his chest. *'We must go quickly if you two care to sssave my worthlesss carcasss. It wasss not Thorn. It wasss the ssshadow of Asssh.'*

Mogon growled and made a fearful growling deep in her throat that raised the hackles of Redmede's neck. 'So – my brother was correct.'

'Ash?' he asked.

Mogon shook her head. 'We have twenty miles to walk before we find warmth and safety, and this night is full of terror, even for one such as I. Let us go.'

Redmede could never recall more than the impression of enormous fatigue and the cessation of warmth. They walked, and they ran – when he lost feeling in his feet, he ran for a while until they hurt, and then he walked again. The woods around them snapped and cracked in the dense cold which came down like a hermetical working, vast and suffocating, and sat over the whole of the forest.

When the first light showed in the east, Redmede was so tired he wanted to lie down on the snow and sleep, but he knew where that would lead.

It was the great Warden, Mogon, who flagged first. She began to wander – in fact, she appeared drunk, and she wove about and made little grunting noises.

Tapio, who had not made a sound in many miles, raised his head. *'Man!'* he hissed. *'She needs fire, or she will die. Very – suddenly.'*

Redmede knew how to kindle fire. And the threat seemed to ignite him – he gathered wood as fast as his feet would carry him, and he found a birch tree, down and dead and still clear of the snow, and he pulled off his mittens, hung them around his neck, and froze his hands stripping the bark. He stripped a mountain of bark, and he piled it under all the branches he'd found – where two dead spruce trees lay across one another at the end of a clearing.

Mogon was keening, and otherwise immobile.

Up to you, Bill Redmede. Fate of the world. Smile when you say that. Tinder box – there it is. Char cloth – good. He laid a piece of the black cloth on his flint and snapped it along his stele. They were warm from being carried next to his body, and the sparks flew.

The char cloth lit. He thought of Bess, that night in the wet woods, and he blew on his sparks and his glowing embers and pressed them into his dry tow. It was cold – but it was dry – and in a moment, he had fire.

He threw the whole burning clump onto his pile of birch bark.

There was pungent smoke...

For a moment, he thought that it wasn't going to light.

And then the birch bark's resin thawed enough to catch, and light and heat exploded into the world – the only magic that Bill Redmede knew how to make, except perhaps a little with a bow. The fire rose and licked at more bark.

'*Nice work, boss,*' said the elk – even as it shied away. Nothing in the Wild loved fire.

The two dead spruce trees caught from the branches and the bark and the fire rose.

Redmede finally had to take Mogon by the hand and lead her to the fire. She would barely stir.

But in minutes, she was herself again.

'Be sure and roast Tapio on both sides,' she said.

The elk turned and presented its other flank to the fire – and then Mogon shook her head.

'One more effort. Thank you, man. You are a useful ally. I missed my moment. I should have built a fire, and I—' She shook her head again. 'Do you know that fire scares me? I cannot remember when I have been this close to one, naked to it.'

She did, however, douse the fire.

And they ran into the cold morning, towards the Hold.

It was late morning when they entered the tunnel, and the heat of the Hold almost suffocated Redmede. But willing hands plucked their lord from the elk and bore him away, and Tamsin placed a warm kiss on Redmede's cheek that burned there like faery fire until he met his own lady-love at the door of their own hut.

She threw her arms around him. 'Merry Christmas,' she said.

Ticondaga – Ghause, Amicia, and Ser John

The road along the lake was yet another military road built by the Imperial legions, and it was good stone covered in good gravel. The wagons moved well, even in snow, until they reached the Break, a three-mile stretch where low limestone cliffs had collapsed into the lake, wrecking the road and forcing a wide detour into the Wild. Those three miles of paths and rutted cart tracks took them two days; they made camp at the edge of a frozen swamp that nonetheless seemed to move, and no one from the lowliest squire to Ser John himself went to sleep.

The woods were alive, despite the season. Ser John's outriders brought in deer, and a cold-slowed boggle; they saw a *hastenoch*, one of the monstrous armoured elk, across a beaver swamp, and every archer in the column cranked his crossbow.

Something low to the ground, black as night and fast, tracked the column, and on the fourth night, despite torches, fires, and doubled sentries, they lost a horse. In the cold light of a frozen morning, the poor horse's shocking wounds suggested that the black thing was huge and very hungry. And that it could fly. The horse had landed a blow and there were long black feathers in the snow.

On the fifth evening, the advance guard caught a pair of Ruk crossing a frozen stream. The giants had to be careful of their footing, and the scouts began to pelt them with crossbow bolts.

As the rest of the company came up, the soldiers crowded to the stony bank and shot volleys of bolts. The men were excited – charged with spirit, animated, eyes glittering as they spanned and shot, spanned and shot, and the men-at-arms awaited the inevitable moment when the giants rushed their tormentors. But the twenty heavy crossbows made short work of the monsters. The larger went down last, screaming with rage, and yet the final look welded to its broad features was one of baffled puzzlement, like an old dog confronted with a strange new thing.

The men fell silent.

Sister Amicia rode up the column, looked at the dead creatures in the stream, and then at Ser John.

'They had to die,' he said defensively.

Amicia met his eye and he flinched. 'If they'd got among us—' he said.

She pushed a tendril of hair back into her hood. 'Ser John, I will not debate military matters with you.' More quietly, she said, 'But the Ruk are as biddable as children, and I could have sent them about their own business as easily as you killed them. They were ensorcelled. I can feel it.' She shook her head. 'It is a crime,' she added. 'A crime to make them into tools, and a crime to murder them.'

The soldiers around her were dismayed, and they reacted in all the ways men react when dismayed. Some grew angry. Others turned their heads away.

Ser John shook his head. 'Listen, sister. I understand – the Wild is not a simple enemy. But neither can we stop to bargain with the Wild.'

'Men are always in a hurry,' she said. 'And they kill what they do not understand.'

The next day, Amicia said mass. It was odd, to say the least, for many of the soldiers to take communion from a woman, but it was odd to be in the Wild in mid-winter and Ser John made no scruple to kneel and take the host from her hands. Her mass was well attended.

The company marched away as the red ball of the sun peeked above the mountains to the east across the lake.

About the time the bells would have been sounding for nonnes at Lissen Carrak, they rolled into a heavy snow shower.

Amicia drew on her second hood, and Ser John reined in beside her. 'We're less than a day from Ticondaga,' he said. 'Can you foretell the weather?'

She steadied herself. 'I can try,' she said. She reached out—

She gasped. 'There is something malevolent – in the woods.' She paused. 'Virgin protect us – they're ahead of us and around us—'

Ser John loosened his sword in its sheath. 'How close?'

She shook her head. 'Let me pray,' she said.

'Stand to!' shouted Ser John, rising in his stirrups.

Conversation stilled. The wagons halted. The Etruscans leaped onto their wagon beds and untied heavy ropes and then lifted wooden shutters into place, making their four wagons into small fortresses full of crossbowmen in the twinkling of an eye. Horse harness jingled, and the bowmen spanned their weapons.

'It is north of here, moving—' She paused. 'Moving west. I hid myself. Ser John – it is— There is already fighting. Hurry.'

'What kind of fighting?' he asked.

'People are under attack,' Amicia said. 'Come!'

She rode ahead.

'Damn it!' Ser John cursed. 'Cover her!'

Amicia bolted away and was lost in the soft curtain of snow, and the vanguard of the column cantered after her.

'Contact!' shouted a man in the main column, far behind him.

'Shit,' Ser John said. He heard crossbows snapping away. Behind him. The convoy was his duty, but the *belle soeur* was his friend.

'Follow me!' he roared, and galloped into the snow after the mad nun and her palfrey into a snowfall that got worse by the second.

Men were riding hard, struggling to get frozen fingers into steel gauntlets as they rode through blinding snow, and none of them had their visors closed. It was a recipe for disaster.

He heard Amicia's shout. Then she said – quite distinctly – *Fiat lux.*

He almost lost his seat at the burst of light. Behind him, a mounted knight and his horse went down on the road. It was as if he was at the centre of the sun.

Something hit him in the head, and darkness brushed his face – he felt a burning, and his sword arm acted. He connected – the thing screamed, his horse reared under him and he managed to get his visor closed by slamming his chin down onto his breastplate as the winged darkness descended again.

He cut at it, wondering what in the name of hell he was fighting.

'Trolls!' shouted one of his knights.

Ser John had time to think that whatever he was fighting was no troll.

He put his spurs into his mount as he was struck a third time – his horse burst forward, and he passed behind Sister Amicia, whose hands were the centre of a circle of radiance. As he rode through it, the black thing vanished from around his head and he caught – in the interrupted peripheral vision of his visor – a glimpse of a wing with barbed black feathers.

There *were* two trolls in the road, towering over a red puddle, and then he struck two-handed and his great sword shattered – but so did the nearest troll's arm. The thing roared, its bottomless violet gullet illuminated by Amicia's working.

Its other fist knocked him from the saddle and he landed heavily. All that saved him was the snow, and even with a foot of the stuff over the rock, he hit hard, there was pain in his back and his head struck a projecting stone hard enough to deform his helmet.

He had no idea how long he'd been out and he made himself move. His back screamed. He couldn't rise to his feet, but had to roll onto his stomach and get to his knees, and with every heartbeat he was conscious that the two trolls were just a horse length away in the snow. Men were screaming, and blood was pouring out of his nose.

Another wave of brilliant golden light. The nearest troll turned and counter-cast a purple-green fog, and where the two workings met they sparkled like metal struck with a hammer on the forge and there was a long *crack* like lightning striking close by – except that it went on and on. Ser John, who was old in the ways of pain, got his left foot under his left hip and pushed himself erect. His horse was screaming, down the bank, its shrill neighs speaking of pain and panic.

His pole-axe was on his horse, and he didn't think he could negotiate the deep snow. So he drew the heavy dagger at his hip, and ploughed forward towards the nearest troll, all the while cursing himself as a fool.

The one he'd wounded was face down in the road. That made him smile despite the pain.

The second one was fully engaged with a blur of gold – the noise the two made was like a hundred savage dogs fighting. Ser John couldn't make out who his new ally was, but he stumbled forward – turned his whole body to look north, in case there was a third – and the black shape descended from the sky.

This time he was more ready. The dagger flicked out and feathers fell to the ground – there was a discordant shriek that pierced even through the awesome sounds the troll and its adversary made.

The great black bird-thing stooped, wings spread, and a thick line of molten gold came out of the snow and struck it in the middle of its black breast. It – *exploded.*

Ser John was knocked flat. This time, he didn't lose consciousness and so he was aware as the whirlwind of the fight passed over him. The troll planted a foot by his head, and Ser John rolled, fuelled by desperation, and he plunged his dagger in behind its hip with both hands driving the hilt. The steel shrieked—

Ser John felt his leg break, saw the armour buckle as the troll's foot flashed out and caught him, but he didn't lose his grip on the dagger, sunk like a piton in rock, and he fell pulling on the hilt with two hands.

The troll toppled. It fell across him, and its arm struck his chest, denting his breastplate and snapping ribs in a cascade of raw pain.

But he saw the troll's end with almost religious clarity. He didn't pass out – that mercy was denied him – and, instead, he was almost preternaturally aware as the troll went into the snow, the heat of its body sending up a cloud of steam and suddenly there was a golden bear in its place gripping a club, or perhaps a warhammer, and it struck so rapidly that its motions were a blur, and so hard that stone chips flew as if the great bear was a mason shaping marble.

There was a final, sharp crack, and the troll shrieked and turned to sand and rock.

The enormous bear stood over Ser John.

'That was unexpected,' it said. 'I think p'raps you saved me.'

Or perhaps Ser John merely imagined that the bear said that. He expected to die.

It raised its hammer again.

The convoy reached the scene of carnage – three dead knights, Ser Anton badly wounded and the others all torn to shreds, and three damp sand-spots, and what appeared to be tens of thousands of black feathers.

Sister Amicia stood over Ser John, who was once again able to speak. She'd flooded him with healing and he was alive. Willing hands got him into a wagon. He was cold – cold all the way through. It had taken time for the bear to break him loose from the dead stone that had been a living troll.

'We rescued bears,' Ser John said. 'Sweet Christ, sister – you risked us all to save some fucking bears.'

'Some day they may save you,' she said, more sharply than he'd heard her speak. 'Now lie quietly.'

'What was the thing with the feathers?' he asked her.

She paused. 'A Bargest,' she said. 'I didn't think they were real.'

The men of the convoy were still in shock. A wave of boggles had struck the column and been defeated, but the shock of the attack and its aftermath – the dozen golden bears trotting along the flanks of the column while Amicia begged the bowmen to hold their shafts – had left men shaken, and some had gagged at the ruin of the knights killed by the trolls.

Amicia had kept them going – she wasn't sure what else to do, and Ser John was so badly hurt that she feared to wake him, and the knights were all too young to take charge – Jarsayans with too little appreciation of the north.

And they all trusted her.

So she kept them moving – the reaction after the fight left men cold, and short of halting and gathering wood, the only recourse they had was food and movement. She ordered them to eat and men did, as if taking orders from young nuns was part of their military training. And when they'd eaten their bread or their bacon or whatever each man had, she ordered the column forward and they marched without much complaint.

Liveried cavalrymen met them – the light-armoured horsemen that Northerners called 'prickers' for their long spurs. They wore the Earl's livery and they were entirely respectful.

'Lady said there was a convoy in trouble,' their officer said after a bow to Sister Amicia. 'I'm Ser Edmund, sister.'

'Your lady was right.' Amicia was very proud of her little army – proud that they'd held together, proud that they hadn't shot a golden bear by mistake. 'But we won our skirmish.'

Ser Edmund nodded. 'Didn't think your lads looked beat,' he said. 'Damme! Is that John Crayford? He looks like shit.'

Alicia raised an eyebrow. 'He's had all the help I can provide,' she said.

Ser Edmund nodded. 'Well, I'm sure we can do better at the castle. I'd best be taking command, eh? You must have been terrified.'

Amicia thought of a number of replies, and settled for one she'd learned from the old Abbess. 'Not at all,' she said. And turned her horse and rode on, leaving the Earl's officer sitting in the middle of the road.

*

Ser John was next aware when he was surrounded by stone – arches everywhere, and a pair of armoured men in green and gold livery.

'Careful, there,' Amicia said. 'If those wounds open—'

'Of course, sister!' one man said.

Ticondaga was built on the same scale as Lissen Carrak – all grey stone and red brick rising into the heavens like a cathedral of war. The courtyard itself was twice the size of the yard at her convent, and the barracks building had the new internal chimneys and a lead roof.

Now safe in the greatest fortress in the north, they sagged to the ground in relief. The knights got themselves off their horses, and their squires – including the squires of the dead men – took their horses and then the castle's men-at-arms flooded the courtyard, and the Earl Muriens was there, barking orders and offering hot stew from a great bronze cauldron which he and another knight had hauled into the yard with their own hands.

'You – lass. Out of those wet clothes,' he barked at her. Then bobbed his head in an insolent parody of a bow. 'Oh – you're a nun. Well – here, drink this and then get out of your wet clothes.' He leered. 'You are the fucking lovesomest nun I've seen for many a year. Are there more like you?' he asked.

He was big, with iron-grey hair and an attitude she knew immediately. The Red Knight might despise his father, but he certainly carried himself with the same air of cocky dominance.

'I'll see to the convoy first,' she said. 'My lord Earl. That worthy knight is Ser John Crayford, and he brought this convoy here to succour the fur trade.'

Amicia watched the old knight being carried into the castle. The Earl walked beside his stretcher for a few paces and said something, and she heard a weak grunt from Ser John.

'That's a fine man-at-arms. He must be fifty! As old as me – a good knight.' The Earl grinned. 'You his?'

Amicia laughed.

The Earl had the grace to be abashed by her laugh. 'Well – there's no fool like an old fool. So you're here for our furs?'

'If we can do it, it will save Albinkirk. As a trade town.' Amicia tried to follow his mercurial changes, and was reminded...

'Might save our trade, too.' Muriens laughed. 'I'll take all the money I can get, but we haven't a tithe of the furs we usually have.

The trade went east to the fucking beg-your-pardon Moreans as soon as folk heard about the attacks in the south.'

'You have no furs?' asked Messire Amato.

Muriens laughed. 'Fucking Etruscans. Of course I have furs. Why don't you all come out of the cold before we start dickering like a man with a whore on a cold night – beg your pardon, sister,' he added with a smile. 'Although, sweet Saviour, you can come and take my confession anytime.'

Amicia smiled right back at him. 'That will be enough of that, Your Grace,' she said.

His mouth moved in a way – a sort of self-aware wryness, an appreciation of his own failures – that she knew so well it almost melted her heart. Then his face cleared and he bowed. 'My apologies, sister. It is just my wicked way!'

Amicia allowed herself to be steered inside, even as she felt the very edge of the *zone* that surrounded beings with great power. She cloaked herself as carefully as she could, using what she had learned from both the Red Knight and Harmodius during the siege, and she kept her eyes down and thought of mice.

This was a mistake, she thought.

A pair of servants led her into the Great Hall and then up a winding stair and along a corridor that went up and then down.

'*Ma soeur*, do you have a maid?' one servant asked.

'No,' she answered.

The woman nodded. 'I'll send you a woman to help. This is the portmanteau from your horse – is there more?'

Amicia looked at the narrow bed with something close to lust. The air of the castle was cold, but not like the open marshes of the Adnacrags. And there was a stack of wool blankets waiting to serve her.

'No more, I thank you. That's all I have.' She smiled. 'I was very much a last minute addition. Goodwife, I am spent. May I lie down?'

The other woman nodded. 'I doubt that Lady Ghause will receive you until after evensong. It is Christmas Eve.' Despite being a senior servant, or perhaps even a lady-in-waiting, the older woman took the time to help Amicia strip.

The moment her soaked undergown was off, she was warmer, despite the frigid air. A pair of servant girls came in, and brought her a wool flannel gown – floor-length, and a lovely blue.

The younger bobbed a curtsy. 'Lady Ghause sends this with her compliments, and says that religious women are all too rare here. She hopes that it suits you.'

The wool was soft and very fine and held a healthy charge of *potentia* like musk.

Amicia pulled it over her naked body, and the older maid pulled the covers over her, and she was asleep.

She awoke flushed and breathing hard, after the most erotic dream of her life. A dream with a very particular focus. She lay in her bed, calming her breathing.

The old Abbess had taught her to make a virtue of necessity. To meditate when only meditation could help. She imagined her knight – still very fresh in her traitorous memory, so she clothed him and armed him and placed his image, kneeling, in a nativity scene – a guard for one of the three great kings who had come to visit the newborn babe.

The nativity played out – the kings gave their gifts, and retreated, and he went with them, his steel sabatons crunching through the snow, and she watched him mount his horse with his usual grace, his annoying, ever-present grace. And she looked back to see the Virgin take up her child from the manger.

She breathed, calm, and centred—

'Time to wake, sister! Time for mass!'

She stretched, at peace with herself, and smelled – perceived – the musk in the real and the touch of *ops* in the *aethereal*. The gown had been ensorcelled.

Honi soit qui mal y pense, she thought and stripped the thing off. She handed it to the maid, who was more than a little shocked at her nudity – and her tattoos.

'Have this washed,' Amicia said. 'It stinks.'

After mass, she followed the housekeeper – the older woman who had led her into the castle – into the Great Hall and up a short set of steps.

Amicia could feel Ghause from across the fortress, and so she was prepared when the housekeeper opened the door.

The woman who sat on the tall chair of dark wood had no embroidery in her lap, and she held her head as few women did – up, with a direct gaze.

'Ah – the nun. My dear sister, it is all too rare to receive a religious vocation here. Are you permitted to speak?'

Amicia thought *so this is his mother. She burns in the* aethereal *like – like—*

'I have no vow of silence,' she said.

'You are the most remarkably attractive nun I've seen in many a day,' Ghause said. 'Watch out for my husband. He doesn't like to take no for an answer. And he likes to break things.' She smiled. 'And people.'

Amicia felt her face burn hot. 'My lady,' she said softly. What else could she say to such a remarkable introduction?

'Are you a virgin, girl?' Ghause asked.

Amicia realised – just in time – that she was in a contest as surely as if she were fighting in the snow. 'That is a rude question, my lady.'

'Oh, I'm a rude woman. You do not fool me, *sister.* You seek to hide your powers, and I can feel them – sweet Christ, girl, you lit the very moon with your sword of light. You are a witch – a very powerful witch. Why are you here?'

Amicia made a good straight-backed curtsy. 'My lady, I am here to help Ser John escort his convoy. As you have apparently seen, I have some skill in working the hermetical.'

Ghause watched her.

Amicia resisted the invitation to talk further.

'You are from Sophie's convent? Eh?' the older woman asked.

Amicia winced at her own foolishness. When she had volunteered to come, she had imagined herself secure. She had imagined that she might look at his father and mother and see the source of his revolt against God. Learn things to his good.

In her pious arrogance, she had assumed that she would be secure and powerful here.

Ghause Muriens wore the *aethereal* not like a cloak or a fog, but like a garment of regal splendour. It was part of her. She *lived* in *potentia.*

Amicia felt naked before it. 'I serve the Order of Saint Thomas,' she said.

Ghause licked her lips. 'At Lissen Carrak?' she said softly. She was beautiful. Amicia had never seen a woman as beautiful. And what she manipulated was not as simple as air or darkness or light or fire.

Amicia nodded. 'Yes,' she said.

'So – you know my son, perhaps?' Ghause asked again. She rested a hand on Amicia's arm, and the nun warmed to the touch. She warmed to her navel, and to the tips of her fingers.

The ring on Amicia's finger flared. Ghause spat – like an angry cat – and started back and Amicia recovered control of her own body and mind. And was only then aware that Ghause had been overwhelming her. Seducing her.

'Bitch,' Ghause said. 'That was unnecessary.' Her eyes narrowed. 'A mere *mind your own business* would have sufficed.'

Amicia's mind reeled. The *ring* had saved her. She took a deep breath, and then another.

Ghause smiled. 'You do know him!' she said. 'Ah – sometimes, I wonder if there is a God after all.'

Amicia had recovered her control. 'Madam, I nursed two of your sons in my place as a novice. And both were fine knights and gentle men.' Her voice was steady as rock, and she had her version of events prepared. She fixed it in her palace, and banished all the rest to the locked box where she kept the Red Knight.

'I am a proud mother, and I was led by false rumour to fear that Gabriel was dead. What can you tell me of him?' Ghause asked.

Amicia shook her head. 'Madam, he was the Captain of a fortress under siege by the Wild, and I was a novice serving in the hospital. Twice when he was wounded, I used my powers to heal him, and I stood by your younger son – Ser Gavin – and saw him fight. Brilliantly.'

'My housekeeper says you have tattoos. Why does a sister of the great order have tattoos?' Ghause smiled like a cat with a bird.

'Once, I lacked the power to stop others from imposing their will on me,' Amicia said gently. 'I no longer lack that power.'

'It pleases you to think you can match me,' Ghause said. 'I know what you dreamed,' she said, almost cooing. 'I watched it.'

'I know of no reason that I should have to match you,' Amicia said. 'If you know what I dreamed, then you also know what I did with it. I am not your foe, madam, but if you attempt to enter my head again, I might feel myself attacked.'

Ghause licked her lips. 'You admired my son.' She put a hand to her bosom. 'This interests me profoundly, woman. Tell me!'

Amicia dropped another curtsy. 'My lady, I am a sister of the Order of Saint Thomas and my only bridegroom is Christ. You may impose on me with your manipulations – I will only see them as torments. I admire your son as a good knight and a good man.'

'By Lady Tar!' Ghause hissed. 'My son Gabriel is not a *good man* or a *good knight*. That horseshit is for the peasants. I made him to be like a god!'

I should never have come here.

The air was full of Ghause's power, and the impulse to speak lay on Amicia like a shirt of heavy maille. But she resisted. *God has the ultimate power. Christ be with me. Virgin, stand with me, now and in the hour of my death.*

'Who gave you that ring?' Ghause asked suddenly.

Amicia opened her mouth to speak, her own will broken by the sudden question, but a voice behind her cut her off ruthlessly.

'Stop bothering the girl. Christ on the cross, woman, you are at her as if she's a maid who's stolen a silver spoon. Never mind the old hag, sister, she likes tormenting pretty women, and look, you are one.' The Earl leaned in the door of the solar.

Trapped between them, Amicia knew a moment of true fear. It was like being a fawn caught between two giants.

'She's no maid. She's a sorceress of immense power, she has more secrets than Richard Plangere, and I think she's lying to me. I wouldn't have let her in my wards, but now that someone else has, I mean to know her.' Ghause stood with her hands on her hips. 'You're no nun.'

Amicia's breath caught. 'My vocation is not for you to criticise,' she snapped.

'Look at those breasts!' the Earl said, slapping his booted thigh. 'Sweet Christ, breathe harder, sweet.'

Amicia stood straight-backed, as if she was the equal of an Earl and the King's sister. 'May I be excused?' she asked. 'If this is your courtesy, I'll stay with the servants.'

She ducked under the Earl's arm and got down the steps to the main hall without a voice being raised.

With help from servants, she made her way to Ser John's room, where the old knight was lying in a closed bed with heavy curtains. His colour was good and he was awake, and his squire was reading to him from a book of chivalry. He rose, but Amicia waved to the young man to sit.

'Do you know Muriens?' she asked.

Ser John shook his head. 'Met the Earl in forty-nine or fifty. We was on the same side after Chevin, and I played dice with him once or twice. That's all.' He raised his head. 'You, my girl, are red as a beet.'

'Lady Ghause has been interrogating me. The Earl would like to peel me and perhaps eat me as well.' She threw herself into a chair. 'I'm a terrible nun. I want to burn her to ash. I need to go to confession for fifty things.'

Ser John nodded. 'Well – you're safe enough in here, and I don't think I could muster an assault on your chastity, even if I was moved that way. How about I'll just tell you my confessions, and then you can give me a nice easy penance. Jehan, go fetch us some nice hot wine.'

'Thanks, Ser John.'

'Think nothing of it.' He managed a smile. 'You save me from monsters, and I'll save you from the Earl.'

She read to him from the gospels – he had a travelling set, writ plain and with no illuminations. After a few minutes, Jehan returned with wine, and sat on the settle near the fire and sewed his master's ruined arming cote. Later, she reinforced all her healing work on him.

The Earl, dressed in green velvet, came to the door. 'There you are,' he said. He pushed in. 'How's your patient?'

Ser John sat up. 'Well enough to tell you to get your teeth out of the nun before I get out of this bed and come after you with a mace.'

The Earl laughed. 'I've heard you are a hot one, Ser John. May I pay her my respectful admiration?'

Ser John looked at the nun and then shook his head. 'I'm thinking the good sister wants no admiration of that sort at all. Having, as you understand, got a bellyful of it from a company of mercenaries during a siege.'

The Earl laughed. 'Damme, Ser John, she must have had them baying like wolves. And full of witch-power, too?' He grinned. 'Sister, I'm not really the spawn of Satan. I'll keep my hands to myself – although, if you ever change your mind—'

Getting no response, he shook his head. 'You're better,' he said to Ser John. 'I gather you went after a stone troll with a dagger and won.'

Ser John laughed. Then he grabbed his ribs and wheezed. 'Sweet Christ, Your Grace, but you can tell it that way. And while the words are true, it'd be just as true to say the evil thing tripped over me!'

The Earl laughed. 'Well – there's a spot at my Christmas high table for both of you. And my wife will keep her place with you, sister.' He grinned at her, and his gaze fell from her face to her breasts, which were, she thought, buried in two layers of wool gowns. But some men—

Supper was served to the three of them without comment. Sister Amicia went to the chapel and prayed with the priest, who seemed distant. She found a clean white wool bed gown on her bed, and she wore it, and the only dreams she had were of swimming in a clear lake under stars so big that they were like berries on mistletoe.

Christmas Day dawned at Ticondaga with a long spell of snow followed by brilliant sunshine. Amicia went to mass, and spent the morning on her knees. As the whole garrison, their wives and sweethearts, processed out of the chapel and through the halls, Amicia found Ghause had left her husband's side and joined her. As Ser John was tottering along at her side, she felt secure from immediate assault. Master Amato was close by, and smiled at her.

'Relax, girl.' The older woman put a familiar hand on her arm – skin to skin – and Amicia flushed. 'When you are old and powerful, you will not fancy having some young sprig burst into your refuge either, dripping with *ops* and smelling of power.' She nodded and arched an eyebrow. 'The more so when the girl is your son's lover.'

Amicia met the woman's eyes. 'I don't plan to have a refuge. I will use my powers for good, and make people happier and better.' She nodded curtly. 'No man is my lover.'

At that moment, there was a pulse in the *aethereal*. The ring gave a flash of heat, and she felt her own store of *potentia* – blessedly unneeded in the fortress of Ticondaga – suddenly expended at a prodigious rate. *Someone* cast a working of healing – she felt it.

Ghause stepped away from her, and put a hand to her jewelled throat. She smiled in triumph. 'But surely that was my son! You two are *linked*!'

Amicia sighed. 'Your Grace, I know your son, and I am fond of him, but he and I have made different choices. I will give my love to all people – not one person.'

'People are generally harder to like than horses or cats,' Ghause said. 'Come – *pax*. Eat with us at our feast – we will have carols.' She nodded to Ser John. 'Bring your patient. My husband wants to know if he really attacked a troll with his dagger.' The older woman's mouth twitched in mockery. 'Men. There are so many more interesting things to discuss than war. Don't you think?'

Liviapolis – The Red Knight

The palace Ordinaries spent Christmas Eve shovelling the snow from the great square, and laying down sawdust, and then rolling mats of woven straw over the ground. Barriers were built, and a mock castle, and four sets of stands in the ancient hippodrome, and then sailors from the fleet assembled canvas awnings from the cellars beneath the stables. Some of the canvas had rotted, but most of it was fresh and white, and in the frozen silence of Christmas morn, they laid it out along the newly rebuilt yards and roofed the ancient hippodrome and its raised timber stands with a great oval of cloth. When the snow began to fall gently outside, the whole hippodrome was covered, and a dozen adepts from the Academy finished the work with a hermetical reinforcement and a layer of sparkling light.

Morgan Mortirmir was assigned to work directly with the master grammarian, which indicated something of the speed with which his studies were progressing. The grammarian watched the workmen assemble the canvas roof far above them.

'You understand the principle?' he asked.

Mortirmir pulled on the beard he was trying to grow and stared at the empty stands. *Was this a trick question?* With the grammarian, you never knew. He looked at the question from half a dozen panicked angles and managed to say, 'Yes?'

'Yes? Or maybe yes? Honestly, Mortirmir.' The grammarian buried his hands in his voluminous fur-lined robe. Mortirmir threw caution to the winds. 'It is not just a single principle, is it?'

Lip curling in disdain, the grammarian raised an eyebrow. 'Explain,' he said.

'The *scutum* or *aspis* spell is among the most basic workings – one that uses *potentia* in a form that is almost raw. But placing the working into the cloth requires a different principle – the principle of like calling to like. The canvas alone would resist the rain or snow for some time, making it a kind of sponge to absorb our working, because our protection has the same intention? And then yet a third principle, because the canvas is woven from flax fibre, and was once alive, and thus is that much more interested in – *harmony.*' Morgan stopped, surprised by the last word. When the grammarian didn't interrupt or blast him to pieces, he added, 'Without the canvas, it would require an incredible effort of will to roof the entirety of the hippodrome and more to maintain it all day. But with the solidity of the canvas here in the real, it is far easier to place our work in the *aethereal.*'

The grammarian smiled. 'Not bad. Here, have some hot wine. Not bad at all. How many workings have you mastered?'

Mortimir winced. 'Four,' he said. 'Fire – as an attack. Light. I have several variations on light—' he went on, but shook his head. 'All of the series of *aspis* or *scutum* manipulations.'

'Hence your presence here,' the grammarian said.

'A lock-breaking conjuration,' Mortirmir added.

'Two of the most difficult manipulations, but not one of the most basic elemental manipulations except fire.' The grammarian nodded. 'Memory problems?'

Mortirmir stared miserably at the ground. 'I practise and practise but things don't stick.'

The grammarian nodded. 'It is hard to come late to your powers. I didn't *really* come to a full memory palace and an understanding of manipulation and illusion until I was in my fifties.' He looked up at the sailors. 'If one of them fell, could you catch him?'

Morgan ran through the sum total of his manipulations. 'Er – yes. I think so.'

The grammarian sipped his bottle of hot wine. 'Would you?' he asked.

'Of course!' Mortirmir said.

The grammarian nodded. 'My pater was a sailor. I hardly knew him. An old priest saw me working power – all green – and sent me here.' He shrugged. 'From then I never left. I like the hot wine. And lights that work. Why am I telling you this?'

Mortirmir managed a smile.

'Can you work this on your own?' the grammarian asked.

Mortirmir nodded. 'I think so. I'm jousting later and I don't want to be weak.'

The grammarian laughed. 'Jousting? You mean that tomfoolery where you ride in a set of iron kettles until you slam into another man? Well, young scholar, your place is here, and if you run out of *ops* you can remember that you have used your powers in the service of the Emperor. Jousting indeed—' The grammarian shook his head, and his brief moment of good will was snapped.

He put his hand on Mortirmir's shoulder. 'Open up,' he said. 'Let me see the prep work on your casting.'

Mortirmir disliked the invasion of his mind by any of the professors, but since the revelation of his powers they were more and more intrusive. And they left echoes of themselves behind – some very dark.

Nonetheless, it was merely part of a scholar's life. He opened his memory palace and admitted the grammarian, who entered as a much younger man in scarlet and cloth of gold.

Mortirmir's memory palace was four columns of the Temple of Athena, and a slightly hasty simulacrum of a blackboard with a piece of silver chalk hanging from a fancy silk cord. There were no seats, and around the four columns there was smooth white marble for a few paces, and then a featureless grey plain stretching to the limits of the *aethereal*.

'Crucified Christ, boy, this is the whole of your memory?' the grammarian looked about with disdain.

Mortirmir shrugged.

The grammarian smelled like heather, in the *aethereal*, a good smell. And his presence was very solid.

He walked over to the sand table that Mortirmir had built in his mind next to the blackboard, and examined Mortirmir's notes. And his grammar.

'Ahh,' he said. 'This is more like it. This – this is the surface area of the hippodrome?'

Mortirmir nodded eagerly. 'I took it from a book of geometrika.'

The grammarian favoured him with a smile. 'You have bettered me, then, young sir. I always meant to, but in the end I always guess.' He ran his slim silver stick along the lines of the working itself, as yet unpowered. 'I see two things that I would do differently,' he said. 'But I see nothing that is wrong, per se. So I will allow you to proceed.'

'Me, sir?' Mortirmir had prepared the casting as an exercise, and only because he'd been told to do so. He'd come to channel power for the master. That's what students did.

'You. There's the Nautarchon waving at us. Let's see it, young man.'

They stood in the real, on the finely groomed sand floor, looking up.

Mortirmir closed his eyes, *and summoned his workplace. The four broken columns stood like a reminder of his hermetical impotence, but he didn't follow that image. Instead, he summoned power – the best of his skills, now – and, flooded with it, began to fuel the first set of his diplomatika.*

At his side, the grammarian murmured, 'Ahh.'

'Look at that!' called a sailor.

Morgan refused the distraction, and ran his fingers over the second part of his working, then dripped his power carefully – the canvas was delicate, and he could burn it.

The canvas took the hermetical power like dye – the golden light of the sun crept across it from the centre to the edges, and each panel flapped slightly as it filled – a line of sparks on the leading edge of the teenaged boy's effort.

'I love this part,' called the sailor. His mate, on the next mast, laughed, and his laughter echoed hollowly.

Mortirmir's first working had actually run lines of power up the masts and across the yards, and now his hermetical dye reached them in a flare of sparks, and the whole glowed a ruddy gold, as if the canvas was afire.

'ASPIDES,' Morgan said aloud.

All nine of the enormous canvas panels froze – the ruddy light flared and vanished. A careful observer could still note a line of light edging each panel, as fine as a thread.

The master grammarian nodded. 'Lovely, Master Mortirmir. Multiple shields, not just one.'

'If one fails, the others will keep people dry,' Mortirmir said.

'And each panel is its own unity,' the grammarian went on. 'Do you see a problem with that?'

Mortirmir shook his head. 'No, Maestro.'

'You've never built a roof, have you?' The master grammarian was smiling, so Morgan began to experience real triumph. The sailors were applauding.

'No, Maestro.' Mortirmir looked up.

The maestro lifted his staff and said, 'Scutum.'

With no flare at all, something changed. Mortirmir ran his tongue over the edges of his working – in his mind. All solid.

'Between the panels, my young scholar. You made every panel whole. But you didn't unify them. Snow would come in between them.

Not much, and to be frank, I doubt anyone would notice. Your work is well done. You understood all of the principles involved, and your grammatical expression was excellent.' The man bowed slightly. 'Mind you, you have good teachers.' He smiled. 'But a roof is always a unity.

Mortirmir sighed. 'I feel like a fool,' he admitted.

The master grammarian nodded. 'Good. That's the feeling we all get when we learn something. I try to experience it once a day. Now go joust. I may even come back and watch.' He paused. 'You really must work on your memory, my boy.'

'Yes, Maestro.' Mortirmir bowed, and the master grammarian returned his bow.

He walked off the sand, and several sailors came and shook his hand. Their praise delighted him.

The Nautarchon bowed to him. 'If you ever pass as a weatherworker, Master, I'd be delighted to have you on my ship.' He pointed above them. 'You treated the canvas – well, I saw it. Lovely. In a storm, a good mage can hold the sails like that – with *ops*. A well-found ship can stand a winter storm with a mage holding the rigging.'

Mortirmir hadn't expected so much praise. He flushed, looked at the ground, and muttered something that he wasn't sure of himself.

And his feet tangled around the blade of his sword as he walked away. Which hadn't happened to him in weeks. He stumbled, looked around, and saw a dozen Academicians standing at the great entrance, in their robes. They were clapping.

Antonio Baldesce was laughing.

Mortirmir didn't blame him. And he summoned up a smile as he crossed the sand, mindful that resentment at the needling he was about to receive would only make the whole thing worse.

Tancreda put a hand on his arm as he walked up. 'He smiled! Gracious Mother of God, Plague! You made the master grammarian smile!'

Mortirmir shook his head.

Baldesce grinned. 'And old Donatedello. He seemed to like you.'

Mortirmir's arm tingled where Tancreda had touched it. He blushed.

'Where are you going?' asked the others.

'I'm – I'm in the Christmas tournament.'

Baldesce laughed again. 'I hope you remember the little people like us who helped you on your way,' he said.

Kronmir read the message written in wax on the blade of a scythe and winced. The code was old and the message was baldly done, the wax visible to anyone, and the messenger – a girl no more than seven years old – had waited in the snow by his inn, thus making it possible for an enemy to take her and her message – and him. It hadn't happened, but he shook his head, patted the girl, and gave her a gold piece.

'Do you have a mother, girl?' he said.

She shook her head. In that head-shake, she revealed the whole of her future – a future Kronmir wouldn't wish on an enemy. Especially not at Christmas.

He added a second gold byzant, a valuable coin. And the thirty copper coins he had in a bag.

'Listen, child,' he said. 'Men will kill you for the gold I've given you. Can you leave the city?'

She nodded.

'Will you go to Lonika, if I send you?' he asked.

She nodded again.

He took a piece of Eastern paper and folded it in a particular way, and wrote on it in lemon juice. 'Take this to the same blacksmith who sent the scythe blade, child.' He put a hand on her head, which was very warm – almost hot. It gave him great pleasure to do such a good deed at Christmas.

However much she might bridle at a life spent in a convent, it would be better than what awaited her in the city, without parents.

When she was gone, he rubbed the wax twice to make sure the message said what he thought it said, and then he tossed the scythe blade in the fire until the wax was utterly gone.

Then he set out across the city to find himself an assassin.

He went to a certain door, and knocked six times, and then walked away. That was all that was required to order the death of the Megas Ducas.

He went back to gather the strands of his extrication network, because in a day or so, a great many of his people were going to need to flee the city.

The assassin watched a mime come along the street, dressed all in red and green, with a wreath of berries in her hair. He had been expecting her – she came each day at the same time, and did the same dance. But today she did a different act, and he felt the spirit of action flood him as she stooped, as part of her dance, and made a snowball of the filthy mush in the street. She threw it with neat accuracy at his shutters. Then she did a cartwheel, heedless of the freezing slush.

She stopped under his window and did a handstand, and then pulled from her bag a puppet dressed all in red, and dropped it in the snow.

And stepped on it.

She left the scarlet thing behind her as she danced away.

He rose from the narrow bed in his garret and pulled on a plain, much-mended dirty-white hood, and then put a tinker's basket over his shoulder.

An hour after first light, the princess processed from the Inner Court to the Outer Court, where she was met by her new Master of the Palace and the Megas Ducas. In the Outer Court the entirety of the Guard stood, shivering and magnificent, in their finest uniforms, a sea of scarlet and purple and gold and shining steel like a mosaic in which each man was a single tessera.

Her Ordinaries and the Nordikans marched to the centre of the Outer Court and the Guard marched out by files from the right and left, and the Imperial chariot – empty, but for a driver – proceeded to the princess.

'I thought that you had betrayed me,' the princess whispered. She was like an icon brought to life – her face as white as milk, her body adorned in stiff cloth of gold encrusted with jewels and edged and accented in pearls.

'Majesty,' the Duke said, very softly.

The procession rolled across the square – a square nigh on packed with the people of the city who followed the princess and her Guard into the great cathedral where the Patriarch said mass.

The Megas Ducas accepted communion and did not burst into flames. Wilful Murder lost a small amount of money over it.

After mass the whole army, with most of the palace staff and the whole of the Academy, instructors, students, and servants in the

Academy's black livery, as well as the greater part of the population of Liviapolis, processed around the city carrying the relics of forty saints.

The aura of *potentia* so permeated the city that when the Megas Ducas was given wine, he could taste the raw power.

After the procession and a snatched meal, eaten cold from golden plates, the Megas Ducas took most of his knights, as well as some Scholae and a dozen knights of the Latinikon to the hippodrome, where heated pavilions had been set.

The crowd was already in the hippodrome – most had gone there straight from mass and the solemn procession. The crowd was so dense that they had raised the temperature inside. The knights were greeted with cheers as they appeared, and then they went into their tents – Ser Michael, as the master of the tourney, had divided them somewhat artificially into two teams.

The Megas Ducas was meant to be last to arrive, and he waited outside the gates of the hippodrome with his retinue of squires and pages; Toby and Nell and Nicholas Ganfroy, his trumpeter, with Ser Jehan leading and his banner carried by Ser Milus, who was a marshal for the day and not jousting. He was dressed from head to toe in scarlet wool and deerskin, with a hat of scarlet leather lined in fox fur and sporting three enormous red plumes. His knight's belt was around his hips, and he wore a small white scrap of cloth pinned to his shoulder with a brooch of rubies and emeralds. At his side was a sword that all but breathed of *potentia* and had a perfection of form that showed even through its red scabbard. The hilt was gilded steel, the grip wired in gold over scarlet deerskin, the pommel enamelled.

There was a great press of people around the gate – at least a thousand men and women, shouting his name. He leaned down from his great horse and kissed a baby – the first time he'd ever done such a thing, and he was rewarded with a warm wet feeling on his hands and a smell, and the mother beamed at him.

Toby handed him a towel and he wiped his hands and grinned at the mother, and then she was lost in the crowd.

The gates began to open, and the wall of sound hit him like a fist. If he had thought that a thousand people packed into the alley by the gate was a huge crowd, what waited for him at the end of the tunnel was twenty times as big, and he reeled as if an enemy had struck him with a lance.

But he got the smile back on his face. At his feet, Long Paw was gently but firmly pushing the crowd back, away from the tunnel into the hippodrome. A few young men and a trickle of older ones squeezed past into the tunnel ahead of the company archers and they flattened themselves against the walls of the tunnel and shouted his style, their cries ringing metallically in the confines of the half-bowshot-long tunnel.

He waved to the crowd trapped outside and made his horse rear a little, and they applauded and he rode into the tunnel. A young man ran alongside his horse, waving, until he tripped on something in the tunnel, and he fell with a shout.

The Red Knight looked down to see what had happened to him. There was a blinding flare of light, something struck him in the chest, and everything went dark.

The Megas Ducas entered the hippodrome last, and he rode in through the Imperial tunnel by the Great Gate very slowly, with great sheets of sound belting across the arena as the city crowd roared for him. But something was wrong – he was very stiff in the saddle, and Nell, the Duke's page, could be seen to turn her horse in the gate and gallop for the palace.

Ser Michael was summoned. He watched a tight knot of the Duke's household push into the Duke's private pavilion, which wasn't what should have happened. He made a sign to Ser Gavin, the captain of the 'Outlander' team, and ran for the Duke's tent.

Inside, he found Toby kneeling by three stools all placed together. Wilful Murder was white as parchment, and Ser Jehan and Nicholas Ganfroy leaning over—

'What's happened?' Ser Michael asked.

The Duke lay across the stools. He had a lot of blood coming out of him. He was talking, but the voice didn't sound like his own. There was blood everywhere, and Father Arnaud seemed to be covered in the stuff. He was mumbling – probably in prayer – and his face looked grey.

'Summon a magister,' the Duke barked. He didn't sound himself. 'A tough one. No – get me that boy. Mortirmir. If he's here.'

Ser Michael knew a crisis when he saw one. He didn't ask. He turned and ran for the defenders' pavilion.

'Messire Mortirmir!' Ser Michael called as he barged in. Twenty men were being armed by forty squires and pages in a cacophony of steel plates and a bewilderment of lost lace-points. Wicker hampers lay open on the sand, and only a few lucky men – and Ser Alison – had stools on which to sit.

Morgan Mortirmir had his leg harnesses on. And he had no squire.

He came willingly enough. 'What's this about?' he asked, and then he paled. 'Shit – it's not the roof?' he asked.

Ser Michael towed him by the elbow out onto the sands, where they received a smattering of applause – Mortirmir was the first armoured man to emerge. The crowd wanted to see some fighting.

Ser Michael was still trying to parse what he'd seen and heard. It seemed to him that the voice that had barked orders hadn't been the Duke's. He'd sounded very much like Harmodius.

Mortirmir was pushed through the knot of men to the foot of the bed made of stools. The Megas Ducas lay on it, covered in blood – his face was crusted in it and his linen shirt was scarlet.

'Jesu Christi!' Mortirmir muttered. 'I'm no healer.'

Shut up and let me in.

Mortirmir might have reacted differently if not for the week he'd just had. He opened his palace *and in strode a tall man in dark blue velvet.*

All the time in the world, now, lad. Is this all you have for memory?

Who the fuck are you? asked Mortirmir, now terrified. He'd let a stranger into his palace. He was, in effect, naked.

Yes, that was foolish of you. Sorry, lad. I'm going to wear you like a shirt for a few hours. You will be supremely tired at the end and – bah. Stop wriggling. Your panic is understandable but a waste of my effort.

Sweet Jesu, you are young. And supple. What a pleasure – there.

Even as Mortirmir attempted to fight the intruder – with no effect whatsoever – the man was using his body. He could feel himself kneel by the Duke's corpse. He could see his arms move.

Most horrible of all, he watched as his memory palace dissolved.

Really, most young people try and build something that is dashing and romantic and far too fucking complicated. The man in blue velvet sketched rapidly with a wand of gold. The gold – its gleam, and its aethereal presence – calmed Mortirmir. The legions of evil didn't wield gold.

You play chess, eh, boy? the old man asked. The floor under their feet suddenly became black and white parquetry – eight squares by eight.

Mortirmir fought the urge to vomit. Nothing so utterly disconcerting had ever happened to him. Even his mind was not his own. His inner vision – in the aethereal – was in the control of this horrible old—

Please allow me to introduce myself. My name is Harmodius.

You're dead!

Hmm. Not exactly. STOP WRIGGLING. There.

Mortirmir's memory palace was suddenly entirely rebuilt as a garden with a giant marble chess floor in the middle. Every leaf on every wild rose bush was more vivid than anything had been in his former palace.

I've never been there – sir – I can't—

Harmodius laughed. No one has ever been here. I made it up. I'm a little busy, lad. Shut up, please?

Chess pieces began to move.

The white queen's head rotated and a line of pure green light shot out of it, touched the golden knob atop the king's head, and turned into a rainbow of colours so vivid they were like a fever dream and Mortirmir wanted to give them new names. The colours focused on a crystal in Harmodius's hand – an artificiality that Mortirmir could never have contrived. The old man nodded.

You are full of power, aren't you, boy? I'm not sure I've ever had access to this much of the raw stuff. He flashed a smile of pure greed. You really are lucky I have other plans, because this body would suit my needs very well. And how your professors would love to have me as a student! He laughed nastily. Worry not. In fact, I suspect I'll prove to be your benefactor.

He tossed the jewel he'd just created in the air, and Mortirmir saw his left hand strip the glove off his right. Saw his own right hand hover above the Duke's side. There was a crossbow bolt protruding just above the heart on the left.

Assassin, the old man said. Very, very close. Another finger's width to the left, and we'd both be gone. As it is we're in trouble, and Mortirmir's finger touched the Duke's side. Power flared as if a small sun had been released. Poison, alchemy, and magick altogether. Someone wanted my young friend to be very, very dead. The sun intensified, and Mortirmir felt all his potential flowing out of him like water from a broken bottle.

It was the most terrifying sensation.

Worst of all, it became obvious to both of them – together, intertwined – that there was not enough potentia *between the three – Harmodius, Mortirmir, and the stricken Megas Ducas – to save him. The power ran in as if into a bottomless pit, and nothing changed.*

Mortirmir felt Harmodius sag in defeat.

His last aethereal *pouch of of carefully hoarded* ops *vanished—*

There was an explosion of pale, golden green light that seemed to come from the mortally wounded man's hand.

Mortirmir's left hand reached in, took the bolt, and withdrew it from the wound with a gentle tug and a horrible wet sucking noise. As the steel head slid free, the skin underneath closed. Perfectly.

Harmodius, deep in Mortirmir's memory garden, stumbled against a stone pillar – the only remnant of the former palace – and shook his head. *By Saint George, young magister. May you never see that again.*

What happened? Mortirmir breathed.

Harmodius stood breathing, like a man who had run a long race. Then he shook his head. *Not my secret to share, young man. He needs to sleep now. How's your jousting?*

Every knight ran three courses. The jousts were arranged carefully – every man knew the order of his opponents, and there were four sets of lists, and squires and pages ran from one to another as Ser Michael directed the whole entertainment.

Ser Alison unhorsed Ser George Brewes, to the crowd's enormous satisfaction. Ser Francis Atcourt unhorsed the Red Knight, who fought with a singular lack of grace, and the princess put her hand to her chest when he struck the ground. But he rose with some of his usual bounce, and improved in his next exchange, plucking the crest neatly off the helmet of Ser Bescanon, whose lance tip scratched across the Red Knight's shield and failed even to break.

Ser Gavin dominated the afternoon. His lance was sure, and it was clearly his day – he dropped Ser Francis Atcourt hard enough to make people in the crowd wince, and he broke a lance on each of three opponents from the Latinikon and then managed a spectacular feat against Ser Jehan, striking his helmet below the crest so that the whole helmet failed along its forge-weld lines and burst asunder. The older man was unhurt, but helmetless, as he rode down the list, and he wheeled his horse and bowed to his opponent as the crowd applauded.

Ser Alcaeus was the crowd's darling, as captain of the defenders, and he dropped three opponents in a row. But the Podesta of the Etruscans, Ser Antonio, knocked him back in his saddle without unhorsing him and was judged the better lance on points. He rode off to stony silence from the crowd, and to the wild celebrations of the Etruscan merchants near the gate.

As the sun began to set, Ser Gavin faced the Megas Ducas, who was riding stiffly. For the first time all afternoon, the Duke was mounted on his new warhorse. Despite his stiff seat, he was technically perfect – as was his brother. They rode the first course, and broke lances on each other. As they walked their horses back to their starting positions Gavin raised his hand and they halted their horses in the centre of the lists, separated by the barrier that kept horses from colliding – and kept them on course.

Ser Gavin leaned over the barrier. 'Is that you?' he asked.

The Red Knight's eyes flashed. 'It is now,' he said.

'Why don't I get to fight someone incompetent wearing your armour?' Gavin asked. He flipped a salute and rode on. 'You're too bloody good.'

On their second course they broke lances on each other. The crowd roared. The small white handkerchief fluttered on the Red Knight's aventail. The knights who were already out pointed and laughed.

Ser Bescanon said to Ser Jehan, 'That was as pretty a pass as I've ever seen. We need an Alban crowd – this is art wasted on swine.'

Ser Jehan handed him a cup of wine. 'He's a brilliant lance,' he admitted. 'Better than I ever was.'

On their third pass, Ser Gavin's lance skidded off the Red Knight's shield and slammed into his left pauldron and ripped it off his body.

The Red Knight kept his seat as if made of iron, but the circular pauldron rolled across the sand like an accusation. The Red Knight paused at his own pavilion to have his visor removed, and then cantered back down the list and embraced his brother, and the two men pounded each other on the back.

'Sweet Jesu, brother!' Ser Gavin said. 'You're bleeding.'

'So I am. But that was spectacular,' his brother said, and they rode together down the lists, saluted the princess, and rode to one of the heated pavilions.

'Melee by torchlight?' Ser George Brewes said, after exchanging a steel hug with his Captain. 'People will die out there.'

Toby got the Red Knight's maille off over his head and they could all see the bandages.

'What the *fuck!*' shouted Francis Atcourt.

'Crossbow,' the Red Knight said. 'It's out and healed. And now I'll get it worked again. Relax.' He waved to Morgan Mortirmir, who was in full armour. The young man looked as if his eyes had been glazed by a potter, but he was adept enough with his healing. 'Poisoned and magicked. Somebody thought it would be a one-shot kill.'

'We didn't get the shooter,' Ser Michael said.

The other knights in the pavilion looked shocked.

The Red Knight took a deep breath as a pair of Academy Scholae lifted his shirt. Blue fire played across his left shoulder. Mortirmir ran his hand over the wound and nodded.

Tancreda Comnena smiled at her Plague. 'When did you learn to heal so neatly?' she asked.

'At the siege of Lissen Carrak,' Mortirmir's mouth said. 'Damn – despoina, please forget I said that.'

She blinked once, slowly.

'You are very beautiful, and I think I'm in love with you,' Mortirmir said.

She flushed.

He knelt with the sort of grace usually acquired by older men. 'My lady, if you would vouchsafe me a token, I would be proud to defend your beauty against all others, taking you and you alone as my lady fair.'

She put a hand on his head. 'What a pretty speech,' she said. 'Does that work on girls in Alba?'

She had left her hand on his shoulder, and he took it, turned the hand over and kissed her palm. And then her wrist.

'Ah!' she said. 'Now that would work on the girls of Alba, I'm sure.' She leaned down. 'Suddenly you are very sure of yourself.' She leaned closer and brushed her lips against his – the lightest of butterfly pressures.

There you go, boy. That's all there is to it. Really, you are lucky I'm giving you back this palace of meat and lust and power. I do this so much better than you do.

When Mortirmir rode out for his last exchange of blows, he wore a magnificent red and purple sleeve on his shoulder. And Despoina

Comnena pulled her cloak tight against her and refused to let her cousin look to see if she had given the sleeve.

In the last courses – mostly retakes from earlier bouts where a run had been missed or a horse or man had been injured – Mortirmir broke a lance against Ser Antonio and rocked the Podesta in his saddle, to the delight of the crowd and young Mortirmir himself, who pumped his fist in the air in self-satisfied glee. But he mastered himself, and the two were seen to embrace. Ser Alcaeus hit Ser Alison hard but didn't unhorse her, and the crowd roared. It was the last pass, between two favourites, and when it was over the two knights met in the middle of the barrier. Ser Alison said something and Ser Alcaeus put his hand on his heart and shook his head, and then the two embraced.

They all rode around the lists in procession, and the princess awarded the prize of honour to Ser Gavin – very much against her will, the crowd could see, and they roared for the Red Knight nonetheless.

And then they trooped back to their pavilions.

'I am so sorry,' Ser Gavin said.

'I'm not – that was magical,' the Red Knight said. 'I think you may be the best jouster I've ever faced.'

Francis Atcourt shook his head. 'Someone stuck you with a crossbow bolt, and you are still jousting?'

The Red Knight winced. One of the two Scholae – young Mortirmir – raised a hand, and a third Academician stepped forward and a line of power connected them – the junior student passing raw *ops* to his classmate.

'I hoped he might be stupid enough to try again,' the Red Knight said. 'Any luck, Morgan?'

The Alban student shrugged. 'We're seeking the weapon, but whoever did this knows enough to break the connection between bow and arrow,' he said, his voice deeper and strangely confident for an adolescent.

Toby, head down and clearly ashamed, said, 'I'm too used to having Ser Thomas. And Ser Ranald. I was lax.'

The Red Knight reached out and tweaked his squire's cheek. 'Horse shit, Toby, we're all a little stretched right now. And this bastard is *good*. He chose his moment well. We covered it.'

'Why do you have to go back out there?' Ser Michael asked.

The Duke's eyes rested on his – sardonic and dark and a little too glittery. And glinting red in their depths. 'Michael – if I go down all hell will break loose. I promise you. If they don't even see me hesitate—' he smiled, '—then they're going to have some fractures of their own.'

'Who is this *they?*' Ser George asked.

Ser Gavin pushed forward. 'Fuck that!' he said angrily. 'This place can burn for all of me.'

The Red Knight shook his head. 'Gentles all, we may have a busy Christmas night. We knew it was coming – Gelfred got a messenger, but there must have been a duplicate.' He sat up. He was very pale. 'However, if I survive the public dancing, we should be fine. If I don't, let me take this moment to tell you all what a pleasure it has been to be your Captain.'

Atcourt turned to Ser Michael. 'He's insane. Make him go to bed. And shouldn't we warn the princess?'

The Red Knight's face closed.

'Warn her?' Ser Michael spat. He turned and looked at Ser Alcaeus, who stood with his arms folded.

The Morean knight shook his head, looking ten years older, but said nothing.

It was Ser Alison who took up the gauntlet. She laughed, and her raucous laugh rang out like a challenge to fate. 'Warn the princess? *She's probably paying the fucking assassin.*'

Harndon – The Queen

The Queen had tidied her apartments with Diota, and she'd busied herself, first meeting with Master Pye, who'd brought her gift for the King, and then wrapping it. Then she'd dressed carefully in brown velvet with bronze and gold beads and emeralds the size of nail-heads. Her belly showed, but Diota had worked a miracle of her own, recutting the brown velvet to match her latest expansion.

'Where is Rebecca? And Emota? And my other ladies?' she asked, as the winter darkness began to roll over the snow. She watched the shadows lengthen – the towers appearing to creep across the dirty snow in the main yard – and thought with a shudder of the other *darkness* in the corridors under the Old Palace.

'Sweet, they're late. Everyone's late,' Diota said, with her usual practicality. 'Because it is Christmas, sweeting, and that's what happens at Christmas.'

'I'm fat,' the Queen said. She glanced at her nurse. 'Emota worries me. She looks ill.'

Diota rolled her eyes. 'You are having a baby, *Your Grace*.' She grinned. 'It's been known to add a few pounds.' She looked thoughtfully at the mirror. 'Emota – I'm a coarse old woman. I'd say she chose the wrong door at the stable.'

'Emota? She is no light of love,' the Queen said.

Her nurse shrugged. 'Men are pigs. And they behave accordingly.'

'What do you know?' the Queen asked.

'Know? Nothing. But I think that one of the Galles has turned her head, and the little bitch has been spying on us for them.' Diota seized a hairbrush and yanked too hard at her mistress's hair. 'I heard one o' they calling her a slut and a whore.'

The Queen shook her head. 'Why are they so stupid? Blessed Virgin – my own husband thinks I was unfaithful,' Desiderata said. Suddenly she sobbed. She hadn't said the words aloud before.

'He's a fool,' Diota said. 'But he's a man, and that's the way of men.'

'How can he even think it?' the Queen shouted. She hadn't meant to shout. The anger appeared, almost out of the air.

The privy door opened, and Lady Rebecca entered. She curtsied, her face as pale as new milk.

'Oh, Becca, what's wrong?' the Queen asked.

Almspend shook her head, pursed her lips and said nothing.

'I command you,' the Queen said.

'It is Christmas, and like everyone else, I am late,' her secretary said. 'Men in the halls are saying endless foul things.'

'You have been attacked by one of the Galles!' Diota cried.

Almspend smiled. 'Unlikely,' she said quietly. 'Or rather, unlikely to happen more than once.'

The Queen sighed. 'If only Mary – bah. She'll come back after Epiphany.' She looked out the window. 'I would give much to leave the poison of this court. To go to a nunnery and have some peace until my baby is delivered.' The thought of her baby clearly cheered her. She allowed a small smile to penetrate her anger.

Almspend made an effort, drew herself together and picked up a brush and began to work on the Queen's hair.

Diota looked at her. The two exchanged glances.

'Where is Emota?' asked the Queen.

Almspend shrugged. 'Busy, I expect, Your Grace.' She was careful, but the Queen's head turned.

'Lying down for her Gallish lover,' Diota spat.

Almspend glared at her. 'That's not how I've heard it,' she said.

'Nurse, do not be crude. Emota is the youngest of my ladies and perhaps not the brightest.' The Queen smiled. 'But she has my love all the same.'

'You should keep it,' Lady Emota said from the doorway. 'I am not bright. I am dull, and stupid, and foolish. And pregnant. Can we share that, Your Grace? Like you, I will bear a bastard child.'

The Queen turned so fast that Almspend's brush tangled in her hair and stayed there. 'Emota!' she said.

Emota pointed a finger at the Queen. 'I am ruined because *you* are a slut. I *believed you.* I believed all that instruction about protecting the protectors and guarding the guardians and all I will have for my idles is a swollen belly and the reputation of being a whore *just like my Queen.*' She burst into tears and threw herself on the carpet.

'What has happened?' the Queen asked. She looked at the other women.

Almspend got hold of the hairbrush and began to work it loose from the Queen's hair.

Diota rolled the prostrate girl over and slapped her – none too gently – on the cheek. 'Get up, you silly woman,' she said.

'He *is* the best knight!' Emota said. 'And he treated me like – like—'

'Are you leman to Jean de Vrailly?' the Queen asked.

'Among others,' Diota spat. 'She's ridden a prize number of war-horses.'

'Aaaghh!' wept Emota. It was as if she'd taken a wound, she cried so hard.

'The Galles will use her against you,' Almspend said, brushing on. 'Her lechery will make you look a wanton, Your Grace.'

The Queen knelt by her lady. 'Emota – I need to know what has happened. But I will not desert you.'

Almspend's eyes met Diota's in agreement for once. 'Your Grace, it would be better if you did desert her.'

The Queen gathered the sobbing girl in her arms. 'Why – because she loved the wrong man? What does it matter?' she asked. 'It is all male vanity and foolishness. All of it.'

Almspend's eyes met her Queen's. 'That's not the argument to use to a court full of men at Christmas,' she said. 'The Galles have us under siege, my Queen. And they have put a sap in through poor Emota.'

'More like a battering ram,' Diota said.

'Be kind. Both of you. What has this girl done that is so bad?' She turned to Almspend. 'I understand your argument, my dear. I am upset too.' She pressed her hand against Almspend's cheek. 'You are angry.'

'More afraid than angry,' Almspend said cautiously.

'What do you know?' the Queen asked, gazing into her secretary's eyes. Almspend's eyes were pale blue and shone like ice on a clear winter day. The Queen's were deep and dark, green and brown and gold, and they seemed to hold secrets – all the secrets of an ancient world.

'What have you learned?' the Queen asked.

Almspend pursed her lips and frowned, and her eyes darted away. 'Not today – please, Your Grace.' She looked at the young woman sobbing on the floor. 'Your Grace – I apologise. Emota is guiltless of anything but having her head turned. I'm sure of it. But the vitriol we will reap—'

'When you call me *Your Grace* this often, I know that something is very wrong.' The Queen smiled. She looked down and put her hand on the girl. 'But no girl who has been raped is guilty of anything, and we will not make her more a victim.' She ran her hand down the girl's back and golden light seemed to fill the room.

'Ahh!' sighed Emota.

The air seemed clear and clean.

Diota breathed in and out noisily, and then sighed. 'Ah, poppet. You have deep places in you, and no mistake.'

The Queen shook her head. 'I *will* make them pay. I will make them pay for Emota and for Mary and for every harsh word they have said. I swear it.'

The lights flickered.

Almspend shuddered. 'That – was heard.'

'*I care not. They would toy with me and harm those I love? I will rip their manhoods from them and blind their eyes with my talons.'* The Queen stood up like a statue of bronze, and she shone.

Almspend stepped back.

The Queen put a hand to her forehead. 'Mary, mother of God, pray for us sinners now and in the hour of our death. Holy Mary, what did I say?'

Almspend shook her head.

The Queen took a little holy water from a vial and crossed herself. Then she took a deep breath. 'I was in touch with something,' she said. 'Becca, you are troubled and you were before Emota came in.'

'Humour me,' Almspend asked without raising her eyes. 'Your Grace.'

'Is it something bad?' the Queen asked.

Almspend raised her eyes. 'Yes,' she said. 'Oh, how I wish I could lie.'

The Queen smiled. 'Let us kneel, and pray to our Lady for succour. And to Christ Jesus.'

Almspend sighed. They all knelt, and prayed.

There was noise in the courtyard, and Diota leaned out to watch. A dozen squires – most of them Galles, but several Albans – trooped by with torches. They stopped in the middle of the courtyard and began to sing a bawdy carol. They were dancing – Diota leaned out further.

Her breath sucked in, and she turned inside.

'They have figures. Made like Your Grace, and Lady Mary, and Lady Emota. In whore's clothes. They are dancing with them.'

The Queen's face darkened. 'Send for my knights.'

'Your Grace, most of your knights were sent north by the King.' Almspend shook her head. 'There's Diccon Crawford and Ser Malden. They can hardly fight all the Galles.'

The Queen's face darkened further.

'And the King has just stepped onto his gallery,' Diota reported.

'He will act,' the Queen asserted.

'I'm sure of it,' Diota said. She came back to Almspend's side, and took up a brush.

After some hooting from the courtyard rose to assail them, the Queen sobbed. The harsh laughter of young men rose to assail them.

And the King did nothing.

'How did it come to this?' the Queen asked.

N'gara – Yule Court

The hall was set with a thousand stars and ten thousand tapers – slight lights of beeswax that nonetheless seemed to burn for ever, while a hundred small faeries flitted from light to light like bees with flowers. The silver sound of their laughter was polyphonic and, against it, Tapio's harper played an ancient lament, the 'Song of the Battle of Tears', which was only played at Yule.

Tamsin sat in state and Bill Redmede, who loved his own lady to distraction, nonetheless found her the fairest being he'd ever seen. Today her heart-shaped face was framed with her snow-white hair and her gown of white wool was embroidered with golden leaves and red berries intertwined with real holly and real ivy, and she wore an ivy crown.

She sat in the centre of the dais with Mogon, the Duchess of the Westmores, as her title was translated, on her right, and a tall golden bear on her left. At her feet was a table full of men – Redmede himself, and Bess and young Fitzwilliam and Bill Alan, and Cat, and the Grey Man. And on the other side sat Outwallers – a very young shaman, an elderly hunter who'd been healed by Tamsin herself, and a handsome man with the strangest skin Redmede had ever seen, blue-black like charcoal, with lively brown eyes and curly hair.

He caught Redmede staring at him, and instead of glaring he smiled. Redmede responded with his own smile.

'Nita Qwan,' the man said, extending his forearm in the Outwaller way, and Redmede bowed his head as Jacks did and then embraced the man. 'Bill,' he shouted over the music. The irks tended to listen for a bit and then wander off into conversation, and the hall was loud, although the plaintive notes of the lament were easy to hear, if you listened. 'Or you may call me Peter!'

'Your Alban is easy on the ears,' Redmede said. He introduced the black Outwaller to Bess, who grinned, and to Bill Alan, who looked at the man's hand for a moment as if it was a precious artefact.

'Was it an accident? Or some monster did this?' Alan asked.

Nita Qwan laughed. 'Where I come from, all men look like me.'

'O' course they do, mate!' Bill Alan said. 'Don't mind me – too much mead.' He raised his cup. 'An' very fine it looks on ye, too!'

'You must be the Sossags,' Bess said.

Nita Qwan grinned and swallowed some mead of his own. 'We must, lady,' he said.

The music changed, and couples – mostly irks – began to rise from the benches. There were enough Western Kenecka Outwallers – with their red-brown skin and high cheekbones – to provide a solid contingent of men and women, and the Jacks and Outwallers were game to dance.

Tamsin came down the dais, and Tapio forward from the tapestries at the back of the hall to bow deeply over her hand. She smiled, as radiant as the brightest mid-winter sun, and the mistletoe in her hair seemed to glitter with life and barely suppressed magic, and Tapio gathered her in his arms and kissed her. And as they kissed, many others kissed throughout the hall, and Redmede found himself lost in Bess's eyes.

And then the Faery Knight took a great cup of beaten gold from one of his knights and walked to the centre of the hall.

'Be free of my hall, all you guests. But be warned that this night we celebrate the triumph of the light over the darkness – whether you choose to call that Yal'da or you celebrate the coming of a blessed babe or you merely yell for the crushing of the long night. If you serve the dark, begone!'

He raised the cup, and light flowed out like spilled wine, and the irks raised a great shout, and all the Outwallers too, and the high-pitched war cry ripped out into the night.

'Now drink and dance!' Tapio said. 'Those are my only commands.'

The wreckage of the hall was fitting tribute to the finest revel Bill Redmede had ever witnessed, or joined, and he himself was almost too drunk to care what happened under the table, behind the tapestries, or on the dais at the head of the hall.

Bess reached out to a beauty – a fair irk woman with a slim figure and a halo of golden hair – and the woman caught her hands and kissed her on the mouth. 'Child of man.' She laughed. 'You taste better than I'd imagined. A bright Yule to you and your mate.'

Bess curtsied. 'You are all so beautiful!' she breathed. 'Where are the hideous irks? The ugly faces and the fangs?'

The irk maid passed her silver fan over her face and there she was, a glowering hag with a nose six inches long and warts with hair. 'Would you go to war dressed for a party?' she asked. 'Or to a party, dressed for war?' she asked, and her face returned to its elfin beauty. 'I have as many faces to wear as a child of man has dresses. Fair is fair,' she added, and kissed Redmede until his head spun. The irk maid spun away on light feet. 'Your mouths are rich, children of men. Be love!'

And later still, when only a hardy few eaters were picking the bones of a deer carcass on the centre table, and a hundred faeries flitted high in the cavernous ceiling, leaving streamers of pale fire as they moved, and half the hall was dancing and the other half was singing or playing instruments – hautboys, sackbuts, and corinettos and oboes and recorders and whistles and lutes and harps and a hundred stringed instruments that Bill Redmede had never seen before – some very small, or possessing just two or three strings, so that the vast cavern that was the Faery Knight's hall seemed to move with the dance – then Mogon came and squatted on her haunches by him.

'The time is now,' she said. 'This is a magic time. The *aethereal* is wide open to the real. Thorn will be blind as a bat, and without high-pitched sounds to help him, and all his little helpers will be deaf until morning.'

Nita Qwan, the Sossag, was resting under the table on the trestle. He emerged with a flagon of Yule ale. Redmede worried briefly what the Outwaller had seen – he and Bess had been a little busy.

'May I see Lord Tapio now?' he asked Mogon.

Mogon nodded. 'You'll see him, as he invites you.'

Nita Qwan and Redmede bowed to their companions – those still upright – and followed the Duchess through the hall. The great warden danced among the dancers, passing light-footed through the intricate whorls and turns of a hundred couples and two different figures.

At the back of the hall hung a tapestry of a unicorn, done in white spider's web on a tissue of spider silk by a thousand faeries. It was so light that it fluttered in the breeze and so vivid that Redmede expected the unicorn to move.

They passed behind it, and the tapestry blocked all sounds – and light. The reverse showed the same unicorn, but with the image turned.

They walked through a broad cavern lit with torches, and into another, and then came to a heavy oak door with decorations wrought in bronze – half moons and stars and comets. Mogon rapped it smartly, and it opened.

Inside was a room that might have been at home in any lord's castle – the whole panelled in old oak, with oak table and chairs and great bronze candlesticks. A fire roared in a huge fireplace that filled one wall – a sorcerous fire, white and blue, and the walls were hung with armour and weapons. And heads. Two Wyverns, a dozen great beasts, an unidentifiable monster – and rows of human heads.

Bill Redmede was arrested by the heads.

'*Welcome, fair guessstsss.*' Tapio put a hand under Redmede's elbow and seated him at the great table. And then he went around. '*Lord Geraaargkh of the Blueberry Moeity, who comes as the Steward of the Adnacrag Bears. Mogon, Duchess of the Western Lakes, and Lady of the Wardens of the Wild. Tekksimark, Marquis of Mound Five and representative of one hive of the Western Boglins. Nita Qwan, for the Sossag – and perhaps for other Outwaller men, as well. Bill Redmede for the Jacks, and perhaps for other men in Alba and the east.*'

There was a sudden, polite babble of complaint – Bill Redmede didn't feel he held any remit to speak for men, nor did Nita Qwan, and Tekkismark chittered animatedly that his hive was one of the smallest.

Tapio swept out an arm in a magnificent gesture. '*I agree that none of us can actually speak for a race. Nonetheless, it is time to act, and when they make songs of us, we will stand for our peoples.*' He frowned. '*If any songs are made in the days to come.*'

Mogon showed her long pink tongue and a smell of burning soap filled the air. 'You are too dramatic, my friend,' she said. 'No matter who wins, there is always someone to make songs.'

Tapio's frown turned to a smile. '*Tamsin and I will have to stand for the irks, although no two Eld folks agree on anything from the best wine to the best way to kiss a mortal.*' He sat, his deerskin shirt glowing from the odd fire. '*I agree that while an irk lives, someone will be making songs.*' He crossed his legs – his legs which were longer than any mortal's. His hose were of deer-skin. '*But we are not here to talk about the vagaries of art, are we? Some of you are already engaged in war, or near war, with Thorn. Others of you are as yet undecided – indeed, one of you is only just discovering the purpose for which we have gathered.*'

'What is that purpose?' demanded Tekkismark.

'*We are here to bring about the defeat of the entity known as Asssh, currently posssesssing the sssorcerer Thorn.*'

The bear growled, then sat back – a very human gesture as it tucked its big arms behind its head. 'What is possessing, in this context?' he asked with a rumble like a cat's purr.

Mogon leaned forward. 'Possession is against the Law.'

Tapio shrugged. '*Isss it?*' he hissed. '*And when doesss Asssh ressspect the Law?*'

Bill Redmede leaned forward, looked at Nita Qwan and met the same incomprehension in his blank stare, and turned to Tapio. 'Lord – who is Ash? What does he have to do with Thorn? What is he to me?'

Nita Qwan nodded his agreement. 'And of what law do you speak?' he asked.

Tapio exchanged a long look with Mogon. Geraaargkh took his clawed paws from behind his head and turned his glistening black eyes on the two men. 'Trust two *men* not to know the Law.'

Mogon shook her great head. 'Why? We take care that they do not learn too much of the Law of the Wild, even when they have lived among us for fifty generations, like the Sossag.' She paused, and the spines on her head raised, the whole crest coming erect with a snap. 'The Law prevents us from destroying each other in times of drought and famine. It was formulated long ago when the first human sorcerers began to manipulate the elements in a way that we had not foreseen.'

'How long ago?' Nita Qwan asked.

Tapio rubbed his bare chin. '*Nine thousand years, as men count time.*' He looked at Mogon, who shrugged.

'There was no time, before men came,' Mogon said. 'It is pointless to count the time since, merely to satisfy the ignorance of men.'

'*There was a great war, that covered all the earth,*' Tapio said very quietly.

'Men against the Wild?' Redmede heard himself ask. He put a hand over his own mouth.

'No,' Mogon said. She stared into the fire. 'Not at all.'

Tapio poured himself more wine. '*When the war was over, the survivors determined that never again would people of power do certain things.*'

Mogon kept looking into the fire. 'All the things the winners had done to win the war were outlawed, of course,' she said. 'Possession. Necromancy. The fire from the sky.'

Tapio added. *'Ash was there. Ash is the greatest of the dragons – and the one most inimical to any rivals.'*

Mogon laughed. 'Ash has no rivals, but he perceives all of us – every sentient being – as an enemy because he understands the potential in every thinking thing to rise to power. Ash desires to be a god. Or perhaps to be God.' Her laugh was bitter. 'I am accounted old at half a thousand years, and I have seen enough to know that the showdown with Ash has been long and long in the making. My father believed—' She looked at Tapio.

Geraaargkh shook himself and hunkered over. 'We were promised!' he said. 'Promised a king. A leader.'

Tapio's smile grew cynical. *'A messiah – isn't that what we were expecting?'*

'Half the Wild thinks it is you,' Geraaargkh said.

'It is said,' Tekkismark spat. 'You are the one. The one who will free us from the wheel and make the gears turn any way they will.' He clashed his forearms together, and they made the same sound, Redmede thought, that a peasant made as he sharpened a scythe.

Tapio looked disgusted. *'I am not your messiah. We need to come down from the clouds and solve this ourselves.'*

Mogon sat back heavily and her big oak chair gave a momentous creak, almost a groan. 'We were promised. By the Lady Tar.'

Nita Qwan nodded. 'Tar is a name I know, even among my people in Ifraqu'ya. But we call her Tara. The Great She-Wolf.'

Mogon's crest was almost a bristle brush – every spine seemed to strain for the beamed ceiling. 'Tar is no wolf, man-who-cooks. Tar is another of the great serpents. A dragon.'

Geraaargkh said, 'Bears call her "The First".'

Tapio sipped his wine and sang a lilting song in an irk language. The pace was slow and steady, and the tuning was alien to human ears, but had a stately dignity that transcended melody.

'First who slipped through dappled glades
First who danced among the blades.'

Nita Qwan cleared his throat in the momentary silence that followed the irk's song. 'So – Tar is good? And Ash is evil?'

Tapio grinned so that all his fangs showed. *'Out in the hall many folk are dancing in the Yule, proclaiming the light against the dark. And despite my love's passion for cleaning, there are small creatures that live in the hall – mice, rats, even some beetles. When the flashing heels of a* dancer slay one such, was the dancer good, or evil? While proclaiming the triumph of light, they may slay a dozen mice and a hundred beetles.'

Mogon extended a long, taloned arm. 'And if the mice and the beetles were to band together and form an army against the dancers would they understand what they were fighting? Would the dancers?'

Redmede felt thick and stupid. He stood up. 'What are we to do, then?' he asked.

Tapio laughed. '*Oh, we'll fight, alongside the mice and the beetles,*' he said. '*Just don't imagine we're the heroes. For all I know, Ash is locked in a valiant struggle with the very soul of evil, and we will provide the tiny distraction that leads to the ultimate triumph of darkness.*'

Redmede grabbed the table. 'Really?'

Tapio shook his head. '*Nay, brother. I am in a foul mood. Listen: west of the Inner Sea everything is moving. Hordes are coming – greater than armies. This is just one tiny part of whatever is going on. We – the mice and the beetles – can only go by what we see. Some dancers avoid us on the floor – some even pick us up and move us tenderly to the wall. Others stomp on us whenever they can.*' He sighed, raised an eyebrow, and looked at Redmede from under it. '*But aren't you Jacks suspicious any time someone tells you that they represent the side of good and right?*'

Redmede nodded. 'That'd be the Church.'

Mogon shook her head. 'No – that's everyone. Once the dispute turns to war, every side claims the others are demons.' She turned to Tapio. 'Can we not approach this Thorn and offer a deal? Or simply make an alliance and use it as a shield?' She nodded. 'And I agree about the west. Someone has kicked all the anthills there.'

'*We can piss on that fire when the flames lick us. As for Thorn.*' Tapio shrugged. '*It is probably worth a try.*'

Geraaargkh said, 'Too late for us. He attacked us. Even now, the cubs of my people are hunted in the woods.'

Mogon was watching Tapio. 'You want this,' she said.

He gave her a wry smile, full of humour and sorrow with a spice of self-knowledge. '*I'm no messiah,*' he said. '*But I'm a pretty fair general. Go to war with Ash? No one will ever forget us!*'

Geraaargkh growled. 'You and your songs will not save the life of one cub, or provide winter food for a starving bear.'

Tekkismark made the scythe sound again. 'Always, my kind are the fodder in the wars of the powers. It would be different to fight on a side we had chosen ourselves.'

Tapio seemed fascinated by his moccasins. '*I'm sure your kind always imagine that they choose their sides.*'

Tekkismark's mouth opened – sideways – and his purple-ichor tonguebeak shot out for a moment. 'No!' he scratched out. 'That delusion is for men. We are slaves to our message breeze, and nothing else.' He snapped the chitinous claws on one delicate hand. 'Coming here, I was against war with Thorn. Meeting you, I war will make. When the spring turns and the hard water softens, then my people will come.'

Geraaargkh snarled. 'My people are at war, although many do not yet know it. But we will have lost the Adnacrags by spring. Where will we make a stand? And how? Thorn's power increases every day, and he gathers men and creatures from many lands.'

Tapio scratched under his chin, a gesture curiously at odds with his languorous elfin dignity. '*Thorn – what a pleasure to say his name aloud – Thorn will have to make war on men to seize the Adnacrags, and men, as we all know, can be brilliant at making war.*'

'The only thing at which they have skill,' Tekkismark said drily.

'They build snug dens,' Geraaargkh said.

'*At any rate, he will have to fight several great battles to take your mountains. We need not hurry. It will take him a long time to reach us,*' Tapio said. He wobbled his head from side to side – not a human gesture. '*A year for him, or perhaps two. And three – at least – before the rising tide out of the West crests and overruns us.*'

Mogon shook her crested head. 'Every victory will make him stronger,' she insisted. 'Even now, Ash has sent him something abominable. When it grows to maturity, it will be mighty indeed.' She paused. 'Is Ash behind the rise of the West?'

'*It flatters me, Duchess, that you ask me about Ash as if he and I were peers. I have no idea what Ash intends. Nor what has happened in the West, where there are powers with whom I, thanks be to Tara, have never contended.*' Tapio nodded thoughtfully. '*But what you say of men and war is fully true, my friends, and perhaps it would suit us to fight like men. And like the Wild, too. Will you have me as your High Constable?*'

Mogon smiled. 'If only my brother had lived. But yes.'

One by one, the others nodded. Tekkismark made an odd sound, and a scent like almonds washed over them.

'He makes the breeze of agreement,' Mogon said.

'*Well,*' Tapio said slowly. '*If Thorn insists on tying himself to an army of men – we can always use the mountains against him.*'

'We could ally ourselves with the men he fights,' Nita Qwan said. Every head turned.

Mogon's head bobbed up and down, and there was a sound like a strong pair of men using a two-man saw. The Duchess was laughing.

'We could go to war, and ally with men,' she said softly. 'We, the last free peoples in the West, could ally with our oppressors to fight off one of our own.'

Tapio met her eye. '*Yes,*' he said. '*Yes, we could.*' He laid a hand on Mogon. '*Victory in war is usually the result of compromising what you want and behaving like those you despise.*'

Later, Bill Redmede couldn't remember a vote, or a show of hands, or even further discussion. Merely that Tamsin came to the door and seemed to bring a scent of peppermint and cinnamon with her, and then they were all in the hall, dancing – men, and irks, and bears, and Wardens and one boglin wight.

All the females formed a circle in the middle, and began to dance widdershins, turning first outward to the males and then inwards to each other, with many a gesture and a twist, while the males circled them like hungry wolves dancing the other way around, clapping and turning as the music rose. Redmede found himself with Bess again, and she grinned at him and he loved her – reached out and took her hand, and she pressed his tight and then swept past as the music swept higher and faster – left to Mogon, nimble on her feet, and right to Lady Tamsin and her entrancing smile.

The males left the great circle, and they formed smaller circles of their own, so that the central figure of women was surrounded by a dozen small circles of men. Redmede found himself behind a short, dark-haired man he didn't know, who was speaking to Tapio, who was next in the progression. The circles dissolved into a promenade, and Redmede caught Bess's hands again as Tamsin laughed behind him.

'It is like the old days,' she said. 'All the barriers are down, and anyone can dance.'

She laughed, and the man with her – the short man – laughed as well, and a trace of smoke came out his nostrils.

Harndon – The Queen

Sometimes, things can be saved by nothing more than custom. The King's indifference – she couldn't call it more than that – might have ripened into something worse, except that it *was* Christmas and he was a great knight, a good king, and a good husband. The habit of being a good husband at Christmas stopped him from taking any terrible action and so the day itself came.

The Queen had sent a dozen notes to her allies. As the war between her servants and those of the Galles at court was nigh on open, she took precautions learned in her father's court to the south, and her training stood up to the test. It began with mass and she attended with Lady Almspend, Lady Emota and ten more of her ladies, all in dark red velvet and ermine as warm as the spirit of fire.

Mass was held in the great cathedral of Harndon, built by six generations of wool merchants, goldsmiths, knights and kings. Its spire towered over even the royal palace; the central window of the martyrdom of Saint Thomas was accounted one of the fairest in Christendom, and with the first light of a winter day shining through the east wall's magnificent depiction of Christ's birth, men might be forgiven for thinking that they were watching the selfsame event as it happened.

A dozen Gallish squires and twenty more Albans who aped their style were waiting in the square outside the cathedral door with buckets of slush and truncheons. They loitered around the Queen's cross, built by the King's grandmother to celebrate the birth of his father.

They thought themselves hidden by the press of the crowd, and for a little while, the mob shouted, 'The Queen is a foreign whore!' and other epithets.

The leader of the squires was disturbed to see a dozen men on black horses, in matching black surcoats, ride down the Cheapside. They filled the mouth of the Cheap from shop front to shop front, their massive horses breathing plumes of vapour like so many equine dragons.

He pointed them out to another squire.

'Time to go!' shouted the second man. 'The bitch has friends!'

But the mouth of Saint Thomas Street was suddenly filled with apprentices, and every man and boy of them had a wooden club.

They came right up to the edge of the mob and halted, very well disciplined.

The mob stopped shouting cries against the Queen.

The trained men came marching down Saint Mary Magdelene towards the square, and the rattle of their drums cleared the mob as fast as boiling water clears ice from a pump handle. There was only one way for them to go, past the King's Arms tavern and along Dragon Street, and so they went. Or rather, some did, and others edged towards the knights of Saint Thomas and away from the noisy squires by the cross.

The square was empty when the Queen passed through. Two hundred shop boys and apprentices bowed deeply as she came, and when she turned and smiled at the trained men, Edmund thought he might die on the spot.

But the Queen herself knew full well that she had not won a victory, but merely set back the day of reckoning.

The King didn't seem to think anything of it, although he did, at the end of mass, comment on the number of militia in the streets. 'A nice demonstration of loyalty,' he said.

The Queen couldn't see whether the Captal was discomfited by it or not.

Later, at the palace, teams of minstrels and jongleurs arrived, and the Queen and her ladies changed hurriedly – although an outsider might have been forgiven for mistaking their speed for something other than hurry. And then, in a long procession led by the Queen, nearly every woman in the palace not actively involved in cooking or laying the Christmas table walked down into the yard with torches and were met there by the King and as many gentlemen, pages, servants and hangers-on, and the whole multitude went out into the streets by torchlight. There was a fair snow falling, and the air was brisk and cold, and the King kissed his wife a dozen times.

'Will we dance?' he asked.

The Queen smiled. 'My lord, if it is your will, we may dance while we carol.'

The King's eye was drawn to something at the edge of the torchlight. 'When I was a boy,' he said, and his voice was far away, 'adventures would come to us at Christmas – giants, and wild men, and once, the Fairy Knight himself, riding on a unicorn, challenging my father's knights to a tournament on the frozen river.'

'Oh!' said the Queen, in delight. 'What happened then?'

'The showy bastard dropped a dozen of my father's best on their arses and we all drank wine and felt like the lesser men. But he gave us the most beautiful gifts, and it was like living a chanson.' He shrugged. 'I've heard – I've heard some evil things recently.' His eyes met hers. 'About you. I don't think I believe them.'

'My lord—' she began, but it was time to sing.

They sang the 'Three Ships' and they sang a carol about the slaying of the innocents, and all the Queen could see in her head was a man-at-arms slaying her new-born babe. Then they sang the 'Agnus Dei' and a mighty hymn, and then the 'Rising of the Sun' and the circles formed to dance, the women as the deer, the men as the hunters.

They were in the great square below the castle, and they danced down the river steps and out onto the Albin, which was frozen six feet thick already and would freeze further before spring arrived. Palace servants came by on skates with warm wine, and then they sang again, this time 'Jesu the Joy of the World' before they were away again in six great circles in the torchlight.

The crowd mixed with the palace servants and the court itself, so that there were apprentices and their girls, knights and their ladies, merchants of the town – the Queen curtsied to Ailwin Darkwood and he turned her sedately and handed her to a tall journeyman wearing an iron badge and steel ring of the armourers' guild.

'What's your name, young sir?' she asked.

'Tom, Your Grace.' He bowed extravagantly to her and vanished down the chain.

As they closed in for the next figure, the King took possession of her and marched her along the shore. A pair of pages held torches so close to them that she feared for her hair, but she looked up into his face and smiled, and he smiled down at her.

'What I was trying to say,' he managed, 'was that in my pater's time, we were much closer to the Wild at Christmas. It was fun. And good for the knights.'

She leaned up, her fur-lined boots secure in the slippery, stamped-down snow, and kissed him on the lips, and hundreds of people close by let out a whoop and did the same.

'The Wild is always close,' she said. 'We are the children of it, not its enemies. You can find the Wild under the floors of the New Palace, and Wild in the woods across First Bridge.'

'What you say is close to blasphemy,' he said.

'Nay, my lord. Simple fact. Feel the air – smell the spruce? You could reach out and touch a tree in the Adnacrags tonight. The world shimmers on the solstice, my lord. The gates are all open, or so Master Harmodius used to say.'

The King stopped and looked up. Behind him, a thousand couples paused, sipping wine or kissing or wondering what the royal couple were about, but such pauses in the dance were not so rare.

'God's truth!' the King swore. 'I've never seen so many stars, that much is true.' He picked her up and spun her. 'By God, madam, why can I not believe you? I want nothing more than a son.'

She put his hand on her belly. 'There is your son, my lord. Feel his heartbeat – feel it beating strongly for Alba.'

He leaned down in the torchlight. 'I cannot believe that you would betray me.' His hand was warm against her.

Then they were moving again, and the procession returned to a circle, and she lost the King in the turnings – in the great chain that some old Harndoners said marked the binding of all the people of Alba, one to another. In a very old way.

The Queen moved on, first turning with a circle of women – there was Emota, her expression strained, and there was Lady Silvia, a new girl from the north, and a trio of red-faced merchants' daughters, giggling with panic at being in the Queen's set, and then she was whirled away into the great chain again, and she touched hands with a young knight of Saint Thomas, who smiled at her with a beatific peace on a heavy, bluff face; on along the chain, a dark-visaged man with dirty hands who nonetheless beamed at her, and a handsome man in a magnificent fur-lined hood, the fabric some sort of Eastern silk worked in figures that flashed in the torchlight. She had a pair of torches by her all the time; despite her elation, she knew that both young men were royal squires, and both were armed. Young Galahad d'Acre alone could handle a dozen footpads or any number of men of ill intent. It wasn't that she was afraid – merely that the last few days had made her uncharacteristically aware of her vulnerability. And her baby's.

Another figure, and she was being turned in place by a man – one of the Galles. He passed her off – somewhat roughly, she felt, but she feared to imagine a slight – and she heard a shout from behind her right shoulder. She reached out a hand and it was taken, and there was the Captal himself. He turned her, his hand not quite resting on hers and his smile fixed in place. His eyes were on the commotion and she turned – it was time for the women to gather in their own circles—

Galahad was down. She knew that from the change in the light. He was struggling to get to his feet and someone hit him.

The snow had extinguished his torches.

She acted, humming deeply in her chest and reaching into the night – and to the stars – and taking what she needed.

The two torches burst into light – brilliant, screaming light.

Galahad caught his assailant a stout blow in the groin with a burning torch and the man burst into flame. He stumbled away into the crowd, and the crowd gave a shriek and parted cleanly before him.

Galahad got his feet under him and raised the torches, ruthlessly illuminating his attacker's last moments. The man burned – his flesh and muscles and fat burned very fast, and his screams stopped, and the blackened sticks of his bones fell to the snow, hissed and went out.

A delicious smell of roast pork wafted over the crowd, and a woman threw up her dinner.

Galahad was weeping.

The Queen looked around her, seeing Lady Almspend close, and Lady Sylvia a little further back. But no Lady Emota.

One of the Galles – the Count d'Eu – took her. 'Your Grace is, I think, in some danger,' he said.

She retreated a step. The Galles were all around her.

'With me, Galahad. Where is young Tancred?' she asked, keeping her voice as steady and light as could be managed.

'Here at your back, Your Grace,' Tancred's high, girlish voice was at odds with his heavy build and single brow.

'Please allow me to escort you to the King,' the Count said. He bowed, and the pressure of his hand on hers was normal. Kindly meant.

One of the Galles wearing d'Eu's colours put a hand on the breast of another Galle and pushed, and the man went down.

The Count's hand pinned hers like a blacksmith's vice and he held her arm under his own as if they were wrestling. He dragged her along. She almost lost her feet and stifled a scream.

'Your Grace is in great danger,' he muttered to her. 'My men are doing their best to foil it, but there is an attack on your person. I swear to you it is none of my cousin's doing. I would know. Come.' D'Eu swept her along the ice, and she was comforted that her two squires remained tight by her sides, both wearing short swords and maille under their fur-lined cotes. Galahad's torches continued to burn more white than red, and the light they cast illuminated the darkness for a bowshot.

'My ladies!' she said suddenly.

The Count paused and turned. 'Monsieur d'Herblay!' he called. 'The Queen's ladies!'

At the edge of the light, a man dressed in clerical black gave a bow and turned. He went back into the darkness with a dozen men at his heels.

The crowd around them began to thicken like ice forming in a bucket. The Queen felt her right hand going numb, so fiercely did the Count pin her hand. She saw concerned faces flash by – the man in the beautiful hat bowed, and then followed her, and then she saw the tall boy, Tom, and he, too, followed.

She saw a dozen torches gathered together on the river, and she knew the King was there, and the relief she felt was so palpable that her knees trembled beneath her.

The King was laughing with the Count of the Borders and the Master of the Staple. He turned and handed her a cup of wine, even while a pretty young woman with red hair plucked at his hand.

'Come, Majesty,' she said.

The Queen took her cup, and the red-haired young woman dropped a curtsey and backed away into the crowd.

The King picked up the tension from her hand, and from the thin set of the Count d'Eu's lips. 'What is happening?'

The Count d'Eu bowed. 'Your Grace, I have no firm idea, but men attacked your squire here, and I feared for the Queen.'

'He was right to do so,' the Queen said. 'I'm sure of it.'

The King returned the Count's bow. 'Then you have my thanks, messire, as always. We must go back to the dance. People will talk.'

He ruffled young Galahad's hair. 'What happened to you? You look white as the snow.'

'I – I struck a man.' Galahad's voice caught. 'And he burned like a torch.'

The King paused, one foot already lifted to walk. 'Did you?' he asked. 'There is a prophecy... never mind now.' He set his face and leaned down to his Queen. 'This is an odd night, and I'll be the happier when we are done with it.'

Then they were back on the river, and she was dancing again. The air became heavy, and she had trouble breathing. There was something in the torches, she thought...

She turned with a stranger, a small man with a pointed black beard. He had a brilliant smile and jet-black eyes.

Behind him in the circle—

Chapter Sixteen

The Red Knight

Liviapolis – Assassin and Kronmir

He sat on the edge of the privy shelf, reassembling his weapon. The crossbow could be taken down into eighteen parts, all made of steel, which he laid on the dirty white wool of his hood. He could wind it by turning a screw built into the stock; he could wield it one-handed, and loose it with a thumb catch mounted atop the weapon. It had been made by a master in Etrusca, and the bolts it shot were tipped in steel. The bow itself was a length of steel spring as big as two spread hands, and it had, in addition to masterful construction, a hermetical device that assisted the user in turning the loading screw.

He cleaned the water and the mud from every bit of the shining steel and oiled it with fine whale oil.

When he was done, he cocked it carefully and engaged the safety on the massive nut that held the string, and then placed it in the tinker's basket on his back. Despite a year of training to use it, he felt real fear in carrying it cocked and loaded, against his back.

But his whole life was about managing fear, so he unbolted the door to the privy in which he was hiding, pulled heavy oiled-wool mittens over the chamois gloves on his hands and settled his basket on his back.

He was very cold, and he knew he was being hunted.

*

Kronmir was waiting, exactly where he said he'd be, under the arch of the ancient aqueduct just as the bells rang for five o'clock. The assassin was a little surprised to hear the sounds of cheering from the Great Square – so loud that they easily carried the mile and more to where he stood.

Kronmir wore a festive Christmas hood and a long robe like a merchant, but the wreath of berries on his head was the safety signal and the assassin approached him with confidence.

'Christos Anneste!' he said. It was the greeting for Easter, not Christmas – a final signal that guaranteed that all was well.

'Christos Anneste!' echoed his contact. 'You missed.'

The assassin paused. 'I beg to disagree. I shot him from very close, and I saw the bolt strike home.'

Kronmir rubbed his chin. 'He's jousting. He appeared and bowed to the princess not half an hour past. I gave up on his death and left the square.'

The assassin bit his lip. 'I suppose you want me to try again? But I have used my contact and my plan. The next attempt will be amateurish by comparison.' He fingered the amulet that Kronmir had given him. 'You will get me out?'

'The best magister in all of the Empire made that amulet. We'll get you out.' Kronmir nodded. 'He has to dance in public. With the princess.'

The assassin shook his head. 'His men are everywhere. And they're looking for me. You think he won't be covered like a blanket? Crowds only protect you when no one is looking for you. And I don't have a second persona – this tinker is all I have.' He coughed. 'I'm sorry. I do not mean to make excuses, but everything about this job has been wrong from the attack on the palace. We shouldn't have failed then, and I shouldn't have failed tonight. It is as if God is against us.'

Kronmir nodded. 'I agree. But I generally do what I say I will.'

'Aye. As do I.'

The two men allowed their eyes to meet. The assassin shrugged. 'Very well. If you can get me out, I'll have another go.'

'Our next rendezvous is at the Silver Stag Inn on Saint Katherine Street. I have a system prepared to extract you from the city. It may not be me meeting you at the inn, so your sign will be a wreath of golden laurels and the password is "stasis".'

The assassin frowned. 'He must have a hermetical aid. My bolts should have dealt with that. Any thoughts?'

'Most hermetical aids take time. Shoot him from much closer.' Kronmir shrugged. 'I am like a student lecturing a master.'

The assassin shook his head. 'I am murdering a man who seems for the most part good – and doing it at Christmas. And I have already failed. I'm not happy; I much preferred slaying tyrants in Etrusca.' He handed Kronmir a small tube. 'This is for my partner, in the event of the worst. Listen – you have been a fair employer, protecting me all that time while I healed up. We will be grateful, however this comes out.'

'That's good,' Kronmir said. 'Because if this goes badly, I'll have to move to Etrusca.' He slapped the assassin on the shoulder. 'Go and get him, and all this will seem like nerves tomorrow.'

The assassin shrugged. 'If it is so easy, why not deal with him yourself?'

Kronmir bowed. 'It is a fair point. If you wish to withdraw, I will not feel you have broken our condotta.'

For the first time, the assassin smiled. 'Now that was fairly said.' He stretched his back and patted the side of his basket. 'I'll get him. I always feel this way before I drop a man. Some feel the sag after the kill – for me, it's before. Bah, I talk too much.' He inclined his head. 'Be well, whoever you are.'

'And you,' Kronmir said, and walked off into the snow.

Liviapolis – The Red Knight

When the snow was swept away, the citizens of Liviapolis began to dance. They turned and swept around, with many a leap, and many a fine ankle displayed under a richly embroidered hem. Women wore hoods, here, in winter, and the men wore fur hats very different from those the Albans wore, and the dancing was different – more athletic. Women leaped while they turned, and landed on one foot. Men jumped, feet slashing high to touch their hands and back down in time to land.

Ser Michael watched it, hand in hand with his Kaitlin whose belly was very big and who still wanted to dance. At her shoulder was Ser Giorgios and his bride. The two Moreans had taught them all the figures.

It was like Alba, and yet very unlike, and Michael was lost in a torrent of thoughts – lost, and yet very much in the present. He leaned over and kissed his wife.

'Is the Captain very much hurt?' she asked.

Michael grimaced. 'I think he's badly hurt and hiding it,' he said, and gnawed on his glove a little.

'They're coming back to the starting figure,' Helena said. She put a gloved hand on Kaitlin's back. 'I hope that I carry mine as well as you carry yours,' she whispered.

Kaitlin laughed. 'Lanthorns are built for making babies,' she said.

Her husband laughed in his glove and turned away. 'In so many ways,' he whispered to her, and she slammed an elbow into him so he slipped on the ice.

The Red Knight appeared among them while they were laughing. He beamed at Kaitlin and kissed her on both cheeks. 'The very image of fecundity,' he said.

She curtsied. 'I'll assume you are trying to be nice,' she said. 'Why don't you go and dance with the princess? Look! She's waiting for you.'

Ser Michael met his Captain's eye.

'Just so,' he said, and went to face the princess.

'He's not very nice to her,' Kaitlin said. 'Yet she's mad for him. Look at her. Will he wed her, do you think?'

Michael pulled her by the hand. 'I don't think so, love. There's things you don't know. I admit I don't know much either.'

'He doesn't exactly have anyone else,' Kaitlin said, and laughed. 'I'm a terrible gossip. But laundresses know these things.'

Michael led her down the steps from the lady's pavilion to the dancing in the square. 'It's politics. There's always more to it – but she isn't mad for him. Far from it.'

'Oh,' said Kaitlin. 'How sad. I'm in love, and I'd like everyone else to be in love, too.'

Michael grabbed her and lifted her in the first figure of the Morean Christmas dance, and she let out a squeal. 'You'll injure yourself – I weigh the earth!'

He smiled and kissed her and she turned and was off into the dance.

*

The Red Knight faced the princess. She stood in the midst of her court, with the Lady Maria at her shoulder, her face framed in a purple silk hood lined in white fur. Her overgown was edged and lined in ermine and the cloth was silk brocade with gold thread embroidery.

She seemed impossibly beautiful. Her pale skin had a gentle flush at her cheeks and her eyes sparkled.

He walked into the torchlight, to the empty space in the snow in front of her, and he lay full length in the snow. His scarlet deerskin looked like a pool of blood in the torchlight and the snow was very cold. He wondered if she would kill him while he lay at her feet, but there was no avoiding this display of loyalty with twenty thousand people watching him.

Lady Maria raised her voice. 'The Imperial princess bids you rise!' she said.

The princess made the motion for him to rise, and he did – first to his knees, where he kissed the hem of her gown, and then to one knee, where he kissed her hand.

He left three spots of scarlet in the snow.

Her right hand was bare, and she gripped his hand hard. And then leaned down to him. 'It wasn't me,' she hissed.

He was warmed by her assertion. He liked her better than he wanted to and while he didn't believe her, he was glad she would go through the motions for him.

He returned the pressure of her hand. 'What wasn't you, Majesty?' he asked. Somewhere in his secret heart he had feared her open hatred, even while his intellect had sought to understand it.

But there were no easy answers. Toby came and dusted him off, and he was handed some hot wine which he traded off with Toby while he hoped no one was looking. They were going to try and kill him. The public dancing was a perfect venue for such an attempt, and yet he had to be present.

He was also bleeding through his bandages and the blood was very cold on his skin.

He wished he had Tom Lachlan at his side.

But he had Gavin, and Gavin's presence warmed him like a hot fire. He bowed again to the princess and turned to his brother. 'Everyone in place?' he asked.

'Ready as we'll ever be,' Gavin answered. 'Master Mortirmir is standing by, as well.'

He was aware of the absence of Harmodius the way a man is aware of the loss of a painful tooth, and he kept visiting his palace and looking about, as if expecting an interloper. And well down in his list of priorities, he was also aware that if Harmodius had possessed the young Mortirmir, something would have to be done about it.

He marked the command post – the invisible place from which the night's activities were being conducted. Mortirmir seemed to have a very slight stoop and wore a cynical smile, and the Red Knight knew him immediately.

I am weak enough to be glad to be rid of him at almost any price, he thought. He sneaked a second glance at young Mortirmir, who stood with a dozen other students of the Academy and with Long Paw, who had his own contingent out there in the dark and his own orders about Master Mortirmir, if things became ugly.

He backed away from the princess and noted that his people were standing well clear of the princess's attendants – and the fissure between them showed. Ser Alcaeus stood between his mother and Ser Gavin, like one fragile link in a damaged chain.

'Gavin – make sure every one of ours picks one of hers and stays close. I mean it.' He nodded. 'Not a breath of suspicion should reach the enemy. They have to think the whole thing went awry. Or better yet, that she's deserted them.'

Gavin's face registered a dark anger, but he nodded assent and smiled a thin-lipped smile at Lady Maria. Before he left his brother's side, he said, 'You know this is all a punishment for how much I loved the court at Harndon, isn't it? This is court life with a vengeance.'

The Red Knight shrugged. 'Trust Alcaeus,' he said. He backed another step into his own men and women and walked briskly to where Mortirmir stood in the snow, handing cups of hot hippocras to revellers.

The young face wore a wry expression. 'Bleeding? My lord?' He made a face. 'Solstice, you know. No hermetical working does what you expect.'

The Red Knight leaned in close. 'It's against the law, Harmodius. And you know what law.'

Mortirmir shrugged. 'I'm bending the rules, not breaking them.

Master Mortirmir has the switch in his hand. He can dump me whenever he likes. You are bleeding. Here.'

He made a sign and said a word, and the Red Knight felt the wounds close. Again.

Long Paw leaned in over the fire. 'My lord. Any orders?'

The Red Knight shrugged. 'He's out there. Do your best.'

Michael and Kaitlin whirled by him. He turned back to the princess and bowed. 'Your Majesty, is it fitting that we join these revellers? And if so, will you do me the honour, unworthy as I am?'

She nodded. 'Let us dance. Is it not this for which we were made?'

He took her hand and they were away.

Moreans regarded their royalty as sacred – almost literally the stuff of saints and God himself, and there was some reluctance to take the princess's hand at first, but the horror of breaking the huge circle – a circle of ten thousand couples or more that filled the whole circuit of the Great Square – overcame the awe and, after some skirmishing, Count Darkhair put himself at the princess's left hand and seemed perfectly willing to hold it against all comers, regardless what the figures of the dance decreed.

They circled for far longer than Albans did, and then they began a hymn – a regiment of monks and another of nuns processed out of the cathedral and the scent of incense filled the square as a hundred censors whirled sacred smoke into the still cold air. The first hymn rose from fifteen thousand throats, and even the ancient statues seemed to raise their voices in hymn to their creator.

And then the dance began again. A snow squall hit – the fine-powdered snow came down hard enough to fill his eyebrows, and he laughed because it was so beautiful. The nuns and the monks exchanged volleys of song. A pair of drummers played back and forth, on horseback, and a single woman's voice rose in a polyphonic descant above the nuns and monks like a personification of ecstasy.

The princess's hand tightened on his. And then she was gone into the snow, as the women formed an inner circle. Most of the other women were as plain as nuns, so that the princess seemed to burn like a star in a dark firmament.

He wondered if she had given the order to have him killed. Gelfred had intercepted the message from Lonika two days before. But spy networks were so convoluted that the order could have originated in the palace. Certainly he had a lot of evidence proving how regularly she communicated with Andronicus by Imperial messenger.

He had plenty of time to think about it as the great outer circle of men moved around the tighter inner circle of women.

The hymns went on, and when he knew the words, he joined in, and sang. Despite the wound in his side and the creeping flow of blood, he was angry.

If I live through this . . .

If I live through this, I must deal with Andronicus, whose army is three times the size of mine. And then I must do what I can for Michael's father and for the Queen, all the while protecting the north against Thorn and dealing, if I must, with Harmodius. If he is turning against us.

By God, if there is a God, I've made so many mistakes I'm losing the thread of my plan. If I ever had a plan. It's more like riding a wild horse than planning a campaign.

I'm a fool. But what a ride!

The man at his right hand broke in on his thoughts. His voice was strangely familiar and sounded clear as bell. 'Do you believe in fate, Gabriel?' he asked.

The Duke's head shot round. He recognised Master Smythe easily enough, and he grinned. 'Haven't we already had this chat?' he managed.

'And we will again,' Master Smythe promised. 'I love the way humans think about time.'

'This is more help than I ever expected,' the Duke said. 'The food – the logistika.'

'Not to mention a slight deflection of a certain crossbow bolt. From which you may assume that things are worse than you imagined.' Master Smythe inclined his head pleasantly, and flashed a flirtatious smile at a woman in the inner circle.

The Duke winced. 'And I thought I was doing so well,' he said with a certain sarcasm.

His partner turned his head. 'You *are*, but our adversary is – beneath his arrogance and pride – very able. Are you ready to be King of Alba?' he asked.

'No,' the Duke said. 'I had planned to build myself a place here. And stay away from there. For ever.' He shrugged and danced a few steps, turned back towards the dragon and nodded to the music. 'As you must already know.'

'But you'll throw all that over to rescue Michael's father and the Queen?' Smythe asked.

The Duke set his face. 'Yes.'

'Even if it means you must go sword to sword with your father?'

The Duke danced a few steps. 'Don't you find it tiresome to ask questions to which you already know all the answers?'

Master Smythe's dancing was a little too graceful. But he nodded. 'Free will generally trumps foreknowledge,' he said.

The Duke flashed a smile as the chorus to a hymn burst from the monks and nuns. 'That is, I think, the best news I've ever heard. I hope you tell the truth.'

'Me, too,' said the dragon. 'Andronicus must go, before Thorn joins hands with Aeskepiles.'

'I agree,' the Duke said.

The dance gathered speed. 'Do you know that everywhere that good men live – and irks and other creatures – they perform this dance at the winter and the summer solstice? Whatever they believe, whatever god they worship, this is the night when the walls are down, and anything may happen?'

'So my mother always said,' the Duke muttered.

'Do you know that there is an infinity of spheres? Of which this one is but one?' Master Smythe asked.

'I try not to think about it,' the Duke said.

'I will leave you in a few moments. Before I do: the Queen's tournament. You know of it?'

The Red Knight nodded. 'Yes,' he said, in case a being with godlike powers couldn't see in the torchlit darkness. Off to his left, the princess was a golden sun of splendour.

'It is a node. So many lines come together there that I cannot see past it, or what is immediately around it. Thorn and his master have their own plans and I cannot see them.' Master Smythe stopped dancing. 'There,' he said, with uncharacteristic satisfaction. 'Time and place. And undetected. My solstice gift to you.'

'Would you tell me if this tournament ends with my death?' the Duke asked.

The dragon paused for a moment. 'It may,' he said. 'Which I would regret. Even to tell you that much is to trespass beyond the borders of the game.' Master Smythe shrugged. 'To be fair, I missed your assassin until he struck. By the way, he's quite close now, and I am not allowed to take action. You seem to understand all this well enough.'

The Red Knight nodded. 'I was born to it,' he said with unfeigned bitterness.

'I know,' said the Wyrm of Erch. He flexed his hands. 'It is so long since I took a direct part in the affairs of men,' he said wistfully. 'What if it proves addictive?'

'Sod off,' said the Red Knight, but he said it very, very quietly.

The men were closing in on the women, and another snow shower hit them – a flurry of flakes all around him, so that, despite the hands on his right and left, he seemed all alone. The snow muffled sound, as well.

He reached out a hand for the princess, and felt a warm hand in his. But to his utter shock – and he was not a man easily surprised – he took the Queen's hand instead.

She paused as he raised her hand. 'You!' she said.

They turned as the music – a polyphony of musics – rose around them, and the snow fell harder. Her hand was light as air. She was obviously pregnant, but she danced with angelic grace. He smiled, and she smiled too.

'Have you come to see my husband?' she asked.

'No,' he said. And he moved on, relinquishing her with a backward glance that met her serene smile over her shoulder.

He turned his head, raising his hand for his next partner, and there was Amicia. He was a beat too late, and she was biting her lip in annoyance, lost in the music, a nun who loved to dance.

Their eyes met. Hers widened, and she caught her breath.

The ring on her finger sparkled.

'You are wounded,' she said. 'Is it you who has been drawing from me all day?' She smiled like the rising of a summer sun and he was flooded with warmth.

He couldn't think of anything to say, so he turned, her hand in his. She wore the plainest brown overgown with a blue kirtle under it – on her shoulder was the eight-pointed star of her order.

'Oh!' she said in delight. 'My handkerchief!'

He opened his mouth, and she danced away into the snow.

His third partner was his mother.

She took his hand and took a graceful, gliding step. 'The walls are truly down tonight,' she said.

He grunted, and looked back over his shoulder.

She laughed. 'You'll have her in the end, I have no doubt,' she said. 'Look at you! The very lord of this world.' She took another pavane step and laughed. 'You are everything I hoped you would be, Gabriel.'

And having sliced him with the razor of her words, she stepped away into the snow.

He might have sagged, but Amicia's touch still burned on his hand, and he took the next three steps the way a trained swordsman will keep fighting when hurt.

Another queen took his hand – not one he knew, but a slight figure in white, embroidered in gold with red berries with her pale hair piled atop her head – a Snow Queen.

'You must be the Red Knight,' she said. 'Ah! We have done it. All the chains are joined this night.' She smiled at him, and whirled in a spray of snow, doubling to the time of the music. 'May light triumph over dark,' Tamsin said, and turned away. 'Let this be a dagger in his black heart!'

He turned outside her and stepped away, wondering and dreading who might emerge next from the snow, but the hand that grasped his was a familiar one, and he found himself turning with Sauce. She grinned. 'Surprised?' she asked. 'I never know which circle I should be—' As she spoke, her face changed, and she stepped past him and threw him to the ground as if they had been wrestling, not dancing. It was all done in time to the music and, surprised, he fell hard.

The assassin was frustrated at the snow and doubly frustrated at the attentiveness of the soldiers, who were, indeed, everywhere in the crowd. After two passes that didn't bring him close enough to his target, he knew that his one chance would be to press straight in. The hymn told him where the dancers ought to be – in a few measures, the men would leave their fifth female partner and come out to the outer circle and turn again with the men.

If he wormed to the edge of the non-dancing crowd, he'd have to be lucky – but if he was, he'd have his shot at arm's length or less. He paused, counted the beats, and burrowed past a clump of goodwives like a mole in the dirt.

But his basket and his relative movement drew the attention of a clump of mercenary archers. He saw them move – saw the change of the glint of their helmets.

If he turned away now, he'd never have another chance.

He pushed harder.

Long Paw saw the man with the basket at the same time as Ser Gavin, and the two moved into the crowd like mastiffs, Ser Gavin leaving Lady Maria standing alone and breaking the circle while Long Paw, half a bowshot away, had the harder journey through a thousand people.

There was a cracking sound, and the snowbound sky was lit by a bolt of lightning. And a sudden play of colours, like a localised aurora.

Morgan Mortirmir grabbed his head as if he'd taken a blow. Then, after a moment's disorientation, he turned on his heel and ran towards the Megas Ducas, dancing with Ser Alison.

The crack of thunder frightened people and they shrank aside. And left a path for the assassin, who strode along the alley so created as if it had been ordained since the dawn of time.

But it was *too* easy, and he was ahead of his time – the Megas Ducas was still turning with a woman, fifteen paces away through the snow.

The assassin threw caution to the winds and burst through the cordon around the dancers and ran for the Duke.

The woman with whom he was dancing saw him and seemed to nod, turning her partner even as the assassin stripped the mitten off his right hand, reached back and caught the handle of his crossbow. He ran at the Duke.

She put her leg behind the Duke's in time to the music.

He was three paces away and it was too late for everyone as he raised his bow and then—

She threw the Duke to the ground.

A great gout of fire struck the assassin's ward, making him stumble.

He whirled and shot his attacker, and the bolt went clean through the young man's hermetical defence and blew him from his feet.

The woman produced a short sword from her skirts and cut at him.

He caught the blow on the arm guard under his peasant tunic and grappled her, expecting an easy conquest and instead getting a knee in his groin and a turn of his own elbow, but he had armour under his clothes and she was hampered by skirts and after a flurry of blows he kicked her – hard enough to snap her knee, but the same petticoats that had saved him now deflected some of his blow.

She fell all the same.

He hit her in the head with his spent crossbow and ran.

He passed the princess, gaping open-mouthed, and then he was in among the statues in the centre of the square.

He stripped the peasant smock over his head, and under it he had the armour and scarlet surcoat of a mercenary archer, complete with sword and buckler. He ran, altered direction by ninety degrees and ran harder, due south, passing through a clump of peasant women and vanishing into the crowd.

Long Paw was fooled, but only for as long as it took him to look at the peasant smock. Then he made a clicking sound with his tongue and followed the tracks through the new snow. He didn't need the peasant women to tell him where the man had gone, and he only paused for three strides to scan the crowd. Even in the flickering torchlight, he could follow the helmet – the one helmet headed *away* from the circle of dancers.

Thunder rumbled overhead like laughter.

Harndon – The Queen

Out in the darkness, a woman screamed.

The Queen had the King by the hand and she froze, her senses a-whirl – for a moment, she had danced with the Red Knight, and with a man like an Elvin prince – she had to ground herself.

Emota was missing.

The King left her side, with a dozen knights at his heels, headed towards the sound of a woman screaming, and the circle was broken while the screams cut through the music.

The power of the circle was shredding away like ice melting on a spring pond. The Queen reached out—

A woman in green and gold took her hand and spat, and she felt as if she'd been kicked in the stomach, and she fell to her knees.

The older woman looked over her shoulder and vanished to be replaced by the same young nun who had healed her on the battlefield at Lissen Carrak. The Queen's head rose.

A woman clad in white leaned over them. 'We cannot let the circle dissolve so early,' she said. Or perhaps she cast her thoughts – it was all so fast that the Queen was suddenly standing with Lady Sylvia's hand in her right and Lady Almspend's in her left, and the three formed a tiny circle and began to turn – and the carollers steadied into their Gloria.

A bowshot away, the King found Lady Emota lying dead in a pool of blood that made the snow look black around her. Her throat had been slashed from side to side the way a deer was ended, or a sacrifice made in ancient times, and then the dagger had been plunged into her.

The dagger bore the arms of the Count d'Eu.

'Why is the Queen still dancing?' the King asked angrily.

The Duke got to his feet, aided by Toby, and extended a hand to Sauce, who was rubbing snow on her exposed knee to the delight of many men.

He looked around. The music hadn't faltered, but the dancers were slowing. Some of the women had stopped and were gathering for protection.

At his shoulder a woman's voice said, 'We cannot let the circle dissolve so early,' and he turned, but there was only the trace of a fragrance of peppermint in the air. But his grasp of the principle was sound enough, and he took Sauce's hand. 'Dance!' he shouted. 'Close the circle and dance.'

The habit of obedience is hard to break. Sauce ignored the pain in her knee and grabbed the hands of the surprised princess and turned her – Lady Maria joined them, and in a moment the women were reforming the inner circle.

Gavin skidded to a halt, and the Duke pushed him into the men's circle. 'Dance,' he ordered. 'Someone is trying to cast a huge working. Breaking the dance is one part of it. Dance, damn it!'

As soon as they stepped away, he dropped to one knee by Mortirmir, who was thrashing, his feet drumming the packed snow, his blood as black as pitch.

The Duke put his hands on Mortirmir's shoulders.

Come on, Harmodius, he said.

And the old magister was there. He reached out in the aethereal *and his hand reached for the Red Knight's hand – the Red Knight stretched, and was led a step closer to the open door – a door that seemed to open on the blackest night, unshot with stars. A blast of cold, a sort of ultimate cold, hit him from the open door.*

The Red Knight stood his ground and leaned forward, straining, into the black-shot aethereal *and got his fingertips onto those of the slim young man in blue velvet—*

There was a sound as of mortal combat—

—and the rising strains of a Christmas carol

a woman's scream

a ship tossed on a storm-wracked sea

an old man in a long beard lying under a quilt

Harmodius shot through the door as if propelled by some outside force, and the door slammed shut behind him. Harmodius lay on the tiled floor of the Red Knight's palace for a moment. He shook his head.

'What the fuck was that?' he muttered.

Gabriel was already up and moving. He pointed at Mortirmir, at the edge of death in the real.

Can we save him?

Absolutely. Bastard thinks he can kill me that easily—

I think I was the target.

Think whatever you like, boy. Christ that was close. Give me . . . ?

Gabriel gave Harmodius his store of *ops*, yet again.

Take that, you bastard, Harmodius said. He opened a link, and cast – the sigils of his palace flashed like the lights of a distant city as he cast *five* complete workings in a single breath.

The blood vanished out of the snow, leaving the snow white.

Mortirmir's eyes opened.

The crossbow bolt protruding from his back flowed away like melted ice.

And something burst in the sky above them, like a firework – a thousand tiny stars lit for a moment and then were dark.

Uh oh, muttered Harmodius. *I just kicked a god in the nuts.*

The Sacred Isle – Thorn

Thorn watched the night play out like a drama. The solstices were always a dreadful time for serious work – neither the real nor the *aethereal* were solid in their spheres at such times, and the simplest workings could miscarry.

His own webs of sorcery hung limp. He feared that the storms of the solstices in the *aethereal* would do them damage without his attempting even the simplest work, and he stood in the snow, dark and silent, contemplating.

If he was silent, others were very loud. Nor did he require nets of spies to see them. The power of their efforts was so great, so vast the expenditure of *ops*, that he felt it from his well of power in the north, where fits and gouts of snow fell into his arms as if he had truly been an old oak tree.

At every pulse of power from the south, the egg at his side burned and chittered.

Something rude, struggling to be born.

A scrap of an old poem, or a prophecy.

To the west, a circle unbroken, and a mighty power proclaimed itself into the heavens like a ring of white fire. Other rings of similar power leaped into the air from many places – from the rude huts of Outwallers, and from the courts of kings and emirs and khans.

But two were flawed, and began to pull themselves apart in the *aethereal*. And something was pulling at them.

Thorn watched with interest, as one predator might watch another stalking its prey.

And then they steadied – both of them together, as if caught in a dance of their own. The white fire died away to a spark, and then leaped again, and the rings flared – there was a burst of power from the east.

Ah, thought Thorn, and the being who rode him said, '*Harmodius yet lives. And has grown stronger. He will make a perfect ally.*'

Thorn shuddered in surprise. '*Why?*' he asked. '*And who exactly are you, sir?*'

'*Any being who achieves sufficient power ceases to be one of them,*' Ash said. '*And becomes one of us.*' The voice rolled on inexorably. '*You have chosen. I have chosen. Now Harmodius has chosen.*'

Thorn shuddered. And wondered – not for the first or last time – what, exactly, he had chosen.

'*I am Ash,*' whispered the voice.

Thorn – who had once been Richard Plangere – knew the name all too well. '*You are Satan's serpent,*' he said.

But Ash said, '*I am in no relation to anything, mortal. I merely am.*'

Liviapolis – Assassin, Long Paw, Kronmir

The assassin emerged from the back of the crowd near the Academy, and he crossed their streets fearlessly, his alumni badge flashed at the portals. As it wasn't actually his badge, there would be no consequence, and he doubted that any of his pursuers had such an item. He had gained himself an hour.

He plunged into the alleys behind the University and moved from alley to alley, pausing only to shed his red surcoat and archer's breastplate. He left them under the eaves of a brothel and ran on into the darkness.

Long Paw came to the wards at the edge of the Academy and cursed. He couldn't pass them, and it was clear from the tracks that his adversary had. He turned back, wasting precious minutes running first north, and then west, where he found Gelfred and Daniel Favour. The two were kneeling in the snow.

'He's cut through the Academy and I cannot follow him,' Long Paw panted.

Favour whistled and a brace of hounds appeared, running over the snow.

'We're casting for a scent,' Gelfred said. 'Let's move south and try again. There's so many people—' He shook his head.

The three men ran south along the avenue that flanked the University. It was well lit with torches on this night, and there were hundreds of people to turn and stare as three armed men ran past them. At the southern end of the University they stopped and cast west, but any hope of crossing fresh tracks was lost in the back streets of the student warrens behind the University.

But a third of the way along Saint Nicholas, the older dog began to keen and whine, and Gelfred let her slip.

'Get him, Luadhas!' he said, and let the animal go. He knelt in the snow and prayed, and then loosed the other animal. The younger male barked, turned in a full circle and ran off in a different direction. The older sprang away towards a low-roofed building with dirty white plaster across the street. He stopped while the three men were in sight, and Gelfred ran to his side and retrieved a soldier's cloak, a surcoat, and a breastplate.

He knelt again, heedless of the weather, and prayed fervently, and then raised his wand and cast, and a silvery fire ran over the brach's limbs and into its nose. It breathed deep the scent on the cloak, and gave a bark of joy, and ran off – into the knotwork of alleys.

The three men followed.

The assassin slowed to a walk well before he reached his haven. He knew the inn, and he didn't intend to blow his new disguise by running in the packed streets, so he emerged into Saint Katherine at a brisk walk, a householder out for a breath of cold air and perhaps a cup of hot wine. He bounced up the steps of the inn like an eager suitor and pushed open the doors.

He scanned the room. There was no one he knew – and so much the better. He crossed the common room and fetched up against a wall – at Christmas there was no place to sit in the whole of the place.

He waited for a contact. For the first time, he let himself think, and he was deeply dissatisfied – what on earth had moved him to shoot the boy when his target was prone at his feet?

But what was done was done.

A middle-aged woman appeared and offered him a steaming cup, which he took with a nod of gratitude. She mimed signing a tab – he nodded. Men in the city were far more trusting then men in Etrusca, but he would honour his payment – it was, after all, Christmas. He closed his eyes and said a prayer for the young man he'd killed.

And opened them when he heard a dog bark.

Dogs. He hadn't considered dogs. Of course, in the snow—

He took a deep breath. A second dog barked.

He took a sip of his hot wine, and reached into his basket, where his short sword rested against the wicker. He took it out as carefully as he could. And began to edge towards the kitchen.

They weren't amateurs. At most he had a few minutes while they gathered their forces.

He looked around for his contact – a wreath of gold laurel – and he saw no one with any wreath at all.

Damning his luck, he put his hand on the amulet, and imaged the sigil of summoning.

Kronmir was two streets west of the inn on Saint Katherine when he saw the men in scarlet surcoats – and the dogs.

He turned away immediately and headed north into the maze of the student quarter. If they had dogs, they'd followed his man to the rendezvous. He didn't even *have* a backup messenger yet – the whole thing was hopelessly ahead of time, and the soldiers already had the inn surrounded.

He thought some dark thoughts.

Behind him, a dog barked.

Suddenly, the alley in front of him was lit by a rising sun of red fire – Kronmir stopped in his tracks, and the blast made him clap his hands to his ears and stumble.

All that saved their lives was Wilful Murder's shrill insistence that they should retreat into the alleys until they had more troops.

'Fucking dogs!' he'd snapped. 'Every bastard in the quarter knows we're here.'

Gelfred knew he was right, and the four of them – five when Bent appeared, and a dozen when his men came at his heels – had retreated into the mouth of the alley known as The Rookery. Favour got his hand on the brach's collar and he silenced her. The younger dog barked again—

And the top blew off the inn.

A wave of fire rippled out from the epicentre like a hermetical tide and burst against the buildings on the other side of the street, and nothing but sheer luck kept the archers in the shadow of the malevolent *potentia*. Gelfred had his ribs broken and was badly burned on his face and hands. Favour was covered by his officer and was merely singed, and Wilful Murder was knocked flat with a broken arm where he'd been pointing. The brach was killed outright.

A hundred and fifty revellers in the inn died instantly.

A dozen houses caught fire. Wilful Murder scrabbled to his feet and ran for the fire company.

Two alleys away, Kronmir leaned against a building and watched the red firelight in the sky.

His mind rattled on with the problem for less than three heartbeats before he drew the obvious conclusion. He tore the amulet from his neck . . . and paused.

And then ran for the Academy. If the thing went off in the alleys then a thousand people would die.

Kronmir ran all the way to the main entrance to the Academy, where the iron maw of Cerberus was a black hole in the night. He sprinted up to the three-headed dog and cast the thing, chain and all, into the open mouth of the nearest head.

The dog gave a cough, like a sick child.

Kronmir stood by it and panted, his elbows folded against his chest. Revellers passed him on either side – across the street, a man stopped and pointed at the red sky. Other people paused, and in the distance he could hear a hymn being sung.

People in the Great Square were still dancing.

He ran the whole strand of logic through in his head – once again. Just to be sure of his chain of causality.

His assassin had been surrounded.

The inn had exploded.

Aeskepiles had expressed surprise that the assassin and the survivors of his team were still alive.

Aeskepiles had made the amulets.

The young man – the young scholar from the Academy – had said that the amulets were surprisingly powerful.

QED.

Aeskepiles had given him devices to kill his agents.

Kronmir stood by the great iron statue of Cerberus for as long as it would take for a nun to say a pater noster.

And then he started across the square.

Gabriel Muriens lay on a cot in the pavilion that had been arranged for him on the jousting field. There were six braziers and a turf hearth struggling to keep the bitter cold at bay, and a closed bed had been moved in.

Ser Michael, in consultation with Ser Alcaeus and Lady Maria, had determined that the Megas Ducas was easier to defend in the middle of the hippodrome.

The Red Knight was sitting up on a dozen heavy pillows, his chest tightly bandaged. Messengers came and went, checked by a series of sentries who were company veterans with orders that only well-known company men could pass. It wasn't fair to the Moreans who were loyal, but it functioned.

'How bad?' the Duke asked a shaken Long Paw.

'Christ on the cross, my lord, it was like—' He shook his head. 'Like the heart of a forge fire, for a moment.'

Young Morgan Mortirmir, standing at the Red Knight's shoulder, gave a slight bow. 'My lord, if you are feeling stable then I'd like to have a look. Any of my fellow scholars could support you in a crisis.'

The Duke frowned. 'What's the Academy doing?'

'Nothing, my lord.' Morgan looked down, as if embarrassed. Perhaps he was. 'They have taken no action.'

The Duke turned his head back to Long Paw. 'What else?'

'We followed the tracks – physical, and hermetical – to the tavern. Wilful got there with some troops, I wasn't keen to take the bastard by myself.'

The Duke reached out and touched Long Paw. 'You did right. Force, especially overwhelming force, saves lives.'

Long Paw looked miserable. 'Tell that to Gelfred – he lost both his dogs and he's like to lose his left arm, too. Or to Kanny – he's dead. Three dead and three more badly burned.' The older man shook his head. 'I'm not cut out for this. I'll cut a throat, but I don't like giving orders. Making the call.'

Ser Jehan held out a cup of wine. 'You did well to come away with anyone alive. But my lord, have you thought this through – militarily? If they have these explosives what else can they do? Can they knock down buildings?'

The Duke gave his mentor a mirthless smile. 'Jehan, a master hermeticist can knock down a city wall in one stroke. They just don't, mostly. It takes time and effort to do, and most of them are playing other games.' He shook his head. 'But this one isn't.'

Jehan drank some wine. 'My lord, I'm always the naysayer – I realise it robs me of – of—' He smiled. 'Of something. But listen – we're on a battlefield of the enemy's choosing, and he's got a new set of weapons and tactics. This is like Etrusca – assassins. Magic. Can we go back to killing monsters?'

'We can't just retreat and regroup,' the Duke said. He grunted as pain hit him afresh. 'Morgan, go see the ruins of the taverna. See what there is to be seen. I'd like to know how it was done so that when I panic, I panic for a reason.' He put his head back slowly. 'Gentlemen, we're building something here. If we beat Andronicus, we'll have plenty of time. We'll have an income base and a series of fortified towns and castles. And allies.'

'Allies?' Jehan spat.

Alcaeus had been sitting on a stool, but now he sat up. 'Yes, ser knight. Allies. Many Moreans are in favour of what you have been doing. Peace – a strong peace, and a fair one, means that our merchants can compete with the Etruscans and Galles, and even the Albans and the Occitans.'

Ser Jehan shrugged. 'While the princess pays Etruscan master assassins to kill us?'

Alcaeus met him, shrug for shrug. 'My mother is doing her best to curb the princess,' he said. 'We don't think she knew anything about the assassin.'

The Duke shook his head. 'It makes no sense. I'm no fool, and I can't even see exactly who we're fighting. Why? Why is the princess sending messages to Andronicus? Why did the court mage betray the Emperor? Why is the Academy standing by and letting people die from a use of the hermetical that – at least in Alba – would get you burned at the stake?'

Alcaeus stroked his beard. 'My lord I grew up here, and I don't understand all the factions. Sometimes every man and every woman is their own faction. As for the Patriarch – who knows what he really thinks – eh? About you as an Alban? About your confessor here?' Alcaeus shook his head. 'I mean no offence, Father, but the Patriarch believes that priests should not fight. Many of our monks and priests are against that, and there has been trouble over it for years – and then an Alban comes with a member of the fighting orders as his confessor—'

'He's not my confessor,' the Duke said. 'I like to keep it all between me and God.'

Father Arnaud was sitting behind the canopy, almost invisible. Now he rose. 'Would it kill you to talk about it? And have you considered that your private quarrel with God may in the end hurt your company? Perhaps it is our business.'

'Perhaps,' the Duke said. 'But you know what? I'm really quite fond of you all – even Wilful Murder. And I'm quite sure that when my little problem with God finally comes to light, you'll all—'

There was a stir, and some shouting out beyond the cloth and the torchlight.

The Duke sat up. 'Michael – see to that,' he said. The Duke had a roundel dagger in his fist.

Michael was in full harness. He and Jehan went out together, and

Toby, also in harness, drew his sword. So did Father Arnaud. Long Paw eased his in its scabbard.

Ser Michael reappeared. 'My lord. It is—' His face was white in the torchlight and his mouth looked stretched tight. 'It's a man who claims to be the head of Andronicus's spy service. He begs an audience with you immediately.'

The Duke's right hand moved, and a glowing green shield came up, a bubble that passed with some attenuation through the cloth of the hangings.

'Michael – strip him absolutely naked. Give him my robe to wear, but take every jewel, every ring – everything. Long Paw—'

The swordsman nodded. 'I'll do it. I've searched a few bastards in my time.'

'If he does anything that seems remotely like an attack, kill him. And until he's stripped, don't bring him within a hundred yards of this tent.' The Duke put his dagger away.

Jehan stood with his sword drawn. 'What if – he himself—'

The Duke's eyes were glowing. 'I can deal with that,' he said.

'Jules Kronmir, my lord,' Ser Michael reported.

Kronmir was brought in. He was surrounded by naked swords, and yet he had a certain dignity. He bowed, very slowly – almost like a pantomime of a bow.

Morgan Mortirmir's eyes widened. 'I know you!' he said.

Kronmir nodded his head, again, very slowly.

'The amulet!' Mortirmir said. 'My lord, I know what exploded. Damn me to hell, I held it in my hand.'

'Not that one, but another,' Kronmir said. 'But yes. You warned me, and I didn't heed you.'

Father Arnaud's sword wavered and then moved to cover Mortirmir's back.

'You two know each other?' Jehan asked.

Mortirmir, apparently too young to understand where this was going, nodded. 'Yes – we met at the ancient temple of Minerva on the hillside, and then later, in an inn. He showed me an amulet.'

He's telling the truth, Harmodius said. *Christ on the cross, I didn't look into his memories. But there he is.*

Kronmir looked back and forth. 'You needn't guess,' he said. 'I'll tell you. But only if you will protect me.'

'You are here to change sides?' the Duke asked.

'This would be an odd method of committing suicide otherwise, so yes,' Kronmir said.

'You'll tell us everything – names, places, dates.' The Duke leaned forward.

'Anything about Duke Andronicus and his plot – yes.' Kronmir bowed his head. 'He has betrayed me. But I will say nothing about any former employers.'

'He's not exactly in a position to bargain,' Long Paw said.

'But you see, my lord, I am,' Kronmir said. 'After all, I know where the Emperor is.'

The Duke allowed himself to sink back into his pillows. He caught Father Arnaud's eye. 'You know,' he said, 'sometimes I have to wonder whether God is really against me.' He turned his head back to Kronmir. 'Put your hands between mine and swear.'

Kronmir knelt. He swore a simple oath, like any man-at-arms joining the company.

'You'll take the word of an assassin?' Long Paw spat.

'Sworn to a mercenary. Are we all not honourable men?' The Duke laughed weakly. 'I need to sleep. Protect Master Kronmir, who I expect will be our most valuable asset. Hide him – most especially from the palace. Long Paw, he's yours. If Gelfred's wounded, who has the scouts?'

'I'd like to try Favour,' Jehan said. 'But he has an arrow in his gut. It's healed, but he'll be as long as – well, as long as you in recovering.'

'Has to be Starling,' Ser Michael said. 'Man's a prick, but he's a competent prick.'

'Make it so,' the Duke said. 'Oh, my God.' He lay back. 'The Emperor. Kronmir – don't get killed.'

Kronmir smiled. 'I don't intend to,' he said.

The Duke's eyes closed, and then sprang open. 'Wait!' he said. 'I have a plan.'

Jehan groaned. 'Here it comes,' he said.

Part Three
Spring

Prince Demetrius

Chapter Seventeen

Sister Amicia

Ticondaga and Albinkirk – Ser John Crayford and Amicia

In the end, Amicia won the old knight over to the notion of passing the Adnacrags again in winter. It took him a month to heal – a month of enduring the ruthless enquiries of a woman untramelled by the least restraint as to manners or morals. Amicia had never known anything like the Lady of the North, and she hoped that she never would again.

On the day when Ser John announced that they would take their merchants and march, Ghause smiled at Amicia across her solar. 'Do you miss him so much?' she asked, and Amicia's heart almost stopped beating.

But Ghause swept on. 'Do you know the Queen's friend, Lady Mary?' she asked.

Amicia was, by this time, adept enough at defending herself. She answered cautiously.

'I met her in the aftermath of the great battle,' she said.

Ghause laughed. 'There are no "great battles", woman,' she said. 'Yon Lady Mary is betrothed to my Gavin.'

'Yes, I believe I knew there was somewhat between them,' Amicia said without lowering her guard, and Ghause laughed aloud.

'This is my dotage!' she said. 'To sit in my solar and gossip about the lovers of my sons.' She leaned forward. 'I like you, witch.'

Those words stayed with Amicia to the end of her life.

*

The Earl of the North sent twenty knights and almost a hundred soldiers to march with the caravan across the winter snows, and they went in sleighs. The Northwallers had many ways of moving in winter that were almost forgotten in Albinkirk, if they'd ever been known there, and the Etruscan merchants were shocked, and a little delighted, to see how fast a horse-drawn sleigh could move along an Adnacrag lake. They could easily make ten leagues in two hours – sometimes more – and then they'd face another weary climb up a ridge to the next lake. Sometimes the military road was clear enough to take the sleighs, and once, they had to unload every bundle and carry it.

The Earl's youngest son accompanied the convoy, commanding his father's men. He was dark and morose, like many young men, and yet Amicia found him easy to like – not just a pale reflection of his older brothers, but a youth already giving signs of being a solemn, cautious man. He found her watching the bundles of furs moved by ropes up a ridge.

'Winter is always with us,' he said. 'We make war in winter, and we travel if we have to. It is the one time that most of the Wild is asleep.' He leaned close. 'What is Gabriel like, now?' he asked.

She closed her mind with a snap and closed her expression, as well. 'He is a good knight, ser. That is all I can say.'

It took them just six days to reach the crossing of the river where the whole adventure had begun, and the sleighs crossed on ice – breaking through in many places, but never so deep as to spill their loads. The wagon beds were shaped like boats and waterproof.

The Northwallers knew all about winter.

And when she could see Albinkirk between her horse's ears, Amicia allowed her eyes to mist over a little.

Riding gave her too much time to think.

She kissed Ser John goodbye in the yard of the citadel of the town, and the thin population cheered their captain, the merchants, and the young nun.

She had a serious meeting with the bishop, and went back to her duties at South Ford.

Lonika – Duke Andronicus

Three hundred leagues and more to the east, servants were removing the spruce wreaths from the beautiful mosaicked hall. It was almost a month since Epiphany. The old Duke of Thrake sat in his Great Hall with his son and a dozen other of his officers arrayed before him like suppliants – including the magister, Aeskepiles, who lurked at the back like a criminal.

'I had to, Pater. He was the very spawn of Satan – he was driving our people out of the city and beating us everywhere.' Demetrius stood straight before his father. He didn't appear to feel any remorse.

Andronicus sat, chin in his hand, on a heavy chair very like a throne. 'You asked me, and I said *no*. Then you went behind my back with that sorcerer and you had him killed.'

'What matters it?' Demetrius asked. 'He's dead and buried. The princess is dismissing his company. She's being careful – wouldn't you, when dealing with such a nest of vipers? But they'll be gone in a few days, and then we can march south.'

Aeskepiles cleared his throat. 'We are months behind our schedule, and we need to move.'

Andronicus raised his eyebrows. 'Schedule? Master sorcerer, I do not have a *schedule*. I intend to save my country from a usurper and from a long reign of bad government. That will take *years*.'

Aeskepiles was very still for a moment, and when he spoke, his voice sounded unctuous. 'Of course, my lord. I only spoke in the most general of fashions. Please forgive me.' He leaned forward. 'I am still surprised at the ease of his unmaking.'

'Ease?' Demetrius spat. 'Three botched attempts and then he was killed when an amulet exploded?'

Aeskepiles smiled. 'I could not have hoped for better,' he said.

Andronicus looked at both of them as if they were children. 'You imagine she will invite us back,' he said.

'If she does not, we can simply tell the people that she betrayed her own father,' Demetrius said.

Andronicus raised his head from his fist. 'And everyone will believe us, of course. Listen, you two fools. What you have done is to win this stalemate – and for *her*. She has the army, now – this Red Knight saw to that. She has her own fleet and it has been paid. The Etruscans, may they be damned to hell, will now pay *her* a tax.' He sat back and rested both arms on the arms of his huge chair. 'In a way – in a strange way – I admire this Red Knight. He did many of the things I'd have liked to do myself.' He looked at Demetrius. 'I suspect that when she is ready, she will offer you marriage, my son. And you will accept it. My titles will be restored, and you will be her consort. If you are lucky, you will be allowed to lead armies. At some point, some impious man will put a knife in her father's throat or wrap a bowstring around it.'

Aeskepiles looked at the old Duke as if he were a pile of dung. 'What foolishness is this? And no man living calls me a fool to my face.'

The old Duke sneered. 'You are a fool. An arrogant, power-mad fool, just as the Patriarch warned me. Arrest him.' He waved at two soldiers. 'Never fear, Magister – I was never going to make you Patriarch anyway.' He turned to his son. 'But what am I going to do with you?' he asked.

Liviapolis – The Red Knight

The company marched out of Liviapolis at the break of day, and it was clear from the moment that they cleared the palace gate that the princess was not going to trust them even in the streets of the city. The Vardariotes took post all along their line of the march, and all the city stradiotes followed at their heels. Two hundred Nordikans rode along behind their baggage train, threatening instant retribution for any misdeed.

Ser Jehan led the column, with Ser Milus at his side carrying the furled black banner. Men wore their scarlet surcoats with an air of surly defiance. Most of the archers glared at the bystanders who came to gape – most of the men-at-arms rode with their eyes down. The company's women rode palfreys, now, and most wore short swords and scarlet cot-hardies too, but uniformity couldn't hide their air of desperation.

The word was that the mercenaries were being evicted unpaid.

Near the gate, a pair of Nordikans saluted Ser Jehan, and Wilful Murder spat.

Just behind him, Nell giggled. As they rode through the great Gate of Ares, she poked Wilful in the ribs. 'You're over-acting,' she said.

'Shut up, hussy,' he hissed. 'You'll wreck it all, and the spies'll hear you and we'll all be killed. Mark my words.'

When the company passed under the Gate of Ares for the last time, the two Nordikans on duty saluted with their axes until the last woman had passed under the iron portcullis. And then they mounted horses already saddled, and joined the company of Nordikans and the stradiotes shadowing the company.

They marched west on the road to Alba. After the crossroads, the pace picked up. A mile past the crossroads, a hundred Vardariotes galloped past them, spraying dust from the newly hardened ground. The snow was already melted in the valleys, although the rivers were full, and there were flowers in the lowest ground. And the sun was rising earlier.

The man-at-arms behind Ser Milus – the only man in the whole column with his helmet laced on – raised his visor and took a deep breath. Toby leaned over and helped him unlace the great helm he wore, and Father Arnaud helped him with the catches.

When it came off his head, he smiled, his black beard framed in the mail of his aventail, and he swept his great horse out of the column and galloped along.

If there had been watchers in the hills, they'd have heard three ringing cheers.

But the scouts and the Vardariotes had seen to that. The Nordikans joined the company columns, and the city stradiotes fell in as well. And six leagues north of the city, Mag waited with Ser Giorgios and forty more wagons, smuggled out of the city two at a time over the last two weeks.

The Red Knight formed his army in two ranks on either side of the road. He rode all the way along their front, so that they could all see him with his helmet off.

'Listen, my friends,' he shouted. They were perfectly silent. 'I'm a devious bastard, and I don't always share my plans. But here's the word – we've slipped out of the city, the roads are hard, and in the next few days we're going to *rescue the Emperor.*'

For the Nordikans and the stradiotes, the promise of heaven wouldn't have been better. A cheer belted out to the sky.

He waited until they were done.

'And then Andronicus will have to come for us,' he said. 'We'll have the better men. He'll have the numbers.' He turned his horse in a circle. 'Every man here, whether a Morean or a mercenary, wants this over with. I intend to force him to commit to a battle. And then I intend that we win it.' He grinned. 'We don't want him to hole up in a fortress. We want him to find us and attack. So follow orders, be alert, and remember – we're going to have the Emperor with us.'

They cheered again.

Gabriel Muriens wondered what it would be like to exert such power over men's minds that they would cheer like that for him.

'March,' he called. And the army swung onto the road by sections, and followed him.

At Kilkis they turned north. Lord Phokus joined them with another hundred stradiotes, and as many archers mounted on ponies, and they didn't march north – they dashed north, into Thrake. On the first day they managed almost forty miles. They made a hasty camp where the scouts led them. Before dawn, a barely recovered Gelfred, still white around his own edges, dashed away, and the army rose in the chilly dark, donned armour, cursed the darkness and did not light a single candle. The ground of their fireless camp was littered with forgotten items – but the army passed over the Thrakian hills that day. They had another day of sun, and the roads stayed hard. They were on the ancient Imperial road and the bridges were stone-built.

On the third hard day they made a camp and surrounded it with felled trees in a long criss-crossed abattis like a temporary cattle fence, and they slept with fires lit. They were only fifty leagues from Lonika, and forty from the coast, through the steepest mountains many of them had ever seen.

That day, the flying column detached from the main army – sixty Vardariotes, a dozen lances, and as many Scholae and Nordikans, all with multiple horses. They crossed a tall bridge of ancient stones that towered over a river rushing black beneath its three arches. Chunks of ice were piled against the bridge, and it shuddered as further ice floes struck it, but the bridge was a thousand years old and an early spring was not a serious threat to it.

They rode east, the Red Knight and Gelfred and Count Zac at their head. With them rode Jules Kronmir. He wore a sword and armour like the rest of them.

After an hour of cantering over winter grass, the column halted and every man changed horses.

Ser Michael was with the priest. He knelt briefly in prayer, and then rose to check his girth. He looked at Ser Michael and raised an eyebrow. 'Why is it that I'm guessing I'm going to hate every minute of the next few days?' the priest asked.

'I don't know any more than you,' Ser Michael said. 'But my gut tells me you're spot on.'

An hour later they emerged from deep fog to find themselves cantering across dead grass and bracken that reached to their horses' bellies. All the Vardariotes but Count Zac and his immediate staff were gone – vanished into the fog.

They halted and changed horses, and they were off again.

At sunset, they stopped long enough to put feed bags on their horses' heads, and eat some sausage. The Red Knight walked from man to man, down the column. He said the same thing to every man.

'We're taking an insane risk, and playing for everything,' he said with a grin. 'No sleep tonight. Just keep going. Ignore the fog. That's what scouts are for.' He passed back up the column, leaving Ser Michael and Father Arnaud to speculate as to what he intended. At the head of the column stood a man holding a pony. The Red Knight bowed to him.

'This is more help than I ever expected,' he said. 'Again.'

'From which you may – again – assume that things are worse than you imagined,' said the guide.

There was a long silence – made more epochal by the totality of the fog and the quiet around them.

He's taking us straight across the aethereal, *isn't he?* asked Harmodius. *Blessed Virgin, think of the power required.*

He's saving us about forty miles of brutal mountains. We'll have to pass them on the way out. Or be trapped against them, unable to manoeuvre, and cut to pieces.

Well, aren't you the optimist?

When they stumbled out of the snowy fog, they were in a broad, flat marsh, frozen solid, at the foot of a ridge that seemed to fill the sky as the sun rose somewhere far, far to the east behind it. A castle stood at the top of the ridge, and well off to the north sat the town of Ermione. The sea was on the other side of the ridge; the Red Knight could smell it.

The Red Knight gathered them all together. 'Now we rescue the Emperor,' he said.

They all nodded.

'Where are we?' asked Ser Michael.

'Eastern Thrake,' said the Captain. 'That's the Imperial castle of Ermione. Last night we moved very fast indeed.'

Count Zac scratched his beard and strove to appear his usual phlegmatic self. 'Where are the rest of my lads?' he asked.

'I very strongly hope that they are storming and holding the high pass for us, and choosing a camp for the main army,' said the Red Knight. 'If not, this will turn out to be a very unfortunate trip.'

Men began to ask questions, and the Captain held up his arms for silence. 'It's not your business if I cut a deal with Satan,' he said coldly. 'It's your business to storm the castle on those heights. I am told that the enemy has a force within a day's march. There will be no siege but we'll only get one shot at this.' He smiled in the growing grey light. 'You'll find if you examine your recent training that you have all practised this.'

Men looked around and realised how many times in the last sixteen weeks they had stormed mock castles.

'How do we open the gate?' Count Zac said. 'Sorcery?'

The Red Knight shrugged. 'Better,' he said. 'Alchemy.'

Ser Michael and Gavin had, as they discovered, practised the whole thing.

Bent and Wilful Murder waited a long time in the growing light at the edge of day, arrows on their bows, watching the men in the towers. It was so cold that the very hairs in your nose seemed to freeze – so cold that sentries kept moving smartly or froze to death. But tired, cold men tend to move in patterns.

Ser Michael opened his mouth, and the Red Knight shook his head and pursed his lips.

The two master archers raised their bows in perfect unison, and all the other archers with them raised theirs, and two dozen shafts flew in the crystalline air. The spent shafts rattled against stone where they missed, but few of them missed.

The two sentries died.

Ser Gavin and Ser Michael picked up the thing like a bronze bell that had materialised at the last halt and ran it to the postern gate of the castle. At their heels came all the men-at-arms, while Count

Zac and his men and all the archers remounted and waited at the edge of the woods.

Ser Michael's hands shook and the backs of his arms and edges of his biceps tingled with what felt like weakness.

The snow crunched under his sabatons, and he made himself run faster.

The two strongest men lifted the bronze bell, mouth to the great iron-shod oak postern door, and seated it against the door.

There was a blur of power, and the bronze somehow mated to the iron on the gate. Ser Gavin let go of the thing as if it was poisonous. Michael backpedalled, almost fell as his heel caught on a piece of frozen dung in a horseshoe print, caught himself with a wrenching motion of his hips that made noise.

'Run!' hissed the Red Knight. 'Here – flat to the wall!'

Twenty armoured men-at-arms held themselves flat to the wooden palisade, just around the corner from the postern gate. The Red Knight's mouth moved.

There was a sound like all hell breaking loose, and the stench of hell, too.

In what seemed like silence, the Red Knight waved his sword and ran into the foul-smelling smoke, and they all followed him in.

Ser Michael's responsibility was the main gate. He led six men-at-arms across the frozen yard and fell flat on his face when the ice under foot betrayed him. Harald Derkensun got him to his feet and the other men passed him. There were men sleeping in the gatehouse, but no guard. They killed the sleeping men in their beds and Derkensun, who knew his way around a gatehouse, tripped the gate mechanism and the chains rattled as the portcullis went up and the two big gates opened on counterweights—

Ser Milus followed the Captain's steel-clad back into the nearest door in the main hall – which proved to be nothing but a covered passage dividing the Great Hall from a barracks area.

'Ignore them!' the Captain said softly and ran through a curtained door into the Great Hall. There were a dozen men sprawled on log benches and two men were awake. One shouted.

The Captain ran through the hall, and none of the Thrakians seemed to see him. So they turned on Milus and Gavin, and the fighting began. Milus set his feet and swung his axe and the Thrakians backed away, and Ser Giorgios ran right past the melee and followed the Captain with two more Scholae at his heels – as they'd been taught to.

Milus's pole-axe caught an unwary Thrakian who didn't know how long his reach was, cleanly severing almost a third of his head as well as the arm he'd raised to defend himself in the last heartbeat. He had enough head left to scream in stupefied horror as the top of his head fell in his lap.

The surprise was over.

Ser Giorgios followed the Captain up the steps of the tower, which twisted like a corkscrew. It was all he could do to breathe, and he was wearing less armour than the Albans.

They reached the top to find four men cramming the landing, using swords to break down the door of the room at the top of the tower.

The Red Knight put one down before the fight started, by slamming his long red sword into the man's unarmoured ankle from three steps down – a long thrust and a wrist cut. It was almost the end of the fight – the man staggered, screamed without comprehending what had happened to him – and fell down the stairs. His death on their swords almost threw the Scholae back, and gave his mates time to prepare.

The Red Knight grunted in exasperation. He leaped up the last three steps, absorbing two heavy blows – one to his helmet and one to his right pauldron – and his basilard clenched in his left fist gutted the nearest man.

Ser Giorgios was so close on his heels that he used the dying man as a shield, shouldered him into the third man on the landing and then stabbed through the dying man – repeatedly – until his adversary gurgled.

The Scholae finished the last man standing when he fell to his knees begging for mercy.

The Red Knight put his gauntleted hand against the door. 'He's in there,' he said. 'Majesty!' he called. 'Open your door! It is your rescue!'

The men pouring out of the barracks had begun to form a line in the icy yard – unarmoured, but with a workmanlike collection of short swords and heavy falchions, sabres and horse bows. An officer shouted, and they raised their shields and gave a Thrakian war cry.

Count Zac led the mounted men through the now-open gates. Arrows flew like snow flurries and the yard, already muddy, turned red-brown. The garrison had nowhere to go, no armour, and no hope of fighting twenty mounted men.

The rest of the armoured men were pouring into the Great Hall to help Milus and Ser Gavin, who had the only serious fighting. Both of them took wounds, outnumbered, fighting alone for as long as it took the sun to rise one finger above the horizon.

Ser Michael had one more duty to perform – a self-imposed one. He collected his team and ran through the bloody yard – the ice was gone – to the kitchens under the eastern tower. The yard door was unlatched, a woman screamed and they were in.

'Lie down!' he shouted. 'And you will not be killed.'

The Red Knight hadn't ordered him to save the women and children, but Michael was newly married, and he had his own notions about war.

Before the last screams were done, the Red Knight came into the yard with Giorgios and two more Scholae carrying the Emperor. Every man in the yard fell to his knees – even the archers, with a little help.

The Emperor smiled. 'Oh, my braves,' he said. 'Please spare the rebels.'

They got him into a horse litter rigged up on the spot.

Milus found the Red Knight with Ser Michael. 'Do we spare them?' he asked.

The Red Knight grinned. 'Ser knight, you have a flap of skin the size of a flapjack hanging off your thigh.' He knelt in the bloody snow and put pressure on a wound Ser Milus hadn't even seen. 'But yes – if the Emperor wants to be clement, I'm not going to countermand him.'

'You said to kill them all,' Ser Michael said accusingly.

'I said that when we were desperate,' the Red Knight said, as if talking to a fool. 'Now we're merely in a hurry.' He glared at Wilful Murder, who was trying to pass unnoticed into the kitchen, and nodded to Michael. 'Saving the kitchen staff? That was well done,' he said. 'I didn't even think of it,' he admitted.

Bent and two more archers were holding Ser Milus, and Long Paw was wrapping his thigh with clean white linen. 'Missed your prick,' the archer said comfortingly.

'If we bind them, they'll be dead in an hour from the cold,' Ser Milus said.

'That's a chance I'm willing to take,' the Red Knight said. 'Sorry. I know you are all gentle, perfect knights on errantry, but I'd rather not see these gentlemen again today. And when Andronicus's relief force reaches here, every one of our prisoners will turn into a blood-mad Thrakian.'

'Emperor said not to kill them,' Ser Michael said. 'If we tie them, the women will just untie them.' He set his hips. 'I won't let you kill the women.'

The Red Knight rolled his eyes. 'I wasn't proposing to kill them, my young idealist. I was hoping you'd come up with some noble, but efficient, way of protecting us – and them from your excellent friends, like Wilful Murder here, who merely want a bit of rape.' He shrugged. 'Very well. Lock them all in the basement of the eastern tower, and let the fates see our mercy.' He leaned over. 'Michael – we did it!'

Michael shook his head. 'Of course we did,' he said.

The Red Knight sighed. 'Sometimes I think you all take me for granted,' he said and went off to wash the blood off his hands.

Father Arnaud laughed so hard that he almost fell down.

Demetrius's relief force arrived at the seaside castle of Ermione six hours later.

His scout officer knew they were too late as soon as he saw the place on the horizon, with no smoke rising from the chimneys, but he kept his mouth shut. Demetrius was in a murderous mood, and looking for scapegoats and victims after his latest savage row with his father, ten leagues behind them with the main army.

They rode into the silent yard and Dariusz busied himself climbing the tower – just in case the guards had followed orders and held the room against all comers. Or killed the Emperor, as they'd been ordered to.

All four guards were dead on the landing – purses empty, weapons gone. The door to the Emperor's room stood open. Dariusz walked around the room where the Emperor had been a prisoner, looking at it with the eyes of a man who analysed things. He came down via the Great Hall, and then walked in – and out – of the gate tower.

By then, Demetrius's Easterners were killing the rescued prisoners, one by one. Demetrius sat his milk-white horse, a beautiful man on a magnificent horse in the midst of a courtyard awash in mud and blood. The men who had been the garrison fell on their knees – some for the second time – in the bloody slush and begged for mercy. This time they found none, and the Easterners coldly shot them down.

Dariusz waited until the worst of it was over, and then picked his way across the yard. 'Sixty men,' he said. 'They took it by coup de main, at dawn. I don't think that they lost a man in the process.'

Demetrius spat. 'Fucking fools,' he said. 'If we kill them all, we make a lesson for the future.' He spat in the bloody snow. 'We *have* to pursue them. We'll lose everything if the Emperor escapes.'

Dariusz looked at Aeskepiles, who was unmoved by the massacre. 'My lord, we have equal numbers and they are hours ahead. If they choose to set an ambush, we'll fall into it. Or we will pursue them too slowly because of the possibility of ambush. Either way, there is no point.' He didn't add that if he'd been the enemy commander, there would be another force – a blocking force – somewhere close by ordered to destroy any pursuit. Or that Lord Andronicus had fielded his entire army in late February, and the enemy's force was as yet undetected.

Dariusz felt something like admiration for the Red Knight. They clearly read the same books.

Demetrius growled.

There were screams. Women's screams.

Dariusz put his heels to his mount so that its head touched the head of Demetrius's horse. To get the lord's attention. 'Spare the women,' he said.

Demetrius laughed. 'Oh, they won't die,' he said.

Aeskepiles drew a deep breath, snapped his fingers and Demetrius's horse tossed him over his head into the muck of the yard.

Dariusz found his hand locked behind his back.

Aeskepiles backed his horse. 'I won't be party to this,' he said. 'Spare the women and children, or by dark gods, I will kill both of you right here.'

Dariusz wondered why the magister assumed that he was in favour of the rape and murder, but he was helpless and unlike many other helpless men, when Dariusz was helpless he relaxed.

Demetrius bounced to his feet. 'You might have just asked, man-witch. Instead, you humiliated me.' He smiled. 'We'll see. For now, they may live, their virtue unsullied.' He rubbed his hip. 'The virtue of some army women, saved by a warlock's honour,' he said. 'You're fools.' He turned to Dariusz. 'I hear what you say, scout. I worry—'

Dariusz shrugged. Since the mid-winter raid in the west, his assumptions had received blow after blow. He no longer assumed that his side was the side of right, and he was quite sure they were the side that was going to be beaten. And the loss of the Emperor—

Demetrius narrowed his eyes. 'I hate to lose,' he said. 'Stay with me, Captain. I'm not beaten yet.'

Twenty leagues south and west of the castle where Demetrius vented his ire on the survivors of the garrison, the Red Knight's army made a camp. Around the commander's tall red tent lay a snug encampment; six hundred tents, each hordled in local brush and wood so that they appeared to be a small forest. A late winter squall had dropped three fingers of snow over them, which insulated the tents, but the army's thirst for firewood had driven every peasant in the village out into the winter, their houses stripped for wood or disassembled, their own crucial woodpiles destroyed as if by incendiary locusts.

Most of the peasants ran to the next village. The poorest died of exposure.

The Red Knight stood over a camp table with his officers gathered around him. The air outside his pavilion was bitterly cold – in the mountains, it was still winter – but inside the presence of fifteen men and five braziers made the air temperature tolerable. At the head of the table, the Emperor sat on a heavy oak chair that Wilful Murder had stripped from the richest of the local peasants, with Count Zac kneeling at his side feeding him chicken, and Harald Derkensun, axe on shoulder behind the Emperor's right shoulder while Ser Giorgios stood at his left. Ser Gavin and Ser Michael stood by their Captain; Ser Jehan and Ser Milus sat on stools, and Ser Bescanon stood with Ser Alison. Gelfred stood at the end of the table, his light helmet under his arm, whispering fiercely with Father Arnaud.

'Now you know why great lords require big tents,' the Red Knight said.

There was an uneasy ripple of laughter, and the Moreans looked pained.

'Gentlemen, thanks to Gelfred's noble efforts, and those of Count Zac and his men, we have the enemy located. They have a strong force at Ermione, and their main army is about thirty leagues to the north, concentrated near the Nemea.' His long finger indicated the towns' locations. He smiled at them. 'Unfortunately, the former Duke's forces considerably outnumber ours, as he has apparently performed a miracle of late winter recruiting.'

Ser Jehan gave a slight shake to his head.

'On the other hand,' the Red Knight said, 'we now have the person of the Emperor.'

Every man present bowed. The Moreans went down on one knee.

The Emperor smiled benignly. 'I thank every one of you for rescuing me,' he said. 'If my legs worked, I would kneel to you. I would, if allowed, kiss the hands of every man and woman in this camp.' He nodded and tears glistened in his eyes. 'But that shocks you, I see. So let me say that your rescue is God's work, and with God at our backs I see no reason why our temporal sword will not triumph.'

The Red Knight's face twitched.

God is on your side, Gabriel.

Harmodius was laughing in his head, and he had a building headache of epic proportions. The truth was that his hours free of Harmodius had taught him that he *had* to rid himself of his guest. Without meaning to, his eyes flicked over to where Morgan Mortirmir stood, behind Ser Alison.

Please leave me alone, Harmodius.

Oh – are we sensitive now? Harmodius laughed. *I have a major work under way now. I'd love to show you what I'm forging—*

Shut the fuck up.

The Red Knight focused on the tent and saw them all looking at him. He forced himself to nod agreeably – he held onto his temper and his irritation about the Emperor's intrusion. Anger would gain him nothing.

Although, in fact, it was increasingly difficult to be chivalrous when his temples seemed to clang against the bones of his skull like loose shoulderplates and his guest continued to indulge in remarks he clearly found witty.

Slow recovery from the wound he'd taken at Christmas – two wounds, really – left him weaker than he wanted to be. His left arm hurt whenever it was cold, and right now that was all the time.

All that, in the blink of an eye.

'As usual,' he said lightly, 'I have a plan.'

*

The ancient citadel of Nemea towered above the plains and looked across a shallow gulf at the beaches of Ermione to the south. The mountains behind Ermione were still capped in snow, but here on the coast, the day was hot and flowers were already in bloom.

Andronicus sat with his chin in his hand, contemplating a variety of futures. His son and his magister had just crossed the town's main bridge.

Andronicus was an old campaigner, and he knew from the postures of the men riding behind his son that they had failed, and the Emperor was free.

Andonicus sighed. He swirled the wine in his golden cup. He smiled grimly at the former Grand Chamberlain.

'My lord?' the man asked. Defeat had not spoiled the man's ability to be obsequious, Andronicus noted with some inner amusement.

Andronicus took a careful sip of wine. 'I'm going to wager that we've lost the Emperor.'

The Grand Chamberlain flinched visibly.

Andonicus nodded. 'Time, I think, to send a message to the city and seek terms.'

The Grand Chamberlain knew that that was a death sentence for him. Andronicus was the Emperor's cousin. He'd have his estates restored, and be slapped on the wrist. But someone would have to be the scapegoat, and the man's fear showed in his eyes.

Andronicus took another measured sip and watched the snow-capped hills. 'Etrusca might be nice,' he said.

He hadn't quite finished drinking the wine when his son, resplendent in golden armour, was announced by his staff.

Demetrius sank to one knee. 'He was gone,' he said. Behind him, the magister, Aeskepiles, entered. The man looked worse than usual – paler, with heavy, dark circles under his eyes.

Andronicus had seldom loved his son as much as he did in that moment. He put out a hand. 'I know,' he said.

Demetrius's eyes were bright. 'Listen, Father. We must crown you emperor. Today. Now. Declare the true emperor dead. And—'

Andronicus smiled. 'No,' he said.

Demetrius shook his head. 'No, listen! This Red Knight has made a fool's error, for all he has the body of the Emperor. He's trapped against the mountains. We have the whole weight of our spring levy. We catch him, crush him, and kill the Emperor.'

'As we should have in the first place,' Aeskepiles put in.

Andonicus shook his head. 'No. Listen, my friends. I wanted to unseat the Emperor to save the empire. He is – a fool.' He looked around. 'But if I lead my levies and my infantry and my stradiotes down into the valleys of Morea to war – who then is the fool? What will we leave? More carcasses for the Etruscans and the Outwallers – and the Albans – to pluck. We threw the dice and we failed. The fool found friends. Now, we are the enemies of our own country.'

'Irene betrayed us,' Demetrius said.

Andronicus's eyes crossed his son's with a little of his former fire. 'I should have been more wary of a woman who would betray her own father,' he said.

Demetrius was still kneeling at his feet. 'I am not prepared to submit,' he said.

Andronicus smiled. 'You are a brave young man,' he said.

'We can win!' Demetrius insisted.

'I agree that you can win the battle. At the end of it, many hundreds of our best men will be dead. So will the mercenary force and many hundreds of the Emperor's best guardsmen. So? *Irene will still hold the city.* The war will go on. But the Empire will be weaker by every man either side loses.' Andronicus sipped his wine. 'Wine for my council. Let us compose our submission.'

Aeskepiles made a motion.

Demetrius was still kneeling by the Duke's chair. 'Father,' he said, and his voice held a rare note of pleading. 'Father!' he insisted.

Andromicus smiled at him.

Demetrius said, 'We will *not* submit.'

Andronicus nodded. 'You and the magister and the Grand Chamberlain?'

Demetrius stood suddenly, towering over his father in his gleaming golden armour. 'Yes!'

Andronicus nodded. 'I reccomend the three of you board a ship, then,' he said. His voice hardened. 'Because, before God, I am the Duke of Thrake. And the army camped outside obeys me.' He caught the movement of the Grand Chamberlain. He frowned. 'Guard!' he roared.

'Father!' Demetrius shouted. 'Stop and listen!'

Demetrius drew the heavy dagger at his hip. He stared at it a moment, as if confused.

Andronicus froze. 'Oh, my son!' he said.

Demetrius was shaking his head. 'I won't!' he cried.

Andronicus had not risen to be the warlord of the Empire by failure to grasp threats. His eyes went to the Grand Chamberlain, already moving to flank him, and to Aeskepiles, who stood silently, by the door, his staff emitting a pair of thick black threads – one to the Grand Chamberlain, and one to Demetrius.

Andronicus didn't flinch or give a speech. He drew his own belt dagger and threw it – at Aeskepiles.

It struck an invisible shield and vanished in a shower of sparks.

Aeskepiles smiled.

Andronicus' throw had got him to his feet and now he stepped to the right, still trying to believe that his son was going to protect him.

Demetrius's dagger went into his left side, under the arm. He felt the blow like a punch – felt the hilt against the silk of his shirt.

Without meaning to, he rotated his son's body and got a thumb onto his son's right eye, even as he realised that he was dead. His sight was going. But the urge to fight back – to kill – was strong.

The dagger had struck straight to his heart.

With his last thought, he released his grasp on his son's head.

'My—'

He hit the floor.

'We need to dispose of the body immediately.' He heard the man-witch say it, as if from a hillside far, far away. He craved to hear something of his son. He willed—

And then he was gone.

A day after the loss of the Emperor to the Red Knight's men, one of Dariusz's patrols picked up a pair of peasants who had a report of rape and murder from the hills to the west. Dariusz lost half a day following these reports up and by the time he made it back to report, the Duke was absent and he was reporting to Demetrius. The Prokusatores officer left Despot Demetrius's tent and approached the khan of Demetrius's Easterners.

The man shrugged and looked away.

Duke Andronicus apparently no longer rode with the army he'd raised. Captain Dariusz knew many of the retainers. Eventually he asked Ser Christos's squire, who shrugged and admitted that the Duke hadn't left Nemea. Many men were aware that the Duke had vanished, and Dariusz kept his ear to the ground, but heard nothing. He assumed the Duke was sick, and his sickness was being hidden, but he had darker suspicions.

He snatched a few hours sleep in the castle of Ermione and then took a powerful patrol west, following the tracks. To his own satisfaction he found the place where the enemy had waited in ambush.

He showed his two best men the place, like a deer lie writ large – snow trampled flat, a small fire, a lookout post complete with closely woven branches and a wall of snow.

Verki – one of his best – stirred the fire with a stick and made a small magic.

'Ten hours. Last light, maybe?' He shrugged, his gesture exaggerated by his long fur coat and heavily padded armour.

Dariusz raised an eyebrow. 'Let's see,' he said.

He followed the tracks left by the enemy horses. They'd done well enough in covering them – swept the snow with branches – but by luck, there hadn't been a snowfall since, and there were places where shod hoof marks showed clear, and where horse dung lay frozen in the snow. Sixty cavalrymen moving quickly are very difficult to hide in a winter landscape.

It was almost noon when they climbed a long ridge. There were horsemen above them, and they had a brief skirmish – a horse died. A man broke his back when another horse fell, and had to be killed.

They seized the ridge top and looked down into the next valley. The enemy rode away.

'You know this country?' Verki asked.

Dariusz shook his head. 'Not really. I've hunted here.'

Verki frowned. 'Something is wrong,' he said. He peered down into the valley. The snow reflected the bright sunlight and made everything difficult to see even though, lower in the valley, the snow was melting and the streams were filling.

Dariusz spotted the walled village protected by a switchback in the winding stream. 'There's the town,' he said.

'With no smoke from the chimneys,' Verki spat.

They looked at the valley for longer, and saw the patrol of enemy horsemen they'd pushed off the ridge riding along the floor of the valley far below. They crossed the stream.

Dariusz put a wrap on the wound he'd taken in the left hand and began to feel cold.

'I've got the bastards. Follow the line of the ford. Look at the ridge top.' Verki smiled savagely.

The faintest smudge of smoke was visible.

Dariusz nodded. 'That must be their camp.'

Verki shook his head. 'Just covered by the ridge. Someone knows his business.'

'Leave a post here. Take two men you trust and get a look at their camp.' Dariusz was breathing easier. The enemy had seemed almost ghostly until now. He still had no idea how they'd got over the mountains. But now he had them fixed in place, and Lord Demetrius would bring up the army.

As he turned his horse and rode east, he had time to consider a number of problems, not the least of which was that he didn't know where Duke Andronicus was.

'You have them?' Demetrius asked. He looked as if he hadn't slept in days.

'We brushed a patrol. We saw the smoke from their camp.' It sounded thin, put that way.

Demetrius glared at the khan of his Easterners. 'Better than anyone else has done. Christ Pantrokrator, one of these fools proposed they'd come by sea!'

Dariusz leaned over the Count's rough map. 'He's trapped against the mountains, exactly as you suggested, my lord, and he'll be out of food in a few days. The villages up there won't feed an army.' Dariusz shrugged. 'I think perhaps we will not even need to fight.'

'You sound like my father.' Demetrius spat.

Dariusz flinched – it was such an odd comment and so uncharacteristic.

Demetrius looked at the warlock, Aeskepiles. And the former Grand Chamberlain.

Aeskepiles nodded. Very quietly, he said, 'As I have said before, we must kill the Emperor. And then we must ensure it appears that the enemy killed him in desperation. I will take care of the latter. But he must be killed, and to achieve that we must attack.' He shrugged. 'If the Emperor is spirited away over the mountains—'

Demetrius laughed. 'Over the Penults? In late winter?' He shook his head. 'A bird would die.'

Dariusz, who had hunted the Penults since he was a boy, disagreed. 'My lord,' he said.

Demetrius raised a hand. 'I'm not interested in your carping. I'm not interested in skulking about in the snow waiting for them to starve. Or worse yet, surrender, so that we have a horde of witnesses.'

Aeskepiles smiled. 'That could be dealt with.'

Demetrius paused. His gaze hardened. 'Warlock, I realise I need you. But have a care. We need there to be an Empire when this is over. If I massacre the guard, who exactly will protect me when I am Emperor?'

'Who will guard your father, you mean,' Dariusz said carefully.

'My father has – hmm – withdrawn from the army,' Demetrius said. 'He has no further interest in this contest, and will enter a monastery.'

For some reason, it was Aeskepiles, and not Demetrius, who looked away.

Dariusz pursed his lips and then nodded. 'I see,' he said.

Ser Christos led the main cavalry force. Every Thrakian stradiote had two horses, and they made excellent time over the snow now the scouts had cleared the ground. Demetrius came in a second division, with all of his father's veteran infantry, and Ser Stefanos brought up the rear with a strong force of Thrakian peasants armed with axes, bowmen from the estates around Lonika, and Easterner mercenary cavalry.

They took just four hours to traverse what the scouts had taken all day to cover. They pitched a hasty camp at the base of the great ridge and made contact with Verki's piquet at the top of the ridge. They stripped the forest for wood and built big fires, protected from view as they were by a horde of frozen sentries and the bulk of the snow-covered mountain between them.

Before first light Verki led the army up the snowy ridge. The moonlight on the snow made the road – if it could be called that – like a black slit of frozen mud in a white wilderness, but they moved fast enough. By the last grey light before dawn, they could just see a line of motionless sentries in red tabards, the bright wink of forty fires, and the smoke rising to the heavens. They could smell the smoke. And they could see the magnificent red pavilion in the middle of camp and the forty heavy wagons of the enemy baggage parked in a wagon fort.

Dariusz had thought the plan rash, and had said so, and now he watched in amazement as Demetrius carefully marshalled his men.

Aeskepiles, at the young commander's request, sent a small fireball whizzing into the heavens.

The Thrakians screamed like monsters out of the Wild. The veterans of Duke Andronicus went forward fast, singing a hymn. The cavalry closed from the flanks.

Off to the east, over the sea, the sun crested the horizon, but here in the mountains behind the coast, it was just an orange and pink outline on the mountains behind them. They crossed the ground, lumbering heavily in deep snow.

Someone screamed – the sound of a man in soul-wrenching pain.

A horse went down.

The enemy sentries weren't moving and weren't calling the alarm.

Another man went down. It happened close enough to Dariusz that he saw the pit open under the man's feet, saw him fall and impale himself on the stakes at the base of the pit. A snow trap.

Dariusz stopped running.

It was a beautiful camp and they took it intact. They took the store of firewood and the fires, which must have been huge, because they had burned down to coals and were still big and warm. They took the wagons – forty beautiful wagons, some full of stores, some full of useful things, including a portable forge for an armourer.

There were a dozen hogsheads of wine, and that wine was open before the officers could get involved.

There was a flash, and a noise like a bolt of lightning in the centre of the camp.

Aeskepiles was seen to hurry there.

Dariusz found Verki watching one of his scouts die. The man had drunk the wine and it was suddenly pretty obvious it was poisoned. His heels drummed on the packed snow, and he retched blood while more leached out of various other parts.

'Fuck their mothers,' Verki swore.

'How long have they been gone?' Dariusz asked.

Verki looked miserable. 'At least two days,' he said. 'The patrol we fought must have been the fire-tenders.'

*

They were negotiating a particularly brutal double switchback, where the Nordikans had to clear the snow with shovels so that anyone could pass, when the Red Knight stiffened in his saddle.

Heh. Harmodius was gloating.

Your little gift?

He'll know it's the same working he used on the amulets.

So now he knows we have Kronmir?

And that he's been had. He'll be mad as hell.

What happens if he turns around? He can still march back to Lonika the long way around as fast as we can go through the hills – probably faster.

In the comfortable room of the Red Knight's memory palace, it was warm. Harmodius sat with his legs over the armrest of a huge chair. He raised a cup of steaming hippocras. He won't. He'll be stung, and his ego will be pricked. And he'll follow you.

Do I sound that cocky to other people?

Harmodius shrugged.

I should stop. You sound so smug I don't care if we win – I just want you to be wrong.

Harmodius nodded. May I show you my finest work? he asked.

The image of the young Captain nodded agreeably. They found themselves in a workshop – an aethereal setting that reflected several workshops that Gabriel Muriens had known. Against the near wall was a bench – a very plain wooden bench lined with tools, each of which had a sigil burning on it.

On the bench lay a sword.

What is it? asked the Captain, through a burgeoning headache.

A Fell Sword, said Harmodius.

For me? asked the Captain. He was suddenly afraid.

Harmodius laughed. It was a dreadful, terrifying laugh.

Oh, no, my boy. I am not that much of an ingrate. He picked it up and flourished it, like a boy with a new sword. It's for me.

Mag missed her wagons. She missed the comfort and solidity of the brutes, but most of all, she missed having dry, warm feet. Sitting on a wagon – even in driving snow or freezing rain – kept your feet out of the wet.

Climbing a mountain pass leading a recalcitrant donkey had a different feel entirely.

John le Bailli was somewhere well ahead of her. The whole army was now a single animal wide, strung out over six miles of high ridges and steep-shouldered mountains. They were above the current snow line, which, in a way, made her life easier, as the ground was frozen. But her toes lost feeling every time she stopped, and she was fifty-one years old, and the great adventure now seemed like a horrible exercise in endurance.

At noon, they came to a stream – or what might, at other times of year, be a dry watercourse or a small trickle of water.

On the first of March, it was a stream twenty feet wide that flowed so fast that small rocks were constantly being rolled along the bottom. While Mag watched, a whole tree from somewhere upstream came by, bobbed, struck a boulder with a resounding crash and continued on its way.

The column was bunching up on the flat by the stream, and increasingly desperate men and women were trying to warm their feet by any expedient they could. It wasn't even a cold day.

The Red Knight had taken most of the mounted across the traditional way – with ropes and horses. Two men had fallen in, and on the other side there were two great fires burning and parties of men trying to save the wet, cold victims.

Mag didn't even pause to argue. She flung three bridges of ice across – one mostly acting as a dam, and the other two with high arches and redundant supports.

Corporals and veterans began to bellow orders. They'd all seen the tree in the current.

'I can get you a horse,' the Red Knight said. He'd ridden up to her where she watched the women crossing.

'Can you get a horse for every woman?' she asked.

He pursed his lips. 'Yes,' he said. 'The ice bridge is a nice trick. I need to learn that better. Mine wastes too much *ops*.'

She met his eye. 'Is this really your plan?'

He shrugged. In full plate, with two great circle cloaks as a sheath of wool, he looked like a giant. The shrug barely raised the magnificent gold brooch on his right shoulder an inch. 'My plan perished when Andronicus fielded five thousand men in the dead of winter. I didn't expect that. This is my – hmmm – my third alternate plan.' Just for a moment, the look of bland indifference he wore all the time cracked.

'I was probably a fool to try this in winter. But – Master Smythe said we had to hurry. And Kronmir said they would kill the Emperor.'

Mag shook her head. People were watching them. 'Another day and we might start losing people. Some of the Scholae aren't used to this kind of life and there's no forage for the horses. We have another day of food and fodder on the mules—'

'—and then we eat the mules,' he said. 'I know.'

But he was as good as his word, and by the next halt, every woman was mounted on a spare horse. Including Kaitlin de Towbray, who had womanfully walked with her pregnant belly all the way up the east side of the mountains.

They didn't stop at dark.

The Red Knight was seen to have a hurried conference with Ser Gelfred; fires were lit, and food cooked – or rather, cold food was eaten and hot tea, or just hot water, drunk in enormous quantities. And then they marched again.

Immediately after leaving their fires, the army started going *down*. They had been up and down the ridges for three days, but now they descended steadily, and the icy track, cleared by the exhausted Nordikans, became a two-rut track with less snow, and then a snow-covered stone roadbed.

An hour before dawn, when Mag was a jumble of old joints, nerves, lack of food and lack of sleep, they turned a long curve on a spur that stuck out from a mountainside – and every man and woman who came to the edge gave a gasp.

On their right side, a cliff fell away. The road continued, with enormous stone arches, buttresses in still more stone, cascading down the hillside like a waterfall frozen in rock, but the cliff was half a thousand feet high and the stream at the bottom was so far down in the darkness as to be lost except for the echoing thunder of its icy passage.

The cliff was imposing, but it was the sight of twinkling lights like distant faery folk that raised the shouts. Somewhere – somewhere within reach, at last – there was light, and warmth.

Aeskepiles looked at the stumps of the ice bridge abutments and cursed.

'How strong is he?' he asked aloud. And after a small ritual of gathering, he built a single bridge.

Demetrius pointed his sword. 'He made three,' he said.

'I must conserve my power,' Aeskepiles said. 'If he squanders his, all the better.'

Amphipolis was the name of the town, and her gates were stormed. The veterans of the company offered no warning and no formal summons to surrender – and the town had no idea that an enemy army was above them in the mountains. The veterans put ladders against the low curtain walls before sunrise, just as if they'd been in Arles. Fifty Thrakian soldiers died very quickly on the wrong side of the main gate, tricked, trapped, and annihilated. Ser Jehan didn't bother taking prisoners.

Father Arnaud and Gelfred sat on their horses in the central square and shouted at the Red Knight until they were joined by the Emperor, and together with a hundred men-at-arms he led them to clear the archers – the victorious archers – out of the streets.

'If you let this town be destroyed, you are no knight,' Father Arnaud said.

The Red Knight leaned over and vomited in the snow.

'Is he drunk?' Arnaud cried.

Toby shook his head.

Ser Michael grabbed the priest's bridle. 'He's tired. And this, pardon me, padre, is war.'

'We don't make war like this on the Wild!' Father Arnaud said.

'The Wild doesn't have silver candelabra or handsome girls,' the Red Knight muttered. 'Damn you and your moral certainty. We are not fucking paladins. We are soldiers, and this town is an enemy town taken by storm. These men are cold, and exhausted, and an hour ago they had almost no hope of warmth.' He pointed as John le Bailli kicked in a door and led three armoured men in emptying the cowering family and their servants out into the snow. Then a dozen of the company's women took the house.

While they watched that drama, Ser Bescanon dragged Wilful Murder out of a building while a dozen other men with leather buckets tried to put out the fire he'd started.

'This is senseless. If I cannot appeal to God, I'll appeal to your basic humanity,' Father Arnaud said.

'Who says I have any humanity at all?' the Red Knight shouted in the priest's face. 'You want me to save the world, and you don't want any innocents killed? It doesn't work like that. War kills. Now get out of my way, because I have tomorrow's atrocities to plan!'

Toby waited until his lord was gone into what had been the mayor's house.

'He's not doing all that well,' he said. 'He's sick, and he's worried. In case you gentleman can't tell. You're all very helpful, I'm sure.' He shrugged, seized an apple from a basket that a looter ran past carrying, and took a bite. Then he followed his lord inside.

After a warm night and a lot of stolen food, the army marched again at dawn.

The town, stripped of preserved food, pack animals, and grain, watched them go in surly silence. Even the presence of their Emperor could not make them cheer.

'If you ever come to rule Thrake, that town will belong to you,' Father Arnaud said, as they rode west.

'Then I'll do something nice for them. Father, I am aware that you are a good man, and, despite appearances, I like to think of myself as a good man. In fact, I pride myself on it. We are, if you will pardon me, in a situation that cannot be resolved by prayer or a noble cavalry charge. So could you, perhaps, leave me alone?'

Father Arnaud smiled savagely 'Never, Gabriel. I will never, ever leave you alone.'

The Red Knight put his hand to his head, which throbbed as if he had spent several nights drinking.

The army marched west, moving as fast as two thousand tired soldiers and their women and baggage animals could manage.

'You swore he wouldn't make it across the Penults,' Aeskepiles said quietly.

Demetrius was looking down at the town below him.

'Now his army is between us and Lonika,' Aeskepiles went on. 'How much of a garrison does your capital have?'

Demetrius chewed on his thumb. He worked on the callus, biting it, chewing the bits. 'Son of a bitch,' he said.

'We have to catch him in the plains,' Dariusz offered. 'The road will be clear, and good.'

Ser Christos shook his helmeted head. 'We're haemorrhaging men.'

'So is he,' Demetrius said. They'd picked up a dozen city stradiotes who'd simply surrendered as soon as they could. They'd already captured almost a hundred stragglers.

Ser Christos let out a long, harsh breath, but said nothing.

'Advance the banner,' Demetrius said. 'Get the scouts well out. Put all the Easterners out. Let us make the usurper's life a living hell.'

Chapter Eighteen

Long Paw

Harndon – The Queen

Four days after Christmas, three ships came sailing in to Harndon port. On board was Ser Gerald Random, and he brought the entire Morean fur trade with him, minus only his concessions to the Etruscan merchants, as well as fifteen tons of Wild honey. The Etruscan banks in the city received into their coffers some thousands of leopards in loans, and trading – gambling, some called it – in the value of some elite commodities changed tenor rapidly.

Ser Gerald was seen to go to the palace and place in the King's hands a quantity of pelts, honey, and gold.

In the great marketplace at Smithfield, outside the western gates of the city, workmen began to construct the scaffolding for a truly titanic set of lists, including bleachers for seats. Loads of lumber came downriver, the great logs simply heaved in and floated down the Albin from the edge of the Wild.

Ser Gerald's furs were sold for good quantities of silver – many to Harndon's Etruscan merchants, who paid a higher price but no doubt had ways of passing the cost onto their customers. But the flow of silver was steady, and, just as the first warmth of spring melts the snow and causes the frozen streams to develop to a trickle, so the silver began to flow into the King's new mint, which bore a startling resemblance to Master Pye's work yard.

The dies were ready, and Edmund began striking slugs of silver as soon as the first shipment reached him. Outside Master Pye's gate, a full company of the Harndon trained men stood guard, less proud now in their half armour than they had been on Christmas night. Keeping a hundred apprentices and journeymen 'idle' so that they could play soldier in winter was expensive and boring and cold.

But there were no attacks on the fledgling mint, and the coins began to flow.

Almost as soon as the new coins appeared – sacks of them – in the trade squares, they changed the nature of commerce. They were solid. They were heavy.

They had an excellent silver content.

The King couldn't share Master Ailwin's triumph as he neither understood it nor, really, respected it. But he did notice the change in the faces of his interior councillors, and he was delighted to hear them vote him the funds to carry on his tournament for the first of May.

If the new Bishop of Lorica listened with a sour face and referred to the whole exercise as 'usury', the King could afford to ignore him.

But if the King was victorious in Cheapside, he was less sanguine about the palace. And the months after Christmas passed in petty defeats for the Queen as her belly grew rounder and her King grew more indifferent. Galahad d'Acre was arrested and thrown in the tower – although no one seemed to actually suspect him of the murder of Lady Emota. Another of the King's squires simply vanished. Some said he'd been murdered, others that he had gone home to his father's estates, afraid for his life and reputation.

The pace of the slanders increased, and the Queen began to seriously suspect that she might have a rival – that the King might have taken a mistress. Such things were done, and it was her duty to ignore such behaviour.

It was not in her character to accept a rival. Nor to accept the staging of a passion play about the whore of Babylon, performed under her window, and loud with the laughter of Jean de Vrailly. And the King. And the Sieur de Rohan, whose hired Etruscan players said the unsayable and sang the unsingable with panache.

Lady Almspend spent her days practising small acts of hermeticism and reading the old King's papers – and those of his hermetical master and several of his other ministers. She declared her reading fascinating, and took copious notes while her royal mistress paced up and down in her solar and Diota cleaned and tidied uselessly.

Eight weeks into the New Year, Desiderata sat down at her writing table – covered in Rebecca's stacks of musty documents and crisp, new notes – and took a sheet of new vellum, idly wondering how many sheep died for her correspondence.

Dear Renaud she wrote. Her brother, hundreds of leagues to the south, in L'Occitan.

She looked at those words, and considered every argument she had made when she had accepted the King of Alba's proposal of marriage. And his replies. His anger. His desire for conflict.

Calling to Renaud for help would be an irrevocable action.

She stared at the words on the parchment, imagining her worthy brother raising his knights and leading them north. Imagining his western mountains unguarded against the Wyrms and Wyverns and worse things that infested them.

Imagining him fighting her husband.

She chewed on the end of her stylus.

'You'll have ink in your mouth, and then what will people say?' Diota asked.

'My belly is as big as a house, woman. No one will look at me anyway.' Desiderata didn't like being pregnant. Things hurt, the morning sickness was oppressive, her bladder was always full and, worst of all, she had lost the regard of the knights of court. They didn't *look* at her. The whispers were bad enough. But the loss of that worship was like torture.

She considered the tournament. The subject made her tired. It had been her idea in the first place, and now—

Now the King's mistress might be the Queen of Love. And she would merely be the Queen. The very heavily pregnant Queen whose husband suspected her of an unspeakable betrayal, and seemed disposed to laugh it off.

She was just framing the thought that she could invite her brother for the tournament when one of Rebecca's dusty parchments caught her eye.

She ran her eyes along the Gothic script automatically. Even without Rebecca's skills, she'd begun to be able to pick up on the hands of the various major players. This was the infamous traitor Plangere.

Her eye caught on the word 'rape'.

She choked at what she read, and closed her eyes and her mouth filled with bile.

She bent over as far as she comfortably could and rested her head on her writing table.

The door to her solar opened, and she heard Almspend's light steps and her intake of breath. 'Oh,' she said.

The Queen made herself sit up.

Rebecca's deep eyes were drawn with concern. 'I'm a fool,' she said. 'I hadn't meant to leave that out.'

The Queen stared at her.

'I couldn't bear to destroy it, because it is history,' Almspend said.

'My husband,' the Queen said. She had trouble drawing a breath. 'My husband,' she said again.

'Madam – it was many years ago. He has doubtless done his penance and made his peace with God.' Almspend held her hands tightly.

But the Queen's world – her very ideas of who she was and who the King was – was collapsing like dams under the force of mountain torrents in springtime. She tried to breathe.

'The King my husband,' she croaked. Her fingers found the parchment. 'Raped his sister. She cursed him for it. Oh, my God, my God.'

Almspend took the document, and smoothed it. 'Yes,' she said. 'He wasn't King yet,' she added. 'He was quite young.' She looked at her Queen and tried a different tack. 'It's only what Plangere writes, and he was a traitor.' She looked at the date on the note.

The Queen put her hand to her chest and sat back. She struggled to pull in a breath. Her hands grew cold. She felt her baby kick, and she cried out, and Almspend put her hand on the Queen's head.

The Queen looked at her, eyes wide as the realisation hit – the moment at Lissen Carrak when— And she cried out again, as if in pain.

'Of course!' she said. 'The Red Knight is his *son*.'

The Imperial Army – as the Red Knight styled their force – arrived on the plains of Viotia as the last snow melted in the shadowy corners of the neatly walled fields. But the frozen ground was still hard as iron, and rang under their horses' hooves.

They swept into the rich lands a day ahead of the enemy, and marched north and west on the ancient stone road.

Eavey – or 'Eves' as the soldiers called it – opened her gates for them. It was not quite the miracle it seemed; the near sack of Amphipolis had grown in the telling. And the Emperor was there in person this time, beautifully dressed in crimson and purple silk over fur. He wore a small gold crown over a magnificent fur hat.

The people came out to cheer him when the gates were open and it was clear that the soldiers were not going to punish them.

The Red Knight went directly to the Ducal residence – one of Andronicus's lodgings, a magnificent forty-room castle with a Great Hall and marvellous woodwork. And ancient sculptures. The chamberlain admitted him, and he quartered the army in the castle.

He summoned Father Arnaud.

The priest came.

The Megas Ducas was sitting with the Emperor, who was dining while the Red Knight served him. Father Arnaud waited patiently to be called forward, as he had studied the Morean etiquette and had some idea what he might be in for.

The Emperor ate as if no one was watching him, and talked – politely – to Count Zac, who poured his wine, and Ser Giorgios, who held his napkin, and to Harald Derkensun, who stood with an axe on his shoulder. There were servants – actual servants – and for each of them there was a gentleman of the Scholae, who watched them the way cats watch mice.

The Red Knight turned and caught Father Arnaud's eye and winked.

Father Arnaud was shocked, but also pleased.

The Emperor discussed the weather, and some differences between Alban and Imperial religious practice. Father Arnaud was surprised to hear how conversant the Red Knight was with Alban practice.

Eventually the Emperor ate something very sweet and sticky, and raised his hand for a napkin. He glanced at Father Arnaud and smiled. 'Ah – the fighting priest. Please be with us!'

Father Arnaud came forward and made a deep bow.

'It is the Emperor's pleasure that you take command of a detachment of belted knights to police the city,' the Red Knight said.

Father Arnaud nodded. 'We intend to hold these walls and force a siege?' he asked.

The Emperor smiled. 'I would rather that my Megas Ducas used our army to force a battle, in which God might show us his mercy. But the commander of our armies has different intentions.'

The Red Knight picked up a dish and Father Arnaud discovered he found it disconcerting to see him waiting on the Emperor as if he was a servant. He bowed, and carrying the plate, which held the remains of two roast pheasants in saffron with their skins gilded so that they shone like birds of solid gold, he walked down the hall's dais and out the door by which the noblemen and women were served.

Father Arnaud bowed to the Emperor, took a serving dish – rapini, or something like it, loaded with garlic – and followed the Red Knight.

The moment he crossed out of the hall, a pair of servants – real servants – took the dish from his hands with the obvious disdain of professionals for amateurs.

'You serve beautifully,' Father Arnaud said.

'I had practice. I was my father's page for years. Ticondaga is too far from civilisation for me to have been fostered, but while there I waited on many famous men.' He followed the servants towards the kitchen, and as they entered he plucked most of a pheasant off the tray and stood in an alcove, eating.

Father Arnaud adapted his actions to his own needs and seized a large piece of slightly used chicken pie, with raisins, spices and sugar, from a serving tray where it sat idle and unwanted.

'There's wine in the pitcher,' the Red Knight said. 'I love kitchens. Well-run kitchens, anyway. I could live here.'

'But we're retreating,' Father Arnaud said.

'Yes,' the Red Knight said. He'd finished his pheasant and now had sticky gold leaf on his hands.

'You could hold this place,' Father Arnaud said.

The Red Knight cocked his head to one side like a puzzled puppy. 'You can't have it both ways,' he said.

Father Arnaud now had hands coated in ginger and sugar. 'Both ways?' he said. Boyhood habits count and he began to lick his fingers. The pie had been delicious.

'You don't want any towns to be sacked. You were right. I was tired and annoyed. And I was wrong. I needed to get my head together and control my men. But – now you want me to hold this place?

Really?' The Red Knight shook his head. 'When we fight, I'll make it as far from here as I can manage.'

'The Emperor seems to think that you – and God – can win.' Father Arnaud couldn't find a cup, so he drank from the jug.

'The Emperor is a kindly man, who is so *nice* that he can't imagine that his daughter sold him out, his chamberlain betrayed him and his magister stabbed him in the back.' He raised an eyebrow. 'Are you staking some special claim to the wine, or will I get some if I'm especially good, or what?'

Father Arnaud handed over the wine. 'He's not a good strategist,' he commented.

'He's not terribly bright,' the Red Knight said. He paused. 'He's not of this world,' he added. 'That's a kinder way of putting it.'

'You *know* that his daughter betrayed him?' Father Arnaud asked.

The Red Knight shrugged. 'I wasn't there. But I'd bet heavily on the notion. I can prove she sent messengers to Andronicus. And Kronmir thinks she was the original betrayer.'

Father Arnaud shook his head. 'How terrible.'

Again, the Red Knight shrugged. 'Really? He's a dreadful Emperor, Arnaud. He cares nothing for most of the things that the others live for – including keeping the Etruscans in line. Imagine living in the palace, watching your father doom your Empire to stagnation and death. Imagine you could stop it. Imagine being trained from birth to respect and adore a thousand years of history that is being destroyed before your eyes.' He smiled.

Arnaud was careful not to move too fast. He didn't want to break whatever spell kept the man talking. 'Is that how your childhood was?'

The other man laughed. 'Not at all. My father was the best soldier I knew, and my mother was the most beautiful woman in the world. We had the best castle, the strongest, the most magical, and it was going to be mine if I proved myself worthy.' He was looking off into the kitchens. 'That's why, when I found out—' He paused. Then he turned slowly and looked at the priest. 'Damn, you are good. Let's just leave it there, shall we?'

Father Arnaud smiled. 'So, I'm the duty officer for tonight?' he asked.

The Red Knight nodded. 'Ser Gavin will take your place at the fourth hour, so you can have two hours' sleep before we march.'

*

'Mark my words,' Wilful Murder said. And this time, he was right. They did march at first light, leaving the most comfortable welcome and the warmest beds. The company had been billeted in the town, and the townspeople had treated them like heroes – scary heroes. Bent and Long Paw shared a bed in a house owned by a wool merchant, and the cook made them bread fried in eggs with maple syrup for breakfast, and Bent shook his head at Long Paw.

'I can't remember the last time someone cooked me breakfast of their own will,' he said. He wiped his sticky moustache on his sleeve.

'Ever think about it?' Long Paw asked.

'About what?' Bent asked, in the way that men do when they already know the answer, but need to buy themselves some time to think.

'Oh,' Long Paw said, and then he got his saddle down off the family's rack – a nice touch, and very helpful on a cold morning. He got it up on his gelding's back. The horse grunted. 'You know. We could have stormed this town. Killed the men. Done the women. Right?'

Bent nodded. 'Yep.'

'We was eating breakfast just now, and she served us on nice pewter plates – you saw that?' Long Paw asked.

Bent nodded, and their eyes met as he flung his own saddle over his horse. 'A few words different, and the Cap'n orders us to storm this place. An' the cook is dead or worse, and I have those pewter plates in my panniers.' Bent got the girth under his horse. 'But no breakfast, eh?'

Long Paw smiled. 'That's just what I mean.'

As the sun rose, it became obvious that the Thrakians had marched all night.

They were just too late to surprise the town – and Count Zac had mounted patrols who reported their approach as the Imperial Army formed up in the town's square.

The Red Knight climbed a tower by the main gate – a laborious process in full harness. Ser Michael went with him, and Ser Jehan too, and they had the briefest of conferences.

And then the army was moving, leaving from the north gate even as the warden of the south gate was opening a parley with the Thrakians.

Count Zac was first out of the gate with three hundred Vardariotes,

Gelfred, and fifty green coated men of the company. They formed in small companies just south of the town and, at a raised hand from the Count, they galloped over the iron-hard fields, right and left around the town.

Next the stradiotes emerged – first the companies of city stradiotes, and then the Scholae, guarding the army's baggage – a long string of mules, some donkeys, a few horses taken at Amphipolis and a dozen new wagons. They passed through the gate one by one. It took a lot of time.

Just south of the city, almost under the walls, Count Zac's Vardariotes emerged from the olive grove and slashed into the vanguard of the Thrakians. They were like a razor cut – they passed very quickly and left blood in their wake.

Demetrius's Easterners countered their charge, emerging from the distant treeline to the south in good order with sabres drawn over their right arms and hilts tucked over their bowstring hands, so that they could loose arrows with their swords ready to hand. Screaming war cries, they went at Count Zac's men. The two forces went right at each other. As it was early spring, there was no dust. The two forces spread out wide, looking for a flank or an opportunity, and then threaded each other, each warrior passing between the charging horses of two enemies.

Both sides rallied instantly. The khan's men had more empty saddles, but they charged again and the much-feared Vardariotes broke and fled. The khan's men harried them, and more than a hundred of the Thrakian heavy horse who had initially been harried by the red-coated Vardariotes now changed direction and pursued the pests who had stung them.

The longbows on the town walls shocked them. The Thrakians had taken for granted that the company archers were already gone, retreating. The flight of three hundred arrows, even at long range, emptied saddles and killed many horses outright.

And then Gelfred struck, leading his scouts in a charge from under the walls to the west. He only had fifty men, but they made a great deal of noise, and the khan's men feared a larger trap – and so they broke.

Instantly, the Vardariotes switched direction – their best trick. Arrows flew in every direction for a moment, but the Easterners were broken. They left two or three dozen dead behind them.

The Vardariotes formed a crisp array, picked up their wounded, and trotted away into the shadow of the olive trees. Gelfred's men took no casualties and melted into the woods to the north and west of the town.

The Red Knight watched the last of the action from the base of a south-facing tower. Then he turned his charger and cantered heavily around the town, in time to see his archers, led by Bent, riding out of the north gate.

Bent saluted, and the archers cheered.

The action lost him forty men, but it bought him another day.

'He is making us dance to his tune every day,' Aeskepiles said.

Demetrius scratched his jaw. 'My men performed well this morning. Those are the Empire's best soldiers – we matched them.'

Aeskepiles shook his head. 'No. We lost.'

'We'll catch him tomorrow,' Demetrius said. 'But our horses need rest, and my men need sleep.'

That night Dariusz doubled the guards on the horse herd. The raid came in the hour of death, when men sleep most heavily, three hours after midnight, and took no one by surprise. The fields were dark, and the woods were darker, and they only found a dozen dead men, but Dariusz slapped Verki on the back.

'It's good to win one,' he said, looking at the dead man-at-arms.

The rest of the army slept. Their horses rested.

At midnight, Gelfred came in from the west and demanded to be taken straight to the Duke, who was awake.

'He looked as happy as his sourpuss face can manage,' Nell muttered to Wilful.

Wilful shrugged. 'We'll be fighting again tomorrow, mark my words.'

Nell slapped him as one of his hands drifted over the treaty line, and he subsided and took a bite of garlic sausage.

Two hours later, Ser Giorgios brought back the raid. He was despondent, having lost almost a dozen men. 'They were waiting for us,' he told Kronmir, who took his horse.

Kronmir nodded. 'They aren't fools,' he said.

'You would know,' Ser Giorgios said. It wasn't accusing, merely factual. Moreans took a different view of these things.

'I would know,' Kronmir said, and went to report to the Duke.

Two hours before sunrise, the Imperial Army had its light horse in motion.

An hour before sunrise, their baggage, all their women and children and most of the non-combatant men, marched away – west. It was the first day they hadn't marched north in several days. Mag knew why, and when she kissed her man goodbye she gave him a hard squeeze.

'What do you know?' John le Bailli asked.

'Same as you,' Mag said. She winked. 'Don't be brave.'

He kissed her again. 'Only the brave deserve the fair.'

'Just my point.' She kissed him again, fought the urge to cry or say something foolish, and pushed him away lightly, her fingers on his cold breastplate.

She climbed back up on her wagon box and looked over her convoy. She pumped her fist once, and the wagons began to roll. West.

The Empress Livia referred to the plains and wheat fields of Viotia as the dance floor of Mars. Both of the major battles of the Irk campaigns were fought there – and two of the three battles of the Second Civic War. There was space on the plains for armies much bigger than the Imperial Army commanded by the Red Knight, but the hand of history was palpable here.

The ground was flat for miles. Lonika rose in the middle distance, almost ten miles away, a forest of turrets amidst the cliffs of crenellated walls.

At the strategic level, the plains of Viotia offered the best manoeuvring space on this side of the Green Hills. He could march his army in almost any direction.

But at a tactical level, they represented a nightmare of hedgerows, small tilled fields, farm ponds and stone walls – some of them ten feet high – stone barns and outbuildings, churches with fortified walls, a monastery as big as an Imperial castle, sheep pens, and streams running so full that they flowed over their carefully tended stone banks, all criss-crossed with excellent roads that had high hedges or stone walls of their own. Most of the fields were quite large, but a few were very small indeed.

His rearguard covered the crossroads where the wagons had

turned west. They waited, a detachment of the company's mounted archers dismounted behind the walls, backed with two squadrons of Vardariotes, until the sun was high in the sky and the wagons were long out of sight to the west. On roads this good, wagons could make five miles an hour.

Ser Jehan kept them in place for another hour. When the first Thrakian scouts came down the road from the south, they received a volley of arrows that emptied a handful of saddles. The Alban mercenaries mounted without haste and trotted away, and the Thrakians kept their distance.

It was noon before Captain Dariusz occupied the crossroads.

He looked west along the old Dorling road and watched it for a while. He could see the enemy army halfway between his horse and the distant loom of Lonika, waiting. He watched them for a bit, too. Then he snapped his fingers.

'Stepan,' he said. 'Inform Lord Demetrius he has his battle.'

Aeskepiles rode into the crossroads and examined the enemy array, and then made a sign, unfolded his hands and produced a shimmering lens of air. He played with it for some time and added a second, and by the time Lord Demetrius came up, he had the thing focused on the enemy.

Demetrius looked through it like a child with a new toy, but his attention was elsewhere. 'Why has he halted? Have they dug traps?'

Ser Christos spat derisively. 'No, my lord. The ground remains frozen. If it wasn't, we'd be fetlock deep in mud.'

Demetrius sat watching. 'Why fight me at all?' he asked. 'The capital is wide open. He can march in and take Lonika.' He shrugged. 'We have no siege equipment.'

Aeskepiles smiled. 'You have me,' he said. 'And your own mages, worthy young men that they are.'

Demetrius shrugged again. He rode west a few paces and turned, looking over the fields from a better vantage point. 'It's not a bad position,' he said. 'He's got his right flank covered against the farm and all those little outbuildings, and his left refused with a nice high wall. A tough nut to crack.' He turned and grinned. 'Let's get him.'

The Thrakians didn't waste time. Their cavalry marched into the field, and then split up into companies and began to form lines. Duke Andronicus' infantry marched straight up the road to a point where their pioneers had knocked holes in the old farm wall. They marched through a gap forty feet wide, with the farmer standing cursing them.

'You fucking— That's a year's work! A *year's* work!'

A spear point licked out and saved him from any further effort. He fell forward, over his own wound, and bled out on the ground he'd tilled throughout his life.

The heavy infantry were almost two thousand strong – all by themselves, they equalled the whole of the Imperial Army. They flew three great banners: the Virgin Mary, Christ Crucified, and Christ Harrowing Hell. They marched in silence, formed up to a few shouted commands, and halted, waiting for the cavalry to form on them.

The Easterners went wide west, galloping away down the road. They were ordered to sweep well out around the Imperial flank on their own left, to fall on the enemy's unshielded flank.

The Thrakian stradiotes formed to either flank of the infantry. The one band of mercenary knights formed to the right of the stradiotes, close to the road. The rest of the left was made up of a thousand Thrakian peasants, all armed with axes and bows.

The Thrakian line overlapped the Imperial line on both flanks. Their line was almost two Alban miles from end to end. The Imperial line had gaps and different depths, and was still only a little less than an Alban mile long.

When the lines were formed, a little less than a mile apart, the Thrakians sang a hymn. It was two in the afternoon, and they raised their weapons and gave a shout that rang off the distant hills.

And then they marched on their enemies.

The Red Knight watched them come and he shook his head. 'He's too damned bold. Didn't he ask himself why I was so eager to fight?' He sighed. 'If he'd waited until tomorrow morning—'

Father Arnaud raised an eyebrow. 'Are we retreating?' he asked.

The Red Knight turned. 'No. We're in it, now. Win or lose, this is our path. But it's going to be tight.' His head snapped around – his helmet was still in Toby's hands. 'No!' he shouted.

The Emperor, mounted on a beautiful white steed, was cantering along the front of his army.

Men cheered.

Then he turned his horse's head and trotted towards the enemy.

'What is he doing?' the Red Knight asked. He put spurs to his great black charger, and he started forward. The Red Knight was thinking of giving this one a name, instead of a number. He'd killed seven chargers so far. But the horse Count Zac had given him—

Father Arnaud cursed. 'He's trying to prevent the battle,' he said, and followed the Red Knight, equally helmetless.

The Red Knight threw himself forward on his horse's neck and the giant horse leaped into a gallop as if they were in a tiltyard. He rode like a jockey in a race, not like a man in full harness on a battlefield. His magnificent warhorse did its best to carry him at breakneck speed.

'Majesty!' he shouted.

The Emperor stopped his horse and waved.

The Red Knight reined in to save his horse's wind and trotted up. 'Majesty?'

'I want them to see me,' the Emperor said. 'If they see me alive they won't fight. *I am their Emperor.* My person is sacred.' He nodded decisively.

The Red Knight felt as if he were arguing with a gifted child. 'Yes, Majesty. But these men have already hurt you.'

The beautiful man turned his head and favoured the Red Knight with the full weight of his magnificent smile. 'No, my lord Duke. Those men are dead. You killed them, and quite justly, before my very eyes. That is the banner of Demetrius, son of Duke Andronicus, one of my most trusted lords. He is my wife's brother.'

'He took you prisoner,' the Red Knight said gently.

The Emperor thought a moment.

Behind them, the centre of the Imperial line started forward.

'He did, did he not?' the Emperor asked slowly. 'How could that have happened? The Logothete warned me – I don't remember. Therefore it cannot be important. Let us ride over and see those gentlemen—'

The Red Knight didn't know why his own company was advancing at the double, but all he could see was disaster. And the unravelling of his plan – his over-complex plan. He took the Emperor's bridle, and turned his horse. 'Those men will try to kill you, Majesty. Come with us – with your friends.'

They trotted along, parallel to the two armies, for a hundred paces, and then the Red Knight turned and led the Emperor towards his own lines. After another hundred paces, he dropped the Emperor's reins, and the man followed him willingly enough.

The Red Knight rode until he met Ser Jehan, leading the company, under his own black banner.

'Looked like trouble,' Jehan said. 'We can turn about.'

The Red Knight shook his head. 'We can't. The city stradiotes only need a feather's touch to cut and run.' He looked at the sun and swore. 'Damn it, Jehan! Now we'll start sooner. I needed *time*!'

Ser Jehan looked away.

The Red Knight looked around. Men were staring at him.

He thought back to his first encounter with them, in Arles, and he laughed. 'Look at yourselves,' he said. He left the Emperor to Toby and trotted to the head of the company. All the men-at-arms except Gelfred's were there, in the front rank, with their squires in the second rank, their archers in the third and spear-armed pages in the fourth. The old way. They were all dismounted, their horse holders well to the rear. Their armour was polished as well as could be expected after a three-week campaign in winter weather, and their scarlet surcoats were fading to a ruddy brown. But their weapons glittered like malevolent ice.

'Look at yourselves,' he shouted again. 'Think of who you were last year. And who you are now.' He turned back to where the enemy lay, having caught in a relieved glance the approach of the Nordikans and Vardariotes, who were reforming the line.

The Scholae came forward at a trot.

He pointed at the enemy, who was marching steadily at them over the frozen fields. 'An archaic scholar once said that the Thrakians would conquer the world, if only they would stop fighting among themselves.' He grinned. 'But he never met you, gentlemen. I will not lie and say this will be easy. I'll merely say that if you hang together for three hours you will be victorious, and the whole of the Morea will be ours.'

They cheered him like a new messiah.

Long Paw, in the third rank behind Ser Alison, said, 'Three hours, against all that? Christ, we're doomed.'

'He's coming right at us!' Aeskepiles said.

Demetrius watched the enemy advance and shook his head. 'He's moving his line forward. What does that mean? He has traps set *behind* him?' He watched. 'Is his line in confusion? Now his left is trailing away – those are the Scholae. And the Vardariotes. I see.'

Ser Christos appeared and raised his visor. 'My lord, many of the levies are anxious. That was the *Emperor*.'

'Merely a usurper,' Demetrius said.

Ser Christos narrowed his eyes. He looked at Count Stefano, who looked away. He turned his horse and faced golden Demetrius. 'Where is your father, my lord?' he asked.

'He is sick, but bravely holding the walls of Lonika with a handful of worthy men,' Demetrius said.

Ser Christos looked at Aeskepiles.

Aeskepiles ignored him. 'Here they come,' he said. He raised himself in his stirrups to cast, but the distance was greater than he had expected and the angle was poor. He put spurs to his horse and went forward.

'Do your duty,' Demetrius told his father's best knight.

Ser Christos nodded. 'Very well,' he said. He took the banner and followed Demetrius into the field beyond the low stone wall, and was the last man to leave the crossroads.

Aeskepiles opened the battle with a set of workings – an illusion of a fireball, a second illusion of a complex net spell weaving its way forward from his feet to the enemy lines, and a third spell, a sweeping organic scythe aimed at bowstrings.

His illusions struck with dramatic intensity, shocking new recruits and peasant levies all over the field. The fireball floated slowly, roaring like a blast furnace, to burst like a terrifying entertainment over the centre of the enemy army.

His string cutter left his hand and vanished into a protection.

The enemy archers raised their bows.

Annoyed, he cast again.

They loosed, and a volley of arrows rose.

He swatted them to earth with a simple wind harness he had prepared, to be safe.

The Thrakian infantry marched slowly forward. Their footsteps raised no dust from the frozen ground, but the ground shook with their matched step. Over to the left, the Thrakian peasants had no order, but they flowed over the ground like thirst-maddened wolves scenting water. The competing wind workings – from both sides of the field – created small vortexes, tiny hurricanes that buzzed as they moved and raised old leaves and mulch into the air.

Demetrius watched the infantry go forward, unscathed, and laughed.

'Oh, Pater. How I wish you'd been here to see this.'

Wilful Murder stood a few feet behind the Red Knight, who had now dismounted and taken his place: at the centre of the line, with the banner.

The line didn't shuffle. The lance points projecting from the pages in the fourth rank wavered – it took real strength to hold a heavy spear this long. And the archers moved. The order had come down to cease fire, but every man had a dozen livery arrows stuck point down in the ground by his back foot.

The enemy spearmen – the same hard bastards who'd almost pounded them at Liviapolis – were coming in untouched by long-range archery while the warlocks and sorcerers fought it out in the air over his head. The Captain had a pair of glowing shields – one of the reasons Wilful liked to be the Captain's archer was that in battle he was covered by the Captain's sorcerous crap.

When the fireball detonated, it was right on top of them. Wilful cringed away – and in the moment after it imprinted itself on his retinas, he patted his forehead and his arms. Then he laughed at the smell.

'Someone pissed their pants!' he called.

Rough laughter. The Captain turned his helmeted head. 'That was just an illusion. There will be more.'

His eyes glowed red. The enemy spearmen were about a hundred Alban cloth yards away.

Bent roared, 'Nock!'

I need you to get closer to Aeskepiles.

Harmodius had been decorously silent since his last burst of humour. The Red Knight had begun to hope – or fear – that the entity was gone. His words were immediately followed by a spike of pain, as if a sword thrust had gone in between his eyes.

Nothing I can do about that just now, old man.

In the palace, things were calm, and Harmodius stood decorously, younger than ever, like a page waiting to serve. He had the Fell Sword in his hand. Aeskepiles has increased in power – again. He has access to

683

something, or someone. He's swatting my wind workings around like a child killing moths, and—

I knew it was mistake to send Mag away.

You said yourself – only Mag can guarantee the safety of our women. Now let me take over.

Don't keep hold of my body when I need to be fighting. Oh – Harmodius, the pain.

Never fear, boy. I'm leaving you soon. I promise. We need to get closer to Aeskepiles. Sweet saviour, where did he get all that power?

Harmodius took control of the Red Knight's body. Without the other presence as an intermediary, he could cast more quickly – more cleanly. And he'd had six months to prepare for this moment. He knew what he wanted, and he knew how to get there.

'Loose!' roared Bent.

The front-rank knights and men-at-arms knelt. The archers leaned forward and loosed. At this range, their shafts had a travel time of about four heartbeats and required very little loft.

Bent was shooting needle point bodkins, cut square, sixpence a head from Master Pye in Cheapside. Hardened steel. The heads were five fingers long and tapered away to a wicked point like an ice pick. He chose his target carefully – the banner man in the front rank. Scale armour, and a magnificent gold helmet. Plate arms and legs.

The arrow weighed three Alban ounces and flew almost two hundred feet in a second. The head struck one finger to the outside of its target's shield and passed *through* a bronze scale and between two iron scales beneath – through the elk hide base, through a layer of linen, through a finger of tightly packed sheep's wool, through a second layer of linen canvas. Through a thin linen shirt.

Through skin into fat, and through fat to muscle. To bone. Slid along the bone almost half a finger and then into fat – and more muscle.

The man fell. The heavy banner fell forward, and twenty hands reached to pluck it up. But the arrow had not arrived alone—

Bent's second arrow was on his bow before the first pierced the banner man's heart. And his third...

Fourth...

'The space between the centres of the two armies was a blizzard of archery, and all the shafts went in one direction. On the Red Knight's left, Demetrius held back his mercenary cavalry for the death stroke – so that the ground in front of the Nordikans was empty.

They began to advance. At a shouted order, three hundred guardsmen raised their axes, screamed a shrill and very ancient cry, and started forward at the distant enemy cavalry. 'The Nordikans were packed so tightly that the man on the right of the line was scraping his magnificent gilded shield against the man-high stone wall of the main Liviapolis-Lonika road at his left shoulder. The Nordikans were only two deep and their line moved with a kind of supernatural precision. Each one of them had a heavy throwing spear – a lonche – with a head that weighed almost a pound, often inlaid in silver or gold or both, the shaft covered in gilded runes, the point of the best steel, blued, running out to a needle. Most of them also had a pair of darts behind their shields – lead weighted, on two-foot shafts. A practised man could hurl them eighty paces.

Fifth—

Sixth—

The Nordikans passed the end of the company line and continued forward, with Darkhair calling time in his own language. His voice had an eerie singing quality to it that rose over the vicious humming of the arrow shafts and the screaming that came from the spearmen.

The enemy spearmen came on through the hail of bodkins and broad heads, despite heavy losses.

The Red Knight was singing in High Archaic, and he had three different moving shields – one lavender, one a very heraldic red, one a blinding gold.

Directly across the field from him was an unarmoured man on a tall grey horse who also wore a succession of shields – green, purple, lavender, red, black. The black shield rose in response to a bolt of levin that came across the field like a cavalry charge. The black absorbed the lightning and it returned precisely down its line of attack.

And met a buckler of the same black stuff – a small shield not much bigger than the palm of a man's hand, precisely focused.

The bolt spat back – to strike the front rank of the spearmen, where a man exploded, his guts emerging as superheated steam and boiled meat. A second man was killed by a piece of his skull.

Seventh shaft.

Eighth.

To the Red Knight's right, the Vardariotes swept forward at the Thrakian peasant infantry until they were less than fifty paces away from the charging mass, and began to loose their own, lighter, cane shafts. Three hundred Vardariotes spread out across the flat plain and emptied their first quivers into men who could not make a reply. And as they charged faster in brave desperation, sprinting at the hornets stinging them with arrows, the Vardariotes slipped away – turning and riding a few paces and loosing another shaft at a range too close for a veteran to miss.

And again.

The peasants were flayed. Twenty of them died with every volley, and the shafts were rolling off the Vardariotes' fingers like coins from a mountebank's trick.

Nine.

Ten.

The spearmen were going to close. They were too brave, too confident to break, or to lie down and die out there on the frozen ground. They'd been shocked at Liviapolis, at the intensity of the archery and the power of the great yew bows, but they'd had six months to chew on their rage and boast of their glory. They took their losses and stepped over them – and over men they'd known for twenty years.

Bent raised his war bow with his eleventh arrow. Experience told him he wasn't getting in his twelfth. He leaned out over Ser Jehan's shoulder in a rhythm that the two of them knew as well as old lovers know the rhythm of their lovemaking – his bow arm well past the knight's right shoulder, his hip against the knight's hip – and shot a veteran of twenty battles just below the bridge of his nose, where the nasal of his helmet stopped.

Bent tossed his bow up and back, over his right shoulder. It would land on the frozen, untilled earth about fifteen feet behind him and he'd find it again if he lived. He passed back a rank, leaving the squire in front of him and the spear of the page passing over his shoulder.

He drew a hand and a half sword from his belt – forty days' pay – and took the buckler off the hilt. And braced his left shoulder against the squire's.

Ser Jehan raised the head of his pole-axe by a distance of about a foot.

Morgan Mortirmir stood in the front rank, terrified. His armour weighed like lead on his limbs, and the spearmen looked like evil gods of war, carrying his doom.

The Red Knight had ordered him to maintain a shield over the whole of the front, and he did so. Well warned, he let the illusions crash among them, although he himself didn't always see the workings as genuine until they were too late.

Stop this one.

Mortirmir threw effort into the pale gold of his shield. Fire roared all along the front of his corner of the battle, and licked both over and under his working. Frozen grass caught fire. He let it burn. The spearmen were closer, the noise was alien and suffocating, and he was desperate to escape the confines of his helmet. He couldn't see anything beyond the hard eyes of the killers opposite him – almost close enough to touch.

His squire – a hard-eyed bastard provided him by Ser Michael – put his shoulder against Mortirmir's back. 'Get ready, ser!'

Mortirmir had decided to fight with sword and buckler. He set his feet.

'Close yer fucking visor, ser,' his squire said. A gauntleted hand slammed his visor down so hard he almost fell.

He looked through the slits and saw—

The spearhead came for him, trying to reap his life, and caught on his chain aventail. He did nothing to parry it – it cut through the aventail, popping rings at their rivets. But the aventail was too big for the fifteen-year-old 'man-at-arms' anyway and the spearhead punched past him, over his shoulder, creasing his round shoulder pauldron and wrenching his shoulder in a way he'd remember in a hundred nightmares.

Mortirmir's training took hold. His buckler flicked out and the steel boss slipped along the spearshaft. He nudged the point of the blade into line.

Phontia! he said.

The spearman burst into flame inside his scale shirt, so that for a moment his face appeared to be that of a daemon from hell.

The old man had told him to remain on the defence. That was, he could see, a recipe for disaster. He pushed into the dead man's place, the smell of burning meat strong in his nostrils even through his visor, and pointed the sword again. He put a quarter of his *potentia* into a single simple working.

Well, not so very simple.

A ball of fire has to emerge from somewhere. Fire, as an element, was parasitic – fire never exists without a source. The source is the hard part – creating the source of a ball of fire requires time and patience and practice. It is much easier if the caster works the source close to himself and much harder if he attempts to do it at a distance – hence, most battlefield casters worked up a heavy shield and then made the ball of fire, fuelled by wood or various gases, appear at arm's length, and then, when they had a satisfactory pyrotechnic, they would move it as they might throw a heavy object. Except worked in the *aethereal*, of course.

This is where education was often a limiting factor on power. A young practioner who has been shown how to create coal oil is far more dangerous than one who has only learned to create beeswax.

A young practioner who has linked to Harmodius has access to a world of substances beyond the ken of most magisters. Rarefied alchemical creations. After all, an hermeticist who knew alchemy need only make a substance in real *once*.

Mortirmir's fireball burned so hot as it ignited six feet in front of him that he flinched away, almost lost his hermetic shield, and lost control of the fire. It drifted away. Then it vanished with a pop as he lost the fine control of his source.

Forty close-packed spearmen were incinerated. The left front corner of the enemy phalanx collapsed.

Ser Michael, who commanded the rightmost battle in the company, pointed his pole-axe – one-handed – at the charred ruin. 'At them!' he roared.

Aeskepiles had ridden his horse closer and closer to the point of impact – so that as the spearmen slowed, aimed and thrust with their spear points and the sound of their impact on the armour of his enemies exploded, he arrived at a point just fifty paces from the combat. He was secure behind the centre.

The closer two magisters were, the less able either was to deflect the castings of the other. At fifty paces—

An enormous ball of white-hot fire appeared to his left. He hadn't felt it cast and hadn't *seen* the caster.

As fast as the flash of terror that rippled through his system – making his horse shy as his spurred heels bit into her sides – he spat five words in the *aether*.

The Red Knight felt the old man leave him as the breaking of a fever and the loss of an unwelcome memory. He wanted to say something. If only to know the man was gone for good.

But the enemy spearmen were two spear lengths away. Cully and Wilful Murder tossed their bows aside and slid back through the ranks – Toby, who fought with a heavy spear, slid it over his head. He raised his ghiavarina. He'd never used it in combat.

He was alone, and the headache was gone.

He took a deep breath. Rotated his hips back. He had the spear, head up, in the spear guard called *dente di cinghiaro*. As his opponent's spear came at him – a long, committed thrust – he cut down into it. His blow should have batted the heavy spear *down* and safely away. Instead, his magnificent, dragon-gifted weapon cut *through* his opponent's spearhead. The truncated, blunt iron end slammed into his helmet, knocking him backward. The force of his cut, which should have been dissipated on his adversary's shaft, sent the head of the ghiavarina deep in the ground at his feet.

He ripped it free, stepped forward, and slammed it into his opponent's head before he was even over the shock of its effect. But it didn't *slam* into his opponent's helmet. It sheared through it, severing the helmet's top four fingers and one finger of the man's skull so cleanly that for a half a heartbeat, brains, skull, arming hood, mail and helmet were a series of concentric circles like some wild nomadic art.

Another spear struck his left pauldron and bounced up and over his shoulder, and a third slammed into his breastplate, but Toby's shoulder in his back kept him on his feet and he struggled to recover from his surprise.

Toby saved his life as an enemy second ranker got a hand on the haft of his weapon – the haft didn't seem to have any special properties – and reached for him with a wicked dagger. It flashed past the bottom of his vision, limited behind his visor, and he felt the blow only as pressure.

Toby rammed his short spear into the man's head. His skull went backwards, Toby passed his knight, stepped long, rotated the spear end for end and pushed the iron at the base of the shaft into the man's aventail and crushed his throat.

The two sides were stable – pushing at each other. Here and there, men fought, but this was what older veterans called *the press*. A deadly shoving match, where the cost of failure was rout and death. The spearmen were deeper. The company had better armour.

There was a titanic flash of yellow-white light in the Red Knight's right peripheral vision.

He tapped Toby with his right gauntlet – not trusting his weapon – and the squire pivoted on his hips, parried a last thrust from their new opponent, and passed back. The Red Knight got his body low and set his feet wide. And cut – small passes. All as precise as dagger flicks. He severed the spear shaft pressing at him, and severed a man's hand at the wrist with the kind of motion that a man might use when fishing.

Then, as his next adversary stumbled back, hand severed and cauterised, the Red Knight stepped forward and swung.

Spears were severed. Men fell forward as they lost the support of their weapons pinned against opponents in the press.

He cut again, as if his sword-like long spearhead was a huge axe, carried by a giant Nordikan.

Everything the spearhead touched was cut – armour, leather, wood, and flesh.

A hole, the width of his swing, opened in the enemy phalanx.

He stepped forward again, and swung at five cringing men. Two died.

The weapon lodged deep in the body of the third. He pulled – and a spear shaft struck him in the back. Desperate, he wrenched at the thing and it slid out like any weapon, shimmering blue red in the spring sunlight.

Whatever properties it had had were used up. And he was six steps deep in the enemy phalanx.

Blows began to fall on him like hail, and he was driven to his knees by a crashing, two-handed blow by a desperate man wielding a spear shaft like a two-handed flail.

The press closed around him.

Another man stripped his weapon from his hands – they were all around him, too close – but he got his right hand on his new dagger hilt and flicked it out.

And then it was just the fighting.

In full plate, he was lighter and more mobile then his adversaries in calf-length chain and scale. They had heavy shields and long spears – some were discarding them and others were not – and as they pressed him down, he burst into the frenzied routines his father's master-at-arms had taught him since boyhood. He caught the right arm of the man who had stripped his spear, rolled him, broke his arm and stabbed him in his unarmoured neck below his ear. Grabbed the next man, slamming his steel fist into the unprotected face, caught his shoulders and used the point of his beaked visor to smash the man's teeth even while his steel sabatons mangled the man's feet and shins. Blows fell on his back – on his right shoulder, exposed in the melee – two blows so hard they moved his whole body and struck his helmet. He was dazed.

His hands and feet kept killing. He kicked a spearman between the legs, the steel point of his sabaton crushing the man's testicles even as he held the man's spear – his right arm shot out, and the hardened steel flange of his own elbow joint ripped the nose from the face of another spearman who was trying to climb his back.

His left leg was caught in something. It threatened his balance, and he was fighting so many men he had no time to spare to free it.

He knew, with awful clarity, that he was going down. The loss of balance was incremental. He got his dagger, point down, into a man's scale-protected back – and the triangular point punched through like an awl through hardened leather.

He tried to use the dagger as a sort of climbing iron to hold himself erect.

Then something gave in his left knee.

Damn it. I tried, he thought, and down he went.

The mercenary cavalry watched the madmen come at them. It was a well-known fact that infantry cannot charge cavalry – that it was suicide to do so.

They came on anyway.

The lead knight – a Southerner from distant Occitan – pointed his lance. 'Sweet friends,' he said, in the language of romance. 'These are brave men and worthy foes. If they want a contest—' He smiled. 'Let us give them their wish.'

He reached up and closed his visor – tossed his head to make sure his great helm was firmly seated in his steel cap. Lowered his lance into his rest. 'For Saint James!' he roared.

The mercenaries were not all from Occitan, and a polyphony of war cries emerged. The knights lowered their lances and rumbled towards the axe-wielding madmen.

The moment of impact was like an explosion of flesh. Axes severed the front legs of warhorses even as lances punched through layered byranies. A generation of Nordikans died in the front rank – a fifth of their number reaped by death in a single instant.

The survivors didn't flinch. The great axe heads swept up again. The horses fought – hooves flashed – and in the centre four friends stood together, the axes had hewn two horses to the ground and the other horses couldn't get past them. That firm point in the centre of the Nordikan line became like the prow of a ship in a storm.

As the knights slowed, their horses became more vulnerable. Lances were dropped, swords swept out.

No shield on earth can stop an axe wielded by a man as tall as your horse. And even when your hardened plate stops the *cut* of the weapon, the force of the blow can still rip you from your saddle.

But while the murderous giant shifts his weight and sweeps the axe up for another crushing blow, he is very vulnerable.

Great men died. Knights and warriors, veterans of a dozen wounds, died in heartbeats, without even knowing their killers.

The horses pressed on. And the Nordikans stumbled back.

The Thrakian peasants broke.

They'd lasted longer than anyone had a right to expect, their bravest men running at a full sprint after the laughing Vardariotes, and dying with carefully aimed arrows in their bodies. The best were killed, and the hesitant and the slow were left. In the end, like scavengers beaten off a corpse, they turned and ran.

The Vardariotes – old hands at this kind of fight – had allowed themselves to retreat all the way back to the stone outbuildings of the isolated farm. They rallied, and changed quivers, and let the remaining Thrakian peasants live.

Count Zac counted the horses. He had lost one man.

'Where's Khengiz?' he called.

'Girth snapped!' an avildahr called out. Men laughed.

Opposite them, they could see the enemy's main cavalry force forming. They had to open the centre of their line to let the peasants through, and that wasn't going well. It was a missed opportunity, but following the peasants too closely could have been a disaster.

Zac shrugged. 'Ready, my loves?'

Their shouts rang in the air.

He glanced left. The Nordikans were in it – they'd die where they stood. The centre of the line seemed to be winning. He frowned.

Ser Giorgios rode over from the head of the magnificent Scholae. 'That was like a textbook exercise.' He shrugged. 'The skirmishing. The—'

Count Zac beamed with pleasure. 'High praise indeed from the Count of the Scholae.'

The enemy was still having trouble with the terrified peasants clumped up in front of their cavalry. *Alas*, thought Count Zac.

'But now,' Giorgios said.

'Bah!' Count Zac laughed. 'Two thousand country cavalry? We have five hundred between us. We can handle them.' He grinned. 'Until their Easterners sweep around these buildings in an hour, and then we all die.' He shrugged. 'I am true to my salt. You?'

Ser Giorgios smiled. 'How shall we begin?' he asked.

'Ah, you grant me the command?' Count Zac was a small man, but he sat up straighter at these words.

'I do.'

'Then we will start with a dramatic failure, I think. Yes?' He laughed.

Ser Giorgios tried to match his laugh.

'Here they come!' shouted Dmitry, Ser Christos's *hypaspist*.

Ser Christos watched the Vardariotes and the Scholae – men he'd commanded on other fields – come at him. The crispness of their lines and the neat precision with which they drew their bows from their bow cases contrasted sharply with his own rural *tagmas*, still struggling with their own peasants. In many cases, their friends and neighbours. A landowner would bend down from the saddle to hear a weeping man tell how his brother had died screaming, gut shot by the red-clad barbarians.

It was all very Morean, and he loved them for loving their men. But he could also see how all this was about to go wrong.

'Look alive, there!' he roared. 'Clear my front! This will be a false charge – see their bows? They will come in, loose arrows, and then run. We will not respond – Hear me, Hetaeroi? Stand your ground!'

The enemy line came forward at a fast trot. Two hundred paces away, as the Latin mercenaries slammed into the distant Nordikans with a sound like their own Ragnarok, the two regiments of the guard broke into a canter.

'Shields up!' Christos roared.

The peasants huddled in front of the cavalry raised what shields they had.

The flight of arrows came in. Some of the Vardariotes loosed arrows with whistles and they screamed.

Those of his own stradiotes who were practised bowmen loosed back.

Men and horses fell on both sides.

The Guard turned together and cantered away, leaving a handful of dead horses and men in their wake. Over the backs of their saddles, they loosed again. Again, the whistles shrieked. It took real courage to stand straight as the whistles came closer – the longest heartbeat of your life. And maybe the last.

There were screams. And grunts.

Ser Christos looked at the sun, which hadn't moved by a quarter of an hour.

Ser Christos thought, *What am I doing here? Why am I fighting these men? This has all gone terribly awry. We were supposed to save the Morea.*

Men were looking to him. His battle plan was simple – to wait for the Easterners to come in on the enemy flank, and only then to charge. With sheer weight of numbers his two thousand horse might break the Guard, but the casualties would break a generation and farms – hundreds of farms – would go back to the Wild. The Guard would not die easily.

Whereas, if they were outflanked, they would retire like the professionals they were. And live to fight for a new Emperor. And his men could vent their rage on the foreigners in the centre.

'Stand fast!' he called again.

Demetrius was winning, he could feel it, and he hadn't even bloodied his sword. He suspected that his pater would have been in the centre with the infantry. Or leading one of the flanks in person.

Dariusz – in many ways, his best man, but an irritating, over-focused man who did not take enough care about how he phrased his criticisms – rose in his stirrups. 'The Thrakians are beaten. Why does Ser Christos not charge through them?' He shook his head.

Demetrius rose in his stirrups and watched for a long time – as long as a priest might take to consecrate the host. 'Go and tell the old man to charge. Now.' He looked at his own right and saw the knights – his best purchase – closing their visors and preparing to charge the Nordikans, whom he feared like other men feared disease and death. The foreigners were too ignorant to know what they were facing, and they were recklessly brave – let them take some time dying, and he'd have the whole battle.

The centres were locked. As he expected. Men died. And other men stepped on their corpses – whether they were alive or dead – and pressed on.

Fifty paces to his front, Aeskepiles sat alone on his pale horse and no light seemed to fall on him, nor did he leave a shadow. He was facing just slightly to the left. He had four shields – one round, one square, two shaped like knight's shields – all a deep black. They moved as he moved.

Whatever he was doing was far, far more spectacular than anything in the previous battle. Lightning of every colour and no colour sparkled among his shields and struck well off to the left of the enemy centre – at the very end of the foreigners, the so-called *company*.

Detonation after detonation rolled against the distant mountains and came back as thunder, and men died every time. Blown to pieces by forces they could not comprehend.

Aeskepiles' shoulders slumped and then rose, as if the man was wielding a great smith's hammer, and he struck again, this time with both hands.

And men died.

Aeskepiles was lost in the great fugue of his borrowed sorcery – aware, at one panicked level, that he was spending his reserves too profligately. Shocked that the young practitioner to his left had such power. Wary that the old one to his right had fallen silent.

But it didn't matter, because his working – his new, unsubtle working – was building to its climax. It built without him, sorcery multiplying upon itself the way living creatures bred and multiplied.

Like a watched pot—

But he didn't need to watch.

The student – he had the boy fixed as a senior Academy student, based on the manner of his casting – produced a very respectable blade of light. Aeskepiles lost two shields, and was aware, in the corner of his mind that was aware of the battle, that the centre was not quite as it should be.

If I do this just right, they will all die – on both sides.

But first, the two who could threaten him. The young one, and then the old one.

Aeskepiles was close – so close that Mortirmir had no chance to parry the attack. The blow from the green-black axe, when it came, collapsed all four of Mortirmir's carefully wrought shields.

John le Bailli died, burned to ash in his armor. Bent died, his lungs on fire inside his body. Ser Jehan died. The company lost a generation of leaders and twenty men in the blink of any eye.

But the main force of the blow fell on Mortirmir.

And it was deflected.

He didn't have time or thought to be shocked.

Move aside, Harmodius said. In the *aethereal*, he took control of Mortirmir's body and his *potentia*. And everything else.

You were just bait, he said. *Now you are the skin of the lion.*

A wall of sparkling white fire stood between them and Aeskepiles. Men screamed – men half burned or caught at the edges of the massive working.

I'm the lion.

Faster than the thought of a mortal, Harmodius rode the casting back to its source – as Richard Plangere had taught him to. He'd declined to do it to a dog – but now—

Instead of casting, he followed the course that Thorn had taught him.

And then Morgan Mortirmir was alone.

The Red Knight had his arms pinned by corpses, and someone stepped on his breastplate. A rib cracked. And he was helpless. Another foot – this time on his armoured shin. The pain was immense, the damage negligible.

He couldn't move.

Panic – blind panic, the panic that comes from helplessness and impending death – was *right there*. And so was death.

He ran, as he had when he was a child, for his hermetical palace, and waited for the end. *Time was different here.*

It is difficult to be panicked when you have time to think.

There was the new statue on the plinth in the middle of his casting rotunda. It had been empty for many months, and he stared at it and realised that he was used to having another mind available to feed him workings.

And then he realised that he wasn't without resources himself.

It wasn't something he had practised. He had to improvise. And he didn't know whether the foot on his breastplate belonged to an enemy or his brother.

In the end, he settled for simplicity. He placed the end of an *aethereal* chain of iron in his left hand. And he pulled it with *ops* – slowly. The sigils whirled above his head – creation, displacement, enhancement, augury (because he needed to know which way to face). He cast the most complex working of his hermetical life – merely to stand.

He stood.

Thrakian spearmen who had seen twenty fights in the Wild and a dozen actions with men fell back a pace. Toby, straddling him, was brushed aside – Ser Milus took advantage of the shock he gave them and cracked a helmet with his great two-handed hammer.

The Red Knight drew his sword. His draw was fluid, his hips rotated – he had seldom felt more *alive*. The great red sword flashed from the scabbard and the heavy point went over the shield of the next spearman.

'Captain's up!' screamed Toby.

There was a sound like a watermill, a roar like a waterfall, and the whole company *pushed*.

The Red Knight disdains to kill his enemies by sorcery. And if I win this, I need as many of them alive as I can manage, he thought. He was under their spears – most of the Thrakians had short swords in their hands. He gripped his sword two-handed, and started hacking men to the ground.

On his left, Ser Milus saw something he didn't and began yelling for men to join on him.

The Thrakians were pushed back another step, and another.

He turned his head – safe for a moment – and saw Milus and Francis Atcourt and a dozen other men-at-arms running to the left.

The company was pivoting on the centre, the right advancing, the left sliding back. And he had no idea why. Trapped in the airless, sweat-stink of his faceplate, he could see nothing beyond the next foe.

He stopped. Pivoted again and let Toby push past. The press was lighter – there was room. A wider space opened in the centre and the Thrakians backpedalled a dozen paces and stopped. Those men who still had spear points raised them.

The centre of the company shuddered to a stop.

Toby stepped past him, and then Cully. And then he was past Nell, who was white-faced and had a red slash from the base of her chin to the top of her left breast – right through her maille.

He had no time for her. He stepped back again. And again.

A boy was holding his warhorse. By an act of pure will he got into the saddle. Flipped his visor back after fighting the buckle. Washed himself in air. Wrenched crisp, clean breaths of it after the foul stuff trapped against his visor—

And saw the Nordikans were dying.

They'd killed a great many knights and more horses, but they were now an island in a sea of cavalrymen. The enemy's stradiotes were mixed in with the mercenary knights – he could see Derkensun's gilded helm, and axes still flashed.

Ser Milus, at the head of a third of the company, smashed into the side of the melee.

To his right, where young Mortirmir should have been anchoring the company shield, there was a light show unlike anything hermetical that the Red Knight had ever seen. Despite which, Ser Michael was far up the field, advancing at a steady walk – so far that he was almost at weapon's length from Demetrius.

The enemy centre was moments from collapse – like his own left.

Aeskepiles – he could just see the man over the swirl of the melee – was writhing like a man fighting a pack of wolves. Except that he was alone, and his shields had all fallen.

And beyond him, further to the right, by the old road to Dorling, there was confusion in the ranks of the enemy's main body of cavalry – confusion that cheered his heart. Even as he glanced that way, the Vardariotes and the Scholae went forward.

One deep breath.

It was all perfectly balanced.

It was not a time for chivalry.

He pointed his sword at the enemy's mercenary knights, and he cast.

The Easterners hadn't appeared.

Count Zac reined in from his latest feigned flight and, while his crack light horsemen rallied on their squadron banners, he cantered around the stone barn and looked west. What he saw made him smile.

He rode back to where the Scholae and the Vardariotes joined. 'Change horses,' he ordered.

Ser Giorgios had an arrow in his right thigh, snapped off short. He waved. He was white, but in charge of himself – to a man like Zac, that was worth high praise. 'You are like one of my own children,' he said.

Ser Giorgios nodded. 'Hurts like poison,' he muttered. 'The centre seems to be holding,' he said. 'What do we do now?'

Zac nodded. 'Now we win,' he said. He pointed with his riding crop, to the west.

Ser Giorgios managed a pained smile. 'I don't see anything.'

'That's why we win!' Zac said.

The horse holders came forward and handed men their remounts. It took very little time for crack troops to change horses.

Opposite them, they only faced the right end of the enemy line. But that end was shifting, trying to remould itself across the road. They were good troops – they weren't in chaos. But they were attempting a difficult manoeuvre in the face of the enemy.

Count Zac watched them for as long as a child might take to count ten. 'Not bad,' he said. 'But wrong.'

He placed himself exactly between the two regiments.

'Walk!' he ordered.

As crisply as on parade, the two cavalry regiments moved forward, horses at a walk.

Zac had dreamed of this a hundred times – a stricken field, against long odds. A fresh horse and a sharp sword.

And an enemy trapped in place. It was the steppe nomad's dream.

'Draw!' he roared. His horse walked six prancing steps before he called, 'Swords!'

Five hundred sabres glittered like ice on a fair winter's day.

The Vardariotes and the Scholae pressed into the centre as they had practised, so that they were a single mass of horseflesh and sabres. Or war hammers or small steel axes, as personal preference might dictate.

The Thrakian cavalrymen opposite them shuddered. That shudder was even visible; their ranks moved.

The Guards rolled forward as gracefully as a dancer at a party. Their precision was inhuman, and they inspired awe.

Zac turned his head and saw movement on the road to the right – a glimpse of steel.

He laughed, stood in his stirrups and threw his long sabre in the air in a great whirling flash – up and up, and then down, and into his hand as if ordained by his own wind-blown steppe gods.

A screech rose in Zac's throat. Unintended.

The Vardariotes answered him, and the Guards put their spurs to their fresh horses, and charged.

And in answer, from the Dorling road, came a great shout that rolled over the field like the hunting call of a great Wyvern or a mighty dragon – 'Lachlan! Lachlan for aa!'

Harmodius stood among the cogs and wheels and foundry runs of Aeskepiles' memory palace. He had time to marvel at the complexity of the man's forming and the strain on it all. There were frayed ropes and chains at maximum tension and leaking buckets, and the water that turned the wheels that drove the workings was sluggish and thick, filthy with unredeemed pledges and treasons.

He flicked his sword, and a massive bellows vanished.

Harmodius allowed himself a grin. A thousand times, it had occurred to him that the hair he'd taken from the cutler in Liviapolis might belong to another man, and not Aeskepiles.

Aeskepiles' aethereal form appeared. He was a big man with a black beard and a scowl, and two heavy black cords ran out of his forehead and away into aethereal space.

Begone! he snapped.

Harmodius smiled.

I am the lion, he said. And severed the chains that powered . . . something.

There was a mighty crash.

Aeskepiles – obviously panicked, even here – raised a wand of iron.

It won't make any difference, Harmodius said. But that's a bad way to go, loosing destruction inside your own head.

He stepped forward.

Who are you? demanded the sorcerer. How can this happen?

I am the lion, Harmodius said, and used his Fell Sword to destroy the sorcerer's soul in a single cut.

Then he opened himself a little, and collapsed the dead man's memory palace, appalled at the waste of energy and potential as the whole of a behemoth spell-working drained away into the aether and the real. He worked fast, scraping it away as a nomad woman scrapes a hide clean of fat.

And then he unpacked his own, neatly. He'd had plenty of time to practise, and it spooled out of his soul into the clean space. Some things fitted oddly. Some things might never be quite the same.

Harmodius remembered his first rooms, when he was a student in Harndon. They didn't match his furniture. But they were his own.

The two black ropes that had been attached to the magister's aethereal forehead remained, dangling, and as his own memory palace materialised around him, they transformed into the black pupil of a golden eye. A golden eye the size of a door.

'Ahhh,' said a deep and pleasant voice. 'I see. I thought you were dead.'

The eye blinked. 'You will not triumph,' the voice said, as if this was the best of news. 'But I grant you, this was clever.'

The sword flicked, and the eye vanished.

And Harmodius stood and shook in the midst of his new home.

When it was too late to matter, and all was lost, Ser Christos stood amidst the rout of his wing and readied his lance.

The Green Hillmen were the Thrakians' ancient foes. They knew each other well. They stood shoulder to shoulder against the Wild, and they hacked one another to pieces over their borders.

The enemy was mostly afoot – big men in ring mail like the Nordikans, and just as ferocious. And they flowed like a tide. And Ser Christos cursed, because on another day, on an open field, he'd have rolled these arrogant clansmen up like a carpet.

But today his men could not fight in two directions at once, and they folded. And in truth, Ser Christos thought, fitting his lance in its rest, in truth, none of them believed it was worth dying for Demetrius, anyway.

One man amidst his adversaries was mounted: a giant man on a giant horse. Ser Christos knew the fate that awaited him, to be executed as a traitor, and determined to give his son a different view of his end.

He put his spurs to his horse.

The armoured giant saw him, and flicked his lance tip – an acknowledgement? And came at him. His horse's hooves skimmed the ground, the sun had melted the surface of the road, and the movement of thousands of men tore the turf down into mud. But he and his enemy were on the road.

He gave his war cry, and his lance came down.

So did his opponent's, and the man roared, 'Lachlan for aa!' and inside his helm, Ser Christos smiled.

They came together like a clap of thunder.

Ser Christos's lance head went through the giant's shield, piercing two layers of oxhide and the carefully laid-up panels of elm underneath – into the mail that guarded the big man's armpit, which it pierced. His lance *bowed* and snapped in three places.

Lachlan's lance struck him full on the shield, and broke it to pieces, and shattered, but the shortened stump of his lance struck the Morean knight's shoulder and slammed him back in his saddle, and the force of the their meeting knocked both horses back on their haunches. Ser Christos's horse was first to recover, and it scrambled away. The bigger horse bit at it savagely while both knights struggled to draw their swords and stay mounted.

The horses circled. Lachlan was bleeding from his right armpit. The Morean suspected that something was broken in his collarbone. He got his sword free and slammed it into the big man's helmet with no obvious effect; a good blow, but nowhere near enough.

Lachlan reeled, and then got his sword free in time to stop a cut to his neck.

For ten heartbeats, both men exchanged blows as fast as their arms could drive their weapons. Sparks flew, and both men were hurt.

Lachlan's stallion planted an iron-shod forefoot on Ser Christos's mount's right front leg, and it snapped. And his horse began to go down. He ignored the pain, reached out left-handed and locked his gauntlet over Lachlan's sword wrist. Then his horse toppled, taking both men with him.

By this time, Ser Christos was the last of Demetrius's men still fighting for a hundred paces in all directions. Men paused – those bent on taking ransoms, or leaning on blood bespattered axes and swords – to watch.

Men who had just surrendered paused and looked.

The two combatants rose together, and Ser Christos planted his pommel hard against Lachlan's helmet, so that the bigger man's head snapped back. Bad Tom retreated a step and his blade snapped forward, staggering the smaller man.

They circled. Lachlan was bleeding from armpit and a hand, and had blood running from beneath his aventail. Christos had only one hand on his sword hilt, now, and blood was running down his left cuisse. He changed guard, rotating on his hips and putting his sword on the left side of his body, point back.

The Hillmen were chanting. Ser Christos had no idea what they were chanting, but he was determined to beat this one man, regardless of the cost. Or he would die trying.

When Lachlan cut at him, a monstrous, overhand cut that seemed to ignore the wounds he'd taken, Ser Christos cut up, into the blow, one-handed.

Lachlan's strike was stopped.

The two teetered, sword to sword, for half a heartbeat.

Quick as a viper, Lachlan reversed his sword and drove his pommel at Ser Christos's face. The Morean knight raised his hands to defend himself.

Lachlan passed his pommel over his opponent's sword arm, locking it down. Then he passed his blade over the Morean knight's head, using the anchored pommel as a pivot, so that he had Ser Chritos's arms pinned against him in the prison of his body and his sword, crushing the man's throat.

It happened so fast that Christos could only struggle, trying to wedge his blade against the giant's crushing grip. He released his sword, the world dimming, and grabbed for his dagger.

The giant swept his feet from under him, so he was suspended in the air.

'Yield,' roared Tom Lachlan. 'Gods, that was glorious!'

Ser Christos coughed. And subsided to the ground.

Bad Tom flipped open his visor and breathed like a bellows. His kerns were gathering over the downed knight. 'Don't kill this loon!' he snapped. 'I want him.'

Demetrius didn't wait for his army to collapse. As soon as he saw the coward Aeskepiles turn his horse and bolt from the field – headed west, of all foolish ideas – Demetrius saw how the wind was blowing.

To the east, by the Lonika road, the mercenary knights had been decimated by a hermetical attack and were now breaking away from the remnants of the Nordikans. The centre was shattered – there was a palpable *hole* in the middle of his father's veteran spear block and the Alban mercenaries were pouring through it. His father's most trusted veterans were throwing down their weapons and kneeling in surrender.

And to the west instead of his Easterners, enemies had appeared.

'Let's get out of here,' he said.

Dariusz shrugged, as if the whole subject wearied him.

Surrounded by his Guard, he rode south.

'Gabriel!'

The Red Knight reined up and waited for the spike of pain in his forehead, but it didn't come.

'Harmodius?'

'I go my own way now. This field is yours – you'll want to stop the killing as soon as you can.'

'Tom will be outraged.'

'I may not see you again. As Master Smythe suspected, Aeskepiles was a tool just as Thorn is. Ash is using them. One of the First. I have done something morally dark. I wish to ask a favour. I think, despite using your body for months, that you owe me.'

Gabriel knew – almost intuitively – what must have happened. Because there was no more lightshow.

'You have taken Morgan Mortirmir's body,' he said.

'No. That option presented itself, and represents a temptation which, thankfully, I resisted. I took Aeskepiles' body. In fact, I AM Aeskepiles. He is not.'

'And your favour?' Gabriel asked.

'Don't pursue me. Our goals are the same.'

Gabriel looked carefully at his mentor. *'You have made a dark choice.'*

'In a good cause.'

Gabriel nodded. 'I will not pursue you.'

Harmodius extended an aethereal *hand. 'You will be very powerful now. Mortirmir – when he regains his wits – will eventually be even more so. With Mag and Amicia and some other allies you may still not last any longer than a candle in a rainstorm against our true foe. But you must try.' The old man's* aethereal *form shrugged. 'You have a sort of ferocious luck that gives me hope.'*

Gabriel nodded. 'Thanks for the good rede, old man.' He reached out, and the two embraced in the aether *– a gesture of trust in that environment beyond the imagining of many practitioners.*

'Where are you going?' Gabriel asked.

Harmodius paused. 'Best you don't know, lad. Desperate times, desperate measures.' He smiled. 'I've left you a set of my guesses as to what is going on.' He handed over a scroll – an aethereal *scroll, a concept that made Gabriel's head ache.*

'Go with God,' Harmodius said.

And then Gabriel was truly alone.

There is a point in a savage action where no prisoners can be taken; where men are too afraid, or too committed to destruction, to give mercy.

But there is another point, where both sides near exhaustion. Then, in sheer fatigue, it is possible to see past the fear and the blood rage.

When one of the captains of Andronicus's veterans held out his sword by the blade Ser Michael saw it. He took the hilt and raised it – both arms high, armpits open to an attack. 'They yield!' he roared.

It took time. For the last man hacked down between Kelvin Ewald and Wilful Murder, it took too much time. Some men in closed helmets couldn't hear. Other men couldn't see.

As the surrender spread, some of the Nordikans had to be physically restrained. Ser Milus had a dent put in his helmet by Harald Derkensun, who was determined to wipe knights – all knights – from the face of the earth. Blackhair lay dead between his feet, pierced through with a mercenary's lance.

The Red Knight sat on his charger, surveying the end. He had only just discovered that Ser Jehan was dead. And John le Bailli.

Ser Gavin caught his stirrup. 'There goes the bastard,' he said, pointing at a golden helm and a white horse, vanishing to the south.

The Red Knight let a moment's rage guide him. 'Let's get him,' he said.

'I'm your man,' Gavin said. He hobbled back into the press of horses and pages behind the fighting line.

To the left and right, the beaten Moreans had slumped down. Most simply sat in the mud and blood. The company weren't doing much better. Half of them were on one knee, or bent double.

Ser Alcaeus dragged himself from the right of the line. 'You *must* finish Demetrius,' he said. 'This isn't done until that imp is dead.' He looked around. 'Thrakians are stubborn, brave men. And we need them.'

The Red Knight looked down at the Morean knight. 'I know,' he said. *Better than you.*

Alcaeus grabbed his horse, and Dmitry, his squire, mounted his. Their horses were fresh; it was the men who were exhausted from forty minutes of fighting.

The Red Knight bent low in the saddle to Ser Michael, who was insisting he would come.

'Shut up,' the Duke said. 'I need you to stay right here and prevent a massacre. We need every one of these stiff-necked bastards. Right? Don't let Wilful and Long Paw decide to "make anything right" for Bent. Got me?'

Michael nodded.

'And get a messenger to Gelfred and the scouts and tell them to get their arses back here.' The Red Knight looked at his brother. Father Arnaud was there, getting a leg over his own jet-black charger.

'Father, fetch Mag. And Father—'

'I know,' Arnaud said heavily.

'She has to be told.' For once, the Red Knight looked young; very young, and not very happy. 'Why does your God allow all this shit, Father?'

The priest's eyes travelled over the line of dead that marked the high-water mark of the Thrakian charge. 'Because we have free will,' he said. 'The shit is ours, not His. I'll tell Mag.'

The Red Knight raised an eyebrow. His mouth opened but his brother leaned over and smacked him in the side with the pommel of his dagger. His mouth closed, and then he reached out to the priest, steel gauntlet to steel gauntlet. 'Thanks. I'll come back as soon as I can.'

There were a dozen of them when they rode. Ser Alcaeus and his squire Dmitry, Ser Gavin, Toby, Long Paw, Nell, Ser Milus, Ser Bescanon, Kelvin Ewald and three pages who had their horses handy and were fresh. Plus one of the Lanthorn boys, and two Morean recruits.

It was a very small army.

Every one of them took two horses, and they took the time to fetch water and food, and most of them were eating cheese or sausage when they trotted out of the battle line, headed south.

They alternated between a fast trot and a canter while the sun set. No one said anything.

Ten miles south of the battlefield, they dismounted while Long Paw looked at a dead horse in the road. It wasn't dark; March in Morea was almost like late spring in Alba, and the red sun threw long shadows. To the west, they could see the broken remnants of the Thrakian left wing being pursued by the Vardariotes, who clearly had not received an order to stop killing.

The Red Knight watched wearily, and sent Ser Bescanon with the two Morean pages as interpreters.

'I would rather go with you, my lord,' Bescanon said.

'Well. I'd rather go drink with the Vardariotes and stop the killing, so we're even,' said the Duke.

Long Paw scratched under his chin. 'They're an hour ahead of us, and riding harder. Galloping, I'd say.'

Ser Gavin nodded. 'If he makes Eves, he'll be a tough nut to crack, and we don't have the men.'

The Red Knight nodded. 'Nothing for it,' he said. And pressed his horse to a heavy gallop.

They changed horses with nothing left of daylight but a red streak in the western sky, so that the spikes and peaks of the highest Adnacrags showed black against it. They galloped on. They could see the acropolis of Eves rising ahead of them, and they could see the black spots of a dozen horsemen riding along the road.

They dashed on, thundering down the road, until the very last light was leaching out of the sky and it was clear that Demetrius's party would make Eves.

And then the Duke reined in.

He rose in his stirrups, and his left hand flashed out. '*Ignem veni mittere in terram*,' he shouted, and a line of fire rose a mile away.

'Jesu!' Gavin said.

'Not exactly,' his brother responded. And pressed his spurs to his horse's side.

They galloped over the darkening fields, and the men they were chasing, trapped on the road by the high walls and the tower of flame, finally turned at bay. There were twenty of them, all professional soldiers. They were in a mix of armour, although they all wore the golden leopard badge of Demetrius. They had ridden away from the flame, which burned like hell come to earth.

Demetrius, in his golden helmet, mounted on his white charger, looked like an angel. But the fire burned too red, and it made him a fallen angel – a rebel. He was in front, and he halted his horse fifty yards from the Red Knight's horse, which was breathing like it was about to founder.

'Warhorse,' the Red Knight said, softly.

Nell brought his horse forward.

He dismounted. 'Single combat,' he shouted. 'You and I can fight for this, Demetrius.'

'I think I'll just surrender and see what my cousin Irene decides,' Demetrius said. 'Or perhaps my guards will take you and your friends. Wouldn't that be a nice reversal of fortune?'

The Red Knight got a foot into the stirrup of his great black charger and pushed with all his might to get himself into the saddle. He failed, and almost fell. But his horse stayed still.

He sighed. 'Look at the pillar of fire that burns at your back, Demetrius. And ask yourself if you can take me – me and my friends?'

'I accept your point,' Demetrius said, his cultured voice light, like a comic actor's. 'I'll render myself your prisoner.'

The Red Knight tried to mount again. His left thigh apparently wasn't doing the job. His armour weighed down like the world on the shoulders of Atlas.

Demetrius laughed. 'Maybe I should fight. I hear you are very good, but you look tired.'

Suddenly, he slammed his visor down, put his lance into its rest and his horse leaped into a gallop. From fifty yards away. A warhorse takes ten seconds to run fifty yards.

The Red Knight leaped, and Nell shoved her shoulder under his left cuisse and pushed. He almost fell, but he righted himself.

Eight.

He got his feet into the stirrups.

Six.

Slammed his spurs into his charger's sides and reached for his sword.

Five.

Grasped the sword as the warhorse exploded into motion—

Three.

Demetrius's lance tip danced in the firelight, but the man was backlit, wearing golden armour, glowing like a creature of hell or one of the old gods, and the Red Knight's draw flicked out—

One—

He cut up into the lance, his sword arm lifting, point dropping so that the lance tip slipped past his shieldless side. Then he reversed the blade, with the full power of his right shoulder, and backhanded the red-enamelled pommel into Demetrius's visor, hooking the pommel on the other man's neck and lifting him over the back of his saddle so that he crashed to earth.

He reined in, only a few paces from Demetrius's men. It was hard to see their faces in the unsealy light, so he backed his horse before turning. But none of them came for him.

He trotted down the road until he came to Demetrius, who was on his hands and knees. He dismounted and walked over to the young man, who was pulling at his aventail, trying desperately to take a full breath through a partially crushed larynx.

The young Count got his helmet free and gasped in a lungful of air. And saw the Red Knight.

'I yield,' he whined, and held out his blade.

The Red Knight had his sword point down, a relaxed grip called *Tutta porta di ferro*. 'No,' he said, and cut.

Demetrius's head hit the ground at the same moment as his body, but they were no longer together.

Far to the north, the Black Knight stood with two of his squires and Master de Marche under the flapping hearts and lilies of Galle. By careful pre-arrangement, they stood on an island in the midst of the Great River. There was still snow on the grass, and the late winter sun shone fitfully on it.

'He won't come,' de Marche said. He regretted that he had become the Black Knight's naysayer. It wasn't a role he relished.

Ser Hartmut Li Orguelleus nodded. 'It was worth a trip here to find out.'

He raised a gauntleted hand. 'Ah! But there he is, messires.'

On the northern shore, a company came into view. They carried four slim boats, and in moments they had them in the water.

It took them the better part of an hour to paddle across. The Great River was feeling the first of the thaws. She was great with water.

De Marche watched Ser Hartmut. The man did move – but it was glacial, and he never seemed to lock a joint. Or tire. De Marche felt the weight of his harness everywhere – his ankles hurt the more he thought about them.

Ser Hartmut merely stood.

Eventually, three of the boats landed, disgorging a hand of slovenly warriors in rusted maille and a handsome young man in what appeared to be hand-me-down armour. His bow was courtly.

Ser Hartmut opened his visor. 'Good day to you, sir.'

The young man rose from his bow. 'You are the Black Knight, I wager. My master has sent me to ask you if you wish to take Ticondaga.'

'I will take it,' Ser Hartmut said.

Suddenly, Speaker was there – cloaked in black, with a tree branch through his midsection and a smell of rot. His once-handsome features were now unmoving. In fact, the body was dead.

Under the body, Thorn was not dead.

'This young man is the rightful heir of the Earldom of the North-wall,' Thorn said. He meant the voice to sound pleasant, but he was out of practice and his puppet's lungs were dead. Flies emerged when he spoke. His puppet emitted a foul reek and a croak.

De Marche retched. And translated.

Ser Hartmut shrugged. 'You are a necromancer,' he said.

Thorn's corpse made no movement.

'What do you want?' Ser Hartmut asked. It was like dealing with Satan himself and a host of his fallen angels, but Ser Hartmut had not come to be called the Knight of Ill Renown without supping with various devils. He'd even allied with other necromancers. He knew the smell.

He knew other things that made a slight smile cross his lips.

Thorn was not, and had never been, a fool. He watched the reactions of the men to his puppet – and cast it aside. He'd been careless, and let the body die. He dropped it, seized one of the slovenly warriors and took him.

The new host was tall and thin. He had never been handsome – his face was too ferret-like – but everything worked.

'There, that will be better,' Thorn said. 'I want an ally in the north. I want the Wild left unmolested by men – all men. Immediately, I will aid in the capture of Ticondaga in exchange for free passage south past its defences and the use of its deep cellars as a source of supply for my army.'

'Your army?' Ser Hartmut asked.

'I will summon the Wild, and it will come. A host of boggles like this world has never seen. An ocean of silkies on the water. Wyverns and Wardens and irks and trolls and things no man can yet imagine.' Thorn spread his arms. 'I will bring down fire from on high.'

Ser Hartmut rubbed the ends of his moustache with his fingers. 'How will you transport this army?'

Thorn shrugged and enjoyed the act of shrugging. 'My captain will take care of the details.' He indicated the young man.

Ser Hartmut nodded. 'On what will you swear?'

Thorn massaged his memory until his puppet produced a lopsided grin. 'My name.'

'On these terms, I am willing to make alliance.' Ser Hartmut turned to de Marche, who was doing his best to maintain a blank expression.

'One last thing,' Thorn said. Ser Hartmut reminded him of all the things he disliked about men, especially fighting men.

Ser Hartmut raised an eyebrow. Inside a bassinet, it was still an expressive gesture.

'I get Ghause. And all the Murienses are to be killed, without exception.' Thorn's voice was like adamant.

Hartmut bowed. 'It pleases me to say I don't even know who Ghause is. And the Murienses—' He snapped his fingers.

More than two hundred leagues as the eagle flies, to the east, Mag was *working*. So was Morgan Mortirmir, and the Red Knight, and every other man or woman who could harness *potentia* and transmit it to those who could heal. The barn stank of shit and blood, and as soon as men were bound up, bones were re-knit, or intestines closed – or as soon as their eyes closed on the pain for ever – they were carried to cleaner places.

Not all of the work was hermetical, far from it. Even with Amicia's support from far off South Ford, even with every scrap of training and working they could muster, much of the blood was cleaned by men and women with their hands. The Yahadut, Yosef ben Mar Chiyya, worked until he fell asleep, rose, and worked again, always carefully using his medical skills to augment his hermetical mastery.

He was not the only practitioner who worked also in the real.

Father Arnaud had not stopped working for three days. And as Mortirmir shook his head over the pile of entrails that had once been a man's digestive tract, and let the man's soul slip away; as Mag sat like a marionette with her strings cut, beyond tears for her love or for any of the boys who were dying in desperate hope as they looked into her eye; as the Red Knight realised that he had struck an absolute wall to his *potentia*, and could do nothing more, he looked up, and saw Father Arnaud bent over Wastewater Will, a boy whose only wound was a simple slash to the leg. It was a slash that had occurred in a barn yard, gone septic, and now would cost the boy his life.

The priest muttered, and shuddered. And raised his hands, and prayed. And prayed.

And the boy died.

Father Arnaud rose from his knees and let a long sigh escape him. Then he made the sign of the cross over the boy's forehead, and said, 'Christ be with you on your journey. Know no further pain, but only joy.' He walked back to another blood-soaked pile of straw, once a man called Lingcropper. But this time he didn't bother to try his injured powers. 'I'll just rewrap that bandage,' he said cheerfully.

Gabriel watched the priest, and wanted to say something. But he couldn't think what it was. So in the end, he only stood a moment with his hand on the man's shoulder. And then he went to find Mag.

Mag was sitting on her chair where she'd collapsed after the last hermetical medical miracle. Her daughter Sukey was by her side; Kaitlin de Towbray held her hand. And of all men, Bad Tom stood at her back.

Mag looked up. 'I'm not going to explode,' she said.

Gabriel Muriens took her free hand. 'I won't pretend that didn't come to my mind.'

Mag looked away. 'It had to have happened sometime. A truly powerful practitioner loses their wits? It would be terrible. Christ defend us.'

He knelt by her a while. Suddenly, and without warning, Kaitlin – heavily pregnant Kaitlin – burst into tears with a great moan and whirl of sobbing, and in a heartbeat Mag and Sukey joined her.

Gabriel Muriens was capable of tears. His weren't very loud, but there were quite a few of them.

But long before the sobs or the Lanthorn keening were done, Tom grabbed his shoulder. 'You need to drink,' he said. He marched the Megas Ducas out of the barn and out of the mud and blood and faeces and into the green fields beyond. The Duke's pavilion was set up on clean, green grass.

Tom guided the Red Knight to a stool and put him on it. Toby came and washed his hands, and he watched the old blood come away. He watched it a bit too closely.

'Blood under my nails, Tom,' he said.

'Aye. Consequence of killing folk,' Tom answered.

Toby poured wine. Others were coming over. He could see Ser Alison, who had, of course distinguished herself in the fighting against the Easterners, and Gelfred, who'd commanded that last operation. His mind whirled a bit. He settled for solid things.

'Why'd you go to Mag?' he asked.

Tom stretched out his legs. 'Oh, comfort the widow,' he said, as if this was a natural thought. 'Offered to marry her,' he continued. 'She said no,' he added, as if miffed.

'Don't tell Sauce,' the Red Knight said. He raised his wine cup.

'Old Gods, you *are* an evil bastard,' Tom said, and slammed his cup on the table. 'This crap's too thin. I have mead.' He walked off as Sauce came up.

'What's wrong with him?' Sauce asked as she ducked under the tent edge. She had been batting her eyelashes at Count Zac, who was performing mounted tricks like a much younger man out in the field.

'You know how he is,' Gabriel said.

An hour later, they were well into the post-battle drink. Bad Tom stood at the table, a great horn of mead in his hand, and his laugh boomed over the camp. 'And then the loon says: stop fighting!' He looked at his prisoner, Ser Christos, who had an arm in a sling and a

713

bruise which covered half his face. 'Mind you, thanks to yon, I was bleeding like a stuck pig. That was a mickle blow, messire.'

Ser Christos bowed.

Ser Michael could see the man was pained, like all of the prisoners, at being present at a victory celebration. His inherent gentility won out over his need to boast. 'Ser knight, there's many of us who'd like to have the power to put a lance in Bad Tom.'

Ser Gavin laughed, and Tom joined the laughter. 'They do!' He laughed. He turned and cocked an eyebrow at the priest, who looked more like sixty than forty. 'And I hear we're all to call him Ser Gabriel now, eh? Not lord high god of all? Not Duke any more?'

Ser Gabriel frowned, and then made himself laugh – at himself. 'I liked being Duke,' he said.

Father Arnaud drank more. 'You'll be a better man as Gabriel.'

Ser Alcaeus looked puzzled. 'You are still the Duke,' he said.

Ser Gabriel was looking at Tom. 'There's men who feel that there is no rank higher than that of knighthood, Ser Alcaeus,' he said. 'And there's men who feel it's time I used my given name.' He looked at Father Alcaeus.

Tom nodded. 'Time *and* time, I'd say. Ser Gabriel. I like the sound of it.'

'That puts me in mind of something,' Ser Gabriel said. 'Toby, fetch my sword!'

Toby went quickly, his face showing a boy who didn't dare to hope. But he was doomed to disappointment.

The Red Knight drew his sword and pointed it at Long Paw. 'Come here and kneel,' he said.

'You wouldn't!' Long Paw said. But he was dragged by other men, nor was it so much against his will. 'You know what I was,' he said, from his knees, with dignity.

'No worse than what any of us were,' said the Red Knight. 'By my knighthood, and the power of my right hand, I dub thee knight.'

'There's another good archer lost for ever,' muttered Cully, but he gave his mate a hug hard enough to hurt his back. 'You bastard,' he said.

After that, there was some serious drinking. Captain Dariusz, who proved to have an excellent singing voice, raised it in an ancient hymn – a marvellous tune, that they all had to learn. Count Zac already knew it, and translated the words to Ser Alison, who grew still.

714

They drank more wine, and debated the strategy of the campaign.

Kaitlin came to see her husband, and looked around at all the men who bowed to her. 'Don't you talk about anything but war?' she asked, cheeks hot.

Count Zac bowed to her when her husband was tongue-tied. 'My lady, we but pour earth and wine on the dead.'

She shook her head.

Derkensun, who was drunker than most of them, grinned at her. 'I have decided to get married!' he said.

Kaitlin smiled politely at the tattooed giant. 'That's different from war,' she said.

When she was gone, Bad Tom licked his lips and grinned. 'You're going to ruin war as a sport,' he said. 'All this *strategia* and *taktika*. What will you leave us?'

'It seemed bloody enough today,' Gabriel said.

At which Tom looked disgusted. 'You're carving the fun right out of war. We outmanoeuvre them. They surrender. Now they fight for us? Christ on the cross. Next we'll settle these things with dice.'

'Don't you have a herd to drive?' Ser Gabriel asked. He sounded better – better than any of them had heard him in months. Despite the dark circles under his eyes. And the impressive intake of wine. Or perhaps because of it.

'Aye. And drive it I will. Being I'm the Drover.' He grinned. 'This was like a nice little rest. No beeves to watch making dung. No sheep – Christ, I hate sheep.' He slammed back his horn. 'Sure you wouldn't like to come to Harndon, now? Ranald is determined to take the beeves all the way. You made him a knight. Now he has another beast in view.'

Ranald coloured, and Ser Gabriel laughed. 'She's not a beast – she's much better looking than that.' He stood up.

Behind him the whole camp was moving. It was three camps, really. The hospital had grown to cover all the buildings of the farmstead, and the defeated army's tentage shared the ground with the victorious army's brush shelters. 'Can I at least ask why we couldn't cut the fucker's bodyguard to ribbons,' Bad Tom asked. 'Fair is fair. They lost.'

Ser Gabriel took a pull of wine. 'They weren't the enemy. They aren't now. In a way they're all my vassals.' He shrugged. 'That's why Demetrius had to die.'

Ser Gavin shook his head. 'It had to be done.' But he sounded unsure.

Ser Gabriel nodded. 'You may have the right of it, but I've a glut of death just now.' His voice was flat. 'It's interesting to parse the morality of the thing. Demetrius was merely Aeskepiles' pawn – but I'd say he murdered his father of his own free will. Where does that put him?'

'Hell,' said Ser Milus. He glanced at Ser Alcaeus. The Morean knight nodded his agreement.

'The Emperor would never have let him reclaim the duchy,' he said. 'His hands were stained with his father's blood. Exile for life was the very best he might have hoped for.'

'Perhaps,' Gabriel said coldly. 'But the Emperor is not of this world. And never is not always a long time, in politics.' He shrugged. 'I had to be sure.'

Toby walked around the table pouring – Gelfred took a little, and Alison, recovering from an Easterner arrow in her left biceps, declined. Derkensun had his poured full.

They were all there, or most of them were. Except, of course, for Jacques and Jehan and John le Bailli and all the others who would never be there again.

The Red Knight raised his cup. 'The Thrakians were never the enemy. Now I hope they're allies. If I understand it – if I'll *ever* understand it – Andronicus intended to rebuild Morea. But Aeskepiles intended to start a civil war which would destroy the Empire's remaining military potential. The Wild is *right there*.' He pointed to the north. 'Imagine the Wild in Liviapolis. Imagine Thorn there.'

The air shivered.

Bad Tom pulled a heavy dagger out of his belt. 'Name him again and let's see how he bleeds.'

Ranald rolled his eyes.

Ser Michael leaned over, a hand in the small of his back. For a moment, with bloodshot eyes and a back arched in pain, he looked like a much older man. 'So we won?' he asked cautiously.

'We certainly didn't lose,' the Red Knight said.

'Now we rebuild the Morean army?' Ser Gavin asked.

Michael looked at his Captain with pleading eyes. Instead of those eyes slipping away, Ser Gabriel met his look and smiled.

'No. We'll leave that condotta to other men. We're going south with Tom. To a tournament. In Harndon.'

'A tournament? What? Fighting for sport? What kind of foolishness is that?' Tom asked, but he was grinning.

'Just so, Tom,' the Red Knight said, and raised his cup. 'We're headed to a tournament of fools.'

Acknowledgements

I'm grateful to Gillian Redfearn at Gollancz for giving me the chance – after twenty years as a writer – to write fantasy – the genre I wanted to write from age 13. I'm also grateful to her colleague Charlie Panayiotou for a great deal of support and a thousand e-mails, and to Shelley Power, my agent; Rebecca Lovatt, my publicist, Dmitry Bondarenko, my graphic artist, Jessie Durham, my web-designer and hostess (is that really the right term) and Steven Sandford, who made the long-awaited maps. All of them are friends, most of them are fellow reenactors and swords-people, and role-players, and fantasy readers. I'm grateful not only for their work and enthusiasm, but for the 'team' aspects of this project. Just as an example, Steve's maps clarified for me some details that – yes, I'm not in denial – I had wrong in geography. Especially in the area around the Green Hills. Dmitry's art has literally inspired – and clarified – not just what people look like, but what some of the Wild looks like, too. Jessie's website has resulted in fan mail which makes all of us feel as if what we're doing has worth – well, mostly – and Rebecca has not only landed interviews that result in me learning more about 'my' world but has also allowed my daughter to concoct an alias. But that's another story.

I'm also grateful to a host of people and places for inspiration and help; I'll hit the high points and forget some truly wonderful people, and I apologise. But in no particular order – Maurizio Oliboni and Giulia Griogoli and all the amazing people who put on the 'Torneo del Cigno Bianco' in Verona; all the members of the reenacting company we call Hoplologia (or maybe the Company of Select Marksmen, or maybe the Companions of St Eustachios); Greg Mele, Tasha Kelly, Nicole Allen, Joe Harley and all the other reenactors/chivalry enthusiasts who pre-read Fell Sword in its various phases; I hope I made all the changes; my sister-in-law Nancy, who tried very hard to improve the copy-editing; Giorgos Kafetsis of Alexandrouplois, Greece, and Giannis, Xsenia and Smaro (and even Hypolita, as yet unborn!) for all-night conversations on the late Byzantine Empire and for an introduction to a 14th century Greek castle – I hope that my fantasy version of Greece and Serbia meets your expectations; all the reenactors, Medieval, Ancient Greek and 18th century, whose work informs my writing, and all the craftspeople whose work fires me at least in part with greed ... JT Palikko, Mark Vickers, Craig Sitch, the folks at Albion and Arms and Armor; Eric Schatzel, Ward Oles, the Brevaks and all the folks 'At the Eastern Door' (check it out for some of the most amazing items) Peter Fuller, Brian Scott Wilson, Christian Darce and Jiri Klepac, Tasha Kelly (now for sewing and not reading) ... really, these people populate my fantasy with artefacts that I can describe, hold, swish through the air or put on my back to keep the rain off or to ward off blows or practise using.

But skills are as essential to descriptive prose as artefacts; so I'd like to thank Guy Windsor, Tom Leoni, Greg Mele and Chris Verwijmeren for lessons, expertise, and authorial support on weapons, techniques, and styles; the folks at Les Maitre D'Armes in Ottawa/ Hull who run Borealis, and the folks at the Chicago Swordplay Guild who run WMAW.

Really, it's too much fun, writing fantasy. Thanks to all. Maybe we should do it again?

Toronto 2013